The Conquerors

A Novel

Achala Moulik

UBS Publishers' Distributors Ltd.
5 Ansari Road, New Delhi-110 002
Bombay Bangalore Madras Calcutta Patna Kanpur London

First Published 1996

Cover Design : UBS Art Studio

Typeset and Designed in 10.6 pt. Times Roman at Alphabets, New Delhi
Printed at Pauls Press, New Delhi

To

The memory of my beloved parents

Leela and Moni Moulik

whose ideals and nobility, courage and generosity

have illumined our lives.

Prelude

The land of India — with its mighty rivers, fertile plains and forests, its gold-towered temples and jewelled idols, palaces of marble and gem, its vast granaries and splendid markets — had always beckoned to those who lived beyond the high Himalayas, eking out a living from their arid plains. They came through forbidding passes and gorges; Caucasians, Scythians, Huns, Mongols and Pathans to encounter a civilisation of lofty metaphysics and erotic madness, exacting logic and fearful superstitions, a love for holiness and a chaotic greed. They were drawn too by whispered legends of fabled wealth, and they came, bringing with them the vibrance of challenge and innovation.

Enriched and invigorated by these invaders, India however soon absorbed their separate identities and became a seashore of humanity — unvanquished.

When the New World was discovered and the sea lost its terror, a new crusade was begun by men in search of dreams — not only of silk, spice and gold — but of new lands to conquer. They saw a great land torn by fratricidal wars and ruinous campaigns. They were eager to trade and grasp the wealth of a wounded empire.

These white, tawny-haired men from across the seven seas, waited patiently, building their clay forts, haggling with local merchants and cringing before the imperial court for firmans or concessions. Their spheres of activity increased and their territorial hunger grew. To these men of Europe's crabbed and confined towns, Hindusthan was a perpetual lure for expansion and enrichment. From sleepy Calcutta and steaming Madras they watched, with veiled eyes, the intrigues, local wars and invasions which left the realm bloodstained and shattered. Slowly, they watched the citadel fall apart, inviting another conquest.

A man of ambition decided to act and mould events to his own desire. Charged with belief in his own destiny, Robert Clive laid the foundations of a new empire.

This empire brought many emissaries. There were the traders who came to plunder and enrich themselves with the gold of India. Others came to offer the challenge of a new civilisation and opened India to the wonders of the west. In time, they were touched by the grandeur of India and were conquered in turn.

This is a story of that encounter.

Contents

PART I

ALEXANDER RUTHVEN

1757 — 1807

CHARACTERS

Alexander Ruthven
Shirin Ruthven
Fiona Ruthven
Liselotte Fremont
Georgiana Ruthven
Andrew Ruthven
Claude Ruthven
Beatrice Ruthven

Ishwar Chowdhury
Indrajit Chowdhury
Bishnupriya Chowdhury
Indumati Chowdhury
Prince Ram Singh

Frederick Manham
Henry Dalrymple
Arthur Latimer

1

A Throne for a Song

The Ganges was no longer a benign lady but the goddess of destruction as she rushed past the high soft banks of Plassey, plucking out great clumps of earth and young trees, on her frenzied monsoon journey to the sea.

In the eerie light of a monsoon dusk, Alexander Ruthven could see the undulating carpet of green rice fields across the river. Men and women bent forward, busy in the task of transplanting rice seedlings. Their lithe, brown bodies moved forward in unison as each row was completed. Women, their saris hitched up to their knees to facilitate movement, covered their heads in modesty. Others, their bodies slim and taut, came to fetch water from the river in brass vessels, carrying their aquatic burden with ease. Sturdy, dhoti-clad peasants drove cows and buffaloes back to the village, pausing to call out to children sporting by the water's edge. Naked little boys, wearing black strings round their waists from which perforated coins hung, called out to little girls whose miniature saris covered bud-like breasts and narrow flanks. Together, they made boats of keya leaves, and perching gingerly on the banks, dropped them into the raging water below. Then they too turned homewards to the darkening village dominated by a grey Shiva temple which stood among earthen, thatched-roof cottages, scarlet gulmohur blossoms and long, swaying coconut fronds.

That evening, the temple bells seemed to ring with greater resonance as if intoning a message of great moment for its devotees. But the deep clear chimes were lost in the growl of thunder reverberating across the leaden sky. It was as if Lord Shiva remained unheard in the ochre, rain-washed stillness of that June day in 1757.

Outwardly, life in the countryside seemed placid. Yet, there was a tremor of disquiet among the people who lived in that rich, verdant country. They knew of the momentous events that were gathering force around them. Such events were not unique in the life of people who had known a millennium of unrest. They had seen invaders come and go — wild, cruel men from Ghazni, Iran and Turan, as well as devious ones from across the seas, who had ruled until a more potent foe came to challenge their might. Now, the Moghul empire was but a carcass awaiting the vulture's touch.

Sitting in the temple courtyard, Ishwar Chowdhury gazed speculatively at the opposite bank of the river. Though he had invoked Lord Shiva's blessings on the terrifying enterprise ahead, he felt a strange dread, almost a sense of doom, envelop him.

Ishwar Chowdhury was one of the many wealthy merchants who had abandoned the nawab of Bengal to assist the East India Company and Robert Clive. He had told himself a hundred times that betraying the nawab was no betrayal at all. He was, after all, an infidel whose people had despoiled Hindusthan for eight centuries, he mused. Had they not razed ancient temples and persecuted our faith? Had not these foreigners fed on the beautiful land, beggaring us? Why not drive out the scions of these Turkish hordes with the aid of these white merchants? And then Hindusthan might once more be free.

Ishwar Chowdhury's thoughts turned to Fort William, the ships and cannons, sepoys and officers of the East India Company. He knew, deep down, that the English would not be so easily evicted. The lust for gold had entered their blood and was not likely to be satisfied except by more gold.

The English had cast their anchor at Sutanati ghat on the bend of the Ganges in 1690, under the leadership of Job Charnock. Driven by marauding river bandits to the safety of Bengal, Charnock of the East India Company built a clay fort. The Nawab of Bengal accorded his thoughtless consent while Ishwar Chowdhury's ancestors sold the Company three strategic villages of Sutanati, Govindapur and Kalighat. The English Company built Fort William and Queen Anne's Church during the reigns of King William and Queen Anne, and conducted a brisk trade in broadcloth, muslin, copper, lead, zinc not only with Indian merchants but with the older Portuguese and Armenian settlements too.

Calcutta expanded and prospered. nawab Murshid Ali Khan was disquieted by the spectacle of the Company's burgeoning wealth, and forbade Indians to trade with the English. His commands were nullified by Emperor Farukshyar who had been cured of syphilis by a Dr. Hamilton of the Company. The exuberant commercial spirit of the Company could not be suppressed.

Plumped by exotic gifts from the English, the next nawab, Alivardi Khan, accorded more concessions to the Company. "The English," he said, "are like bees. Press them gently to extract honey but do not get stung."

The bees, however, soon became eagles that could not be dislodged, as Alivardi's grandson, Siraj-ud-doula discovered. Lacking any apprenticeship in statecraft, this headstrong nawab fell headlong into conflict with the devious and calculating Colonel Robert Clive of the East India Company.

His rough imperiousness made enemies of his own courtiers as well. By and by, these men joined Clive in a conspiracy to depose the nawab. Some, like Amirchand, merely wished for a handsome bribe while others like Jagat Seth wished to trade with the English. And Ishwar Chowdhury dreamt of regaining his lands.

"Will the conspiracy succeed?" he wondered. "If not, I am lost—for I have staked everything on this enterprise. If Clive wins, I will get back my ancestral lands. If not . . . why, the Nawab will sever my head from my shoulders!" The zamindar closed his eyes, almost feeling the cold blade of the executioner on his neck. "Is it worth it?" he asked himself for the hundredth time. "But of course.

Has not this Nawab's grandfather taken our lands? Has not this Siraj despoiled our sacred Nadia where the godly Chaitanya sang a message of hope to our anguished people? Has not Siraj insulted Jagat Seth in court? Why shouldn't I, Nanda Kumar, Amirchand and Raja Krishnachandra turn to Colonel Clive? He will not bring back our Hindu kings — that the great Moghul will not allow — but he will have a complacent puppet to rule; Mir Jafar, the trusted uncle and general to Siraj-ud-doula!"

Ishwar Chowdhury laughed softly. Siraj was no fool. He had sensed that a conspiracy was afoot, had taken Calcutta and ransacked the treasury of Fort William. And now he was marching again — aided by the French, "to put" as he said, "that shopkeeper, Clive, in his place."

The zamindar peered through the hazy screen of rain that all but obscured the frantic activities of the two armies at Plassey, on the right bank of the Ganges. Torches and flares pierced the clouded twilight, as Siraj-ud-doula's vast army prepared for battle. Ishwar Chowdhury rose from the damp stone steps and descended to the ghat where the wild water swirled around him. "Victory. I pray for victory," he murmured, gazing unblinkingly at Shiva's trident silhouetted against the leaden sky.

On the opposite bank Alexander Ruthven stood at his post, his gaze shifting from the turbulent waters to the furtive movements around him. Like the Brahmin aristocrat on the other bank, young Ruthven knew that an event of great portent was about to be enacted. He, a mere lieutenant of the Company's army, could not know or even guess the cat's cradle of chicanery that had preceded and would ensue after the battle. Yet, the sensations he had experienced twelve years ago, in the days following the battle of Culloden, returned, threatening to revive long suppressed memories of despair.

The rugged grandeur of the Scottish highlands, covered by heather and gorse, the wide sweep of sea and moors seemed far from the warm, fertile valleys of Bengal. But the memory of a lost battle against the English army, the burning of rebel villages, the screams of people still had a painful proximity. He could see even now the figure of a blond Redcoat shoot his father, and violate his young sister before his stunned eyes.

Alexander was roused from his sombre reveries by a commotion on the river below. Boats drew up along the banks; the sounds of marching feet and cannons being dragged competed with the steady growl of thunder. Robert Clive stepped ashore, and stood in the rain, scanning his assembled army speculatively.

"Has the Nawab's army taken up position?" Clive asked Colonel Stringer, shaking off his rain-soaked cloak.

"They are within three miles, Sir," Stringer replied and paused before continuing, "six thousand men are in position. A larger force is following. Heavily armed with French ammunition ... under the command of St. Frais."

Clive nodded, a frown creasing his wide-domed forehead, a cynical smile playing on a face already hardened by ambition. "Very well. I will require five hundred men — both Indian sepoys and English soldiers. We will adjourn to Plassey House to await His Majesty, the Nawab."

Clive's officers laughed, accustomed as they were to their commander's impudent gestures. Plassey House was a lonely brick villa surrounded by a high brick wall where Nawab Siraj-ud-doula held mushairas and carousals. Nothing, Clive knew, would enrage the nawab more than to hear that the English commander had entered its guarded portals.

The colonel's astute eyes fell on the young Scotsman who stood watching him impassively.

"You ..." he snapped, jerking a forefinger at Alexander Ruthven. "You may accompany me. You seem to have an unblinking pair of eyes. Perhaps you'll keep watch better than the others."

Bowing in acquiescence, Ruthven picked up his matchlock and wordlessly began walking towards the hunting lodge. Clive watched him with a frown, shrugged and walked slowly towards the house.

All night, Alexander Ruthven heard the sound of arriving sepoys and soldiers. Rain fell in torrents, flooding the rice fields and swelling the turbulent waters of the Ganges. The soldiers bivouacked among the dripping mango trees, now laden with ripe, heavy fruit. Ruthven sat under a cornice of Plassey House, huddled against the damp chill air, staring at the flaring torches glimmering between tents and trees. Sudden flashes of lightning lit up the stormy sky, the fury of the river and the men of the East India Company poised for battle. And then, from a cluster of huddled soldiers came the unmistakable sound of a familiar refrain.

You take the high road, I'll take the low road
But I'll be in Scotland before ye
For me and my true love will never meet again
In the bonny bonny banks of Loch Lomond.

Alexander Ruthven stiffened in surprise at the pain that surged through him. A pain induced by that well known tune that resurrected long-banished memories.

Memories soon dissolved amidst the excitement of the present. Marching up and down the rain-drenched garden of the lodge, young Ruthven caught glimpses of Robert Clive pacing restlessly in the spacious halls of Plassey House. He saw the commander occasionally pause his frantic pacing to peer into the rain-lashed landscape lit by flashes of lightning.

All night the Commander pondered over the forthcoming battle, torn by indecision. Could it be that I, son of a humble lawyer in the obscure village of Market Drayton, have been chosen to lead a victorious army? Or am I doomed to failure? he agonised to himself. He sat still for a few moments only to spring up again and begin pacing. Ruthven watched, surprised by this new aspect of the man who seemed outwardly so assured. As he too paused and paced, Ruthven heard a medley of strange sounds emanating from the mango grove in the nawab's camp — of drums and horns, the neighing of disquieted horses and trumpeting elephants. In the English camp, an uneasy silence prevailed. The silence of men uncertain of the enterprise that lay ahead.

The sun rose over a bank of clouds, its fiery rays glittering on the turbulent river and green rice fields, on the two armies poised for battle and on the villagers who had ventured out in the eerie stillness of that morning.

Bleary eyed and weary, Robert Clive came out onto the terrace of Plassey House and trained his glasses on the spectacle of the nawab's army, spread out in the fields beyond. Ruthven saw him stiffen in surprise before he slowly lowered his glasses and handed them to the young lieutenant.

The army of nawab Siraj-ud-doula looked splendid in the ochre sunlight. Heavy cannons drawn by oxen, richly caparisoned elephants and horses, were arrayed as impressively as soldiers armed with swords and matchlocks.

"Formidable, is it not?" Colonel Clive asked grimly.

No one spoke. Then Major Lawrence, hero of the battle of Trichnopoly, said, "There is a multitude and there is pomp. But we have nothing to admire or fear from the Nawab's army. Redcoats never lose. Remember Trichnopoly, Colonel?"

Clive sighed, unaffected by his comrade's enthusiasm. "We must give them the best fight we can during the day and at night sling our muskets over our shoulders and march back to Calcutta. We cannot win against the impressive cavalry of the Pathans, the heavy artillery and French officers under command of Monsieur de St. Frais."

Abruptly, he turned away. "Let us begin. Our soldiers must now leave the mango grove and take up their positions."

The army of the East India Company began to move. Clive led the cry in the name of King George. The soldiers cried, "Clive Saheb Bahadur Ki Jai!" Victory to the valiant Clive! And in response came the cry of the nawab's troops, "Saheb Jung Bahadur Ki Fateh!"

The salutations were drowned by a burst of artillery fire from the nawab's army, under the guidance of the generals Mohanlal and St. Frais. The deafening roar of cannonade shook the mango trees and obliterated all other sounds. Clive watched in dismay as line after line of his soldiers fell in the relentless firing. "Retreat behind the grove!" he shouted.

Retreating to safety, Alexander Ruthven aimed his fire at the enemy with a strange detachment. As the bullets flew and reverberated around the grove, he wondered, not for the first time, why he was fighting the nawab and his French allies. He saw enemy soldiers fall before his aim and continued in his duty, with neither thought nor sentiment.

At midday, the fighting remained indecisive. Clive summoned his officers to hold their positions and decided to attack the enemy camp after nightfall because he could no longer resist the relentless fire of the nawab's men.

"Why are you turning back?" General Mohanlal of the Nawab's army taunted Clive. "Have you found the men of Hindusthan too strong for your taste? Stay back, foreigner, and fight!"

Clive rode ahead, leading the retreat.

Then the sun disappeared behind the clouds and the heavens spilled a monsoon shower on the two sides. The English covered their ammunition with tarpaulin. The Nawab's army waited for the deluge to cease as they helplessly watched their ammunition become sodden. Realising their plight, the Nawab's men began to retire to their camp.

In vain did Siraj-ud-doula order his commander in chief, Mir Jafar, to send reinforcements. He exhorted Rai Durlabh, another general, to go into battle. But neither moved their soldiers. They had formed part of the conspiracy to assist Clive. They watched impassively as the emergent Company troops scattered the nawab's forces.

Only General Mohanlal remained loyal to the Nawab. Bloodstained and weary, he cried, "Take heart, my men! Do not flee! The battle is not yet lost! We have fought mightier foes! Take up position and charge!"

Mohanlal regrouped and led a desperate charge against the Company's forces. His cannons were useless, his gunpowder soggy but he continued to fight, his brandishing sword flashing valiantly in the sunlight.

Clive watched the advancing soldiers with a grim face, recognising in Mohanlal a desperate valour that could turn the tide. "Open fire!" he ordered. "Draw out the Nawab's soldiers from their entrenchments."

General Mohanlal fell in the reckless charge. Other officers followed their commander in death, under the unceasing hail of bullets from the Company's army.

"We are lost!" cried a young officer. "We have been betrayed! The battle is lost!"

The mighty army of Bengal retreated.

Seeing his army routed, the Nawab of Bengal removed his turban and offered it to Mir Jafar, imploring aid and advice. "Send an order to withdraw the soldiers. Tomorrow, we shall see," the traitor replied coldly.

It was a tomorrow Siraj-ud-doula never saw. Certain now of betrayal and defeat, the young king collapsed on the silken divan of the royal tent, remembering the fakir's prophecy of doom. "He had warned me!" the nawab cried, tearing his embroidered tunic. "The fakir had warned me that I would be betrayed, that I stood in peril, but I refused to believe him! In rage I cut off his ears. Oh wretched me, why was I so heedless of advice?"

"Your Majesty!" a loyal soldier cried, rushing into the tent, "the Company soldiers are advancing here!"

The Nawab stood up swaying on his silk-slippered feet, his eyes bulging out of their sockets. "They will kill me! Yes, they will murder me! Here, get me a horse ..."

"The horses have scattered ..."

"A camel then ... anything ... to escape!"

Remembering the old king, Alivardi Khan, who had shown him kindness, the old soldier hurried to summon a swift camel from the melee outside. A camel and mahout were soon procured. The old soldier knelt before his young king, grandson of the master he had loved. "Godspeed, Sire," he murmured.

Siraj-ud-doula leapt up from the divan, trembling and frantic, barely acknowledging the old man's salutation. "Take me swiftly to my capital," he half-commanded, half-implored the mahout. "For there I will be safe."

Siraj-ud-doula, the once arrogant and headstrong king of Bengal, sped on over muddy rivulets and deserted rice fields, aware of his hopeless position. Rain lashed his bare head and soaked his rich vestments but the camel galloped on, faster than an Arab steed, sensing his ruler's plight. Perhaps Siraj-ud-doula thought of his wayward youth, his mother's admonitions and finally the fakir's prophecy. It was too late for regret, too early for hope. He had first to escape from the foreigners and from the traitors in his own ranks.

Exhausted, the camel collapsed gracefully on its knees before the grand palace of Hazar Duari, or the thousand portals. Stumbling as if in a delirium, Siraj-ud-doula rushed through the guard room to his own opulent chambers.

Begum Lutfinissa, a beautiful girl of twenty years, stood before him. Slowly, she sank to her knees in a gesture of homage. "My lord," she whispered, her voice quivering, through a haze of tears. "My lord, we must flee!"

Siraj-ud-doula stared at her, the wife he had neglected, who now wished to share his misfortune. "Hide? With me? No, Begum, you will stay here . . . they will not harm you. I will return to regain my kingdom!"

The dowager Amina Begum entered the chambers, heavily veiled. "My child! Oh my wretched child! You must flee at once! The traitor Mir Jafar has ordered your arrest."

"How? How could his orders reach before me?" the Nawab cried, swaying on his feet.

"A carrier pigeon landed here this morning — in the bazar! Go. My child, go soon! A boat awaits you — near the moat. Nazir, who loved your grandfather will take you away. Go ... it is already late."

The old begum stretched out her arms to hold her star-crossed child in a last embrace. As she watched his retreating figure she whispered, "My wretched womb! What sorrow you have brought me!"

Lutfinissa covered her face and began to weep. Her daughter

nestled in her arms and began to cry strange, uncomprehending tears.

Siraj-ud-doula's dinghy was lashed by the wild, white waves of the Ganges until it crashed on the banks, splintered by the raging waters. The nawab barely managed to swim ashore. Nazir lay on the wet ground, too exhausted to move. Trudging across the rain-lashed countryside with his once frenetic energy, Siraj-ud-doula finally reached a hamlet of thatched houses. "Here will I hide and rest ... and somehow plan to get to Delhi to seek protection of the Emperor ... or to Lucknow where my French friends will aid me!"

He came to a hut and called out for help. Slowly, the door opened. Before the Nawab stood the fakir who had prophesied his end and whose ears had been cut off in punishment. Siraj-ud-doula stepped back, stifling a cry of surprise. The fakir came forward. "My prophecy is fulfilled," he smiled, bowing in mockery," Your throne is lost. Now, my lord, you too are a fakir!"

2

A Star of Fortune

The victorious army of the East India Company marched towards Murshidabad under clouded skies, reaching the fallen capital on the 28th June amidst tunes of horns, fifes, drums and bugles. The city which greeted the foreign army was silent, curious. Quivering shafts of monsoon sunshine glinted on matchlock and sword hilts as the procession moved through the streets. The Bengali populace watched in enigmatic silence: for five centuries they had seen new rulers come and go.

Ishwar Chowdhury stood on the balcony of his temporary habitat, along with a few Seth bankers.

"It is not the first time foreigners have intruded in our affairs," he told a banker friend. "The Portuguese did so much earlier and then there were the Dutch and French."

"Quite so," the man responded, smiling. "These firingis are but our agents." He turned to the patrician landlord. "It is you and I, Thakur, and others like us who call the tune ... and choose our nawabs."

"Of course," replied Chowdhury with an alacrity that concealed a growing unease. This time it is no different. A Muslim nawab to rule as viceroy of the Moghul emperor. More trading rights for the company . . ." His gaze fell on the inscrutable face of the colonel riding past, a strange smile on his cold face. "Is it only that?" he asked himself, "Or have we mounted a tiger?"

Robert Clive glanced around him, satisfied with the lush grandeur of the Bengali countryside and the opulence of Murshidabad. "Yes," he thought, "it has been worth the deceptions and intrigues."

Mir Jafar was waiting richly dressed, with other noblemen and merchants in the Durbar Hall, for Robert Clive. He was restless, uneasy, over anxious to please his sponsor. When the Englishman entered, Mir Jafar hurried to greet him at the end of the glittering audience hall.

"Take your place on the masnad of Bengal," Clive told the old man.

Mir Jafar bowed slightly. "I request you to escort me, Clive Saheb . . . for it is you who . . ."

A sardonic smile lit up Clive's cynical features. Bowing, he led the usurper to the throne of Bengal, and in compliance with the custom of Moghul India, made his submission before the new nawab with the traditional pieces of gold, the nazrana. Mir Jafar was thereby pronounced the new Nawab of Bengal.

The ceremony over, Robert Clive took a leisurely tour around the treasury of Murshidabad. He was not displeased by the vaults of gold and silver coins and plate of treasure chests heaving with precious gems and gold cloth. "It is not as much as I expected," he confided to Watts, the chief instigator of the conspiracy, "a mere million and a half pounds."

"It is adequate, Clive Saheb . . . to pay our agreement," Mir Jafar, the new nawab hastened to assure him. "And there will be more . . . much more . . . after merchants settle their . . . promises."

If Robert Clive was surprised at the directness of speech from a man known for his ambiguity, he did not show it. After all, it was better to be clear about future expectations.

Mir Jafar hurried on, "I have decided to confer the zamindari of 24 Parganas on you. The annual revenue from this fertile district will be handsome." He paused, then added, "This will be in addition to a salary of rupees four hundred thousand."

"That should be adequate," Clive murmured as calmly as he could. "I will have more revenues than a rich duke in England," he thought to himself with satisfaction.

In the evening, the conspirators met in the house of the great banker Jagat Seth to celebrate their victory and settle their dues to one another. A sum of rupees two and a half million was comfortably distributed in reward for English support and cooperation. One of the conspirators, Amirchand, had been cheated by Clive and Watts, by writing his share on a paper which was later exchanged. Clive received £235,000, members of the Council got £8,000 each. The army and navy shared £400,000 between them. Everyone was well satisfied as they sat down to drink claret. The Hindus avoided drinking with the foreigners.

The celebrations were followed by a sumptuous dinner at the palace of Murshidabad where more wine flowed, and choice courtesans sang and danced to amuse the foreigners.

Alexander Ruthven had been taken in the entourage of "Stringer Lawrence" who liked the competence of the taciturn young Scotsman. Ruthven was glad to exchange the moist darkness of the lamp, around which frogs and crickets kept up a steady duet, for the brilliance of the palace. His blue eyes widened in astonishment as the party made their way through corridors of marble tracery, past walls hung with the famed silk tapestries of Murshidabad. Mirrors ensconced in jewelled frames and filigreed brass lamps lent a shimmering quality to the halls. The diwan-i-khas, the audience hall, where Siraj-ud-doula had once dispensed a capricious justice, was ablaze with candles and redolent with the scent of jasmine. Courtesans scattered rose petals on the guests and sprinkled them with rose water. Ruthven paused to stare at the women, their legs in tight churidars, their knee-length dresses designed to draw attention to their breasts and waists. At the far end of the hall sat the musicians playing the tabla, dhol and shehnai while nautch girls danced slowly and sensuously to the music.

The prettiest dancer showered her interest on Robert Clive. He tossed a few gold coins at her. She flung them aside in mock outrage, her kohl-lined eyes smiling meaningfully at him.

Alexander Ruthven watched, fascinated by the nautch girls. There had been a few in Madras, where he had served earlier, but he could remember none that had been as enticing as the apricot-skinned, firm-bosomed damsels that knelt, pirouetted and pranced now before the guests. He leant back against the silken bolsters to watch the dance, sipping at claret, until his eyes fell on Prince Miran, son of Mir Jafar.

"A dark horse," Major Lawrence muttered, following young Ruthven's gaze. "As bad as Siraj, if you ask me. Look at 'im eyeing the singer."

"She *is* lovely," Ruthven replied, staring at the voluptuous girl. Lawrence laughed. "Hindusthan has many such." He bent closer to Ruthven. "They are even better on closer scrutiny."

The bacchanalia continued, and young Ruthven soon wearied of the singing. The nautch girls ignored him; his shabby coat and greyish linen bespoke his impecunious circumstances. Suddenly he noticed Prince Miran conferring with an attendant and then stealing away furtively. On a sudden impulse, Ruthven followed.

He took care to pause behind pillars and alcoves as he followed the prince. They ascended a wide, curved staircase, dark but for a brass lamp and proceeded down another corridor, until at the end of it, the prince flung open a door. A flurry of activity greeted his arrival as attendants scurried around. Afraid of being discovered, Ruthven slipped into the next chamber.

"Bring the lady Lutfinissa here," he heard Miran order the eunuch who guarded the Begum's chamber.

"The Begum has . . . retired," the eunuch muttered. Miran laughed. "Then I will join her . . . in her retirement!"

"Your Highness," a veiled lady spoke up. "That gesture will not enhance your prestige."

Miran stepped towards her. In silence, he stared at the thick black lace that covered her figure.

"Dare you advise me, you old hag? Call Lutfinissa! Tell her that the future nawab of Bengal summons her. She has much to lose if she does not please me."

The veiled figure stood motionless for a moment. Then she turned and went inside the Begum's chamber where the deposed Siraj-ud-doula's wife sat on a divan, red eyed and weary. Seeing her cousin enter, Lutfinissa asked eagerly, "Is there some news of my lord? Has he returned? Perhaps the French are preparing to fight?"

"No, my lady. No news of the ... Nawab. But the new king's son is here ... asking for you. I beg you to be careful."

Lutfinissa retorted, "Tell Prince Miran to look elsewhere. I am Queen of Bengal. I do not entertain a usurper's son!"

The inner door flew open. Prince Miran entered, ignoring the protests of the zenana ladies. His eyes burned like live coals as he beheld the fair young begum. "Her beauty has not been exaggerated," he thought. Aloud he said, " Lutfinissa ... you are no longer the queen of Bengal. You are nothing, in fact. But if you obey me ... and please me ... as you evidently pleased the deposed nawab ... I will make you my queen."

The former queen was so enraged by the man's presence that she replied hotly, "I will never be your queen ... you traitor's spawn!"

Miran's eyes narrowed. "You will not find the dungeons a better place, fair lady. That will be your fate if you display such unseemly hauteur."

The veiled lady turned and involuntarily raised a hand towards the former queen, as if to caution her.

As she did so, Miran's eyes fell on that hand — long, pale and slender. Instantly he stepped forward and tore off the lady's veil, to the dismay of the other ladies. "You cunning maiden," he laughed cruelly, "pretending to be an old hag! Why, you are as delicious as the begum herself!"

The young lady stared back at Miran with terror-stricken dark grey eyes.

Slowly, Begum Lutfinissa drew her veil aside, revealing a face of exquisite beauty. In fact there was a close resemblance between herself and the other lady. They had the same grey sloe eyes, smooth oval faces, rosebud mouths, complexions of alabaster.

"Shirin Bano is my cousin, and therefore a member of the royal house of Alivardi Khan. Nay, more, Shirin Bano's mother was a princess of the Timurid dynasty, a distant kinswoman of our Moghul emperor. It would be unwise to offend her," Lutfinissa said.

Miran's thin lips stretched into the travesty of a smile. "Indeed? But the mighty Emperor Shah Alam is far away. When he could not keep Siraj-ud-doula on his throne, how can he keep Shirin Bano from . . . my . . . arms?"

A heavy stillness throbbed in the lamplit room. "No one can help Shirin Bano except the British and they will not concern themselves over a kinswoman of Siraj-ud-doula!" He paused. "Come Shirin Bano, let me while away a few hours with you until . . . the lady Lutfinissa agrees to be my begum. Why, I might even keep you both in my harem!" He chuckled lasciviously.

Shirin hesitated for only a moment, as she read the resignation in the other, now unveiled faces. Then, suddenly like a gazelle, she sprang forward and ran out of the lamplit chambers. Slow to react, Miran watched her go and then began to pursue her down the corridor.

Alexander Ruthven stepped out into the corridor through the little arched door of the antechamber, watching the flight of the young woman and the prince. Her cries of "Mujhe bachao!" — Save me! echoed helplessly through the corridors. The Scotsman told himself that he was only a hired mercenary, a soldier of fortune. The plight of conquered women was no concern of his. Yet her cries were strangely similar to the ones he remembered hearing twelve years ago, after the battle of Culloden, when his sister Deirdre was dragged out of their house and raped by English soldiers.

"Mujhe bachao!" screamed the girl in one last despairing cry. Then Ruthven heard the sound of ripping silk. Reluctantly, yet swiftly, he ran down the maze of corridors to see Miran fling down the semi-naked figure on the marble floor and collapse over her inert body.

With one clenched fist, Ruthven struck the prince's jaw, stunning him. With another blow, Miran toppled over and lay unconscious next to the terrified but dazed Shirin Bano.

"Get up! Disappear! Your life is forfeit!" Alexander Ruthven tersely commanded the young lady.

"Go where?" she whimpered, rising, drawing her torn tunic over her bare breasts.

It was the first time in many years that Alexander Ruthven had seen a naked woman. In fact, not since that day when he set sail from Marseilles three years ago. And never had he seen a woman so clean or comely. The sight of her small round breasts, the rounded arms and willowy waist stirred his blood. He had not experienced desire until now.

Prince Miran stirred and moaned. Alarmed, Shirin Bano clutched Ruthven's arm. "Help me to escape, foreigner, and I will repay you with rare jewels!"

Ruthven grasped the girl's hand and ran down the corridor until they came to the unguarded door through which he had entered. He did not stop running until they were out of the palace grounds and into the hot, starlit darkness. Shirin Bano's breath came in ragged gasps when they stopped before a country lane.

"Come with me," Ruthven said brusquely. "I will present you before one of my officers and secure your protection."

"Will ... the English protect me? I am of ... Siraj-ud-doula's family," the girl asked numbly.

"My seniors need not know that. Don't speak. I shall speak on your behalf."

Alexander Ruthven led Shirin Bano to the camp of the East India Company, now lit by flaring torches and bonfires. Rain fell intermittently, cooling the fragrant, humid night. Ruthven strode ahead of the young woman, not exchanging a single word, while she, dazed, bewildered and afraid, half ran to keep pace with his long-legged strides.

"Is Major Lawrence here?" Ruthven asked a sepoy, stopping before a tent.

"Aye. Awaiting the Colonel Bahadur Saheb," the Indian sepoy replied.

"Tell him . . . Lieutenant Alexander Ruthven seeks an interview."

"Go in, Saheb. The major is ... relaxing."

Hesitantly, Ruthven entered and greeted the intrepid Major Lawrence who had fought the French in South India before accompanying Clive to Bengal. He listened to Ruthven's version of the episode, of how he had been strolling in the palace grounds when this young lady rushed out, pursued by a courtier. Major Lawrence listened with an understanding smile, as his eyes took in the comely woman before him. Ruthven sensed his attitude and improvised again.

"The courtier is one of Siraj-ud-doula's followers. Can we not give this lady protection from such a person?"

Major Lawrence no longer smiled. "Yes, of course. But where could she stay? Surely not in this camp!"

Alexander Ruthven turned to Shirin Bano and asked her the same question in broken Urdu. She hesitated a moment before replying.

"Allow me to hide in the dowager Begum's house. She ... did not approve of her son ... and will look after me ... especially if the Major Saheb recommends."

There was something in her manner which made the major scrutinise her more closely. Was it her air of self-assurance and hauteur? he wondered. "Very well, we will have you escorted to Amina Begum's house. Do not leave until ... things settle down." He turned to Ruthven. "You may escort her to the Begum's home. Take a few sepoys with you."

Amina Begum had foreseen the tragic events which had overtaken her son. As astute in statecraft as her father Alivardi Khan had been, she had urged Siraj-ud-doula to avoid confrontation with the English while building up the strength of his army with the French. She had interceded with her son on behalf of the East India Company several times. Now, even when Siraj-ud-doula was deposed, Amina Begum remained unmolested. It was to the security of her home that Shirin Bano fled.

At the gate of the Begum's mansion, now guarded by East India Company sepoys, Shirin Bano regarded Alexander Ruthven with a proud, wilful expression. "I am deep in your debt, Officer. Will you meet me again so that I may repay you ...?" she asked.

Ruthven smiled. "Certainly, Bano," he replied.

The young woman paused before continuing. "They say the firingi male is gallant to womenfolk. I thought that you had rescued me from Miran Beg out of a sense of chivalry."

Alexander Ruthven stared at the haughty noblewoman. Her opaque grey eyes were cold, and seemed to have a separate existence from the rosebud mouth and long nose. His glance moved downwards to her pale, slender neck, and the embroidered dress which had been torn across her firm breasts. He remembered the sudden flaring of desire at the sight of her flesh and the anguish of her cries, reminding him of Deirdre. But the intervening twelve years had taught him the religion of self-preservation.

"No, lady," he said with a sardonic smile, "it was, I think, the promise of jewels that prompted me to help you. So I shall come to collect my dues when you are ready to receive me. Good night."

Astonished and troubled, Shirin Bano watched him go. She was certain she had seen a tremor of desire in his eyes when she pleaded for help. "Apparently, I do not know how the firingi reacts," she thought. "Maybe they are more ardent about gold than they are about a woman's charm."

Alexander Ruthven returned to camp, immersed in his thoughts. The young Bano had, despite her coldness, excited his imagination.

Two days later, Murshidabad was restless with news of Siraj-ud-doula's capture and return. The fakir had sent word to Prince Miran whose men had swiftly ridden to the town of Rajmahal on whose outskirts the deposed nawab had sought shelter in the house of the fakir. Siraj-ud-doula had been brought under cover of darkness to the capital — unkempt, wounded and almost insane with rage and despair. People did not see him but they heard of his plight.

Though he had been a cruel and capricious ruler, they could not help but pity his wretched condition.

In the palace of Hazar Duari, the new nawab Mir Jafar held frantic consultations with his courtiers. The older noblemen who had served Alivardi Khan were reluctant to kill his grandson who had been entrusted to their care. But Miran Beg was stubborn. "Spare the fugitive, Siraj-ud-doula and he will continue to depose you, Your Majesty," the prince warned his father.

"The former nawab is now a prisoner in chains," an elderly aristocrat reminded Miran Beg. "How can he depose Mir Jafar?"

"Yes ... but the French are nearby. Monsieur St. de Frais will not relinquish his hopes of leading the Bengal army. He will attempt to reorganise his men and put Siraj on the throne." He paused. "Why, even the English may take pity on him and let him retire somewhere. Who can foretell what may happen then?"

Quietly, behind closed doors, the new nawab approved the murder of his predecessor. Since no courtier or soldier would perform this supreme act of treachery (though they had been willing enough to defeat Siraj-ud-doula by betrayal), a professional executioner was found to strangle the crazed prisoner, in the very same dungeons which he himself had crowded with hapless prisoners.

In the afternoon, the corpse of the former nawab was flung across an elephant and paraded through the streets of Murshidabad. With its strange memory for events past, the elephant halted at the very place on the road where two years ago, it had seen the murder of a nobleman on Siraj-ud-doula's orders. The man had been the lover of Ghasita Begum — aunt of Siraj-ud-doula and sister to Amina Begum. As the elephant paused, drops of blood from the Nawab's dead body fell on the road.

As the procession passed the house of Amina Begum, she ran out weeping, forgetting the strict code of seclusion, and flung herself before the elephant.

Another heavily veiled figure rushed out, and dragged the bereaved mother away, muttering consolation. She stopped just once to glance at the group of East India Company officials watching the grim spectacle. Flinging aside her veil she cried, "You have had your sport. Now leave us to bury the dead." She turned and hurried inside.

The officials of the East India Company turned away, no longer interested in the spectacle. Only Alexander Ruthven continued to stand there, staring after the retreating figure of Shirin Bano. The elephant moved on, down the road lined with people on both sides. "The tyrant is dead!" some cried. "Long live Mir Jafar! Long live the Honourable Company Bahadur!" Alexander Ruthven wondered how deep ran the antagonism towards the deposed nawab. Had he been cruel enough to merit this inglorious end? Or had he been unlucky in his advisers who had betrayed him to the East India Company? And did the people of Bengal really prefer the veiled rule of the East India Company to that of their nawab?

Sitting in the house of Jagat Seth, the merchant banker who had conspired for the downfall of Siraj-ud-doula, Ishwar Chowdhury discussed the consequences of British victory. In a few weeks it had become evident that Mir Jafar was not very different from his predecessor. The same air of suspicion and intrigue, the same arbitrary methods of government had returned. Men whose loyalties were suspect had been assassinated by the new nawab. The kingdom of Bengal was unquiet with rumours and dissatisfaction. Many local zamindars and rajas were disturbed by the implications of Mir Jafar's victory and the eminence of the East India Company.

"Well, my friend?" Ishwar Chowdhury asked Jagat Seth. "Was it worthwhile?"

"We have rid ourselves of one nawab. We can depose this one too — if he should become arbitrary." Jagat Seth spoke gravely.

"Will Robert Clive remove his puppet?" Ishwar Chowdhury asked, helping himself to the sweetmeats and sherbets that were served by bare-chested servants in the lamplit reception hall of the banker's mansion. Sandalwood incense sticks burned to keep away the swarms of mosquitoes that flourished with the monsoon.

"Robert Clive needs us — his partners in trade. He will cooperate as long as we are useful. The East India Company is interested in trade. So are we."

Chowdhury waved away the mosquitoes singing around his ears. But if a day should come when our interests differ . . . or clash . . . the Company will not hesitate to dispossess us."

"We must take care not to clash. As it happens, Colonel Clive has asked me to proceed to Delhi to secure imperial approval of the accession of Mir Jafar as Viceroy of Bengal. At the moment we are interacting well." Jagat Seth's tone was calm and confident.

Ishwar Chowdhury laughed. "Did you not obtain the Emperor's approval for Siraj's accession too? Little good it did him!"

"Siraj opposed us. His example is before Mir Jafar," Jagat Seth snapped. "Let us hope it will serve as a lesson."

"For a wise man, Seth Saheb," Chowdhury said gently, "you have missed a point. It is Clive Saheb Bahadur who is asking for the emperor's approval — for Clive's appointment of the Emperor's viceroy. Is that not sheer impudence? I trust the Emperor Shah Alam will appreciate that it is the East India Company and Clive who now rule Bengal — and send empty homage to Delhi."

A slow smile appeared on Jagat Seth's harassed, plump face. "What difference does it make to us, Ishwar Babu, who rules Bengal? Did we benefit much under the Moghuls? We Hindus have always been persecuted by these infidels. The English want trade and we can give them that — and make some profit for ourselves. Let us follow Clive Saheb. He is a man of destiny."

The significance of Clive's victory at Plassey was acknowledged even in Delhi. Emperor Shah Alam, presiding over a phantom Moghul empire did not hesitate to confirm the English victory at Plassey by the imprimatur which gave legitimacy to Mir Jafar — an imperial firman. If the emperor regarded Clive's letter asking for recognition of Mir Jafar as an act of impertinence, he was in no position to say so. In fact, Shah Alam made Robert Clive a nobleman of the Moghul empire and conferred lofty titles on him. Jagat Seth returned triumphantly from Delhi, and his alliance with Robert Clive was cemented by the bonds of gold.

Bengal, "an inexhaustible fund of riches . . . with money and provisions in abundance" was now in English hands. Robert Clive realised that the future success of the East India Company in India depended on its power in Bengal and strove to keep it as the citadel. His difficulties now, however, were of a different kind. Until Plassey, the English presence had been commercial and concerned with profit and even plunder. Now Clive sought to give English presence the dignity that comes from political power. But men of the East India Company, who were accustomed to enrichment on private trade, were not willing to shed their old ways.

Alexander Ruthven had looked forward to the life of a private trader. The desire had lured him like a magnet from the shabby attic in Marseilles to journey to India for nine months, across unknown and interminable waters. As the boats carrying gold from Siraj-ud-doula's treasury sailed down the swollen river to Calcutta, young Ruthven remembered the journey. And his past.

Ironically, he had heard about India from a French sailor in Marseilles where he worked. They spoke of Dupleix, the great French general and head of the French Company in India, who strove to make India a part of France, and of the riches that awaited whoever conquered India. Young Alexander was not lured so much by the fabled wealth as by the prospect of liberation from his dreary work as a clerk in a warehouse near the dock.

Alexander's father, James, had been a staunch Jacobite. His devotion to the cause of Charles Edward Stuart or Bonnie Prince Charlie ultimately led to his death and to the flight of his widow and children to France. To support the survivors of the family, Alexander had begun to work at sixteen. His wages were barely enough to keep body and soul together. India seemed the answer to his poverty and misery. Against his mother's advice and ignoring her pleading, eighteen-year-old Alexander left Marseilles and set sail for London. There he went to the office of the East India Company at Leadenhall Street and enrolled as a sergeant in the East India Company army. India House, as the building was called, had a partiality for young Scots who had always proved to be hardier than the others. Ruthven concealed the fact of his six years' exile in France and his father's participation in the Jacobite Uprising of 1945.

The East Indiaman, with its great masts, cargo and guns along the ship's bulwark, set sail from Gravesend. Merchants muffled in cloaks and mufflers boarded the ship along with grizzled sailors sporting rings on their ears. Lastly came the autocratic captain who would be the arbiter of their destiny for many months.

In a few days the ship landed at Marseilles where the passengers eagerly alighted to purchase fashionable French clothes. Ruthven laughed when be saw them duped by French tailors who sold them high-waisted coats, short kilt-like skirts, breeches of scarlet satin, waistcoats hung with spangled lace and absurd hats. "The latest from Versailles," the sartorial experts informed the credulous customers. "Now for you, Mademoiselle, how about a fantastic hat, designed by Madame de Pompadour? And you Madame, you must wear tiers of side curls to hide your wispy hair!"

Alexander had hurried along the steep hilly road, which led to the tall, narrow house in which the surviving Ruthvens lived. Beatrice, the mother, embraced her son and wept. "Don't go," she begged, "I cannot survive without you!"

"Hush Mama! You must survive — for Alistair and Fiona's sake — even for Deirdre, should she ever need you. I will return Mama, to keep you in comfort and educate the little ones. Truly I will! You must believe in me!"

"Oh my darling boy, I want nothing but to keep you three close," Beatrice sobbed. "I have lost enough already."

Alexander gently released himself from her arms. "I want a great deal, Mama," he said grimly. "I want to avenge Papa's murder and Dierdre's shame. I want to keep you in style ... and give Fiona and Alistair everything they could want. Yes ... I want a great deal .... and I mean to have it!"

Beatrice Ruthven gazed, astonished, at her son. Terror sparkled in her blue-green eyes. "Why, child, you are mad! How can you do all this?"

The blue-green eyes of her son were strangely unchildlike as they gazed back at her, calm but intense. "I will, Mama. In a few years, I will be back ... I promise you!"

Two days later, after tearful farewells, Alexander Ruthven stepped out into the autumn afternoon as church bells chimed the vesper hour. He looked around him, over the tiled rooftops, the steeples of churches and monasteries, and towards the blue Mediterranean. Abruptly he ran down the hill, never once pausing to look back.

As the East Indiaman moved into the Mediterranean, heading for Madeira, gulls hovered over the great white sails swelling in the wind. The rigging seemed to be singing. Alexander Ruthven stood on the deck, watching the familiar coast of France fade into the violet evening sky. He had never felt more alone. Yet there was considerable merriment on board. He soon joined his fellow passengers for dinner in the second deck. Loyal toasts to George II were drunk. Captain Digby noticed that the young East India Company cadet instead of drinking the toast merely touched the glass to his lips. Later, he joined the others for coffee and tea in the "round house". At night, while the passengers danced on the upper deck or roistered in the "round house", Alexander learnt to play whist, faro and backgammon.

He was always correct, always courteous, but never intimate or even cordial. Indeed, sometimes he preferred the noise and discomfort of his cabin in the lower deck where he taught himself Persian, the official language of Moghul India.

As the ship left Madeira and then the Azores, a sense of isolation settled over the passengers. The western coast of Africa was inhospitable and uncharted. The isolation turned into hopelessness when passengers and sailors developed scurvy because of the daily diet of salted beef. Alexander watched grimly as bodies of the dead were cast into the sea.

He still remembered the relief it had been to land in the Cape of Good Hope where fresh vegetables, fruits, milk and eggs had been available. He remembered too how he had been struck by the austerity of the Dutch settlers and their subjugation of the "kafirs".

The journey over the Indian Ocean was fraught with dangers of pirates and privateers. Whenever an unidentified ship was sighted, the women and children were hastily hustled below deck. Ruthven's journey, however, was singularly uneventful. When his ship anchored in the mouth of the Hughli, Alexander felt an overwhelming emptiness as he gazed at the wild new landscape of the Bengal delta. It was almost with a sense of homecoming that he arrived at Fort William to take his place among the other humble soldiers of the army of the East India Company.

Now, sitting in his tent, preparing for the march back to Fort William, Alexander Ruthven realised with horror that three years had passed and he had saved hardly enough to pay for his journey back home. The prospect of an interminable existence as lieutenant or captain in the 23rd Bengal Native Infantry was bleak. Yet he had found no alternative.

"A message for you, Saheb," a little man murmured, bowing low.

Alexander stared at the Muslim emissary. "A message?" he asked.

The emissary carefully brought out a paper scroll from his tunic. "The lady Shirin has sent this, Saheb."

Perplexed, Ruthven took the scroll and held it before the candles. With some effort he read the message in Persian, requesting him to meet her at a particular place. He looked at the emissary. "Is this a ruse? Why does Shirin Bano wish to see me?"

The old man bowed. "She is in trouble, Saheb, and needs your help. If you will trust me, I shall lead you to the place where she waits."

Alexander Ruthven hesitated. "Why should she not be at Amina Begum's place? Our Company sepoys have been posted on duty there."

"Shirin Bano will explain. Can you not trust her word?"

Alexander Ruthven shook his head. Trust was a mirage, easily lost.

"Then I will not trouble you further." As the old man turned away slowly, Ruthven said impatiently, "Very well, take me to her ... but if this is a ruse, your head is forfeit. He picked up a pistol for good measure and followed the old man into the stormy night. Procuring a horse, Ruthven rode with the emissary towards Moti Jhil, a moated palace some miles out of Murshidabad where Siraj-ud-doula's aunt had once fled with her lover. The palace was silhouetted darkly against the lightning-streaked, monsoon sky.

There now, Shirin Bano waited, a black burqua hiding her rich clothes. The veil was lifted over her pale, imperious face. "So you came, Saheb. I didn't think you would."

Alexander Ruthven smiled wryly. "You were certain of my coming, Bano. Otherwise you would not come so far to await me."

Shirin Bano smiled now. "True ... I knew you would not ignore my appeal. Come inside .... it will rain again."

The hall was large and elegantly furnished, though dust lay thickly over the carpets and divans. Shirin Bano placed a brass oil lamp on a carved table and stared at it for a long moment. "Help me to escape, Saheb," she said finally, looking up at Ruthven.

"Escape? From Murshidabad?" he asked, suddenly tense.

"Yes ... and from Miran Beg. He ... wishes to take me as a ... concubine."

"Is it not a predictable fate for ladies of the Moghul court?" Ruthven asked lightly.

The opaque, grey eyes glittered in the pale haughty face. "You dare speak lightly because you find me in this plight. Do you know my past?"

Alexander Ruthven shrugged his shoulders. "No," he muttered impatiently.

"Then let me tell you. My mother is a kinswoman of the emperor and I was to have married Shaukat Jung ..."

"Shaukat Jung?" Ruthven looked surprised, "Was he not a cousin of Siraj-ud-doula and a rival for the throne?"

Shirin Bano nodded. "Yes. He almost became the nawab ... but Siraj had him murdered when their aunt Ghasita Begum took up Shaukat's cause." Shirin paused, and her cold eyes lit up briefly. "We used to come here ... and plan our future with Ghasita." She turned to Ruthven abruptly. "You realise, don't you, that I, who could have been Begum of Bengal, cannot be a sport for that beast Miran Beg! Today I would have been a queen if my kismet had been different!"

"And what would you have done to Begum Lutfinissa?" Alexander asked dryly.

Shirin Bano shrugged her shoulders. "I'd be kind to her ..."

"As she has been kind to you," Ruthven retorted coldly.

"Lutfinissa needed me ... as an ally. I was her friend. Her life was not easy with Siraj."

"Why does she then not marry Miran Beg and secure her future?" Ruthven asked.

"Because she is a fool! The idiot lights candles by Siraj's grave and spurns Miran's overtures with reckless remarks like 'one who has mounted a horse cannot ride a donkey'."

Ruthven smiled. "Yes, she is a fool," he murmured, the irony in his voice lost on the young woman. Then he said briefly. "Well, lady, why did you summon me here?"

Shirin Bano regarded him with her opaque, inscrutable eyes. "Take me to Calcutta with you."

"To Calcutta?" Ruthven laughed derisively. "You are mad. How can I take you, a member of the royal household, with me, a soldier of the East India Company? Why, Miran Beg would ensure my dismissal!"

"Make me your wife. No one can interfere then." Ruthven stared at Shirin, speechless.

"I have a fortune in jewels... a portion of what Ghasita Begum took from the state treasury before coming here to Moti Jhil. It is all here . . . hidden under the pillars. Take me as your wife and it will all be yours."

Alexander Ruthven shook his head. "Impossible!" he muttered and turned to go when Shirin grasped his arm. "Listen," she said urgently. "You need not be a soldier — risking your life. My wealth will bring you more — as a trader. I know many merchants who will help. My family members in Oudh and Delhi will be your allies."

"You are mad," Ruthven retorted, staring at the woman.

"Wait," Shirin said and drew out from the folds of her burqua, a handful of gold mohurs and cut diamonds. "These are mine ... and I have many more! Miran Beg wants these for his coffers. But I would rather die than relinquish this. Even Siraj-ud-doula could not lay his hands on them.!"

"Show me more," Ruthven said. "I wish to see for myself."

Shirin's eyes narrowed. "You doubt my words?"

Ruthven nodded. "I trust only my own eyes."

"Come then," she said coldly and led him to a small opening in a corridor. Slowly, she prised out a stone and drew out a casket. Glancing at him, she opened the lid. Ruthven drew in a breath of amazement, and then met the challenge in her eyes.

"A small fortune," he muttered to himself. "To begin life ... to buy boats and hire men for trading ... to keep Mama and Fiona in comfort ... to live in comfort ..." He turned to her. "Why are you offering me this?" he asked. "Why not to one of your own kinsmen?"

"No kinsman will defy Mir Jafar and his evil son ... but you ... a foreigner ... you are not afraid."

Alexander Ruthven looked around him, at the stormy twilight, and the dark lowering clouds. His regiment was soon to leave for Calcutta. He had very little time to decide.

"Miran Beg will soon be here," Shirin said dully. "You must decide quickly."

"Come then," he heard himself say, "hide in the camp until we are ready to go. I will arrange for your safe travel."

Shirin Bano tucked the heavy casket in the folds of her burqua and glanced at him sombrely. "It is settled then?"

Alexander Ruthven nodded.

"Insh 'allah," Shirin Bano murmured, following the Redcoat out of the deserted mansion and into the stormy night.

3

The Agent of Bishnupur

A furious monsoon storm lashed Calcutta. It battered violently on the closed window panes of the little room atop a house in Alipur where a Muslim agent of the East India Company lived. Several candles spluttered in the stray gusts of wind that reached their feeble flames but still managed to illumine the satin quilt strewn with jasmines. Alexander Ruthven stared at the singular nuptial couch and then at his bride with a sense of unreality. Shirin Bano sat on the floor, her voluminous gharara revealing little of her slim, taut body, a gauzy veil covering the dark hair. Several necklaces of pearls and diamonds glittered at her throat.

Sensing his unease, Shirin whispered, "I am as afraid as you are ... but together ... we need not be afraid. We might even ... prosper."

She put into words the ambition and insecurity that had brought two such unlikely people into matrimony. Had there been no English victory at Plassey, the Muslim noblewoman would have adjusted to or perished in the new regime. But Clive's pre-eminence meant safety with a Company official. A safety she had chosen. Alexander Ruthven, seeing no end to the bleak and dreary existence of a petty officer, had gambled too on an alliance with Shirin Bano.

None of these considerations, however, could ease the tension of their first encounter. Alexander had been to the houses of pleasure that had mushroomed around Fort William, snatching relief, if not pleasure, from the shrill, brassy females who clamoured there. None of them had possessed Shirin's inbred composure and lightly veiled hauteur that chilled him now.

"Yes," he murmured, sitting down on the thick satin quilt spread on the stone floor, and pulling off his boots and then the only decent evening coat he possessed. Pale but composed, Shirin began to unpin her coiled hair. A gust of wind blew out the candles, leaving the room in darkness. For a while neither spoke or moved. Then, Ruthven knelt and drew his bride down on the quilt. They groped in the jasmine-scented darkness until instinct and a desolate hunger gave them sight and touch, quickening their dormant desires. There was no need for a display of tenderness — for neither felt it — but they relied on a fugitive courtliness to give them time to prepare for pain and pleasure. The solitary window swung open admitting a spray of rain and the scent of wet earth as Alexander Ruthven made Shirin Bano his wife.

She woke at first light to stare at the tall, sinewy figure stretched out beside her. A novel sensation of passion stirred within her, and with it a craving to give her body to him once more. The rough and hesitant coupling had unleashed unknown hungers buried deep within. Tentatively, she placed a hand on his head of flaming hair, and scrutinised the long high-bridged nose and thin, wide lips. Her touch disturbed his slumber. Opening his eyes slowly, Ruthven saw her face flushed by desire.

"Still afraid?" he asked.

She shook her head. "A little ... uncertain."

"So am I," he admitted, smiling ruefully but drawing her down towards him once more, taking his pleasure hurriedly while the Moghul noblewoman blinked back tears of mortification at his lack of sentiment.

The days that followed were crowded with events. Alexander was, despite his stubborn detachment, caught up in the excitement and speculation that followed Plassey, In the officers' mess at Fort William, the men talked of Clive's efforts to restore normal trade, and the haggling over prize money or compensation to the conspirators: £400,000 to the army and navy, £150,000 to the Select Committee of Six, £50,000 to the members of the Council. Bengal seemed like a golden goose, ready for picking. The officials of the Company discussed the prospects of making quick fortunes as their superiors had done, by receiving gifts from those in need of Company favours. They talked also of participation in private trade, and of taking advantage of the unlimited credit available to Company officials.

"Colonel Clive has got a jagir worth £30,000 a year," one officer said, "in addition to the £234,000 already taken. Can we lieutenants and captains not expect half that?"

Laughter greeted the officer's remarks. "Indeed we can!" responded another. "I have a preference for the factory at Patna."

"And I for the residency of Murshidabad!" declared another.

More laughter followed as drink loosened tongues and banished inhibitions. "And I for the residency of Murshidabad!" retorted another.

Glasses clinked in more toasts amidst raucous laughter. Alexander Ruthven listened, barely touching the wine glass to his lips when toasts were drunk to King George of England, Scotland, Ireland and Hanover. "They are drunk with triumph and a new sense of power," he thought soberly. "They are no longer mere traders but have become arbiters of politics. Well, I too shall make use of the English victory to my own purpose."

Shirin Bano listened to his descriptions of the officers' celebrations. Despite her fragile appearance, he grew to recognise the steely woman, notwithstanding the frilly gharara and lacy veils, who could discuss trade and politics with surprising facility. He was amazed by her knowledge of the procedures for obtaining a favour. "Take Karim Beg with you," she advised, pulling out a sizeable ring from a thin, fair hand and holding it up to the flames of several candles. "He will take you to the officer who is in charge of giving agencies. Ask for Bishnupur. It is a rich place."

Ruthven stared at her, bewildered. "Agency? But I am not a

trader ... I may have to go somewhere else if the army moves!"

Her grey eyes were cold. "I crave indulgence, Janab. I presumed that you had finished with the life of an impecunious soldier."

"Have I?" he asked quietly, remembering his resolve to return laden with riches to Marseilles.

"Was not that the reason you married me?" she asked, her voice toneless. He glanced at her, remembering the haze of numbness, even incomprehension which had led him to acquiesce in the proposals of this imperious woman. Had it been the lure of jewels that had driven him into this unknown journey with her?

"I ... am still uncertain of what I wish to do," Ruthven said, parrying her question, which could have been answered only by sacrificing either truth or courtesy.

Shirin's rosebud mouth tightened. "Take this ring," she said solemnly. "It will ease the way."

And so it did. Karim Beg guided him through the tortuous procedures but in the end he received the agency of Bishnupur for private trade, offering the sizeable ruby as homage to the senior Company official who gave him the dastak, the certificate that would enable him to trade, both for the Company as well as on his own account. Shirin Bano packed once more but this time she did not have to hide her casket inside trunks full of old vessels and clothes. This time she rode in a litter drawn by two horses while her husband rode beside her on a newly purchased Arab steed. Behind them came a cart drawn by bullocks, carrying their belongings over the fertile land from Calcutta to the banks of the sacred Bhagirathi, a tributary of the Ganges that flowed across Bengal until it reached the sea.

The agent's house was a modest rambling bungalow set on a flat terrain bordered by a cluster of shirish trees whose filigree of leaves stirred with the slightest breeze. It had been built by the Company almost half a century earlier, at the time of Job Charnock, when textiles had been the main industry of Bengal. The architectural vogues of an England ruled by a Dutchman had thus found their way to this busy Bengali village on the banks of the Ganges.

In the months that followed, Clive was busy restraining Mir Jafar's greed which stirred discontent of the populace. The Dutch at Chinsurah watched for a good opportunity to intervene while the English traders took full advantage of the troubled time.

The traders of the East India Company found unlimited opportunities for private commerce to plump their purses. That it would eventually bankrupt the Company troubled them little. Thus they traded duty free while Indian merchants had to pay 40 per cent ad valorem.

Alexander Ruthven lost little time joining the fray, as the accredited agent of the Company at Bishnupur.

Bishnupur was a prosperous centre of textile manufacture, rice, tobacco and the saltpetre so prized by Europeans for making gun-powder. The hinterland provided betel nuts, sugarcane and coconuts. The new agent's trading took him across Bengal — from Dacca, near the confluence of the mighty Meghna and Padma, to the arid regions of Birbhum. He bought cheap and sold dear, mapping a sizeable profit each time. The dastak from the Company gave him the right which his ubiquitous gomasthas, clerks, enforced.

Across the river was the famed town of Shantipur, the centre of fine cloth weaving as well as cultural activities. Further north was the more celebrated town of Nabadwip, where the great saint Chaitanya had revived Hinduism reeling under the onslaught of Afghan proselytisers in the fourteenth century. South of Shantipur was the rich village of Mayurganj where Alexander Ruthven went one summer day in 1859.

Riding over the sun-hardened ground, smarting under the harsh glare, he glanced around at the verdant landscape. Clusters of thatched cottages stood behind vast expanses of paddy fields broken by patches of cotton and sugarcane. Beyond stood bamboo groves which provided cane.

Upon reaching the village, he dismounted and turned to glance at his sepoys and gomasthas. "The village is quiet," he observed. "Have we arrived on a feast day?"

"They have gone indoors, Saheb ... to avoid us. But we will win them over. After all, they will have to buy opium and salt, tobacco and betel nuts."

Ruthven looked around the silent village. "Perhaps they resent paying higher prices than ..."

"Sir! Please! Let us not consider that again. The country traders could not have charged less!" Pyarelal was indignant. "Let us go to the headman's house. He will summon those who wish to trade."

Meanwhile, the rough sepoys went around, knocking on a door here, shouting there, to drum up business for their firingi master. The villagers came, reluctant and uneasy, scanning with anxious eyes the Company's ubiquitous traders.

"We have nothing to sell," their spokesman said. "There was problem in shipment of our sugar and rice. The barge carrying them was waylaid by dacoits ... so we lost our money. We can neither buy nor sell."

Ruthven shook his head. "My information is that this village is rich in sugar and rice. We will buy these from you ... and you can buy from us the much-awaited opium."

"At what price?" one villager cried. "You sell us opium three times dearer than what our own merchants sell it! We will have no traffic with you!"

Ruthven nodded slowly. "Very well. If you don't sell rice and sugar, we will go elsewhere. But no one from our Company will buy your products either."

The villagers were adamant. So was Alexander Ruthven. He shrugged and mounted his Arab steed, and nodded once more to the sepoys. They nodded in acquiescence. As Ruthven moved away, under the shelter of a banian tree, the sepoys fell upon the villagers with their matchlocks, delivering a blow here, a cuff there, battering down the doors of fragile warehouses where the precious rice and sugarcane was stored. Bullock carts were waiting to carry away the commodities — to be sold to areas deficit in rice and sugar at twice the price of what country traders charged. When the menfolk physically resisted the loading of their produce on the carts, Pyarelal asked one of the sepoys to fire in the air. This action had the desired effect. The villagers hurriedly dispersed. In the ensuing silence, Pyarelal announced the price he was willing to pay for the rice and sugar. It was one-third of the market rate. Protests were ineffectual and had been made before. Seeing no alternative, the villagers came forward to accept the pittance for their summer crop.

The evening shadows had lengthened over the village pond and rice fields when Alexander Ruthven set off to camp for the night in a nearby serai. He was well satisfied with Pyarelal's performance for the day. He was riding along, deep in thought, when his path was barred by a group of men. At their head was a youth of not more than sixteen mounted on a white horse. Alexander wondered why the face was familiar. He had seen that straight nose, wide, heavy-lidded eyes, and compressed, sensual mouth somewhere else.

"Alexander Ruthven?" the youth asked brusquely. Alexander nodded, eyes narrowing in a flicker of irritation. "Why are you obstructing my way?"

The youth sat erect on his horse. "I want to know why your gomasthas molested my father's tenants?"

A slow smile lightened Ruthven's sombre face.

"Molested?" he echoed. "But I only traded with them."

The youth's pale olive face flared into red.

"These are sad times when dacoity masquerades as trade!"

Colour suffused Ruthven's face. His right hand went ostensibly to the pistol at his belt. "Choose your words with care, boy," he said.

"Listen, firingi," the youth replied, "my father owns this village. He is the zamindar of Mayurganj. I say what I like. Our Nawab may be Clive's puppet, but my father is still free!"

"Indeed?" Ruthven asked, raising an eyebrow. "You surprise me. I thought Clive owned all of them."

The youth brought out a pistol from the belt of his dhoti. "Don't come here again, Ruthven, if you care for your life. Mayurganj will not be your loot as long as the Chowdhurys are here. Dastak or not, you shall not rob our tenants."

Ruthven stared at the boy, for he was not much more than that. Despite a momentary fury, he felt a grudging respect for the stripling who had dared to defend his land. It brought to mind his own words to the English soldiers who had poured into his village after Culloden. He smiled. "Well, young Chowdhury, how will you guard your estate each time a Company trader comes?"

"I shall continue to do so — somehow or other,"

Alexander Ruthven shook his head. "You will not succeed. The Company has given us the right to trade freely." His blue eyes swept over the youth appraisingly and then flicking the reins of his horse, Ruthven urged it into a trot.

Indrajit Chowdhury watched him go. "Robbers and dupes!" he muttered under his breath. "Did my father and his friends not realise what the outcome of their conspiracy would lead to? Did they mount a tiger believing it was an ox?"

The tenants looked up at their lord's son, so unlike his placid, devious sire. They often wondered if it was the boy's mother who had transmitted some hidden fire to her child. "Go home, little lord," an elderly villager said. "These firingis will go also — as others have gone."

"After they have plundered us — like the others?" Indrajit retorted.

"Yes, that too, after they have had their fill. But we will remain forever, on our dear land near our holy river."

Twilight was falling as Indrajit glanced over at the sacred Bhagirathi, on whose calm bosom glided slender fishing boats as well as ships of the Company. "No, it must not continue like that. This time, it must be different," he said as he slowly turned homewards.

The serai had been constructed by a long dead ruler — Sher Shah — an Indian prince who had tried to nip the Moghul empire in the bud. He had built the Grand Trunk Road to link central, eastern and northern India. The serai at Goalpara was one of the taverns along this road. The place where once Moghul, Pathan and

Hindu traders and officials had halted for the night was now the meeting place of East India Company officials traversing Bengal for trade.

Alexander Ruthven greeted his fellow travellers with a nod. Even now, in the midst of hectic commercial activity, he kept aloof from the English officials of the Company. Tonight, as lanterns were lit and tables spread with colourful cloths, the conversation turned to the difficulties of trade.

"I hear Ellis has taught them a lesson," one official remarked.

"Indeed he has!" replied his companion. "We ought to emulate him. Can you stomach such insolence? The village chief threatened Ellis that he would be reported to the Nawab!" The man laughed.

"And what did the Nawab do?" asked his companion, also laughing.

"Actually, Mir Jafar made some sort of protest, I believe. Said he was losing revenues and therefore couldn't pay his dues to the Company and Clive. But of course nothing was done. When Ellis met the Nawab's officers at Kasipur he defied him — openly."

"So we can expect to be left alone now?" asked the other.

"I think so." He looked at Ruthven sitting on a low stool, while a servant poured him a drink in a pewter mug.

"How have you fared, Sir?"

"Satisfactorily," came Ruthven's laconic reply.

After a few more unsuccessful overtures, the Company official did not pursue further conversation with the taciturn Scotsman but turned back to his eager companion.

"We may have trouble again. It seems Colonel Clive is dissatisfied with nawab Mir Jafar's delay in settling dues to the English."

"Clive would not tamper with so complacent an ally. After all he made Mir Jafar the nawab."

"Let us see."

Supper — a tasty meal of rice, mutton and country fowl — was served by the caretakers of the serai while the servants of the Company officials poured out wine from bottles immersed in water.

Ruthven ate, listened to the conversation of the other travellers and then turned in for the night. He would have to rise early to reach home before the heat became too oppressive. The servants had set up his tent in the serai courtyard and built a small fire to keep off wild animals. His six sepoys reposed on their straw mats, chatais, matchlocks ready for any eventuality. Ruthven lay down, face turned upwards to the clear summer sky. A vague uneasiness stirred within him, keeping him awake. Yet he could not pinpoint the cause of this sudden restive mood. It was as if there was some discord within himself, but he did not know whence it sprang. "That boy ..." Ruthven mused. "Why has he affected me thus? Why must he stir my memories ... and certitude?"

Jackals howled in the nearby bamboo thickets, echoed by village dogs. An owl sitting on a tree overhead, hooted. Ruthven tossed and turned, trying to keep his memories at bay. Finally, he dropped off to sleep lulled by a light night breeze.

By noon he was back home in Bishnupur.

Alexander dismounted and paused for a while, staring at his house. He was not yet accustomed to the altered circumstances of his life. The impulsive decision taken at the moated palace near Murshidabad seemed, in retrospect, judicious and profitable. Yet it had left him dazed, as if the will to shape his own destiny had been taken from his hands and passed on to another. He recalled the hasty ride from Moti Jhil to the British encampment in Murshidabad and the hurried, almost frantic arrangements to meet Shirin Bano in Calcutta. Shirin Bano had gone separately to the capital dressed as a man, accompanied by two old retainers. With her went a casket of jewels set comfortably in a trunk filled with old clothes, pots and pans, quilts and shawls so that an impatient robber might reflect before proceeding further with the search. Alexander reached Calcutta ten days later with his regiment — the 23rd Native Bengal Infantry — and they met at the house of Karim Khan, an adherent of Shirin's family, to be married.

Pausing now before his bungalow, Ruthven then walked slowly towards the door. In two years, the bungalow had been repainted and repaired, the vigorous mildew of the monsoons removed, but it still looked shabby. What compensated for the drabness of the house was the luxuriance of the garden, its wild exotic blooms and massive, ancient trees extending their shade over half the grounds.

Two servants hurried out to remove his boots and coat and take his pistol. Hot and dusty, he entered the large, cool room which served as the main bedchamber. There Shirin Bano sat awaiting him.

Two years had transformed the pale cameo of her face. Sunshine had never entered the royal zenana, thus making the women shadowy figures. Like a flower suddenly exposed to the sun, Shirin had wilted at first, losing the delicacy of skin and form, then the heritage of her Turkish-Afghan ancestors had taken over. Roughened by the harsh sunlight and the altered circumstances of her life, Shirin Bano took command of her household, and her husband's fortune.

She rose from the divan and nodded curtly to the waiting women in dismissal. "How was Mayurganj?" she asked quietly.

Alexander Ruthven never failed to marvel at her avid interest in his trading ventures. Sometimes he wondered if it was her compelling desire for wealth that drove him from one district to another, though at the same time he was aware that the determination to wrest a fortune had lain dormant within him for several years.

"It was profitable," he said. "The sale of rice and sugar in the western districts will provide a comfortable margin."

Shirin nodded thoughtfully. "Perhaps we can buy back my house ... sequestered by Mir Jafar's courtier ..."

Alexander Ruthven glanced at her, feeling a strange affinity to her: they both had the same determination to wrest back what had once been theirs.

"That may happen sooner than you think, Begum," he said quietly.

"How so?" she asked, suddenly alert.

"I hear ... that Colonel Clive is not happy with his protege ... Nawab Mir Jafar who has not fully settled his dues to the English."

A slow, cruel smile flitted across Shirin's statuesque face, "I am glad. I hope Mir Jafar is deposed. He deserves such a fate."

"Would Miran Beg make a better nawab?" he asked ironically.

The calm, mask-like face was suddenly troubled. "No ... that would be much worse! He would ... he would ..." she paused and then shook her head. Mastering her panic, she continued, "He could not do anything now ... could he? After all, I am the wife of an East India Company official ... Mistress Ruthven .... Is that not what I am called?"

Alexander laughed. For all her cynicism, Shirin Bano could often be very child-like. "I prefer to call you Begum ... it is more suitable to your person." Then he said quietly, "I do not think Miran Beg would dare molest you again ... he knows that the jewels are in my custody."

"Who would replace Mir Jafar?" Shirin asked anxiously.

Alexander shrugged. "Who knows? There are so many claimants." He paused to look at her intently, "If Prince Shaukat was alive ... he might have been chosen as Nawab. Though a brother of Siraj, he did not approve of the nawab. Isn't that so?" He watched her, waiting to see if the name of her once-betrothed would evoke pain and regret. If Prince Shaukat had been alive, he might have been nawab of Bengal and Shirin his Begum.

Shirin lowered her gaze at once, to shut out thoughts of what might have been. Yes, the prospect of being queen had once thrilled her ... until she had seen the fate of her kinswoman, the ill-starred Begum Lutfinissa, wife of Siraj-ud-doula. "Your servants are waiting ... to attend your bathing," she said, in subtle dismissal of her husband's conversational gambit.

Without a word, Ruthven went to the adjoining room where a servant waited with a set of fresh clothes, while another brought in buckets of water from the well. He divested himself of his dusty, sweat-stained clothes, allowing the servant to pour water on him. Another retainer appeared, to soap, scrub and massage the sunburnt flesh of the white saheb. Then a flurry of towels, and soon the trade agent of Bishnupur was ready to face the rigours of a hot afternoon.

Begum Ruthven, as Shirin liked to call herself, was at the

square table, where Alexander had his meals. As befitting a high-born Muslim, Begum Shirin did not eat with her husband but sat by his side, lightly veiled, while the khidmatgar, the butler, served the dishes brought in by the bawarchi, the cook. In the background stood the patient punkah-puller, negotiating with ropes the huge flaps of cotton that served as ceiling fans.

In the beginning, Alexander had remonstrated with the Moghul lady, asking her to dine with him but true to her upbringing, she refused. Only when he had eaten and gone to his study to look at his papers would she sit in her room and pick daintily with her fingers at whatever took her fancy. Despite her fragile exterior, Shirin kept a hawk's eye on the servants, curbing extravagance and exacting obedience more effectively than an Englishwoman could have done. Coming upon her reproving an errant retainer, Alexander Ruthven had often to compose his spontaneous urge to laugh.

Today, Shirin sat distracted, staring at the brass dishes oblivious to the servants, unaware even of their performance. She played nervously with her many rings and bracelets while Ruthven ate veal chops, roast pheasant and washed down curried lamb and rice with a bottle of warm claret. When the meal was over, he went to his study to calculate the profits of the transactions in Mayurganj and plan the sale of the purchased commodities in arid Birbhum.

It was late evening when Alexander returned to their bedchamber, after a vigorous ride by the verdant fields, ripe with rabi, the summer crop. Another bath was followed by a light supper of chicken cutlets, curried vegetables and rice, a sorbet of chilled, pulped mangoes, bowls of sharp-tasting jamuns and a bottle of Madeira. Thereafter, the little boy whom Shirin had trained to serve as hookah-bardar brought in the elaborate hookah — an invention of coiled pipes and water bowls for drawing in scented tobacco fumes. Alexander sat on a divan on the back veranda facing the river and addressed himself to this pleasant recreation.

The scent of aromatic tobacco and bubbling water filled the dark veranda. Not far away, the river Ganges, called the Hughli here, flowed slowly by on its way to Sagar Dwip, the majestic estuary where the great river met the sea. Dhoris and bajras sailed by, dark shadows against a starlit sky. From the servants' quarters nearby came the sound of hushed conversation and occasional laughter.

It was during this haunting hour that Alexander Ruthven wondered what he, a boy from the highlands of Scotland, a refugee of Marseilles, was doing in Bishnupur. Five years had passed and he was nowhere nearer to fulfilling his pledge to his mother. Letters had come — seven in all — telling him of his younger brother and sister and their life in Marseilles and then Paris where brother Alistair had acquired the post of tutor to a merchant's son. His mother had written that sister Fiona was a wayward girl who caused her great concern. "Not at all like my darling Deirdre whom we have lost forever. Sometimes I wonder if I should go to London and search for my child. Is she well? Is she alive? Oh Alex, my son, if only you could find her or get news of her! I cannot die without knowing what has become of my angel!"

Tonight, Alexander Ruthven remembered the anguish of the latest letter from home, which had taken eight months to reach him. "It is time I went back to them ... they need me. The meagre fortune I have got is enough. How long must I save and toil like this?"

"Have you gone to sleep here, Janab?" Shirin asked gently, using a Persian term of respect.

"What? Oh no ... I ... was thinking ... "

"Of what, Janab?" she asked.

"Of ... home ... and my family," he said sombrely. He did not wish to tell her now of his desire to see the beings dearest to his heart. Nevertheless, his words sobered her and put a distance between them.

Nodding slowly, she murmured. "Yes, it must be dreary for you to be here ... far from your native land and your family."

The poignancy in her tone made Alexander look up. In the darkness he could see only her shadowy form, the sequins on her odhni glinting like glow-worms. "I think the hookah has cooled. Let us go in."

"It is hot inside and the punkah-walla makes so much noise,"

Shirin replied.

"We shall send him away and open the lattices. Come, Begum, it is late." Suddenly, Alexander was afraid of his memories and his yearning for home which now often submerged him in anguished waves.

"I have something to tell you, Janab," Shirin murmured as she laid aside her finery. She was wearing a muslin chemise that revealed every part of her pale, slender, almost virginal body.

"Yes?" he asked, alerted by her tone. She sat at the edge of the bed, silent and motionless. He sat at the other end. "Well, Begum, I am waiting."

"I am ... with child."

It was not more than a whisper. Yet the words filled the room like an explosion. Alexander Ruthven sat as motionless as her, staring at her. "A child ..." he echoed at last. "My child."

Shirin rose and came timidly to him, all hauteur gone. The three candles in the Moradabad holder revealed the anguished uncertainty in her face. "Tell me you are glad, Janab," she whispered, kneeling before him.

Slowly, he lifted her back onto the bed, laying her down among the pillows and bolsters. "Of course I am glad, Shirin Begum! How could I be otherwise?" He paused. "I ... had begun to think that you ... were barren."

"Allah is merciful," she whispered. "I prayed for a child to ... make you come closer."

The long held back words were out. She had tried to suppress, even destroy, the passion that he had roused in her but it had only grown with his polite indifference. It had been an effort for her not to cry out for tenderness each time he took his pleasure and left her aching for more. She had feigned an indifference to match his loveless lust while in actuality a searing passion engulfed her.

Alexander bent his head towards her, regarding her face in the flickering candlelight. "Shirin ..." he said gravely, "our lives are irrevocably linked together now."

Her thin hands, aglitter with rings, reached up to his neck, drawing him close, tantalising him with hands that had learnt in the zenana how to please a man. Alexander allowed himself to be drawn into that whirlpool of delights, and when he had been satiated, he did not draw away but laid his head close to hers, his hand on the belly where his son grew.

"I was thinking of going home ... when you told me about our child," he confided.

Shirin forced herself to be calm though panic eddied around her. "Tell me about your home, Janab," she pleaded.

For the first time in many, many years, Alexander Ruthven reminisced about his home. And with the memories came the pain and anger that lay coiled deep within him.

He described his home near Inverness, a place of lakes and streams, where trout and salmon leapt, of the misted highlands where thistle and heather grew tenaciously over ancient rocks of the laird's sombre, massive castle amongst those peaks. He had been their protector and defender as well as their exploiter in the true feudal spirit. It was he again who had taken up the cause of Prince Charles Edward Stuart, or Bonnie Prince Charlie, when people tired of the Hanoverian usurpers on the. British throne.

The Stuart dynasty had rallied the people of Scotland from where they originated and had their followers in England as well. James Ruthven, Alexander's father had joined the cause of the dispossessed prince in the uprising of 1745, and had been wounded in the decisive battle of Culloden.

"I remember him returning home," Alexander reflected grimly. "Word of Scottish disaster had preceded him, accompanied by accounts of the atrocities perpetrated by the Duke of Cumberland, the butcher of Culloden. A strange stillness fell upon our village, as if in anticipation of the devastation that was to follow. My father was wounded, a hunted man, but he came to have a last look at my mother and us. She would not let him go and almost dragged him to the hayloft where she tended to him for several days."

Alexander Ruthven paused, as if struggling against apocalyptic visions of bloodthirsty Redcoats pouring into the rugged, tranquil highlands. Cumberland's men hunted down the rebels and arrested them on grounds of treason. Then they set fire to the cottages."

"Tell me ... what happened?" Shirin asked timidly, afraid of the expression on Ruthven's face.

"My father was shot for high treason. And my fourteen-year-old sister Deirdre was abducted by one of the officers — to provide sport for himself and his men. They did not even spare my poor mother. That was their idea of justice."

Alexander left the bed and stood by the window, staring into the dark gardens sloping down to the eternal river. Even after fourteen years, he could remember the torment and anguish of those days. Father dead. Mother violated. Sister outraged and abducted. Home set on fire. And then in the dead of night, leaving on a flat boat for France — to avoid more retribution at the hands of the triumphant Hanoverian supporters.

The widowed Beatrice Ruthven had landed in France with her three children, eleven-year-old Alexander, eight-year-old Alistair and four-year-old Fiona. They had roamed from place to place, supported at first by sympathisers of the Jacobite or Stuart cause, and then gradually left to fend for themselves. The lovely Beatrice, once a prosperous farmer's wife, now became a seamstress to support her family. In time, Alexander and Alistair took odd jobs to supplement the meagre family income. They learnt the meaning of poverty and humiliation.

Shirin left the bed now and laid her head against his chest. "Please, my lord," she murmured, "don't torment yourself with memories. Forget all that."

"Forget?" he shouted in the silence of the night. "I shall never forget! How dare you tell me to forget my dear ones."

Shirin stepped back, horrified. Not once in these two years had she heard this aloof and taciturn man raise his voice.

"I shall remember," he said through clenched teeth, "because if I forget, I cannot help them. I must go back and look after them ... and one day ... set the balance sheet right!"

"Yes ... of course," Shirin murmured anxiously, as fear tugged at her heart, "but till then, remember only the gentle things ... not the terrible ones."

Alexander sighed deeply, and turned to her. "Help me to forget ... for a while," he said gravely. "Help me to dream of glory and wealth ... and, perhaps, even a little happiness."

4

Heir and Heirlooms

Despite her joy at the forthcoming arrival of her long awaited child, a sense of unease gripped Begum Shirin Ruthven. She was now afraid that Alexander Ruthven might decide one day to return to his native land. There was, she felt, only one way to keep him and that was to urge him on in his quest for riches. "That was, after all, my reason for marrying him; to secure a promising future, to acquire wealth and power," she mused. She would not acknowledge to herself that she needed Ruthven to satisfy something more than just a desire for security. Raised in the cynical environs of a palace where fratricide and treachery were routine, Shirin refused to allow herself to believe in sentiments even when she felt them surge within her. She stayed in the orbit familiar to her: the world of intrigues and negotiations; of merchants and power brokers, using the arts she had learned under so capable a practitioner as the Princess Ghasita of Bengal.

Alexander Ruthven watched her with a detached curiosity, surprised by her competence to haggle and dissimulate. He watched with a kind of fascination too when she suddenly flung aside her veil in the midst of commercial negotiations to admonish a recalcitrant trader or clerk. As he saw her pore over accounts, and check inventories, he marvelled at her enthusiasm and was grateful for her assistance. She brought out a piece of jewellery now and then to tide over a lean period, pausing to gaze at the casket. Shirin held on to it as a link with the world she had left behind but which was truly hers. Though her father had been a rude soldier, her mother had been a descendant of an effete Moghul prince who had perished in one of the perpetual fratricidal orgies that plagued the Moghul court. Shirin's mother, Zobaida, had acquired a sautoir of pearls that had once embellished the throat of Empress Nur Jahan. When Shirin had shown them to Alexander, he had stared wide eyed at their blinding brilliance.

"This could buy me another barge for trading, a phaeton and pair and ..."

Shirin snapped the box shut. "These," she said brusquely, "will go to my son's wife ... perhaps a princess like Ghasita or one like Nur Jahan."

Alexander Ruthven regarded her with some surprise. "Despite her earthbound mind, she still dreams," he mused with a smile. Aloud, he said, "Do you not know what is happening to the Moghul power? The Emperor counts for little and Mir Jafar is shortly to be deposed. He has failed to pay his debts."

"Indeed?" Shirin asked grimly. "And who is to be his successor?"

"His son-in-law, Mir Kasim," Ruthven replied.

"So the poisoned cup returns to the lips of the one who made it," Shirin observed drily.

"Quite, and justice is usually done."

"Is it?" she asked harshly. "Siraj and Mir Jafar have paid for their sins but will Shaukat Jung come alive?"

Alexander Ruthven's jaws tightened. "Begum," he said, rising from the divan, "methinks you still hanker to be a queen! Or is it that you care for the dead prince?"

Shirin nodded, her grey eyes dull as glass. "Yes, I would like to be a queen, Janab. And I shall be one — someday. You, Janab, will bring me the crown."

Alexander Ruthven stared at his wife, bewildered. "Is she mad?" he wondered. "Or does her ambition have no bounds?"

News of Mir Jafar's deposition and the accession of his son-in-law, Mir Kasim, was a source of consternation in some quarters and of joy in others. The Hindu merchants who had sponsored the puppet nawab were now anxious, fearing that they too might find themselves out of favour.

Jagat Seth, however, was satisfied and celebrated his newest victory at his palatial mansion in Calcutta. As an ally of the East India Company, the great merchant naturally invited his foreign friends to dinner. In the few years of his intercourse with the firingis, Jagat Seth had observed their customs and habits and adopted their ways while entertaining British guests.

His Bengali guest, Ishwar Chowdhury, however, had not yet grown accustomed to the strange manners of the foreigners. It was therefore, with considerable effort that he sat through dinner with them. To decline the invitation for Jagat Seth's dinner would have been unthinkable for it would have been construed as an insult to the powerful men who now manipulated the affairs of Bengal. Nevertheless, the hours of watching those red-faced men drink bottles of blood-like liquid called claret, and hock, while evening silk jackets became stained with sweat, upset the fastidious Brahmin in Chowdhury.

That summer evening of 1760, Ishwar Chowdhury sat, immaculate in dhoti and kurta, awaiting the ordeal. Jagat Seth chided him for his squeamishness. "If you want to trade with the firingis and build a mansion like mine, you will have to accept their ways. After all, what have I lost?"

"Strictly speaking, Seth-ji, you have lost your caste by sitting with the British gentlemen when they partake of not only meat but beef," Ishwar Chowdhury retorted.

Jagat Seth smiled condescendingly. "For a Brahmin you do not know your scriptures well. The ancient Brahmins ate meat. What do you suppose the Ashwamedha Yajna was? The imperial horse was sacrificed and roasted for the delectation of the Aryan-Brahmins."

Ishwar Chowdhury shuddered at this latest affront to his sentiments. "Then why did we fight the Muslims for eating meat?" he asked wearily.

Again Jagat Seth bestowed a wan smile on his Brahmin guest and colleague. "We fought the Muslims because they usurped our power — the power of you Brahmins and us Banias, not to mention those numbskull Kshatriyas! Do you not see how we merchants have again manipulated events? What does it matter which fool sits on the throne of Delhi or Bengal if we can plump our profits? We must be free to trade and if the firingi facilitates our pursuit of wealth, well then, we must aid him! Mir Jafar resented the influence we exerted on the state of affairs and so he connived against us. But we have managed to have him set aside. Mir Kasim is not antagonistic to us Hindus. He knows that we have influence with the British."

"Mir Jafar has been set aside because he did not fulfil his pecuniary obligations to Robert Clive," Ishwar Chowdhury persisted.

"No ... Clive Saheb also knows that Mir Jafar does not enjoy our support," Jagat Seth retorted.

"Let us hope Mir Kasim will be more to our taste," Chowdhury replied sarcastically. "From what I have seen of him, he has a mind of his own."

Jagat Seth laughed, a laugh of the indulgent contemptuousness that a clever man has for a stupid follower. Then, hearing the sound of carriages, he straightened his silk turban and long muslin kurta and proceeded to the front veranda to welcome his British guests. Robert Clive led the party, dressed with quite elegance, his unhurried manner betraying little of his inner turmoil. Other officers from the Company and its army followed. There was one face which he did not recognise but which arrested his attention. The cool scrutiny of the blue eyes bored straight into his own dark, piercing ones. Noticing Jagat Seth's brief interest, Holwell, a senior official of the East India Company hastened an introduction.

"Allow me to present Alexander Ruthven, our accredited trader at Bishnupur — who is here in Calcutta on business. I took the liberty of bringing him along."

Jagat Seth welcomed him with the courtesy for which he was renowned. Alexander bowed respectfully and joined his palms in the Hindu greeting. "I have heard a great deal about you from my wife — a lady from Murshidabad. I wished therefore to meet the one whom they call 'Banker to the world'."

Jagat Seth smiled, now mollified. "Indeed? It is a high epitaph for a humble broker."

"No, Seth-ji," Ruthven murmured. "It is rumoured that you will go to the emperor once more — to petition for recognition of the new nawab. One who meets the Badshah of India so often can hardly be a humble broker."

Jagat Seth was on his guard now. There was a glint in the young man's eyes that caused him disquiet. He waited for the firingi to make the first move, and in the meantime, led his guests to the jalsha ghar, the pleasure hall, where a bevy of comely girls sat on a soft plush carpet, flanked by half a dozen musicians. "For your entertainment, I have procured the best courtesans of Lucknow but our singer is the nightingale of Bengal. So sit down gentlemen and spend a pleasant evening."

The British officers sat on comfortable divans while dhoti-clad servants brought in trays of Madeira, claret, Rhenish and hock. Emulating his British friends, Jagat Seth raised a toast to the King of England and nawab of Bengal but did not sip even a drop. Ishwar Chowdhury declined to accept a ritual glass and averted his eyes when the Seth's servants carried in silver tureens of kababs and curries for the assembled sahebs who fell upon the Moghul delicacies with considerable gusto.

Soon a noted singer began to strum the strings of the veena and raised an invocation to Saraswati, the goddess of learning and music.

Alexander Ruthven strained his ears to listen and soon found an answering chord. The low octave of the singer reminded him strangely of the monotonal lullabies he had heard as a child. As soon as the invocation was over, the tabla gathered momentum and Rehana, the dancer, burst into the room from behind silken curtains.

There was a pause in the hum of conversation as the dancer's skirt fluttered, revealing a pair of shapely, golden legs, slender ankles bound by silver chains and tiny bells. The girl leapt and pranced, swayed and shook as dictated by the music of Tara Baiji. Her movements drew the spectators' eyes to her smooth arms and neck and the swell of her generous bosom, outlined suggestively by a jewelled bodice. Her bold brown eyes moved from Clive and Holwell to the junior trade agent, Ruthven, who stood out apart from the rest by his tall, supple figure, mane of red hair tied back by a black velvet ribbon and a pair of blue eyes that appraised her with a calm but appreciative gaze. His attention encouraged her to dance with greater enthusiasm, engaging in overtly sensual movements. Inflamed by wine, the guests cried "Shabash!" in appreciation. Rehana smiled and swayed, and as the tabla and shehnai gathered speed, as Tara Baiji's voice rose to a crescendo, the dancer's body vibrated provocatively, hushing the men into a throbbing silence. They stared at the dancer with bleary but hungry eyes. Rehana's eyes, however, kept returning to the taciturn young agent who stood silently watching her.

When it was over, the British guests applauded and scattered coins on the carpet, at her feet, in the style of Muslim courts. Rehana bowed low, smiling, touching her right hand to her forehead in a salaam. Then she smiled, specially for Ruthven, and disappeared once more behind the curtains.

Jagat Seth clapped his hands and half a dozen servants bearing silver hookahs entered and placed them in front of the guests. Alexander had learned to appreciate the rich aroma of the tobacco as it filtered through attar-scented water. It was better than smoking a pipe of the English style, especially when the hookah-bardars placed a whiff of opium in it. Now pulling at the thick coiled pipe, young Ruthven felt at ease, almost soporific.

"So the colonel is leaving for England?" Jagat Seth asked Robert Clive who nodded, smiling. The smile, everyone noticed, never reached his shrewd blue eyes.

"Let me hope your successor will be a little like you. Bengal needs a firm hand. The misrule of Mir Jafar and the skirmishes with the Dutch Company and the imperial crown prince have left us weary," Jagat Seth observed.

Clive smiled again, remembering Jagat Seth's brief flirtation with the Shahzada, the Emperor's son, when that prince had come seeking the throne of Bengal. "I dare say Mr. Vansittart will be as capable as the situation requires. He does of course have an inclination to be over righteous about minor issues."

"We will miss your guidance ... and daring," said Jagat Seth.

Robert Clive inclined his head in mock humility, causing Alexander Ruthven to smile. "No doubt the colonel knows his departure will create considerable difficulties," he thought. "Indeed he is anxious to leave before the situation deteriorates further. The nawab's treasury is empty and private trading has caused loss to the Company.'

Ruthven paused in his reflection to study the "heaven born" general of William Pitt's tribute. "This is a man who pursued an idea, who dared to act in the face of odds and who wrested for himself and for his country a substantial prize." Ruthven felt a surge of admiration for the older man and with it came a desire to emulate him and make conquests in the rich and vulnerable land awaiting the invader's embrace.

It was as if Clive felt waves of sympathy emanate from the young Scotsman and sensed the ambition and turmoil beneath Ruthven's polite and taciturn exterior. "You have prospered, Mr. Ruthven," the commander said with a twisted smile.

Alexander bowed. "You have made it possible, Sir. Without Plassey, I might have continued as a lieutenant, moving from fort to fort until ..."

"Until victory was yours," Robert Clive interposed, his sudden smile banishing the solemnity of his mien. "We are, Mr. Ruthven, descendants of the Normans and Saxons, and of men such as Drake and Hawkins. Never forget that." Clive stopped abruptly, afraid as always that he had said too much. He left Ruthven to unravel the perpetual enigma of the commander.

When the evening's excitement was over, Alexander waited for the senior directors to leave before he summoned his syce and horse. A servant of the Seth bowed and murmured, "Tara Baiji asks you to come to her apartment — in the adjoining house here."

Surprised, Ruthven hesitated. Then remembering Rehana's dancing, he smiled and followed the servant to the adjoining house where other officers of the Company were present. Divested of their jackets, they sat on the floor attended by Rehana and her companions. Hookahs were brought in once more, with chessboards and dice so that the guests could gamble in soporific ease. Seeing Ruthven enter, the nautch girl stepped forward, dressed now in a flimsy silk robe.

"You liked my dancing, Saheb. I wanted you to see more," she said gaily, without a touch of coquetry.

Ruthven smiled, delighted by her candour. "More dancing, Baiji?" he asked lightly. "Or something else?"

Rehana giggled and taking his hand, she led him to a small room where the combined aroma of tube roses and incense made his head whirl. Thick, padded quilts bordered by bolsters and cushions were placed on the floor.

"Sit down. Take off your jacket and shoes. There is more wine and a hookah for you," the courtesan said as she helped him to peel off his coat and the jabot of lace at his throat. Then she lit his hookah and flung off her wispy dress.

Ruthven put down his goblet of wine with a gasp. He had not seen a more voluptuous body nor one more ornamented to excite the senses. Her firm, heavy breasts were scented with attar, their tips tinted with henna. A gem was embedded in her navel. Slowly, she sat next to him and laying her skilful hands on his chest, slid them down with the ease of one accustomed to such tasks. Suppressing a moan, Ruthven lay down while she explored his flesh with finger and tongue. Groaning, he flung her down and leapt over, her, but she laughed and struggled, pressing her legs together. "Not yet, my fire-bird," she whispered, "I have still to show you more."

Ruthven lay without volition while she played her erotic games with him, arousing him to a fiery craving until finally he pressed her down and thrust himself into her with a hoarse cry for mercy. Now she yielded to his invasion and let him flood her with his desire.

He got up at first light, inert and in a stupor. Rehana lay back, smiling. "You will come again, fire-bird?" she asked.

"Tonight," he muttered, staring at the golden body. No woman had delighted him so. Other courtesans had provided him transient relief but this one ... she filled him with a maddening craving that remained unsatiated.

She rose and stroked his damp, red hair. "Come soon, my fire-bird. I shall be waiting."

In the days that followed, Ruthven came every evening to Tara Baiji's pleasure house, where Rehana carried him into a whirlpool of delights as he lay marvelling at her infinite variety of skills and her inexhaustible energy. His trading activities suffered but Rehana would not free him from her thrall. He began to come in the afternoons too when she took him to purchase silks and trinkets or of a dusk to visit the temple of Firingi Kali built by Job Charnock where the British officers freely joined the Indians in sacrificing goats and pigeons to propitiate the goddess for favours. The Brahmin priests raised no objections to the entry of the white mlecchas in their sacred territory. Ruthven smiled at the chaos and clamour and happily prostrated himself before the black stone image, as did other Englishmen and Scotsmen in their pursuit of fortune. He smiled too when a Company official said, "Kali listens to prayers accompanied by goats." Ruthven knew that there was no one who listened to prayers. Every man was alone.

Only the hours spent with Rehana made Alexander forget his exile and his ever present loneliness. Indeed, so warm was his gratitude for the vibrant hours with her that one day he gave her a ring of rubies surmounted by diamonds. "Take it, lovely witch," he said sleepily, laying his head on her heavy, scented breasts, his limbs twined around hers. "I have a pair of earrings to match."

Rehana's smile deepened. "So, my master was right," she thought, staring at the rare red gem which only the Begum of Bengal possessed. "But how do I get to the rest of the jewels?" Aloud she said, caressing his hair, the long neck and hard chest. "A rare gem, fire-bird. Where did you get it?"

Ruthven laughed softly as her cunning hands glided down his body, dissolving him into a stupor of delight. "My Begum ... she took it from her lady Lutfinissa." Rehana's hand paused in its progress for a fraction of a second. "But you, lovely witch, shall have it. I have many more." He rose and pulled her down. "Now, Rehana," he muttered thickly, drugged by the opium in the hookah, "come." She complied and let him visit her waiting body. "Tomorrow I will tell my master," she mused. "Your company has bled him enough without your purloining Lutfinissa's little treasures."

Rehana's master was none other than the new Nawab of Bengal, who had paid a heavy price for winning the throne. He was a son-in-law of the unprincipled Mir Jafar and cousin to the ill-starred Siraj-ud-doula. He had agreed to the deposing of Mir Jafar by Clive but in his heart was the resolve to wrest Bengal from the vice-like grip of the Company. But first he needed the cooperation of the foreigners. He agreed to pay £200,000 to the Calcutta Council and assign the rich districts of Midnapur, Burdwan and Chittagong for the maintenance of the Company troops. Unwittingly, he mortgaged his future for the throne.

Mir Kasim began by obtaining the imprimatur of approval of his succession from the fugitive Emperor who was repulsed in Bihar and then reinstated in Delhi. After Clive's departure, the new nawab secured the removal of Clive's protege from Bihar in order to gain access to the Patna treasury. The new nawab was deep in debt to the Company.

He was not indifferent when Rehana, an old favourite, informed him of the jewel-nest in Begum Ruthven's possession. So Rehana continued to entertain the taciturn firingi until suddenly, Alexander Ruthven tired of Rehana. He always grew weary of routine. One day, he abruptly left her to take up trade again. He obtained a dastak for duty free trade. At the riverside he met Ishwar Chowdhury the zamindar of Mayurganj with whom he traded in goods. "So Zamindar Saheb," he taunted, "you do not protest? Have we finally become masters of Bengal?"

What he traded for the company was far less than that for himself. Some of the directors of the Company were puzzled by the loss of revenue but Calcutta was far from Leadenhall Street. In fact, so profitable was the free trade in salt, betel nut, and tobacco that many traders resold the dastaks to Indians at exorbitant prices. Everyone wanted to join the plunder. Alexander too resold his dastaks at steep prices to Indian traders and with the proceeds bought a barge for trading in the fertile lands of eastern Bengal where fish, rice and jute grew as richly as the rivers.

Ishwar Chowdhury was one of those who felt the price was too high, but he purchased the dastak all the same.

"You will recoup it in time," Alexander assured him. "The trade in saltpetre will bring immense profits."

"Yes," Chowdhury said bitterly, " it is kind of you, Mr. Ruthven, to let me trade in my own land."

Ruthven looked at the zamindar, a sardonic smile lightening his cold blue eyes. "Did you not invite us, Mr. Chowdhury, to deliver you from Siraj-ud-doula's depredations?"

"Aye," Chowdhury replied, "we invited you, wretched fools that we were." He paused. "If it had been Mir Kasim instead of Siraj, we would not have chosen that path."

Alexander nodded. "Perhaps. However it is too late to regret. Mir Kasim too will abide by his promises."

The zamindar smiled, gazing at the busy river scene before him, crowded with barges and boats, fishermen and bhatials. "Do not rest on that thought too much," he said. "Mir Kasim is not Mir Jafar."

Then bowing, he lifted up his dhoti pleats and picked his way through the sun-baked banks towards his palanquin. Ruthven stared after him and then shrugging, went to his own palanquin, vaguely troubled, looking at the newly developing area of the "Strand", the warehouses, toll booths, brokers and moneylenders, noisy with the babble of a myriad tongues. Today, this bustling scene did not divert him. The bullock carts trundling past irritated him, and even his own palki-wallas seemed to be walking like drugged troopers. "Ought to have taken my horse," he grumbled, though he knew that the desire to emulate a genteel zamindar had got the better of him. "Besides, the sun is unbearable."

Indeed, summer burned the new houses of the traders, and set fire to the thatched houses of the poor. Leaves crackled on trees and even the Ganges slowed down, dusty and thinned by the hot winds that swept down from plains and deserts. The scent of mangoes on vendors' baskets filled the air. "It is time to go home, to Bishnupur," Ruthven thought wearily.

A month had passed since his departure but it seemed like an age. Bishnupur was far away, in another time. Even the crumbling bungalow looked unfamiliar. Dismounting swiftly, Ruthven went inside to be greeted by a strange sight. The women retainers were huddled together, whispering and waiting in turn. The men stood behind, anxious and helpless. Seeing Ruthven, they came forward, hands clasped.

"What is it?" Alexander asked, checking that familiar throb of panic in his chest.

"Saheb ... the Begum ... is ..." The khidmatgar, the major domo, could proceed no further.

Clenching his hands, Alexander went to the main bedchamber. There lay his wife, ashen faced and hollow cheeked. A woman servant fanned her with a cluster of large, stiff palmyra leaves. Another pressed damp cloths on her forehead. Seeing him, she beckoned. He went quickly to her side.

"You have come, Janab. I am glad. I held on — just to see you." She paused, licked her cracked lips with a fuzzy tongue and went on. "Take your son ... and care for him, if you wish. He is a child of misfortune."

Great tears slid down her wasted cheeks. Alexander turned around and saw an infant lying peacefully in a cradle. His wispy hair was like copper silk and the half-opened eyes were a deep blue. The skin was cream and gold. Without thinking, Alexander picked him up, and peering into the squinting blue eyes, laughed in joyous delight. "My son," he said, in wonder and joy. "My son! A true Ruthven!"

Shirin stared at him, troubled and confused. Then a faint, reluctant smile stretched her dry lips. "He pleases you?"

"Of course! Are you not as pleased?" Alexander cried, rocking the child exuberantly until the ayah, the nurse, protested.

"I wish ... he had not been attended by misfortune," Shirin whispered.

"What misfortune?" Ruthven asked quietly, handing the infant back.

"The day after his birth ... dacoits came ... and stole some of my jewels ,.. the ones I took from Begum Lutfinissa," Shirin cried.

Slowly, Ruthven sat down on the rumpled bed, gripped by a sudden remorse, that he had been carousing with Rehana while his wife had given birth to his son, and while robbers had invaded his house to deprive him of a modest fortune in gems. "Rehana," he thought, "how she lured me ..." Slowly, another thought formed in his mind, of Rehana enquiring about the jewellery in his wife's possession. "Had she then arranged the theft?" He rose abruptly, avoiding Shirin's opaque but sapient eyes that seemed to divine his thoughts.

"If only you had been here, Janab!" she reproached hoarsely.

"I was ... engaged in ... selling and buying dastaks and arranging trade in the eastern districts. It was imperative for me to stay!" Ruthven's curt rejoinder seemed more like a defence than an explanation.

Shirin Begum turned her face away, mortified. He seldom spoke thus and she knew why. Noticing traces of dissipation on his face, she wondered which woman had made him forget his duty. Ruthven was now angry with himself for having been duped by a dancing girl. "Fool!" he abused himself. "How could I believe in the affections of a whore? How could I so ill judge the dancer's motives and fail to see her game?" But he knew why. Rehana was the most erotic woman he had encountered. Anger at his own folly filled him.

"I will compensate the loss of your jewels ... in trade. Do not I pray, distress yourself," he said gently, his glance moving from the sick mother to the sturdy child sleeping peacefully in the ornamented cradle. "We have a deeper bond now, Shirin, and a reason for success."

In the months that followed, Alexander Ruthven addressed himself even more vigorously to his commercial ventures. The country boat, the bajra, he had purchased enabled him to extend his activity to the richer districts of eastern Bengal whose fertile deltaic soil yielded a luxuriance he had never seen elsewhere. Here, in the lands bordered by the turbulent rivers Meghna and Padma, cotton was raised in abundance. Though the staples were shorter than the American crop, and resulted in waste during manufacture, the cotton was useful for manufacture of coarse cloths. A small hand-gin or wooden cylindrical machine had been used from antiquity to clean the staples. These were purchased from the cotton farmers and conveyed in boats to Calcutta. Like other traders, Ruthven sold the cotton bales to the Company who put the produce in cotton screws and shipped them to England.

Of the cotton sold to the Company, the best was grown by the farmers in Dacca and woven into the famous 'malmal' or muslin which had no equal elsewhere. The traders purchased these at low prices and sold them to the Company who shipped them to England, where the affluent paid a fancy price for the famed Dacca muslin.

Shirin Begum told her husband of the silk farms in Murshidabad, the capital of the nawab of Bengal, and urged him to trade in this commodity, though the Company exercised monopoly rights. To inaugurate this venture, Ruthven took his Begum back to her old haunt. Heavily veiled in her silk and lace burqua, Shirin summoned trusted retainers of Begum Lutfinissa who had been banished to Rajshahi and instructed them to show "Sikander Saheb" (as Alexander was known) the farms where mulberry and silkworms were reared. They showed him the white mulberry leaves imported from Italy, the purple variety from China and the indigenous green leaves. Alexander learned the methods of picking leaves, feeding the silkworms and the immersion of cocoons in boiling water.

Seeing the possibilities of this trade, Alexander Ruthven determined to apply for appointment as a "Commercial Resident" who paid advances to the middlemen, the pykārs, on behalf of the Company. A commission of 2½ per cent was given to the Resident by the East India Company which then sent the silk to be reeled by Bengali workmen to then be woven in the Company's factories. He saw no reason why he should not establish a small factory and produce silk cloth for export.

Within a year, Alexander Ruthven had widened the scope of his operations. Trading in cotton, silk, sugarcane and saltpetre had brought him substantial returns. Indeed, he was one of the many East India Company officials and British residents who were wresting benefits and privileges from a province where the East India Company had established its authority.

Ploughing back profits into commerce, Ruthven purchased a farm and factory from a bankrupt Muslim entrepreneur and in Murshidabad embarked on a lucrative trade.

5

The Master of Mayurganj

Sitting in his new capital of Monghyr, the nawab of Bengal fumed over the transgressions of the East India Company officials and agents. It was a time of unbridled economic freedom for them and they were determined to make private fortunes as Clive had done. Their insistence on tax-free internal trade affected Nawab Mir Kasim's revenues and his independence. Mir Kasim needed money to fight the growing encroachment of this Company and this was what seemed impossible to combat.

Ishwar Chowdhury came to the pleasant hill town of Monghyr where the Nawab had moved his capital in order to reduce the interference of the Calcutta Council of the East India Company. Bowing low before the Nawab, the zamindar folded his hands in despair.

"Save us, Your Majesty," Chowdhury pleaded. "We, who had a thriving business in cotton and silk, have become virtual dependants on the Company, which decides arbitrary prices for these products. The worst abuse is here — perpetuated by the gomasthas, the Indian agents of the British traders."

"I sent my revenue officers to deal with these gomasthas," the Nawab replied heavily.

"We know, Sire, but your men are unarmed while the Company sepoys carry matchlocks. Your revenue officers are molested and put to flight."

The Nawab regarded the zamindar with cold, hooded eyes. "Was it not you and your friends who called in these people? Siraj-ud-doula was a wayward youth but he knew the British game. That is why he fought them — but you bankers and landlords betrayed him. Are you not satisfied?"

Ishwar Chowdhury shook his head. "We thought them to be only traders, jackals who wanted our leavings from the carcass. We did not know we had mounted a tiger."

The nawab nodded, grim faced. "But the tiger must be put to flight — or else we will perish."

"What shall we do, Sire?" the zamindar asked humbly.

"Nothing! You sold your freedom for trade only to find it wrenched from you. I will have to meet the new Governor of the Council."

Henry Vansittart was made of different stuff from Robert Clive. He had the sound, frugal taste of his Dutch forbears and carried with him the racial memories of Spanish oppression of the Netherlands. He did not believe in the unbridled rapacity of merchants. To bolster his view, he had an ally in Warren Hastings, the Company Resident at Murshidabad, who also wished to curb the growing intransigence of the trade agents. Both men set off for Monghyr in the autumn of 1762, to parley with the Nawab.

The monsoon had ended, leaving the Gangetic plain lush with verdure. Beyond Burdwan, the hillocks of Bihar appeared on the rim of the flat paddy fields ablaze with ripening rice and the famed pulses, the dals of this area. The feathery plumes of sugarcane stirred in the warm scented air. Vansittart dozed in the carriage while Hastings pored over the lyrical poems of the Bengali mystic, Ramaprasad. As the evening shadows gathered, silence fell upon the villages as the carriage trundled over the Grand Trunk Road, postillions riding ahead. From afar the passengers could see fires being lit from whence woodsmoke emanated. Warren Hastings nodded to himself, as if in confirmation of his thoughts. "Ramaprasad or Chaitanya, Tulsidas or Tukaram," he murmured, they are all the same; sons of a perennial mother force — Hindusthan."

Vansittart opened a delft-blue eye. "And Mir Kasim, Mr. Hastings? Is he part of this perennial force?"

Hastings sighed. "They all are. Even we have unwittingly become a part of it."

Vansittart shook his head, gazing into the darkening landscape. "We must remain detached — as traders who come and go."

Hastings' impassive face registered surprise but he said nothing. He closed his book as the carriage drew up to a dak bungalow.

Monghyr had sprouted like monsoon grass from the obscurity of a provincial town noted only for its excellent pulses and grams to the eminence of a kingdom's capital. The townsfolk were not displeased by the burgeoning business brought to it, and displayed on its river ghats and wharfs. The Nawab's presence meant the expenditure of a court and the extravagances of its nobles. They looked with considerable interest on the two white sahebs who rode on horses towards the Nawab's hilltop palace, reassured that the Company did not rule Monghyr as it ruled Calcutta.

Mir Kasim did not share the sanguine optimism of his subjects. He had known Hastings at Murshidabad and judged him to be an able man, but he was not certain of his ambitions. Vansittart was more reassuring.

"We wish to trade, Your Majesty," Vansittart said courteously. It is not our aim to disrupt the trade of your people or to affect the revenue of your kingdom."

Mir Kasim nodded, relieved. "Then the taxes must be increased for your traders."

Hastings produced his proposals. "We suggest a 9 per cent ad valorem duty on European traders' goods. They will be subject to the local foujdars, your police, in cases of disputes."

"That seems reasonable," the Nawab said quietly.

"Let us hope there will be no violations hereafter."

The three men sealed the Monghyr pact in the beautiful garden, drinking wine and sherbet while unseen musicians played from the high-pillared halls.

"What has Vansittart done?" Alexander Ruthven cried in dismay to Hay and Watts of the Calcutta Council. "We must reject the agreement. It is dishonourable to us! We cannot have the Nawab dictating terms. Why should we traders not enjoy the conditions assured by Clive? Those must not be choked by taxes!"

Warren Hastings and Henry Vansittart sought in vain to reason with their colleagues.

"We are not here to interfere in the affairs of the country nor to sanction oppression committed under the English name. From such irregularities the country people are habituated to entertain the most unfavourable notions of our Government." The Governor spoke with his habitual composure.

"The opinion of the people, Mr. Hastings, is not a matter of concern to us. What interests us is the advancement of the Company's commerce. Was it not for this that Colonel Clive fought the Nawab?" Ruthven retorted.

"Trading privileges do not imply the despoilation of a province!" Hastings exclaimed hotly. "The conduct of the British traders cannot fail to draw upon the Company the severest resentment. If our people, instead of converting themselves into lords and oppressors of the country, confine themselves to the lawful authority of the Government, they will be courted and respected. The English name, instead of being a reproach, will be universally revered."

Mr. Ellis, an assertive company trader greeted this with derisive laughter. "We seek no reverence from the people — only their rupees!"

Many joined in the laughter. The Calcutta Council rejected the Monghyr agreement, despite Governor Vansittart's and Councillor Hastings' pleadings.

Later, in the Fort William mess with its raftered ceilings and polished silver, Alexander Ruthven learned of the news with relief. "It would have been awkward if the Council curbed our enterprises now!" he confided to a fellow trader.

"Indeed it would. One wonders why the Governor defends the nawab's interest!" his companion responded.

Alexander smiled. "It is rumoured that Mr. Vansittart has been bribed by the Nawab! In Hindusthan, the impossible is attained by bribes."

General laughter followed his remark with speculations about the amount. "poor Mir Kasim! The bribe was to no avail! Wonder what the Nawab will do now?"

Nawab Mir Kasim did something totally unexpected and unprecedented. In order to safeguard the interests of the Indian traders, he abolished all taxes due to him, thereby nullifying the privileges wrested by the Company's traders at the expense of Indian traders.

The indignation among the Company traders was widespread.

"The Nawab grows more insolent every day," remarked a senior member of the Calcutta Council. "He would do well to remember the fate of his kinsman, Siraj-ud-doula."

He is astute and resourceful. Moreover, this Nawab enjoys the loyalty of his people. It will not be easy to find another party to oust him," Ruthven observed. He had seen the respect accorded to Mir Kasim during his trips to Murshidabad.

"In that case, we shall fight him ... and put a man of our choice on the throne of Bengal."

Mir Kasim was determined not to let such a fate befall him. He persuaded the Moghul Emperor, Shah Alam, that the growing tentacles of British trade would one day endanger the Moghul throne and what remained of Moghul territories. Another nawab — the ruler of the rich province of Oudh — had also grown to fear the East India Company. Together they formed an alliance and prepared to deal with the menace of the East India Company.

The British colony in Bengal began to feel uneasy. Alexander Ruthven rushed to Bishnupur where Shirin Begum and their two children, Andrew and Beatrice, lived.

"Is Mir Kasim preparing for war?" the Begum asked anxiously.

"No, he is not preparing for war... but we are. We do not intend to relinquish the privileges gained from Plassey," her husband replied. You had better prepare to come to Calcutta ... where we shall be safe within the walls of the Fort."

"And you, Janab?" Shirin asked. "Will you not be there as well? I would not ... feel comfortable ... among your people."

Alexander Ruthven stared at his wife of seven years, the woman who had fled the seclusion of the royal zenana to share his disordered existence; who had guided him through the labyrinthine intrigues of trade, and revelled in his plunder. Never, in all these years had she expressed a thought or interest contrary to his.

"My people?" he asked quietly. "Surely they are yours now. Have you not identified yourself with our cause?"

Shirin fidgeted with the lace trimmings of her voluminous skirt, the gharara. "Indeed I have ... but would your people ... consider it so?"

"As long as you do not profess any loyalty to the Nawab, no one will question your bonafides," Ruthven replied. He paused, peering into her opaque grey eyes. "I trust there is no residue of ... old sentiments for Mir Kasim?"

Shirin shook her head. "No ... there are no sentiments for Mir Kasim. He was a distant kinsman of my mother's ... no more."

"Then no more is to be said. We will leave for Calcutta in a few days. This house will be guarded by my own sepoys until we return."

"Will you be in the Fort, Janab?" Shirin asked, sensing a new restlessness in her husband.

He smiled. "No, Begum. I have of late tired of trade and crave action ... the excitement of battle. Perhaps I will join the Company forces against the hosts of Shah Alam, Mir Kasim and Oudh."

Shirin stiffened. She had not known that the Emperor would join the war: Badshah Shah Alam, the symbol of Moghul glory ... whose blood flowed in her veins. Or so she had been told by her mother.

Ruthven observed the manner in which her pale face became ashen. Rising from the high-winged chair where he sat, Alexander Ruthven came to his wife. "Can it be that you have still some sentiments for the Emperor?" he asked quietly.

Shirin met his challenging gaze with her cool, inscrutable one.

The old emperor Mohammed Shah had been kind to her father, an able Afghan mercenary, and had given his kinswoman, Princess Zobaida to Shacoor Khan in marriage. Zobaida had been granted an estate in Bengal. Her husband had been introduced to Alivardi Khan, nawab of Bengal, who made him a general of his army. "But that is all over and done with," Shirin reflected. "I owe his grand-nephew, the Emperor, nothing ... nor do I owe anything to Mir Kasim. This firingi on the other hand has made me rich and I have borne him children. With him my future is assured."

"No Janab," Begum Ruthven replied gravely." I have no sentiments for the Badshah. I broke my allegiance to him and to the Nawab of Bengal when I ... left the palace with the Begum's jewels." She did not intend to let Ruthven forget his debt to her.

Ruthven laughed softly. "We are well matched, you and I. We both know where our interests lie." He paused and added. "We are both mercenaries." It was the first time Ruthven saw his Begum's pale face turn crimson with fury. She turned away and went to begin packing.

In Calcutta, the British were furious over the intransigence of Mir Kasim. "Master of his own house!" Hay exclaimed at the Fort dining hall. "The Nawab forgets who made him master!"

"Ellis, our agent at Patna, will make sure he remembers," Watts mused, "and will surely provoke him to fight."

In the summer of 1763, the smouldering hostilities broke into an open war between the Company forces and the Nawab's army. Ruthven had joined the Company forces under General Adam. He felt a keen desire to see the destruction of the impudent Nawab whose effrontery was affecting their trade. It was also exciting to be back in battle, amidst the crack of gunfire and smell of smoke. General Adam engaged the Nawab's new army under the command of a German, Walter Reinhardt in several battles. Ruthven came near enough once to see Walter Reinhardt gaunt face which had earned him the name of "Sumroo", an Indian version of sombre.

Tales of Sumroo's wealth and power stirred new ideas in Ruthven's mind. "Why not be a mercenary," he thought, "and hire out my sword to a bidder? But not now, not until Mir Kasim is taught a lesson!"

Reinhardt was no match for Adam. His army lost in four pitched battles. Mir Kasim fled to the neighbouring kingdom of Oudh, where Wazir Shuja-ud-doula ruled. Reinhardt recouped his honour by executing British prisoners.

Alexander Ruthven remarched with his soldiers towards Patna, in the heat of the smouldering summer.

Long ago, in a Marseilles tavern haunted by declasse intellectuals who were addicted to recitals of classical poetry, Alexander Ruthven had heard of Dante's Inferno. The description of hell had seemed the extravagance of a poet embittered by exile. Now in the north Indian summer, Ruthven realised that the Inferno existed not only in the imagination but in this very world. The sun threw out tongues of fire that enveloped the ground, scorched his skin and pierced his blood-like fangs, driving him to a deadening exhaustion. Ruthven felt as if he had reached hell without experiencing death. But this Inferno was different from Dante's; he mused, it had stately palaces, that sent slender minarets to the sky and mosques that drew pilgrims and pigeons into their cool cavernous interiors. Here were gardens and fountains whose crystalline drops evaporated in its dance. Nevertheless, this was an Inferno, burning up dreams and memories and leaving intact only a fiery desire to triumph!"

"And triumph we shall!" General Adam shouted, leading the victorious army to the capital. "A pity the Nawab has fled. I should have liked to stick his head on a pike," Adam cried.

The army returned to Calcutta to recoup its strength but General

Adam, stricken by fever, died. News of a combined imperial army reached Calcutta by early 1764, sending ripples of disquiet among the Indian soldiers, the sepoys of the Company army, who were reluctant to fight the Emperor of India.

Twenty-one-year-old Hector Munro quickly took command of the Company army.

"No doubt our troops wish to join them," Munro said, as he quickly selected twenty-eight of the chief mutineers for a drumhead court martial and ordered thereafter the time honoured execution in which the men were placed over the muzzles of field guns in which the charge was ignited. A muffled lament went up as the execution was carried out.

"That will teach them the futility of rebellion," Munro observed.

Accustomed as Ruthven was to bloodshed and violence, this particular punishment made him recoil in horror.

"The native rulers use the same method," Munro said by way of explanation. "It chastises the spectators as well."

"I dare say," Ruthven murmured, turning away to stare at the lush green fields stretched out before them.

The monsoon had come and gone leaving the Gangetic plain heavy with the kharif crop. So distant from the scenes of headless bodies and mutilated corpses, were tranquil rice fields, glinting gold and green in the capricious sunlight.

"Discipline must be restored, Ruthven," Munro retorted, leaving his companion to contemplate the price of rebellion.

Briefly he remembered a highland village set to flame, its men hunted and massacred. "And now, the boy who had sworn revenge for his father's murder and sister's dishonour is here, trying to subjugate an alien people so that his people may act with impunity!" Ruthven mused.

By October 1764, the two antagonists prepared to meet. The Company army marched against Oudh and was met by the combined imperial forces at Buxar. As it had been at Plassey, the battle began at daybreak and ended at dusk. Hector Munro proved himself a great commander. He neither saw nor counted the dead though the casualties on both sides turned the river red. There was so much bloodshed that Alexander Ruthven wondered if he would remain in these verdant fields to rot until the next monsoon. The vast army of Shah Alam advanced like an endless wave and with ceaseless fire, it mowed down the small Company forces. What Ruthven did not know was that Munro had a secret arrangement with the Nawab of Oudh who held back his forces until Mir Kasim's men were annihilated.

The battle of Buxar was a triumph for the East India Company. For the first time the "inviolable" Moghul Emperor was engaged and defeated in battle. The Nawab of Oudh, his vazir and principal ally, was in flight, knowing that it was a matter of time before Oudh met the fate of Bengal.

Ishwar Chowdhury sat staring at the river, head between his hands. "Mir Kasim has lost," he said to his son, now a youth of twenty. "The Nawab attempted to stem the tide of the Company's power but failed because his allies were undependable. Mir Jafar is back on the throne."

Indrajit's dark eyes narrowed. "So you gambled twice — and lost twice!" His voice was low but hard.

Ishwar nodded, eyes dimmed by tears. "I have eroded your inheritance, my son," he said in a quavering voice. "I can only ask your forgiveness."

Indrajit felt a tremor of pity for the ageing man who sat disconsolate on the roof garden of the new mansion at Mayurganj, the zamindari having been restored to the Chowdhurys after the depredations of Alivardi Khan and Siraj-ud-doula. Here they had lived since the fifteenth century when the celebrated Muslim king, Nusrat Shah, had ruled Bengal. That noble and tolerant monarch had ordered the composition of a Bengali version of the epic, Mahabharata. A Brahmin scholar had begun the task. Pleased by the Brahmin's scholarship, Nusrat Shah had conferred upon him the jagir of Mayurganj and the title of 'Chowdhury' after the family name, Acharya.

"Will forgiveness redeem our debts?" the son's voice was like a whiplash.

Ishwar shook his head, staring down at the river, dotted by boats. "No. Mir Jafar will not help. The Emperor has conferred the diwani of Bengal, Bihar and Orissa on the Company. Apart from rupees twenty-five lakhs to be paid as tribute, the rest is loot for the Company."

"Precisely. Your intrigues have made the British masters of Bengal. They started by being traders and manipulators. Now they rule — with unbridled power. We have not stemmed the abuses but we have incurred the hostility of the Company." He waved his hand at the verdant land stretching to the rim at the horizon. "All this is ours — but endangered. Out cotton and silk weavers are in despair."

Ishwar rose and met his son's derisive scrutiny. "I have failed, Indrajit. I admit it. What more can a father do to make amends?"

Before the son could speak, a girl of sixteen stepped out onto the roof terrace. Frail and pretty, she carried a casket of jewels. The anchal, the end of her sari, partially covered her silky head, but failed to conceal the indignation in her large eyes.

"Father," she addressed Ishwar, head bowed, "my jewels are at your disposal. Pay your debts and tell those robbers to leave us alone!"

Ishwar Chowdhury stared at his daughter-in-law, Bishnupriya. "Bow-ma," he said, rising hurriedly, "you must never say such a thing! Take these jewels back. They are yours. No one must touch them."

"What good are my ornaments if you are to suffer?" the girl asked. "Take them, Father, and settle your debts."

The zamindar's eyes glistened with tears as he gazed at the frail girl. "Little mother," he said softly, "you are truly Bishnupriya, the goddess Lakshmi, come to my house. Bless you. Bless you a thousand times." He glanced at his son. "Such a bride is worth many hundred acres of land."

Indrajit glanced at his wife of four years, a sickly wife who had failed to give him an heir. But his father was devoted to the girl and would not hear of a second marriage.

"What acres remain is yet to be seen," Indrajit retorted as he left the roof terrace.

The zamindar sat back wearily. "Little mother," he said sadly, "I have made a mess of matters. What shall I do?"

Bishnupriya sighed. "It will work out in the end, Father, you'll see."

"Sing a song, little one ... to comfort me."

Bishnupriya cleared her throat and began to sing the songs of Shri Chaitanya who had lived nearby, in Nadia, three centuries ago. Ishwar listened, eyes closed. "One must not lose hope," he consoled himself.

Hope receded for the Indian traders and craftsmen as the Company exulted in its triumph and burgeoning power. The theoretical authority of the Moghul emperor had been eroded. The independence of the nawab remained less than a myth. The Company ruled Bengal and its officials plunged into an orgy of plunder. In fury, Indrajit recounted these depredations to his father.

"James Rennell, the Surveyor General, is aged twenty-two and enjoys perquisites of £1,000 a year while his salary is £900. He boasts openly of being able to make £ 6,000 in a few years." Indrajit paused, eyes flashing. "Rennell is a modest man. There are others who hope to make £50,000 in a few years."

Ishwar nodded, head bowed. His son continued. "Did none of you — the wily Jagat Seth, and others — anticipate what would happen when you called the Company in to intervene in our realm? Was it not better to endure the wild Siraj, who in any case would have been eventually deposed by a cousin, than to have our trade ruined, our revenues despoiled?

Ishwar nodded again, his head sunk on his chest, his visage so desolate that his son paused for a moment. "Well, enjoy the

Company's rule!" he snapped unkindly.

The Company's rule alarmed the directors at Leadenhall Street in London. There had been a decline of remittances from 1758 but there was little they could do to control the men whose plundered wealth enabled them to buy company stocks and with them, accompanying votes. So they continued to reap a rich harvest in inland trade, fixing arbitrary prices for goods and selling them at exorbitant rates. The farmers, weavers and craftsmen had no court of redressal and were unable to resist. The emperor was a phantom power, the nawab a puppet.

The Chowdhurys of Mayurganj fell on bad days. They could not sell rice, tobacco, cotton, betel nut or mustard seed at the former prices. Their farmers were able to keep very little as surplus. Faced with hunger and penury, they acquiesced to the terms offered by the Company's traders, which only deepened their poverty. Ishwar summoned his munshi, the accountant, to see what lands could be sold. He had received an offer from one Henry Dalrymple, a trader who had garnered the fine cotton of the area and was looking for land to erect a mill.

In vain did his daughter-in-law plead with him to sell her jewels to pay the arrears. Ishwar would not hear of it. "There is enough land," he said wearily. "nawab Nusrat Shah had been very generous to my ancestor. We can lose a few acres without much harm."

Indrajit fumed. "How complacent and foolish you are!" he stormed at his father. "Dalrymple will not stop at a few acres! He will encroach deeper — as our finances dwindle. You have, as our people say, cut a channel to let in a crocodile!"

Ishwar did not reply. There was little he could say in his defence.

Alexander Ruthven returned to Calcutta from his campaigns in North India as the cold air of December blew over the city and its environs. He was in time to celebrate Christmas with his compatriots.

The British had much to celebrate that year. The victory at Buxar had given them a sense of omnipotence as the Company could now command the revenue of Bengal for its own use. Farmers could be told what to produce.

One of the East India Company traders, Henry Dalrymple, who was a guest at Ruthven's Christmas dinner, expanded on the theme. "Saw a pretty stretch of land up north, near Nadia. The landlord is in debt and has agreed to sell a few acres."

"A trader become a farmer, are you?" Ruthven joked as he carved the wild roasted fowl and goose spread on huge silver salvers.

"Why not, Sir?" Dalrymple asked, licking his thumb to savour the brown sauce spiced by onion, garlic, fenugreek, ginger, asafoetida and bay leaves. "Intend to put up a mill for cotton and indigo."

Ruthven paused for a moment to consider the matter. "It's easier to trade, Mr. Dalrymple. Bengal is about to be the Company's diwani and with the defeat of the French in the south, the Carnatic is open for us as well. Think how that will expand our trade!"

"Do you think so?" another trader, Ralph Fullerton, asked. "It is said that Robert Clive is returning here — to change matters."

"Change matters?" Dalrymple cried, helping himself to fresh fish from the river and chops of lamb killed early that morning. Two khidmatgars brought in cakes heavy with nuts and fruits and served wines to suit every palate. "Why he started it ... showed us the way, so to speak!"

Ruthven smiled dryly. "Nothing like a poacher who becomes a gamekeeper!"

The men laughed. Little Andrew or Andraz as he was often called, sat listening wide eyed. Every so often, his father patted him fondly on the head. Alexander doted on the boy.

Begum Ruthven sat in her room with her daughter Alice or Alia as she called the three-year-old, listening to the masculine conversation. She was gratified that her husband approved of the Christmas dinner which if not very English, was certainly sumptuous. She had also learned how to decorate a fern tree and fill Alexander's stockings with gifts. This Christmas, she had parted with the last of her purloined diamonds to make his coat buttons. He had been overjoyed indeed and had taken her at once to the canopied bed to express his appreciation. Outside, in the cold morning light, English children sang carols as the mist rolled in from the river. Andrew had run out singing, to join the group.

Now, Shirin waited for her lord to join her, to talk and perhaps to make love once more. His waning desire for her had revived after the military campaigns.

As at all of Ruthven's parties, only gentlemen were invited since Begum Shirin refused to sit with the foreign menfolk. Alexander was therefore restricted to ask only his bachelor colleagues for these gatherings. As time went by, the bachelors became married men and joined other groups, leaving Ruthven feeling alienated. Though he was invited to join these groups, the reluctance to offend his Begum made him, more often than not, decline the invitations.

The brief winter's day was over when the guests left. Ruthven went to the Begum's chamber where his hookah and port were brought in. Servants lit candelabras and lamps as dusk fell. Around them, in adjoining houses could be heard choruses of English voices singing Christmas carols.

The Begum knew that these festivities made her lord homesick but she feigned ignorance. Today, however, she read something in his eyes that made her uneasy. Hoping to distract him and lighten his mood, she asked him how the Company sahebs had liked the Christmas dinner and the gifts of silk, silver ornaments and ivory that she had packed for each one.

He nodded absent-mindedly, as he sipped his port. And she prattled on, with an unaccustomed gaiety that told Ruthven that she was prepared for an announcement.

"Shirin," he said quietly, reclining on a chaise-longue. "I want to go home."

Shirin knew the long-awaited blow had fallen at last. She had been dreading it for seven years, but after the birth of Andrew, she had hoped to bind her restless husband. "And I thought he loved me more," she mused, "now, especially today when he took me ... ah, treacherous firingi! To reward me like this on his own feast day!"

Ruthven puffed on the hookah, glancing at her ashen face. Andrew and Alice sensed thunder in the air and stole away.

"Home?" she echoed at last. But *this* is your home!"

Alexander Ruthven stirred on the chaise, pulling at the lace jabot of his throat. "How can this country ever be my home?" he asked grimly. "I came here to make a fortune — and have done so. But it is not my home — only the scene of my adventures. I have no roots here, no fond remembrances of childhood nor the bonds of race and family."

"What about your children? Do they not bind you here?" Shirin asked with quiet fury. "If your native land was so full of sweet remembrances, why did you come here, Alexander Ruthven?" Ruthven rose from the chaise, staring at his Begum whose pale cheeks were flushed with indignation.

"Why did I come here, Begum? To shake the pagoda tree — as so many of my countrymen have done. A task in which you have helped me, Shirin ... no doubt for our mutual benefit."

His words angered her further. "You came here because you were banished from your land, by the very nation which you so faithfully serve!"

He laughed to disguise his own anger. "I serve no one but myself, my lady. Like you, I pursue my own interests, without a thought for others. That is how we have made a modest fortune, Begum."

"Which you will now squander in your native land!" Shirin cried in utter despair, flinging herself on a divan. "And forget us!"

Alexander watched her for a while, almost enjoying her misery. It was so rarely that she gave vent to the emotions which he knew lay beneath that ritual courtesy that always governed her behaviour. Even in bed, she remained in command, enacting the appropriate gestures but without any spontaneity. That he clung to her cool, impassive body was because he suffered from an aching loneliness in the paradisical remoteness of Bengal.

Now her distress stirred him. Going up to her, he said, "No

my dear, I will not abandon you nor squander our fortune at home. I must go and see my family without further delay. Ten years is a long time. My mother pleads for my return in every letter. Will you wait and look after our estates while I am away?"

Shirin nodded, partially relieved, though she could not quell her rising apprehension at his departure. It was what she had feared all along. Uprooted from her own society, Shirin had no illusions about her position if Alexander Ruthven abandoned her. She would be an outcast amongst her own people who had begun to realise the folly of calling in the Company to arbitrate in their disputes.

Alexander found an agent who could look after matters and assist Shirin during his absence. The traders of the Company realised that they had to be careful now. Clive, invested with authority and an Irish Peerage had come back to take over command in May 1965.

A new puppet nawab, Najiu-ud-doula, sat on the throne of Bengal and the Company had, in exercise of its de facto powers, appointed Raza Khan as the naib or deputy nawab.

The Council urged Clive to take Oudh and march to Delhi. "No power can resist us now!" they exulted.

"True," Lord Clive mused, smiling wryly at his colleagues, "but can we fight the Jats, Rohillas, Marathas in the vast land upto the Delhi Doab? Better to concentrate on the kingdom of Bengal and leave Shuja-ud-doula of Oudh to stand as a buffer between us and the others. Likewise, the authority of the Emperor must be maintained since it is he who gives us legitimacy."

Thus it was that the Emperor conferred legitimacy on the Company which now further enmeshed the powers of Hindusthan in its web.

Clive had been charged with the task of controlling the abuses of inland trade and receipt of presents. Though he did manage to do this to a certain extent, it was not effective enough. Nor would the Company directors in London, when addressed, agree to Clive's suggestion to increase the salaries of East India Company officials. Thus the old customs persisted: officials covertly received shares in salt monopoly or commissions on revenues, thus opening the floodgates to extortion.

Many landlords were ruined and farmers were left on the verge of starvation. The Chowdhurys of Mayurganj did not resist when Henry Dalrymple came to buy the lands on which he had set his eyes. Young Indrajit watched the florid-faced, thickset man ride away towards Dab Tola, coconut corner, where tantric sadhus held their new moon rituals. Seeing his grim face, his wife Bishnupriya laid a timid hand on his. "You will retrieve Dab Tola one day," she said softly. He turned his smouldering eyes to hers. "When?" he cried angrily. "Don't you see that they are taking over everything? Not only revenue but law and justice is also in their hands!" He paused and said hoarsely, "Bishnupriya, we are now virtual slaves!"

6

Pomp and Circumstance

Alexander Ruthven sorted out his affairs and in June 1765, boarded one of his flat barges to take him to the estuary where an East Indiaman waited for cargo and passengers for that long and uncertain journey over tempestuous waters. In that interminable journey, he thought more often of his wife and children, particularly his beloved Andrew, than the family he had left behind ten years ago at Marseilles. He worried too about Shirin's capacity to manage the silk farm at Murshidabad, the trading activities in sugar, cotton and saltpetre. Though he had left behind a trusted agent, Ruthven wondered if the man would prove reliable. Then he smiled to himself. Begum Ruthven would be a match for any agent!

Paradoxically, as the ship advanced closer to Europe, Ruthven pushed away memories of the past — of Culloden and Cumberland's atrocities, of the dispersion of his family. A well of guilt lay beneath, questioning his long absence and his heady obsession with making money. A nagging voice reminded him that he ought to have gone home much earlier, but he ignored it, dwelling instead on thoughts of the future and what his wealth would do for his family.

Like many weary Jacobites, the Ruthvens had returned to the scarred remnants of their highland home, to resume a disrupted existence. Twenty years had passed since Culloden; the Hanoverians were seated firmly on the English throne while Prince Charles Edward, last of the Stuarts, had returned to the French court of Louis XV. The Scottish people had turned their energies from rebellion to commerce; the Dundee recruit of the East India Company was foremost.

Alexander Ruthven arrived at Inverness where his family had now settled, since their land had been forfeited to the crown for James Ruthven's treason. The town looked no different from what he remembered of it twenty years ago when they had taken a boat to France. The medieval streets were narrow and cobbled, the houses dark and the Clyde side as dismal as any port could be.

Descending from the carriage, Alexander knocked on the door of a modest, newly painted house, waiting with a throbbing heart for the door to open. When it did, he stood motionless and tongue-tied, staring at the grey-haired woman in a black dress who stood before him. She too looked back at him silently. Gradually, the astonishment turned to recognition and then joy. Finally, Beatrice Ruthven drew her son to her breast, to weep tears of mingled emotions.

In time came Alistair, a clerk in one of the Clyde-based shipping companies, and sister Fiona, who was a tutor to the children of a prosperous family. They sat together for hours, talking endlessly, haphazardly, to capture the past. When evening fell and candles were lit, Beatrice ordered the maid to lay the table for supper. Glancing around, Alexander felt satisfied that his remittances home had kept the family in modest comfort though it had not raised them to their former prosperity. Fiona, an auburn-haired, green-eyed woman of twenty-two was a spinster and likely to remain one. Twenty-seven-year-old Alistair was pale and studious, unlike his bronzed and dashing brother. Ruthven found his thoughts straying to his long-lost sister.

At supper, he finally summoned enough courage to ask. "Did you ever come to hear of ... Deirdre?"

For moments no one answered. Then Beatrice Ruthven spoke. "Yes. We heard of her when we were in France — through other exiles. It was for her sake that we returned to Britain. We stopped in London to take her with us."

"Where was she?" Alexander asked, tense and eager.

Beatrice stared at her plate. "Deirdre was in the house of Walter Manham, the Redcoat major who executed your father ... and violated Deirdre."

Alexander felt his hands go cold. He glanced at his brother and sister, who looked back at him stony faced.

"Deirdre had served her purpose for Manham. She had borne him a child and together the two stayed in that house as servants — even after Manham married."

"You ... brought her back ...?" Alexander asked.

Beatrice nodded. "We brought back her living body. Deirdre — the one we knew ... so full of grace and kindness ... she had perished in Manham's house. The child died a few years later."

Alexander rose abruptly, sending the chair clattering to the floor. "Where is Deirdre now?"

"She lives in a convent with the good sisters of St. Clara. There she makes garlands for the altar, roams around the garden, laughs and sings and weeps as her mood dictates. The good nuns know her grief and the cause of her madness. They treat her kindly."

The next morning, Alexander went to see his sister, the beloved companion of his childhood. She met him, blinking watery blue eyes in bewilderment. How could she recognise in the tall, elegantly dressed man of thirty-one, the boy of eleven who had watched her screaming as a Redcoat fell upon her? She herself had changed beyond recognition. The auburn hair was grey streaked and the slender, flawless-skinned girl was now a pockmarked, heavy woman, exhausted by childbirths, domestic labour and terrifying memories of degradation.

Alexander was speechless. He stared, horrified, at the picture of devastation before him. What he saw was not only a tragedy but the symbol, in his eyes, of what subjugation of one race did to another.

Deirdre turned to glance at the man who stood at a distance.

There was terror in her eyes; her vagrant mind conjured up visions of another such well-dressed man who had treated her with brutal indignity.

Finally, Alexander spoke. "Can you not recognise me, my dear love? I am your brother, Alexander."

She frowned and smiled wanly. "Alexander? No ... he is a little boy ... in France. He and Mamma left me with Manham ... they forgot me. I was sick ... and tired ... but they stayed away ..." She looked around, frightened. "Manham is looking for me," she whispered hoarsely, "but I will escape him this time. Mother Celeste will protect me. Will she not, Sister Angelina?"

The nun nodded impassively. The story and the anxieties of the sick, mad woman were not new to her.

"If you see my brother Alexander," Deirdre whispered, "tell him I ... want to play by the stream again ... and catch trout there." She laughed suddenly and turned away towards the grilled door.

Sister Angelina bowed and led her charge away, leaving Alexander desolate.

On the way back home, Alexander felt searing remorse for not having returned to Europe earlier, for not rescuing Deirdre from Manham's brutality before she went mad. As his smart carriage ran over wet cobbled streets, the feverish lust for amassing wealth in India suddenly seemed insignificant weighed against the tragedy of his sister. He vowed to avenge Deirdre's ruin and neglect of his family.

"I am thrilled ... Alex ..." Fiona Ruthven murmured, gazing out towards the distant shoreline of Bengal harbour, as the East Indiaman ran seven knots an hour under topsails and foresail. "I hardly believe it is true."

Alexander Ruthven smiled indulgently at his youngest sister. "I trust you will not be disappointed, my child. India can be a trial."

After seven months at sea, Fiona Ruthven still looked as fresh and robust as she had in Scotland. There were changes in her appearance however; the satin dress she wore was hooped wide, with bows and lace, and her hat was wide brimmed and loaded with flowers. Several ornaments of gold and pearls adorned her wrists and neck. "No, I shall not be disappointed, Alexander," she assured him, gazing once more at the creamy, frilly breakers extending way out, before they broke with immense fury. A light south west breeze sprang up, carrying them to Balasore Road where the ship *S.S. Falmouth* dropped anchor, off Sagar Dwip or "Saugar Island" as the British called it. Here the blue turbulent waters of the Bay of Bengal received those of the amber Ganges, laden with silt. Here the passengers transferred their persons and luggage to a panchway or five-laned boat which took them to Calcutta. On the way they stopped at a grimy tavern in Culpee where the dirty mattresses were overshadowed by the feast of excellent fresh river fish, tender fowl, bacon and eggs, hot brown bread, and the claret and Madeira which attended the meal. After the meal, the men played billiards on an improvised table and Fiona slept fitfully on the mattress as mosquitoes serenaded her. The silence was punctuated by sounds of baying jackals. The next morning, they boarded the panchway and resumed the journey.

The swift tide bore them quickly past the village of Ulberia until they were at Garden Reach — a colony erected by the East India Company to accommodate its highest officials. The bank stood thirty feet above the river, surrounded by the luxuriant verdure of tropical gardens. Above them rose clusters of magnificent mansions, built by the East India Company's officials and traders. On the wide expanse of water floated ships of many sizes and further up were the wet and dry docks built by the Company. Clustered around were shops owned by blacksmiths and sailmakers, naval stores, warehouses for timber, cables, canvas and anchors. At the bend of the river stood Fort William, citadel of the growing British power.

The ship anchored in the dock, and while Ruthven's minions

came to take charge of the luggage, he and Fiona boarded a phaeton. They drove by the busy, crowded Strand dotted with wharves and thatch-covered warehouses and then on to the Esplanade whose whitewashed offices and shops stood back from the wide boulevard. Scores of carriages clattered past.

Fiona sat on the phaeton, glancing around her with evident excitement and wonder. The office buildings on the Esplanade with their Romanesque facades seemed at variance with the warm sunlight, the vivid tropical flowers and the dark, lithe figures that flitted past. Smart carriages and colourful palanquins jostled each other on the wide, shady roads and vendors cried out their wares in a tongue that was as different from the highland burr as the budding mango blossoms were from heather. She leaned out perilously upon seeing an ash-smeared naked sadhu stride past, a trident held aloft, followed by ochre-robed disciples beating cymbals. Alexander Ruthven chuckled, seeing her amazement. "An ascetic who has renounced all vanities," he said, in explanation.

"Heavens!" Fiona cried, "what bold men!" She turned to her brother. "This is a strange, amazing place!"

Ruthven nodded. "That it is, but don't be afraid, my dear. You will get accustomed to it all soon enough."

"I am not afraid, Alexander. Indeed, I am filled with wonder."

Smiling, Ruthven drove towards Alipur. Riding between houses girded by tall, spreading trees, they stopped before an imposing white mansion built in emulation of the classical style, its facade Romanesque, the wide verandas supported by Corinthian pillars. "Welcome, my dear," Ruthven said with a smile, pleased by his sister's wide-eyed admiration.

"This is yours?" Fiona murmured. "Your own house?"

"This is the house I commissioned Tisetta to design and build before I left," Ruthven said dryly.

Fiona stared at the mansion, at the young coconut saplings lining both sides of the gravel path, the old trees encircling the large garden. Slowly, she alighted from the phaeton and ascended the shallow marble stairs leading to the cool, shaded veranda where a dozen servants stood watching her with candid interest.

Alexander Ruthven followed and then led her to the vast drawing room with its circular bay windows and gilted ceilings. "Bare, is it not? Never mind, we shall soon set it right. Tisetta has discharged his duties well." He left the drawing room to walk into the dining room whose French windows looked out into the garden. Quickly he strode to other rooms, checking and appraising until he came to the wide, curved staircase leading upstairs.

"Is the Begum in her chamber?" Ruthven asked the major domo, a quiet and competent Hindu.

"She has been waiting, Saheb ... since your ship was sighted at Sagar," the servant replied.

Ruthven glanced at his sister. "Wait in the drawing room, my dear, and take some refreshments. I must go up to greet my wife."

Fiona nodded as Alexander made his way up the staircase, its design copied from a Renaissance palazzo. He glanced with satisfaction at the Persian carpet placed over the marble flooring and then strode to the main bedchamber on the landing.

Begum Shirin Ruthven sat on a chesterfield recently shipped from England. The entire room was furnished in the style of a Moghul palace. The figure of the Begum in brocade kamiz and gharara, laden with heavy jewellery merged with the room. She rose as Ruthven entered, a slow colour spreading over the pallid cheeks. Involuntarily, she stepped forward, then retreated, as she remembered that it was he who must make the overture.

His eyes swept over the plump cheeks, the lines along the rosebud mouth and grey sloe eyes, the heavy breasts which had once been taut. The supple waist and arms had thickened as well. Only the hands were the same slender, satiny ones he had first seen in the palace of Hazar Duari ten years ago, after Plassey. She still retained the impassive beauty of a Moghul noblewoman but Ruthven saw that her youth had begun to flee.

"Janab," Shirin whispered, no longer able to maintain the aloof dignity of her legacy and frightened by the scrutiny of his cold blue eyes. "I have waited and prayed for your safe return."

Sudden compassion for his Begum and gratitude for her past support made him put aside his infidel thoughts. "Begum," he murmured, stepping forward to take her in his arms, "I am glad to be back."

The embrace, begun with kindness, soon turned to an eager, impatient craving for her body. Roughly, he pulled away her voluminous skirt and short tunic, and laid her on the huge satin-covered four-poster bed. Now he saw that her trim, tense body had become plump and flaccid but her hands could still conjure up the old magic on his body and excite him to a frenzied desire. As he thrust himself into her, she fought free, murmuring hoarsely, "Not so soon, my Sikander, not so hastily please! Twenty months I have waited for you ... for this moment. Treat me sweetly ... as you used to ... and take me ... with love."

Alexander Ruthven saw tears rise to her grey eyes, no longer opaque and inscrutable but filled with the anguish of doubt. She had waited ... and borne him a son in his absence while he had caroused in Edinburgh and London and Paris, sampling women from taverns as well as country houses. On them he had squandered baubles and received tributes to his manhood.

Gently he drew her close, savouring with his tongue her rosebud mouth, and the sweet heavy breasts, kneading the soft plump flesh with his hard competent hands, until she arched beneath him and whispered hoarsely. "Yes, my Sikander, now I am ready ..." Slowly he entered her, aware of her great hunger and the passion he had never perceived in her hard, younger body. It grew with her movements, so frantic and urgent, so pitiful and unashamed, until he responded as fiercely, their bodies coalescing in satiation.

Some time passed before Ruthven got up and began to don his clothes. "My sister ... has been waiting downstairs ... shall we go down together to welcome her?"

Silently Shirin got up, dressing hurriedly, a strange fear clutching her. Together they entered the drawing room. Begum Ruthven stared at the slender, comely woman who bore so striking a resemblance to her husband. Shirin's body eased into relief. "The firingi woman is not his concubine," she thought with a surge of joy. "Ah Allah, praise be to you! When I heard that a firingi woman had come with him, I felt it must be a concubine!"

Fiona Ruthven stared at Shirin, tongue-tied and bewildered by the oriental dress and jewels and curious of her brother's relationship to this lady. In eight years, Fiona had learnt to accept a "Moghul" sister-in-law but face to face with this noblewoman of Afghan ancestry, Fiona lost her composure. It was as if she had been transported to a world of exotic fairy tales, peopled with princes, genies and dancing girls. Only this "princess" did nothing to break the ice. The cold, kohl-lined eyes were more veiled than her colourless, impassive face.

Alexander Ruthven chuckled, amused. "Ladies, you will continue to pass the afternoon scrutinising each other. Need I formally introduce you?"

Shirin read the warning in his voice and slowly advanced towards Fiona. "Welcome ... to our home ... to Calcutta," she said solemnly.

Fiona came forward and kissed Shirin on both cheeks. "I am glad to meet you, Begum. I hope we will be good friends." Her voice shook with uncertainty and fear.

Begum Shirin smiled, touched by Fiona's maidenly behaviour. "We shall be more than friends, Fiona Bano ... we shall be sisters."

The ladies embraced with tears and smiles while Alexander looked on as if it were all a joke.

Fiona Ruthven was launched into Calcutta society at a ball given by no less a personage than Lady Impey, wife of Sir Elijah Impey, Chief Justice of Calcutta High Court. She had earlier held the ceremonial breakfast at which all newcomers to Calcutta were introduced. Here Fiona met distinguished lawyers such as Sir George Shee, Leonard Collins, Edward Hay and Peter Moore all of whom were polite to an upcoming "nabob" like Alexander Ruthven.

The ball was not quite what Fiona had visualised or heard about from the gentry in Scotland.

Guests assembled at Sir Elijah Impey's home in Chand Pal Ghat — on the riverbank — at dusk when the cool February air wafted into the long rectangular rooms. Lady Impey, like many other rich British residents in India, had had shiploads of furniture transported from London or even Paris. Huge chandeliers from Antwerp hung from the high ceiling. The house too was built in the new classical style favoured by the Adam brothers in England. The rich Persian and Kashmiri carpets, brocade covers for settees and chairs, and heavy silk curtains gave an Indian touch to an essentially English house. As did the vast retinue of Indian servants in colourful "Moorman's trousers" tunics and turbans. Lady Impey complained that she could "barely manage with eighty-five retainers."

After introductions and sherry, the guests assembled in the dining room where tables had been set for a hundred. Dinner consisted of ten courses: soup, fish, fowl or pheasant, mutton, beef or veal, curries of various vegetables with pullao, and finally dessert, and an assortment of cheese with biscuits, concluded by coffee or tea and brandy or port. "Just a little party," Lady Impey informed the haughty Begum Ruthven and Miss Fiona Ruthven.

Alexander Ruthven watched his wife with satisfaction. Fiona had persuaded the haughty Moghul lady to make her appearance in British society. For years, speculation had been rife about "Nabob" Ruthven's Begum. That she was descended from Moghul emperors (albeit through concubines and bastards) on the maternal side was no longer doubted; the imperious cast of her pale face, the opaque grey eyes and high cheekbones betokened Turko-Afghan ancestry. Of her wealth there were no questions; her person glittered with jewels of size and brilliance. Her husband's devotion to her was borne out by his attentions. When she spoke, in halting English, Lady Impey strained to listen and agree charmingly. She had great expectations from friendship with such a Begum. Alexander Ruthven was vastly amused by his wife's haughty, condescending stance.

He was less amused by Fiona's bewilderment as the guests, intoxicated by Rhenish and Madeira began to pelt each other with pellets of crushed bread from their plates. Fiona could not know that this was a fashionable game at British parties in Calcutta. The champion of this sport, General Barwell, kept up a relentless fire across the table, occasionally hitting Fiona.

"Damn you, Barwell, this goes too far!" Captain Morrison exclaimed as a handful of pellets spun into his glass of Madeira.

"Far? Indeed, Morrison, you do not know how far I can go!" Barwell retorted, laughing and rising from the chair to address the hostess. "My lady, I will now demonstrate my other prowess. Allow me to snuff out your candles from a distance of four yards."

Long accustomed to such boisterous manners, Lady Impey sighed and nodded. General Barwell stepped back and stood at a distance of four yards. Then filling his chest with air, he emitted it back with full force, extinguishing three candles.

"Splendid!" Mrs. Grover cried, rising to kiss the champion. Their kiss was interrupted by a flying leg of mutton, staining the gallantuomo's satin jacket with a thick butter and cinnamon sauce, and splashing the lady's malmal dress.

The burst of laughter at the champion's plight faded as Barwell strode with grave dignity towards the English trader who had flung the missile.

"I call you out, Sir," he shouted.

Mr. Grover bowed. "My pleasure, Sir. When shall we commence?"

"Right now, Sir! Say your farewells ... for you shall not last the night!"

A troubled silence fell upon the noisy revellers as the two men prepared to leave the room. When Lady Impey made a movement of protest, Sir Elijah shook his head. Fiona, who had read of duels in story-books, stared white faced at the two men. She was shocked to find a sardonic smile on her brother's face. Begum Shirin murmured with a sneer. "Moghul durbar me aise nahin hota tha," — Such things did not happen at the Moghul court.

"The dessert!" Lady Impey's voice broke the silence and galvanised the butler who had also been standing transfixed, into action. He scurried out to summon the servants to produce sorbets of pomegranate and tangerine along with the barfis and halwas so favoured by the British.

Fiona stared at the sorbet, straining to hear the sound of swords when her brother said quietly, "They will be near the Maidan. You will not hear them from here."

The sound of galloping horse hooves was soon heard in the ensuing silence, as Colonel Barwell and Mr. Grover rode away to fight their duel.

Mrs. Clorinda Grover stood up, wild eyed and dishevelled. "Someone must stop my poor husband from fighting Barwell! He cannot survive that man's aim," she cried.

"Indeed, Ma'am, you should have considered the danger earlier when you encouraged Barwell's dalliance," retorted a shrivel-faced lady.

"Ah! It is intolerable!" Clorinda cried, clutching her bosom. "I will then go alone to the Maidan!"

Fiona Ruthven stood up, pale but composed. "I shall accompany you, Mrs. Grover," she said quietly as she followed the distracted woman towards the door.

Begum Shirin glanced hastily at her husband who stood up to detain his sister but could not stop Fiona's swift flight to the Grovers' carriage.

The roads were dark and deserted. The only sound was the soft lapping of the river on the pebbled shore nearby. As the carriage left Alipur and approached the Maidan, the shrieking jackals and wild cats made Clorinda pause in her weeping.

"Is it safe, Miss Ruthven? Should we return?" she asked in a high, shrill voice.

"How can you, Ma'am, when your husband is in peril?" Fiona reproached tartly.

Clorinda put her head between her hands and moaned in despair, until a burst of gunfire shook the dark stillness. "Mr. Grover!" she screamed. "I fear he is dead!"

Fiona did not contradict her, though she was puzzled by the swift succession of shots. A duel would not call for more than four. She sat still, peering into the darkness as the carriage rattled forward towards the sounds.

Two men galloped forward on horses and brought their carriage to a lurching halt. One masked man held aloft a flaring torch as he peered into the faces of the two astonished women.

"Ah! Two lambs to fleece! What astounding good fortune in one night!" The Englishman turned to his Indian comrade who wore a Moorman's coat and turban. "See here, Gopaldas, what a haul we have on milady's throat."

Gopaldas chuckled softly. "Almost as good as Barwell's pocket," he replied. "But let us not tarry here, Howard. Barwell will recover presently and give us a merry chase."

"Barwell is wounded then?" Fiona asked, recovering from the shock.

Howard laughed. "Not from his opponent's pistol, to be sure. That man cannot shoot at even an arm's length. No my lady, it is my pistol that has winged the redoubtable colonel."

"And my husband?" Clorinda Grover asked in a choked voice.

A smile lit the masked Indian's eyes. "He lives ... as we prevented Barwell from his sport."

Clorinda burst into tears. "Oh Sirs! How shall I ever repay you?" she asked.

"Simple, Ma'am," Howard replied softly. "The bauble on your pretty neck should suffice."

Clorinda tore off the diamond pendant and handed it tearfully to the English bandit. "Thank you, Ma'am," he said smiling. "It is little enough for saving your husband's life."

"But enough to cut short your precarious lives!" Fiona burst out. "Dacoity is not a safe sport."

Howard nodded. "Agreed — but how else can an impecunious writer of the East India Company supplement his income except to join the fraternity of Indian dacoits?" He turned to his comrade. "My friend Gopaldas is well versed in the trade. I am safe in his company," He paused. I would caution you not to reveal our names, Ma'am. We hurt no one if our demands are met. Should you however reveal our ... er ... meeting, we would not balk at ... abducting you for offerings at our new moon ceremonies."

Laughing, both men spurred their horses and disappeared as abruptly as they had appeared. Slowly, the carriage trundled forward to rescue the two duellers who stood, dishevelled and indignant, in the darkness.

Their arrival at Impey's house occasioned only mild laughter. Such occurrences were frequent. Besides, by ten o'clock the ball began with the arrival of another hundred guests. Many came already inebriated.

A Mrs. Gordon glided towards Alexander Ruthven who was taking a pinch of snuff. "Why, Mr. Ruthven, how nice to see you again! When did you return?"

Though Ruthven replied politely, his eyes sparkled in amusement at her dishevelled coiffure and crumpled skirt. Noticing his look, Mrs. Gordon said,"Do you know we could hardly reach here ... what with bad, unlighted streets! As for Mr. Howard, his phaeton collided into a tree!"

Ruthven nodded. "Indeed, Calcutta gets more chaotic every year."

Mrs. Gordon pouted and smiled. "You are quizzing me, Sir! Now, ask me to dance the cotillion and describe the latest fashions in London and Paris. Is it true that Madame de Pompadour has set a new style in dressing?"

As Alexander Ruthven danced with Mrs. Gordon, he enlightened her about European fashions while Begum Ruthven watched from a settee, eyes narrowed, her pale hands clenched over a sandalwood fan. When a Company official came up to her, inviting her to dance, Shirin lifted her fan and answered in chaste Urdu, "In our country only nautch girls dance." Flushing a vivid scarlet over a face already coloured by claret and hock, the gentleman bowed and withdrew. At once, Fiona rose and offered shyly if she would suffice and during the dance, took pains to explain that oriental women brought up in seclusion were not as free in society as European women.

The lawyer smiled sarcastically. "Indeed Miss Ruthven? I am reassured to hear of the delicacy of their conduct and sentiments. However, I happen to know that the Begum has considerable talent in trade ... and politics."

Fiona was silent. Her sister-in-law was an enigma to her — almost as much an enigma as her brother.

The dancing gathered momentum as the February night turned cold, with mist rising from the Ganges nearby. Above, a million stars shone through a veil of wispy clouds. Below, on the garden paths and balustrades coloured lanterns spluttered and were extinguished by the night wind. Fiona Ruthven looked around the ballroom to find only very young people dancing to the tune of two bands. Many of the unmarried gentlemen had slipped away to anterooms to keep assignations with ladies of their choice while the husbands sat playing cards. She paused to watch and was surprised to find the men playing for extremely high stakes. Mr. Gordon had lost a small fortune to General Barwell, and vowed to recoup it at the "Whist Club" next week. In another well-appointed room, Sir Elijah Impey was deep in discussion with Alexander Ruthven and other officials of the East India Company.

"Colonel Clive has been assiduous in his efforts to control our commercial ventures," Sir Elijah said. "As you know, he has ordered the curtailment of presents for officials and double batta for our soldiers. Moreover, he resents that men below the rank of field officers have money to squander."

Ruthven nodded. "There is pressure from Leadenhall Street to curb our fortunes. During my sojourn in London last year, I was dismayed to find that the directors of our Company resent the fruits of our enterprise."

"Ah, they are only dismayed that we earn it and not they! There is a clamour too among our nobility to share this wealth. Sons of dukes and earls, not to mention Princes of the Blood wish to come to India. Clive has joined the chorus. He was heard to say the other day to a visiting nobleman, "The East India Company is a group of merchants whose servants have lately exhibited in these realms the magnificence and pageantry of sovereigns to the disparagement of the ancient nobility."

"Ancient nobility!" Ruthven retorted. "The ancient nobility has been dispersed. Is there a Plantagenet or Stuart family left in Hanoverian England? We have only Germans and Dutchmen!"

"Aye ... that is so," observed the astute Impey, noting Ruthven's sympathy for the Stuarts. "But Clive's Covenant ... what shall we do about that?"

"Ignore it. How can he prevent our ventures? Has he not dipped deep into the nawab of Bengal's treasury every time he installed a new usurper? Has he not permitted private trade in saltpetre to continue? And what of his own jagir for which the Company pays him a rent?" Ruthven spoke with controlled disgust.

"I hear ... though it is as yet unconfirmed, that Parliament is going to order the Company to pay £ 400,000 to the treasury." Elijah Impey sounded distraught. "How shall we raise the amount?"

Ruthven leaned forward and spoke softly. "How, Sir Elijah? Through increased private trading, through taxes on Indian merchants and landlords. This country is rich enough."

Sir Elijah nodded, looking at Ruthven with new perception. "How is your own private trade, Ruthven?"

Ruthven took a pinch of snuff from a tiny jewelled box. "In my absence, the silk farmers I had employed became impudent. They began to weave silk for selling to the Company. I hope I have taught them a lesson by cutting off their thumbs." He paused and smiled. "It is a pity, however! Their skill is peerless. But our English factories need Indian silk and cotton yarn only

— not manufactured goods. Our Bengali farmers refuse to forget their skills!"

Laughter vibrated in the room as the men rose to adjourn to the drawing room to drink more wine and partake of the cakes and cold meats now being served.

Fiona slipped away before her brother saw her, to a secluded corner of the wide balustraded terrace which descended in long, shallow steps to the river. She could see the most determined guests dancing to the point of exhaustion. "A guest was almost killed in a duel, a lady has collapsed from exhaustion ... and still they go on," she thought in bewilderment.

A pale but glowing winter sun rose over the river when Alexander Ruthven found his sister, sleeping wearily, muffled in a shawl. Coffee and tea was being served. The party was ending.

7

Dark Indigo

"I had a different image of my brother," Fiona reflected, sitting in her newly furnished room. "This aloof man with his air of detachment and sardonic smile has little resemblance to the kindly, intense youth who was our anchor in Marseilles. Until that night at Sir Elijah's house, I had no idea of what trading they did and of how the nabobs acquired their wealth. That these rough and coarse men come to flaunt their riches in England ... ! No, but I must not express such sentiments before my brother ... or to his Begum, for that matter. They are ... drawn together by a love of riches ... a bond as strong perhaps as love itself."

The riches had come now from England: furniture from London, Staffordshire pottery and Sheffield cutlery, clothes from Bond Street, silver tea sets and candelabras. Fiona had been charged with the task of decorating the rooms in English style while Begum Shirin grumbled and insisted on retaining Persian carpets, silk curtains, Moradabad lamps and jugs. As a result, Ruthven House became a medley of styles, with neither elegance nor character.

Though Alexander Ruthven displayed indifference with regard to house decoration, he insisted on Fiona's obedience in the social life he planned for her. He was pleased by Fiona's success in Company circles and gratified that she had persuaded Begum Shirin to forsake the purdah and enter Company social life. He enjoyed the effect that Shirin's jewels and imperial pretensions had on his colleagues. Begum Shirin Ruthven attracted the naive Britons with stories of the Moghul court, its intrigues and fratricidal wars. She told them of her Afghan father, a mercenary general whose ability pleased Nawab Alivardi Khan of Bengal so much that he selected a lady of the Moghul court as wife for the Afghan general. "My mother," Shirin liked to relate, "was descended from Emperor Jahangir."

At this point Alexander Ruthven always bestowed a sardonic smile on his Begum who had not concealed from her Scottish lord the fact that her mother's grandfather was one of the numerous bastards attributed to that licentious emperor. If Begum Shirin intercepted Ruthven's ironical countenance, she reacted by thrusting aside her veil or beatilah to display the long rope of lustrous pearls which cascaded over her bosom. "These," Shirin would declare haughtily, "were once the possession of Jahangir's celebrated Empress, Nur Jahan."

"Purloined, my dear, from the casket of Begum Lutfinissa of Bengal," Ruthven thought with a chuckle. Nevertheless, he was gratified to see how the story of Shirin's imperial lineage impressed his British colleagues. "It confers a new dignity on me," thought Ruthven. But it did more than that. It sowed in his mind inchoate and restless dreams.

If Shirin formed part of those dreams, Fiona was to serve other designs. To reduce her resistance and make her pliable, Ruthven surrounded her with the gaiety and luxury of a "Nabob's" lady.

Fiona was woken by a posse of servants, announcing that the night had ended. The maidservants massaged her with scented oil, scrubbed her with loofah, a dried fibrous vegetable, poured cool water on her and then helped her to don one of the ethereal dresses made from Dacca muslin and designed by a growing tribe of "Memsaheb's Darzi" or tailors for white women. They could copy any style to perfection. After dressing, Fiona sometimes went to greet her brother who sat on a high leather chair while his barber shaved his cheeks, cut his nails and cleaned his ears. Two more servants came to bathe and dress him.

After a breakfast of papaya, fruits, lamb chops, omelette, fried fish and toast, Alexander sat reading the *Calcutta Gazette* while his hairdresser cleaned and combed out a wig to put on the Saheb's head. With tea came the hookah-bardar. After a leisurely puff on the hookah, Alexander announced his intention to go to the Company Kacheri or Writers' Building, the red brick Georgian-Gothic structure built by the East India Company to house its many 'writers' and officials.

Fiona watched the imposing procession from the upper balcony. When the mood dictated, Ruthven was carried to the office on a palanquin by four bearers. Preceding him were two subedars, six harkaras or announcers dressed in scarlet coats, loose blue trousers and white turbans. "Rasta, rasta..." the six harkaras shouted, to clear the progress of the nabob. If he rode, two scyce or grooms ran with him, gasping all the way, under spreading shirish trees.

To while away the mornings, Fiona joined other British ladies for phaeton drives around the flat open plain or Maidan. They would stop at the vast race course to chat and then return home to wash and change, in readiness for visitors. Attracted as much by the enigmatic Begum Ruthven as by Miss Fiona, many visitors called.

The older group came to meet the Begum, who received them with a graciousness tinged by condescension.

"Their manners," she explained to Fiona later, "are far from those expected of the gentry. In our courts, no one talks or laughs so loudly. A man who slaps his thigh is considered vulgar. As for that man who aimed bread pellets at that lady's bosom ... in a Moghul court he would be executed." Though inwardly Fiona agreed that the conduct of the Company officials and their wives was crude and boisterous, she felt constrained to defend her compatriots. "You must not judge our countrymen or women by the Company officials. Our aristocrats would grace the Moghul court."

The visitors, Fiona observed, were restrained in the Begum's presence but once she left to await her husband in their apartment,

Fiona would be inundated with anecdotes and jests about the previous night's party.

"You will not credit this, my dear Fiona, but Mrs. Apsley actually removed her overdress to dance," one lady informed her. Another related how a Mrs. Fenn was mortified by Lieutenant Brooke's behaviour when the band struck up in the mess of the Bengal Native Infantry. "As they played 'Kiss My Lady', he kissed Clorinda Grover, and Mr. Grover could do nothing about it but stomp out. So they called him 'cock tail'. Is that not mortifying?"

Fiona nodded wearily. "Very. I do hope that Captain Fenn will be more firm in future with his subordinates."

"And Evelina Mandeville? Did you see her? She ate two pounds of mutton at dinner and washed it down with a bottle of medium claret."

Mrs. Mandeville's complexion was also discussed. "No doubt she does not care to trouble herself," commented one visitor. "In this season one needs to add a touch of colour. 'Venus Bloom' and 'Marshall Powder' repair the damage wrought by the heat. You should try these, Miss Fiona, as well as Hungary Water, Lavender and Bergamot for shoulders and hands."

Fiona eagerly noted the names. The summer heat and monsoon sultriness had already taken their toll on her fresh complexion while frequent washing of silks and brocades had taken the shine off the fabrics. The solution, one lady indicated, was to have a very large wardrobe. "My husband, for instance, possesses seventy pairs of breeches, eighty waistcoats and a hundred shirts. Thank heavens that dimity, nankeen and malmal are cheap. Whatever should we have done otherwise?"

Tea, wine and sweetmeats were brought in by a bevy of servants. As doctors believed in the antiseptic value of port wine, it was drunk on all occasions as a talisman against disease.

Gossip was then concluded for the day as the ladies dispersed to await their menfolk for lunch. Lunch was elaborate, no matter what the season. The Muslim cooks competed with one another to produce their version of "Angrezi khana" or English cuisine, which was in fact a fusion of English, Moghul and Portuguese styles. An abundance of wines accompanied these heavy meals.

Fiona lay restless on her wide bed upstairs during the long siesta hours. She heard her brother working in the study across the landing while Begum Shirin had herself massaged to sleep. There was an unreality about this existence which troubled her. These wild parties and interminable dances had no resemblance to the austere routine of her Inverness days or the bleak exile in France. Inured to hardship, she wondered how long this pleasure-filled opulence would last.

Before any answers could come, it would be dusk — heralded by the appearance of the French hairdresser who charged a steep price — rupees four — to pile her hair on a frame, twist it like a turban and embellish it with ribbons and flowers. Alexander Ruthven wore his red hair unpowdered, and tied back with a black velvet ribbon, while his Begum preferred to have her dark hair plaited and coiled and pinned up with jewels with the help of her favourite serving woman, Salima. In time, when this servant learned to do Fiona's hair with all the intricacy of a Versailles paruchiere, the Ruthven ladies kept the matter a great secret though Alexander jested, "I shall hire out Salima to Lady Impey for a steep price."

Dressed in lace, spangles and foil, the ladies, in their hooped skirts of taffeta or brocade, the men in their vivid coats of Indian silk, went out on phaetons or palanquins to meet in the Maidan or by the river. There, they exchanged the day's news and then adjourned to attend the numerous parties thrown by bored, rich ladies.

It was at one of these gatherings that Fiona was introduced by her brother to Henry Dalrymple, a rich indigo planter. Alexander left them together, admonishing Fiona to be amiable with Dalrymple. "He came, like me, as a soldier in the Company's army but has made his fortune in land."

"How so?" Fiona asked softly, scrutinising the thickset man in his silk coat and diamond buttons.

"He has been judicious in his purchase of lands— sold in auction by the Company when the Indian landlords could not pay taxes."

Fiona became solemn. "How unfortunate that we, who are foreigners here, should have the power to take over their lands." She paused. "It was what happened to Scotland after Culloden." She glanced at her brother with some trepidation." Should we ... perpetrate the pain that was inflicted on us?"

Ruthven's lips tightened. "You can return to Inverness any time you wish, dear sister. Alistair will not, however, keep you. He is my agent in Leadenhall Street and Mama is in his home. They will not cross my will."

Fiona flushed, her small bosom heaving with suppressed fury. "Perhaps I may do that ..." she said, turning away. Ruthven caught her slender wrist in an iron grip.

"Until then, be pleasant to Mr. Dalrymple. We are to visit his estate next week." His voice was like a whiplash.

Fiona breathed deeply to choke back a cry of protest and allowed herself to be led to the eagerly waiting Dalrymple whose bleary eyes devoured the slender, nubile, young woman before him. Candlelight glimmered on her Titian hair, and turned her blue eyes to fiery sparks. He ran his tongue over dry, thick lips in anticipation of the kisses with which he planned to arouse the grave-faced lassie.

Fiona sat frigid and grim in Henry Dalrymple's veranda, pretending not to hear his conversation with Alexander Ruthven, as the men drank a pre-dusk rum.

"The Chowdhurys are resisting my demands," Dalrymple observed. "Not the father so much as that irascible son. Damned stubborn fellow!"

Ruthven nodded. "That he is. I remember seeing Indrajit Chowdhury about nine years ago when I came here to trade. A stripling he was but ordered me off his lands." Ruthven paused to laugh softly. "I would like to order him off now." Dalrymple joined in the laughter — more loudly. "Yes, that would be a delight. And it won't be long before he will cringe to sell the other lands ... at the rate that our Company Bahadur is collecting revenues."

Ruthven raised his glass. "To richer revenues!"

"To more lands!" Dalrymple rejoined, laughing still louder. The rum was beginning to take effect.

In the silence that followed, Fiona glanced towards the distant, slow flowing river where shallow dinghies glided past, nets held aloft by fishermen who sang a mournful dirge of boatmen.

Dusk will soon fall
And I will be alone
Empty and poor
On Mother Ganga's Bosom.

Fiona drew in her breath, moved by the lament that needed no words of translation to stir memories of loss. She felt a surge of anger and fear mingle within her as the men continued their conversation.

"The only problem is the damned sadhus," Dalrymple resumed, refilling his glass. "They used to worship in the coconut grove at the edge of the river yonder. After I came, I pushed them out, but they come back on new moon nights."

Ruthven nodded. Though flushed by the punch, he showed not a trace of inebriation. "They do not take kindly to displacement."

Dalrymple drew his chair nearer and glanced apprehensively at the darkening grove one furlong away. "They ... are a wild lot, Ruthven. I .... am ... er, not quite easy with them. You know about the tantrics?"

Ruthven nodded. "Vaguely. I gather they practise strange rites of sacrifice and orgy."

Dalrymple nodded. Beads of perspiration glistened on his florid face. "It would be ... interesting to watch," he mumbled.

Ruthven rose. "I would not do so," he said quietly. "Leave the Hindus to their rites. We need have no concern with their customs. So long as they give us our taxes." But his eyes were on the distant coconut grove. "I will change for dinner. No doubt you will do the same, Fiona."

Fiona stood up rigidly and was about to follow her brother when Dalrymple interposed. "Let me take Miss Fiona for a stroll ... just to show her my estate ..."

Ruthven seemed to hesitate before saying, "Very well — just for a while."

Fiona strode on ahead, refusing the offer of Dalrymple's arm. The front garden was wild and unkempt though traces of its former beauty were still visible. The house was new and garish, like Dalrymple's clothes. They strolled across the compound and went into the land lying in a haze of misty grey — the terrible indigo fields. Fiona saw men working on them — blackened by the sun, shrivelled by hunger and now intimidated by the appearance of Dalrymple. They paused briefly in their work to glance at their master with apprehension.

"Why do the farmers look upon you with such fear?" Fiona asked her host.

Dalrymple's jovial countenance underwent a sudden change. He stared at Fiona with a strange anxiety. "Fear? Yes, I suppose they do fear me. Why should they not?"

Fiona stared back with hard eyes. "They should — if they have cause to fear ... your cruelty," she said evenly.

Dalrymple flushed, his hands clenching in anger. "I shall trust you not to concern yourself with matters not connected with you."

"Certainly," Fiona replied with a smile. "It is no concern of mine. When I return to Calcutta, I assure you I shall not give the matter a thought." She turned towards the house, but glanced back again at the wizened men working in the indigo fields. "Of course, it will be difficult," she murmured, "to forget the fear and revulsion on their faces." Fiona turned and strode swiftly towards the house. Dalrymple followed, his gait loping and unsteady.

Dinner was a stilted affair. Both men were suddenly aware that Fiona was not the pliant and timid woman they had assumed her to be.

Next morning, before the men were awake, Fiona dressed

hurriedly, and snatching up a wide-brimmed hat, went out into the pale glitter of an October dawn. On both sides were dark expanses of indigo plants, interspersed with slender bushes of poppies — the two products on which Dalrymple had made a small fortune. His tenants were at work already. They paused briefly as she approached, and waited in anxiety for her to say or do something. Uneasy, Fiona strode on ahead until she came to the boundary of prickly mehendi hedges that marked the limits of Dalrymple's lands.

In the midst of ripening rice fields stood a tall, lithe-figured man, dressed in a dhoti and kurta. A servant held up a large tasselled umbrella over the young man's head as he stood watching his peasants, his face reflecting mingled pity and impatience. "This will not be enough to pay our taxes," he said gravely, appraising the paddy in the fields.

"This is all we can do, Babu," a peasant said wearily. "There has been less rain ... and we could not dig more channels or buy the oxen we planned to get ... it is all we could do."

Indrajit Chowdhury sighed deeply, in silent understanding and made a move to go. Then his eyes fell on the young woman standing at Dalrymple's boundary, on the lands which his father had sold two years ago. He noticed the flame-coloured hair and the blue eyes, the small freckled nose and full, wide lips. Suddenly, he remembered a British trader who had visited Mayurganj nine years ago who had resembled the woman.

"What do you want?" Indrajit asked curtly. "This is the boundary. Do not stray beyond this ... Dalrymple has not grasped this as yet."

Fiona felt a swift rush of blood to her face and would have retreated at once but for the strange magnetism emanating from the hostile young landlord. She saw the supple muscular figure which the folds of the dhoti could not conceal, the harsh, chiselled face and olive-coloured skin. His eyes were dark and compelling. She moved forward, almost without volition.

"Did you not hear me, Madam?" Indrajit asked icily, in English.

"Or is Dalrymple now using women for his nefarious designs?"

"I am a visitor here, Sir," Fiona replied indignantly. "I know nothing of Dalrymple's designs."

"If you are Dalrymple's guest then stay within his boundaries," the young zamindar retorted.

Trembling, Fiona walked towards Indrajit Chowdhury. His haughty face registered surprise as she said, "I do not wish to encroach upon your land." She paused and met his cold gaze. "I wish however to know — for reasons of my own — how Dalrymple acquired your lands?"

Indrajit smiled bitterly. "Innocence incarnate," he murmured to his munshi, in Bengali. "This firingi has all the cunning of a courtesan."

Fiona could not understand the words uttered in chaste Bengali but she gathered the implication. "Your attitude is offensive," she retorted hotly. "It is clear you are ready to condemn me as well!"

Indrajit regarded her with astonishment, his anger suddenly subdued by the fiery blue eyes that held an inexplicable plea. His cold glance moved to her flame-coloured hair that seemed to be woven out of the rays of the sun rising over the rim of the fields. Involuntarily, he moved a step forward and spoke.

"We have tried not to condemn all the British ... but the exceptions are few," he said slowly. "When we see our lands confiscated and auctioned on frivolous pretences, our farmers forced to grow indigo instead of rice; when our weavers, famed for their skill, are deprived of their thumbs in order to prevent them from manufacturing Dacca muslins and silks ... what are we to think?" He paused to essay a bitter smile. "Twelve years ago, my father Ishwarnath Chowdhury joined the Company of Robert Clive, against Siraj-ud-doula. He paid the Company officials in the hope that Bengal would be free of arbitrary nawabs ... but no nawab — not even Siraj-ud-doula — brought Bengal to so complete a ruin as has the Company Bahadur. Thirty million people in Bengal, Bihar and Orissa are taxed beyond endurance in order to enrich a foreign trading company." Indrajit glanced around, his bitter eyes sweeping over the land. "This year, the company — now the real Nawab of Bengal — has imposed an impossible tax demand on us. Most of my farmers are penniless. I too am on the verge of ruin. If I do not pay the required tax ... this land ... held by my forefathers for three centuries... will be auctioned. Either Dalrymple or his friend Ruthven will then be its owner."

Fiona started. "Ruthven? Is he also interested?" she asked agitatedly.

Indrajit nodded slowly. "Oh yes, he has cast his covetous eyes here ever since the time he was the Company's agent after Plassey. I remember how he came here nine years ago to trade, bullying our tenants to sell their goods cheaply. I was a boy of sixteen and longed to evict him ... but my father held me back."

Fiona heard the outburst with intense shame. "I am Ruthven's sister," she said quickly, meeting his eyes.

Indrajit nodded. "I guessed it to be so," he murmured. "I am ... grieved to hear of your tribulations. If only you could petition the Government in England ... Or should I inform my brother what their actions have led to?"

Indrajit shook his head. "I have preferred an appeal to the British judge at the Calcutta high court — a creature and puppet of the Company. They will do nothing. As for your brother, he will only laugh at your piety. However," Indrajit said, eyes hardening, "you can congratulate both Ruthven and Dalrymple that their greed and avarice has been the cause of my father's death." He glared at Fiona now, once more aware that she was British ... and Ruthven's sister as well. "Go back to your friends, Madam. That is where you belong."

Fiona gazed at him for a long moment. "Strange," she murmured, "that our lives should have a similar pattern. My father ... was killed by Redcoats ... and our property ruined ..."

Indrajit stared at her and then as he tried to speak, Fiona turned and began walking towards Dalrymple's bungalow. The sun was orange now, a glowing orb rising over the shimmering rice fields, gilding the fronds of coconut palms and grey plumes of sugarcane. The fields were awakening with the murmur of peasants and lowing of cattle. Women came out with their vessels to fetch water from the river bank. Indrajit remained staring after the retreating figure of Fiona Ruthven, until she disappeared from view.

At home, in the mansion built by his father, Indrajit was confronted with aggravating domestic problems. "It is enough to worry about the estate and crops, taxes and food, without having to settle servants' disputes and measure butter!" he shouted.

The munshi bowed his head. "We try to help ... but ..."

"Yes, but there is no lady of the house!" Indrajit exploded. "My mother dead, my wife ..." he stopped, remembering that he now had two wives; the frail, childless Bishnupriya, now a woman of twenty, and a robust bride of ten named Indumati.

The child-bride had been selected from amongst many candidates by Indrajit's uncle who was anxious to save the Mayurganj Chowdhury line. The little girl had a glowing olive skin, sturdy bones and a ready smile, but Indrajit could not imagine her as the mother of his children. He had, however, been too beleaguered with tax matters to make any effective protest when Indumati Chattopadhyay was brought from Nadia where her father was manager of one of the temples. "Some say she is a descendant of the saint Shri Chaitanya," the uncle said. "Imagine, what a rare find we have!"

"Yes," Indrajit thought bleakly. "What a find! A merry little girl of ten who has not a thought or care in her head!"

Little Indumati came towards Indrajit that bright autumn morning with a platter filled with fruits and a jug of milk. She wore a sari with difficulty; its folds were tucked hurriedly, revealing a tiny waist, slim shoulders and a chest with no hint of maturity. Her little wrists jingled with gold bracelets and a huge red bindi dominated her small, smooth forehead. Indrajit sank onto the divan on the veranda, weary and despondent. "Is this infant to be my chatelaine?" he thought miserably. "Why, it will be years before she is a woman!"

"There," Indumati announced, placing the platter on a low table. "Didi said to give you this ... and milk." She wrinkled her nose. "I loathe milk."

Indrajit stared at his child-bride, as she selected a guava and began nibbling at it. "So innocent, no unaware, so unconscious of her position and relation to me!" he reflected with an ironic smile. The little wife turned around. "Ah, there is Didi."

Indrajit also turned and saw his first wife Bishnupriya standing at the entrance of the circular veranda that was poised between the two wings of the mansion like a huge cupola. He smiled benignly at his wife, inviting her to join him. Bishnupriya came up, hesitant and uneasy.

"Did ... our little bride ... serve you properly?" she asked, still standing, as Indumati negotiated a railing post to climb onto the balustrade, as expertly as any boy. Two lithe little legs were revealed and hastily covered. Bishnupriya sighed, head bowed. "She is such a baby, really. I told Uncle that ... a ... bigger girl ..." Bishnupriya began to laugh.

Indrajit stood up impatiently. "It was going on as before. There was no point in bringing home this infant who is a naughty tomboy to boot!"

Bishnupriya's eyes filled with tears. "But you must have a son ... many sons ... and daughters. What will happen to Mayurganj if you ... are childless?"

"What will happen to Mayurganj?" Indrajit cried, raising his voice. "Mayurganj is going to that evil man Dalrymple or his devilish accomplice!"

"No!" Bishnupriya cried, clenching her fist. "Never!"

"Yes! And very soon! I can already see the failure of the crops. The harvest will be poor and we have little to give as taxes. So I will have to leave my ancestral home — the place where my great ancestor composed the Bengali Mahabharata! So why weep over your barren stock, Priya? To go as a mendicant with one wife is bad enough but to be saddled with a mulish little girl as well!"

Bishnupriya began to weep disconsolately. She loved Indrajit and Mayurganj beyond pride, perhaps beyond life.

Indumati climbed back from the portico, her sari everywhere but on her heaving little chest, her silky hair dishevelled. Approaching her lord, the little bride's eyes glittered. "Why are you shouting at my Didi?" she demanded in a clear, ringing voice.

Indrajit stared astonished, looking from one wife to the other. Bishnupriya's tearful eyes also widened.

"Aren't you ashamed to shout at Didi? She is not well, you know, and has this cough. Why, I made a clove and ginger syrup to relieve her. Not a servant here knows how to make it!" The little girl went up to her rival. "Didi," she said gently. "Come and lie down. Let me tell you a story ... one which my father told me."

Bishnupriya allowed herself to be led away by the little girl, the one who had come to take her place in Indrajit's life. Watching them, Indrajit understood why his wise old uncle had selected Indumati. "She will be a fine lady of the home one day ... but until then ..."

The ritual of life continued on the estates as autumn turned to winter. Indrajit supervised the harvest operations with suppressed panic. The poor monsoon had devastated the crops. "How shall I pay the dreaded supervisors?" he wondered in despair. Bishnupriya was in fever again and Indumati stayed by her side, telling stories, concocting syrups or singing the devotional songs of Chaitanya. These diversions calmed Bishnupriya but left Indrajit as despondent as before. His only hour of peace was in the one before dawn, when he went down to the bathing ghat beside the stone Shiva temple built many centuries ago by an unknown devotee. There he stood, waist deep in the cold water, to petition the gods for mercy. It was the only serene time of his day, though that was soon to change.

Fiona began coming to the bathing ghat every morning when the orange sun glimmered over the white waters at dawn. Though ostensibly, she came to ride along the low bank of the river, where ancient ashwath trees sprawled like primeval animals reverently holding up a canopy of interlaced green branches over the terracotta temple of Shiva, in actuality she came to see the young zamindar perform the ancient Vedic rituals. She watched his lithe, golden, graceful body plunge into the river and heard his incantations to Surya, the sun god, Vayu the wind god and Varun the rain god. She realised that he prayed fervently for their help in sustaining the earth goddess who lay reeling under an ominous season of drought. The sonorous cadence of the Sanskrit verses reminded her of the Latin chants she used to hear long ago in the Cathedral of Sacre Couer.

One morning, Indrajit Chowdhury finally acknowledged her presence, as she leaned against a bamboo tree, as slender as her own pulsating body, a wide-brimmed hat in her hand. Neither spoke. There was no need to communicate with words when eyes expressed eloquent messages of empathy. He filled a copper kettle, a kundali, with water from the holy Ganges and waded slowly through the rippling river, frowning, until he stood before the intruder.

"No one but a Hindu can come near this temple," he said brusquely.

"Is it forbidden to hear you chant that lovely prayer?" she asked with a smile.

A reluctant smile touched his dark, anguished eyes. "You, a mleccha — a foreigner. What can you understand of our faith?"

"Only that the words stir some chord in my heart ... even if I do not know their exact meaning. Yet a prayer is the same everywhere — a petition for divine mercy, a request for peace."

Indrajit gazed at her in surprise. No woman had seemed so wise and so vulnerable as she seemed to him. Her blue eyes were bright and freckles sprinkled her glowing cheeks. His gaze moved to her breasts which rose and fell quickly. Abruptly, he turned away, saying coldly, "Don't disturb my worship again!"

"Do I disturb you then?" Fiona asked softly. "I am glad!"

Indrajit Chowdhury clenched his free hand, loath to acknowledge her power over him, a power which made the words of the Sanskrit sloka already a blurred memory. "Go back to your people," he retorted in a low voice. "There is no place for you — amongst us."

Fiona watched him go, but knew that he would be waiting for her as well as for the sun god, the next morning.

Fiona's visits beyond the boundary to the river ghat did not remain a secret to Alexander Ruthven, who had watched her saddle a mare at dawn and ride southwards towards the Chowdhury estate. His keen, sapient eyes noted Fiona's heightened colour, as well as her air of subdued excitement after these visits. He saw too the growing repugnance his sister felt for Henry Dalrymple, and her visible shudder when one of his large, raw hands encircled her waist or caressed her cheek. Dalrymple must have noticed it too because he told Ruthven one day, "It's time you made up your mind. You shan't regret it."

"No," Ruthven replied slowly, his cold blue eyes on his associate. "I dare say I shan't."

"Nor will Miss Fiona," chuckled Dalrymple. "She may even like a rough coupling."

Ruthven did not answer. He closed his eyes briefly, as if to obliterate an old and banished memory of his fourteen-year-old sister lying beneath a Redcoat in a smoking Highland village.

That night, when an inebriated Dalrymple had been carried to bed by his servants, Alexander came to his sister's room. Fiona sat by the window, staring out at the distant flare of torches near the coconut corner, Dab Tola. The impenetrable silence of the dark autumn night was occasionally broken by the muffled sound of cymbals and drums.

"The sadhus are trying to frighten Henry out of his land," Ruthven observed. He could not see her face in the darkness but he sensed her anger.

"His lands? Why, he has wrested them from Indrajit Chowdhury's father! The sadhus were here long before ..." She stopped abruptly.

"Pray continue, my dear," Ruthven said, snapping open his enamelled snuff box. "I did not know you were an ardent champion of the zamindars."

Fiona felt her hands chilling. Ruthven took a pinch of snuff and then put away the box. "I came to inform you that ... Henry Dalrymple offered for you ... and I accepted."

Panic knotted her stomach and choked her throat. "Marry Dalrymple?" she asked hoarsely. "But I ... he is ... oh no!"

"Was not that the intention of our visit here? It is indeed generous of Dalrymple to offer for an undowered woman. But then he is as rich as a nabob."

"And you both will grow richer on indigo that ruins the peasants here!" Fiona stormed, battling with tears of impotent rage.

Ruthven's eyes were veiled. "Indeed we shall. Indigo is a prized produce and in great demand in England. Since the trouble in San Dominigo in the Caribbean, Europe looks to us to supply their demand. With our brother Alistair established at Leadenhall Street, Dalrymple and I do not anticipate any problem with the Company directors."

Fiona's eyes smouldered until it seemed, even to the imperturable Ruthven, that the fire in her eyes had set ablaze the fire of her hair. "What if I refuse to do your bidding, dear brother?" she asked icily. "What if I do not wish to serve your purpose?"

Alexander pondered the matter briefly. "You will return to Inverness — to resume your duties as tutor to a petty timber merchant. The *Hero* sails in a fortnight from Saugar."

In the years ahead, whenever Fiona's tender heart grieved for her brother, she steeled herself to remember this scene, so that her pity changed once more to the incandescent anger she felt now. "Very well. You have vanquished me, Alexander. But let me congratulate you."

"For what?" Ruthven asked, puzzled.

"For being a good Redcoat." She paused, satisfied by the angry flush that flared across his bronzed face. Then she delivered a Parthian shot. "Our father would have been ashamed of you." Fiona left the room to stand on the grilled veranda and stare at the distant torches of Dab Tola, wondering if Indrajit was there tonight.

Ruthven forced himself to breathe deeply and calm himself before repairing to his own room, where he lay sleepless, remembering his father who had thrown away life and security for fealty to his leige lord. James Ruthven seemed to belong to another age.

Fiona Ruthven became Mrs. Henry Dalrymple a few days later. A pastor from Bandel was summoned to perform the ceremony. He surveyed the ad hoc arrangements with evident distaste.

"Could the marriage not have taken place in church? There is one several miles down the river," Arthur Latimer observed.

"We ... had little time," Alexander said quickly. "I must leave for Calcutta soon."

"Yes," Dalrymple added, glancing at his ash-faced bride. "I am in great haste to bed the lady."

Reverend Latimer frowned and looked away from the trio, his distaste now palpable. Even Alexander's impassive face registered uneasiness.

"Then let us hurry," the young pastor muttered. "I have no wish to tarry here."

The ceremony was saved from being a total travesty by the presence of Reverend Latimer whose low, clear voice gave a transient dignity to the vows uttered with levity by an inebriated Dalrymple. Fiona's responses were so reluctant that Reverend Latimer glanced at her over his half-moon spectacles in query. "If you are uncertain, Miss Fiona," he said gravely, "do not take these vows."

Fiona cast a startled glance at him, as if reprieve lay in those words, but Ruthven was beside her at once. "The *Hero* sails in a week," he muttered through clenched teeth. Fiona repeated her vows in a strangled voice. No sooner was the ceremony over then

Dalrymple crushed his bride in an embrace.

Reverend Latimer closed his eyes to shut out the spectacle, and snatching up Bible and hat, rushed to fling himself on a pony, and be off. "Wretched girl!" he muttered to himself. "I wonder if she is with child?"

Alexander Ruthven drank two bottles of Madeira at the wedding lunch, and then intoxicated for once by the vast quantity of wine, lumbered into his barouche. "Dear child," he said hazily, "it is hard, I know ... but try to be ..." He shook his head and laughed strangely.

"Will intoxication deaden your remorse forever?" Fiona asked coldly as he stared at her for a moment, before driving off.

"Come," Dalrymple spoke, his tongue slurred, his eyes bloodshot. "I cannot wait till night ... besides I want to see you by daylight and ascertain matters for myself."

"No!" she cried, her pent up horror and revulsion breaking open. "I will not come!" Wrenching herself free from his embrace, Fiona began running headlong towards the boundary of prickly mehendi bushes. Dalrymple tottered after her, swaying and shouting obscenities, but the vast quantity of claret had fogged his brain and stiffened his limbs. He fell upon the hard ground, growling in impotent rage.

Fiona ran along the boundary of the Dalrymple estate until she came to the thick coconut grove, which lay swathed in darkness. A thatched pavilion stood in its midst. "Dab Tola," she murmured, "let the sadhus kill me in human sacrifice! I will not return to that beast!"

The rustle of muslin skirt and swift slippered feet crushing dry leaves, made several figures emerge from the pavilion. The sadhus stared at one another, until one of them came forward. The startled look on his face changed slowly to one of pleasant surprise. Seeing him, Fiona stopped.

"You?" she cried hoarsely. "Why are you here?"

"'Tis better you explain your presence here," Indrajit Chowdhury replied, horrified by her dishevelled hair, the torn bridal dress, its hoops missing, the panniers torn. He sensed that she had taken flight on her wedding night.

"I ... cannot endure ..." Fiona murmured, as sobs rose in her throat. Seeing the other sadhus watching, Indrajit led Fiona to a hut nearby. "Well?" he said grimly.

Fiona looked at him desolately. Slowly, he went to her and tentatively took her hand. She responded to his hesitant touch and both found each other in a desperate embrace.

"This is madness!" he whispered hoarsely, caressing her cheeks and hair. "You are a wife now — bound to a man by vows."

"I do not believe in vows forced from my lips!" she whispered, lips parted for him.

Indrajit released her suddenly. "Nevertheless, you took them," he said gravely. "You must keep them ... as I must keep mine."

"Yours ... To your sick wife and little bride!" Fiona asked, bitter tears coursing down her cheeks.

Indrajit shook his head. "No, Fiona, not to them, or to any woman." He paused. "I have taken a vow of service — to Mother Bengal. Until these depredations cease, I shall not return to my home or family ...."

"You have abandoned them!" she asked, surprised.

"No ... they are safe with my uncle in Burdwan. My house is empty now. Wild guards watch over it. I ... am now ... a vagabond sadhu." He led her out into the starlit winter darkness. The sadhus were getting ready for their midnight ceremonies. Fires were lit and floral offerings made before the black stone image of Kali, the goddess of destruction.

Fiona suppressed a shudder. "Is it true that tantrics perform bloody rites and orgies?"

Indrajit shook his head. "The depraved do ... but the real tantrics seek to raise their level of consciousness ... and by mastering their bodies, strive to control the external world. We seek inner power — by renunciation."

"Let me share your efforts," Fiona pleaded. Indrajit shook his head, gazing at her in mute yearning. "One day, when you are ready to renounce your bonds, I will let you come ... but now ... return to your world."

"One day, I will come," she said, struggling with tears of misery. "Do not spurn me then." She turned back only once to see Indrajit standing by the sacrificial fire, in the saffron dhoti of renunciation. Her whole being longed for him. "But he has sent me away," she said to herself, "to my doom. Oh dear Lord, how shall I endure the terrible years ahead!"

8

The Sanyasi Rebellion

The times indeed were terrible. A conspiracy of nature and men from a distant island had brought grief to Bengal's once-verdant country. One-third of the cultivated lands had been laid waste by drought. Landlords and peasants had suffered alike; they had no money to plough into the land. Production had dwindled dangerously. Husbandmen sold their cattle and implements of agriculture. They had, in their hunger, to eat their seed grain. Watching their children starve, fathers sold them to anyone willing to feed them. When things became still worse people ate leaves of trees and grass from the fields. Ponds and tanks dried up and pestilence broke upon the starving populace. They left their stricken villages and converged upon Calcutta, Murshidabad, Bandel and Burdwan in search of a few morsels. Many fell in the desperate exodus and their bodies were left there, to await the vulture's claws.

Amidst this, the Company supervisors collected land taxes with cruel severity, adamant against remission. Many zamindars became destitute as their estates were sold and the peasantry reeled in a whirlpool of destruction.

Fiona stood on the balcony of Ruthven House, trying to obliterate from her mind scenes that seemed to have seared themselves into her memory during the journey from Mayurganj to Calcutta. The spectre of hunger, disease and death had swept through the province.

She had seen deserted villages where the only sign of life was at the cremation grounds.

The strains of a cotillion drifted up to the balcony. Alexander Ruthven was celebrating the tenth birthday of his son and heir, Andrew. Senior officials of the Company and officers of its army had come to enjoy Ruthven's hospitality. The mahogany table in the wood-panelled dining room groaned under the weight of roast ducks and chicken, roast suckling pigs with apples in their mouths, huge broiled hilsa fish, lamb cutlets and an assortment of pullaos and curried vegetables. On one sideboard were lined bottles of claret, Rhenish, hock and Madeira. On another were juleps and sorbets, mangoes, lichis, jamuns from the trees in the garden.

In the drawing room, ladies chattered gaily about the new consignment of dresses that had arrived by the latest Indiaman. "The panniers get broader," one complained, "and the skirts shorter," said another.

Begum Shirin Ruthven sat on a sofa, resplendent in a brocade gharara, the celebrated pearls of Empress Nur Jahan, and a tiara of diamonds. Every plump finger flashed with a superb ring. A little girl fanned the Begum's heavy body and flushed face. "Purchased her in Murshidabad," the Begum informed an English guest. "Her parents could no longer feed her."

"Really? How nice. I hope she appreciates her good fortune," responded the lady. The Begum blushed.

Fiona Dalrymple's eyes blazed with blue fires, but she had learnt to hold her tongue. The outbursts had proved futile against the indifference of her brother and the brutality of her husband. She went to the card room where Dalrymple was losing at faro, and then wandered to the ballroom where couples executed steps of the cotillion. An officer of the Company's army claimed her for a dance. Fiona let herself forget recent events as she danced with others, until the heat overcame her and she excused herself.

The young officer followed. It was not a frequent occurrence to find an attractive and well-bred woman in the society of upstart "nabobs" in Calcutta. Besides, Fiona was an enigma to her peers. Those who remembered her as a blithe young woman soon after her arrival three years ago noted the change now. She did not enter into the round of morning calls, or drives along the Maidan, nor the hectic dances and dinners at twilight. She had, however, developed a partiality for cards and liked nothing better than to play for high stakes at the faro or whist tables. It seemed to please her when Dalrymple fished into his pocket at the end of such an extravagant evening to fling a bag of coins at her.

"You will ruin me," he usually raged on the way to Ruthven House.

Fiona nodded, smiling derisively. "I married you Mr. Dalrymple, so that I could live in style. Yet you grudge me a few thousand rupees on cards."

"Aye," he snapped back, "I married you to give me pleasure and breed sons. But you have done neither."

Fiona blushed but never replied on this score.

"Lying with you, Madam, is like lying on a slab of ice," her husband retorted. "And your womb is barren. So why should I pay your card 'debts'?"

"Don't," Fiona replied. "I shall find a protector to do so."

Dalrymple's florid face contorted. As much as he hated Fiona, possession of her as his wife conferred a dignity on him. She was a lady.

"You will be a carcass the day you get a protector," Dalrymple informed her.

Fiona had no desire to take a lover. All taste for physical pleasure had been killed on her wedding night when Dalrymple had taken possession of her as if she was a harlot. "So you are a virgin!" he had chuckled as she had lain bruised and bleeding by his assault. "Never believed Ruthven when he told me you were a virgin. Thought he was getting rid of a tramp. Well, this is a surprise!"

Fiona had turned her face to the wall to weep in abject misery at her fate. Dalrymple had clutched her fiery tresses and turned her towards him. "Seems you don't fancy me, eh? Well, Madam, I wanted a lusty wench ... not a snivelling lass .. which is what you are, for all your carrot mane. But you'll have to give me pleasure, understand? No shrinking or snivelling. Buried two wives already. So give me an heir — soon!"

The heir had not materialised in a year, despite Dalrymple's repeated, rough assaults on Fiona. She was glad. Motherhood through his courtesy, she thought, would have been degrading.

Now in Calcutta, Fiona indulged in her fondness for cards and masculine conversations. Dalrymple did not cross her will often and Alexander thought it prudent to humour the sister who was mistress of an indigo estate. Alexander watched Fiona sit at a table with her friends, to play a round of whist and discuss the state of affairs.

Thomas Beecher, a member of the Calcutta Council liked Fiona's company, and shared her sympathies.

"Who would imagine a famine is sweeping over Bengal?" he asked. "We act as if there is nothing wrong. Life goes on merrily with balls, races and gambling."

The army officer shrugged. "How are we concerned, Mr. Beecher?" he demanded.

Beecher bestowed a withering glance on the young captain. "As it happens, we, of the East India Company, who hold the diwaniship of Bengal, are doing nothing to stop this province's ruin. The first concern of the Company has been the raising of large sums to answer the pressing demands of Leadenhall Street and defray the large expenses there."

The officer laughed. "Do enlighten me, Mr. Beecher. Is the Company here to disburse charity to the people of Bengal?"

Thomas Beecher bristled in irritation. "You are obviously ignorant of the responsibilities of governance."

Sighting a young lady in search of a partner for the quadrille, the officer retreated hastily. Mr. Beecher stared after him. "It is a pity that our people do not appreciate their responsibilities in

Bengal. Nor, I am afraid, do our directors."

Fiona fanned herself slowly. "We are traders, Sir. The Company is not a government." She paused, debating a point and then proceeded. "Even in the midst of famine, the Company traders are speculating on rice and wheat, selling at steep prices."

Beecher nodded. "I am aware of it, Mrs. Dalrymple." He too paused. "I hear that both Mr. Dalrymple and Mr. Ruthven are engaged in these speculations."

Fiona nodded, staring at her fan. "I am afraid so," she murmured. Impulsively, the councillor laid a hand on hers. "I am glad to find in you a degree of compassion lacking in others." He paused, groping for words. "Can you not spend more time in Calcutta, instead of the countryside? You would be an ornament to our society here ... such as it is."

Fiona laughed, pressing his hand. "Indeed I would prefer to be in Calcutta than at Mayurganj. Here I can select books from the Company's library, collect journals, see a few plays ... whereas there is little for me to do in my husband's estate."

"Then persuade him to rent a house in town for the summer," Beecher urged. He wanted to see this woman often; he thought she could cure the sense of futility he had often felt since his arrival in Bengal.

"That can be done," Fiona mused, "for Dalrymple likes nothing better than to behave like an English lord. But my reasons for staying in Mayurganj are ..." She halted. "No," she thought, "I cannot tell anyone, not even this kind and wise man, why I am staying on in Mayurganj ... in the vain hope that one day my zamindar will return home."

Thomas Beecher sensed her hesitancy, and did not pursue the point. "The quadrille is progressing well, Mrs. Fiona. Shall we try our feet at it?"

Fiona nodded and was happy to spend the next two dances in his company. Together, they smiled at the overheated ladies who went out now and then to splash water on their faces and necks before continuing their hectic movements. They laughed at the invariable game of "pelt my lady" that went on among the guests leading to a fracas or two. The ladies goaded the gentlemen on in setting right imagined assaults to their honour. Miss Samantha Bailey insisted that Mr. Egbert Frobisher had thrown bread pellets between her breasts. "It is incumbent upon my host to avenge my honour!" she wailed.

Alexander Ruthven entered the music room where the outrage had been perpetrated. His ten-year-old son Andrew stood beside him, a replica of his sire except that his eyes were a deeper blue and the fiery hair was more copper. Two khidmatgars stood behind, trying to assume an air of indifference to the proceedings.

"Frobisher, did you offend the delicate sentiments of Miss Bailey?" he asked sharply, though his lips twitched.

"Delicate sentiments, Mr. Ruthven?" exclaimed the young man. "Why Miss Samantha played footsie with me at dinner. I thought she wanted to be pelted."

Ruthven tried to look severe. "This is hardly a chivalrous mode of address, Frobisher. You must make your apologies to the lady."

Frobisher grinned. "Calm down, Samantha dear," he said in a broad Midlands dialect. "I meant no harm. 'Twas in merriment ..." he paused and glanced at her decolletage. "And you are so provoking ..."

Miss Samantha picked up a Moradabad brass plate and hurled it towards Frobisher's head. "Bounder!" she screamed as she stormed out of the room.

Fiona sighed. "Dear heavens, where do they find the energy in this heat for such behaviour?"

Samantha's indignation was somewhat mollified by the courtesy of her host, who danced a quadrille, a cotillion and then a Roger de Coverley with her until she was forced to sit and gasp for breath, her fine muslin dress soaked with perspiration. Alexander left her in the anteroom to recover, promising to send a cup of punch to revive her. In the clamour of the party however, he quite forgot to do so, as Begum Ruthven was waiting for the elaborate birthday cake to be cut, and toasts to be drunk to the long life and health of her eldest son.

Fiona watched her brother's children by the Begum with pride, tinged by envy. Andrew, his sisters Alice, Clarice and Beatrice resembled their father while four-year-old Louise was like their mother, hazel eyed, brown haired and pale skinned. "If only I could be happy like the Begum!" she thought wistfully as Thomas Beecher led her in to dinner.

The older members of the party discussed the famine and the effects of the starvation deaths upon the economy, while others analysed the intrigues of the Marathas and Moghuls in north and Central India.

The next morning, Fiona was wakened by a piercing sound of wailing. Snatching up her dressing gown, she rushed across the corridor to the Begum's open door. Alexander sat motionless while his Begum beat her forehead repeatedly. "My little Louise is gone," she sobbed when Fiona entered. "Taken ill at night ... and we never knew!"

"The English lady brought the contagion," the child's nurse cried. "She has been found in the anteroom — cold and stiff."

Fiona went down to see poor Samantha Bailey lying dead in her sprigged muslin dress, a bread pellet nestled between her cold bosom. Frobisher's last missile. Slowly, Fiona covered the wretched girl's body and sent for the young blade who had driven her to a frenzy yesterday. Upstairs, she could hear the preparations for Louise's burial which the Begum insisted should be in the garden, where she could watch over the child. No matter what Alexander said, Begum Shirin was adamant. Louise would not be banished to a cemetery.

Henry Dalrymple was beside himself with terror. "Contagion?" he shouted. "Of course there is contagion here. Two people have died! I will not stay here! Let us leave for Mayurganj at once!"

Fiona's protests were of no avail. "Pestilence is stalking the entire province. Where will you hide? The Crown Prince of Bengal has died recently, behind his secure palace doors. It is no use escaping.

Let us stay here. Shirin is crazed with grief!"

Dalrymple fixed wild, terror-filled eyes on Fiona. "We leave at once. Do you hear? You will be ready in an hour!"

Dalrymple boarded his carriage even before earth was scattered over the little coffin in the Ruthven garden. Fiona barely had time to console her stone-faced brother and shattered sister-in-law before she was hustled into the coach by her terrified husband. The coachman too was harried to push forward as if the hounds of hell were behind him.

Calcutta fell far behind as the coach bounded forward over the ochre, parched land, past the great river banks baked hard by the sun. They halted at night in a dak bungalow and set off again for Nadia district. By now, Dalrymple had recovered his equanimity; the terrors of a pestilential fever had waned before the prospect of acquiring an auctioned estate.

"I think," Dalrymple said with a twisted smile, "that Indrajit Chowdhury will have to sell his estate this year. He is heavily in debt, and his plea for remission of revenue has been rejected."

Fiona paled under the golden tan she had acquired, from working outdoors.

"Does that distress you, my dear?" Dalrymple asked in a low, smooth voice. Fiona felt drops of perspiration prickle her forehead and throat. Dalrymple went on with that same twisted smile, "Perhaps I shall offer him the post of a munshi. He is educated enough for that."

Fiona leaned back against the leather seat, staring into the burnt, arid landscape of abandoned villages and fallow fields. There is no hope for Indrajit, she thought in despair.

"Well woman, why don't you speak? I weary of seeing your whey-faced countenance. Would it please you if I took Chowdhury as my munshi, eh?"

"Chowdhury left his estate almost a year back," Fiona replied coldly. "He will not be available to accept the exalted post you offer."

"Then he will beg, borrow or steal," Dalrymple retorted, "or he will die in the famine."

Fiona lowered her eyes, afraid that he would see the fury in their blue depths. "I think he would prefer to die ... than become your munshi," she said quietly.

"Indeed, Madam? Well, we shall see! Within a few months the zamindari will be mine ... and the haughty Brahmin aristocrat will come begging to me — just to live!"

Death was a reality now. She could see corpses on village lanes and by dried ponds, in front of thatched cottages. Dead cattle and sheep scattered the once-verdant plain. The stench of decay rose powerfully from the luckless earth.

"Bad, eh?" Dalrymple asked his wife. "Well, we are saved. We have enough stocks of rice to last us till the next season." He paused and glanced at the chest tucked beneath the leather seat. "Got a nice price for the indigo this time. More than I expected. Thanks to the trouble in San Dominigo, their indigo is unavailable so we can quote our price."

Fiona glanced at the chest which she knew to be full of golden pagodas. She resisted thinking of how it was all acquired.

"Must lock up my grain house," Dalrymple muttered, looking at the corpses. "Can't have them loot my grains."

"Loot," Fiona murmured softly. "That is a word you are familiar with."

As he reached out to strike her, the carriage lurched violently and shuddered to a halt. The liveried postillions ran away into the forests amidst deafening cries of "Hare rere re! "— Here we come!

From out of the cerulean horizon materialised a group of saffron-clad men, their heads shaven, brandishing swords as they rode towards the carriage.

"Egad! The sanyasis!" Dalrymple shouted in panic, struggling to bring out his pistol with trembling hands. By then the sanyasis, ascetics, had converged around the carriage.

"Hand over your plunder, Saheb," a young sanyasi commanded Dalrymple. His face was covered by a saffron shawl, his dark, sombre eyes visible.

"Plunder? What plunder?" Dalrymple shouted in a quavering

voice.

"The loot that came from destroying your farmers and other landlords. Hand it over quickly. We have other people to ... visit."

Dalrymple glanced wildly around until the pearl chain with its gold crucifix reposing on Fiona's throat caught his eye. It was the only jewellery she wore because it was truly hers, inherited from an affluent grandmother. Tearing it from her neck, Dalrymple handed it to the sanyasi leader. "Take this. It is worth a small fortune."

The sanyasi smiled and handed it back to Fiona. "Keep it, lady. We do not attack women or take their trinkets. Now Dalrymple, hand over the chest containing money from your ill-gotten indigo ... at once. We know how much you have extorted from them." Slowly, the sanyasi drew out a pistol from the folds of his saffron robe and aimed it at the indigo magnate.

Seeing no option, Dalrymple indicated the chest by his side, watching with a furious countenance as the sanyasi leader counted the gold mohurs.

"This will go back to the peasants whom you have robbed and bled white this year. They owe you nothing — yet you plunder them until they are at death's door. But we shall redress the wrongs, check the untrammelled plunder of Bengal, Dalrymple ... or die in the process!"

Fiona stiffened. Though the voice was muffled by the saffron shawl swathing the face, she knew too well the cadence of his speech, the timbre of his voice. It was almost a year since she had seen him last, in the darkening coconut grove, in a bitter mood. Soon after, she had heard that he had left Mayurganj, presumably to join his two wives in Burdwan. How often had she saddled her horse to ride along the boundary of the coconut grove which was the boundary between the two estates, in the futile hope of seeing Indrajit — but in vain! The ornate mansion stood deserted amidst the groves of mango and jamun, its garden run to weed and wild growth. Rough, strange men haunted the grounds, refusing to answer her questions. "He is gone," she told herself repeatedly as a sense of emptiness washed over her.

Now he sat on a black horse, revealing only those proud, sombre eyes that had stirred her being.

"Indrajit," she whispered and then clapped a hand on her mouth, but it was too late. Dalrymple spun around in rage.

"So you've turned a robber, have you Chowdhury?" he asked, sneering. "Couldn't pay your taxes?"

Another sanyasi levelled his pistol at the indigo magnate. "Silence!" he commanded. "We can take you with your chest ..."

Fiona sprang down from the carriage and went towards Indrajit. "Why have you done this?" she asked, bewildered and anguished. "Why have you, the embodiment of pride and honour, stooped to this way of life?"

Indrajit glanced down at her, his eyes softening at her reproach as he studied the amber sunlight on her fiery hair and blue eyes. He seemed to hesitate only a moment before he lifted up her slim body onto his horse. Then addressing a few commands to his followers, the sanyasi-zamindar rode away into the coral-coloured horizon. Henry Dalrymple stared after them in stupefied silence, and recovered only when the sanyasis dumped the contents of Dalrymple's treasure chest into a sack. His screams of impotent rage were drowned by the thunder of horse hooves as the sanyasis rode swiftly away behind their leader.

They rode over withered fields of paddy, plains of fissured earth, abandoned villages that were a song of desolation. The sun slowly dipped behind an endless burnt-ochre horizon, that seemed to merge with the ochre robes of the sanyasis. Then the terrain changed; first tall grass and then thick trees fringed the forests. Slowly, they entered its dark, cool depths. Fiona was not certain whether the darkness was caused by the departure of the sun or the impenetrable vegetation of the forests. Only when the moon lit the narrow path did she know that the day had ended.

Deep in the forests was a clearing where stood an ancient temple dedicated to Lord Shiva and his consort, the goddess Parvati, untouched by the iconoclastic invaders from the northwest. Indrajit gestured to the others to ride on, while he dismounted and then helped Fiona to alight.

She said nothing. Her astonished bewilderment had deprived her of speech, though her startled eyes were full of questions. Indrajit led her to the temple whose cavernous interior was illumined by numerous earthen lamps. At the entrance, he touched the pendulous bell whose clear peal seemed to reverberate around the blanched forest. It seemed to Fiona as if Indrajit was announcing his submission to the gods before the dark mystery of the forests. Slowly, he turned around to face her questioning eyes. "I brought you here so that you may understand ... and judge justly," he said severely, though his eyes were pleading.

"Judge? Who am I to judge?" Fiona asked with a tremor in her voice.

His eyes softened for a moment, but his voice remained severe. "Your countrymen judge us all the time — in their courts of justice."

Fiona shook her head. "I cannot speak for their actions. I ..."

"You are a compassionate woman," he said in a strange voice. "I seek your ... approval."

"Is ... that all you ... seek?" Fiona asked, almost inaudibly. Indrajit turned away from the radiance of her eyes and the allure of her lips to contemplate the stone pillars. "That is all I seek," he replied gravely. "Your ... understanding .... of my action."

"Then tell me what this is all about and why you have adopted this life?"

"We follow the Sanathan Dharma and dedicate ourselves to the oppressed and down trodden .... and honour women ... even those of our enemies. Our aim ... is to ... rid Bengal of the Company's rule so that misrule and plunder of her people may cease."

Fiona was visibly troubled. "Then I fear for you. The Company has a trained army and controls the trade of this province. How can you fight gold and guns with austere vows?"

His eyes glittered and his finely impassive, chiselled face was suffused by intensity. "Did not your Christ fight a mighty empire with goodness? Can the East India Company be more powerful than the empire of Caesars?"

They stood motionless, close in sudden understanding. Then Fiona said dully, "The Redcoats are powerful. My father perished in that unequal struggle." She paused and met his ardent gaze. "I would not have you destroyed as well. Let us leave ... and seek sanctuary somewhere ... in Oudh or Mysore .... before our days are cut short ..."

Indrajit took both her hands in his. "I must stay here ... with my brethren until our work is done, Fiona. And then ... if you are still waiting ... my life is yours."

Tears glittered in the depths of her cerulean eyes. "When? It may be so long ... and by then I ... may not be ... existing. What will I do until then?"

Indrajit wiped away the tears from her dust-streaked cheeks. "I will find you, wherever you are; in this world or that ... have patience, my ... dearest one." He paused, divesting himself of his saffron shawl and handing it to Fiona. "I wanted to see you desperately ... before ... anything happened ... and now that you have come, let me show you our community so that you may know that I have not stooped to anything low."

He led her deeper into the forest, both of them pausing now and then to gaze upwards at the vaulted, velvet sky iridescent with winter stars and falling meteors. It seemed to them as if they had merely to reach out to the stellar paths glittering above.

It was midnight when Indrajit took Fiona to the temple deep in the forest where the sanyasis worshipped the goddess of power. The cavernous gloom of the temple was illumined by a hundred and one brass lamps, and scented by marigolds and jasmines. On special festive days a hundred and one lotuses were brought from the distant lake as on offering to the goddess Durga.

Indrajit left her at the platform, shrouded in a sari, while he went in to join the others in meditation. Several hundred men were gathered there, silent and determined, drawing strength and

inspiration from ancient Sanskrit verses admonishing them to uphold the thorny path of dharma.

Strength is in your hand, Mother
Devotion in your heart
Your image I built in every temple
To lead me towards victory.

The celibates sang softly in one voice, renouncing riches and power, love of life and all bonds of the flesh until their land was freed of the depredations of the foreigners. Thus charged with the magic of mantras, the sanyasis filed slowly back to their cottages, to rest before the next day's adventures.

"Is it incomprehensible to you?" Indrajit asked a wide-eyed Fiona, as she stared at a jewelled idol of the mother goddess, Durga, her ten hands stretched out, each one and its ornament a symbol of power. There was fire in her dark, doe eyes and mystery in the third eye on her forehead.

"What does the goddess symbolise?" Fiona asked.

"She symbolises strength and power. Look at the trident, sword and mace in her hands." Indrajit replied.

"She also holds a lotus and conchshell," Fiona rejoined. "Are they not symbols of benevolence?"

Indrajit smiled. "Yes, I see you understand the duality of Durga's personality." He paused. "She is a mother too — like your Virgin Mary."

Fiona nodded. "There lies perhaps the common need of us all — to find an anchor and a refuge."

"Come," Indrajit said softly, "the puja is over."

Pale winter moonlight illumined their path as they walked slowly back to the deserted pavilion at the edge of the forest. All sounds of human habitation disappeared. Even the nightjars and owls settled down on their boughs. Only the cool breeze rustled through the thick foliage.

"I have brought food for you ... and a quilt for you to sleep

on. By first light you must leave," Indrajit said quietly.

"Leave?" Fiona asked. "Did you bring me here only to send me off so soon? Surely I could stay a few days?"

"Even this has been a transgression of the rules, Fiona," he replied, "but I wanted you to see for yourself, lest you give credence to the lies that must surely be said of us."

"I would never believe ill of you, Indrajit," she said softly, reaching out her hand to touch him. "You can do nothing ignoble."

The moonlight illumined his bitter smile. "Except to desire another man's wife."

Fiona's hand tightened on his. "We ... were drawn together before I married. I cannot consider it a sin to ... love you," she whispered.

Indrajit drew her close for a brief embrace and then abruptly released her. "I cannot consider such a thing ... I have vowed to love no other than the land of my birth and dream of nothing but her liberation. Until then ..."

"Until then ..." Fiona repeated dully, "we must bury our dreams and burn our youth. Is that what you have vowed?"

Indrajit nodded. "It may be a long wait, Fiona. Do not wait for me. I may never return."

Fiona sensed his sorrow as also the quiet resolve in those aquiline features. He reminded her of a Scottish fugitive rebel in Paris who had also taken an impossible vow. Suddenly, a wave of love and pity surged within her. "I shall wait, my love," she whispered. "Even on the other side of paradise."

Indrajit bowed over her hand and gazed at her in silence. Then as an old woman came near, he murmured a farewell and left.

Fiona spent the remaining hours on the quilt, gazing at the sky, thinking of the sanyasi rebel to whom she had given her heart. "And how shall I return to that odious man now? How can I endure his touch when I know what love can be?"

It was evening when Fiona reached Dubb's Point. The old woman and her son had escorted Fiona to the nearest village in a bullock cart, and then left her to continue the journey alone on foot.

She arrived at the house to find it dark and deserted. Uneasy and bewildered, she went in and heard Henry Dalrymple groaning in the next room. Puzzled, Fiona went in and found him tossing in high fever.

"Caught the contagion," he said hoarsely, through cracked lips. "The damn child gave me the pestilence ... but I shall live ... have no fear ..." His eyes glittered in helpless rage. "Returned, eh? The thief-zamindar cast you off, eh? Not to his taste, eh? Well, I don't want you either ... you whore!"

Fiona turned to go but he screamed hoarsely. "Water! Give me water, you hussy. Have you no heart, no shame, no gratitude, eh?"

Silently, Fiona poured water into a glass and gave it to Dalrymple, who drank it greedily. "Food! Get me food! And a glass of hock. Then lock up the house ... the bloody servants have fled. Rascals, deserting me now!"

Fiona brought a dish of bread as there was nothing else in the house. Then as she locked the doors a squall rose, gathering momentum. Windows and doors rattled and flew open, as candles were snuffed out. From the darkness, Dalrymple gave a choked cry of fear mingled with pain. Then he rose, tottering, and shouted, in a delirium. "My indigo! Get my indigo! No? Why, I'll thrash you to death!"

Fiona turned in horror to see him approach her, arms outstretched, muttering incoherently. Then as another gust of wind blow, he turned back to his room and lay down, crying for indigo. When she went to him a few moments later, she recoiled in terror. He had renounced both his indigo and his life at once.

9

Lucknow Adventure

Fiona sat immobile before the inert body of Henry Dalrymple, unable to believe that the man who had raged with a rough zest for life was now lying cold and stiff. She tried to summon grief and was ashamed that she could not. The malodorous body swelled in the heat, drawing hordes of flies. Fiona knelt down to pray, searching her dazed and weary mind for the right words. None came. "I never loved him," she thought. "Indeed he repelled me in mind and body. How can I feel grief now? But he was my husband and somehow I must accord him the honours due to the dead."

Numbly, she got up and went into the unkempt garden, to pluck a few flowers to lay upon the dead man. She was aware of the unseen presence of the servants who had returned to see their dead master. If only they would come and help! she thought. I feel so helpless in the vast solitude of this famine-stricken land!

"Memsaheb," an old retainer murmured, emerging from the tangle of a croton bush, "What shall we do?"

Fiona indicated a barren stretch of land beyond the garden. "Dig a grave.... for the master."

The retainer nodded, with a twisted smile. The master was to dwell forever with his beloved indigo.

A storm swept over the flat sun-baked terrain, mowing down trees and the thatched roofs of deserted homes. Fiona paced the cool, dark hall wondering how the last rites could be performed in the midst of such a deluge. A vague terror gripped her. It seemed as if amidst the turmoil, Dalrymple would rise to torment her. She closed her eyes and struggled to be calm. As lightning streaked across the sky, the front door flew open. Fiona stared wild eyed at the heavily cloaked figure, a scream of panic rising in her throat.

"Mistress Dalrymple?" he asked gravely. "I heard of the .... sad event from your old retainer." His grey eyes rested briefly on the bloated body. "When the storm abates, we shall perform the ceremony. Now," he said divesting himself of his wet cloak and three-cornered hat, "would you get me candles and oil?"

Fiona continued to stare at the spare young man who began to draw out a Bible, incense sticks and a crucifix from his pocket. His calm eyes intercepted hers. "You do remember me, Mrs. Dalrymple? I performed your wedding ceremony."

"Reverend Latimer," Fiona murmured hoarsely, tears pricking her eyes in relief and gratitude. "How did you ... where ..." Her voice caught in a web of misery.

His simple, kind face regarded her with compassion. "Your good servant came to summon me last night. He told me you were all alone ... so I came. But I must return to Tamluk where ... my work ... is unfinished."

Fiona nodded and stood aside as Reverend Arthur Latimer read the funeral service to the accompaniment of a Kal-baisakhi or black April storm. She listened and thought how those tranquil words of solace and submission that seemed so appropriate in a verdant English churchyard seemed so bizarre in this dark and sultry bungalow in rural Bengal.

Arthur Latimer, however, read on, with a kind of detached reverence. His task completed, he gave instructions to the reassembled servants for the burial to begin.

Fiona stood on the front veranda while Reverend Latimer led the funeral cortege in the midst of the storm. She watched the young pastor aid those whom Dalrymple had used so cruelly.

"Does life end thus?" she asked Latimer when he emerged in

fresh, dry clothes. "A place in the earth and imminent oblivion?"

Arthur Latimer regarded Fiona with a stern countenance. "It must seem so if you lack the strength of faith."

"Do you regard it otherwise?" Fiona asked.

Latimer nodded. "Life, as we call it, is a halfway house to the unknown." He began to gather his possessions. "It is late. I must leave for Tamluk at first light."

The servants brought in a simple meal of spiced lentils, vegetable and rice and requested the Reverend and their mistress to eat. Fiona sat, toying with her food. Latimer pretended not to notice as he glanced frequently at the darkness outside.

"Reverend Latimer," Fiona said at last, staring at her plate. "Do you listen to confessions? If you do, I should like to unburden myself."

Arthur Latimer rose abruptly from the small table. "I am a Protestant, Mrs. Dalrymple. But if it would lighten your burden, let me hear.'

Fiona continued to stare at the plate. "I married Henry Dalrymple without regard or affection ... and despised him ... and feel ashamed of my inability to feel grief." She looked up to meet his calm countenance.

"I know, Mrs. Dalrymple. It was evident to me at your wedding ... that your ... affections were engaged ... elsewhere."

Fiona felt a warm flush on her cheeks. The pastor continued. "But that is over. A new chapter begins for you. Shall you be staying on, Ma'am?"

Fiona shook her head. "I ... am contemplating going to Calcutta ... it is quite solitary here ... on my own."

Latimer nodded. "Yes ... and the sanyasis are on the rampage."

Fiona dared not look at him. He knows, she thought, but he must not know more ... not of their forest retreat or of their vows to liberate this province.

"Go with escorts, Mrs. Dalrymple. The road is not safe. I can accompany you a little of the way — for I must be back in Tamluk soon."

"Do ... you not ... fear the sanyasis?" Fiona asked, meeting his eyes. Reverend Latimer shook his head. "I am too well acquainted with them to fear them. In my work, we are engaged in constant friction."

"Indeed? How is that, Reverend?" Fiona asked with quickening interest.

Latimer smiled wanly. "It is a long, story, Ma'am, but suffice it to say that Reverend William Carey and I come into conflict with the orthodox Hindus when we oppose their obscurantist ideas and ... cruel practices. The Brahmins exercise absolute dominion over the minds of their fellow Hindus. So our task is to convince people that divinity does not have to be propitiated by sacrifice of female children."

Fiona listened with uneasy anxiety, wondering if Indrajit belonged to this group. of people.

Latimer went on. "We also try to alleviate distress but the people regard us with suspicion." He paused. "It is to be expected. All they see are Company traders hurrying to amass wealth ... with indigo, muslin, silk, tobacco, sugar."

"Are there none who are interested in remedying matters?" Fiona asked.

Latimer considered the question thoughtfully, as if searching his memory for a few names. "There are a few persons, I believe, who would like to regulate British conduct in India ... but they are few. We missionaries have been asked to operate outside British territory since our Christian .. teachings may offend the Hindus and Muslims.

"To hear of Christ's message? Dose it not offend them when they see their estates seized, their artisans despoiled?" Fiona asked hotly.

Reverend Latimer looked at her thoughtfully. "I see, Ma'am that you have an understanding of matters. May I therefore make a plea?"

"Certainly."

The young pastor paused once more before saying, "May I suggest that you grant remission of taxes to the hapless tenants on your land? Your late husband ... taxed them beyond endurance. Yet... these lands were theirs ... before the advent of the Company.

"Do you suggest that I bear the taxes, Reverend?" Fiona asked curtly, irritated by the pastor's visible disapproval.

Arthur Latimer's grey eyes twinkled. "Why Mistress Dalrymple, I could hardly suggest a better gesture nor one more imbued with Christian charity." He paused before saying, "You would assist our work, Ma'am. If Christianity is to appeal to the people of Hindusthan, then Christians must be seen to be people of nobility."

Fiona inclined her head. "I appreciate your sentiments, Reverend, but it is doubtful if we could all turn sanyasis," she said crisply.

"No?" Latimer asked softly, looking at Fiona. "But I understand that sanyas or renunciation is a phenomenon you ... admire."

They stared at each other appraisingly. Then the young pastor bowed and left the young widow to collect her chaotic thoughts.

The next morning, Fiona set off for Calcutta. The bungalow had been locked and the keys handed over to Bansi, the chief servant of coconut corner, or Dubb's Point as Dalrymple had renamed it after the Bengali Dab Tola. Instructions had been issued regarding cultivation of rice instead of indigo, but Fiona had neither the means nor the aptitude to supervise the agricultural operations. She hoped that the peasants would know what to do, and shedding all responsibilities, she prepared for her flight to Calcutta.

She was afraid of the solitude of Dubb's Point and dreaded the silence of the night when crickets and frogs kept up a steady duet. It seemed as if Dalrymple would awake any moment to re-enter the world he had so reluctantly quit. "If ... Indrajit had been at his estate," Fiona mused, "I would have stayed ... but he will not come for some time ... and I cannot wait forever. I must live before I too am claimed by a sudden fever and eternal oblivion."

Calcutta was another world, far removed from the solitude and harshness of the famine-mocked countryside. Here, Fiona saw her compatriots live in heedless pleasure, grabbing every day as if they could hear the muffled drums of a funeral cortege on their trail. The parties were as boisterous as ever, and both men and women donned their best clothes, and danced until they were exhausted. Rhenish and Madeira flowed with the merry chatter, and helped even the diffident to explore forbidden paths. Ruthven House was full of great expectations.

Alexander Ruthven had made a tidy fortune during the famine, by profiteering in necessities. Rice and wheat had been sold at exorbitant prices to those of the populace who could afford to trade gold for survival. Fiona arrived in Calcutta to find him irritable and preoccupied, and not at all pleased by her advent. "You ought to have stayed in Mayurganj and looked after your property. It is worth a fortune."

Fiona enlightened him, not without malicious pleasure, of the sanyasi raid and the chaos in the indigo plantation since Dalrymple had become an opium addict in the last year of his life.

"I shall have to send a manager there, then, to put the estate in order. It is too valuable to be neglected." He paused and smiled ironically at his sister. "You are now a widow of substance, my dear. Offers will come for your hand. Let me select a husband for you once more."

"Someone like Henry Dalrymple?" she asked tartly.

Alexander Ruthven shrugged. "He proved to be a wise choice, you will admit? Better to be a rich widow than an impecunious spinster."

"I will sell my property in Mayurganj and return to Inverness," she said, turning away. "I can no longer endure this place!"

"With Warren Hastings in India I may follow you," he said wearily. "That man will be our ruin yet!"

In the days that followed, Fiona heard of no one but Warren Hastings, the newly-appointed Governor General of Bengal. Begum Ruthven and the British ladies met to discuss the scandal about the new Governor General's wife.

"Bought her for £10,000 from her husband, Baron Imhoff. Can you credit such a story?" a lady asked Shirin Begum.

"Yet it is true. Maria Imhoff was only too willing to be bought. Would you refuse such a position?" the Begum asked sharply.

"So indelicate," whispered another lady. "On the ship at that ... with all the world watching!"

"Yet he dares to be self-righteous," protested another lady. "My husband says he will erode the power of the Company."

Pouring tea into fine English china cups, handing around scones, crumpets and iced cakes, Fiona heard of the new Governor General with avid interest, and decided to call on Mrs. Hastings, the erstwhile Baroness Imhoff at the graceful, two-storeyed house in Alipur where Hastings now resided. Begum Shirin Ruthven was also eager to go, but her husband forbade her. "Wait until we see what he is like," he said.

They soon discovered that Hastings was a man who meant business. The misrule of the East India Company had generated immense criticism in London, leading to the appointment of Hastings who was charged with the task of assuming control over the civil administration of Bengal, collection of taxes and maintenance of law and order.

Realising that Company officials could not collect taxes effectively in remote, water-logged or forest-encircled villages, Hastings charged the zamindars with this task.

The Moghul system of revenue, established by the great emperor Akbar, had disintegrated in the chaos of the early eighteenth century. The traditional zamindars had lost their lands to plundering adventurers, dacoits or river pirates. Many ancient and illustrious families had auctioned their lands and fled to Calcutta for security.

Hastings sought to weed out the usurpers and bring back the older class, whose loyalty would thereby be assured. Gradually, these landlords began to claim hereditary rights and became the buffer class between the British rulers and the Indian peasants.

He gave fixity of tenure for five years and expected the zamindars to collect a fixed, specified amount. This saved the zamindars from the Company's extortion and the peasants from the zamindars' greed. The Bengal Presidency was brought under six Revenue Boards which looked after several districts. Auctioning of estates was stopped and taxes determined on fertility of land.

It soon became clear that Warren Hastings sought to consolidate power in his own hands, to control the Council and the jobbery of Company directors. Europeans were told to stay in Calcutta where their conduct would be under the jurisdiction of the mayor's court. He wrote to the board of directors in Leadenhall Street that, "Investment is desirable but cannot supersede the happiness of people who are now subjects of the Company and whose lands and revenues must be restored. India does not exist merely to enrich England or the Court of Directors."

A storm of protest was evoked by this letter, not merely from the men at Leadenhall Street but by every trader, soldier and official of the East India Company. Their ire deepened when Hastings ordered a ban on ostentation and display among Company officials. Ignoring their resentment, the new Governor General turned his attention to the systematisation of revenue, administration of justice in civil and criminal courts and the establishment of a police force to check dacoities and piracy which had made life a continuous threat for common people.

"The halcyon days are over," Alexander Ruthven announced to his Begum one day, late in 1772. "The proposed Regulating Act will end our activities. No more free trade and amassing of wealth. Now Hastings will decide everything."

"And Marian of Alipur will be Poolbundhi. It is rumoured that she is the receiver of bribes. Does Hastings Saheb know of his beloved's activities?"

"It is no concern of ours. We must revise our thoughts for the future."

Begum Shirin laid aside a piece of intricate golden embroidery which she was doing on the kameez of her youngest daughter.

Her eyes were thoughtful as she looked at her disgruntled husband.

"I too have been musing over the future, Sikander Saheb," she said slowly. "So long as traders were head of the Company here — Clive, Verelst, Carter — we had no problem but now ... it is a different matter." She smiled drily. "The days of trade are over."

"Indeed, Begum?" Ruthven snapped. "And what is your suggestion for the future?" He sat down on a brocade-covered divan, and loosened the jabot of lace at his throat. Begum Ruthven rose and glanced out of the windows into the mellow autumn afternoon. Her boudoir admitted a little of this light through the trellised shutters. It touched the fine wooden screen from Kashmir, the rugs from Lucknow and glimmered on the silk curtains of Murshidabad. Here and there a Moghul miniature lightened the heavy, ornate room diffused with the scent of attar and musk. Alexander's senses had adjusted to these colours and scents. Yet there were moments when he longed for the fragrance of mimosa by the sea or thistle on windy hillsides.

Shirin poured him a silver goblet of thick Turkish coffee, before standing behind him so that her heavy breasts touched his head and neck. Her fingers ran through his flaming hair and loosened the black velvet riband that held the hair tuck. Alexander stirred uneasily; her hands had not lost their cunning even if her body failed to delight him. "Come, Begum," he said, guiding her to the seat beside him. "Drink a cup of coffee with me. And then tell me if you have any alternative plans."

Shirin sighed and sat down on an opposite divan, piqued by his subtle rebuff. He now rarely responded to her overtures. In the five years since his return, she reflected, I have had only one child. But now I have a plan to arouse his interest.

"My plans for the future, Sikander Saheb, are bound with the past — and of course the present."

"How so?" Ruthven asked, opening his jewelled snuff box to take a pinch before drawing the fragrant hookah towards him.

"Take a look at the situation in Hindusthan. Since the sack of Delhi by Ahmed Shah Abdali in 1757, continuous chaos has reigned. The Emperor Alamgir was killed, his son driven out until the Marathas came to the aid of the Moghuls, leading to the battle of Panipat. A Rohilla chief, Najeh-ud-doula ruled Delhi for nine years. There is no real power in the north except the Marathas."

Ruthven pulled on the coiled pipe, while the aromatic water of the hookah bubbled. "That is so," he thought, reflecting on the situation in northern India. "The Moghul empire has ended as an effective power. The Emperor Shah Alam rules by courtesy of either the Afghans or Marathas though the Moghul vazir, Najaf Khan tries to retain independence. Yet the kingdom of Bengal-Bihar has passed to the British, and even Oudh has come within the orbit of British power since Wazir Shuja-ud-doula sought Company aid to expel the Rohilla hordes. The Rajputs are disorganised and disunited, ignoring the Moghuls and fearing the Marathas."

Laying aside the coiled pipe of the hookah, Alexander said slowly, "The Marathas are in resurgence. Their defeat at the battle of Panipat subdued them temporarily. Five years ago they crossed the Chambal and have spread out faw-like in several directions."

Begum Ruthven smiled, folding a betel leaf stuffed with shredded areca nuts and scented nicotine. "That is what I was coming to, Janab," she said. "The Marathas have become powerful, but each military chief wants to be free of the central authority of the Peshwa at Poona. The Gaekwar's seat is at Baroda, the Bhonsles govern from Nagpur, the Holkars at Indore and the Sindhias at Gwalior." Shirin paused to smile, the folded pan poised in her plump jewelled hand. "The Marathas broke the empire of my ancestor, Aurangzeb, but their own conflicting ambitions will destroy Shivaji's empire."

Ruthven smiled. "Still loyal to the Moghuls, my noble Begum?" he asked lightly.

Shirin's smile disappeared. "No, Janab," she said softly.

"I am loyal only to you and my Andraz." She paused. "It is because of this I make a suggestion."

Ruthven nodded, lulled into a euphoria by the scented tobacco water of the hookah.

"The Maratha magnates are looking for European generals. They lost their best men at Panipat. Now mercenary soldiers and commanders are filling their armies." She paused, aware that her lord's relaxed body had suddenly tensed.

"So?" he asked quietly.

"Why ... do you ... not hire out your sword as commander to one of these Maratha chiefs?"

Alexander Ruthven rose from the divan and paced the room in his stockinged feet. "As a general? But I have been out of battlefields for ... seven years, since Buxar. What would I do?"

Begum Ruthyen rose slowly and stood before her husband. Her once bright grey eyes, were bleary now and lined by fine wrinkles which even the skilfully applied kajal could not conceal. Yet they had a certain power to hold and compel a man's attention, even a man as restless as Alexander Ruthven. "Go to Lucknow, my Sikander," she said, lowering her voice to a whisper. "Meet the Frenchman, Claude Martin, who is the practical vazir of the Nawab. He knows of all the plots and intrigues afoot in Hindusthan. He will guide you ..."

Ruthven stared at his wife. "You are ambitious, Madam," he said softly. "You never cease to plan, do you?'

"For you, Janab," Shirin murmured, "and for our heir Andraz."

"Have we not enough?" he asked drily. "Have we not come far from the bleak days in Murshidabad, fifteen years ago?'

"No!" Shirin whispered fiercely. "I dream of bigger prizes ... not only of wealth but ... power ... as well. I want you to carve a kingdom for yourself as Martin has done and as de Boigne and George Thomas are planning to do. You can lead armies of Hindusthan and extract the obedience of petty nawabs and rajas. You can ..."

Ruthven laughed derisively and turned away. "You dream too high, Begum."

"No!" Shirin retorted, pulling him roughly to face her glittering eyes. "These are not dreams! I have thought of this since you returned from Europe. You can be a power in a princely court." She paused. "You must do it not only for yourself but for Andraz ... in whose veins runs the blood of Tamerlane and Akbar!"

It had been many years since Ruthven had seen his Begum so animated. Indeed, she looks almost like that imperious and compelling girl I knew fifteen years ago after Plassey, he thought. Slowly, he went close and ran a finger over the kohl-lined eyes, the rose-tinted lips, the fussy lace and silk bodice, the tiered necklaces and sequinned veil. "My Shirin," he murmured, kissing her lightly, "you are no placid lady of the zenaṇa ... but a true daughter of Tamerlane who swept over Hindusthan in search of riches and glory."

Shirin held him close. "Go to Lucknow and find out which ruler wants a general. Name your price and carve out a kingdom for yourself. I want you to be a real nawab — not like the gaudy, vulgar Englishmen who call themselves 'nabobs'!"

"Very well," Ruthven said, clasping her hands tightly in his own. "I shall go to Claude Martin and try my luck." He paused and added grimly, "Warren Hastings has left me no alternative.

Shirin nodded. "You will triumph, Janab Sikander," she murmured. "The star of fortune is yours. I saw that long ago — in the palace of Murshidabad."

The royal court of Oudh was a luxurious and dazzling place. Nawab Asaf-ud-doula was a man mild in manners, polite and affable in his conduct, possessing no great mental powers but well disposed towards the English who had sent an astute Resident to keep the

Nawab, in turn, well disposed towards the Company Bahadur and to indulge him in his passion for western goods. The king of Oudh annually spent £200,000 on his whims. His curios ranged from a priceless Louis XIV ormolu clock to a wooden cuckoo. He had built a splendid Residency at the capital, Lucknow, and financed an equally impressive villa for General Claude Martin who was the liaison between the Nawab and the Resident.

Martin had served in the French army of Comte de Lally and following the defeat at Pondicherry formed a Company of Chasseurs which served the East India Company. He worked as surveyor general in Bengal, engineer and architect, cartographer and ballistic expert, watchmaker and indigo farmer. In Lucknow, he had started a money-lending business and indigo trade which was to bring him a handsome fortune. Already, plans for his fantastic houses, Farhad Baksh and Constanta, were afoot.

The French general met Alexander Ruthven in his lovely house by the Gomati river. At once, the Scottish adventurer realised that Martin was his ideal — the multifaceted Renaissance man who was both scholar and soldier, engineer and banker, condottiero and liberal benefactor of the poor. Ruthven realised too that he could not hope to achieve in one lifetime all that Martin was doing. Yet some affinity drew them together. The two men talked of and remembered France with a reluctant nostalgia.

The atmosphere of Claude Martin's house was a blend between a Renaissance palazzo and a seraglio. Here he sat at the head of an immense mahogany table and held discussions on history and archaeology, engineering and warfare, while Muslim footmen in impressive liveries served French and Moghul food. Santerne, Bordeaux and Orvieto accompanied every dish. Martin's wives sat with him; as exquisite and well trained, as any sultana. Their children flitted through the large spacious rooms, happy and carefree, yet aware of the enormous importance of their father who virtually ruled the kingdom of Oudh.

Alexander Ruthven acknowledged the validity of Shirin's ambitions. "This is the life I want," he thought, staring at his versatile host. "Not only a life of riches but of power ... and eminence!"

Another man, equally enamoured of glory and grandeur, was also present. Benoit de Boigne was a Savoyard, astute yet addicted to daydreams. Alexander Ruthven listened and learned a great deal at the gifted Frenchman's table. Then hesitantly, the Scotsman told the Frenchman of his quest.

"The Maratha chiefs have begun to move away from the Peshwa at Poona," Claude Martin said to Ruthven as they paced the colourful gardens of the general's residence. "Sindhia and Holkar, particularly, want to build up armies."

"Whom do they wish to fight, Your Excellency?" Ruthven asked.

Claude Martin chuckled. "You may well ask, Monsieur. Perhaps they want to avenge Panipat, or overcome the feeble Emperor."

"But Delhi is stable under Vazir Najaf Khan. And the Afghans retreated many years ago."

The general stopped to glance at the Gomati river where barges glided towards the city of Kanpur. Fisherfolk squatted at a distance mending nets, while the buxom women of mingled Hindu-Muslim blood came to dip their pitchers in the clear waters. Slowly, he turned to the Scotsman. "Perhaps they will seize Delhi," he said, "or perhaps they will fight each other. That is why they want strong armies to spread their individual domains." He paused. "One day they will come into conflict with the British as well."

"The British?" Ruthven asked. "But the Company is a trading concern!"

Martin laughed. "Mon ami, you have not then assessed Monsieur Hastings. He has larger designs. Were he a mere trader, he would not try to change Company rule in Bengal."

Ruthven frowned. Martin continued. "If the Marathas come into conflict with the British, you, a Britisher will be caught in a dilemma. Have you thought of the consequences? What will happen to your silk and cotton factories in Bengal, your trade in saltpetre and tobacco?"

"Yes, I see," Ruthven said, sighing in visible dismay.

"But I have another ruler in mind, Monsieur. A Rajput prince at Ratangarh who trembles at the growing menace of Sindhia and Holkar. Would you wish to train his army?"

Ruthven was silent. Claude Martin went on. "The Rana of Ratangarh is of proud and ancient lineage. At one time, his forefathers gathered other states into its fold. The great emperor Akbar sought the Ratangarh Rana's hand in alliance and his niece Jia Rani became Akbar's Hindu empress. Their domains stretched once to the Jamuna but repeated wars with the Marathas and Moghuls shrunk the state. The present Rana plans a revival and a reckoning with the Maratha menace. For that he needs a modern army and a good general."

"Ratangarh," Ruthven murmured, staring at the river. "The jewelled fort." He turned abruptly to General Martin. "Yes, I will go there and offer my services."

"Good. I shall inform the Rana of your visit. Until then you are my welcome guest."

While the letters of introduction were being written, Alexander Ruthven roamed the exotic city of Lucknow, the citadel of Moghul-Indian culture with its elaborate villas, lush flower-filled parks and canals that flowed below aristocratic homes in summer. The bazars were noisy and colourful, the people effusive with poetic salutations. Courtesans waited in balconies for upward glances while wayward youths waited in shadows for their favours. The exquisite mosque, Imambara, dominated the city.

Returning from one exploration of the city, Ruthven strolled across the velvety grass towards the veranda where the General usually met his guests for tea. On the way he passed a bower of madhavri and champa plants. A young woman sat under its dappled shadows, mixing paint and water on a much used palette. A canvas stood on an easel with a half finished portrait of a little girl who could only be one of Claude Martin's numerous daughters.

The sound of Ruthven's footsteps made her glance up at him. Then she looked around the garden. "Ou cest vous?" she cried to her vagrant model. A little girl emerged from a bush, laughing. "Here I am Liselotte!"

"I will not paint you if you run away again!" the young woman exclaimed as her slim, deft fingers began moving over the canvas. "How difficult it is to work here! I marvel that Messiers Zoffany and Renaldi could have the patience to paint."

Ruthven watched the artist add a subtle stroke here, a vigorous brush there, until the child's image was captured in its fresh bloom. Once more the child leapt up crying — "Cakes! Salim has brought in my favourite cakes!"

The artist shrugged a pair of slim shoulders and gathered the tools of her craft, apparently unconscious of the tall, flame-haired man watching her. She ambled gracefully across the lawn to the veranda where General Martin had gathered his guests. Ruthven went slowly back to his room.

They met for dinner at General Martin's opulent dining room. Alexander Ruthven was surprised by the easy conviviality among the guests who came from various stratas of society: a Muslim moulvi, a Hindu zamindar who did not touch food or drink, European army officers in search of employment, musicians from the town's taverns, a famed Urdu poet. Conversation was lively and well informed. He was surprised to find the lady artist participate with ease. Finally, Claude Martin addressed her.

"Well, ma petite, did you have a fruitful day?"

"Toinette was naughty — as usual. I despair of completing her picture but Wazir Khan — ah, he was more tractable!"

A ripple of laughter flowed over the ornate table. The artist's cheeks dimpled into a merry smile. "The Nawab sat quite still while I did a preliminary sketch."

"He was bewitched by Mademoiselle Fremont's talent," the Urdu poet ventured, devouring the young lady with his kohl-lined eyes.

The general laughed. "If it is only her talent he admires!'

More laughter followed this remark. Alexander Ruthven felt uncomfortable and glanced at Mademoiselle Fremont. Her gay, hazel eyes met his brooding, blue ones. "Surely the Nawab was equally polite to Renaldi and Zoffany when they came to paint him? And you, mon generale, did you not sit for these gentlemen as well?" Liselotte asked nonchalantly.

"My third wife did," Martin said, "causing constant discomfiture to that provincial Englishman."

Liselotte Fremont caught the Scotsman's gaze once more and smiled at Ruthven's discomfiture.

After dinner, the party adjourned to the ornate drawing room where furniture of the era of Louis XIV jostled with Kashmiri rugs and Moradabad lamps. Potted palms and malati creepers lined the room while paintings of Renaldi and Zoffany shared the walls with priceless Moghul miniatures of Emperor Jahangir.

"Now, play for us, Liselotte," General Claude Martin said, settling down on his favourite settee flanked by his two wives.

"What shall I play?" she asked, sitting before the pianoforte.

"One of your Provencal chansons."

She sang the song in her clear contralto voice, conjuring for the exiled Frenchman, the verdant river valleys of the Loire, the matins ringing at dawn, the scent of myrtle and mimosa on balmy summer nights, the taste of warm bread and full bodied wines and images of castles where troubadours sang for ladies.

Alexander Ruthven listened, smitten by an overwhelming nostalgia for the France he had known as a boy, where he had eaten the bitter bread of exile, to escape the wrath of a Hanoverian monarch. And now that France beckoned to him like the mirage of a well beloved. His brooding blue eyes moved from the lines of the singer's supple body to the gleaming brown hair curled around her head, revealing a long neck, slim shoulders flowing into slim arms. Her wide, hazel eyes gave warmth and mobility to her face.

The clash of cymbals and drums broke the spell as a celebrated nautch girl came in to the sound of jingling bells on her ankles. She knelt before the general, waving her jewelled hand thrice in salutation whereupon he gave the signal for the dance to begin, to the accompaniment of tabla, sitar and tanpura. The Europeans watched avidly; the Urdu poet now devoured the dancer with hungry eyes. Liselotte lowered the lid of the pianoforte and went into the adjoining balcony. Slowly, almost without volition, Ruthven followed.

The luminous spring sky was a mantle of lilac sprinkled with stars. Against it, the dome of the main mosque glimmered like a vagrant moon, its four minarets like jewelled posts. The muezzin cried to the faithful as night deepened, admonishing gorgeous Lucknow to shed its voluptuousness in anticipation of the austerities of approaching Ramzan.

The cameo of Liselotte's profile, her high forehead, uptilted nose, curved lips and brown curls threaded by velvet ribbons seemed incongruous against the Lucknow skyline. She belongs to the land of the troubadours, he thought, not this royal court. Indeed, her singing has opened the floodgates of forbidden nostalgia for my lost world. She reminds me of the Europe I had glanced at, behind gleaming windows as I trudged the streets of Paris and Marseilles; of people in satin and powdered wigs dancing to the minuets of Haydn and Mozart in warm candlelit rooms. He felt a keen craving for that world as an old desolation swept over him.

Liselotte turned as Alexander Ruthven's long shadow fell across the white balustrade. "You are not interested in the nautch? Soraya Bano is a celebrated dancer — and a favourite of the Nawab."

Ruthven shook his head and stood by her in silence, staring at the stars and silhouettes of mosques. "Do you not get homesick, Mademoiselle?" he asked at last. "This hardly seems to be the place for you."

Liselotte's merry laugh seemed to drown the hectic dance music beyond. "Home, Monsieur?" she asked, vastly amused. "But this is the only home I have known since my father was killed at the battle of Wandiwash. I was thirteen then. My mother ... accepted the ... protection of General Martin. I grew up here."

"And before that?"

"Before that? I was born, I am told, in Provence and came with my parents to India in 1750. I was four years old and remember nothing of France. The Carnatic was my first home and now Lucknow."

Ruthven looked at her. "You ... have ... made me nostalgic

for Europe," he said gravely.

"Oh ... I ..." Liselotte was not prepared for such an admission but Ruthven's searching eyes brought a surge of anticipation to her placid nature. Her bright hazel eyes noted the richness of his apparel, his air of authority. "Do you miss Europe very much, Sir?"

Ruthven nodded as his mind formed a swift plan. "I liked your drawing of Martin's daughter. I wonder if you would consider painting a portrait of my wife.

"Your wife?" she echoed, wearily.

"My Begum," Ruthven said, looking evenly at her. "You might enjoy painting her. She is descended from one of the Moghul emperors on the maternal side and was a maid of honour to the late Queen of Bengal."

Liselotte was bewildered. "I do not know if I could do her justice," she murmured.

"The commission will be handsome, Mademoiselle," he said quietly and saw her stiffen in indignation.

"I have no need of commissions, Monsieur," she said, turning towards him. "I have enough for my needs." Without a word, Liselotte Fremont snatched up her shawl from the balustrade and made a move to go. He stopped her, laying a hand on her cool, slim forearm. "You may not realise until it is too late what your needs are." She tried to free her arm from his grip but he held it, feeling the texture of the firm young flesh and the supple hand which he brought to his lips. He was rewarded by her astonished look and a sharp intake of breath. Then it was he who turned and strode back to the brilliantly chandeliered hall, leaving her to sort out the strange new sensations that assailed her.

Armed with letters of introduction from Claude Martin, Alexander Ruthven left for Ratangarh a few days later. Passing the river-girt district south of Lucknow, he came to the once sprawling state ruled by an ancient Rajput dynasty. They clung tenaciously to their domain, in the face of the Maratha expansionist policy. The old Rana had therefore sent word to General Claude Martin to find him a European commander. Perhaps the Rana believed that the general himself might come, leaving behind the gilded fripperies of Oudh and the intrigues of the Company Resident for the more challenging task of raising an army. Martin had sent instead a fiery-haired Scotsman "who had wearied of trade and thirsted for glory."

Rana Ram Singh was not disappointed in the Scotsman. His tall spare figure, the cold, resolute, blue eyes and firm mouth offered hope of finding a brave and bold commander. He named a salary that was a quarter of what Ruthven made from his trade, but both men knew this was only a prelude. Ruthven knew he could expect more once the campaigns began.

Ruthven stayed for a fortnight at Ratangarh to acquaint himself with his task before the die was cast. "It is not easy," he wrote to General Martin, "to change from an employee of the Company. I have served under British officers — to advance the interest of the British Company. Now I am to lead a disorderly and turbulent Rajput army against the disciplined Marathas under Sindhia and Holkar. I think of your admonition to remember the brittle pride of the Rajput race and the fact they will not respond to the court orders delivered to the sepoys of the East India Company. It will be futile and perhaps even perilous."

Indeed, the disorderly warriors of the Rana reminded Ruthven of the feudal Scottish chiefs who failed to keep pace with advanced British methods. "These men wear yellow tunics, called the marancha poshak, or costumes of the dead — as a symbol of their readiness to die. They carry obsolescent arms and have no idea of drill or discipline. The only tactic known to them is to surround the enemy in a circle or gol until he flees or perishes."

Ruthven learnt that the Rajputs had successfully resisted the Turko-Afghan hordes in the middle ages. Even the mighty Moghul army had been routed by the reckless valour of Rajput lords. Standing together on the highest tower of the citadel that looked down on a plain of green and brown patchwork, Rana Ram Singh displayed his soldiers before his crew commander.

"They are brave men, Ruthven Saheb, but valour cannot prevail over howitzers and bayonets. I realised this as I saw state after state fall to the French and British. That is why I want my army modernised and trained." He paused, and directed half-closed eyes at Ruthven. "If we lay siege to territories coveted by the Marathas in the Doab, the lush valley between the rivers Ganges and Jamuna, then we shall enrich ourselves on that revenue." He paused again and smiled from behind enormous drooping moustaches. "Some of it will be yours, Ruthven ... perhaps a jagir — like Lord Saheb Clive."

The old Rana observed that the Scotsman's habitually impassive countenance became animated for a moment. Alexander Ruthven was thinking of his Begum's dreams. She has made this dream within the bounds of reality, he smiled to himself and reflected. Would it not add another pattern to the Indian tapestry if I, a fugitive Scotsman, should carve out a principality for my son in whose veins the blood of Turkish nobles and Scottish farmers runs?

The pact was sealed under the pale windy sky of a Rajasthani winter day, when the pink-grey towers of the citadel glimmered in the pink-grey twilight. Alexander Ruthven bridled his horse, wondering why Ratangarh drew him like a magnet. "Have I been here before, as the Hindus believe, or will Ratangarh be a part of our future?" He was in a thoughtful mood during the long journey back to Calcutta.

Calcutta had a surprise awating him. Arriving at his large mansion, Alexander Ruthven found his Begum in a stormy mood. For the first time in fifteen years, she did not rise to greet him nor make the customary obeisance to her lord when he entered her chamber. Nor did she thank him when he held out a square leather box to her. Amazed, he asked, "Is there something the matter, Begum Shirin?"

She rose from the satin covered sofa and faced him with cold grey eyes. "Who is this woman, Janab, that you have invited without even the courtesy of a consultation?"

"Which woman do you refer to, Begum?" he asked, irately.

"The firingi is downstairs, awaiting you. She assured me you had invited her. She says she is to paint my portrait."

Alexander Ruthven could not credit her words, nor check the spontaneous pleasure that suffused him. "She is here?"

The Begum nodded icily.

He composed himself, chilled by his wife's expression.

"You will like your portrait done, Shirin," he said, taking her hand. "Our grandchildren must remember us in our glory." He paused to take out his jewelled snuff box. "Sit down, Shirin, so that I may tell you of the handsome offer I have received from the Rana of Ratangarh to train his army."

She was pleased despite herself. "So General Martin helped?" she asked excitedly. "I am glad! But why a Rajput? Why not a nawab or the nizam himself? That would have been preferable."

"The Nawab of Oudh and the Nizam are employing well-known commanders — who have made a mark on the battlefield. The Rana had found no one." Ruthven paused. "He is ambitious as well. It is his plan to reclaim the territory taken by the Marathas in the last century."

Shirin grimaced. "Still, the Rajputs fought the Moghuls."

"No, Begum. They were also partners of the Moghuls, especially of Akbar. Rana Ram Singh's ancestress was Jia Rani, Akbar's consort.

A strange look come into Shirin Ruthven's grey eyes. "Then she was my ancestress as well," she mused softly.

Ruthven nodded sombrely. It no longer amused him to see this daughter of an Afghan adventurer pose as a Moghul princess. He felt a twinge of pity for her pretensions, for her desire to be recognised as a descendant of Tamerlane and Akbar. "Yet," he thought, "had she not nursed these impossible dreams, I would not have gone to Claude Martin or to Rana Ram Singh."

"If we succeed, dear Begum," Ruthven said softly, "the Rana may go to Delhi and become the vazir of the Emperor. And I will get a jagir — for Andrew."

Shirin's opaque eyes blazed with excitement. "This is what I had hoped for all these years," she whispered intently, "ever since the masnad of Bengal slipped from ..."

"Shaukat Jung," Ruthven interposed with a sardonic smile.

The Begum nodded, unembarrassed. "Yes ... that is so But now I do not grieve for that dead prince ... for you will make good what I lost with a masnad for my Andraz!"

She flung aside the heavy brocade and clapped her hands. "We will celebrate with a feast tonight, Janab," she said resolutely. "We are on the road to glory!"

Ruthven smiled and bent low over her plump hands, whose soft satiny texture he still enjoyed. "Take these jewels, my Begum. I bought them from the jeweller to the Nawab of Oudh."

Shirin snatched the box and snapped open the lid, crying with delight at the string of pearls that held a pendant of diamonds, rubies and emeralds. "Put it on me, Janab," the Begum said in a husky voice. Alexander placed it on the thickening throat and slowly drew her close to him.

"My lucky talisman," he murmured. "Together, we can achieve our dreams." His hand moved over the swell of her heavy breasts and thickened waist. Her ageing body no longer pleasured him so he closed his eyes to remember the slender, imperious girl who had fled from the dangers of Plassey to seek refuge with him. He thought back to their first passionate encounter. He realised that he felt a sense of deep gratitude to his wife, and bent his head to kiss her paan-stained lips. Gratified by the gesture, Shirin responded warmly, her senses roused by his touch. She even forgot the intruding firingi woman from Lucknow who waited below.

Ruthven however had not forgotten her. Indeed, he wondered

if his sudden tenderness towards Shirin was impelled by his desire to allay suspicion. He therefore did not meet Liselotte that evening as he and his Begum celebrated their new venture in her heavily scented boudoir, rounding off with one of those carnal encounters that left his Begum breathless but satiated and himself tense and dissatisfied. He could now meet the lady from Lucknow without unease, and he chose to do so in his Begum's presence, in the ornate drawing room.

"So you came, Mademoiselle? I am glad." He turned to his wife. "Begum, this is Mademoiselle Elizabeth Charlotte Fremont, ward of General Claude Martin. She is to paint your portrait."

Begum Shirin Ruthven nodded with the half-smile of condescension given to a hired painter, but her eyes met Liselotte's hazel ones with a quiet scrutiny.

"When shall we begin?" Liselotte asked hastily, uneasy with the Begum and disturbed by the proximity of Alexander Ruthven.

"Begin today. I will be leaving for my new assignment at Ratangarh within the month and wish to take the portrait with me. Perhaps you could do a miniature of me as well — for my Begum to keep?"

Liselotte nodded, wondering if she had heard a note of irony in his voice. Did this cool condottiero truly long for his ageing Begum? But then Reinhardt adored his Begum and Claude Martin loved his. Perhaps these women knew how to keep their men's attachment. Aloud she asked, "How would you like the Begum depicted? With her beatilah removed so that you may see her fully?"

"Of course ... and in all her finery. Shirin, wear the Empress' jewels, and the pendant I brought for you from Lucknow."

Shirin nodded, puzzled. "My Janab speaks to her as if to a waiting woman. Could I have suspected him wrongly? Can she be just like a dressmaker or masseur?" She addressed her husband so that the painter understood as well. "If only this lady could paint me as you first saw me ... on that stormy night in Murshidabad."

Ruthven saw the plea in the grey eyes and the hectic flush on the flabby cheeks. "I can still see you, dear Shirin, as you were — your gharara torn, your veil awry ... but so lovely! That is how I always think of you."

Liselotte glanced from one to the other, puzzled by their exchange yet conscious of a bond deeper than she had realised. "This bond," she reflected, "will survive boredom, the waning of desire and even infidelity. What, I wonder, is the secret of their closeness?"

Alexander Ruthven turned to Liselotte. "Make your portrait worthy of my Begum, Mademoiselle." He paused and added, "The commission will be handsome."

Flushing angrily, Liselotte Fremont began her work. "The upstart," she thought in fury. "He is only a vulgar upstart! How foolish of me to have disobeyed Uncle Claude and come here!'

The days passed. Liselotte Fremont settled down to her commission like a pacified bird after it has ruffled its angry feathers. The leisurely pace of the cool days brought a new bloom to her sallow cheeks. Here there was not the rush and bustle of Lucknow, no guests of the general to entertain, no assignments thrust on her. Here she woke late and strolled around the flowering garden until the aroma of coffee and rolls drew her to the dining room where the master of the house usually read the *Calcutta Gazette*. He sat in silence, in shirtsleeves, his fiery hair unpowdered, speaking only occasionally to his beloved son, fifteen-year-old Andrew, while fourteen-year-old Alice, twelve-year-old Beatrice and seven-year-old Clarice chatted softly among themselves. They regarded Liselotte with curiosity. Only Alice sensed something that made her suspicious. After breakfast, Liselotte worked on the portrait, then lunched and took a siesta. In the evening, she went for a ride or a walk and had dinner with the children at eight since the Begum would not permit a hired painter to join them for the more formal meal of dinner.

Liselotte did not object. Indeed, she seemed to enjoy making preliminary sketches of the plump, imperious woman with her heavy, glittering jewels. Shirin held a fan in one hand in western style and a rose in the other, imitating Empress Nur Jahan. However much Mademoiselle Fremont tried to give the sketches a western character in the manner of Madame Vigee Lebrun, something oriental emerged. It was as if Begum Shirin imposed her Moghul legacy on the very paper and crayons held by the Frenchwoman. Nevertheless, she fought the Begum, striving to keep her own style.

One morning, Alexander Ruthven dropped in to see the painting. Glancing at the sketches, he asked, "Who is your teacher, Mademoiselle?"

Elizabeth Charlotte Fremont continued to paint. "Madame Vigee Lebrun. My guardian, General Martin, sent me to Paris five years ago to study under her. Madame is highly regarded, as you know, being both the friend and portrait painter of Queen Marie Antoinette."

"Vigee Lebrun," Ruthven repeated vaguely. "I do not recollect that name. Certainly it is unusual to find a woman painter."

The Frenchwoman laughed, not pausing to mix paint or paint. "Then you are ignorant, Monsieur, or you are out of touch with Europe. Madame Vigee Lebrun is famous. Perhaps you have lived too long in India."

"Yes," Ruthven murmured, staring at the picture she herself made standing before the large canvas, dressed in a yellow starched muslin dress, that revealed the round curves of her youthful body. Her light brown hair was tied back with a yellow ribbon, unpowdered and uncurled. Her slender hands moved deftly over canvas and palette, almost as restless as her bright hazel eyes that moved from the easel to the model.

"It is time for a holiday," she continued in that light, merry tone which he found so refreshing. "Take Madame Ruthven with you. It will be an experience for her." A smile of gentle mischief dimpled one smooth sallow cheek.

"Yes," he replied. "I would love to see that world again."

Now she paused to glance at him, struck by his nostalgia. "Why Monsieur, you are very homesick!" she said in French, not wishing to offend the Begum.

There was a long silence as the young woman resumed her painting. The Begum stirred and shifted, irritated by their incomprehensible exchange, as the koels and maynals chatted and chirped loudly among the freshly verdant branches outside, from whence emanated the happy cries of Ruthven's five surviving children.

"Yes, Mademoiselle," Ruthven replied in French. "You have made me thus." He met her startled gaze defiantly, bowed, and left the sunlit morning room.

Mademoiselle Fremont paced the terrace of a small bungalow in Garden Reach two days later, pausing now and then to look at the river where flat barges with tattered sails glided past, alongside sturdier boats. As twilight fell, fishermen spread out their nets in the topaz-coloured water, hoping that the night would bring in a good haul. They sang a poem of praise to Mother Ganges, pleading her assistance. Then, as the stars came out in the velvet sky, she heard footsteps on the veranda.

They faced each other across the length of the veranda, each preparing a defence, hoping to project an aura of innocence and spurious dignity, until Alexander Ruthven said, "It was good of you to came, Mademoiselle. I have looked forward to the evening."

"Your invitation was ... unusual ... and I was bored alone in my room," she responded instantly.

"Come ... let us go to the side veranda where dinner is being laid. We can watch the river and talk of Europe."

The evening slipped by and night deepened, bringing a heavy stillness broken only by the sound of water lapping on the bank beyond. "Do we ride back ... or go by barge?" she asked as they rose from the table.

He stood before her, grave yet gentle. "I had hoped ... you would ... stay the night ... with me."

The Frenchwoman shook her head. "No, Monsieur, I cannot do that," she spoke boldly.

"Why?"

"I could not accept such a role."

"Yet you came to Calcutta? Was it not in search of such a role? Surely you realised my interest in you in Lucknow?"

"Indeed I did," she asserted, a swift colour suffusing her sallow cheeks. "That is why I came to see the situation here." She overcame her diffidence and looked at him with an unwavering gaze. "I did not realise the strength of your attachment to your wife. You would not discard her for me, would you?"

Ruthven sat down, staring at the dark river beyond. "No, I will not discard her. She has been a good wife — to whom I owe much."

"Do you not love her?" her words were coolly challenging.

"I needed her once and now she needs me. Is that a kind of love?" He sounded weary. She moved to another part of the veranda, and stood staring at the river. Ruthven came towards her. "Mademoiselle Fremont, what I seek from you is companionship, the gaiety and lightness which is in your music and painting." He paused. It is my only link with my lost world." He paused and moved away, his face averted. "If I made you comfortable, would you consider it worth your while to accept the ... position I offer?"

Elizabeth Charlotte Fremont started and stared at the sombre man.

"This is the house I will enlarge, furnish and embellish for you — attended by servants, equipped with a carriage and four, a barge, and a generous allowance for clothes and trinkets."

"In return for what, Monsieur?" she asked, almost inaudibly.

"To be my ... companion ... and mistress."

Elizabeth Charlotte stared at the taut handsome face of the Scottish adventurer, seeing in it a loneliness that he was perhaps himself unaware of. She checked back her impulsive words of kindness.

"What you offer is tempting but it is not acceptable."

He turned abruptly. "Why?"

"Why?" she echoed gravely. "Perhaps I may prefer the dignity of a wedding ring and the legitimacy of my children ... to the allurements you mention."

"Why did you not accept the offers of marriage and dignity made to you? General Claude Martin mentioned those offers. Were they not attractive enough?" His voice was harsh.

She shook her head as tears filled her eyes. The injustice of fate struck her once more. Before her stood a man to whom she would gladly have given herself ... but with honour ... while those who had offered her an honourable proposition had left her unmoved.

"It is late ... it would be best if we travelled by barge with my sepoys. The road is infested with sanyasi rebels." He spoke curtly and turned away with a lantern. Liselotte stepped before him abruptly and held up a hand in despair. "No," she said dully, "we will stay here ... together ..."

Dawn was breaking over the Ganges, scattering its coruscating colours on the breeze-rippled surface when Alexander Ruthven asked, "Liselotte, will you come with me to Ratangarh?"

Elizabeth Charlotte Fremont glanced at the man beside her with a smile. "Did you offer me this villa, servants, a carriage and four, as the inducement to be ... your mistress?"

Ruthven raised his head from her breast to scrutinise her pale heart-shaped face, its wide soft lips and small pink-tipped breasts. Slowly, he ran his hands over her and then explored her mouth with his own. The night of wild passion had not slaked their mutual thirst. They joined together once more. Relieved at last of the burden of chastity, Liselotte plunged into her passion for Ruthven with the same gusto with which she painted pictures or played Haydn. Ruthven was surprised and pleased by her playful carousal.

"I could leave you here, mon amour, but I would prefer you to accompany me ... we will be quite alone and undisturbed ... and the Indians do not care about the legalities of marriage. They would accept you as my ... wife."

Liselotte sat up, disengaging her supple body from his embrace. Her hazel eyes brimmed over with tears. "How splendid!" she exclaimed bitterly. "They will perhaps be persuaded to call me Madame Ruthven, yes? A beautiful name is it not — Liselotte Ruthven?"

Alexander Ruthven sat up, aware of the pain he had caused. Gently, he drew her close and began to kiss her fiercely. "Yes ma chere, one day you will be my wife ... I promise you ... Will you believe me?"

Liselotte sobbed. "I have thrown away ... all my hopes ... for you ..." Ruthven laid her down on the bed and gazed intently at her tearful eyes. "I will make it worthwhile, Liselotte, truly I will!"

With a sigh of despair she drew his head close to receive his kiss and to let him plunder, once more, her eager, waiting body.

10

A Sword for Hire

The fort of Ratangarh dominated a range of hills overlooking a dusty plain. Built in the halcyon days of Rajput glory, this citadel had withstood the attacks of Turks, Afghans and Moghuls until a niece-princess of Ratangarh married the great Emperor Akbar. Palaces, villas, offices and arsenals were perched on the fortified hills, more it seemed for defence for than easy living. Sparse woodlands lay in between and a mountain stream had been harnessed to provide a lake in the lower hills.

Alexander Ruthven rode slowly, his keen eyes following the contours of high walls and towers pierced with arrow slits and crenellated parapets. He passed the Suraj Pol, the sun gate, and two other gates which could be defended from square holes by musket fire. The Sun Gate led to Jaleb Chauk, the first court of the citadel opening onto the Chand Pol, the moon gate. Beyond lay the sombre yet graceful fortress-palace. Ruthven was stirred once more by the power and majesty of the ambience, the stamp of indomitable pride.

Awed, Liselotte sat in the carriage, glancing around uneasily. This was not a scene she was prepared for; the dense wooded hills, the windswept towers, and the strange silence. The cool, aloof man astride his chestnut horse also seemed alien and unfamiliar, not related to the ardent lover of the previous night.

They had left Calcutta separately in order to avoid arousing the suspicion of Begum Shirin, who had, nevertheless, sensed her husband's hunger for the "firingi". Liselotte had waited for her lover in Lucknow and after spending a few idyllic days there, they had set off for Ratangarh — a journey of two days.

Now the guards of honour saluted the new general of the Rana's army, and watched him alight. The entire palace watched in silence, openly or from behind latticed windows, as the tall, flame-haired man in a blue coat and white breeches strode up the high steep steps to the diwan-i-am. There Ruthven bowed deeply before the Rana of Ratangarh.

"Welcome, Ruthven Saheb," the Rana murmured from behind enormous drooping moustaches. "I am glad you have come ... and with your wife?"

A slight suffusion of colour told the Rana that his general was discomfited thought he replied equably. "My wife, Begum Shirin, is forced to remain in Calcutta to watch over my various interests. I have therefore brought my ..." Ruthven paused, at pains to choose a word. Then remembering that he was in the orient, he said, "A concubine."

The Rana nodded in understanding. Recovering from the momentary vexation, Ruthven glanced around the opulent rectangular hall, encircled by a veranda with a double line of sandstone columns, their capitals carved with elephant heads.

Without wasting any time, the Rana plunged into a discussion of their strategy. "Madhaji Sindhia of Gwalior has employed Benoit de Boigne to train his army. No doubt Tukaji Holkar of Indore will do the same. Why, even that low nautch girl, Begum Samru, has got George Thomas to organise her brigands. Why should I not do the same?"

"Why not indeed, Your Highness?" Ruthven asked with a smile that concealed the deep unease he suddenly felt. Could he, a soldier turned trader, train a disorderly Rajput army to withstand the undoubted talent of Benoit de Boigne or the brilliant but erratic Irishman, George Thomas.

"That is why I appointed you. You must organise several battalions for me. I do not lack funds." He paused to glance through hooded eyes at the outwardly impassive Scotsman. "My treasuries are hidden all over my realm. It is futile for anyone to search." Ruthven nodded and the Rana continued. "It is imperative that the Rajputs make a concerted effort to check the Marathas. Even now, twelve years after their crushing defeat at Panipat, they have ambitions to rule Hindusthan. Madhaji Sindhia does not even conceal his scheme to seize the poor Badshah, Shah Alam, at Delhi and make the hapless Emperor his 'puppet'. Then that race of brigands and hill rats will overrun Hindusthan!" He paused and pulled at his moustaches. "Tell me Ruthven Saheb, what will your cunning Governor General do then? Will he not stop it?"

Alexander Ruthven stared at his new master, unable for a moment to believe that one Indian prince could so hate another that he would prefer a foreign power to usurp the central authority vested in the Emperor.

"Well? What does Hastings Saheb contemplate?" The Rana's voice boomed in the audience chamber.

"Mr. Hastings will continue to administer Bengal which is granted to the East India Company by the Emperor. What happens to the Emperor's remaining domain is of no concern to the Governor General," Ruthven replied.

"Bah! Don't talk like a Company clerk, Sir! You know as well as I do that Warren Hastings will want no single power to threaten British interests." The Prince paused, and narrowed his eyes to scrutinise his commander more keenly. "Should it be necessary for you to lead my army against the British forces, would you decline the honour, Ruthven Saheb?"

Memories of Culloden and a childhood vow of revenge sprang before the Scotsman's eyes, obliterating all other predicaments — until he remembered the fate of Walter Reinhardt. "May I be permitted to postpone that decision until the situation arises, Your Highness?"

Rana Ram Singh nodded, a frown deepening between his straight eyebrows. "For the time being, however, we fight the Maratha brigands. That should not distress you. We will start tomorrow. I will ask my chamberlain to show you to your quarters."

The house of a former minister or general had been set aside for the new commander of Ratangarh's army. It was on a terraced slope within the fortified hills, where the Rana could keep a vigilant eye on his general while offering him the security of his walls. A pleasant garden surrounded the house which was built in Rajput style with chatris or round topped balconies, courtyards and a graceful tower on the roof. From here, the plain below could be seen for miles; pink at dawn, ochre at noon and tawny at dusk. Pale green patches of barley and millet grew in between. A wood stood behind, offering shade from the glitter of the Rajasthan sun. From below came the soft murmuring of the mountain stream.

Liselotte's uneasiness evaporated on seeing the white stone villa, its pillars draped with vivid purple and gold bougainvillaea. The furnishings were oriental: silken divans, mirrored cushions and bolsters, low, polished tables, rugs of thick cloth and curtains of silk. Statues of Lord Shiva and his consort, the goddess Parvati, the presiding deities of Ratangarh, were carved along the walls.

"Ah, my first own home, my own home," Liselotte murmured as she stepped into the garden. Her bright hazel eyes suddenly clouded as she thought, "Yet this is a home without a husband ... the home of a concubine."

Ruthven saw the change in Liselotte's countenance. Ignoring the presence of Rajput courtiers, he picked her up in his arms and carried her across the wooden threshold. "Ma chere," he murmured, brushing her lips with his own, "we are one now ... and this is our home." He gently set her down.

"Truly, Alexander?" she asked, her hand on his chest.

"Truly, ma petite," he replied, kissing her hand.

They went into their room where an ornate, canopied bed stood amidst low stools, carpets and an armoire. It had an adjoining balcony with a magnificent vista of the tawny hills and distant towers. A low, long, polished table stood at one end with matching stools.

As Alexander glanced around appraisingly, Liselotte said, "It is a pretty house ... and comfortable as well. Let us hope to be happy here."

Alexander's ironic smile puzzled Liselotte; she had not guessed the range of her protector's ambitions. "Yes," he added hastily, "let us hope we are."

Liselotte fell upon her task of homemaking with a joyous animation that touched Ruthven. She took particular care to make his "studio" attractive, with a sofa and secretaire brought from Lucknow, local brass lamps and carpets. She hung her paintings on the bare white walls so that he might see diverse landscapes — as diverse as the Loire from the Ganges, when he glanced up from his work.

Work for the commander of Ratangarh was arduous. He woke in the early hours of dawn to inspect the soldiers in the plain below. "These feudal pikemen," he was told by the Rana, "have to be made into skilled artillery men using grape. Teach them the use of bayonets in assault, and the reloading of guns during attack." Ruthven taught them the imperative of flexibility in manoeuvers, unwavering progress in assault and immovability in defence. "Learn the basic rules of Dundas' Manual," he told them in Hindusthani. "You must keep the ranks and file closed so that you can proceed without interruption if the first line falls."

The Rana often came to watch. "What about my battalions?" he asked impatiently.

"In time, Your Highness. They will learn to integrate the artillery into the battalion, and then develop the separate seize train of heavier battering guns."

The plains rang with musket fire and bugle calls as the proud warriors in yellow tunics were introduced to novel methods of European drill and attack. "They think it is a game," Ruthven thought, exasperated once by deliberate disorder. "They will learn of its gravity when they face the superior Maratha forces."

Liselotte watched sometimes, sitting on a hill, where she came to paint or chat with the Rajput women who had been assigned to wait on her. Filled with pride, she thought, "Why, he looks like Alexander the Greek, commanding the men of Hindusthan." With pride came a demon of fear. "If he becomes mighty and famous, will I still be needed?"

At the moment, however, she was needed. When he returned at noon, dusty and weary from the morning manoeuvers in the dusty plains or wooded hills, he was glad to let her pour water on him as he bathed, and then have lunch on the high balcony. While Liselotte read and rested, Ruthven worked on his papers, enumerating requirements of supplies, sorting out accounts. "One of the main factors of disaffection," he once told Liselotte, "is arrears of pay. This leads to treachery and mutiny. Regularity of pay is as necessary for discipline as drill."

"And something else," Liselotte murmured, timidly, "something that my guardian Claude Martin told me."

"What is that?" Ruthven asked, glancing up from his papers.

"The Rajput soldiers cannot be taught by abuse or harshness. They are proud and intractable. You have to respect them."

Ruthven regarded her with a strange smile. "So too believed the highlanders of Scotland until they saw the English Redcoats."

The better part of the year slipped away. Rana Ram Singh was well pleased with his mercenary general. Ruthven's salary was increased; gifts of jewels and silks came for "Liselotte Bibi" a term that had no nuances of legality. The Rana's chief Rani, Gouri-bai invited the general's lady to the zenana where they amused themselves by dressing Liselotte in a colourful Rajput skirt and choli, and painted her hands and feet with intricate henna designs. Ruthven was not amused. "I have one wife who uses henna," he said curtly. "I want you to remain a Provencal." Liselotte laughed at his anger glad that he preferred her as a Frenchwoman.

The zenana ladies however became protective when they discovered that Liselotte was with child. The laughter and games changed to concern and care. The ladies made an ornamental cradle and a swing for Liselotte, sent her sherbets and fruits and Rani Gouri gifted the general's lady with a diamond locket.

Timidly, Liselotte announced her condition to Ruthven. He nodded. "I had guessed," he replied.

"Yet you said nothing?" she asked, offended and hurt.

"I waited for you to tell me," he said sitting beside her.

"What will happen to the child?" she asked, her anger intermingled with injury.

"Have I not told you that your children will be looked after?"

"And your Begum? Will she not create a furore? I hear she wants to join you here!"

Ruthven stood up abruptly, irritated. I have written to the Begum not to come. She will obey." He paused and added, "Indian women are less demanding than European women."

Liselotte turned to him, flushed and trembling. "Why then did you not take an Indian concubine, Monsieur de Generale?"

Ruthven shrugged. "I hoped to find a companion — not a consort."

Liselotte burst into tears and fled from the room.

Liselotte's temper did not improve with the passage of time. She even deserted the Rani and often went off to paint landscapes from the high ramparts. To win her back, the old Rani asked the general's lady to make a portrait of her, thus ensuring Liselotte's presence in the security of the zenana. The Rani told her of the Ratangarh dynasty while Liselotte painted.

Another woman watched the proceedings with a sardonic smile. Chandrika was an illegitimate niece of the Rana by a courtesan. She had fully inherited her mother's gifts and before long had lured the Rana's general to her chamber where she entertained him with dances and ribald stories. Ruthven was careful; he realised that Chandrika was a spy, charged with the task of gleaning Ruthven's future plans. However, the temptation of spending a few carefree hours with the courtesan, while Liselotte sulked, was not to be resisted.

"If only Liselotte were as sensible and obedient as my Begum!"

"They are not like us," Chandrika said.

"She was gay and amusing — until she conceived. I think imminent motherhood has made her morose." Ruthven drank the goblet of wine in one gulp.

Chandrika's hand was poised over his head. "Foolish woman," she muttered. "She should be happy to bear you a child!" She paused, her fingers running through his hair. "I would gladly give you a child."

Ruthven pulled her down beside him on the silken divan on the veranda of the courtesan's room, letting the stars alone be witness to their revelry.

In the meantime, Begum Shirin wrote flowery and fulsome letters to her Janab expressing anguish at their separation, taking care to conceal the fury smouldering within her for the intrusion of Mademoiselle Fremont into her husband's life. It was one thing for Ruthven Saheb to amuse himself in the pleasure houses of Calcutta with nautch girls. It was quite another to set up a parallel household in Ratangarh with a firingi concubine. Shirin ended her letter with an exhortation "to remember your beloved son Andraz, for whose future I am enduring the anguish of separation. If he can inherit a masnad, however small, my sacrifice will be worthwhile."

"Damn these women!" Ruthven exploded, tearing his Begum's letter to shreds. "Nothing but complaints and lamentations!"

It was with relief that Alexander Ruthven heard of the preparations of war being made by the Maratha chief, Madhaji Sindhia, who had become emboldened by the deterioration of the imperial authority of Emperor Shah Alam II. The Moghul Emperor was now a mere cipher with neither power nor prestige. His fate was decided by whatever faction was in power. Yet he had remained till now, a symbol of the imperial unity and cohesion that Akbar the Great had established in India. But now, the Moghul Emperor had ceased to be even a symbol. He had become a phantom — more dead than alive. Nevertheless, anyone who occupied the imperial throne could attempt to exercise the fast fading authority.

With this end in view, the Maratha prince, Madhaji Sindhia marched with his army of Hindusthan led by the Savoyard, Benoit de Boigne. Reaching Delhi, Sindhia placed the Emperor under his protection and assumed imperial power. The disappointed Moghul nobles and Rajput chiefs decided that "the Maratha upstart" must be taught a lesson. While they conspired, Madhaji sent de Boigne to teach the Rajputs a lesson. The two forces met on the Rajput plains at Lalpat.

Alexander watched the yellow-robed, plumed, helmeted and jewelled men of Rajputana clash headlong with de Boigne's brigade of cavalry, infantry and irregular light horse. With sudden despair, Ruthven realised that the Rana's soldiers were no match for the men trained by de Boigne, who sat alone on his horse in the centre of his square formation, looking around at the hedge of bayonets. His officers, both Indian and European, stood in the fighting line on the right of their respective commands.

Ram Singh's young son led the charge before Ruthven could stop him. Screaming "Jai Kali!" the Prince brandished his ancient jewelled sword and advanced towards de Boigne's army.

The French commander of the Maratha army gave an order to the front face which turned sharply, wheeled by sub-divisions, and fell back through gun intervals. They "unmasked" the eight and six pounders which were free to fire to their front. The European gunners stood ready, with their match burning. As the jewelled, yellow-jacketed Rajputs advanced recklessly towards the square, the eight guns went off in a single crashing salvo. But the inspired, reckless warriors moved forward, undeterred. At that point, de Boigne raised an embroidered gauntlet which signalled the release of volleys of three hundred muskets at close range.

Terrified by smoke and fire, the heavily caparisoned Rajput horses galloped around in panic, throwing off their riders. Their reckless, orderly squadrons broke up. The hapless Rajputs, blinded by smoke and gunfire, scattered before the inexorable Marathas who now advanced shouting "Har Har Mahadev!" While one side invoked the assistance of Kali, the other sought the assistance of Kali's consort, Shiva or Mahadev.

Alexander Ruthven galloped forward, trying to halt the paincky retreat. "Turn back!" he screamed. "Re-form yourselves and attack! Remember to charge — with bayonets levelled!"

His admonition fell on dead men mowed down by de Boigne's artillery. Nevertheless, he rode around the Rajput groups, in an effort to rouse them for a last desperate charge. His black horse became almost indistinguishable in the black smoke belching from cannons. "Turn back!" he shouted again and again. To no avail. Even if they had wanted to, the warriors of Ratangarh could not turn back to fight. The Maratha infantry pursued them across the plains of Lalpat like the horsemen of the Apocalypse, until their path was marked by dead men and horses.

Alexander Ruthven took the route of retreat cut off earlier by the Marathas. Galloping swiftly through smoke and random musket fire, he saw Benoit de Boigne watching the spectacle of the Rajput debacle with a triumphant smile.

"I will return!" Ruthven shouted hoarsely to the Savoyard. "It will not end here!"

"Ah bien! de Boigne laughed. "Vediamo!"

Thus did the two mercenary generals from Savoy and Scotland decide the fate of the Marathas and the Rajputs. Pushing back Rajput resistance, the Maratha army of Madhaji Sindhia pushed forward towards the imperial city of Delhi, to take possession of the phantom emperor.

Ratangarh lay shrouded in gloom. Rana Ram Singh berated his general and his son in the audience hall. "My men died for nothing! You allowed those hill rats to insult us!"

"The crown prince did not wait," Ruthven replied bitterly. "He rushed forward without a thought, and ignoring all my instructions, approached the enemy. No doubt they were numerous but our tactics were better. If only the Prince had listened, Your Highness!"

Bharat Singh, the heir, turned on Ruthven in fury. "That is how the Rajputs have always attacked! That is what I shall do again!"

Ruthven bowed before the Rana. "Give me leave to retire then, Your Highness. It will be futile to continue. If you wish to battle the Marathas under de Boigne, you will need to adopt his techniques. He will not be intimidated by hordes of screaming warriors!"

The crown prince and the general glared at each other across the vast audience hall. "Your Highness must decide whom he wishes to command his army," Bharat Singh said grimly. "It is clear that there is not room for us both."

The Rana's bleary eyes surveyed the grizzled old nobles and warriors who had led and fought for Ratangarh. They were sombre and motionless as the two younger men duelled with words. Slowly, he rose and sighed deeply. "Go to Deogarh, my son, and guard the citadel. It is the entrance to Ratangarh. Ruthven Saheb will command the army."

The cool months passed. For a while, people forgot the ferocious heat of Rajputana. Tentatively, flowers bloomed on the arid hillsides. Tended by the water of underground springs within the fortress-palace, a profusion of flowers and shrubs sprouted along the marble terraces, and around the stone fountains. The sky was a canopy of pure azure; distant and unattainable, the place from where the gods and goddesses would not deign to come.

Alexander Ruthven read despatches from the two English officers under his command. The Maratha army, or the Army of Hindusthan as Madhaji Sindhia liked to call it, was advancing towards Delhi, quelling all opposition under the superb leadership of General Benoit de Boigne. The Moghul Emperor sat in the imperial capital, awaiting his conqueror and deliverer who would save him from the treachery of his own Moghul general, Ismail Beg. The Emperor, whose ancestors had scattered pearls and diamonds as largesse, was now on the brink of penury, uncertain where the next meal would come from.

The Rana laughed derisively when his mercenary commander informed him of the news. Laying aside his hookah, the Rajput said, "So the Badshah is awaiting the Maratha's embrace! How very sad, my general! You, a European cannot know what happened a century earlier between them ... but I do. Shivaji was the great leader of the Marathas; bold and ruthless and more than a match for the bigoted, cruel Emperor Aurangzeb. They fought a deadly duel; no trick or tactic was omitted in this feud. Murder, treachery, insult and broken promises were all in order. Aurangzeb took Shivaji prisoner but the Maratha leader escaped ... and from the forts and hills of the Deccan, his nimble warriors harassed the Moghul army. Aurangzeb emptied his treasury and bled his subjects white with taxes to defray the cost of this life-and-death combat. To no avail. He only weakened the empire ... an empire we Rajputs had helped consolidate." Rana Ram Singh paused to stare at the fountains before continuing with a whimsical smile. "My mother, a princess of Jodhpur, was connected to the Timurid dynasty by blood. Her great-great-grand-aunt, Jijabai, was Akbar's empress. Badshah Jahangir had married a Rajput princess. Aurangzeb's blood was half Hindu yet his fanatical hatred of the Hindus destroyed the empire. And now the Marathas are going to rescue Aurangzeb's descendant from Muslim generals!"

"Alliances change, Your Highness," Ruthven offered, trying to soften the Rana's bitter mood. "The English destroyed my country and family. But I fought for the English for many years."

Abruptly, the Rana looked at him. "Do you have no loyalties then — beyond yourself?"

Ruthven laughed harshly. "Have I not hired my sword to you, Sire? What loyalty can a mercenary general afford?"

Rana Ram Singh picked up the hookah with a frown, troubled by a vagrant thought. "Will you betray me then — for a better price."

Alexander Ruthven felt a swift surge of shame, a phenomenon he had not known for many years. It was with shock that he realised how degraded he must seem in the eyes of men who gave their lives for honour. For a brief, blinding moment, he thought of his father, James Ruthven, who had given his life for a cause. He had come far from that ethos. Pushing back pride and summoning a nonchalant smile, Alexander Ruthven said,"I shall try not to, Your Highness."

The Rana's dark eyes bored into Ruthven's, as if to penetrate their hidden thoughts. Abruptly, with a shrug, he turned away. "We cannot stop the Marathas from taking custody of the emperor in Delhi but we can harass their vassals on the way and cut off supplies. Plan this campaign well, Ruthven Saheb, and I will reward you well!"

While practising and drilling his soldiers for the forthcoming campaign, Alexander Ruthven was summoned from his camp to his villa. Liselotte had given birth to twins whom she had chosen to call Claude (after her illustrious benefactor, General Claude Martin) and Lucille, after her mother. She sat on the low, wide bed, pale and timorous, uncertain of the reception her children would get from their father.

Touched by her fragile countenance, Ruthven hurried to her side and gathered her in an embrace. Contact with her soft, slender body once more aroused his desires and the sight of his illegitimate twins lying in the large ornamental cradle stirred his more tender sympathies. After kissing his mistress's pale lips, he inspected the twins — red headed and blue eyed like himself. Laughing, he said, "No one can question their paternity. They are true Ruthvens."

"Will you always remember that, mon ami?" Liselotte asked tensely. "You will not abandon them ...?"

Ruthven walked back to her bed, where they had enacted such passionate encounters. He cupped her swollen breasts in his hands, satisfied by the shiver of delight that ran through her, and slowly pushed her back on the pillows. "I will not abandon you or your children, Liselotte," he whispered thickly, a hand sliding down to her now flat belly and to her firm, smooth thighs. "Get well, soon, ma chere, so that we can return to our pleasures — before I go in pursuit of the Marathas."

That day the Rani came to Ruthven, her mirrored odhni, her veil, drawn back from her head. It was the first time Ruthven had seen the imperious lady. Instinctively, he bowed low.

"Your lady frets for your love, Ruthven Saheb," the Rani said gently, while Liselotte blushed and murmured incoherent protests. "It seems the customs of your country prevent you from taking several wives. Not so with us ... As you have seen here, your master has many women though I came first — as his queen. Adopt our ways, Ruthven Saheb." She paused to pull Liselotte gently closer. "Dip your forefinger in vermilion and put it on her forehead. Then exchange these garlands I have made for you. You are then married ... in the Gandharva style."

Surprised yet pleased by the Rani's interest, Ruthven did as directed. Liselotte followed. "Go back to your house," the Rani whispered, "and be happy."

That night, the Rajputs celebrated Holi with music and dancing that went on long into the night. They began as the moon, a golden platter, arose from the hills, at first silhouetting the ramparts and then bathing them in silver. Every feature of the fort, the hills and trees stood out clearly in the brilliant winter moonlight. The Rajputs sang of Lord Krishna and his beloved Radha with an intense tenderness that stirred Liselotte deeply and affected even the cynical Ruthven. In this mood of desire and longing, he took his mistress back to the villa to enjoy her slim, yet mature body, to feel the changes ushered in by motherhood. He discovered she was as pleasing as before, more generous in her gestures, more bold in her overtures, as if she knew that she must delight him if she wanted to keep him near.

As the golden full moon dipped behind the wide lake, their bodies exploded in a burst of physical ecstasy. The bridal garland she had worn all day had been torn during his exploration of her body and the vermilion bindi on her forehead too had been effaced. She knew in her heart that she remained his mistress, a creature to whom he would turn for companionship and pleasure; but she was not his wife.

A few days later, the Ratangarh army led by Alexander Ruthven left the fortified city to begin the assault on the Marathas. In a year, the mercenary commander had made the wild warriors into disciplined soldiers, well versed in techniques of assault and retreat. They rode for several days, through stony hills and over sandy plains, where cities had been built with stones, where kingdoms had flourished and perished with the abruptness of desert storms. Dwarf trees and stunted scrub sprinkled the hard, arid land. The harsh, white glimmer of sand and sunshine coated everything, until it seemed that even the sky had taken on the colour of the sandy plains. Ruthven rode in silence, thinking of verdant Bengal which he suddenly missed, and of the Scottish highlands where gorse and thistle grew and where the heather glowed purple in the last flourish of the autumn lights.

At last, one afternoon, they sighted the imposing ramparts of Deogarh, now held by a vassal of Madhaji Sindhia. Here they stopped and waited for nightfall.

Two hours before dawn, when sleep was the deepest, the cannons were placed around the main front walls and a severe bombardment began, setting the town on fire. As the walls were breached, Ruthven and his soldiers rushed in, swift and brutal in their assault.

The Marathas were unprepared for this sudden onslaught, especially from the defeated Ratangarhis, a disorderly Rajput clan. Paradoxically, it was now Rangoji Rao, the commander of Deogarh, who acted with disorderly valour. Shouting a summons to the Maratha warriors, he led a charge on horseback against the Ratangarh forces whose ready and relentless musket fire mowed down the Marathas. Alarmed by the reaction of his soldiers, Rangoji Rao mounted his elephant and led a desperate charge through the Ratangarh forces, as usual, crying, "Har Har Mahadev!" For a moment, he burst through the ranks and scattered them. Watching his progress, Alexander Ruthven took careful aim with his carbine on the Maratha general. Rangoji Rao shuddered in one last convulsion of pain and fell, without a cry.

Despite the training imparted to them by Benoit de Boigne,

the Marathas scattered in disarray when they saw Rangoji Rao's riderless horse. The Ratangarhis pursued them, giving no quarter and slaughtering as they went to the cry of "Jai Bhavani!" They were ruthless even with their own wounded since Ruthven had ordered that the momentum of attack should not be impeded by rescuing the wounded. Unfettered thus by chivalry, the Rajputs of Ratangarh rushed on, seizing cannons not yet ready to defend, killing surprised and unprepared Maratha soldiers who had once routed more formidable Moghul foes.

By early afternoon, Deogarh had been taken by the Scottish mercenary general of a Rajput army. The surviving Maratha commanders were rounded up or brought back from where they had fled, to be executed before the townsfolk. "They will think twice about rebellion now," Ruthven said solemnly as preparations were made to behead the enemy commanders. Then his eye fell on a young man, barely past adolescence, with a smooth, sallow face and fierce, hazel eyes.

"Take him away. He is Rangoji Rao's son," Ruthven ordered.

"I wish for no mercy!" the youth cried. "I shall be happy to meet my father in heaven!"

Ruthven's lips twisted into a smile. "I dare say. However, we have better use for you." He paused and asked softly, "Are you not also Madhaji's nephew by marriage? Your uncle will pay a high ransom for so brave a warrior." He gave the signal for the executions to begin.

The gallant Rajputs watched the massacre of their valorous countrymen with cold, impassive faces.

That night, the townsfolk murmured, "A red devil has taken our city." Accounts of Ruthven's ruthless strategy spread like wildfire. "A veritable demon," they told each other, wondering if an exodus would be advisable. Their decision was delayed, for they too were soon caught in the net of the Red Devil.

To safeguard the hinterland, Alexander Ruthven decided to capture the surrounding countryside, the countless villages that lay in the no man's land, belonging neither to the Rajputs nor the Marathas.

Stationing the main army to guard Deogarh, Ruthven led a few handpicked warriors and cavalry soldiers to raid surrounding villages. Huts and hamlets were set on fire and cattle seized. Small brass lotas or jugs and plates were taken, to be cast as cannon ball. Resisting men were killed, the women raped. The luckier ones escaped to the safer company of desert jackals and hyenas.

There were others who also saw the opportunity to loot and plunder in this area of chaos. These were the Goshais and Bairagis, violent sects dedicated to plunder and rapine. In times of trouble, both the Marathas and Rajputs had called upon these sects for assistance. Now, these sects decided to act on their own and seize what they could from the hapless peasants. Bodies smeared with ash, without a shred of clothing, these "sadhus" raged through the countryside, plundering and killing with unbridled daring. They were not afraid to die since salvation lay in death. They rode into camps at night, stealing horses, cattle and utensils and setting fire to cannons. They killed with gusto, and the very sight of their naked, ash smeared bodies, tangled hair and bloodstained swords terrified soldiers and peasants alike.

Alexander Ruthven watched their raid into his camp only once. He recognised their ability to terrorise his soldiers and decided to act.

Several nights later, Ruthven rode at the head of a hundred handpicked soldiers, naked and smeared with ash. His red hair, normally powdered and tied back with a black riband, was tangled. Holding aloft a trident, he plunged shrieking into their firelit camp, deep in the hills. The Goshais were enjoying ganja and bhang, the essential opiates for divine revelation. Their mellow mood was shattered by the tall, broad, fiery-haired, naked sadhu brandishing a trident. "I come from the Lord of Tangled Hair," he shouted in Hindusthani, "with a demand for your co-operation. Cease to trouble the Rana of Ratangarh's army, for he has pleased Lord Shiva with human sacrifice. Turn your attention to the Marathas who seek to ally themselves with the Moghuls! Destroy the army which goes to help the Badshah!" He paused, his blue eyes ablaze. "Should you fail in this task, the Lord of Wrath will accompany me and hand you over to unclean rakshasas!"

Ruthven swung back on his horse and rode away, accompanied by his naked, ash-smeared Rajput soldiers screaming "Rudra Narayan Ki Jai!" — Victory to the Lord of Wrath!

The Goshai depredations ceased for a while, and the Ratangarh forces were free to pillage village after village and take a few more forts on the way. The Rana's territory had extended now by a hundred miles, and he had assumed the title of Maharana or the Great Raja. Locked in a grim struggle with rebel Afghan generals who had imprisoned the Emperor, Madhaji Sindhia had no resources to resist the ambitions of Ratangarh.

Leaving adequate forces at each of the four forts he had wrested from the allies of Madhaji Sindhia, Alexander Ruthven returned to Ratangarh after an absence of ten months. Rana Ram Singh waited to welcome his intrepid commander. There was something heady in the respect accorded to him by the proud Rana, and the adulation of the people of Ratangarh.

'I have known success," Ruthven contemplated, "but this is an entirely new sensation." He wondered briefly if this was what his father had felt when he embarked on that desperate fight for Bonnie Prince Charlie. Despite the December cold, people stood on the windswept hillside to pelt him with flowers as he rode up the steep road, past the sun gate and moon gate to the citadel of Ratangarh. With slow, measured steps, Ruthven walked across the diwani-i-am, until he came to the throne where Ram Singh awaited him. Ruthven bowed, but the Rana noticed that the gesture was a mere formality, a beau geste, from a conqueror to his titular lord. The Rana rose and stepped down to the marble floor. He held out an ancient jewelled sword. "Take this, Ruthven Saheb," the Rana said in a strange voice. "It was last used by my great ancestor, Maharana Kumbha, when he defeated the mighty Moghul. No one since then could aspire to use it." He turned to his minister who held a massive key on a gold plate. "This is the key to the fortress of Deogarh and the lands that belong to it."

For a moment Alexander Ruthven lost his composure. "Key, Your Highness?"

The Rana smiled indulgently. "The key to your little kingdom, Ruthven Saheb. You are now Fateh Jung Bahadur or hero in war. You shall be addressed as Bahadur Saheb." He paused, a mischievous twinkle in his eyes. "I wanted to gift you with a Rajput wife ... but my Rani tells me that you already have a European lady here. However, if you wish, she is yours, a woman of half-royal blood."

Alexander Ruthven stared wordlessly at the Rana, who informed him of the handsome revenues to be derived from Deogarh, the soldiers who would be in his army, the taxes he could impose and so on. The Scottish adventurer listened in a daze, and then gradually drifted away to another world, to the time when he had, as a little boy, gazed up in wonder at the laird's sombre castle in the Scottish highlands. "That I, a crofter's son, who had starved in exile and worked as a footman in a French household should now be ... Bahadur Saheb of Deogarh!"

Forgetting all the pride of a conqueror, Alexander Ruthven bowed low before the Rana in obeisance and kissed his hand in profound gratitude.

The festivities to celebrate the "Bahadur Saheb's" conquests were brief but lavish. In deference to his employer, Ruthven refrained from calling himself "Rana". However, he accepted Chandrika, the niece of the Rana, as a wife. She had already delighted him when Liselotte had been morose and moody during her pregnancy and the Rana gifted the girl to his general in the hope of retaining Ruthven's loyalty. Braving Liselotte's stormy eyes, the commander of Ratangarh went to take possession of Deogarh. He had seen it before, as a prize for battle, but not as his own domain. Studying its grim grandeur, he felt a thrill of pride and accomplishment run through his being.

The fortress of Deogarh was not as impressive as Ratangarh but it acted as a gateway to that Rajput state.

It also commanded a spacious plain where maize and barley were grown by the hardy peasants. Its value lay, however, in the mines which yielded quartz and mica — and many tribes had fought for its possession in the middle ages. Ruthven knew he could expect a substantial revenue from this jagir and he set about to assess its yield of crops, quartz and mica before fixing the rents on the tenants, who only wished for peace and order.

Chandrika provided a glittering diversion when he returned to the citadel. With the help of artisans and craftsmen from Ratangarh, she had managed to bring an air of luxury and comfort to the austere apartments of the fortress. Here Ruthven retired in the evening to hear her sing or dance or lie in her arms to savour her charms. Sometimes, she spoke of beginning a dynasty with her son. "We will call him Prithviraj, which means lord of the world," she said. Ruthven listened with a smile, lured by her plans. "Yes," he replied. "We will start a new line."

Liselotte remained behind in Ratangarh, a silent and solitary figure who strolled through the villa gardens at dawn and dusk, lost in reveries. The old Rani sometimes joined her, heavily veiled, and pleaded with to her shrug aside her lover's inconstancy. "All men are feckless," she consoled her. "But we women have homes to protect and children to cherish. Think of them and be reconciled to your husband."

Impatiently, Liselotte turned to the Rani. "He is not my husband! Were he my husband, by European laws I would have dealt appropriately with your niece! But I have no status except that of a concubine and no claims except that of the heart!" She covered her face and wept brokenly.

The Rani's eyes brimmed over with tears. She struggled to restrain the impulsive words of sympathy that came to her lips reminding herself that Ratangarh's interest always came first, before the sorrows and joys of people. "He will return," she told Liselotte. "He will tire of the courtesan. Never fear. She cannot hold him."

Liselotte shrugged. "Does it matter? He will always stray. Inconstancy is in his nature — and also ambition."

The people of Ratangarh became accustomed to seeing Liselotte sitting on the hillside before an easel, painting pictures of the harsh landscape. A vast hat almost covered her face, now tanned as dusky as any Rajput girl's. Sometimes the Rajput nursemaids brought her children there and she painted them against the ramparts of the citadel. This was the only way she could keep herself occupied; the only way she could lessen her sense of betrayal and loneliness.

But when she found she could no longer endure this existence, Liselotte made preparations to depart for Lucknow.

News of her plans must have reached Ruthven in Deogarh. He sent an emissary to bring her, Claude and Lucille to his domain. Liselotte demurred. "I will not go," she declared. "I intend to return to Lucknow and to my foster-father."

"Go, my child," the Rani advised sapiently. "He needs you now."

On entering the fortress, Liselotte soon guessed the cause of her lover's hasty summons.

Begum Shirin Ruthven had arrived four days ago. Clad in the full regalia of Moghul court dress, she looked massive and magnificent. Purloined jewels from an Empress' casket now coruscated on her ample bosom, arms and hands. Even Alexander Ruthven seemed awed by her haughty mien. Next to him stood their son, seventeen-year-old Andrew Ruthven, so excited by the prospect of inheriting Ratangarh, that he seemed oblivious to his parents' hostilities.

"It is almost a year since you came to Ratangarh ... and yet I was not informed," the Begum spoke in a low, menacing voice.

"I was preoccupied ... it was my intention to send for you eventually," Ruthven replied with a nonchalance he did not feel.

"You ought to have sent for me immediately ... to enter Ratangarh in triumph by your side." Her opaque eyes glittered, boring into his. "Was it not I who spurred you on to this road of glory? Was it not I who told you to meet Claude Martin and seek your fortune in war and plunder?"

He nodded. "It was only you," he said quietly.

"Have I not waited for three years in Calcutta, burgeoning

profits in our estates, giving bribes to Company officials and sending money for your fancies? Her voice rose, shrill and strident.

"Yes, that too," He paused and asked softly. "How much is there in our coffers?"

She laughed. "Ten lakh rupees, Janab ... all safely hidden in various secret places."

Alexander Ruthven knew he was trapped. He had left his Begum to manage the finances and she now had the whip hand. But he the conqueror of so many Maratha forts, could not cower before an ageing virago.

"I too have made a fortune here, Begum," he said smoothly. And a jagir to boot."

"Which Andraz your heir, will inherit," she said grimly.

"Of course," he replied, glancing at his son, so like him in appearance and yet so different in spirit. Andrew lived in a dream world of Saadi's and Firdausi's poems, Jalaluddin Rum's philosophies, and the music of Tansen. Yet who had greater claim to succeed to his wealth than this son, born of his union with the Moghul lady? Or would he breed a dynasty of half-Rajputs on Chandrika Bai?

Begum Shirin was satisfied. She smiled at her Janab. "Then we are agreed. I shall stay here and manage affairs while you go on with the Rana's work. Andraz shall learn how to be a nawab.

"Rana," Ruthven corrected with a sardonic smile. "The Rajputs will not have a 'nawab' on their sacred soil ... even though they support the Emperor."

The Begum's red, betel nut-stained lips tightened. "Very well, Rana, then. But when the Badshah of Hindusthan conquers once more, the Rana of Ratangarh will be glad to have the Nawab of Deogarh as an ally."

Ruthven laughed. "Dear lady, you live in the past. Your Badshah is now besieged by his treacherous Afghan generals. One of them has plucked out his eyes, with the point of a dagger even though the Emperor pleaded with him not to tear eyes which have meditated on the Holy Koran. Ruthven waited to see the effect of his words on his wife. Her face blanched and after many many years, he saw real tears in her grey eyes. "Shah Alam will be happy to accept the protection of Madhaji Sindhia who is now at the gates of Delhi, and will soon be the virtual ruler of Hindusthan."

"That Maratha jackal!" she hissed. "Because of de Boigne!" She paused and spoke deliberately. "Why do you not try your luck against his? The Emperor would prefer a Rajput army to a Maratha one."

Ruthven laughed and drew his wife close to him. "You do not cease to plot and plan, do you, Shirin?"

She quivered at his nearness. He was as attractive now as when she had first seen him nineteen years ago. Probably more so. She longed for his touch, for his caresses, for his invasion of her body. So the words tumbled out, without her volition. "All plots and plans are for you, my Sikander .... my love."

Alexander Ruthven stood motionless. Long ago, he had tried to love her — harsh, pretty and sensuous as she had been. It had been a long time since she had aroused his desire now. Yet it was obvious she still hungered for him. Pity and gratitude washed away his impatience and anger. He drew her fat, rippling body close and kissed her lips. "Tonight we will love again, my Begum. He released her and said briskly, "But now I will show you our domain."

Liselotte's appearance four days later raised no storm. The Begum of Deogarh had already taken command. She had been satisfied by her lord's lust on the night of their union when he had entered her vast flaccid body with the gusto of a bridegroom. The next day, she had sat down to work on the accounts and calculations of what the jagir would bring. "It will be considerable. But more important, we will bring our products here. These arid, austere cities will snatch up our fine rice, silk and muslin, tobacco and betel nut. We will take back to Bengal the stones from these mines and sell them to Europe and Calcutta at thrice the price."

Ruthven smiled warmly, realising what had kept him bound to this hard, ruthless woman. She was his Lakshmi, the goddess of fortune, his talisman of success. For her, he was ready to sacrifice the gentle, lovely Liselotte and the delicious, charming Chandrika.

He met Liselotte in a high sunlit balcony, surrounded by wild flowers. He noticed her thinness, the hectic flush on her sallow cheeks and the glisten of moisture on her forehead. Had she succumbed to consumption, he wondered, with sudden dread. "Ma chere," he said, "I wanted you near."

"The Begum, your wife, has arrived," Liselotte replied dully. "What was the need for me to come?"

"You could not stay indefinitely at Ratangarh, ma chere. Your place is here."

"With the Begum?" Liselotte asked, her merry laugh not disguising her anxiety.

"With me, Liselotte," he murmured, drawing her close. "I cannot do without you. For a while you will stay here and then return to Calcutta with me."

She waved her hand wearily. "Let me live in peace — with the children, Alexander. I cannot combat your Begum or your Rajput concubine."

He nodded. "That is what I have planned, Liselotte. You will go to Calcutta and live in my villa at Garden Reach — with every comfort. It has been expanded and you may decorate it as you wish. I will come whenever I can ... to enjoy your company."

Liselotte nodded with a sad smile. "It all began there, Alexander. Do you remember? How I resisted this role ... from which there is no escape now."

"Wait, Liselotte. You are young — not yet thirty. We will be married one day. I promise you."

She nodded again, laughing bitterly. "When we have half a dozen children?"

"They will be well loved," he assured her.

"More than the young Nawab Andraz?" she challenged.

Alexander Ruthven was troubled. "How well she knows me, this gentle, wayward, vagabond. Yes, I love Andrew best, though Liselotte's children were created in joy." He silenced her with a kiss and carried her inside, resisting, to the warm, cosy room where a brazier burnt. A large canopied bed was covered by a thick, bright quilt and cushions of many hues. Low wooden chairs covered by cushions and woven rushes helped to take the chill out of the stone floors. Laying her on the bed, he peeled off her voluminous, hooped dress and unpinned her high pompadour coiffure. Then he took possession of her, unhurried and gentle, tender yet lusty, breaking her thaw in the warmth of his desire. He had revelled for nine months in Chandrika's skilful sensuality; her henna-tipped breasts and jewelled navel, musk-scented hair and supple, fragrant body so wise in its work. But now Liselotte's simple passion, her wistful smile and unadorned body was like clear water after heady wine. And yet, he wanted all three.

"Every ruler has a harem," he told a furious Begum Shirin, "especially men of your faith. Is is not appropriate that I, Bahadur Saheb of Deogarh, should have one?"

Shirin's eyes were as dull as glass. "To think I saw in you a different being, Ruthven Saheb. A noble, brave foreigner!"

Stung by this novel reproach, he flung a jewelled tiara at her. "A noble foreigner would not have procured a jagir for your son nor a coronet for your head!"

The tiara lay at her feet, glittering in the lamplight, like a jewel that was gone forever from their lives.

A few months later, the Rana of Ratangarh came to see his vassal and commander. He was happy to see his mercenary general exhilarated by his little kingdom, his army, his subjects and his harem. With considerable nonchalance, Bahadur Saheb Ruthven displayed all three women at the large, high-roofed hall that served as an audience chamber.

Begum Shirin left no doubt as to who ruled the present ruler. Indeed, she brought a touch of the phantom Moghul court to the ambience of Deogarh. Chandrika had, to Ruthven's surprise and relief, relinquished her paramountcy to the Begum and enacted the role of the "Choti bibi" or junior wife with sweet decorum, deferring always to the wishes of the "Begum Saheba". Shirin had no idea that Chandrika evoked gales of laughter among her women by mimicry of the consort. Liselotte maintained an air of deliberate detachment as she played the part of concubine, but within her raged a storm of resentment at Shirin's paramountcy and Ruthven's obvious delight in Chandrika's drollery.

Nevertheless, all three "bibis" walked by the small lake on the foot of the fortified hill, listened to music together, dined together and occasionally rode on a richly caparisoned elephant. They played cards, trying to outwit each other, in order to retrieve a trinket gambled away the previous day, or told each other mendacious stories of past triumphs. It was only at night, when the revelries of the warriors ended that Ruthven decided with whom he would spend the night. Suddenly, the day's superficial camaraderie would be obliterated by the ensuing resentment. But, even here, they shared. Each knew that the chosen of tonight would give way to the chosen of tomorrow.

Thus did the wily Rana Ram Singh of Ratangarh keep his formidable general from mischief and from joining the all-conquering Marathas under de Boigne. Suppressing his distaste of Begum Shirin, the old Rana subtly tutored her to consolidate her position as he sang of the riches of Deogarh. He hinted too at the perils of Ruthven's ambition. "Let him not stay too far from here or from you," he often warned Shirin. Chandrika was his secret ally, and kept him informed of Ruthven's schemes. The Rana knew she would alert him at the first hint of mutiny.

The Rana left Liselotte to her own devices; the Frenchwoman was an enigma. Seldom had he seen a woman as heedless of the future or as carelessly tender. "Had I not feared my general," he confided to Chandrika, "I would have taken the endearing creature for myself. But I need Ruthven. The effulgent Maratha sun is rising once more, scorching Rajput dreams. We must prepare for a last engagement with Madhaji Sindhia before he becomes the virtual ruler of Hindusthan."

11

The Zamindar's Ladies

"It is true then? You have returned?" Fiona asked, pausing in her ride across the yellow fields covered by a flush of mustard flowers. Her wide straw hat hung back on her neck, revealing a tawny, freckled face and fiery locks that glinted in the autumn sunlight.

"Yes. It is true, I have returned," replied the young zamindar of Mayurganj. "I have been away long enough. My estate was falling into disrepair."

Fiona nodded, her blue eyes held by his dark, heavy-lidded ones. He seemed to her to have become even more attractive in the three years that had passed. There was about him now the quality of tempered steel, an air of quiet resolve that had been absent in the impetuous man who had raged against Dalrymple's depredations and the company's arbitrariness.

"I am glad you have returned," Fiona murmured, almost without volition. "I have ... missed you ... these years."

Startled, he glanced up at her. His retainer shifted his feet, thereby moving the huge white umbrella held aloft over the zamindar. Indrajit Chowdhury hesitated, as if trying to select the right words. "Your ... husband died ... soon after that night when I took you to our forest ashram."

Fiona nodded, remembering the strange night in the forest hideout of the sanyasis, the return home where Dalrymple lay dying of a malignant fever, and the quiet years that had followed.

Indrajit glanced away into the distance, narrowing his eyes to look at the thick coconut groves, the fields of paddy and mustard which grew in place of the hateful indigo.

"Your estate has changed," Indrajit said quietly. "I hear your revenues have lessened since you ceased to grow indigo."

Fiona nodded, a smile quivering on her wide mouth. "Is this not what you wished?" she asked.

The zamindar's eyes held hers. "Did you do it to please me?" A flush of colour suffused her tawny face. "Neither denial nor affirmation sprang to her lips. He watched her intently before saying, "I am glad for my former tenants. They have at least been restored to their former position ... though the land is no longer mine. Henry Dalrymple ... and the brigandage of your countrymen saw to that."

The colour on Fiona's face faded, the freckles standing out against the paleness. "I am ... prepared ... to ... make amends for that as well," she murmured in an unsteady voice.

"Fiona!" he exclaimed, stepping forward abruptly to touch her hands clenching the pommel of her horse. "I ... "

"The sunlight, Babu," the retainer said thickly, "I cannot extend the umbrella further."

The zamindar of Mayurganj swung around, his eyes blazing at the retainer's impudence. "How dare you!" he said raising a strong hand to strike the elderly chatradhar, the umbrella bearer. Suddenly, his glance was caught by the estate accountant, a thin and embittered Brahmin. There was such derision on the munshi's face that Indrajit suddenly dropped his hand. "Leave me," he said hoarsely. "We have inspected enough for today."

The umbrella bearer remained motionless, still holding aloft the silk-fringed canopy.

"Go," Indrajit said. "I do not need you."

The retainer bowed and moved away. "The sunshine is strong, Babu. Let it not scorch you."

Slowly, Fiona dismounted as the retainers moved towards the

zamindar's mansion, leaving Fiona and Indrajit alone in the stillness of the morning air.

"Fiona," he said gravely, "tell me why you are willing to relinquish so much ... It is yours by law now."

"Yes," she replied sombrely, "but I do not consider it mine, because your ancestors were given this land and my ... er ... Mr. Dalrymple bought it from your hard-pressed father."

"Is it only that which makes you want to return it?" he asked, looking intently at her. She shook her head, her blue gaze level on his dark, brooding one. "No ... I want to ... lessen your ... bitterness."

Indrajit reached out and clasped her hand tightly in his. "You have done so already," he said in a low husky voice. "I am thankful for that. Keep your land, Fiona ... so that you are near."

Instinctively they drew close and without willing it, were in each other's arms in a brief and searing embrace. It was Fiona who withdrew. "Your people disapprove ..." she said quietly, "even your retainers."

"Let them!" Indrajit retorted, as he held on to her firm, cool hand that seemed to send the blood pounding to his head. "I ... want you ... near." He paused, as if to get back his breath. "I will visit you in the evening. Go back now ... the sun will scorch you."

Mayurganj was soon aghast by the conduct of its zamindar. "That this man who had joined the sanyasi rebellion to fight the Company's oppression should now pollute himself with a foreign woman!" was the unworded protest in everyone's mind. It was not so much the zamindar's relationship that struck his subjects as dishonourable as much as the status of his mistress — a firingi and a widow — two unpardonable states of being.

In the cool halls and chambers at the zamindar's mansion, there was a warmer indignation, led chiefly by Indrajit's second wife, Indumati, now an unfolding fifteen-year-old beauty. The zamindar's first wife, Bishnupriya was twenty-six, with two daughters whose births had enhanced her frailty. She was often in bed, sick or tired, and looked upon her virile lord's liaison with the firingi widow as the result of her own inability to satisfy her husband. Indumati, a spirited girl with a formidable will, regarded the liaison as degrading but logical. "My older sister has been ill," she said of her husband's first wife, "and I have been a child for so long. But we will not allow the matter to go on thus!" She examined herself in the long mirror, noting her budding breasts and developing roundness of hips and arms. "I am not ready yet," she told herself, "but in the meantime ..."

The matter was discussed in the zenana where Indrajit's aunt presided, as alarmed as Indrajit's wives and retainers by his passion for the firingi widow. It was decided to accept Indumati's suggestion to bring in a buxom village girl to satiate the zamindar's carnal propensities.

Kamalakshi was of poor Brahmin parentage which had prevented a suitable early marriage for her, but she had the requisite robust body and eagerness to please. She entered the household unobtrusively and was sent to please her master one night. Indrajit was pleasantly surprised to see the buxom girl whose full, breasts rippled under the thin chemise, and whose full, wide lips parted in an inviting smile. "I am to be your new wife," the girl told him with such candour that he called at once for the household priest to join them in a brief ceremony. Then, he took Kamalakshi as his wife.

The zamindar was satisfied; he stayed home the following night, awaiting Kamalakshi's generous body. Indumati and Bishnupriya embellished their protegee with scents and jewels and left her to plan her own strategy of seduction. Indrajit revelled in his new wife and stayed home the entire week. Then a note came from Dubb's Point; an epistle of gentle reproach of neglect. Indrajit hurried that evening to Fiona Dalrymple's bungalow beyond the coconut grove.

He stayed one night and into the next afternoon, immersing himself in her intense and fiery passion. It seemed at times as if they were united by the external elements. "My sun goddess," Indrajit murmured, drifting into sleep upon her alabaster breast. "Did I know you would come in this form when I called out to the sun god every morning in the holy river?"

Fiona caressed his bronzed features, and sinewy limbs, noting the fairness of skin where the deltaic sun had not burnt it brown. "You are the wind and rain clouds," she whispered, smiling, "as dark and tempestuous."

Night fell. Starlight glinted on dew drops and called up the spirits of lovers long gone, to deepen the hunger and ecstasy of the two figures moulded together in the shadowy room. They rose before dawn to bathe in the river, offering oblations to the deities that had brought them together. When they parted at first light, it was with the assurance of meeting again.

"It is rumoured that our husband is planning to bring the widow into the house," Kamalakshi announced, bursting into Bishnupriya's chamber one sultry afternoon. Indumati glanced up from the marble pestle in which she was powdering a medicine for the eldest wife, her huge eyes narrowed in apprehension.

"Is that true?" Bishnupriya asked, laying aside her embroidery with a startled air.

"He has taken the widow on his bajra ... to show her the forests of the Sunderbans and the sea," Kamalakshi said, puffed with fury. "He plans to install her here ... over us all. So our priest says."

Bishnupriya gazed beyond the curtained window to the haze of the summer sky. "It is a long time — perhaps ten years — since I boarded the bajra." She paused, "I was young then ... and healthy." Tears danced in her deep, pain-dulled eyes.

Indumati embraced the elder lady. "Didi, do not lament so." She paused, and continued, "he will be made to return — to you — and conduct himself as a respectable householder." She rose and sent for the munshi. The priest, the thakur came in his wake, muttering about the calamity that would befall the Chowdhurys of Mayurganj if the zamindar brought in a mleccha widow into the ancestral home.

"How bad is the situation?" Indumati asked the astute manager.

"Bad, Bow-ma," he repeated. "The zamindar has lost interest in the estate; he has taken the tenants' taxes and has sent a man to Calcutta to buy jewels and clothes for the ... woman."

The muffled sound of Bishnupriya weeping broke the stillness of the Antah-Mahal, the ladies' apartments. Kamalakshi sat there, furious. Indumati reflected before saying, "Have the tenants prepared the land for sowing the monsoon crop?"

"Not yet. They will start as soon as the heat abates and clouds gather near the estuary," the manager replied.

Indumati nodded. "Tell them to abandon the fields for a few days. Let them not work. Let them disappear for a while."

The munshi was puzzled. "But why, Bow-ma?"

"Do as I say, Chakravarty-babu. I have a plan. Our zamindar has to be confronted with a calamity."

The elderly Brahmin bowed before the young chatelaine. "Mayurganj has a master again," he said, deliberately insulting the absent zamindar. "I am honoured to serve you, Bow-ma."

Indrajit Chowdhury returned after a few days. His advent had a strange effect on his household. The wives withdrew, the retainers hurried away and even his children by Bishnupriya scattered like pigeons when his footsteps echoed across the mosaic floor. His imperious and defiant countenance forbade familiarity. Going into his room he flung himself onto the huge four-poster bed and called for his personal servant, Banshi.

Indumati came in instead. "You called?" she asked.

Indrajit sat up, briefly puzzled by the apparition of the slim, glowing-faced maiden, whose silky black hair fell around her face like dark clouds, and whose eyes were like those of the goddess Durga.

"Who are you?" he asked, frowning.

The doe eyes narrowed in derision. "So addle-pated that you cannot recognise your bride?" she asked tartly.

Indrajit stared at her, surprise changing to anger. Slowly, he rose. "How dare you talk to me that way! You who shelter in my house!"

"As your bride, Sir, not as your whore!

Indrajit raised his hand to strike her. Indumati stiffened and all colour left her glowing face. "May your hand wither for assaulting a chaste wife," she said calmly. He stepped back, stunned, his hand dropping limply to his side.

"You will be sent back to your father. I have no use for a wife like you," Indrajit stormed.

Indumati nodded. "I came to ask just that, Zamindar Saheb. When can I go back?" She smiled sardonically as his lips parted in surprise. "You see I would rather live as a widow in my father's house than lose caste here." Slowly, she began removing the jewelled bangles and necklaces he had given her on their wedding day when she had been a child of ten, and wiped away the vermilion on her hairparting.

"What are you doing, you mad woman, you inauṣpicious female?" he shouted as a superstitious dread filled him at the sight of his bride removing the symbols of marriage and good fortune.

"Preparing myself for the imminent calamity, lord," she replied grimly. "Soon Mayurganj will be a cremation ground. Already, the peasants have fled. They say their grain-seed are withering because of the mleccha. Maybe the rains will fail or the lands will be drowned by floods. The munshi and thakur are seeking employment elsewhere. The servants refuse to serve you. Didi is becoming weaker and Kamala fears her child will be deformed. I must flee before this place becomes the habitation of vultures and ghouls."

Indrajit stared at her, astonished, as she stood unadorned, like a widow, before him. "You can live here then, in peace with your widow!"

The zamindar, in a blind rage, pulled her roughly and struck her on both cheeks. Indumati bit her lip, and controlling her tears, glared at him, eyes glittering. "Mayurganj will soon be razed to dust ... and vultures will take the place of peacocks!"

She turned towards the carved door, and almost flung herself out.

For seven days, the mansion lay in an eerie silence, as the

servants cowered in terror of their lord. But they feared the second wife or "Indu-bow" as they called her, more. Some said she was an incarnation of a goddess. Her radiant looks confirmed the theory. Bishnupriya sat trembling while the timid Kamalakshi whimpered. The munshi and thakur had left for the next village as instructed. The peasants had disappeared as commanded. The estate seemed abandoned ... almost desolate. It was a fearful sight.

Indrajit paced the floor of his chamber, where he emptied bottles of claret but still found no respite from the dread that overwhelmed him. His once-bright, vibrant home, had become a dark prison. No one lit lamps or blew conches at dusk. No one scattered Ganges water on the threshold at dawn. The only face he saw was that of the frail Bishnupriya, who, heavily veiled, came and left his food on a table in silence. He was afraid to leave the house and seek solace in Fiona's arms; afraid that he might return to a ghost house. He sat and thought of all the Chowdhurys who had striven for centuries to make it bloom. "And I, who became a soldier, have brought it to this!" he reflected morosely.

At last, when he could bear it no more, the zamindar confronted Bishnupriya. "Tell the priest I am ready to be purified," he said in controlled fury, "then ask the munshi to call back those who have left. One day I swear I shall teach them a lesson!"

Bishnupriya bent down to touch his feet. "Forgive me," she whispered, "I did not wish to hurt you."

Indrajit raised her to him and was shocked by her wasted appearance. "Priya," he cried hoarsely, "you are ill!"

"I have grieved for you," she whispered. "You are my life ..." Indrajit embraced her gently, feeling her frail body against his own lusty, virile one. He felt ashamed now. "You are truly Bishnupriya," he murmured, "my own Lakshmi. Forgive me."

They stood thus in gentle embrace, her head on his shoulder, until Bishnupriya said, "I must light the lamps and blow the conchshell, and summon the gods back to our house."

Indrajit watched her go. Later that evening, sitting wearily before his desk, he wrote a letter of farewell to Fiona Ruthven.

It was many months before Fiona recovered from this blow. "I loved him well enough to enter his house and take my place with the other women. I was prepared to defy my brother and anyone else who objected. But he has retreated before the onslaught of his own people. He did not care enough," she concluded.

She tried to immerse herself in the work of the estate, in a piece of embroidery or she sat alone, staring at the river brimming with life and activity. She thought of the ecstatic nights she had shared with her zamindar lover, the nocturnal walks when they had gazed up to identify the stars and planets which fascinated Indrajit. She recalled the idyllic sailing on the zamindar's barge towards the turbulent estuary. "It seemed that bliss would last forever ... and we would grow old together. Instead, I am left with a sense of terrible emptiness, all the more intense because I know what might have been."

These moods brought on at times an immense surge of anger against the society that could so enthral a man in superstitions.

Fiona often drove to the nearby villages to watch and assist Reverend Arthur Latimer. He had few resources apart from what the American Baptist Mission gave him and he had, therefore, to travel a great deal to raise funds for building a church. Land was a problem, since the Company frowned upon missionary activity and no local landlord would part with dearly bought lands. Fiona decided to offer a corner of Dubb's Point for building a church and a thatch-roofed pavilion for the village children.

Arthur Latimer was perplexed. "Will you not require it to grow crops?" he asked.

Fiona shrugged her shoulders. "The place is swarming with coconut palms. Nothing grows in their shade, but your church would be cool under its leaves.'

"Yes ... it would be beautiful. Now tell me, Mrs. Dalrymple, should we have a graceful Italianate facade or a simple square Norman one?"

"Perhaps a Norman tower would be incongruous but I should prefer that," Fiona said. "After all, the Normans were great travellers."

"Quite, quite," Latimer replied, busy sketching an edifice with twin square towers.

The church had been his dream ever since he had come to India ten years ago. The life of a wandering missionary had left him with a sense of vagrancy and alienation from both his own people and those of Bengal. While the former scoffed his reformist efforts, the latter hated him as a mleccha, an alien, who interfered in customs sanctified by time and necessity.

Recently, there had been trouble at Sagar Dwip on a full moon night when the sandbanks and swollen waves had provided the pilgrims the perfect setting for their bizarre ceremonies. Those whose prayers had been granted came on that summer night to offer infants in thanksgiving. Holding aloft those infants to the sky, they chanted incantations.

Latimer had rushed in with his followers. "Stop!" he had cried out, over the roar of waves."Your gods do not want your children!"

A priest had stepped forward, his face contorted by rage. "Dare you interfere, firingi, in our customs? Your Company has forbidden you from trespassing in our domain."

"I obey no one who perpetrates barbarism, Thakur," Latimer had replied. "Especially when your customs are an affront to the Almighty in whose name you perform these ceremonies!" He moved into the group which stood motionless, astonished by his effrontery.

The chief priest had nodded and issued swift commands. Men materialised from the crowd and pounced on Latimer and his followers, bound them and thrust them onto the sandbanks. The swollen waves began to carry them towards the open sea. Latimer struggled with the ropes that bound him, his eyes on the dozen infants who had been set adrift into the swirling waters. Their feeble cries were drowned by the waves crashing on the shore.

"Bless us, oh gods," the pilgrims cried, "we have given you our children."

Latimer saw the tiny forms raised on breakers before they vanished into the moonlit maelstrom. In one last spurt of fury, he tore asunder the ropes and made his way back to the shore just in time to see the last pilgrims leave.

The next time he and his followers came armed with pistols and shot dead the master of ceremonies. As the participants scattered, Latimer gathered up the infants and wrapping them in cloaks, rode back in his bullock cart to a village which had sheltered him.

As he saw the children grow, he wondered if he had given them back a life that would be more a burden than a gift. "If only I could make a home for them," he often thought, "what would I not do for them! But I have no home ... I am as lonely as they are ..."

Then he thought of the comely, courageous Fiona Ruthven Dalrymple who obeyed only the rules dictated by her heart and who too had cut herself adrift from both worlds. "Together," he thought, "we can find significance and purpose in all this suffering."

He came infrequently to Dubb's Point, pausing on his old horse to watch the progress of the little Norman church. Sometimes he hesitated before dropping in to call on Mrs. Dalrymple, who seemed pleased to see him One morning, a hasty summons brought him rushing to Dubb's Point. "Mrs. Dalrymple?" he asked Fiona standing on the high porch, "what is wrong?"

Fiona pointed a sturdy, bronzed hand at a youth in the distance who was bridling a wild horse. "My brother has sent his heir to be educated by me." She laughed. "Is that not amusing?"

Arthur Latimer screwed up his grey eyes to scrutinise the tall, flame-haired youth, struggling with and finally mastering the wild stallion. "He could be your son," the Reverend mused. "He looks so much like you."

"That is the Ruthven heir, Reverend Latimer. Watch him at closer quarters. You will also see the Afghan in him. It's there in the way he handles the horse, the way he ... scoffs at feminine authority." Fiona's tone was troubled.

"Yet Mr. Alexander Ruthven wishes you to make him an Englishman? Latimer asked sardonically. "I hope you will succeed."

Fiona sighed. "My brother is in Ratangarh. He has been given the jagir of Deogarh. Andrew must therefore be educated to be a jagirdar. I would have thought his mother, the Begum, would be a better tutor than I." She glanced at Latimer. "Reverend, I need your help to educate Andrew."

"Andrew?" Latimer repeated.

Fiona shrugged. "His name is Andrew but his mother calls him Andraz. She does not like infidels. But we will treat him as a Christian. He is going to be an Englishman after all."

The education of Andrew Ruthven brought his mentors closer. They taught not only him but other village boys converted to the new occidental creed. And when Latimer went to Serampore or Sagar Dwip to continue the struggle against Hindu superstitions, Fiona stayed back to do his work.

She heard through the villagers, of the zamindar's involvement in his estate, of the improvements he had undertaken at the behest of his munshi. She heard too that the real motive force came from the lissome young woman who was Indrajit's second wife. Curious, tormented by a strange pain which Fiona refused to acknowledge as jealousy, she strolled along the river bank one day, crossing the boundary that separated the Chowdhury estate from the Dalrymple's until she stood beside the black stone temple of Shiva, where once she had come to see her lover, the young zamindar.

Indumati was there now, standing waist deep in the river, lifting her cupped hands full of water to murmured incantations. Fiona saw her finely carved profile silhouetted against the iridescent dawn sky and felt a chill of dread.

"This child-woman is my adversary," she thought.

Fiona turned and ran over the soft earth, leaving her footprints indented in the clay.

"Aunt!" Andrew cried from the river, sailing a fisherfolk's dinghy.

"Come for a sail. We will catch fish. Latimer Saheb is here as well."

Blinking back tears, Fiona sailed with the two men, bravely hiding her sorrow from them.

Fiona received a summons from her brother later that year, inviting her to bring Andrew for inspection to Ruthven House. "I have returned to Calcutta for a sojourn and to satisfy myself that my commercial interests have not suffered during my absence in the north, he wrote. "Moreover, I intend to settle Liselotte and her children at Garden Reach before I leave again for Ratangarh where my Begum is managing matters. Our daughters, Alice, Clarice, and Beatrice are here but will be joining their mother shortly. I would be glad of your company."

Fiona laughed. "Glad of my company indeed! What he wants is my assistance to manage his numerous progeny by three women!"

Arthur Latimer was grave. "Why not assist him? After all, you are not burdened with a family of your own."

Fiona's azure eyes darkened. "Yes," she said dully, "that is all I can do — tend to others — since I have no life of my own."

"It is a noble life that lives for others," Latimer said with a faint smile. "You will find that a life of service brings peace to people."

"I do not wish for peace!" Fiona exclaimed, rising from the bamboo chair on the porch and gazing into the darkening smudges of trees, huts and the opalescent river at sunset. "I have yet to live ... to enjoy the ordinary joys of life! I will not renounce all hopes for that even though ..." Her voice shook and she bit her lips to choke back angry tears.

"Even though you have been twice grieved," Latimer interposed softly, rising to join her. "Choose wisely next time."

She turned to him. "And suppose the next time too, I am proved wrong?" He turned away from her incandescent gaze, afraid of its power, yet stirred in a manner that broke through his inflexible resolve. "You can only hope," he muttered and left in the swiftly falling dusk.

Calcutta seemed different to Fiona now. The city had recovered from the scare of the famine of 1770, and was prosperous once more. The Governor General, Warren Hastings, had brought an air of solemn dignity to the company diwani, just as his Act of Regulation had done away with the rough commercial atmosphere in the Company domain. Hastings had imposed order and stability in the diwani, while the rest of India still seethed with the turmoil of internecine struggles.

The Regulating Act of 1773 had created a new post of Governor General of Fort William in Bengal as well as a Council of Four. The Governor General was given authority over the two other Presidencies of Bombay and Madras, making Calcutta the capital of British India. Though the dignity of the Government in Bengal was enhanced, the internal squabbles within the Council were no different from those between the Marathas and Moghuls. The only difference was that Warren Hastings proved more than a match for his adversaries, General Clavering, Colonel Monson, Richard Barwell and finally, Philip Francis.

The Council resented the immense power of the Governor General and the patronage he conferred. They resented the secrecy with which he acted, and his reluctance to take them into confidence. This was first demonstrated during the Rohilla wars and then in the episode over the Begums of Oudh.

In 1775, the Nawab of Oudh, ruler of the largest kingdom in India, had died. Three of the Councillors had forced the new Nawab to cede the vital zamindari of Benaras to the East India Company with an indemnity of Rs. 600,000. Reduced to penury, the nawab could not pay his troops, who mutinied. A massacre followed. Though Warren Hastings opposed this policy, he was overruled by the directors in London.

However, help came to Warren Hastings in the person of Sir Elijah Impey, appointed Lord Chief Justice of the Supreme Court in Calcutta that had been established by the Regulating Act. Not only was Sir Elijah a friend of Mr. Hastings, he was a staunch ally of the Governor General's lady, Marianne, with whom he shared the spoils for contracts on roads and bridges. At the outset, the charming Mrs. Hastings was called "Poolbundhi" or agent for bridges. Hastings received Rs. 150,000 from the Rani of Burdwan as a bribe to keep off her state while the dowager Begum of Bengal arranged lavish entertainments for the Governor General.

Alexander Ruthven, like many Britons in Bengal, was drawn into the conflict over Warren Hastings' treatment of Nanda Kumar, the Indian merchant-prince who had always served the British cause faithfully. For some reason, he turned against Hastings and joined Francis, Clavering and Monson, the triumvirate in the Council who sought to contain Hastings' power. With the aid of Sir Elijah, the flexible Chief Justice, Hastings brought charges of forgery against Nanda Kumar. The trial was a farce, and the sentence death, even though forgery was not punishable by capital punishment in India. The jury recommended mercy on the grounds of Nanda Kumar's rank and past record of service. Hastings and Impey rejected the appeal. The old man died with dignity and courage, insisting on his innocence and denouncing Hastings to the end.

Calcutta was aghast at the cold-blooded nature of the act, but no one dared to voice an effective protest, certainly not the cynical men who had instigated Nanda Kumar. Arthur Latimer, however, who was visiting Calcutta at the time, cared little for discretion.

"It's scandalous!" he thundered in the Ruthven house in Calcutta. "After committing forgery against Amirchand, Clive was made a Lord, while an Indian has been sent to death for the same alleged offence! Hastings is iniquitous, a blot on the fair name of Britain!"

Alexander Ruthven smiled, as he toyed with his wine glass. "Reverend Latimer," he said with elaborate politeness, "the fair name of Britain has been blotted many times over, but her power grows. Obviously, morality and success are separate functions of politics."

The young pastor flung his napkin on the damask-covered table. "That, Mr. Ruthven, is what you would like to believe. But it is not so! Why, there is an outcry everywhere! Hastings will be recalled. Already Clavering has been appointed Governor General, by the Council.

"Mr. Hastings will not resign, rest assured," Ruthven replied, unmoved by Arthur Latimer's indignation.

Fiona looked alarmed, glancing now at her brother and then at the man who had become a regular visitor to her house. She had found herself getting gradually drawn to the pastor who had helped her through the bleak period following Indrajit's farewell. Indeed, Fiona enjoyed listening to him talk about his exploits in the remote parts of Bengal, and about the brave William Carey, Arthur's friend and mentor. Such talk appealed to her and satisfied her need to believe in heroism.

Alexander Ruthven did not fail to notice the respect in his sister's eyes, nor the protective tenderness apparent in her concern for the pastor. He though Latimer was a fool and William Carey a busybody. But he knew Fiona had to be handled tactfully. She was, after all, an affluent widow of thirty with no children. If she remained an unmarried woman, her not insubstantial estate would go to his children, perhaps little Claude or one of the daughters.

"We must visit your parish, Mr. Latimer," Ruthven said, in an attempt to divert the subject. "Fiona tells me you have built a church and an orphanage."

Latimer's grey eyes rested warmly on the attractive widow. "Helped and inspired by Mrs. Dalrymple," he said in a low voice.

"Indeed?" Ruthven asked sharply-glancing at his agitated sister.

"Oh yes," Latimer enthused. "Mrs. Dalrymple presented Reverend Carey and me with a handsome amount for the two buildings — on her land. Even now, she assists us regularly."

Ruthven stared at his sister who met his gaze with eyes once similar to his yet so different now. "Well, Fiona?" he asked coldly, "is this how you have handled your affairs while I have been away?"

Reverend Latimer flushed in indignation. "I must protest, Sir!" he exclaimed hotly. "I do think ..." Fiona raised a hand to silence him as she held her brother's gaze with her own.

"It is my estate, Alexander, and therefore I do as I wish. Further, in view of Reverend Latimer's efforts to improve the mind and manners of your son, Andrew, you ought yourself to contribute something to his cause."

Liselotte, who had been listening in bemused silence till now, emitted a delicate laugh. Her lover's warning glance failed to check her amusement. Sensing an ally in her, Fiona continued, "For a year, Arthur and I have sought to guide your son and educate him as an English gentleman. Without Arthur's help, I would have failed. The Begum resisted every effort of ours." She rose abruptly from the table. "This is as good a time as any to announce my intention, which your absence has so far prevented me from doing."

Arthur Latimer rose too and going towards Fiona said, "Do not be so agitated, my dear."

Alexander Ruthven stared hard at them, wondering what was their intention when Fiona said quietly. "Arthur and I are to be married."

Ruthven wanted to protest, even forbid the action but he recognised in Fiona a determined adversary. In the seven years after her arrival in India, Fiona had matured into a competent and resolute woman. "I wish you joy," he said, not without a touch of irony. At the back of his mind arose the mildly consoling thought that if the lusty Henry Dalrymple had failed to beget children on Fiona, the gentle Arthur Latimer might be just as unsuccessful, thus leaving the estates for his own progeny.

Liselotte rose and embracing Fiona, wished her happiness, her warmth unfettered by any of the thoughts that plagued Ruthven.

In the days that followed, Alexander Ruthven tried to subtly dissuade his sister. While offering no direct objections, he said, "I earnestly hope, my dear Fiona, that the Reverend Latimer has a genuine attachment for you."

"I think he does," Fiona replied, remembering their hours

of conversation, their walks in the garden, the times they had sat by the river, discussing the alien land which they both loved and feared.

"A woman possessing some fortune can be led to believe in a man's affection," he said softly.

Fiona glanced at him with a derisive expression on her face. But her voice remained level as she said, "I too had similar apprehensions in the beginning but in these few years I have come to know how lofty is his character and ideals."

"Men of the church can appear so," Ruthven said in the same smooth tone.

Fiona laughed, amused now by her brother's fencing. "Indeed so. Arthur, however, did things to prove his nobility." She paused and looked at her brother. "He asked me to give up indigo farming on my estate and allow the peasants to revert to their former cultivation of rice, sugar and cotton. He asked me to build storage huts for their grain, and to lower my demands on their produce." She paused, lowering her eyes and clenching her hands.

"He also asked me to sell back the lands wrongfully acquired by ... Henry Dalrymple from the ... zamindar of Mayurganj."

Ruthven stiffened. "Did you?" he asked curtly. Fiona shook her head, her eyes on the linen table cover. "Dalrymple had bought the zamindar's land for a song when ... Indrajit Chowdhury had been unable to pay the exorbitant taxes levied by the Company's agent who was in collusion with Dalrymple. It was only right that the lands be returned at the same price ... Arthur could not build a church, he said, in the proximity of stolen and seized property." She paused, and continued softly, "However, the zamindar would not ... take back the lands."

A terrible silence ensued. Coming upon them in the morning room, Liselotte paled and retreated. Fiona raised her eyes. "So you see, dear brother, Arthur is truly a man of god — like Reverend William Carey."

Alexander Ruthven rose abruptly, sending his chair crashing

to the ground. "You are a damned fool, Fiona!" he said in a low, furious voice. "I came to this benighted land to build a fortune for myself and my family. I brought you here to marry well and prosper. All you have done is destroy that — by listening to a whey-faced parson!" He left the room, banging the door behind him.

Fiona remained seated, a smile on her lips. She would not tell her brother about Indrajit and how sweet could be the love between a man and a woman. If Dalrymple had remained her only mentor, she knew she would have felt degraded and sullied forever. Now that she knew what love was, she wanted to offer some of its radiance to dear, unworldly Arthur.

Alexander Ruthven was diverted from his irritation over Fiona's behaviour by the gathering clouds of distrust and discord between the Governor General and the Council which opposed Hastings on all important issues, leaving him no alternative but to use his casting vote to decide all issues. The situation was fraught with deep tension. People wondered if Hastings would be able to stand the strain of the attrition.

He did, and in fact, it was his opposition which began to crack. In September of that year, 1776, Colonel Monson died. Informed of the Governor General's arbitrary conduct, King George III and Parliament demanded the recall of Hastings. General Clavering was appointed to take Hastings' place but the Governor General refused to resign and was supported by the board of directors of the East India Company and the Supreme Court.

From across the Atlantic, came news of British reverses against the American colonies. "We need a man of resolution to save at least our eastern territories," was the general opinion. So Hastings continued in his post and unable to bear the strain, General Clavering died soon after.

Ruthven was discomfited to find that his mistress had developed a friendship with the mistress of Philip Francis, the chief enemy of the Governor General. Francis' mistress, Madame Grand, was a Frenchwoman. It was natural that the two French ladies should be drawn together by mutual affinity and common problems. While Ruthven did not wish to forbid Liselotte the friendship since it was not known who would eventually prevail in the Council, he suggested that Liselotte visit Fiona and her new husband in Mayurganj.

The monsoon had retreated, leaving the fields ripening with paddy, pulses and mustard under skies the colour of the blue lotuses that floated in the brimming ponds and tanks. Fisherfolk glided down the gilded waters of the river, their nets afloat.

Fiona was surprised one evening to find Indrajit at her door. "I have come to invite you to attend Durga Puja in my house," he said gravely.

It was the first time they had met after her marriage. Indrajit noted that the once restless Fiona was more serene now, as if she had found an anchor in Arthur Latimer. Her figure had filled out in anticipation of childbirth.

Fiona smiled. "Of course we will come. My brother's ... Liselotte will be arriving shortly. She will be happy to come as well."

Indrajit nodded gravely. It irritated him to see Fiona calm and composed. "Has she forgotton everything in the arms of that padre?" he wondered. Aloud he said, "I am glad to find you looking well, Fiona."

"I am well, Indrajit," Fiona said, suddenly sombre. "The ... disquiet of the last years was a burden on me." She paused and glanced at him before gazing away at the coconut grove that dominated the boundary. "I want to settle down ... and find peace," she said. "I am busy all day ... helping Arthur in the school and church."

His eyes went too to the low, graceful church with square Norman towers and stained glass windows. It seemed incongruous against the tropical verdure of coconut palms, paddy fields, flimsy fishing boats and dusky peasants. Its bells chiming compline, matins and vespers sometimes clashed, sometimes blended with the bells of the zamindar's Shiva temple. It was, he thought, a pattern of the discordant times, this clash of two civilisations confronted by one another. "You struggle in vain, Fiona," he said. "Our Hindu faith will not be destroyed. Many invaders have come and gone, some more cruel and disruptive than others but they could not impose their ways on us. Tell that to the Reverend Saheb."

Indrajit's anger against Latimer amused Fiona. "So he still cares," she mused. Aloud she said, "Arthur does not wish to impose his ways on you ... but he wishes to open the doors of understanding and light up areas of darkness." She paused, hoping to win support for her husband. "Arthur goes to Sagar to dissuade people from sacrificing female infants and maidens. He preaches against the immolation of widows. Is that wrong?"

Indrajit frowned. "Why does not Reverend Latimer try to improve the morality of his compatriots? Even the great men of the Council are providing a rare spectacle for us."

"Will you not support Arthur?" Fiona asked quietly. "It would help him."

Indrajit shook his head. "I shall not assist the spread of an alien faith — not while I wear this sacred thread of a Brahmin."

Her blue eyes searched his intently. "Have you then retreated so far from me?" she asked softly. "Once we were ... almost one."

He sighed deeply. "Once, we were willing to abandon our own worlds for each other ... but now, we have been summoned back to our own orbits ..." He took her hand and kissed it briefly. "Command me in any way you want, dear love, but do not ask me to forsake my beliefs. I have suffered enough for that."

"Dear, sweet love," Fiona murmured, gazing up at his troubled face, "I am at peace now — with you."

Liselotte arrived with her twins, Claude and Lucille on the new moon night of Mahalaya, as the preparations continued in the zamindar's house for the recital of the Puranas, the ancient scripts depicting the triumph of the goddess Durga over the demon world. The chief priest was seated in the centre of the roof garden, and as the fine sliver of the new moon rose behind the coconut fronds, the chanting began.

Fiona sat in the veranda, longing to be on the roof terrace with the man who had moved so far away from her path.

That year, 1775, the zamindar of Mayurganj invited Warren Hastings to the grand Puja which lasted for four days. No one was surprised when the Governor General gladly left behind the intrigues at Calcutta, the despatches from the Bombay and Madras Presidencies, to enjoy a few days of lavish hospitality in the Chowdhury house. He had made it clear that the British had no interest in interfering with the religion or customs of India. He had even opposed the transplantation of English jurisprudence to India on the ground that it did not suit the genius of the people.

So when buffaloes and goats were sacrificed to the loud chanting of ancient Sanskrit prayers, Warren Hastings stood nearby, in his stockinged feet, watching without flinching. Indeed, he explained to Liselotte the significance of the sacrifice since the buffalo, the attendant of the demon Mahisasur, represented lust, greed and violence. In slaying it, the mother goddess Durga cleansed the world of evil. Fiona stood nearby, half listening, and remembering how long ago on a starlit night, Indrajit had told her the same things as they had sat close together on the warm stone steps of the temple, deep in the forests.

As conches blew and drummers beat frenziedly on dhols, elongated drums, boys danced with brass incense burners before the massive statue of the ten-handed goddess astride her lion and surrounded by Lakshmi, the goddess of fortune, Saraswati, the goddess of learning, Ganesh the god of enterprise and Kartik, the god of war. Priests recited mantras, holding aloft lamps and lotuses to the effulgent goddess. When the prasad, the oblation, was given to the worshippers, the Governor General accepted it with every sign of reverence.

"Tell your husband, Ma'am, that there is much to know about the Hindu faith," the Governor General told Fiona as they sat in the flower girded veranda of the zamindar's sprawling mansion. "I have read some of the texts and find them both moving and inspiring."

Fiona bowed her head in acquiescence, thankful that her impulsive spouse was not there to read Mr. Hastings a sermon on political morality. "Apparently the Governor General saw no discrepancy in reverence for Hindu civilisation and waging war against the most militant representatives of this culture — the Maratha confederacy," Fiona reflected to herself.

He took a little longer to give his second piece of advice. "I hear your brother, Colonel Ruthven, is back from his exploits in Rajputana."

"That is so, Your Excellency. He has left his Begum to administer the jagir given by the Rana of Ratangarh," Fiona replied with natural familial pride.

Mr. Hastings nodded. "Then he will be kept occupied. It would be a pity if he accepted the invitation of either Sindhia or Holkar against our efforts."

"I have suggested that we should go to Europe for a long sojourn," Liselotte said, quietly. "Perhaps Your Excellency can give him an assignment which would take him there."

Warren Hastings smiled. "I think that can be arranged, Madame," he said. "The sooner the better."

The Governor General left for Calcutta on the day after Vijaya Dashami, when the images of the goddess and her companions were immersed in the swift flowing Ganges. Indrajit Chowdhury presented Warren Hastings with gold plates and bolts of silk for Marianne Hastings. The Governor General reiterated his good will and support for Chowdhury. In those tumultuous times, such good will was worth many gold plates.

Fiona watched these courtesies from a distance, her eyes not on the men but on the three young women who stood heavily veiled and jewelled, behind their lord. The Governor General bowed to all three and exchanged a few words with them in impeccable Bengali. He paused longest with the young woman who stood in the middle, a girl with a complexion of rose and honey, large lustrous eyes and an imperious countenance. Turning to the zamindar, the Governor General said in English, "Your second wife illumines your house." Then he moved on.

Indumati's eyes met Fiona's and then her full lips quivered in a smile. Fiona wondered whether it was in fact, a smile of triumph.

12

Mirages

A year after Liselotte's sojourn in Mayurganj found Alexander Ruthven in a state of suppressed excitement. He had received, he said, a cryptically couched message from the Maratha Holkar chief to lead one of his battalions against the Regent of the Maratha kingdom, Raghunath Rao.

"Are you going to accept this invitation?" Liselotte asked, her hand trembling as she poured the tea. This was what the Governor General, Warren Hastings, had warned her against, and while she had formulated a vague plan of action, she could think of nothing else to say.

Ruthven lifted up the light china cup to his lips and smiled at his mistress. "It will depend on what the Holkar has to offer." He paused. "You see, the Maratha chiefs, Holkar and Sindhia, are anxious to throw off the authority of the Peshwa at Poona. The Regent of the Maratha king had sought the aid of the Company last year, and the Bombay Council agreed to send troops in return for Salsette and Bassein. The campaign cost the Regent, Raghunath Rao, a sum of rupees six hundred thousand. The Governor General has repudiated the Treaty of Surat and asked for a fresh settlement. The Company directors in London wish the campaign to be revived in favour of the Regent."

"Will the Governor General send an army to aid the Regent?" Liselotte asked.

"Hastings can hardly refuse to obey the directors of Leadenhall Street."

Liselotte put down the fragile Sevres teapot and clenched her hands on her lap, so that Ruthven could not see them shake. Slowly, she said, "Is it wise to fight for a Maratha chief who may oppose the Company?"

The hookah-bardar entered the morning room and installed the hookah on a carved table, uncoiling the pipe and lighting the charcoal. Bowing, the servant handed the mouthpiece to Ruthven who gazed meditatively at the hookah. Liselotte waited, tensely.

"If I can amass a fortune by helping Holkar, why not join him?" he said idly.

"Can Holkar withstand the British forces?" Liselotte asked.

Ruthven burst into laughter. "Ah, ma petite, you are acting out of character! Since when have you been interested in Marathas and armies?"

Liselotte felt a swift rush of colour to her sallow cheeks and saw his blue eyes harden. "Has he heard of my conversation with the Governor General at Mayurganj?" she wondered. Tossing her head of ringlets, Liselotte exclaimed with spurious hauteur, "You forget, mon ami, that my foster-father, General Claude Martin, has taught me to be interested in the armies of Hindusthan!"

Alexander Ruthven nodded, smiling indulgently. "That is so, but do not become too involved in these themes, Liselotte."

"I understand," she said coldly. "These lofty subjects are to be discussed only with your Begum."

Ruthven laughed again. "True. My Begum understands politics, intrigues and power. She was once close to a glittering throne. In fact," he said, laying aside the hookah to sip another cup of tea, "Shirin has informed me that my liege lord, the Rana of Ratangarh, wishes me to return and take command of his army soon. With Ratangarh lying close to the rump of Maratha territories, the Rana has suggested a rearguard movement; to pursue Holkar and Sindhia from the west and seize a chunk of their lands while the British march from the east." He paused. "I can then name my price — possibly another jagir adjacent to Deogarh." He paused and added, "For Claude."

Liselotte stared at her lover, startled, and then rose suddenly. "Are you in earnest?"

"Why not? Andrew has a large jagir already. My second son is dead. That leaves only Claude. He too should inherit from me."

Liselotte knelt at Ruthven's feet, her hands on his knees. "I will not ask for more, mon ami," she murmured huskily.

Ruthven took her hand and brushed his lips over them. Ma chere, don't make hasty promises. You will ask again." He paused. "Do you not wish to be Madame Ruthven one day?"

Liselotte shook her head. "I am happy as I am ... if I am loved by you... but if you recognise Claude as an heir ... I will ask for nothing more."

Ruthven nodded. "I have given you my word." He rose, suddenly impatient. "Now, let me go and read my letters. And you, Mademoiselle, had better attend to the house. Decorate it ... refurnish it ... I wish to come here to Garden Reach, to relax."

Gladdened by the prospect of Claude's ownership of a jagir, Liselotte forgot Hastings' warning for Ruthven. She now actively encouraged her lover to consider the prospect of leading the armies of either Holkar, Sindhia or Bhonsle, since this course of action would guarantee spoils of war. In the meantime, she threw herself enthusiastically into the task of furnishing and decorating the riverside villa. Summoning the gifted local carpenters, she showed them designs of the light, graceful furniture then in vogue in Paris. She sold the heavy damask hangings favoured by Begum Ruthven and put up silk curtains in their place. Orders were sent to purchase porcelain and china ornaments from Sevres. Ruthven gave her a handsome allowance for clothes and jewels; he provided her with servants, a carriage and four but he did not take her into the official circles of Calcutta. He felt that Shirin Begum still ought to be regarded as his wife, a semi-royal consort who had been close to the masnad of Bengal. In the upstart world of the nabobs, a wife like Shirin had more dignity than a pretty mistress like Liselotte Fremont.

Liselotte smarted under the subtle indignity but was soon able to find her own distractions. She made friends with Madame Grand, the notorious woman who had left her French husband, Colonel Grand, to become the mistress of Philip Francis, a member of the Council and Hastings' determined enemy.

Ruthven was annoyed when be heard of the friendship. "Do you know of the scandal caused by your friend?" he asked in the astringent voice that Liselotte dreaded.

"Yes," Liselotte replied. "I remember it very well. Monsieur Grand was informed by a servant that Francis had climbed into her room at night and proceeded to sue the Councillor for a million rupees." She laughed. "I remember the moral homily given by Judge Chalmers before he awarded a damage of rupees fifty thousand to the betrayed husband."

"It was all rather shabby," Ruthven said. "The Governor General felt embarrassed."

"Indeed?" Liselotte asked, hazel eyes glittering. "Did not your exalted Governor General purchase his precious Marianne from Baron Imhoff? How could he be embarrassed by the emulation of his Councillor?"

"Liselotte," Ruthven said patiently, "I would advise you not to discuss the Governor General in this manner. He is a powerful man. The even tenor of our days depends on his good will."

"Does that mean I cannot be a friend to Madame Grand?" she asked defiantly.

"It might be advisable not to be over intimate with a woman whose ... protector is an adversary of the Governor General."

"Even if I am happy and amused in her company? Do not forget, she is also a Frenchwoman exiled like me ... and in a position of indignity." Liselotte was glad to see Ruthven's face flush in vexation. Emboldened by his discomfiture, Liselotte plunged into an attack. "These mutual dishonours draw us close together. If Mrs. Hastings would receive me once as a guest in her drawing room,

I would not feel so distressed. But she will not do so."

The man who fearlessly led armies into battle felt a quiver of disquiet when faced by his mistress' smouldering resentment. "Mrs Hastings treats me as if I am an outcast!"

Ruthven did not reply; he had not realised until now how deep was her indignation of the status he had conferred on her. "I did not know you minded so much," he said at last, distressed by her stormy countenance.

"Did you not? Did you think I enjoyed my role as concubine and that Mrs Hastings' insults amuse me? I was not, to begin with, a demi-mondaine like Marianne Hastings or Madame Grand. I had hopes and dreams ..." Liselotte bit her trembling lips and blinked back tears.

Moved, and deeply disturbed, Ruthven came up to Liselotte and held her hot, flushed face between his cool, firm hands. "Ma chere, my sweet Liselotte," he murmured, I shall compensate you for the misery you have endured. I promise you that."

"How, Monsieur Ruthven?" Liselotte cried. "Five years have fled. I am thirty now. Soon I shall be old."

"I shall think of some way, ma chere," Ruthven said, looking at her intently. "Perhaps we shall go to Europe for a holiday ... when the situation settles down."

"Oh Alexander, you are not jesting?" Liselotte asked, between a laugh and sob. "Will we really go to Europe together? To France, to Provence, my birthplace! I will enjoy showing you Paris and Versailles, and the Castles in the Loire ..." She stopped, puzzled by the sombre expression on his face. "What is it, mon amie?" she whispered.

"I will show you the hovel in Marseilles where we all lived in exile — after Culloden," he said in a strange voice. "Perhaps then ... you will forgive me."

Liselotte clasped him close, as if to brush away his grim memories. "Do not think of all that ... it is over," she murmured, her lips on his cheek. "And you do not need my forgiveness ... you have ... made me so happy at times"

Ruthven held her close. "Liselotte, my dear, sweet one," he whispered, "I am fortunate to have found you."

Guilt softened him, and made him eager to please Liselotte. He dropped his objections to her friendship with Madame Grand, and indulged her in many other ways too.

Madame Grand fascinated Liselotte. Bold, unashamed and extravagant, the mistress of Philip Francis had a considerable following in Calcutta, particularly among those who resented Hastings' complete authority over policy matters. Madame Grand organised supper parties al fresco in her riverside villa not far from Ruthven's country house. Here she entertained lavishly and joined her lover in making fun of the Governor General. Sometimes Ruthven accompanied Liselotte to these parties and found himself drawn into something more than frivolous pastimes.

"Hastings wants to wage wars," Philip Francis declared angrily at the faro table. "He is not content to guide Company affairs. His ambitions will destroy the gains consolidated over the years."

"The Maratha Confederacy is posing a threat," Ruthven reminded the Councillor.

"As did the Rohillas?" Francis asked sarcastically. "Oh no, Mr. Ruthven. It is only the will of your Governor General."

Ruthven looked up from the cards in his hand. "Why do you not oppose him, then? After all, you all supported him to reject the action of the Bombay Council."

Francis' mouth tightened. "Hastings' casting vote overrides our decisions. Besides, our directors at Leadenhall Street have begun to listen to the bombast. We will have to fight the Maratha Confederacy — and face the consequences."

In another room, Madame Grand made fun of Madame Hastings. "My lady is nicknamed 'Poolbundhi'. She is the collecting agency for all contracts and licences." She emitted a silvery laugh and fluttered a white hand. "Perhaps the lady has reimbursed Hastings the £10,000 he paid as bribe for a divorce to Marianne's first husband!"

Liselotte laughed; she was happy to join the ridicule against

Mrs. Hastings who was of dubious background but who regarded Liselotte as unworthy of her drawing room. "It is incredible," Liselotte told her friend and compatriot.

"Ma chere, it is your fault. Can you not persuade Ruthven to retire his fat Begum and marry you? Are you not a daughter of Provence, in whose veins the blood of troubadours sings?" Madame Grand pouted her lips in mock exasperation.

Liselotte sighed. "Alexander is loyal to the Begum."

Madam Grand's soft malicious chuckle was almost inaudible. "That is reassuring. After all, he must be loyal to someone!"

Ruthven was silent as he walked back to his villa with Liselotte, who sensed that the conversation at Francis' house had given him food for thought. She did not, however, press him for details. Since the outburst a few months ago, he had been more attentive and considerate to her than before, and drove down from Calcutta to spend half the week with her and their three children — the four-year-old twins Claude and Lucille and one-year-old Alexina.

Now, he was immersed in his own thoughts. Two servants strode ahead, swinging large lanterns while another followed, clapping his hand to disperse reptiles or rodents that might be lurking on the path. Above, the summer sky was a bowl of white stars glistening through a haze. In the distance could be heard the lapping of water on the low banks.

When they reached the house, Ruthven lead Liselotte to the airy drawing room where a lamp still burned, casting shadows on shimmering, silk-covered chairs and gleaming tables. "Ma chere," he said quietly, "I must return to Ratangarh. The Rana will be waiting to mobilise his army. The Maratha Confederacy is girding itself for a confrontation with the Company forces, and his territory lies on their path."

Liselotte searched his face intently, looking for the real motivation behind this decision. But his countenance was inscrutable as usual, his eyes aloof and cool. "Why, mon amie?" she asked. "You owe the Rana no loyalty. To enter the fray now would be dangerous."

An ironic smile lifted his lips. "As you say, ma chere, I have no loyalty — to the Rana." He paused. "Perhaps to no one. Is that not what your friend Madame Grand thinks?" He saw her blush even in that meagre light. "She is right."

"Then why are you going to Ratangarh?" Liselotte's question echoed in the silent, sleeping house.

"I am restless — and in need of adventure once more. Buying and selling of saltpetre, silk and tobacco no longer holds my interest. Besides, I must protect my jagir."

"Andrew's jagir!" Liselotte snapped, furious with the dissimulation.

Ruthven's eyes leapt into blue fires. "Andrew's then, if you wish. I must protect it from both Maratha and Company depredations."

"Go then," Liselotte whispered hoarsely. "I have little to say in the matter!"

Andrew Ruthven glanced at his aunt and uncle, barely hiding his impatience at their homily. "It is impossible to communicate with Aunt Fiona," he thought angrily. "She will not appreciate the fact that I am of nineteen years and weary of the classroom!"

"It is my intention to send you to Oxford or Cambridge," Arthur Latimer said. "There you will learn of the ancient classics and modern sciences."

"I tell you, I have no desire to be a scholar like you, Uncle Arthur! These three years have been tedious enough!" Andrew exclaimed.

"A good ruler must be educated," Reverend Latimer insisted.

"A good ruler must know how to protect and defend his territory. The pundits can learn the scriptures for him!" Andrew retorted.

Fiona Latimer rose from the armchair. "It will soon be dusk," she said. "I must superintend the lighting of the lamps. Nitish does not trim the wicks daily." It was clear she was weary of arguing with her stubborn nephew, though she felt a secret sympathy for his impatience and restlessness. "Dubb's Point is no place for a youth with hopes and energy," she thought, as she watched Nitish trim wicks and clean the glass globes of lanterns. Parul, the ayah, made the beds for the Latimers' two children. The door closed as Reverend Arthur Latimer went to the little church for evening prayers. Vespers rang in the sultry air, buzzing with mosquitoes.

Fiona stood on the porch to murmur a prayer, before the steeple disappeared in a bank of monsoon cloud. From across the fields came the sound of bells from the riverside temple, where the zamindar's three wives went to pray every evening. She had stopped going there for over a year now — ever since that morning when she had seen Indrajit Chowdhury standing waist deep in the glittering waters, his hands cupped with water and flower petals, as oblation to the five elements. Near him had stood a girl of seventeen, as radiantly beautiful as an image of the goddess Durga. Her pale-honey complexion seemed to blend with the dawn light, and her dark hair streamed around her like the river.

"Give me a son, Indu," Indrajit had said after his prayers were finished. "Mayurganj has no heir. Let it not fall to any but our blood."

Indumati had sighed. "It is in the gods' hands. One of us may bear a son."

Indrajit's eyes were on his second wife. "I want a son only from you. Such a son will be worthy of this zamindari."

Indumati bowed her head, trying to hide her smile; a smile of triumph, Fiona had thought with an ache that she refused to recognise as jealousy. The little girl of ten who had come as a bride for the exasperated Indrajit was now a comely woman. She had become the chatelaine of Mayurganj — proud, imperious but also graceful and generous. She subdued men as much by her beauty as her competence, while the womenfolk were won over by her generous kindness. Indrajit, Fiona realised, adored his second wife. Bishnupriya had retired in peace to her apartments, consigning the care of her growing daughters to Indumati. Kamalakshi, the third wife, had no choice but to accept the imperious girl as her superior.

It had been dark when a servant came from Mayurganj with a basket of fruits and sweetmeats. The zamindar's emissary had smiled happily. "Indu-ma has given birth to a son," he had informed Fiona. "The Zamindar Saheb asks you to rejoice for him."

Fiona had nodded, chiding herself for the sudden pain within her. "Tell your lord and lady that I am glad," she had said slowly. Watching her from the veranda, Arthur Latimer's eyes had darkened in pain. But he had come in and increased the flame of the lantern. "Chowdhury will be a happy man now," he had said, without looking at his wife. "Perhaps one day his son and our Ian will be good friends."

Fiona had nodded, gazing at the silhouettes of coconut groves in the distance, where, as a youth, the zamindar had held tantric rituals, and where Dalrymple had stalked with his gun. "One day, the zamindar's son and the Reverend's son would walk over these grounds, unaware of the past," Fiona thought. "Time is slipping away."

Andrew Ruthven burst into the lamplit drawing room, jerking Fiona back to the present. "I am leaving at daybreak," he informed her. "The zamindar's agent told me that a battle is brewing in the west. The zamindar is offering pujas for the victory of the Marathas." Andrew saw his aunt pale suddenly. "He feels that this may be a decisive war in Hindusthan. I wish to join my father." He came and embraced his aunt. "Thank you for everything, Aunt Fiona. You have been like a mother to me, but it is time now for me to go."

Alexander Ruthven had delayed his departure to Ratangarh on account of the illness of his son, Claude, who had caught a contagion while playing with his friends by the riverside. In the meantime, a barrage of letters arrived from the Rana of Ratangarh, urging him to lead his armies — not against the Marathas — but against those of the Company.

"A new feeling has arisen among the rulers of western and central Hindusthan," the Rana wrote. "We wish to combine and drive out the armies of the Company, which are encroaching into our domains. Perhaps we shall not get another chance such as this. Salsette and Bassein are gone. The Marathas wish to regain lost terrain — and I a Rajput — am afraid of losing mine in this forthcoming conflagration. Make haste to come soon."

Begum Shirin supported the Rana, if only to make the jagir of Deogarh safe for her son Andrew.

Alexander Ruthven was surprised but not reluctant to go. Leading the armies of Ratangarh or Holkar or Sindhia was an honour not to be taken lightly. Victory against the Company's forces of Redcoats would, in some way, he felt, wipe off the blood of Culloden, spilt thirty-three years ago. He prepared to go, lured not merely by hopes of gain but by anticipation of excitement.

"Father!" a high cry shattered the stillness of the hot, inert air of Garden Reach.

Alexander Ruthven put down his cup with a clatter and stared at Liselotte opposite him. "Who was that?

Before she could answer, the door was flung open and young Andrew Ruthven stood there, flushed and breathless. Alexander rose at once, and came to him, puzzled, but pleased to see his best-loved child. "Andrew! I thought you were studying with your aunt at Dubb's Point."

Andrew laughed. "So I was, Father ... until two days ago."

Father and son embraced. Liselotte watched, afraid yet fascinated. Andrew was the very image of Alexander; tall and spare with a headful of red hair tied by a black riband and blue eyes as determined as the sire's. There was no trace in him of the Afghani mother's watchful mien nor the subtle hesitancy that hid a simmering ambition.

Andrew's gaze travelled to his father's mistress, who stood

framed by the window. She saw then the youth's resemblance to Begum Shirin — in the outwardly calm countenance that hid a hundred emotions. He bowed deeply, and she, brought up in the studied mannerisms of Lucknow, bowed back, smiling as warmly as she could. "You are welcome, Andre," she murmured, not daring to offend Alexander by slighting his son.

"Thank you. I trust you are in good health, Madame?"

Liselotte nodded, colouring, because those sapient eyes observed her enciente condition. "How are my dear brothers and sisters here?" Andrew asked with the ingrained Moghul disregard for sincerity.

"Claude has recovered from his fever and Lucille and Alexina are well." She paused and asked, "How is the Begum? And Alice, Clarice and Beatrice?"

Andrew nodded. "Mama's last letter informed me that she and my sisters are well and thriving in the cold of Deogarh's winter."

Alexander led his son to the linen-covered table where a prodigious breakfast had been served. Andrew sat down eagerly to sample the French rye-bread, rolls sprinkled with aniseed, mushroom omelettes, sardines marinated in a sauce of tomato and coriander, and ginger and orange marmalade.

"What a change from Aunt Fiona's porridge or Mama's parathas!" the youth exclaimed, glancing at Liselotte appreciatively.

"Liselotte rekindles my memories of France with this fare," Alexander told his son, as he watched him thoughtfully.

Liselotte poured coffee in three cups and waited. Andrew put away his fork and knife. "Father," he said softly, "I came to ask your help ... to join the Company army as an officer."

An uncomfortable silence vibrated over the table. Koels and parrots flashed past fruit-laden trees.

"Why should you do that? You are a ... jagirdar ... not a paid soldier of the Company."

Andrew looked intently at his father. "I wish ... to be ... a true Englishman."

Alexander stiffened. "But you are British ... and my son and heir."

"No ... I wish to be a true European, not just in name or even in colour, which I am ... but in mind, manners and ... loyalty." He paused and added softly, "I do not wish to be a half-Moghul nawab or a half-British trader."

Alexander stared at his son for a long time before lifting the heavy Jacobean silver pot to pour himself a cup of coffee, taking time to summon the right words. "It is your mother's ambition and mine that you should be the ruler of a principality. It is something like a legacy — because your maternal ancestors were of the house of Tamerlane. In these troubled times you may annex more land to Deogarh ... and establish a princely line of your own."

"I wish to be a British officer, Father, not the descendant of an Afghani adventurer. I wish to fight under the Union Jack and be part of the new regime!"

Alexander rose from the table. Liselotte watched them with bated breath. She was too bewildered to consider the implications to her progeny if Andrew Ruthven became a British officer.

"What will happen to Deogarh? Who will rule it and collect the revenues?" Alexander asked coldly. "Did I build up all that only to relinquish it?"

Andrew turned to Liselotte with a smile. "Claude Martin Fremont Ruthven would be a good nawab, would he not? Especially if little Claude has in his veins, the blood of his martial grandfather, General Martin."

Liselotte blushed. "So he too believes me to be the illegitimate daughter of Claude Martin," she thought. Suddenly, Alexander turned around, his blue eyes fierce. "I forbid it! Return to Dubb's Point! Or better still, take charge in Deogarh!"

Andrew shook his head. "No, Father, I will not. I will join the Company's army."

The two men stared at each other in a moment of bitter antagonism, but Alexander saw the cold, determined gleam in Andrew's expression that he recognised as his own, and felt a shiver of foreboding, as if someone had walked over his grave. Suddenly, inexplicably, he relented. "Very well, join the Company army and learn to be a good commander so that you may lead your own army one day. I will speak to the Governor General."

Andrew embraced Alexander. "Thank you. I will try to be a credit to you. I hope to make you proud of me in the battlefield."

Alexander nodded but could not shake off that inexplicable sensation of doom, as if Andrew had embarked on a perilous journey by refuting his mother's Moghul heritage.

In mid-1778, Warren Hastings heard of the dissension in the Maratha capital of Poona and in November, the Bombay forces of the Company took the field to restore Raghunath Rao as Regent of the Peshwa, Madhav Rao. The military command was placed in the hands of Colonel Egerton, who soon resigned, handing command to Cockburn. The two armies met on hilly terrain at Telgaon and were pursued by the combined forces until they were scattered at Wargaon. There, Cockburn agreed to the restoration of all territories taken after 1773, the restoration of Broach to Sindhia and the withdrawal of the advancing army from Bengal.

By then, the Bengal army under Colonel Goddard was already making its way across Central India. It marched past fields ablaze with ripening jowar and bajra, favoured by the hardy peasants of Central India. Andrew Ruthven rode on a chestnut charger, gifted to him by his father. He felt a sense of exhilaration as the horses trotted over the hard ground, and the cool air, washed of the summer dust by the late monsoon, sang past him. Tawny hills ringed the plains, interspersed with crenellated walls of forts from where the Marathas watched the British advance. "I have a new identity," Andrew thought proudly. "No more need I hear Mama's exhortations to be a nawab or uphold the traditions of a Timurid line, which came from Samarkand to chastise the infidel hordes of Hindusthan. Now, I am British. I belong to a race that will soon rule Hindusthan."

Goddard's army stormed through fort after fort, taking

Ahmedabad, overrunning Gujarat and Surat. Popham took the impregnable fort of Gwalior by escalade. Sindhia, the leader of the Confederacy, soon realised that retreat was essential. While he agreed to negotiations with Goddard, he also attempted to mount one more concerted effort.

It suddenly dawned on the warring Maratha chiefs that their real enemy was not each other but the cold and ruthless Englishman who ruled from Belvedere. In haste, they patched up their differences to corner Goddard. It was decided that Madhaji Sindhia and Tukoji Holkar would attack Goddard's forces, Bhonsle would prepare to invade Bihar and Bengal, the Nizam would grasp the Madras Sircars and Hyder Ali the Carnatic. Alarmed at the prospect of the princes combining forces, Hastings began negotiations separately with each, offering them substantial portions of each other's territories.

Thus divided, the Marathas, Mysore and Nizam split once more, enabling Goddard to march to Poona, the seat of the Peshwas.

Andrew Ruthven's daring at the siege of Gwalior earned him words of appreciation from his commander, and when he threw himself with energy and passion into the siege of Bassein, the commander admonished him to act with greater caution. Dust-smeared, bloodstained and exultant, twenty-year-old Andrew Ruthven gloried in his battle scars and worshipped the general who broke through the concerted cordon around the British army.

The Maratha hosts swept down the arid hills, materialising out of scarred forts and scrublands and charging towards the motionless men who waited, matchlocks and bayonets raised, under a fluttering Union Jack. "Har Har Mahadev!" they cried above the thunder of their matchless steeds, invoking the name of the lord of destruction. The mercenary troops of Goddard waited, breathless until the signal was given, and then they plunged into the Maratha ranks, mowing down with bayonets and carbines whatever lay in their path. Andrew ploughed through the Maratha infantry, his sword raised, shouting to his men in Hindusthani to follow. Heedless of danger, he broke through the enemy formations and scattered their ranks, leaving the artillery to complete the destruction.

Warring armies had regularly traversed these fields, leaving bent and bowed heads of grain in the wake of their horses' hooves. Peasants watched the armies in despair. Accustomed as they were to such depredation, each battle weakened their bodies and strengthened their belief in the futility of an existence that gave them little joy. Now they stood on the fringe of these vast despoiled fields, staring at the hordes who swept through in a mood of destruction. It mattered little to them whether the men were white or brown. They were all harbingers of doom.

In Calcutta, Hastings was tense with anticipation. He had resolved on this course of action as a means of strengthening British presence. He realised that unless Madhaji Sindhia and his confederacy was controlled, the prospects of British expansion mere dim. As news came of triumphs, Hastings selected Alexander Ruthven, the taciturn, neutral adventurer to represent his progress to the board of directors at London.

He arrived at this decision despite Alexander Ruthven's indirect connection with Hastings' antagonist, Philip Francis. It was no secret to the Governor General that the French mistresses of both these British 'nabobs' were friends. However, since it was his wish to separate the two men, he decided to do it by displaying unequivocal trust in the Scottish adventurer.

Ruthven met the Governor General at his residence, Belvedere, a house built in the simple yet stately proportions of the neo-classical style. Ruthven mused with pleasure that his house, Bellevista, set amidst a wide expanse of green lawns, a grove of banian trees, and coconut palms, was more impressive. The interior, however, did not equal Belvedere in elegance and style. Obviously, Ruthven reflected, Marianne Hastings had the taste of a lady, even though she possessed the morals of a roguish broker. And the man who had set the course for such a grand enterprise as the expansion of British rule, looked more like a solicitor's clerk than a Governor General. His dark, opaque eyes expressed nothing more than polite interest and his stern mouth widened in the briefest of smiles. Anyone looking at the two men might have wondered why the imperious Ruthven, in his blue satin coat fastened by sapphire buttons, his hand sparkling with priceless gems, bowed deferentially to the insignificant looking man in the grey broadcloth coat and breeches.

"Mr. Ruthven," Hastings said quietly, indicating a tapestried Hepplewhite chair, "we are pleased to hear of your son's daring deeds."

Ruthven coloured and bowed from his seat. Nothing could have pleased him more than to hear of Andrew's gallantry.

"A mere boy, I think," the Governor General said, "but so clever and intrepid. Colonel Goddard has recommended a decoration for him. This will be one of my recommendations to the board of directors."

Moved and surprised, Alexander Ruthven rose from the chair. "I am indeed very grateful, Your Excellency," he said with a humility he had never showed to the Governor General.

Warren Hastings nodded his head. "I understand your sentiments, Mr. Ruthven. It is good to have a brave son." He paused and added, "I lost mine many years ago." Then he too stood up and paced the room, his small feet tapping out a firm, measured rhythm. "There is trouble for Britain in the New World. General Borgoyne has surrendered at Saratoga to the American colonists. It is imperative to protect our Indian possessions. France has aided the American colonists; they are waiting to aid the Indians against us. French agents are everywhere. We must have a free hand here. I want you to impress upon the board of directors the necessity to continue the war against the Indian princes. We need money and men. We cannot give the Company the stipulated £400,000 without weakening ourselves here. Then we may lose what we have. Will you convey this to the directors, Mr. Ruthven?"

Alexander Ruthven was taken aback. "Would the directors be inclined to take congnisance of my opinions, Your Excellency?"

"They will, when they know of your status as a successful commander of a Rajput army and the jagirdar of Deogarh," Hastings replied with a smile. "They will realise."

There was no more to say. The Governor General asked Ruthven to meet him again after a week by which time the necessary letters and reports would be ready. In a fortnight an Indiaman was to sail for England.

Begum Shirin Ruthven arrived within a few days. With unerring prescience, she had guessed that her husband was to cross the seas, and wished to berate him for allowing her darling Andraz to go into battle. She stormed through Ruthven House like a galleon in full sail, threatening and accusing her silent spouse.

"My Andraz is to be a nawab, not a ragged Company soldier!" she cried.

"He will be both, Shirin. In battle he will learn to be a man, and a leader of men. He will then be a better nawab." The Scottish adventurer paused. "Did your great ancestor, Emperor Babar, stay in Ferghana or did he come to Hindusthan to found an empire? And did I, a rebel crofter's son, fritter my youth away in Paris or come to find my luck in India?"

Begum Shirin's ample bosom heaved with indignation. She hated being outwitted by her low voiced, imperious Janab. "But Andraz has everything! Why should he risk his life? And that too, before he could marry the Nawab of Oudh's niece? Is not that the way in which to start a new dynasty? Should he go into battle without leaving a child behind?"

"I did not have a child when I fought at Plassey," Ruthven replied.

"You, Janab," Shirin said scornfully, "were not the prince of Deogarh!"

The Scottish condottiero's eyes were like ice. "I am the ruler of Deogarh, Begum," he said in a low voice. "I won it by conquest. You are merely my representative — and execute my orders. As does Andraz." Ruthven was satisfied to see the pallor of his consort's face. The harsh, aquiline features had thickened with age and an inordinate partiality for halwa or Turkish delight, but the opaque eyes remained as haughty as ever. "Andrew says he wishes to be a true European. Perhaps he would rather marry a European than a niece of Oudh."

"My Andraz will never become a firingi! Rest assured, Janab, the blood of Tamerlane and Akbar will not blend with that of firingi traders."

Husband and wife faced each other in wordless antagonism. Then suddenly, Shirin sat down with a moan. The pallor of her face increased. Alarmed, Ruthven came to her. "What is it, Shirin?" he asked, "are you in pain?"

Shirin shook her head. "It will pass," she whispered hoarsely.

Ruthven sat beside her and held her icy hands in his. "How long have you been in pain?"

"For some time ... after going to Deogarh. The harsh air ..." she murmured, massaging her breasts, "I become breathless at times."

"Shirin," Ruthven said gently, "I want you to be in Calcutta with our daughters while I am away. The Marathas are waging a bitter battle with the Company forces in that area. It is not safe for our girls. When the war ends, Andrew will take charge. Until then, my agent, one Major Sullivan, will act on my behalf."

Shirin nodded, gazing at her husband of twenty-two years. "Return soon, Janab," she whispered. "I am afraid this time."

Ruthven frowned. "Afraid? But why, Begum? Of what are you afraid?"

"I do not know, Sikander," she murmured. "It is just a strange ... foreboding." She clutched his hands. "Come back soon. Do not tarry in Vilayat."

"Shirin," he said gently, "you are the mother of a warrior — one who will bring us pride and glory. I go to England to bring more honours for him on the recommendation of the Burra Lat Saheb. He will be a fine nawab and our girls will marry well."

"Do you remember that stormy night when we married?" she asked.

Ruthven nodded. She went on. "Let me not lose you, Sikander."

"I am yours, Shirin," he said softly, kissing her attar-scented lips, "always yours."

It was more difficult to persuade Liselotte to stay behind. "Stay behind?" she cried. "But it was my idea to go to Europe. I planned and hoped for years that we would go to France and England together. For seven years I have waited — in arid Rajput forts or in this lonely villa."

"This time it is difficult," Ruthven said, trying to draw her close, "I cannot take you this time."

"It is always difficult!" Liselotte cried, freeing herself roughly from his embrace. "You are always holding out promise of a next time! But this time I will not wait. I will go back to Lucknow. General Martin's home is still open to me!"

"I could not bear that, ma petite," he said, taking her in his arms. "You are my refuge from storms. No one can soothe me or divert me better than you can. You cannot leave me, ma chere. Besides, how can you travel with little Lucille or frail Alexina? Let them grow up, Liselotte, and we will make a Grand Tour of Europe one day — you and I — Claude and Andrew, and my six daughters."

Liselotte chuckled. "And the Begum? Will she not deign to come?"

Ruthven looked sombre. "Ma chere, look after my Begum. I fear she has not long to live."

Liselotte's smile vanished. She too had observed the signs of a malaise. "I will, my love," she said gently, and paused. "The Begum is still dear to you, isn't she?" Ruthven nodded. "She changed my life, ma petite, and gave my vague ambitions a direction. I cannot forget my debt to her."

Liselotte nodded, resigned to her own nebulous status.

"You are dear too, Liselotte. With you, I find peace ... and my broken links with Europe ... and home." He paused. "Live in harmony with the Begum and my daughters. I leave them all in your care until I return."

Liselotte smiled sadly. "Have I ever crossed your will, mon amie?" she asked.

Two weeks later, Alexander Ruthven boarded an Indiaman at Sagar Dwip to travel over the waters to England.

13

Revenge

London was becoming the greatest city in the world, governed by her own magistrates, guarded by her militia and enriched by her merchants. Even the seats of power at Westminster and St. James respected the independence of Londoners. But it was a city of contrasts, a city in which dockers and unskilled labour of a port-metropolis lived under appalling conditions of filth and squalor; as also a city that was home to the burgeoning class of skilled craftsmen and merchants whose activities enriched England, and who beautified London with their homes. It was also the centre of intellectual life where leading thinkers, writers and lawyers met to forge the new Age of Enquiry and Enlightenment. Beyond them lived a vigorous aristocracy, with its vigilant eye on both power and wealth, patrons of art and letters, who built spectacular houses in Piccadilly, Bloomsbury, St. James's Square, Covent Garden and Westminster. The monarchy had become, after the boisterous Tudors and fascinating Stuarts, a dull Germanic establishment, whose inability to speak English stimulated parliamentary democracy, leaving government in the hands of a balanced aristocracy and bourgeoisie.

The majestic Thames, still flowed on, as commanded by Spenser, and was the most vital of the city's highways. Boats and barges carrying merchandise plied the murky waters alongside pleasure boats transporting the nobility and traffic boats which ferried passengers to the numerous landing places along the North and South Banks. Ferries took coaches and horses across the river, to Lambeth or to Parliament. The two picturesque bridges of London and Westminster spanned the river, though occasionally hindering high-masted riverine traffic.

Sailing up the Thames, Alexander Ruthven felt as awed by the great metropolis now as he had been twenty-five years ago when he first came to the city to enlist as a cadet in the East India Company. Now he came not as a supplicant, a fugitive or rebel's son but as an immensely wealthy 'Nabob' and jagirdar with the newly-won status of emissary of the Governor General. He intended to make his presence felt both in Leadenhall Street and London society.

This purpose was facilitated by the cordiality of one of the directors, Thomas Bennet, who wished to learn more about the Company's affairs and make political capital out of his revelations. Secretly, Mr. Bennet envied Warren Hastings his power and success but the exigencies of Company interests and British sentiments necessitated the extension of support to him.

Mr. Bennet moved in the circle of prosperous men who, having made their fortunes in overseas trade, were aspirants to participation in political life. After the decline of Dutch power in the 1700s, London had become the centre of European finance where capital flowed in more freely than anywhere else in the world. The joint stock company had suffered a setback after the South Sea Bubble in 1720, but since it was suited to a patrician commercial environment, the landed gentry could meet a banker and broker and combine to influence politics; the growth of provincial banks providing a further impetus to agriculture and industry. The Jews had moved from Amsterdam to London, bringing with them the international commercial network through the houses of Giddeon, Goldschmidt and Rothschild.

While this circle did not consist of the aristocracy, it was to them that the nobility came either for assistance in their activities or redeeming them from financial distress.

Thomas Bennet soon realised that 'Nabob' Ruthven would be an invaluable asset to him. He had the means to purchase a parliamentary seat, and to be a partner in Bennet's proposed venture of establishing cotton mills in Lancashire. With fine cotton staples coming from Dacca, and silk from Murshidabad, Bennet hoped to compete with entrepreneurs dealing in more expensive cotton from the former American colonies. Hargreave's 'Spinning Jenny', and Artwright's and Crompton's inventions in previous decades had shifted the hitherto cottage industry to the 'satanic' mills.

However, Bennet observed that Alexander Ruthven was awed by the glitter of London. He invited him to his spacious suburban house at Chelsea, which, like Hampstead and Walthamstow, was a favourite retreat of the merchants. There, Bennet introduced Ruthven to other city merchants, aspiring politicians and a few aristocrats, like Lord Rockingham, the patron of Edmund Burke.

In that house of simple and noble proportions with its tall windows and doors, and gilt-engraved ceilings, Ruthven saw elegant Chippendale chairs and cabinets, jasper ware and porcelain from Staffordshire made famous by Wedgewood, as well as acquisitions from Derby and Worcester, Meissen and Sevres. Mrs. Bennet explained how the newly discovered ruins of Pompeii had provided a new inspiration in porcelain and furniture design. Ruthven gazed at everything, bemused.

The Bennets introduced their friend to others of their own class in whose homes Ruthven saw private art galleries boasting paintings by Gainsborough, Crome, Reynolds, Girtin and Turner. Books well bound and tooled in leather, covered vast walls, painted a fashionable pale green.

At Lord Rockingham's country house Ruthven met the fiery parliamentary orator, Edmund Burke, who, despite his meditative air, was quick to extract information about Warren Hastings, as the house party trampled through wet grounds and woods of beech and oak in search of partridge, snipe, ducks, bitterns and ruffs. Returning at dusk, Ruthven was struck by the location of the house, set high on a hill to command a "prospect". The formal Dutch gardens of King William's reign had been swept away to make way for parks, grassy slopes and high trees. Under the influence of Capability Brown, artificial ruins, which in imitation of Pompeii, ornamented the gardens, halls and vestibules of these patrician dwellings. On other days there were long rides across the open country, on horses of Arab and Berber blood introduced by the horse breeder, Godolphin.

After game-shooting and fox-hunting, the guests assembled in the Palladian style drawing room to hear the ladies sing or play on the harpsichord, before adjourning to partake of a Lucullan dinner that comprised of soup, slices of sauted cod, shin of mutton, pigeons with asparagus, fillet of veal with mushrooms and high sauce, roasted sweetbreads, hot lobster, apricot tart and in the middle, a pyramid of syllabubs and jellies. A dessert of fruit followed, accompanied by Madeira, white port, claret and champagne.

Late at night, discussions continued on politics, literature, history and Classics. Ruthven felt himself at sea among these men who spoke with ease and familiarity of great philosophers like Rousseau and Locke, poets of antiquity as well as Pope and Goldsmith, of Parliament and the colonies. Eager to participate, he was soon drawn by Burke into revelations regarding the activities of the East India Company officials and the Governor General. Ruthven answered Burke's searching questions regarding the execution of Nanda Kumar, the explosive Rohilla War, the pensions of the Begums of Oudh and the annexation of the holy city of Benaras. Burke spoke softly, reasonably, drawing out the awed nabob. The great orator soon realised that Ruthven was a source of valuable information. From the grand house of Lord Rockingham, Burke adjourned to the more heady ambience of Ashville, the estate of the Earl, Roger de Courtney where he hoped that, warmed by the attention of the Quality, the rustic Ruthven would forget to be discreet about Warren Hastings.

Here, Alexander Ruthven saw traces of an England that lived in legends; the ancient Plantagenet castle turned into a manor house of the fifteenth century, with Tudor wings, mullioned windows and Stuart facades. Formal Dutch gardens graced the front while Tudor herb gardens were walled in by mellow, old bricks. Behind the castle stretched the woods of Ashville where the Courtneys of Plantagenet times had fought duels or hidden in the times of trouble that beset England periodically. Here, Ruthven met the jovial Lord Roger Courtney, his robust wife, the Lady Arabella, and their five children who filled the house with laughter, music and vivacious conversation.

It was the Courtneys' earthly exuberance which caught Ruthven's attention. They were Whig landowners, who had governed England for most of the century, dominating the House of Commons and producing more ambassadors, ministers and secretaries than any other class. The Courtney sons he was aware, had gone on a Grand Tour after learning Classics at Eton and Oxford. The daughters had learned French, manners and deportment. They had learned to "admire the grand style in painting, the correct in letters and Latin oratory." Polished and precise, they shunned the vagaries of philosophy, the austerity of religion and the pomp of the Hanoverian royal court.

Among the younger Courtneys, he observed two other people who bore a close physical resemblance to them but who were, in some subtle way, different. They attracted him in some strange way.

The youth had full, almost fleshy lips, a Roman nose, and sea-green eyes. He played faro and loo late into the night. The young lady danced gracefully, sang and played on the pianoforte with a polished precision that was symbolic of the very ambience of Ashville. She had, Alexander Ruthven observed, a distinct partiality for the Earl of Ashville's heir, Viscount Robert de Courtney. He watched them with a fascinated eye, as the young lady danced the cotillion with Robert and wondered how long the young man would resist the charm of that fresh, cream and rose complexion, the golden tresses around the shoulders, the straight nose and curved, if heavy, lips. Her figure was Junoesque, its sensuality enhanced by a lacy and low decolletage that revealed the swell of alabaster bosom. The sea-coloured eyes were bright and inviting. Ruthven could hardly take his gaze off her.

Lady Arabella observed the fascination in Ruthven's countenance and smiled kindly. "Lovely, is she not? We hope Robert will choose her ... Georgiana is after all, half a Courtney." She paused and added, "Her mother, Lady Orinthia Courtney, was Walter Manham's second wife."

Alexander Ruthven stared at Lady Arabella. "Manham?" he repeated in a choked voice.

Lady Arabella nodded. "Do you know Sir Walter Manham? Made a reputation in the Rebellion of Forty-Five. Was, I believe, the Duke of Cumberland's trusted lieutenant." She stopped, astonished by the expression on Ruthven's face. Touching him gently on the arm, she said, "Are you quite all right, Mr. Ruthven? Would you like to sit down?"

A deathly pallor spread over the nabob's bronzed face. He felt as if the musician's gallery above was swaying towards the hall where people were dancing, and as if the massive chandelier was circling crazily. He swayed and caught at a nearby chair with white knuckled hands.

"Mr. Ruthven, do please sit down ... let me get you a glass of wine ... ah Robert," she said in some agitation, "pray get a glass of wine for Mr. Ruthven ..."

Through a haze, Ruthven saw Robert de Courtney turn towards the dining hall while Georgiana Manham came towards him, puzzled.

"Are you unwell, Sir?" she asked in her rich, throaty voice.

Ruthven shook his head, staring wildly at her carnal radiance. "Manham," he whispered, "daughter of Manham."

Georgiana glanced at her aunt, frowning, and then seeing Robert, she said, "Ah, Robin, do come and let Mr. Ruthven get a breath of air."

Alexander Ruthven took the proferred glass of wine and then rose to his feet. "I ... am ... quite recovered, my lady," he said to Lady Arabella. "I had better stand on the terrace for a while."

From the terrace, Ruthven watched the Courtneys in the brightly lit hall, his eyes following Georgiana as she circled, pranced and bowed with her partner. "Is this why I was drawn to her?" he asked himself. "Did I feel a strange link with her ... because of ... the blood that lay between us? Or is it because I see in her ... the fairy princess of my boyhood dreams when I stood outside the windows of great houses, stunned and shivering — as I do today?" He closed his eyes to quell the wave of bitter fury that lay deep in him but it rose, slowly and inexorably, obliterating everything else except the memory of a hawk-nosed, fleshy-lipped, blond man shooting his father, molesting his mother and raping his sister Deirdre before his own innocent eyes. He could hear once more the screams of the womenfolk as the victorious Redcoats under Major Walter Manham let hell loose on the tranquil Scottish highlands.

"Are you recovered, Mr. Ruthven?" Thomas Bennet asked, closing the terrace doors behind him. "Perhaps the chill of the English countryside is unwelcome after the heat of Bengal."

"That must be so," Ruthven said, hastily composing himself.

"Come to the smoking parlour, then. We can talk quietly there."

"Before that, Mr. Bennet, I would be obliged if you could tell me about the ... Manhams."

Thomas Bennet smiled sympathetically. "Certainly, if it pleases you ... but ... Miss Georgiana is almost betrothed to the earl's son and heir, Robert de Courtney."

"I know," Ruthven said grimly. "I am not ... interested in the young lady ... but in her ... father."

Thomas Bennet frowned but nodded. "Walter Manham became the Duke of Cumberland's trusted aide after Culloden and rose high in the army." He paused. "Walter Manham's father was a Hanoverian clerk in the German entourage of George I. The family name originally was Manheim — changed to Manham. Enriched by royal patronage after Culloden, Walter Manham settled down to a life of ease and enjoyment. When his first wife died, he married Lady Orinthia de Courtney, daughter of the old Earl of Ashville and sister of the present one. But she too died, leaving Frederick and Georgiana, and Manham married again, though he had several mistresses as well."

"Is ... Frederick ... the fair haired youth who is ... often seen at the faro table?"

Bennet grinned. "That is Frederick ... and he lives in a grander style than his sire. At twenty-four, he has run through four mistresses, fought half a dozen duels in Leicester Fields behind Montaigne House and has run up a debt of £20,000, but he keeps on gambling in the hope of retrieving a fortune."

"A gambler," Ruthven murmured, almost to himself, and as he smiled slowly, the fury in his heart gave birth to a plan. "Let us go in, Mr. Bennet. I crave to dance with the Quality."

Georgiana Manham was polite but detached as she executed the measured steps of a quadrille with the "nabob", making appropriate observations about the state of the weather, partridge-shooting and music. Ruthven wondered if it was the fragrance of lavender in her dress or the proximity to her glowing flesh that disquieted him so much. "Or is it becuase she is Manham's daughter?" he wondered.

The dancing over, Georgiana returned to talk with her cousin, Robin, as she tenderly called the Viscount. And Ruthven went to join Frederick Manham at the faro table.

'Freddy' Manham looked a proper London bean in a coat of dull gold brocade, with stiffly whaleboned full skirts. Large cuffs turned back to the elbow, revealing a quantity of Mechlin lace frothing at the wrists. Freddy wore a patch in the corner of his full mouth and another on the cheekbone. Yet there was a calculating gleam in his eyes as he surveyed the "nabob" in his opulent but outlandish clothes. Indeed, his restless glance took in the diamond buckle in the velvet riband that tied back the nabob's dark red, unpowdered hair and the immense diamond ring on his left hand. He noticed that the buttons of his green brocade coat were large emeralds while more uncut stones studded the buckles of his shoes. Freddy Manham suppressed a desire to laugh. "Rich Ruthven may be," he whispered to cousin Robert de Courtney, but he is a bizarre and vulgar man!"

Alexander Ruthven intercepted both the glance and the words, and retorted in a tone of offended bumpkin dignity. "I may be from Calcutta and you, Sir, from London, but I assure you I am an ill pigeon for plucking."

Manham chuckled softly. "The bumpkin is afraid, after all! What a pigeon to pluck!" he muttered once more to Robert as he got up to pour himself a glass of Madeira.

"Indeed he is, but do be careful, Freddy. These nabobs are no fools, even if they dress gaudily. Further, it might be worthwhile cultivating his acquaintance. Papa would like to send my younger brother as an officer in the East India Company."

Freddy returned to the faro table where Alexander Ruthven brooded over the cards. "Rest assured, Sir," he said, suddenly sober, "I am no hawk."

"Just as well. Will you cut?" Ruthven asked, in obvious relief.

The game was played. Alexander Ruthven lost badly. Manham goaded him to play once more. "Retrieve the thousand pounds, Sir," he said silkily to a sullen Ruthven who lost once more. Manham was jubilant. From faro they went to piquet. Ruthven lost some three thousand pounds to the gleeful beau. Word soon went round Courtney Hall that the "nabob" from Calcutta was a lamb for fleecing. Ruthven played on, despite the admonition of both Mr. Burke and Mr. Bennet, and finally, lost to both Robert de Courtney and Georgiana.

At that point, Thomas Bennet insisted on returning to London with his protege. Edmund Burke shook his head. "On this man, I had placed hopes of gleaning information about the infamous Hastings."

"You may yet do that," Bennet assured him. "We will entertain him in London."

Thus it was that Alexander Ruthven visited the famous coffee houses of London: White's Chocolate House in St. James's, Street where the beau monde gathered and where young lords were ruined by gamblers and profligates, Cocoa Tree House for the Tories, St. James's Coffee House for the Whigs, Wills, near Covent Garden, for poets and litterateurs, and Trubys for scholars and clergymen. Here Ruthven heard lofty ideas discussed and books analysed. He got news of commerce, finance and shipping, and he went through it restlessly, waiting.

Frederick Manham followed him to London and invited Ruthven to White's Chocolate House, where he had often been fleeced by skilled gamblers. Georgiana accompanied her brother, looking lovely in a dress of hooped lavender satin with a pink bodice, which enhanced the vernal radiance of her body and face.

Ruthven smiled, almost to himself, admiring the young profligate's cunning. Immersed in the contemplation of Miss Manham's fresh beauty, her refined manners and patrician poise, he lost a considerable sum of money to Freddy. Georgiana seemed embarrassed by her role in the game. As if to compensate for the transgression, she asked Ruthven to the Manham's mansion at Cavendish Square for dinner.

Alexander sat awake that night, gazing at the Thames following past Chelsea embankment, thinking of the Ganges, of his two women awaiting him and of his numerous devoted children, both Moghul and French. "How would it be," he wondered, "to mingle one's blood with the aristocracy descended from the Plantagenet-Norman barons who shaped English history? Would that not be the final victory?" He thought of Georgiana's beauty and accomplishment, remembering the sheen of her golden tresses and the laughter in her sea-green eyes.

It was with a specific purpose that he went to the Manhams' house the next evening. He was determined to ruin Frederick in a game of cards.

Ruthven shuddered imperceptibly as he entered the mansion. "This," he reflected grimly, "is where my sister Deirdre was brought, dishonoured, betrayed and discarded by Walter Manham thirty-six years ago." Deirdre had been a child of fourteen and had borne Manham a child. Now Deirdre was a tubercular lunatic of fifty in an Inverness convent. An old fury and grief exploded within Ruthven, and once more, the Adam staircase and chandeliers swayed crazily before him. Frederick's face blurred and became the face of Walter Manham as he destroyed the Ruthven family in an hour.

He began playing in earnest now, using every card trick he had learnt from the desperate Griffins, Factors and Writers of the East India Company. Ruthven carried his own cards and was so well trained in sleight of hand that Frederick did not even guess. Yet he played on, with all the optimistic obduracy of a born gambler.

At midnight, Georgiana began to get alarmed. She implored them to cease, but they played on, like two men possessed. One had to retrieve the vast sum lost. The other thirsted for revenge. At dawn, they finished. Frederick had now a debt of fifty thousand pounds to be given to Ruthven. He made the mistake of calling Ruthven a cardsharper and cheat whereupon a duel was called at Leicester Fields. For the survivor of Plassey, Buxar and Maratha wars, the dandy Manham was a jest. The clatter of steel went on for a while until Ruthven brought the cold tip of the sword to Manham's throat. "Apologise," he muttered hoarsely, "and pay your debt of honour. Otherwise Manham House is mine."

Polite society was agog with the news of Frederick Manham's ruin and disgrace. The older aristocracy were delighted by the upstart family's humiliation but many close to St. James's Court and Westminster were distressed by Ruthven's ultimatum. Particularly King George III who had a special regard for old Manham, his grandfather's favourite and one of the heroes of Culloden. Emissaries were sent to mollify Ruthven, pleas were made to him to relent and show mercy. Even Thomas Bennet and a few directors of the East India Company asked Ruthven to waive the debt. To no avail. Ruthven wanted full repayment of the debt of honour.

After an appropriate wait, however, he sent an emissary to Frederick Manham. The debt would be waived if Georgiana Manham accompanied Alexander Ruthven to India as his mistress and if Manham House was renamed Ruthven's Den.

At first, the Manhams were outraged and stunned. Frederick shouted and stormed through the house, vowing to murder Ruthven. The two younger Manham daughters, Margaret and Henrietta sat immobile in the morning room while Georgiana wept, trembled and acquired a high fever. Then Walter Manham, old and broken, emerged from his room to tell his children the story of Culloden and Deirdre Ruthven.

"He has planned this revenge for years. I still remember him as a boy of ten vowing revenge." Walter Manham paused and stared out of the window. "Deirdre called down a curse on my house the day she was taken from Inverness to London. She assured me my wickedness would not go unpunished. Now, after thirty-six years, nemesis has caught up." He paused and looked bleakly at his favourite child.

"I had dreams for you, Georgiana. I had hoped that you would marry Robert de Courtney, your cousin, and become the Countess of Ashville one day. But Freddy has ruined that chance."

"I?" Frederick Manham shouted. "I have done nothing! You have brought this about. You wicked and lecherous man!"

Walter Manham nodded, his rheumy eyes filled with tears. "True, my son. I am vile. But now, my beloved Georgiana must pay the price ... in return for Deirdre Ruthven's misery."

There was a palpable stillness in the room as the Manhams gazed in horror at one another. "Yes, child," the father said brokenly. "You must go with Ruthven. He has indicated that nothing else will satisfy him."

"Sell everything!" Georgiana screamed. "Pay your old debts and sins!"

"And destroy us all?" Frederick retorted. "Beggar us all?"

"You should be sacrificed, Father, or you Freddy — not I!" Georgiana screamed. "I will not go to the wilderness of India with Nabob Ruthven as his mistress! Never!"

"You will go, Georgiana," Frederick replied. "Otherwise you will leave this house forever."

Old Walter Manham left the room, trembling, and the faces of her brother and sisters told Georgiana that she had no choice. Even then she made one desperate bid for escape; she wrote to her cousin and almost betrothed, Viscount Robert de Courtney.

"Marry me now Robin, and this terrible man cannot harm me further. Frederick and Father will have to deal with him. Save me, darling, from a life in death!"

It was the enlightened Whig lord, Roger de Courtney who replied to his niece, apologising that Robin had gone to the Continent and could not reply to her letter. It would be better if she went with the nabob, because Robert could not risk his future in the House of Lords, burdened with such a scandal. Lord Roger de Courtney bade good-bye to his niece with reluctant sorrow.

Everyone in London seemed to know of Ruthven's revenge. Manham House had been renamed Ruthven's Den, even if only for a fortnight, when Ruthven saw the new brassplate installed. Friends came to see Georgiana who had shut herself up, refusing visitors, as she quivered in pain and fever. The coffee houses were full of ribald jokes and the most hardened gamblers avoided Frederick Manham — the man who had sold his sister to pay his debts. The aristocratic Courtneys closed their doors to their degenerate nephew and innocent nieces. George III terminated Walter Manham's honorary position as Gentleman of the Chamber. The Manham family's disgrace was complete.

Alexander Ruthven and Georgiana Manham set sail in a huge Indiaman from Liverpool. Georgiana watched the shoreline of England receding into the grey skyline. She stood without cloak or shawl, hoping to die of fever. But her young vigorous body withstood these mortifications and as darkness fell and drunken sailors appeared on the deck, she went in dread and horror to Ruthven's cabin.

He was dressed in shirtsleeves and breeches, and sat drinking port and reading despatches from Leadenhall Street to Warren Hastings. He glanced up as she entered, cold and hostile.

"You missed dinner. I have ordered nothing more. Take a sip of port if you wish," he said curtly, "then undress yourself so that I may make you a mistress — or is it a whore — before a sailor does."

It was then that Georgiana realised how deeply he hated her

as the flesh and blood of Walter Manham. But it was in bed when he plunged into her virginal body, without passion and without desire, perhaps even without lust, that she realised how little he cared for her comely body. He invaded her flesh with a brutality that stunned her and made her scream in pain for mercy. Not for a moment did he show a shadow of tenderness or even desire, but when she resisted his violation he pinned her down roughly and possessed her again. Then, as she lay, bruised and bleeding, he left her on the bunk, saying. "You are now free to drown yourself Madam, or go to the sailors' quarters. I have no further use for you."

"Then why did you bring me?" she whispered through cracked lips.

"To settle the score with your father. My sister was violated by him and my father murdered — before my very eyes." Ruthven paused. "I have a wife of noble Moghul lineage and a lovely mistress. You are quite redundant. Indeed, you would shame me before them, you child of a rogue!"

The ship kept good time while it crossed the Channel, and the Bay of Biscay and glided over the summer brilliance of the Mediterranean. Georgiana strolled the upper deck, pausing now and then to gaze at the flying jib, the main skysail, the various topsails and the foresails which determined the direction. Sometimes a grizzled sailor explained to her the structure of the ship, pointing out the wheelbox, rudder and sternpost. She learnt the difference between a sloop, a schooner, a brig when they passed the *Crocodile*.

The sea exhilarated her; she let its sharp salt spray wash over her as if its elemental force would cleanse her of Ruthven's degrading violation. Even when the ship tossed and rolled, Georgiana stayed on deck, to gaze at the endless blue or at night to stare at the stars as if their patterns would reveal the fate that awaited her. Sailors passed by, not daring to insult the "nabob's muslin".

After the first brutal encounter in the cabin, Ruthven did not touch Georgiana again. He allowed her, as if on sufferance, to share his cabin but did not exchange a single word with her. He forced her to accompany him to the captain's table where other traders, and officials of the East India Company sat. It was soon evident that Nabob Ruthven had purchased a mistress from Quality. While the women avoided her, the men eyed her with a frank interest that brought a deep colour to Georgiana's cheeks. Ruthven remained unperturbed.

It was in the Cape of Good Hope that Georgiana could no longer hide from herself the terrible truth. She had conceived on that horrifying night, the child of Ruthven. A fierce pride would not allow her to mention this to him, so she kept the terrifying discovery to herself. Sometimes she contemplated suicide and sometimes a means of aborting the child burgeoning within her. Often when she sat at the captain's table, she considered taking up the carving knife to plunge it into Ruthven's heart. When the *Crocodile* passed the ivory coast of Africa, Ruthven saw at last what was happening to his captive. He smiled in satisfaction. His sister Deirdre had borne a child created from degradation. And Manham's daughter would now do the same. From Mauritius Ruthven sent a letter informing Walter Manham of the fate that had befallen his daughter.

"I must either kill him or myself," Georgiana kept saying as the ship ploughed through the hot Arabian Sea. "I will not endure this degradation!" But some vagrant hope for life and happiness, some desperate yearning to return to England and to Courtney Castle prevented her from throwing herself into the shark-infested sea.

Eight months later, the Indiaman arrived at Sagar Dwip at the mouth of the Ganges, where monsoon storms brought down the sails and lashed the ship's stern. Georgiana had never before witnessed the fury of nature as she did at the landing place. She was carried by sailors from the ship to the small boat which had been sent down from Calcutta to receive the passengers of the *Crocodile*. Rain lashed at the small boat as it tossed and rolled on the turbulent Ganges towards Calcutta.

Couriers had ridden swiftly over the mud and water roads to inform the family of the arrival of Ruthven Saheb ... "and ..." they began, but could not summon enough courage to continue.

Begum Shirin Ruthven had worn the full regalia of Moghul

court dress, an egret feather held by a diamond clip on her head, and the imperial pearls on her vast bosom. "And what?" she asked the khidmatgar, with a thickly beating heart.

The retainer bowed his head, refusing to meet the eyes of the imperious Begum. His silence told her that something, indeed, was wrong. It was Liselotte who turned from the contemplation of the rain-drenched garden to challenge the old retainer. "And what, Abdul? Tell us — so that we may be prepared."

Abdul the Bulbul, as he was called for his singing prowess looked first at the Begum and then at "Madame" as Liselotte had begun to be called. "Our Janab comes with ... a ... Memsaheb."

The welcome party seemed to disintegrate in an instant. The Begum and the Madame stared at one another. How strange, thought Liselotte, that we should have become friends and confidantes in the last twenty months and shared our common loneliness at Alexander's absence, to cherish each other's children and look forward to this day, only to have it shattered. Slowly, she went to the Begum who had sunk onto a sofa and laid a hand on the heaving shoulders. "Ma chere," she murmured, "this is no way for the mistress of the house to behave ... for you are the chatelaine. Nothing can change that!" Shirin glanced up with terrified eyes at her one-time rival. "What God wills," she whispered hoarsely, clutching Liselotte's hands.

The Ruthven girls — Alice, Clarice and Beatrice by the Begum, Lucille and Alexina by Liselotte — stood motionless, watching their mothers in anguish. Finally, twenty two-year-old Andrew Ruthven broke the silence by saying to his ten-year-old half-brother Claude, "Let us go for a ride in the Maidan." The hero of the siege of Gwalior found it difficult to confront his father with a new concubine.

The house was silent and inert all day until the sound of a barouche racing up the driveway was heard. Everyone stiffened and rose like bent grass to meet the master of the house. He entered, elegantly dressed and coiffured but the tidiness of his apparel did not blend with his wild and triumphant appearance. Behind him came the intruder, the Memsaheb. They stared at her heavy body, at the golden locks tied by ribbons and eyes blazing with bitter fury. Their shock changed to amazement when Ruthven came forward to kiss the Begum's hands and lips.

Shirin was the first to recover; she came from a race of woman which had learnt to accept the indignities imposed by their menfolk. "Janab," she murmured, bringing her right hand to her forehead in salutation. "I and your second wife, my sister Liselotte, bid you welcome. Our prayers are answered. You have returned home."

Liselotte stared now at the Begum who had never in ten years accorded her the status of a wife. She smiled at the Begum's ingenuity and took the hands that Ruthven held out to her, with a warm, almost tender smile. He kissed her hands and embraced her swiftly so that tears sprung to her eyes. The girls came one by one to kiss and salute their father.

Georgiana stood as motionless as a statue, and as lifeless, her eyes vacant. When all greetings were done, Ruthven turned at last to glance at his captive. "I purchased this woman in England. Teach her how to conduct herself in our society." He paused and added grimly. "Her father was the man who killed my father and destroyed my sister."

A strange atmosphere enveloped the mansion in Alipur Road. Ruthven's Begum and mistress spoke in whispers, afraid of his whims. They felt they had nothing to fear from the handsome young woman who had shut herself up in the room allotted to her on the second storey. "Her purchase is his revenge," Liselotte repeated to the Begum who shook her head and murmured, "Yet she bears his child." Liselotte shook her head. "But he does not visit her, nor asks for her — even for a moment. Is that the way of love?" The Begum sighed deeply. "I am afraid, Liselotte!" she repeated. "Why, Begum?" Liselotte asked. "Your Janab has been good to us since his return."

Indeed he had. There were trunkloads of dresses for Liselotte, ordered from the best shops on Bond Street and dresses too for his five daughters. Bolts of satin and sarsanet, Mechlin and

Valenciennes lace, were presented to the Begum. Trunks full of clothes of all sizes were displayed; shawls of Merino wool, satin fans, band boxes of wide-brimmed hats with long ribbons made fashionable by the Duchess of Devonshire and Lady Bessborough, high-heeled satin slippers, ermine trimmed velvet cloaks, cameo lockets. Ruthven smiled as the Begum and Liselotte exclaimed in pleasure and his daughters pirouetted around with excitement. His own pleasure deepened when he presented silver stirrups, Moroccan saddles, Toledan swords and English pistols to his two sons.

Andrew Ruthven was as bewildered as the others by his father's inexplicable behaviour. He had not come to greet his father until late at night, and then too, with considerable agitation. When he did it was to encounter a father who loved him as deeply as ever. "Andrew," he said slowly after exchange of greetings, "I know your mother wants you to be the ruler of a principality but I ... want something else for you."

"What, Father?"

Ruthven thought of the majesty of the houses of Parliament and of the great houses in London and the countryside. "I want you to sit in the House of Commons, and ... marry an English noblewoman."

Andrew's face was illumined by joy. "But that is what I dream of, Father! That is why I wanted to join the Company army. Even now I wish to return there ..." He paused. "I am British, Father. But will your people accept me as one?"

Alexander Ruthven gazed at his son; at the dark blue eyes, the chestnut hair and ivory complexion, the tall, lean body full of suppressed energy. "You would grace any nobleman's house," he said.

Andrew grasped Alexander's hand tightly. "Father, I am fortunate indeed to be your son."

Some strange sensation stirred within Ruthven. "May you always feel that way, Andrew."

"But of course, I shall!" He paused, colouring slightly and looking away. "What pleasure you take with ... ladies ... is not my concern ... I only wish that my mother ... is not dishonoured."

"I have not dishonoured her, have I?" Alexander's voice became cool.

"No. You have treated her with greater dignity than would have been accorded by a nobleman of her race," Andrew replied gravely.

"Ah, Andrew," Alexander murmured, embracing him, "we must always be united thus."

"We shall be, Father. We shall be."

"Insh'allah," murmured the Scottish nabob.

Georgiana listened to the sounds of Ruthven House with a sense of unreality. There was the cold, imperious voice of the Begum, the light melodious one of Liselotte, the high pitched and soft, clear ones of the daughters. She recognised Ruthven's deep voice but was puzzled by another, similar to his and yet different — gentler, smoother and more sensuous. She sat by the window, staring at the lush garden below, or stared at her canopied bed, the damask-covered sofas and chairs, the cupboard full of her clothes and at the women who waited on her. She raged at the fate which had brought her to this alien, sultry land and cursed the father and brother who had ruined her.

She waited for her gaoler to come and enquire after her but he remained aloof. She would have preferred the brutality of their only carnal encounter to this terrible indifference. "I will die here," Georgiana thought dully. "I will die in childbirth amongst these hostile, alien beings. And that will be my deliverance."

Alexander Ruthven had not forgotten his captive in the corner room on the second floor. She haunted his thoughts daily, but he chose to ignore her and the sensations she had roused in him. To do so he flung himself into his work and his new interest in politics.

The Governor General waited to meet his emissary to England. The high point of the crisis of attrition was over. By a twist of fate, Hastings' opponents in the Council — Monson and Clavering — had died. Furious with these developments and thwarted by the indifference of the new Councillor, Sir Eyre Coote, Philip Francis provoked the Governor General to a duel on the grounds of Belvedere. Hastings was an intrepid marksman. He 'clipped the wings' of his foe, maiming Francis' left arm for life. Francis left India, resigned to his defeat at the hands of a foe.

Alexander Ruthven met him now in Belvedere, the powerhouse of British India. They sat in the spacious lawn, under a spreading shirish tree, that allowed flickers of sunlight to penetrate its gossamer leaves. The monsoons had left the land moist and lush; the sky a canopy of blue, flecked by retreating white clouds.

Warren Hastings listened as Ruthven described the atmosphere of London and the attitude of Parliament to both the East India Company and the Governor General. "There is growing resentment against your power and the man who leads it is Edmund Burke."

Hastings had anticipated this. "My two antagonists," he said bitterly, "are the Parliament, which understands nothing, and the Supreme Court here, which is arbitrary. Between them, they force me to tax the Indians in our territory and impose a system of jurisprudence entirely alien to them. Far from safeguarding justice, the Supreme Court has perpetrated action which has ruined zamindars and the ordinary folk — whom I have had to bail out. But I shall not allow the Supreme Court to interfere in revenue administration. That is my domain," Hastings said decisively.

"I believe an Act has recently been passed to define the powers of the Supreme Court. It was the subject of much discussion in London. That and the establishment of civil courts in Calcutta."

Hastings nodded. "You see, Mr. Ruthven, India is a turbulent nation. Only great emperors like Ashoka, Harsha and Akbar were able to impose law and order here. We, the British have, by a twist of history, inherited the legacy of the imperial Mauryas, Guptas and Moghuls. We must unify and tame these talented but turbulent people. Law is one road surely — but administration — the implementation of law — is the crucial force."

Alexander Ruthven felt, despite his greater height and physique, dwarfed by this slight, insignificant looking man. Warren Hastings had ideals and visions of India, which he, Ruthven, knew he lacked. His life as a trader, a military adventurer and even as a nabob suddenly seemed hollow before Hastings' understanding of the country in which they lived. The Governor General continued, "The Moghuls had no police service. I have introduced it — with the foujdars. "Even then, the zamindars keep their hired goondas to guard their land. Villagers are kept in terror and relinquish a portion of their produce. It is feudalism at its worst at work. While you were in England, I initiated a new measure. Covenanted civil servants are vested with magisterial powers and may commit cases to the nearest Indian criminal court. Eventually, an administrative cadre will be created to dispense law and justice." He paused, anticipating Ruthven's query. "Yes, Mr. Ruthven, in time, Indians will also form part of this structure, particularly the Brahmins. With their gift for memory and metaphysics, English jurisprudence will pose no barrier for them."

"You are attracted to Hindu culture, I understand," Alexander Ruthven ventured, as he was leaving the Governor General's residence, after handing over the various despatches sent by the directors of the East India Company in London.

"Indeed I am. It is more profound than either Greek or Roman civilisation, and yet it is as alive today as it was two and a half thousand years ago when the great Upanishads and epics were written." He smiled at Ruthven. "Why not attend one of the soirees in my salon next week? You may find considerable stimulation in meeting some scholars and musicians."

Ruthven thanked him and rode home in the barouche that had accompanied him from England, musing over the complexity of the Governor General's character. The man who could vindictively and cold bloodedly execute Nanda Kumar, who could unscrupulously seize the territory of Raja Chait Singh of Benaras and extract double the tribute paid by him — this same man was a lover of India's ancient heritage.

Nor did subsequent events resolve the contradictions within the Governor General. He pursued an aggressive policy not only in

Bengal, Bihar and Oudh but in the Carnatic as well. Here, deftly bypassing the webs of deceit and network of intrigues between the Nawab of Arcot, the Nizam of Hyderabad and the Nawab of Mysore, Hastings steered a single-minded course — the expansion and consolidation of British territories. He did this not only by defending British territories but by carrying the war into the territories of the Indian princes. To implement these bold policies, Hastings appointed Hector Munro, the hero of Buxar and Sir Eyre Coote, a veteran in Indian battles whose armies swept through Mysore, Madras, Mangalore, the Coromandel and Malabar coasts, establishing the prestige and power of the East India Company and British arms.

In the midst of such turmoil, Warren Hastings maintained an open house once a week at Belvedere where his astute and attractive wife presided over the social ceremonies. Marianne of Alipore, as Mrs. Hastings was called, had an insatiable love of beautiful things and to nourish this, she was compelled to accept tributes from those who sought her intercession — contractors, shipbuilders, traders, lawyers, aspiring Residents and hounded zamindars. It seemed perfectly proper to her that they should thank her for advancing their ambitions and aspirations. It pained her that English ladies twittered behind her back, that the spectacular Madame Grand, who was more scandalous than her, should pronounce sanctimonious homilies on her. But safe in the unswerving direction of her brilliant second husband, Mrs. Hastings moved in Calcutta society with the aplomb of a queen.

The Governor General's lady had heard, along with many other people of Calcutta, of Ruthven's "purchase" of Miss Georgiana Manham, daughter of a general and niece of an earl. "No one has seen her as yet," Marianne Hastings told her friends, "but descriptions of her beauty and spirit have percolated outside the walls of Ruthven House."

"Spirit?" a lady asked. "What girl of spirit would consent to be the mistress of a man twice her age, with two wives and seven children?"

Marianne Hastings smiled strangely. "That will be explained

later, my dear." She paused and lowered her voice. "Miss Manham is ... enceinte now ... but we shall meet her in due course."

•

Georgiana gave birth to a daughter on a cool October day. Hearing her cry of agony, Begum Shirin defied her husband to assist the intruder and assuage the pain that ripped through the robust, young body until Georgiana lay white faced and spent on the vast bed, her green eyes feverish as she stared at the Begum, "You should have let me die," Georgiana said, through cracked lips. "Life is quite unbearable for me."

Shirin stared at the young woman, at a loss for words. "That is in the hands of the Almighty," she said. "Let him decide what he has in store for you."

"Emptiness, humiliation, misery," Georgiana murmured, tears spilling on to her ashen cheeks.

Begum Ruthven picked up the new-born infant and gazed for a moment at its red-gold hair and blue-green eyes — the mingled colours of the Ruthvens and Manhams who had destroyed each other and whose scions had met in a brutal carnal encounter at its creation. She carried the infant to Georgiana, who recoiled from her child.

"Take it away! I do not wish to see it — ever!"

"It will die if you do not nurse it!" Shirin cried.

"Let it!" Georgiana screamed. "I want it to die!"

The door opened and the tall figure of Alexander Ruthven stood framed at the entrance. Silence fell upon the apartment as he slowly walked towards the bed where his latest child lay. "A special child," he thought, "born of hatred and revenge." He felt no tenderness on seeing the infant and even less as he beheld the mother. If he felt any emotion, it was one of triumph. The tragedy of Culloden, of his father's murder and Deirdre's ruin, had been avenged at last. Walter Manham had died of a broken heart soon after Georgiana's departure and she herself was ruined forever.

"Well, Miss Manham," Ruthven said coldly, "what will you name your ... bastard?"

Georgiana bit her bloodless lips to choke back a sob. Even the Begum looked away. "Would it be appropriate to call her Deirdre after the woman whose ruin I have avenged?'

Rage glittered in Georgiana's eyes as she nodded and whispered hoarsely, "Yes, that would be appropriate indeed." She paused, then said, "And let this Deirdre bring you even greater sorrow. Is not Deirdre the symbol of grief among your tribe?"

Ruthven stepped back as if stung. Out of the woman's spent face, two green eyes blazed with hatred. Abruptly, he left the room and took refuge in Liselotte's arms. But Liselotte, too, was bewildered. There was something terrifying in her lover's hatred for the girl who had borne him a child of hatred. It puzzled her when he came to her every night, revealing a passion he had never shown before, murmuring incoherently as he caressed and explored her. Gone was the light tenderness, the gay sensuality that had been there between them. She wondered if he did love her at last and asked him so.

"Of course," he said softly. "You are sweet and gentle, ma petite."

"More than your Begum?'

"I care for her too. She is my Andrew's mother."

"And Miss Manham?' Liselotte murmured hesitantly.

Ruthven sat up. "Never mention her to me again. I wish ... she had died on the ship." He held Liselotte close, as if to banish a phantom. Liselotte's hazel eyes searched his haunted ones. "Why does he need us all now, this man who was always so self-sufficient?" she thought to hereself in confusion.

Georgiana recovered sufficiently to leave her room and walk on the veranda adjoining her room. Her corn-coloured hair streamed around her shoulders, catching the clear autumn sunbeams. She paused sometimes to gaze at the cupolas and spires on the skyline of Calcutta, dotted with tall coconut palms, shirish and gulmohur. The garden below lured her with its profusion of dahlias and marigolds. As she looked down one morning, she saw a man who seemed Alexander Ruthven's replica, except that he was younger, slimmer, not so tall, and he had none of his sire's harshness. "It is," she thought, "as if sunlight had spilled onto a highland scene."

Conscious of her presence, Andrew glanced up and met her intent gaze. He felt a tremor pass over him, tinged with nebulous, undefined emotions. Hastily, he turned and fled inside. Georgiana stared after him, blushing, and then she laughed, very softly, compelling her two servants to ask for orders.

"Go to your master and tell him I require a carriage ... or better still, ask the Begum. I want to see the city ... and breathe fresh air."

Begum Shirin was glad to oblige. "It will be less oppressive if the Memsaheb leaves the house." She paused to glance at Liselotte who was teaching Ruthven's daughters the art of water colours. "I cannot bear her pacing the corridor all day."

Liselotte nodded. "I too have heard her, Begum," she said, mixing colours on the palette. "Let her go out ... and see the world."

Ruthven's eldest daughter, Alice, stopped sketching. She had resented Liselotte's entry into their lives ten years ago but now her mother's alliance with the Frenchwoman had reconciled her to Liselotte, who was content to be a concubine, to honour Shirin's children and treat them with warmth. Alice was furious with the new intruder, who was almost her own age. "Arrange for her to be abducted," she said, "or killed."

Liselotte spilt the colours on her muslin dress, her hazel eyes wide with terror. "Never let your father hear this," she said gravely.

Alice tossed her red hair. "Why not? He hates her. He wishes to destroy her."

"Does he?" Liselotte asked, her eyes lifted to the sky. "I wonder."

The Begum pricked her finger on a piece of Lucknawi embroidery and shook her head.

Georgiana began to go out on drives to see the city — the ornate mansions on Chitpur Road, occupied by Indians and Britons and offices of British traders, the warehouses not far from the river.

The Begum's cabriolet and driver took her past the graceful buildings on the Strand, the medley of windows, turrets and facades that comprised Writers' Building, the Secretariat of the East India Company. Beyond lay open parkland and the Royal Calcutta Turf Club. She returned to Ruthven House, in a pensive mood. One day, she went to Belvedere and left a card for Mrs. Marianne Hastings.

Three days later, Georgiana was summoned to the study where Alexander Ruthven paced the parquet floor. He turned as she entered and for a moment was wrapped in a strange silence. Georgiana glowed with health and energy. Her golden hair hung in ringlets and curls, threaded by a riband of green velvet. She wore a dress of apple-green satin with white panniers. Lace frothed at her bosom, suggesting their swell. But her eyes were as cold as dull emeralds. Only her lips twitched in remembrance of her ordeal.

Ruthven was agitated but remained outwardly composed.

"How have you managed to meet Mrs. Hastings?" he asked coldly.

"I have my ways."

"You are quite resourceful — even from a chaise longue," he taunted.

"True, but it was not my wish to lie on the chaise longue. Even now ... " her voice softened in a plea ... "you can let me return to England."

He smiled. "Return to England, Miss Manham? What would you do there — now? Your father is dead, your brother running from the duns, your sisters living on my charity — in my house in Cavendish Square. What could you do?"

His derisive tone brought a swift colour to her cheeks. "I will live the life of a fashionable demi-mondaine. That is what you have left me suitable for. But let me go."

"And your child? Who will care for her? My Begum and Madame have no obligation to look after her as they are doing now."

"Throw her in the Ganges. I hear the Hindus make sacrifice of female infants."

His eyes darkened. "You are as heartless as your father."

Georgiana shook her head. "I take after my mother, Lady Orinthia de Courtney. But that is besides the point. I am repelled by the child ... and by you."

Ruthven's jaws tightened. "The feelings are mutual, Miss Manham. But you will stay here ... until I permit you to return."

Georgiana nodded. "Very well ... but I will not be confined in your house. I must be free to amuse myself."

Ruthven said nothing. It was as if he was trying to remember Georgiana Manham as he had first seen her on a mellow autumn afternoon, two years ago in Ashville when she sang and played on the harpsichord, then got up to pour tea for the guests. Robert de Courtney had come in after a ride and asked her to play again. The poignant tones of Mozart's Divertimento had filled the comfortable afternoon room. "Was it then that I realised how little I knew of the life of the heart?" he mused.

The strange look in his eyes made Georgiana uneasy. Hastily, she dropped a curtsey, almost in mockery, and fled to the safety of her room.

Andrew Ruthven met his father soon after. "I am joining my regiment, Father," he said. "Sir Eyre Coote is advancing towards the Carnatic." He paused. "If we are fortunate, we will subdue Tipu Sultan and the Nizam, as we subdued the Maratha Confederacy."

"And then, Andrew? Will we go to England and pursue our projects?" Alexander asked, embracing his son.

Andrew nodded. "But before that please settle my sisters. Alice is twenty-one, Clarice nineteen. Little Beatrice is also growing up. Once they are married, I shall feel free."

"What of your mother?' Alexander asked, curious.

"Mama is ... frail and sick. Her days are numbered." On an impulse, he clutched Alexander's hand. "Father, be kind to her ... whatever happens."

Alexander Ruthven nodded, solemn faced. He felt as if someone had walked over his grave.

14

The Nabob's Lady

Georgiana Manham had managed an entre to Mrs. Hastings' morning room, not as an honoured evening guest with the luminaries of Calcutta but as an interesting visitor, who could describe London society, the policies of the Whigs and the Tories, the prevailing fashions in letters and painting. It interested Marianne Hastings to find that Miss Manham knew Edmund Burke and Lord Rockingham, and that the critical Whig peer, Lord Roger de Courtney was Georgiana's maternal uncle. Wife of the most powerful man in India, Marianne nevertheless felt awed before this poised and polished woman who hailed from England's aristocracy. Despite her exalted rank, Marianne Hastings recognised her social deficiencies which she felt Georgiana could rectify. The awe turned to a deeper interest when Georgiana told her of the intrigues of Burke and Rockingham and their potential danger to Warren Hastings.

Georgiana was then elevated from the rank of an occasional visitor to that of an honoured guest. She was invited to quiet dinners with Marianne and Warren Hastings at Belvedere. There, while cicadas and crickets kept up a steady drone outside, massive silk punkahs stirred the hot air, and candles sputtered in the river-scented breeze, the Governor General listened to Georgiana's assessment of political reaction in England to events in India. Convinced of her value as a source of information, the Governor General extended courtesies to the disgraced young woman. Marianne found another interest in supporting Miss Manham; it was a way of putting Mademoiselle Liselotte Fremont in her place as penalty for fraternising with Madame Grand, mistress of Hastings' enemy.

Realising that the Hastings' valued her acquaintance, Georgiana seized the opportunity to obtain Marianne's reluctant assistance to find separate lodgings for herself. As protegee of the Governor General's wife, Georgiana knew Ruthven would not force her to remain under his roof.

In the months that followed, Georgiana Manham acquired an identity of her own. She was to be seen at soirees at Belvedere, at the Hastings' villa in Garden Reach and hunting parties in the Governor General's lodge in Barasat on the fringe of the swamps of the Sunderbans, where deep tangled forests seemed to float on the marshy backwaters of the Bay of Bengal.

The evening soirees were particularly enlightening for Georgiana. This was the time when Belvedere was transformed; the time when the despatch boxes and legal documents were laid away and the candelabras and lamps brought in to the wide, spacious drawing room. British scholars sat with Indian pundits, discussing and analysing, arguing and reciting.

It was at one of the soirees that Georgiana met the brilliant cluster of scholars that the Governor General had gathered around him. Under the erudite Governor General, Halhed was studying Hindu law on a Persian treatise, translated from the original Sanskrit by ten pundits. William Wilkins was immersed in the study of Sanskrit; he had read the two epics of India — the Ramayana and the Mahabharata, and was then engaged in translating the Bhagavad Gita, the central spiritual message of the Mahabharata. Sir William Jones was a famous jurist who had joined the Supreme Court in Calcutta, but he too had become fascinated by India's ancient civilisation and its immense heritage of astronomy, mathematics, literature and philosophy.

Hastings moved from one group to another, talking or listening, contributing a thought here, an idea there. They would all assemble in the dining room late into the night, still deep in discussion until Mrs. Hastings brought them back to their environment from the lofty, remote world of the epics or Classics.

Georgiana listened, bewildered, because she had not known that India had an ancient and rich civilisation or that Sanskrit was a great language, older, Hastings said, than Greek or Latin.

"It is more stately than Greek and more precise than Latin, more melodious than Italian, more polished than English," Sir William Jones told her once.

"Perhaps that is because it has always reflected a complex, sophisticated civilisation," Wilkins remarked. "The Greek produced the Iliad and the Odyssey which are superb works of drama and literature but where is the timeless message of the Ramayana and the Mahabharata? They have no Bhagavad Gita to guide man to his ultimate destiny."

"Nor a code of laws as enshrined in the Manu Samhita. Roman jurisprudence came two thousand years after Manu, the lawgiver of Vedic India," Halhed offered.

"The Vedas are unsurpassable," Hastings observed and turned to William Wilkins. "Mr. Wilkins, do recite, I pray you, for the benefit of our new friends, a few lines from the Rig Veda." He turned to Georgiana. "The Vedas are the oldest literary and religious works in Sanskrit, composed by the Aryan tribes who came to India some four thousand years ago. There are four Vedas of which the Rig Veda is the most poetic, both in its description of the physical universe and its quest for the unknown."

The heavy silk punkahs moved back and forth over their heads as night deepened. The bustling city fell asleep, but Belvedere remained illumined. Wilkins recited in a sonorous voice, the famous Hymn to Creation.

Nor Aught nor Nought existed; yon bright sky
Was not, nor heaven's broad roof outstretched above.
What covered all? what sheltered? what concealed?
Was it the water's fathomless abyss?

There was not death — yet was there nought immortal,
There was no confine betwixt day and night;
The only One breathed breathless by itself,
Other than It there nothing since has been.
Darkness there was, and all at first was veiled
In gloom profound — an ocean without light —
The germ that still lay covered in the husk
Burst forth, one nature, from the fervent heat.
Then first came love upon it, the new spring
Of mind — yea, poets in their hearts discerned,
Pondering, this bond between created things
And uncreated. Comes this spark from earth
Piercing and all-pervading, or from heaven?
Then seeds were sown, and mighty powers arose—
Nature below, and power and will above —
Who knows the secret? who proclaimed it here,
Whence, whence this manifold creation sprang?
The Gods themselves came later into being —
Who knows from whence this great creation sprang?
He from whom all this great creation came,
Whether His will created or was mute,
The Most High Seer that is in highest heaven,
He knows it — or perchance even He knows not.

Georgiana listened, mesmerised by the cadence of the lines. She understood not a word but she was sufficiently acquainted with Latin to grasp the stately vigour of the poem. "So strange ..." she murmured, "and yet so grand." She turned to Wilkins. "Would you translate it so that I may share the meaning?"

Sir William Jones had been watching the golden-haired, voluptuous woman. "Proserpine," he thought to himself 'but no, there is no innocence in her. Juno, more likely ... cool yet sensual, with a desire to dominate."

"Would you care to learn Sanskrit, Ma'am?" the scholar-judge asked. "If you know Latin, you will take to Sanskrit with ease."

"I learn Sanskrit, Sir William?" she asked. "But of course, I would like to learn. Can a teacher be found?"

Sir William Jones nodded slowly, his wise eyes on her. "I shall begin your lessons and then my friend Gopal Chattopadhyay will take over."

Gopal Chattopadhyay, a learned and erudite Brahmin scholar, nodded uncertainly. "How can a woman learn the Vedas?" he murmured to Warren Hastings in Bengali.

The Governor General smiled. "Leelavati, Kathyani and Gargi were women, were they not? Savithri too, who turned away the lord of death by her logic."

The Brahmin sighed in resignation. One did not argue with the Burra Lat Saheb, even if one knew better.

Thus, a vast, strange world was opened before Georgiana Manham. She learnt from the scholarly judge about India's ancient civilisation, its polyglot cultures, its faith covering a vast spectrum — from worship of stone to adoration of the Unknowable One. She learnt of its festivals, attuned to its seasons, and the need of the Indian people to celebrate life; to cherish it even in the midst of suffering. Georgiana waited eagerly for the two days in the week that Sir William Jones met her in his gracious bungalow, where a bewildered Lady Jones presided over the tea table, longing for the cool, soft air of Durham where she grew up as daughter of the bishop.

Georgiana attracted the brilliant judge by her quick intelligence, her greedy erudition and an air of patrician poise. He enjoyed opening up a new world of ideas and traditions before her. He saw that she was often awestruck by the dimension and immensity of Indian civilisation.

"I feel, Sir William, that I have lost my bearings ... and stand in danger of surrendering my identity," she told him once. "I was brought up in the Whig household of my uncle, Lord Courtney of Ashville, where logic and reason were all that mattered."

"Surely you believed in a Supreme Being?" Wilkins asked sharply.

Georgiana glanced at the scholar who was immersed in translating the most venerated of Hindu books, the Bhagavad Gita, The Celestial Song.

"Yes, in an abstract, businesslike manner. One did not seek to know Him or to renounce the world." She paused and smiled sardonically. "In Ashville, everyone was sensible ... and practical. Enthusiasm was not encouraged ... nor were passions."

"Except the passion for hunting, eating and ... love making," Wilkins retorted. He was vaguely irritated by this gorgeous demi-mondaine and kept her at arm's length. "A nabob's concubine masquerading as a sensitive scholar," he scoffed inwardly.

"That is true. And because they are so eminently sensible, they do not suffer," Georgiana replied. "But you, Mr. Wilkins, do you find peace in reciting the Gita?"

The scholar's grey eyes were as luminous as stars. "Peace, my dear lady? Oh no, it is not peace I find!" Wilkins exclaimed. "Reading the Gita, and understanding its message of loving detachment, its compassionate intelligence and liberation — it brings you a sense of wonder, of being on the fringe of eternity!"

Georgiana nodded. "How fortunate he is," she thought ruefully. "He can believe in such beautiful things."

"You see, Miss Manham," Sir William Jones continued gently, "Indian civilisation is like an onion. One can feel layer after layer of experience from the very physical to the pure metaphysical ... where your very existence is questioned as part of Maya or cosmic illusion."

Georgiana nodded. She had begun to see only a glimmer of what the other India was about; "the India that Nabob Ruthven does not know about, the India which he has missed in his quest for trade in muslin, silk, saltpetre, sugar and tobacco," she thought. "He has built a fine mansion and acquired a jagir but he is still a primitive highlander living on blood and tears."

Alexander Ruthven heard of his captive's success in the unconventional cosmopolitan society of Calcutta where quick wits and erudition, boldness and beauty were admired more than pedigree or status. The mixed disorderly world of adventurers, mercenary generals, unscrupulous traders and Company officials eagerly accepted Georgiana Manham in their fold. Poised and cultivated, this lady of the Whig aristocracy was as enigmatic as themselves. Often they attempted flirtations with her but were puzzled by her refusal to engage in anything more serious. However, dancing in moonlit gardens, wading in eddies of water, and going to the Kali temple to watch the sacrifice of goats were episodes of frivolity in which she freely indulged. She raced men on swift horses, exulting in the sense of freedom and space as she thundered over the turf of the Maidan.

Stories of Georgiana's escapades regularly reached Alexander Ruthven. When the Governor General held his next dance, Ruthven ensured an invitation for himself at Belvedere.

Georgiana was there in a gown of deep rose with wide panniers and a pelisse of white brocade. Her golden hair was in ringlets, unpowdered, and threaded by strings of jasmines. Unadorned (since brother Freddy had sold the family jewels), Georgiana wore a cluster of white roses on the lace froth of her bodice. Ruthven halted, dazzled. She met his eyes across the crowded hall and waited. He walked slowly towards her, a dazzling figure in a blue satin coat and white silk breeches, the diamond buttons on his coat and shoes glittering.

"How are you, Miss Manham?" he asked gravely.

"Well, as you see, Mr. Ruthven," she retorted coldly.

"I came to ask you for a dance," he said, summoning a smile.

"You are quite shameless, Sir."

He shook his head. "No, Madam. I am quite within my rights." He paused. "Your family's house in Cavendish Square is now mine. If you do not wish for your sisters to be turned out by my agent, you had best remember the terms of your ... sojourn in India."

"You are a fiend," she whispered furiously.

He inclined his head. "As was your father, Ma'am."

For a moment, her green eyes smouldered, and then, slowly, furiously she curtsied and offered Ruthven a gloved hand. They danced the minuet to the music of Haydn, with a dignity that made others pause and smile. Neither Miss Georgiana's history nor her relationship with 'Nabob' Ruthven was unknown to the Governor General or his circle. She bore their sapient glances and insinuating smiles with a smiling fortitude that puzzled Ruthven more than anyone else.

It was Georgiana's enigmatic attitude that drew Alexander Ruthven to yet another gathering where he expected to find her. If it irked him to see his captive free and gay as a butterfly, he contained his frustration in a surge of stubborn interest in this woman who could flaunt her defiance before the world while shrugging him off with polite indifference.

With each encounter, in fact, Georgiana's temper improved, as if she had forgiven Ruthven's "bad taste and boorish conduct." Indeed, halfway through the stately steps of a cotillion, or a spirited conversation at a dinner table, Ruthven found her watching him with a strange speculative smile. One night, after dinner was over at Belvedere and the card tables were laid, Alexander Ruthven persuaded Georgiana to accompany him for a stroll in the vast, lantern-lit gardens, where they talked in earnest for some time.

Ruthven returned from these excursions to his mansion, moody and taciturn. Begum Shirin gauged him with her sapient, watchful eyes, aware of his turmoil. Never in the twenty-six years of their marriage had the Begum seen him so distracted. There had been, she knew, many women in his bed who had caroused and gone away, leaving him lighter in heart and purse. His liaison with Liselotte Fremont had angered her when it began, but like a wise woman, she had soon accepted his need for another woman. The Rajput girl, Chandrika, had been no problem at all, though for a while, Ruthven had been besotted by her, lavishing jewels, palanquins and clothes on her. "But I always knew he was mine and would return. Above all, I know he loves Andraz best and I, as the mother of his beloved son, will be always honoured," she had consoled herself.

Looking through a half closed door at Ruthven now, when he returned to the vast, silent mansion, Shirin saw a terrible shadow fall across her life. In despair, she turned to Liselotte. "What has made him so remote and distracted?' she asked her one-time rival. "He seems to be like a ghost ... haunted by some terrible predicament."

Liselotte nodded. Her own friends had not failed to keep her informed. Above all, Mrs. Marianne Hastings had ensured that the Frenchwoman, who had been a friend of Madame Grand, should know why Alexander Ruthven went to Belvedere and other places where he could meet the Junoesque beauty. "I know," Liselotte murmured, "he sees Miss Manham."

"But he can bring her and keep her as a concubine!" Shirin wailed.

Liselotte sighed. "It is, I fear, more complicated." Her hazel eyes darkened in pain. "Miss Manham is not a fool like me, Begum."

Shirin shivered. "I will have it out with him. I cannot bear this torment of watching him drift away." She paused and asked, "Liselotte, does ... our Janab ... love ... this woman?"

Liselotte's eyes filled with tears. "Have you known him to love anyone, Begum?"

"He loves Andraz," insisted the Begum.

"Then ask his intentions about Andrew. That will tell you how the land lies," Liselotte said grimly.

It was however, Alexander Ruthven himself who summoned his Begum one day to the library not long after. Shirin went to embrace him impulsively, shocked by his sunken eyes and hollow cheeks, a hectic flush on his face. Ruthven held her back with a cold hand.

"I wanted you to know that I am making a will, a secret will, which will remain with you. In it I am designating Andrew as my chief heir. He will be the jagirdar of Deogarh, and will inherit this house and my estate in Murshidabad." He paused, took a deep breath and continued, "Claude shall inherit Garden Reach and my silk factories at Murshidabad. For my five daughters, I am leaving £25,000 each as dowry."

The Begum stared at him, puzzled. That nameless shadow again made her shiver. It is generous of you, Janab," she said unsteadily.

"I have ... a condition however, Begum."

"What is that, Janab?"

Alexander Ruthven turned away to look out of the window below. There, in the garden, sat Liselotte with her two daughters and the Begum's three daughters. He could hear her instructing them in Renaissance painting. Begum Shirin waited, hands clenched, until he turned once more to her.

"Will you go to Deogarh — as my agent — and administer it until Andrew returns?"

Shirin knew now that the shadow was real. "If I refuse?" she asked quietly.

"If you refuse?" he echoed coldly, his blue eyes sweeping over her in disdain. "I will then have to endure your presence."

Begum Shirin choked back a sob. "You will not punish Andraz?"

"Punish my son?" he cried in exasperation. "Why should I do that? I would rather die first!"

Shirin did not wipe away her tears. "Then I will go to Deogarh. Indeed, it is time I left. I was quite happy there ... it is only you who summoned me back." She rose heavily from the chair and looked at him. "It seems a long time, does it not, since that stormy night in Moti Jhil, twenty-six years ago when we ... made a pact ... to help each other?"

Ruthven closed his eyes, shutting out those memories — of that stormy night, and his early life with the slender, attractive, indomitable Shirin who was now a fat, gouty woman with tear-bleared eyes. He opened his eyes and came to her. "You will always be my Begum. And Andraz will be a true nawab ... a better, purer one than me. I swear this, Shirin, on my father's soul!"

She saw his anguish and turmoil, the hint of tears in his eyes. She went to him and kissed him, this time not in joyous passion but in sad farewell.

Liselotte waited, her hands poised over the piano keys, when the house was silent once more. Shirin came, her steps heavy, and sat down. "Go to your villa at Garden Reach. It will be given to Claude. There will be no room for you here. Take your little girls too. He will provide well for you, if you obey his wishes."

Liselotte's head bowed over the piano. Tears fell on her fingers as she sobbed. "I remember, Begum, the idyllic days at Ratangarh when I thought he loved me ... and when I ... gave him my young body ... my laughter and love ... and trusted him with my dreams." She paused to glance at the distraught Begum. "Do you know what he used to say? 'Have patience, Liselotte. You will be Madame Ruthven one day'."

Begum Shirin rose, clutching her heart, closing the door upon Liselotte's unbridled grief.

"Ten years," Liselotte thought, "in which I bore him five children. Even now I carry his child, created during those tempestuous nights after his return from England ... when he came to me every night, wild yet tender. I thought he loved me at last, but no it was a prelude to his farewell. It is time I end my bridal dream! My radiant, heedless youth has passed in waiting. And now I have nothing but the bondage of motherhood and dependence."

Only when the vast mansion was cleared of wife, mistress and children did Alexander Ruthven go to Georgiana Manham and ask her to return there.

She regarded him with little surprise and less emotion, although his wild eyes and frenzied speech were entirely novel to her. She remembered his cold disdain and hatred on the ship, his mechanical coupling on the hard bunk. And now that man was asking her to be his wife!

"What about your Moghul Begum?" she asked in a detached tone.

"She ... has left for Deogarh ... in time ... when she recovers from the journey ... and the sadness ... I will give her talaq." He spoke hurriedly, disjointedly and in obvious pain.

Georgiana nodded thoughtfully. "And Mademoiselle Fremont?"

"She has been sent to my villa at Garden Reach. She can be no impediment." His voice was unsteady, almost weary, as if he had fought a battle and lost.

"Quite so," Georgiana agreed sardonically. "Past affections and commitments, shared experiences and memories can hardly be construed as impediments." Inwardly she thought what a vile man this was.

Ruthven did not reply. She had indicated her terms when he had asked her to return to him during a stroll in Belvedere. He had executed her wishes with the single-minded determination he had always displayed to attain goals. After humiliating Georgiana and punishing her father, he had wanted her, with a hunger that was almost a madness. To possess her, he had agreed to her terrible terms.

"Very well. Let the marriage be performed in St. John's church." She paused and said softly, "Your ... er ... marriage with the Begum was not, I gather, solemnised in church?"

"No."

"Not before a British magistrate either?"

"No."

"Then we need not consider it a marriage."

Ruthven did not reply. He would deny his very existence if it was necessary to possess Georgiana Manham.

Mrs. Georgiana Ruthven was, after the Governor General's lady, one of the most honoured women in Calcutta. In a year, she had transformed the trader's mansion into a house of English aristocracy. Furniture, tapestries, paintings, porcelain, pottery and silver had come from England in the Indiaman which came regularly to Calcutta. Walls were now painted in white and gilt or the pale blues and greens decreed by the Adam brothers. Fireplaces were installed in styles designed by them. Heavy Moghul ornaments and furniture were banished to make room for light, classical commodities from England and France — Aubusson carpets, Hepplewhite chairs, Chippendale tables and cabinets, tapestries from Lisle and Tournai, Queen Anne silver, Murano glass figurines from Venice and leather-bound books. Paintings by Turner, Gainsborough, and Reynolds covered the walls. A grand piano was installed as well, with room for other musical instruments. Outside, the luxuriant tropical garden was uprooted and a disciple of Capability Brown came from England to lay out vistas and follies, formal gardens and careless walks.

Adornment of Georgiana's residence was accompanied by adornment of her person in wardrobes sent from London and Paris and complemented by jewels made in India.

Scholars such as Sir William Jones, Charles Wilkins, Halhed and Colebrooke, judges like Elijah Impey, adventurer-soldiers like Benoit de Boigne and Eyre Coote, officials and merchants were glad to receive invitations to Mrs. Ruthven's soirees and dinners where all courtesies were observed, and where conversation was as sparkling as the imported champagne. Here, boisterous games of bread-pellet throwing, frenzied dances, or indecorous jokes and innuendoes were not permitted by the patrician hostess. Here conversation centred on politics, the classics both of Europe and India, linguistics, mythology, music. News from Europe was discussed without nostalgia but with interest. Events in India excited more animation.

Warren Hastings came when he could take time off from his numerous preoccupations, accompanied by an awed, hushed Marianne Hastings. He announced one evening that the war between Britain and France was over. "Now we may have respite in the Carnatic and Hyderabad," the Governor General said. "The skirmishes of the Madras and Bombay Presidencies put a burden on our resources. With France at war against us, we faced additional strains."

"Especially when the French produce a brilliant admiral like Baithe de Suffren," Mrs. Ruthven spoke from the head of the table.

"Indeed so, Ma'am," the Governor General replied courteously. "However, we have Eyre Coote at the helm and he has already given the French a bad time. Suffren, of course, retaliated by attacking Cuddalore."

"Who will you combat now, Your Excellency, that the French are no longer enemies?" Georgiana asked with a smile.

Warren Hastings gazed at the dazzling figure at the head of the table. The emerald tiara on her golden head was designed to echo her eyes, and the white satin dress seemed an extension of her sculptored, marble body. "Had I not been so devoted to my Marianne," he mused, "I would have become as madly enamoured of her as Ruthven has become."

Aloud, he said, "We will attempt to curb the ambitions of the Mysore rulers. Hyder Ali died last year but his son, Tipu Sultan, is no less ambitious. I have sent Mathews to harry him at Mangalore. Macartney has already taken Dindigul and Dharmapuram. Macleod is advancing towards the Malabar coast, to seize Cannanore and Palghat." He paused and glanced at the assembled, immaculately dressed guests sitting around the glittering table. "You will understand the circumstances which prompted, indeed compelled, me to take action against Chait Singh of Benaras and redistribute the pensions of the Begums of Oudh."

No one spoke in affirmation. Hastings' treatment of Chait Singh of Benaras appeared arbitrary, even to British eyes. His conduct towards the widowed Begums of Oudh was no less authoritarian. Accounts of these actions had been transmitted to London with no loss of colour.

"The Begums did not require those vast estates. Nor should Nawab Asaf-ud-doula be denied his legacy," Hastings said intently, trying to impress upon all present the urgency of his position. He paused, and looked around with a sardonic smile. "That we sit here, ladies and gentlemen, in comfort and conviviality, without anxiety about our safety is due to the success of Company arms. If we are to continue and prosper, we shall have to defend our territories with many such wars. For that, revenues are essential."

Georgiana nodded assent. "Your Excellency is most eloquent. No one here would dissent or disagree with you." Later on, taking him aside after the men had drunk their port and Madeira, Georgiana informed the Governor General that Fox and Pitt in London were preparing the India Act, and that he was likely to be disturbed in his office. "You must muster support, Mr. Hastings," she said gravely. "I have written and despatched a letter to my uncle, the Earl of Ashville, to support your cause in the House of Lords. As a Whig peer, he can restrain the other Whigs who seek to slander you."

The Governor General bowed deeply. "I wonder if Alexander Ruthven realises his great fortune?" he asked, as he kissed her slim hand. Georgiana Ruthven laughed lightly. Warren Hastings took his seat in the elegant drawing room to hear his hostess play a Mozart sonata. His hand once went to his lips, to reassure himself that his lips had not been frozen by the steely touch of Georgiana's fair hands. Gently, he took his wife's hand in his. It was a corrupt hand, but a gentle and kindly one.

Early in 1784, Georgiana gave birth to a son whom she, with her usual sardonic humour, called Charles Edward. "After all, our marriage occurred due to an old Jacobean-Hanoverian feud. And since the Jacobean won, should not his cause be remembered by calling his son after Bonnie Prince Charlie?" she remarked, laughing.

Ruthven smiled, neither entirely displeased, nor amused by her sarcasm. A daughter had been born before but she had died soon after and it astonished him when Georgiana previously so cool and detached, came to give him pleasure in bed. Their coupling was like the mating of animals — fierce and brief. And when it was over, it was Georgiana who turned away, while he continued to fondle her breasts, caress her hair and kiss her body. Then, as soon as she had conceived, however, she locked the door of her apartment at night. Sometimes, on those nights, Ruthven reined his horse and rode furiously to Garden Reach, to find consolation and release in Liselotte's arms. Sometimes, lying with her, he yearned to take her back to Calcutta to regain the lost joy of his life. But the lure of Georgiana drew him back, hungry and mesmerised.

Georgiana watched over little Charles Edward like a hawk, not trusting wet-nurses or ayahs. For a while, she disappeared from social life, concentrating her entire energy and attention on the little boy with his reddish-gold hair and blue-green eyes. Even then she saw that while Charles had acquired some of her colouring, he was cast in the Ruthven mould. Indeed, she thought, he could be the brother of Andrew, son of the Begum. For daughter Deirdre, now two, she had little interest or affection. She was the child of her degradation. Yet Alexander Ruthven adored the daughter who was named after his beloved sister and who was growing up to resemble so closely that tragic figure. Yes, Deirdre among his daughters and Andrew were his favourite children. It gave Georgiana Ruthven food for thought.

When she turned her attention back to social life, Georgiana continued to play the part of a leading hostess in Calcutta society. She had taken care to keep in touch with the intellectual men who had been her first and most valuable friends. When Warren Hastings and Sir William Jones established the Asiatic Society in 1784, Georgiana not only attended the opening ceremonies swathed in silk and lace, but also cajoled Ruthven to contribute handsomely for its functions, thereby strengthening her friendship with Sir William Jones, Wilkins and Halhed. Indeed, it was her intention that, in time, Ruthven House should take the place of Belvedere as the most cultured salon in Calcutta. Only then she felt she could lay to rest the ghosts of her degradation, in the ship's cabin en route to India. Alexander Ruthven, however, fumed.

"What is the purpose of establishing the Asiatic Society and the Muslim Madrasa?" he asked his wife irately, as the last carriage rolled away after a dinner to honour the scholars, both Indian and English, who formed the nucleus of the Asiatic Society.

"The purpose, Mr. Ruthven? Why, I thought that was evident enough. Mr. Hastings and his kindred spirits feel that the storehouse of Indian civilisation should be opened, and its possessions understood."

Alexander Ruthven waved his hand dismissively. "Does Hastings care a damn about Indian civilisation?"

"The Governor General has a great love for it," Georgiana said loftily.

Ruthven laughed. "Indeed? He shows it in a singular fashion, then. The annexation of Benaras, the harassment, arrest and eviction of Raja Chait Singh from his own kingdom, the subsequent bleeding of that state accords ill with Hastings' professed love for India and her culture."

Georgiana regarded her husband's derisive countenance with a cool, astringent smile. "Have you not, Mr. Ruthven, loved what you sought to subjugate?"

Alexander Ruthven's smile vanished. He moved forward, stretching his arm towards her. "Georgiana, my darling," he said hoarsely. "I ... did ... love you ... even before ... I asked for your ..."

"Degradation," she concluded harshly.

"Whatever it was ... but I seek only ... your heart now," Ruthven continued, clasping her cool, jewelled hand.

Georgiana nodded, an ironic smile on her wide lips. "Of course." Then, abruptly, she turned. "The last guest has gone and the servants are waiting to extinguish the chandeliers." She left the pillared veranda and entered the vestibule, and then the drawing room which she gazed upon with satisfaction. The servants were busy plumping cushions, dusting carpets and tables, removing glasses and cups. It was her standing instruction that the house should be clean and tidy by first light. Leaving the retainers to their task, Georgiana left the room and swept up the wide, curved staircase, with Alexander Ruthven following, holding up a candlestick.

An old khidmatgar, remembering the once imperious master who had kept wife and mistress under dominion, sighed. "This Mem," he whispered to a colleague, "is from a race of rulers. She has conquered her master."

The colleague laughed softly. "The master is ageing. It is not difficult to rule an ageing lord."

Georgiana glanced down once, her eyes narrowing, but quickly moved forward again in a rustle of silk, pretending she had not understood. The next morning, the old men, followers of Begum Shirin, were dismissed from employ.

Georgiana's warning to Warren Hastings did not prove to be

a false alarm. Whig disapproval of his methods and acts led to the Tory Pitt's India Bill in August 1784. Though the British Prime Minister opposed Fox's proposal for the direct management of India under Parliament, or by the Crown, he recognised that the growing British possessions in India could not be supervised by the East India Company alone. The new Board of Control was vested with powers shared by the Court of Proprietors. The President of the Board of Control became, in effect, the minister responsible for conducting the affairs of the East India Company. The powers of the Governor General were defined and enlarged but were brought within the purview of the Crown.

The man who had come to India as a 'griffin' of seventeen years in 1749, left it as Governor General, having altered the nature of both British possessions and Calcutta as the seat of a nascent empire.

Georgiana Ruthven gave a reception in February 1785, to the departing Governor General. "If he knows of the relentless campaign that awaits him in London, he gives no indication of it," Georgiana reflected, as the cold and aloof man moved among the assembled guests. His thin lips may have stretched to smile and jest but his eyes held a simmering resentment. Only with Georgiana did he unbend sufficiently to say, "They may now deny the Company its pre-eminence but it is the Company which won and established territories for Britain in India."

"The Whigs clamour for national interests rather than narrow commercial ones," Georgiana soothed. "It is not a personal matter."

"Fiddlesticks! That hypocrite, Burke, has begun the noise. Why? Because he could not dip his family finger deeper into the Indian pie."

"Come, let us not whisper together. Let the guests come to bid you farewell," Georgiana said gently.

Those who had come to Hastings for advancement had already turned to Macpherson, who was to fill the gap until the new Governor General arrived. Hastings had seen enough of the vagaries of human nature to ignore the slight but his own cynicism had not inured him to the cynicism of others.

Warren Hastings left Calcutta as the mango blossoms appeared under the deep blue skies of falgun, when the air is balmy and clamorous with the songs of nightingales. He had been in India for thirty-six years and had become an Indian — almost.

For a while, British India suffered a corrupt and venal Governor General in Macpherson, who defied the Board of Control by virtue of his friendship with the Prince Regent of Britain. By September 1786, however, Lord Cornwallis arrived in India, ending an inglorious period.

Georgiana Ruthven lost no time in making acquaintance with the new Governor General. With her acute perception, Georgiana realised that this aristocrat was entirely of a different breed from Clive or Hastings. Of him it was said, "There were no broken forces to be mended, no avarice to be gratified, no beggarly kinsman to be provided for." Sincere and incorruptible, the man who had lost the battle of Yorktown and surrendered to the American colonists was determined to succeed in India.

He succeeded to a considerable degree. Georgiana and her friends watched with great interest as Lord Cornwallis began undoing the work of Hastings. At one of Georgiana's dinners, he announced his intention to allow the princes of India to live in peace, without fear from venal Residents. The first to feel Cornwallis' stern hand were the Residents at Benaras and Oudh. Though they were given handsome salaries, they were at the same time warned not to accept gifts or bribes. Nor were they permitted to speculate on trade. The Governor General also made no attempt to hide his contempt for the mercenary European soldiers in the employ of the Company. "The Duke of York did not exaggerate when he said those men are the riff-raff of London streets, got together by the crimps and gleanings of the different gaols," he said, one day.

Alexander Ruthven flushed in anger and Georgiana, stirring

uneasily in her seat, tried to divert him with a beatific smile. At once, the old mercenary was soothed. His attractive, young wife could thus control his moods.

The Governor General continued, "Give me the native sepoys any day. Honest, dutiful men. They don't betray their officers."

"Does not the Prince Regent prefer Europeans to natives?" Ruthven asked sombrely.

Now it was Cornwallis' turn to flush. "I dare say, Prinny may think so. But I never favour a man for his colour. It is character that counts." He paused and stared with vivid blue eyes at the Scottish nabob. It is time we showed the Indians that the British race is not entirely corrupt and avaricious!'

No one spoke. Many present at Mrs. Ruthven's table were men who had made their fortune in speculation, and unbridled trading privileges. There was an Englishman who had accumulated a fortune as a Resident by bleeding a Raja white. None dared speak before this blunt and brave aristocrat.

Travelling through British territories in India, observing the society of Calcutta, Cornwallis realised that India had paid a heavy price for her weakness and chaos. It was his ambition to cleanse the administration. Recognising the need for an honest and able civil service, he wrote back to London, urging the formation of a civil service for India. "Let us recruit educated young men of good families, not traders graduated in chicanery or grown grey in fraud and corruption." London agreed and to India came the embryo of the famed Indian Civil Service.

Cornwallis was no less ruthless with private trade. He abolished the system altogether. The trading community of India heaved a sigh of relief after four decades of persecution. Local civil courts were established to make possible the luxury of justice. No one, Cornwallis declared, European or Indian would be spared if they violated the laws of the land.

Work went ahead for the establishment of courts of circuits and courts of appeal. The Governor General appointed Sir William Jones, the great scholar, to codify all existing Indian laws with regulations. District collectors were compelled to learn these laws so that they might dispense justice more effectively. English judges were later appointed to supercede the collectors.

Honest and well meaning, Lord Cornwallis did not, however, always see the implications of his actions. He embarked on an enterprise that was to affect the prosperity of rural Bengal for a century.

15

Things Fall Apart

Indrajit Chowdhury, the zamindar of Mayurganj had heard of the terms of the proposed Permanent Settlement. He personally had no cause for worry. Hard work and prudence had made his lands yield, and he took care never to be in arrears with the revenue department. The spectre of 1770, with its famine and devastation had remained vivid in his mind. However, his friends, the zamindars and rajas of Dinajpur, Nadia, Rajshahi and Bishnupur would fare ill by the Settlement and it was on their behalf that he set out on a cool autumn day for Calcutta.

Indumati, now a woman of thirty-one, stood under the ornamental portico to see off her husband. Despite her many child bearings, she retained a look of perennial youth in the glow of her pale gold complexion, the tautness of her ripe figure and the sparkle of her dark eyes. While the robust Kamalakshi had died in childbirth, her "Didi", Indrajit's first wife, Bishnupriya, had defied all predictions of brief longevity to reach middle age and lived to enjoy Indu's ordered dominion.

Consigning the heavy burdens of housewifery to the younger wife, Bishnupriya spent peaceful days reading the scriptures or holding soirees in which the songs of the mystic-poet Ramaprasad were sung, accompanied by dhols and tanpura.

Had I but dived deeper
Into the sweet waters of faith
Rich would have been my find

Indrajit came to hear, and afterwards he sat with his first wife, discussing abstract notions of life, destiny and death. Others watching Indrajit with his two wives called him Yajnavalkya, the philosopher of ancient times whose wives were a perfect foil to each other.

"Fortune has smiled on Indrajit Chowdhury," they said. "He has everything."

Indumati managed the household with a strong but kindly hand. The only person who eluded her authority was Indrajit, now a grey-haired man nearing fifty. He was, however, dependent on her and attached to his eldest surviving son, Brajesh, who now prepared to travel with his father.

"Do ensure his safety," Indumati told her husband. "I do not trust the dak bungalows on the way."

Indrajit smiled. "We will be safe enough. If Brajesh is to enter school in Calcutta, he will have to become accustomed to this journey."

"Brajesh will not enter school now," Indumati replied firmly, and added, "whatever may be Mrs. Latimer's opinion."

Even now, sixteen years after their brief affair, Fiona Ruthven Latimer remained a friend of Indrajit Chowdhury, and gave him advice on the education of his children.

Indrajit sighed. "We shall see," he parried, fully aware that the imperious chatelaine would cast the decisive vote, "but now we must go to Calcutta to see the school and of course, visit the Lord Saheb."

"And meet Fiona Latimer," Indumati thought with a twinge of jealousy, though Fiona was now as grey as Indrajit. But somewhere under the ash and embers, Indumati wondered if the fire still glowed.

The carriage trundled out of the circular portico, and over the long driveway towards the high wrought iron gates. Indumati stood on the veranda watching the two beings so beloved to her, go away. She sighed and turned to go inside where a hundred tasks and decisions awaited her. Indumati's daily duties included supervision of the twenty household servants, the conduct and studies of her own four children and Kamalakshi's two, and occasionally, a discussion regarding the affairs of the estate with her old friend, Munshi Chakravarthy. She felt oddly cheated; having rescued her husband from perdition by a liaison with Fiona, Indumati had hoped to draw closer to Indrajit, who, however, remained elusive. They had lived as man and wife now for fifteen years but he was still as remote as before, except for the brief and passionate interludes in her apartments, when he left her feeling ecstatic. For all her intelligence, Indumati did not realise that Indrajit, in the high summer of his life, had become deeply attached to the high spirited, comely woman who had come to his house as a little girl. But a stubborn pride kept him from acknowledging her triumph since he had condemned her once for defying him — something no woman had ever done — not even the flame-haired foreigner, Fiona.

Indrajit turned back once to see his second wife, standing motionless on the veranda, her vast eyes fixed on his carriage. As the rice and sugarcane fields, coconut groves, clusters of areka trees, tanks and lotus ponds, thatched huts of the peasants sped past, Indrajit thought of Indumati. A person as warm and intense, as stubborn and imperious as himself. A surge of passion swirled within him, even making him toy with the idea of turning back, to spend a night with her and confess to her in the lilac hour before dawn that she was his best-loved woman, more dear to him than the gentle Bishnupriya, or the voluptuous Kamalakshi, dearer even than the passionate and tender Fiona. These women had been the joys of his youth. Indumati was the peace of his autumn.

The carriage sped swiftly over the hard autumn roads, skirting the river, passing the tranquil towns of Nadia, Nabadwip and Krishnagar, the citadel of Bengal's culture, the storehouse of her poets and mystics. Seven-year-old Brajesh stared at the passing landscape, awed and thrilled by his first journey out of Mayurganj. His father watched him with a smile, confident that this bright son would one day be able to manage Mayurganj.

But for that, an education was necessary. Fiona had persuaded him that a sound western education was indispensable for an Indian who wished to rise in the Bengal ruled by the East India Company. Remembering his youth spent in futile rebellion against the might of the foreign rulers, Indrajit had decided that Brajesh would make peace with reality and be a part of the Company milieu.

His own temperament, however, had still not changed, he thought ruefully. "Otherwise, why should I be going to Lord Cornwallis to protest against the proposed Settlement?" He sighed, wearily, wondering when this ceaseless combat would end.

Fiona Ruthven Latimer awaited him at her brother's house in Alipur.

"Ah, Indrajit, you have kept your promise!" she exclaimed, hurrying towards him with outstretched hands. He stood on the pillared veranda of Ruthven House, a slim figure in a spotless white dhoti and kurta, an exquisite shawl folded on his shoulder. His greying hair added distinction to the chiselled nose and mouth, the wide brow and the intense, dark eyes.

Indrajit lifted her hands to his lips, his eyes on her vivid blue ones. He remembered their relationship of the past with surprise. "How strange," he thought, "that I can greet her calmly now, and touch her without the madness of those years! Was it this same Fiona that I loved? This heavy, ageing woman with streaks of grey in her flaming hair?"

"Are you tired after your journey?" Fiona asked, unsettled, as she always was by the touch of his fair, sensitive hand, the introspective gaze of his wide, slightly slanting eyes. Fifteen years of marriage and two children had still not cooled her ardour for this patrician Brahmin.

"No, I rested at my house in Chitpur Road." He paused. "The second storey is coming along well."

"I am glad. You need a pieda terre in Calcutta." Fiona replied.

He nodded, smiling. "You know all my needs, Fiona," Indrajit murmured.

Fiona regarded him solemnly. "That I do, Indrajit," she said sadly, "but I have not the power to satisfy them — not any more."

Her reproach hung between them as she communicated wordlessly that while she still hungered for him, she realised that he had found a new anchor in life. Fiona knew by instinct of his attachment for Indumati.

"I still need you, Fiona," Indrajit said softly. "You must guide me regarding my son." He glanced at little Brajesh who stood behind him.

Fiona turned to the boy and her eyes suddenly filled with tears. Bending down, she gathered him in her arms and kissed his smooth, pale-olive cheeks. Surprised but not displeased by this gesture, Brajesh smiled at Fiona who hugged him tightly and whispered, "He might have been mine!"

Indrajit watched, at a loss for words, and was grateful when another little boy ran from a corner of the garden shouting, "Auntie, do stop Deirdre from hurling stones at me! Why does she always fight me?"

Brajesh released himself from Fiona's embrace to stare at the boy with red-gold hair and blue-green eyes who had rushed to his aunt's side in agitation. Fiona rose and glanced at the two boys. "Charles Edward," she said with mock solemnity, "you have a visitor, Brajesh Chowdhury, from Mayurganj. I hope and trust you will entertain him while I converse with his father."

Charles Edward Ruthven glanced at the patrician figure of the zamindar and then at his contemporary. Advancing a few steps forward, he extended his hand to the father and then to the son. Then, abruptly, he asked Brajesh. "Do you play cricket?"

Brajesh shook his head, not comprehending English.

"Kya khelta hai?" Charles Edward tried again in Hindi.

"Onek khela jani," Brajesh replied laughingly, in Bengali.

"Achha, tab chalo!" Charles responded grabbing his new friend's hand and sprinting towards the smooth green lawns beside the house.

Indrajit and Fiona gazed after them, as if they knew somehow that theirs would be a friendship fraught with events.

A large party set out late in the morning for the Governor General's office in Belvedere, where Lord Cornwallis conducted affairs of the Company's rule with the same tragic honesty and stupidity with which he had mismanaged the American War of Independence.

The Permanent Settlement was his pet project. As a landowner, he felt an affinity with the zamindars of India, assuming them to be counterparts of British landlords. He felt that annual leases should be abandoned for more permanent revenue collections, which would be the responsibility of the zamindars. They would pay nine-tenths of the revenue collection to the government through collectors while smaller landlords or talukdars would pay directly to sub-collectors. In so doing, he intended to protect the peasants or ryots from the oppression of the Company's collectors.

Indrajit realised the pitfalls of the proposed legislation and discussed it with fellow zamindars who had similar reservations. They converged at Calcutta to remonstrate before the Governor General.

Lord Cornwallis met the zamindars in his simply furnished office. "Apart from a predilection for port and pretty faces, His Lordship is a blunt and genial country squire, not particularly burdened by intelligence," Fiona murmured as she walked sedately beside Indrajit Chowdhury, who soon understood why the English had coined the phrase "the road to hell is paved with good intentions."

"The system will not have flexibility," a zamindar of Nadia protested to the Governor General. "If the assessment is high, there is no form of redress." He paused. "Your revenue men believe I can pay higher than what I am doing now."

Lord Cornwallis' solid face showed no trace of softening. He stared at his quill with pale, protruberant eyes.

"In the present system, we landlords do not face confiscation of our lands if the jama or assessment is not paid."

Lord Cornwallis glanced up, his lower lip jutting out. "You face the indignity of flogging and fines."

"We prefer that, Your Excellency, to confiscation," another zamindar protested.

Lord Cornwallis did not flinch. "That may be so but I cannot countenance such customs. The landlord class must be given prestige and responsibility." He paused and added, "I fail to understand why you remonstrate against the system. Most landlords are satisfied."

Indrajit Chowdhury spoke now. "Those who are satisfied do not realise the implications, Your Excellency. The landlords will have to deliver the assessed rent regardless of their peasants' capacity to pay. In our land, the monsoons are fickle and may disturb cultivation patterns. What can the peasants do if their fields are fallow? And if they cannot pay, how can the zamindar?"

"Peasants can pay," Cornwallis insisted. "This is a fertile land."

Indrajit's face darkened with memories of the famine of 1770. "Yet we have had famines that have devastated the countryside and carried away one-third of the population," he retorted. "Now they will have no relief if they cannot pay."

"It is not our intention to oppress the peasant, Mr. Chowdhury," the Governor General hastened to placate the zamindar who spoke slowly and clearly in English.

"It is what you have achieved, nevertheless. In fact, you have broken the tie of cooperation and interdependence which was the basis of the Indian system," Indrajit replied coldly. "I pray you reconsider the matter." He rose and signalled to the other landlords.

Cornwallis remained seated, annoyed. "Jonathan Dundas and John Share have bestowed their attention on the matter. It has been the dedicated work of many years. I see no grounds for retraction of the proposed laws." He paused and said, "We landlords of Britain had hoped to find mutuality of interest with the landlords of India."

"Then you have not understood our differences," Indrajit replied, and bowing, left the Governor General's chambers. As soon as he came out, Fiona rushed in from an anteroom. "What did His Lordship say?" she asked anxiously.

Indrajit shook his head. "The law will be decreed soon. We have failed to convince the Lord Saheb." He paused and said, heedless of who may hear, "Cornwallis is honest and high-born, with no fences to mend or nephews to accommodate. However, these qualities are no substitute for intelligence and imagination."

Fiona laid a warning hand on his arm. "Let us go, my friend," she said and pulled him gently forward along the red-carpeted corridors of Belvedere. The other zamindars followed suit and boarded their carriages in silence.

Indrajit watched Fiona drive her brother's phaeton with surprise. Her strong, slim hands guided the two Arab steeds for a soothing drive across the Maidan, the river embankment and on to Park Street, where shops were reopening after the long siesta. Coloured palanquins glided along the shaded streets, drawn by dark, breathless men. Fiona then turned back to Alipur and stopped before the wall of thick trees behind which stood Ruthven House, bathed today in a golden autumn light.

Georgiana awaited them in the drawing room, dressed in a crepe dress that was moulded close to her voluptuous body. Her hair was swept up in a Grecian style and held up by a velvet band sewn with pearls, leaving her round, white neck as well as a portion of her gleaming bosom in full view. She smiled at Indrajit Chowdhury, interested by the tales she had heard of his earlier rebellion and his carnal relationship with her sister-in-law. It amused Georgiana that "dear, simple Fiona", tall and spare, with freckles on her nose, could rouse an aloof and fastidious Brahmin to such madness. "Are the men of the Orient bewitched by us?" she wondered with a strange smile. "Can we really hold them in our thrall?"

She greeted them both cordially and invited them to sit by the French window, where tea was laid on a round table.

"Mr. Hastings would not have committed this stupendous blunder," she exclaimed, pouring tea for her visitors from an exquisite Queen Anne teapot. "He would have ascertained the extent of individual holdings of the zamindars, the average yield per acre, and hereditary claims and titles before making such wholesale changes. Ignorance of local conditions, ownership and customs has made this legislation inequitable and unjust."

"You are loyal to your friend," Indrajit Chowdhury observed, looking at the alluring woman who seemed to have descended from another world. Despite her elegance and splendour, he did not feel at ease with Georgiana Ruthven. Beneath the surface softness, seemed to lie a steely will and determination. Involuntarily, he glanced at Fiona. The years of strife and hardship had not hardened her. She had acquired a strength and sweetness which was stamped on the pale, freckled skin of her face and which illumined her blue eyes. Her tall, slender body retained a touch of innocence despite its knowledge.

A shadow fell across the elegant Adam-style room. Georgiana glanced up, and when she saw Andrew Ruthven pause by a mahogany cabinet, her hand trembled. Quickly, she put down the Sevres cup on the table and, in a gay voice, invited her handsome stepson to join them. He stared at her, his blue eyes never wavering as they swept across her white neck and shoulders and the gleaming half-exposed breasts surrounded by a foam of lace. Then he saw Fiona and the strange look gave way to obvious delight.

"Aunt Fiona!" he exclaimed. "How glad I am to see you! I did not know you were in Calcutta. When did you come? How is Uncle Arthur?" Without waiting for a reply, he bowed and shook Zamindar Chowdhury's hand.

As they talked, Fiona's wise eyes kept straying to her nephew and to her sister-in-law. She was filled with dread of what she saw. It was something she could not mention, even to Indrajit, from whom she had no secrets. He would, she knew, recoil from the horror of it. Or he might, Fiona thought, divulge all to Alexander Ruthven.

"Back from Deogarh, dear Andrew?" Fiona asked gently, defying Georgiana. It had pained her to see Shirin banished from the house she had helped to build.

Andrew nodded, as if reluctant to talk of Deogarh and his mother but Fiona persisted. "How is your Mama? And the girls?" She paused. "I have not heard from them for so long."

Embarrassed, Andrew glanced at Georgiana who bowed her head, and blushed, remembering her harshness.

"Alice is married to the Nawab of Jaunpur. She is now Begum Alia. Clarice is married to a landlord of Oudh. She is now also a Muslim. And Beatrice is at home ... with Mama."

Fiona nodded. "I am glad my nieces are settled. I ... am sorry they have rejected our faith ..."

No one spoke. Everyone knew why Ruthven's daughters had renounced their British father's creed and embraced their Muslim mother's heritage. Yet, Andrew remained strangely unmoved by references to his banished mother and embittered sisters. His gaze was fixed on his beautiful stepmother.

At dinner, Fiona watched them as unobtrusively as she could. For one who had endured the torment of a forbidden love, it was not difficult to read the signs and symptoms of such a passion. Fiona had loved Indrajit with the same futility. He, a Kulin Brahmin, had already had a wife when she, an unmarried British woman, had met him by the temple. And she had had a husband when she gave herself to him in the forest temple, on that magic night. She regretted nothing of that encounter. Henry Dalrymple had had no emotional claims on her. But when she married Arthur Latimer, she had consciously transformed her passion for Indrajit into an inalienable devotion, which could hurt or offend no one.

"But between Georgiana and Andrew ... there is something wrong. Andrew is betraying his own father, the father who loves him so deeply. Georgiana owes Alexander no loyalty — she has suffered at Alexander's hands ... but Andrew?"

Fiona tossed and turned on her bed. Should she tell Alexander, who had gone to inspect his silk factory at Murshidabad, or should she warn Andrew about the disaster he was inviting? "Tomorrow," Fiona thought, we will see Brajesh's new school and then return to Mayurganj. I do not like the ... atmosphere of this house anymore."

Fiona spoke to Andrew before she left for Dubb's Point, but he only laughed. "Auntie," he taunted gently, "you are a reformed romantic. Did not the zamindar bewitch you once?"

Fiona flushed and replied. "He was ... not ... my stepfather."

Andrew blushed.

"That makes everything different," Fiona continued. "Take care and be wise, dear child. I do not want any sorrow for you."

An autumn dusk settled abruptly over the city, silent but for the distant rumbling of thunder. In a flurry of panic, ravens and koels, pigeons and sparrows drifted to their foliaged retreats in the Ruthven garden. The myriad barefooted servants walked silently, carrying silver candelabras to various rooms in anticipation of the darkness. By tacit agreement, no one entered the music room where Georgiana Memsaheb had recently removed her piano and harp and where she now sat alone, yet expectant, playing a Mozart sonata.

Its stately simplicity reminded her of evenings spent in Courtney Hall, where she had played this piece for her cousin Robert de Courtney, whom she had hoped to make her husband. Robert had had the hauteur of one who was assured of his own perfection. Georgiana felt they would have been well suited to each other, both in the salon and boudoir. Robert seemed to have thought so as well. He approved of her cool intelligence and ironic humour. He had sampled too the curves of her breasts and the taste of her strawberry lips. Though brother Freddy's raffish friends had attracted her, Georgiana had kept herself chaste, well aware that the future Earl of Ashville would not countenance a "soiled muslin" for his bridal bed.

Suddenly, she stopped playing the piano. "To what end have I been chaste?" she asked herself bitterly. "To experience the violence and degradation of an ageing nabob's assault in a musty ship's cabin? To feel my flesh torn; to be despised and to create in those moments of horror, a child; a child of a man who hated me and my family?"

Rising, she went to the tall, arched windows, thinking of her vow to substitute success as an antidote to her broken dreams of happiness. "For six years I have done just that. Mrs. Georgiana Ruthven is one of the most admired women in Calcutta, with a beautiful home, luxuries to indulge in, interesting and powerful friends, and a rich nabob for a husband, who is her slave." She paused and thought of her ageing husband, who repelled her.

The door opened. Georgiana did not have to turn to know it was Andrew. She sensed his presence at once by some alchemy of passion. Slowly, she turned and saw him silhouetted against a side window. The livid colours of a September sunset lit his face with violent hues of orange and purple and turned his red hair to green. They stood motionless, each in their own corner, regarding each other with the wonder and awe of a newly-discovered passion.

"A storm is brewing ... over the river," Andrew Ruthven said, coming towards her silhouette. "But why did you stop playing? I like listening to Mozart. Liselotte has taught me to appreciate its beauty."

Georgiana's lips tightened for a moment. Liselotte had to be banished — totally. As had to be the Begum. But Andrew, her sweet Andrew, was the Begum's son. "It reminds me of my girlhood ... of dancing the cotillion on a winter's night with ... my betrothed. I prefer to forget that life," she said sharply.

"Does it still hurt so much?" Andrew asked. When she did not reply, he sighed and said. "Perhaps loved memories hurt." He came close, grasped her shoulders and looked into her glittering, green eyes. "Will memory of our time together too ... hurt one day?" Georgiana nodded, allowing him to draw her close so that she could feel his sinewy arms enclose her aganist his hard chest. She opened her mouth to receive his slow, sensual kiss.

"Come," he whispered. "We do not ... have much time." He led her out of the room and through a side terrace to the dark garden lit fitfully by sporadic lightning. They paused to look at each other, frightened and excited by each other's expressions. Then they hurried across the thick, springy grass towards the folly set on a mound. Though it was dark inside, a thick quilt had been spread earlier. They rushed in and closed the door.

They had met every evening since Alexander Ruthven had left for a tour of his silk factories at Murshidabad. Nothing had happened suddenly. For eight years they had been attracted to each other but their relationship — that of stepmother and stepson — had held them back until finally, their passion had overridden their fears. Freed of restraint, they had become lovers on a stormy night when the candles had been blown out in the music room. They had embraced there and closed the door on the world.

Thereafter, they met wherever possible, snatching moments together in quiet frenzy. He had long been fascinated by this Junoesque woman who had banished his Mama and Aunt Liselotte but he could not summon up the hatred he wished to. She was his fairy princess, with golden hair and pink cheeks, the English girl he had vowed to marry. Unjust fate had made her his stepmother ... but that could not be helped. He made love with his virile young body and thrilled her with his Persian couplets. She, starved of fulfilment with her ageing and hated husband, responded to Andrew's tender passion with a madness that knew no cure.

Sometimes, lying spent and fulfilled at night, Georgiana wept in his arms at the futility of it all. "Let us go to Ratangarh, beloved," Andrew begged. "We will ask the Rana for support and my mother for her pardon. I will lead the Rana's armies. I will keep you safe and happy."

Georgiana had sat up, golden hair falling in a sheath around marble shoulders, green eyes wide with sudden hope. "Can we escape ... Alexander Ruthven?"

"Yes, my love. We can escape him. He has betrayed the Rana over the Maratha wars. No one will find us there." The young warrior drew his mistress closer, his lips brushing her full, ripe breasts, the supple waist and hips. She opened up like an unfurling blossom, quivering in anticipation of his coming. He parted her legs and entered her as she cried out in exquisite pleasure, and their bodies were convulsed by a terrifying force.

"Will you come?" Andrew asked, as they lay in silence.

"Can I relinquish the glory of my position, the honour of society, this house and possessions and the privileges I enjoy ... for Andrew's love? For the ecstasy of our union," she wondered and then turning, kissed her lover's eyes and hair. "Let us wait, my darling. There is no need for haste. We are happy enough like this ... we are often alone." She laughed softly. "Send him to your mother. She will detain him."

Andrew sat up, abruptly releasing her. In the candlelight his blue eyes were like steel. "How dare you involve my mother in our intrigue! You, who threw her out ... my mother who shared his ordeals and triumphs for a quarter century. My mother would be horrified if she knew of our ... liaison!"

Georgiana's hand stopped his words. "I wish I could undo all that, beloved!" she cried. "I wish I could have run away with you on the first day I saw you ... in the garden yonder." Her voice quivered in a sob.

He gripped her shoulders. "We can still do that! Let us throw ourselves at the mercy of my mother. Will you do it Georgiana? Will you, my love?"

Georgiana trembled at his fierceness and at the consequences of the step he was suggesting. A concubine again, she thought, adrift in the world and dependent entirely on a lover's mercy. Bidding farewell to Ruthven House and to the glittering society of Calcutta. No longer playing hostess to the Governor General, great scholars and soldiers and condescending to a haughty Brahmin aristocrat like Indrajit Chowdhury. Then she thought of lying beside Alexander Ruthven, his cold, tired body demanding passion.

"Let me think!" she cried hoarsely.

Andrew leapt up from the tumbled bed. "Then think!" he cried. I will come for your answer in a few days. "I will not behave like a thief. I will defy my father and be disowned but I will not deceive him further!"

In the next few days, they met each other in company — at dinners and dances, card parties and boat rides. Both of them were stiff and formal with each other. Then Georgiana drew him aside. "Come to the folly three days hence — before ... he ... arrives. I will tell you then ..."

Deirdre Ruthven had been watching her mother for some time now. Ever since her little brother, Charles, had told her that he had seen Andrew kiss Mama. She followed them thereafter, in smouldering rage. She had always resented her gorgeous mother for neglecting her, indeed, for shrinking away from her. While Georgiana caressed and cuddled Charles, she avoided closeness to Deirdre. It puzzled Deirdre at first and then she learned, through the innuendoes of the old servants who had been loyal to Begum Shirin, of the circumstances that had attended her creation. She had ceased to be a child very soon. And now she had lost all innocence.

"There, Papa," she said to her father, who had returned unexpectedly a day earlier. "Mama is there in the folly with Andrew."

Alexander Ruthven frowned, uncomprehending.

Deirdre nodded. "They are always together... when you are away." Alexander stared at his ten-year-old daughter. He had grown to love the child over the years, as his passion for Georgiana deepened. "What are you saying, my angel?" he asked, incredulous. "Go Papa ... and see them ... as I have ..."

Alexander Ruthven stared wildly at the clear, starlit autumn sky. Cold and trembling, he took stiff and halting steps towards the folly. His legs moved without his volition, impelled by a primordial fear. The garden inspired by Kent and Brown of England was redolent with the scent of roses and jasmines. From the bough of a spreading shirish tree, koels and nightjars broke the silence. At Ruthven's approach, they fluttered and flew away. The weary man looked around, knowing suddenly that life would never be the same again.

The house was wrapped in the shroud of a deathly silence the next day. Servants, normally curious, had disappeared to their corners and kitchens, terrified. Guests had left their cards and gone away in their carriages, puzzled by the stillness of Ruthven House. Meals were served to an empty table and taken back thrice. Deirdre sat before the window, smiling to herself. "Mama has been punished," she thought. "She will not be unkind to me agian." Little Charles Edward sat stiffly, trying to write his alphabets but the sense of impending doom overwhelmed him. He wept in his ayah's arms. The luminous autumn light changed colours before dissolving into a many-hued dusk, leaving the garden starlit once more. Candles were lit and placed in the various rooms except in the library where Alexander sat huddled before a window, and the bedroom where Georgiana Ruthven sat at the dressing table, staring at her white, terrified reflection. Andrew Ruthven paced his room, staring wildly around him until a servant, grown old in Shirin's service came in to say, "Janab, your father asks for you."

"You called me, Father?" Andrew Ruthven asked quietly as he entered the room. Alexander Ruthven stared at his palms for a long time. No fortune-teller had ever forecast this disaster to him. Andrew stood motionless before his father. Finally, Alexander raised his old, blue eyes to Andrew, who was shocked by their swollen redness. An impulse stronger than pride or fear made him rush and kneel before Alexander.

"Father, forgive me," Andrew whispered, convulsed by sobs of remorse and anguish. "I deserve to be beheaded."

Alexander swallowed his tears, staring at the bent red head so like his own; at the fine long hands that clutched his feet. Was this his Andrew, the son who would continue a noble line of conquerors in India, who bore in his blood the lineage of mighty Moghuls? Was this the boy he had loved and pampered, for whom he had dreamt glories greater than for himself? This Andrew, who had been seduced by his father's young wife and had wallowed in carnal ecstasy with her? Rage and grief tore at him as sharply and completely as it had forty-three years ago, when he had seen his father shot before his innocent eyes. But now, unlike that cold autumn day, he wanted no revenge. Revenge had brought him this grief. Revenge against the Manhams had destroyed him. He would not be able to hope or love again.

"Start for Deogarh at daybreak," Alexander said in a voice hoarse with grief. "Take money for your needs. Tend to the jagir ... and to your mother. Both need care and attention. Come back only when I call you ... not before. Is that clear?"

Andrew clutched his father's hand. "Father, forgive me. Tell me to kill myself and I will do it gladly. Don't, I beg you, treat me like a leper. I am ashamed, dearest Papa, so very ashamed of myself! ... Please do not hate me!"

Alexander released his hand and laid it on Andrew's head. "I am trying to forgive you, my son. I am trying to understand because ... I love you."

Andrew brought his head down to his father's feet and wept silently.

"Yes, Andrew, it is true. If I could hate you, as I have tried to, all last night and today, it would have been easier. But you are bound close to my heart. It will take time to forget ... and to let my anger cool ... but it will, in time. Return then, my son, and we will be at peace."

Alexander Ruthven sat in silence for a long time, thinking of his past life, of his actions and deeds. It seemed at last that there was sense in the theory of karma. As one sows, so one reaps. No one else was to blame. His own actions had set in motion a chain of events from which there was no escape. Or was there? Could one atone for one's sins and be redeemed? "Go, my son," he said at last to the son who had fallen asleep, exhausted, at his father's feet. "Dawn is breaking."

Alexander Ruthven stayed on in Calcutta, attending to his commercial work, taking renewed interest in his estates, sending letters of instructions to Begum Shirin about collection of taxes from the peasants of Deogarh. If the news of his son's liaison with his wife had percolated to Calcutta society, no one found vestiges of sorrow or anger in the elegant nabob's demeanour as he received guests or attended dinners and dances. He looked more sombre, certainly, but then Ruthven had always been so.

Georgiana waited for some drastic action, some gesture of rage or disgust but nothing happened. Alexander Ruthven accorded her all the courtesies due to a wife in public. But he moved to a separate apartment in the Ruthven mansion, and avoided all contact with her in private.

Outwardly, everything remained the same. Georgiana continued to preside over dinners and led the cotillion and quadrille at dances, played faro and desquenet for high stakes, gambled away her handsome allowance at the races, laughed and flirted with young officers and merchants. Boat rides on the Hughli and hunting expeditions to the Sunderbans continued. Ruthven escorted her everywhere, but spoke not more than a few words to her. Sometimes, she caught him staring at her with a wild, brooding expression. At others, he was cold and indifferent. He lay awake every night, alone on his big bed, wracked by a hunger for Georgiana's warm, firm body and then remembered that that body had been offered to Andrew, his son. Together, they had gratified their lust on his bed. He was certain that the child Georgiana now carried was Andrew's. Fresh waves of rage and pain hit him, making him half mad.

It was at a dinner at the Governor General's that Alexander Ruthven heard about his son.

"Young Andrew has been an invaluable officer for us," Lord Cornwallis addressed Alexander Ruthven just as the simple meal ended and the ladies were preparing to retire to repair their coiffures, lip salve and rouge. Georgiana sat stiffly, staring at the Governor General while her husband looked completely bewildered.

"In what way, Your Excellency?" he asked, recovering his composure.

The bluff soldier did not notice the sudden interest everyone displayed nor did he see the ladies watching Georgiana with strange smiles.

"Since the young gentleman is half-Moghul and speaks perfect

Urdu, he is able to perform certain delicate tasks for us ... among the enemy. In fact, he has met Tipu Sultan several times in the guise of an Afghan general, offering to lead the Mysore armies against the Company." Lord Cornwallis laughed. "Fortunately, your son looks more like you than an Afghan so the cunning Sultan of Mysore ordered his arrest."

Georgiana struggled hard to control herself. Alexander Ruthven paled but showed no emotion as he asked, "What happened after that, Your Excellency?"

Lord Cornwallis frowned. "Has he not written informing you of his assignment?"

"Andrew ... is a poor correspondent," the father said with effort, while Georgiana stared at her gloved hands.

Silence reigned for a few moments at the Governor General's table. Even he, usually unperceptive and blunt, could sense vibrations of tension. Too polite to cause embarrassment, the Governor General said," Er ... quite. Well, young Ruthven has been promoted as major, and will be my aide de camp when I go south to take command of our armies shortly. At the moment, the Mysore army is gaining ground against us. But young Ruthven is fighting them bravely."

Rage did not permit Alexander Ruthven from participating in further discussions about the ambitious and able Tipu Sultan of Mysore, who had roused Cornwallis' ire by attacking the Raja of Travancore, an avowed ally of the British. War had begun six months ago, and Andrew Ruthven had joined at once, Cornwallis informed him. Returning home that night, Alexander wrote a letter to his son demanding an immediate explanation.

Several months later, a sealed letter arrived from Bangalore, which town Lord Cornwallis had seized from Tipu and now made his army headquarter. Andrew Ruthven wrote asking his father's pardon, not only for his previous actions but also for his present disobedience. "However, it is imperative for me to obliterate my shame in battle, so that you may regard me with pride and affection once more."

The older Ruthven read the letter several times with tears in his eyes. And without wasting any time, wrote back asking Andrew to return soon, since his father had forgiven him and was proud of him once more.

The war in the south, however, raged on. Lord Cornwallis had come to India, forbidden to wage war against "the country powers" or to conclude treaties with them. This was the purpose of Pitt's India Act of 1884. But the men in Westminster did not realise that the very nature of the British status in India demanded interference, if British possessions were to survive. Despite the Regulating Act of 1772, the Madras Presidency behaved independently and aggressively, provoking the Nizam of Hyderabad to join forces with Hyder Ali of Mysore and Sindhia of Gwalior against the Madras government. From then on, Hyder Ali expanded his realm and his son Tipu Sultan consolidated the gains. He saw in the Company's power, the impediment to his own plans of expansion, and the fulfilment of the dream of a renewed Muslim empire. Able and tolerant of Hindus, Tipu was able to muster the support of southern Hindus to establish his kingdom. He knew that the Company was biding its time to attack. Regarding offense as the best defence, Tipu Sultan attacked Travancore and his agile army cut off General Meddow's heavily encumbered Madras army.

Cornwallis assumed command and soon took Bangalore, Tipu's summer capital. He then marched towards Mysore, but Tipu compelled him to retreat by cutting off supplies in a series of swift strikes. The Governor General fumed, and blamed the Madras army for its clumsiness. General Meddows was obliged to remind him of Saratoga and Yorktown, where Cornwallis had been flayed.

"We will plan an advance...rest assured, gentlemen," Cornwallis shouted. "Tipu Sultan shall not harry us further."

In March 1792, Cornwallis marched once more, traversing the undulant, verdant terrain that lay between Bangalore and Mysore. Andrew Ruthven rode on a spirited charger, occasionally glancing around at the stony hills that ringed rice and ragi fields, ripe with the summer harvest. "Father will be able to forgive me now," he thought. "I have washed away my shame by shedding blood for his honour." The night before the assault, sitting by a campfire in a field not far from the market town of Mandya, Andrew Ruthven wrote a long letter to his father, promising to return as soon as the war against Tipu was over. "Take me back as your son," he ended.

Winter came and went, followed by spring. Leaves unfurled to reveal mango and jamun blossoms in the garden. Nightingales clamoured loudly and incessantly on warm, fragrant nights. Alexander Ruthven paced the lawn, restless and anxious for news of his son. Georgiana, who had recently given birth to a daughter, found she loved the child, because it was the fruit of her love for Andrew, created in joy and pleasure. She could not, for all of Alexander's hostility and contempt, regret the experience of fulfilment she had shared with his son.

Cornwallis was successful in the third advance as the Madras army laid siege to Tipu Sultan's fortified citadel at Seringapatnam. Andrew Ruthven rushed forward recklessly in the front line of cavalry, determined to drive back the Sultan's army. Tipu's territories were annexed; an indemnity of £3 million exacted, and two of Tipu's sons were taken hostages. However, Tipu was allowed to continue as ruler in preference to restoring the inept Wadiyar dynasty to Mysore's throne.

On a hot summer day, when blazing sunshine and hot winds turned even the Hughli into a liquid sheet of fire, an officer from Lord Cornwallis' establishment came to Alexander Ruthven carrying a letter. It was a personal condolence from the Governor General who expressed grief over for the death of Andrew.

"Promoted, to the rank of colonel, much decorated and honoured for his reckless gallantry, you will be comforted to know that Andrew died a hero's death in the battle for Seringapatnam. He knew our position to be hopeless, thwarted as we were by shortage of men and supplies, but Andrew, with a chosen few, decided to ford the swollen river Kaveri and find a breach in the fort walls to facilitate our entry. He was shot by Tipu's soldiers on the rampart."

Alexander Ruthven cried out in agony, causing Georgiana to run to the library, to snatch the letter and read it, in rising pain, until she could endure it no more. Sobbing, she fled to her room to release her grief in heart-breaking tears.

Alexander Ruthven was broken by this blow. His son's betrayal had stunned him, but his son's death left him no hope of reconciliation. He sat for days on the terrace, impervious to the heat of summer, or the duststorms that swirled and eddied around him. For hours he recalled Andrew playing in that lawn, climbing the giant banian trees to explore a raven's nest or succour a squirrel, attended by a cluster of adoring sisters. Andrew growing up to manhood, fighting for fun in the Maratha wars, learning dancing and French from Liselotte ... and then ... Georgiana Andrew, who was to establish a new house of mingled Scots and Moghuls, and who now lay under a tree in the verdant fields skirting the Kaveri in far-away Mysore. He had recovered his honour. His father would always be proud of him.

Alexander Ruthven set out in the midst of that merciless summer for Deogarh. Now, in his wild grief, Alexander Ruthven wanted no one but his Begum, who had borne him the beloved son he had lost. Shirin, he knew, was made of steel and blood. She would console him even when her own heart was breaking. She had spurred him to success, inspired by memories of racial glory and an obstinate ambition to recapture that past glory. Yes, she would tell him what to do, how to recover from this terrible blow.

Deogarh lay blistering in the summer sun. The rocks and stones were ablaze with heat. Alexander rode up to the fortress, eager to fling himself into Shirin's arms, Shirin, who had been his companion of three decades.

Beatrice, his youngest child, received him at the hall. White skinned, blue eyed and auburn haired, she looked incongruous in the Moghul dress. But she was embittered already and had no desire to be British. "Where is your mother, child?" Alexander cried. "Tell her I've come ... with a broken heart. Tell her to forgive me ... tell her to console me now. I can no longer endure this pain!"

"You come too late," Beatrice said coldly, staring at her father.

"Too late?" Alexander echoed, shivering despite the heat.

"Mama died ... after hearing the news of Andraz's death."

"Dead? Shirin?" Ruthven cried shrilly.

Beatrice nodded grimly, glaring at her father. "Why the grief, Janab?" she asked in Urdu. "Did you not send Andraz to battle so that he could die? So that the whore's son could inherit everything?"

Ruthven sat down, trembling and exhausted. "I never sent Andrew to war. He went of his own accord ... to please me, he thought ..."

"No! To retrieve his honour!" Beatrice screamed in rage. "Honour! Because he had lain with his father's whore! It is she you should have banished, not your son! It is she who enticed and snared him to her bed, because her old husband could not satisfy her lust. But no, you are blind to your whore's misdeeds."

"How do you know all this?" Ruthven asked wearily. Beatrice laughed bitterly. "Mademoiselle Fremont keeps us informed. You see, she too was banished for Madame Georgiana."

Alexander rose from his chair. Deogarh ... His proud acquisition, surpassing all his dreams. This was to have been Andrew's home, where he would bring a noble wife and breed children of royal blood. It seemed now like a tomb for his dreams, for all his work. Shirin dead. That relentless, tireless, it seemed, deathless Shirin, who could never accept defeat. Dead from grief and despair.

"Georgiana Manham. What a cursed day was it when I decided to make her pay for her father's sin. Henry Manham not only killed James Ruthven but has from his grave, destroyed both Alexander and Andrew Ruthven," the broken man mused.

For interminable days he sat on the ramparts of the old fort, staring vacantly at the plains below. His thoughts became confused and he could not separate the past from the present. Sometimes he called out to Shirin, sometimes to Andrew, unwilling to acknowledge that both were gone. In a few months, his fiery hair, specked with grey turned white and his piercing, blue eyes seemed always bleary with tears.

Beatrice watched her father and suffered. Her dashing, resolute father had always been the mainstay of her life. Even after he had banished Begum Shirin from Calcutta, Beatrice was secretly proud of her father; proud to be his daughter, unlike her sisters who had banished their father from their hearts. Now to see that dazzling, protean figure prostrate with grief brought out all the inherent kindness in Beatrice's nature. Tentatively, hesitantly, she tried to console the desolate man.

For Alexander, it was a journey of discovery of his daughter. Beatrice reminded him of Shirin. She had the same strength and passion though she also possessed an impulsive kindness, akin to Fiona's. He stayed on in Deogarh, remembering the years with the Begum and their children; their common conquests and triumphs.

In the winter of 1793, Claude, his son by Liselotte, arrived in Deogarh to end the voluntary exile of Alexander Ruthven. "It is time to return to your world, Father," Claude said. "Life has to go on — and though Andrew and the Begum are gone, my mother and your other children remain. Will you renounce us again?"

Alexander Ruthven gazed with dull eyes at his illegitimate son, searching for signs of Andrew in Claude's slight figure, the red-brown hair and grey-green eyes. He found none. Claude was as unobtrusive as Andrew had been flamboyant, as if perpetually apologising for his birth.

"Return to what?" Alexander asked, ignoring Claude's subtle reproach.

"To everything that you built and achieved. That cannot be destroyed by anyone," Claude replied quietly.

Alexander Ruthven nodded. Yes, his heart yearned once again for his home and his many enterprises. He was weary of Deogarh's desolate splendour, especially when the night wind sang a dirge to his dreams of Andrew.

After an absence of eight months, Ruthven returned to Calcutta, to the vast mansion at Alipur where Georgiana waited in dread. She saw him alight from the carriage, aged and broken, and felt a surge of pity, even of remorse, for the man she had hated for so long. The retainers welcomed him in silent homage for they dared not speak before his obvious grief. Claude followed him, unobtrusive but watchful ... and waiting. He had no doubt now of his father's intentions. "It will be interesting to watch," he mused.

Alexander's son by Georgiana too watched the altered being that was his father. Charles Edward had guessed that some terrible episode had altered the happy days of his childhood, and that his gorgeous mother was guilty of some nameless sin. Yet, his admiration for the imperious figure of his father had not dimmed. Unable to contain himself, the nine-year-old burst into the library where Alexander sat at his desk. "Papa!" he said in a quavering voice. "I am glad you have returned. I have ... missed you!"

Alexander Ruthven stared at the little figure in breeches and ruffled shirt, the red-gold curls, his eyes as green as his mother's. Georgiana's son, he thought, the one whom she had planned would be heir. Submerged by a wave of rage, Ruthven said coldly, "I do not wish to see you."

Charles Edward stood frozen on the carpet, his hands clenched. "Papa," he began, but a sob choked him.

"Go away from here."

Charles Edward felt the room sway crazily around him. Biting his lips to stifle tears of anguish, he fled to his ayah, unwilling to see the mother who had contrived to bring misery into his life.

"What happened?" eleven-year-old Deirdre asked. She was now frightened of her father, and appalled by the enormity of what she had done. Yet she was not sorry to have punished Mama, who had always treated her coldly. Did Deirdre know of the violence and hatred which had attended her creation and which had twisted her mind from the first flicker of her life? Unwittingly, she had fulfilled Georgiana's curse, "May this Deirdre bring you greater sorrow."

It was evening when Alexander Ruthven finally summoned Georgiana to the library which she had refurbished in the style of Courtney House in London. He did not look up as she entered, a beautiful and contrite figure, eager to make amends. Staring unseeingly at the ivory mantelpiece where priceless jade statues and Meissen figurines reposed, he spoke in a dry, toneless voice.

"I am making arrangements for you to leave for England with your children. You may stay at my house in Cavendish Square until you have found rooms elsewhere. My agent in London will make payment of your allowance every month." He paused and glanced at her briefly before continuing, "If you agree to a divorce, a handsome settlement shall be made."

Georgiana stared at her husband, the man who had been besotted by her only a few months ago; the man who had delighted in gratifying her every whim. Could he really be asking her to leave him? She watched him in silence until he was forced to look at her. In his cold, antagonistic eyes she saw the Alexander Ruthven who had regarded her with the same expression in London in 1780; the man who had waited a lifetime for revenge.

"What if I refuse?"

"You cannot refuse. I do not wish to keep you as my wife anymore ... not after you ..." Even now, he shuddered at the remembrance of what she had done.

All the pity and remorse she had felt for him throughout the day vanished. "You are not free, Mr. Ruthven, to dispose of me as you wish. Not anymore. You brought me to India as a hostage, a means of satisfying a revenge. You violated me and brought me shame, to avenge a wrong which was done before my birth. I left your house to fend for myself in Calcutta. And then you came to offer marriage on my terms. You cannot ask me to leave now. I am your legal wife ... the mother of your only surviving, legitimate son."

Alexander Ruthven stood up, suddenly straight. "You are quite shameless. But I can still divorce you, on grounds of adultery Madam, and disinherit your son!"

"Can you?" Georgiana asked, eyes glinting with green fires. "Can you divorce me without dishonouring the memory of ... your first-born son?"

Alexander Ruthven stood trembling, clutching the ruffles of lace at his throat, as if he was choking, trying to cry out in pain but all he could do was stare at the dazzling and defiant figure of the hateful woman who had destroyed him and his best-loved child. Suddenly, he wanted to flee from her, from the lure of her gorgeous body, the very house which was the scene of her betrayal and corruption.

"The Manhams are a vile breed! Stay then ... but not here! Ruthven House is closed to you. Go to Garden Reach and spend your days there. I shall not come near you!"

Georgiana trembled. There was a cold finality in his tone. She knew she had lost her dominion over him forever. "Was the world worth losing for a moment's joy?" she wondered, as she climbed the wide, curved staircase to her own room.

Georgiana moved to the villa at Garden Reach with her son and daughter. Though Alexander had wanted to seal Ruthven House, Liselotte pleaded with him to reconsider. "It was our home," she said gently, "where we were all happy once ... yes, mon ami ... the Begum and I, with our children and loyal servants ... our cherished objects. To close the house would be to uproot ourselves."

"I cannot live there again," Alexander observed grimly. "Not after ..."

"Quite so, you and I shall go away for a while ... but let all the children make it their home ..." she paused and said, "and that includes Charles Edward and Deirdre."

For the first time in twenty-one years, Liselotte saw tears in Alexander's cold eyes. Tenderly, her sensitive artist's fingers brushed them away, over the hollowed cheeks and thin, bitter mouth.

"We will go to Deogarh, mon ami, and recapture our youth," she said softly. "And remember all our old dreams."

Alexander Ruthven rose from the chair and placing his head on Liselotte's frail shoulders, wept silently.

Liselotte moved into Ruthven House with Claude, Lucille and Alexina. Later, Alexander coaxed Beatrice, his daughter by Shirin, to join them. Though Liselotte tried her best to create a happy atmosphere in the house, she was not wholly successful. Begum Shirin's mementoes were everywhere as were those of her son. Alexander brooded on them and on the havoc wrought by Georgiana.

Banished to Garden Reach, Georgiana contrived to make herself comfortable in the villa, tended the garden and supervised the education of Deirdre and Charles Edward. Little Adrianne, whom she believed to be Andrew's child, had died soon after birth. Georgiana knew that she must bide her time, as she had once before, but the days seemed interminable now. She was twelve years older and approaching her autumnal years.

The uncertainty of the situation in Europe following Britain's declaration of war on revolutionary France was reflected in India. The rulers of Mysore, Hyderabad and the Maratha principalities intended to use Britain's reverses to their advantage. Tipu Sultan prepared for war with French assistance.

Sir John Shore, the new Governor General was not the right man to deal with this turmoil. Cultured, urbane and incorruptible, he preferred the study of Indian civilisation to the tangled webs of Indian politics. For this reason, he sought the company of Georgiana Manham at her retreat in Garden Reach.

It was a life Georgiana had envisaged; this tranquil, leisured existence, though the dream had been bound with Robert de Courtney, in the Earl's estate of Ashville, as a respected leader of society. Garden Reach, the sultry climate, the fisherfolk and boatmen, wharves and cotton mills, ships carrying merchandise to Europe were all alien to the world she had once cherished. Yet, determined not to acknowledge defeat, she played her role with steely grace, organising soirees and dances, picnics by the riverside, boat rides on moonlit nights, and forays to the Governor General's house to meet the important and the powerful. It gave her a twist of pain to pass Ruthven House in her smart cabriolet, wondering how Liselotte's children lived while she herself yearned to take her place at the head of the table in the yellow, silk-lined dining room.

New houses had come up in the once silent street, shops had grown in number at Park Street; Calcutta seemed to be busier and more prosperous. Returning to her riverside villa after these excursions, Georgiana tried not to succumb to a deep melancholy at the gradual shadowing of life's light.

The advent of Richard, Marquis of Wellesley did not improve matters. Haughty, self-willed and remote, he strove to enact the role of a Roman consul in India.

Richard Wellesley was an aristocrat and an autocrat. The people of Calcutta, who came to call on the new Governor General, returned subdued and perturbed. Georgiana scrutinised the short man with the sharp-featured face that bespoke an imperious temper, ambition and restless energy. His keen eyes observed the assorted society of Calcutta: "the British adventurers aping aristocrats," "the blowsy and overdressed European women," "the bizarre Indians with singular customs." Shrinking from contact, the haughty Lord Saheb decided "to entrench myself with forms and ceremonies and introduce much state into the whole appearance of my establishment and expel all approaches to familiarity."

Bizarre as he considered Indian customs, Wellesley had, nevertheless, the European's fascination for oriental ceremonials. But first, he needed an appropriate backdrop. The magnificent new Government House, designed on Keddleston, became thereafter the citadel of British power. Here, he ruled in solitary but Moghul splendour with guards posted at every gate, liveried servants at every door. When he rode a phaeton or coach through the streets of Calcutta, the populace scattered like pigeons on hearing the hooves of horses ridden by half a dozen dragoons.

The pose of a Roman consul that Wellesley adopted was possibly a residue of his classical studies at Oxford though his actions accorded well with the mood of Roman legions which traversed Europe, establishing Roman rule. Richard Wellesley believed that the Indian princes were incapable of maintaining the stability or tranquillity necessary for the conduct of British commerce. The Nizam, the Peshwa, the Ranas and Nawabs were perpetually at war, seizing and reseizing each other's territories, or threatening Britain's. Paramountcy of British power was imperative. He prepared to meet the challenge.

Twenty-five-year old Claude Ruthven watched these events with growing fascination and determined to be part of the circle which had gathered around the new Governor General. He had grown up in the shadow of his elder half-brother, Andrew, whose future had so concerned Alexander Ruthven. But now, as Alexander's heir, Claude decided to further his own prospects. Obtaining a recommendation from his godfather, the aged General Claude Martin, now living in his exotic villa, Farhad Baksh at Lucknow, Claude Ruthven waited impatiently for an audience with Wellesley.

The Marquis regarded Claude as one of the "adventurers" whom he distrusted though the connection with General Martin intrigued him. It was a time of hired mercenary generals. Benoit de Boigne, George Thomas and Perron were carving out territories for their princes and for themselves. Wellesley deemed it judicious to offer an opportunity to a young man so eager to serve and who had a renowned general as a relative to boot.

Claude Fremont Ruthven soon became a favourite of Wellesley, particularly after his exploits in Mysore during the final battle with Tipu Sultan in 1798. He returned to Calcutta with the victorious army, eager to relate his exploits at Seringapatnam, which had now extended British hegemony to the Carnatic. What he omitted to mention was that he had seen the son of Andrew by a Mysore noblewoman. "If my father finds out about the existence of Andrew's son, I will be set aside. I shall not return to the shadows again!"

Nor did he. Claude Ruthven became an important man in Calcutta and was considered for appointment as Resident to Mysore or a Maratha prince, while the aggressive Governor General pushed forward his plans for subsidiary alliances, whereby protection would be given to those Indian rulers who recognised the Company's suzerainty. While Claude exulted in Wellesley's policy, Liselotte smiled ironically and commented, "It is strange that the Governor General, a fervent opponent of Bonaparte, should follow the latter's policy."

"It will unite India," Claude retorted.

"No one, except Emperor Ashoka, has ever united India," old Alexander Ruthven murmured.

Claude now dominated Ruthven House. His new social status enabled his two sisters to marry well. Alexander and Liselotte retired to Deogarh, leaving Claude to enjoy the wealth and position he had craved for twenty-six years.

Hearing of these developments at her Garden Reach villa, Georgiana at last resolved to return to England. "There is nothing more to be hoped for," she told a friend. "Once Claude succeeds his father, my position will be precarious, if not desperate." She wrote to Alexander Ruthven, agreeing to a divorce in return for a handsome settlement and was immensely relieved when her husband replied, agreeing to her terms. "I thank you," he ended, "for this small mercy. I can now honour my dear Liselotte with the title of "Madame Ruthven" — a promise made but denied for years through my folly. I will ensure the comfort and prosperity of you and your children in England. God speed you on your journey home."

Georgiana left for England in the winter of 1801, twenty years after her arrival in India. The child she had then carried within her now stood beside her, a wild and beautiful girl of twenty years, distorted by secret grief and fury. On her other side stood sixteen-year-old Charles Edward, sombrely watching the shoreline of Calcutta recede as the barge glided down the Ganges towards the open sea. The only relatives to see them off had been

Fiona Latimer and her son, Ian. Otherwise, Georgiana left as lonely as she had arrived, in the ship "*Crocodile*" twenty years ago. As the ship floated downstream, Georgiana was suddenly aware of her attachment to that vast and verdant land that had served as the backdrop to her joys and sorrows, her triumphs and ordeals. "It is not as if I am going back home," she murmured to her silent children. "It is as if I am leaving behind something well loved and familiar for a great unknown."

PART II

CHARLES EDWARD RUTHVEN
(1807 — 1847)

CHARACTERS

Charles Edward Ruthven
Lady Eleanor Ruthven
Lady Cressida
Catherine Ruthven
Julian Ruthven
Ian Latimer
Brajesh Chowdhury
Indumati Chowdhury
Annapurna Chowdhury
Sudhir Chowdhury
Rana Nahar Singh
Rani Urmila

16

Return of the Native

Georgiana Manham Ruthven stood at the head of the wide staircase to receive the visitors to her 'at home'. Though she smiled warmly at each of the announced guests, her emerald eyes held a flicker of impatience as they swept over the titled or important personages. She craned her long neck slightly to glimpse occasionally the next approaching figure. A shadow of disappointment crossed her face, only to be replaced by a winning smile as she exclaimed, kissed and curtsied, only to wait again.

Then he came, an immense and opulent figure, affecting a majesty that eluded him. Georgiana sank like a swaying flower on her knees, bowing her golden head. George, the Prince Regent of Britain, smiled appreciatively, his pale, protruberant eyes reposing on the lady's swelling bosom, bare, gleaming shoulders and shapely arms. When she kissed his hand he held them tightly and pulled her up, to plant a kiss on her reluctant lips. Georgiana coloured prettily, not because the Prince Regent had kissed her but because Lord Moira stood behind the Prince, with a sardonic smile on his handsome face. Then he moved forward and kissed her hand. Now her hands lingered on his. They smiled at each other and then Lord Moira moved on, into the splendid drawing room.

Regency England provided Georgiana with an appropriate background to her personality and aspirations. "Nabob Ruthven", as she now referred to her husband, had enabled her to set up house in Cavendish Square, in a beautiful red brick Jacobean mansion, which had belonged to a Scottish laird before 1745, and had then been forfeited and presented to Walter Manham for his 'valour' at Culloden. In1781, the house had passed to Alexander Ruthven, after his success at faro and desquenet tables against Freddy Manham. Ruthven had changed the name of the house, emblazoning his name and that of the abode — Ruthven's Den — on the brass plate, but he had never lived there. It was the home of his father's murderer, the scene of his sister's degradation. It had fallen vacant in 1790, with the death of Freddy and the marriage of the Manham sisters.

Georgiana came back to Cavendish Square, not as Manham's daughter but as Ruthven's wife. She brought to it the splendour of her Indian sojourn; imparting to the elegant baroque house, the opulence of gold candlesticks, ivory statues, silver plates, brocade curtains, peacock-feathered fans, and copper braziers — just as she had once brought the elegance of Nash and Adam to the ornate Ruthven House in Calcutta. Georgiana held court, attired in Benaras brocade in the evenings and diaphanous Dacca muslin in the morning, with flowered Murshidabad silk for an afternoon ride in her high phaeton. Berber and Arab horses bred by Godolphin drew her coach or cabriolet. Six Indian servants dressed in immense turbans, ballooning pantaloons and waistcoats clashed with the more sober cockney servants recruited locally. Her jewels never ceased to elicit exclamations from women and speculation by men.

Fables of her wealth drew impecunious and handsome men, stories of her connections attracted the ambitious while her rich, mature beauty dazzled others. She swept through London society in triumph; from the feminine effusions of Devonshire House to the masculine stimulations of Holland House, the political activities of the Cecils, the intrigues of the Melbournes and the extravagance of Lord Moira.

It was he who had introduced Georgiana to the Prince Regent, but the friendship had proved costly; 'Prinny' liked Lucullan feasts and Oriental homage. Nor was he averse to 'touching' her for a loan, sending Georgiana in panic to the elderly Lord Moira.

A wise and patient man, Lord Moira valued Georgiana's friendship. He found her widely read, well informed, and with an intuitive judgement of Indian affairs. He was impressed too by her devotion to Warren Hastings, whom she entertained on her return, and he laughed when she imitated Wellesley's haughty demeanour. Through Lord Moira, Georgiana entered the world of politicians and generals caught in an epic struggle against Napoleon Bonaparte. Yet, a part of her remained attached to India, to the events on those sultry plains. She read of Lord Minto's rule with mixed feelings but she could not help respecting him.

When Minto was still known as Sir George Eliot he joined with Edmund Burke to impeach Warren Hastings who, however, emerged exonerated in 1795. Georgiana's gratitude to the former Governor General had not endeared her to the Whig gentleman whom she had met at the Melbournes' or Hollands'. Yet, in time, she recognised Lord Minto's humanity and liberality. Like many brought up in the spirit of the enlightenment of eighteenth century, Lord Minto believed that progress could be achieved by rationalism, education and the curbing of unbridled power. As an Englishman, he wished to safeguard British interests in India but as a humane, intelligent man, he could not ignore the injustice prepetrated at times by the policies of the East India Company. The Governor General's hands were full with the rise of Maharaja Ranjit Singh in Punjab, mutinies in Bombay and Vellore, the French occupation of Mauritius and the depredations of the Pindaris in Central India. He tried to check the aggressive missionaries, who had begun a campaign of revilement of Hinduism. Lord Minto did all this with an elegance of manner and quiet humour, which smoothed his path. He encouraged and gathered around him young men of talent such as Metcalfe and Mountstuart Elphinstone.

Georgiana learned too that Lord Minto had been kind to Alexander Ruthven and to "Madame Liselotte Ruthven". He had recognised the undoubted talents of Claude, who was a hero of the second Maratha war. Sighing with resignation, Georgiana stifled her feelings of anger and vexation, recognising the fact that Liselotte and her son had long waited for such honours, while she, Georgiana, had wrested them in Calcutta and was doing so in London once more.

Perhaps the greatest honour was the triumph over the Courtneys of Ashville. Her maternal cousin, Robert de Courtney, was now the Earl of Ashville: florid, gouty and bleary eyed, with a pretty but insipid wife from the Tory landed gentry. His first wife had died long ago in childbirth. Looking at him, Georgiana wondered how she had ever persuaded herself to love him. The Whig Courtneys had, to be sure, lost the eminence they had enjoyed in the eighteenth century. Constant warfare with France and continental blockades had impoverished their bastions — their vast estates. Moreover, the French Revolution had produced a reaction in England against the spirit of the Age of Enlightenment represented by the eminent Whig families. Prince Regent depended on the Tories and excluded the Whigs from positions in government. The descendants of Norman-French barons were now gratified to claim Georgiana Ruthven as a kinswoman, because even though she was a woman with a nebulous past, and dubious morals she obviously had glittering prospects.

Georgiana stormed Courtney Castle as a medieval knight may have done. It was the place she had cherished and coveted in her youth but it was also the place that closed its doors on her after Alexander Ruthven created a scandal, thereby sealing her fate. Now those heavy, brass-studded oak portals were opened to her as she drove up in her dark blue barouche one spring day in 1804.

The medieval baronial manor of the de Courtneys had been built in the thirteenth century, a crude stone edifice with square Norman towers, arrow slits and keeps from where missiles were shot and hot oil poured upon a rival baron's soldiery. The graduation of the robber barons of Plantagenet times to earls under the Tudors brought changes in the castle. A wing was added in imitation of the Florentine style, and embellished further with the gaiety of Jacobean baroque. The facade was inspired by Adam.

Georgiana let her gaze wander from the huge rambling edifice to the woods and downs surrounding it, the lake and unused drawbridge. She remembered halcyon days spent in the enchanting place when her mother, Orinthia, daughter of the old Earl Geoffrey, had brought Georgiana there for holidays; when she had begun to dream of being the chatelaine here, as wife of Robert de Courtney. Now he stood before the massive oak door to welcome his never-to-be bride and "dear cousin".

Lord Robert's kiss was like the brush of a dead leaf on her cheek. It roused nothing but waning memories of vernal desires. His wife, Lady Clarissa, a pretty, pouting woman, surveyed the "nabob's lady" with envy and awe. In twenty-five years, Georgiana's escapades had become family legend.

Georgiana soon realised the immediate provocation for the effusive welcome. Cousin Robert, who had rejected her as a bride, sought her as a mother-in-law for one of his three daughters: sixteen-year-old Lydia, fourteen-year-old Eleanor by Robert's first wife and the beautiful eleven-year-old Cressida by Lady Clarissa.

Georgiana played the game, receiving the homage of her aristocratic relations with the graciousness of a monarch. If she felt a brief pang of regret that Clarissa was the chatelaine of this ancient house and its traditions, as time went on, she realised that her turbulent and colourful life in India had certainly been more satisfying than Clarissa's sedate and predictable existence.

Once news of the de Courtneys' rapprochement with Mrs. Ruthven spread, other conservative blue-blooded families opened their doors to the flamboyant "nabob's lady" from Calcutta. That she wore diaphanous dresses over a splendid voluptuous figure or that she had numerous lovers, seemed of little consequence when she was an intimate of the Prince Regent, a friend of Lord Moira, and known to the prime minister. Her singular habit of chewing betel nuts, taking a pinch of snuff or smoking a hookah were considered an essential part of her exotic personality. Yet amidst the gaiety and glitter of Regency London, Georgiana missed her Calcutta house, the burnished gold of the autumn light, the cloudless, azure skies as well as the violent Kal-baisakhi storms of April and the clamour of birds at night. She had left a part of herself behind in the hot, humid valleys by the Ganges.

Twenty-three-year old Charles Edward, however, shared little of his mother's sentiments. Uprooted from the land of his birth at sixteen and lost in the alien world of Eton, the "nabob's" son had determined to forget the land and people and assumed the airs of a cold, aloof Englishman. He was happy in the cloisters of Oxford, where he excelled in Classics and languages, his eclectic ears facilitating the learning of Sanskrit and Persian.

"Do you disapprove of me as well?" Georgiana asked with a sardonic smile.

Charles Edward regarded his mother with something between impatience and compassion."Of course, I disapprove of you, Ma'am. Do you think it pleases me to hear of your flirtations with bloated satyrs or young adventurers, or hear innuendoes of your past?"

Georgiana lost her insouciant expression as she advanced towards her son, standing cool and aloof before her. "Have you ever thought what I endured in Calcutta, as a ... captive concubine of Alexander Ruthven, and how I finally got him to offer marriage?'

Charles Edward retreated before her smouldering gaze. "I was miserable, boy," she said softly. "And yet I carried on, determined to succeed...until I fell in love ... with my stepson."

"Stop!" Charles shouted.

"No! You must hear so that you know ... and do not judge me as your father has done."

"I refuse to hear!" Charles retorted through clenched teeth.

"You shall hear, my son! I loved Andrew who was of my age... a handsome, kindly, generous man. We laughed and conversed in joy and made love in joy. I bore him a child ... oh yes, your sister Adrianne was his. Alexander Ruthven guessed that. But I could not go away with Andrew ... I wanted to be a grande dame ..." Her voice broke as she struggled for composure.

Charles Edward had taken refuge near the marble fireplace,

where he stood staring at the flames. Deirdre born of violence, he out of loveless lust and Adrianne, out of illegal love. Deirdre had died soon after arriving in London. Georgiana had not grieved for her for long. Deirdre had been the cause of her grief. "If only the girl had been stillborn ... or better still, never born at all!" Georgiana thought bitterly. "What a family! How little the world knew as they courted the London Ruthvens."

"So, I shall be a grande dame, my son ... and run through my settlement! And you ... will wed my beauteous niece, Lady Cressida de Courtney, daughter of an earl and granddaughter of a duke. Then you may wash away all the squalor and scandals of the Ruthvens!'

Charles Edward coloured. The reference to Cressida quickened his pulse. How astute his mother was, he thought ruefully. She knew everything. Coldly, he replied, "Cressida de Courtney will have more eligible bachelors to choose from." He paused. "Besides, I am joining my future regiment in a month or so."

Fear tore at Georgiana. Until now she had not realised how deeply she loved her son. "Where will you go?"

"Spain, Ma'am."

Georgiana turned away. Suddenly, the glitter of London wearied her. Life without her son would be fearfully lonesome.

"Must you go, my son?"

"Yes, Mother, I must. I ... do not wish to live under the shadow of Alexander Ruthven. If I make a name for myself ... you will be proud of me."

Georgiana smiled, her eyes bright with tears. "I am already proud of you, Charles Edward. Your performance at Oxford was excellent. People speak of you with respect. Lovely Cressida pines for you. What more could I ask ... except that you be a little generous and forgiving to your mother?"

Charles moved towards her, taking her hand to kiss. "It would be impertinent of me to forgive you — a woman of so much courage and spirit. Look after yourself, Mama. I will be home soon."

Before leaving for Spain, Charles Edward visited Courtney Hall to see his second cousin, Lady Cressida, whose brilliant eyes and corn-coloured hair had ensnared him. In this pursuit, at least, he knew that he had his mother's approval as Georgiana thoroughly approved of such a bride for her son.

Sixteen-year-old Cressida was a gay, vibrant creature with a saucy tongue and ready wit. She made her older half-sisters seem insipid and insignificant when she led the dance at Courtney or at London. Sometimes, watching her, Charles Edward saw a reflection of his mother as she must have been at Cressida's age. She had, he soon discovered, the same capacity for passion, as her lips discovered his, and her hands caressed his temples and throat. At twenty-four, Charles Edward was still innocent. Cressida's carnal allure affected him like a heady wine.

"Marry me now, Charles!" Cressida murmured, kissing his mouth hungrily. "Why should we wait?"

Charles Edward released himself with a great effort. Those wild green eyes — Courtney eyes — dissolved his will. "What would you do as my wife while I am at war, my sweet?" he asked hoarsely. "It is better that you enjoy yourself while I am away. We will marry when the Peninsular Campaign is over."

"I want you now," she whispered, her hands moving along his neck to his shoulders and chest.

He laughed shakily, amazed and yet pleased by her candour. "We will marry, I promise you, as soon as I return."

Charles Edward was away in the Iberian Peninsula for the next three years, sharing the hardships of his men, learning to endure hunger and cold in wordless acceptance. But sitting by the campfire at night, while the Spanish zhitanos sang mournful gypsy songs, Charles Edward wrote long passionate letters to Cressida de Courtney, and lying in a snow-bound Pyrenees village, he shut out the scenes of war and bloodshed by conjuring up visions of Cressida dancing or Cressida riding over the turf at Ashville on her wild mare.

Charles Edward made a name for himself in the Peninsular Campaign. His commanders were as impressed by his valour and enterprise as by his spontaneous kindness which was belied by the habitual aloofness he assumed as a shield against the world. His men adored him and were ready to follow him on any daring escapade in the Pyrenees to confound the French. Recognition in the war gave Charles Edward a new identity of his own, one that had nothing to do with his nabob father or extravagant mother. In the wilds of Iberia, amidst the harsh landscape and inflexible Spaniards, he even schooled himself to forget India, though at times the heat, star-strewn sky and mournful songs recalled to him the land he had vowed to forget.

In 1811, Charles Edward obtained furlough to visit England. The joy and excitement of homecoming was dimmed at finding his elder half-brother Claude Fremont Ruthven visiting Cavendish Square. Georgiana was civil but Charles saw that she was visibly distraught by his visit. Claude was, however, quite entertained by her discomfiture. He was now the heir of Alexander, while she, who had banished both the Begum and Liselotte, had herself been banished to a life of dependent frivolity.

The brothers Ruthven faced each other. They had not met before. Claude had been nine years old when Georgiana sent him and his mother to the Garden Reach villa. Now, after exactly thirty years, he had come to vindicate his position. Charles Edward met Claude's veiled eyes with his direct gaze, seeing in them a legacy of past hatreds and resentments. More than ever he wished to distance himself from the turmoils of his Indian psst.

Georgiana seethed in fury that Alexander's illegitimate son by "the Frenchwoman" should be the heir to the Ruthven fortune instead of his legal son. Charles Edward reminded her of his Manham blood, "A disqualification, surely in my father's eyes."

Claude Ruthven had set up residence on Half Moon Street, entertaining lavishly and being entertained. "The young nabob," polite society whispered, "is looking for a suitable bride."

Georgiana spent a few moments remembering the pretty and gentle Liselotte who had managed to be happy in the end — as "Madame Ruthven". Content to love, eager to please, yearning for security, Liselotte was Alexander's anchor. Cast aside, she offered no resistance, taken back, she showed no reluctance. "A water hyacinth," Georgiana mused, "forever bending to the flow of water around her ... and thereby surviving."

Charles Edward lost no time in visiting Courtney House in Berkeley Square. He had dreamt of this visit for three years, envisaging how he would be united with the desirable Lady Cressida.

Cressida met him coldly. The young girl who had quickened his desire with her ardour now took refuge behind form and procedures, refusing to ride with him in Hyde Park or meet him at Almacks or even to invite him to Courtney Castle in Ashville for a few days. Unable to contain himself, Charles Edward asked, "Cressida, what is the matter? Why have you changed?"

The green eyes were derisive now, and the perfect features seemed pinched. "Have I changed, Mr. Ruthven? Indeed, it must be so. For that, you have only yourself to blame."

"What have I done, Cressida dearest? Tell me at once and I will remedy the matter!" he exclaimed, bewildered.

Her laugh was mirthless. "The matter is certainly beyond remedy, Sir."

He caught her wrist and pulled her close. "Tell me! Whatever it is, I will set right!"

Cressida wrenched her hand free. "You cannot set right the fact that your-half brother, the illegitimate son of your father by his French mistress, is the heir to the Ruthven fortune."

Charles Edward stared at Cressida, who went on. "Why did you not tell me before?" she asked sharply.

"I thought you knew." He paused, then asked in a strange voice, "Was it important?"

Cressida was taken aback by his tone. The ardour was gone from his blue-green eyes. Had she known the notorious "nabob" Ruthven, Cressida would have recognised the same hardness in Charles.

"Yes, it matters," she whispered at last.

"I see."

Cressida did not dare to look at him now, fearing the effect of his handsome, tender face on her. Her eyes were level with his chin and she glanced at the chiselled mouth which had kissed her ardently not so long ago. She wanted to feel his strong, gentle arms around her body and feel the response of her flesh to his. Cressida had often imagined erotic scenes where he, her eager, tender lover would possess her. But now she steeled herself to forget those cravings. He was a man without a fortune and no future except as an officer of the Hussars. She turned away abruptly.

"Am I to understand that you do not wish me to ask for you in marriage?" Charles Edward asked in a toneless voice.

Cressida nodded. Charles Edward stood for a long moment, staring at the beautiful girl he had dreamt of for three years: beautiful, passionate, impulsive Cressida who had turned out to be cold and calculating.

"Rest assured, Ma'am, that I will not vex you further with my attentions. Good afternoon."

Cressida watched him go and stared out of the bay windows as he leapt onto his horse, a tall, imposing figure with reddish-gold hair and chiselled features. A Plantagenet prince, one of her stupid sisters had said. Yes, he could be one, but for the fact that he had no throne to inherit and no largesse to disburse.

Anyone watching Charles Edward Ruthven galloping across Hyde Park and across crowded Bond Street, would have considered him mad, as he rode recklessly between speeding phaetons and coaches. He was quite unconscious of his surroundings, thinking only of the girl who had spurned him with so little ceremony, the girl for whom he had craved through blizzards and cannonades.

"Fool that I am!" he muttered, colliding into a brewery cart drawn by heavy dray horses, and knocking out a few casks of ale. "Watch it guv!" the whiskered carter shouted. "A fancy cove like you won't be smart with ale on your breeches!"

Charles Edward muttered a curse and rode more slowly, thinking now not of Cressida de Courtney but Claude Fremont Ruthven who had contrived to cast a shadow on his life. A new rage surged within him, as he dismounted before Ruthven House and strode up the stairs to his room.

Salim, the Indian footman, a Bengali Muslim whom Georgiana called "Suleiman the Magnificent" bowed, but glanced apprehensively at the butler, who murmured, "His Nibs is in high dudgeon."

Salim lost no time in informing his Memsaheb of the Master Saheb's temper. Georgiana came with some trepidation to the room where Charles Edward was flinging clothes into several valises.

"What are you doing, my love?" she asked, eyes wide with astonishment.

"Returning to Spain, Ma'am," Charles replied through clenched teeth.

"But why? You have an entire fortnight left! Why, you have just arrived!"

Charles Edward suddenly stood motionless and looked at his mother. "There is no purpose in staying. You see, Mama," he said grimly, "I came to ask ... Cressida for her hand." He stopped, unable to continue.

"Has she ... ?" Georgiana did not dare utter the word. Charles nodded. "Refused ... me ... "

"But why! She has been ... so ... enamoured of you!" Georgiana cried.

Charles Edward's handsome mouth twisted into a bitter smile. "Old sins have long shadows, Mama. Your father set into motion events which have now overtaken me; his brutality, my father's revenge, your disgrace and Claude's triumph." He paused. "This is Father's final revenge, you see, to cut me off from what I cherish."

Georgiana stifled a cry of pain upon seeing her son's desolate face. "My love, it is Claude who has done this mischief — not your father," she said.

Charles Edward shook his head. "It is all the same," he muttered, "and I am weary of it all. Perhaps one day I will forget the Ruthvens and Courtneys."

Georgiana shook her head. "They are in your blood. You are both," she whispered.

A day before Charles' departure, Salim the footman ushered in a young woman into Georgiana's drawing room at Cavendish Square. She stood by the tall windows, her intense gaze moving from the ivory statues of Hindu gods, to the brass jugs, Rajput miniatures, to the carved sandalwood tables. Drawn by the novelty of form and colour, she moved closer and was lost in contemplation when the door opened.

Charles Edward started; at first sight she resembled Cressida yet she was different. The eyes were dark green, the hair a deep chestnut and her slim, graceful figure lacked Cressida's Junoesque charm. Lady Eleanor de Courtney turned, and seeing him, dropped a brief curtsey.

"Good afternoon. My mother is not at home; she is visiting Princess Esterhazy." He spoke curtly, without intending to.

Lady Eleanor nodded, her pale cheeks afire with vexation. However, her eyes, wide and dark green, remained calm. "I am aware that Aunt Georgiana is out. It is you I came to see."

Charles Edward was surprised. "What can I do for you, Lady Eleanor?" he asked stiffly.

"May I sit down?" her voice quavered.

"Please do. Would you care for refreshments?" he asked in an attempt to amend his rudeness.

"Thank you, but I too must hasten to attend the tea party at Princess Esterhazy's. I came for only a moment to speak to you."

Charles Edward's face remained impassive, hiding the turmoil within. Lady Eleanor was not beautiful as Cressida; indeed, her clean-cut features had more character than beauty but her eyes had depth.

"What can you have to say to me, Lady Eleanor?" he asked quietly.

Eleanor paused, hands clenched tight on her flowered silk dress.

"I ... came ... to ask you to ... pardon my sister for ... her conduct." Her voice was almost inaudible but Charles heard, and felt his breath catch in his throat.

"Cressida is young; merely nineteen ... and much accustomed to being admired and pampered. She did not intend to be ..."

"She did not intend to put matters so bluntly!" Charles interposed with a sardonic smile.

Lady Eleanor coloured again. She had heard Cressida speak to Charles Edward Ruthven and had been mortified that her sister, albeit half-sister, could use words so coarse.

"I can only plead for her, Mr. Ruthven, and beg you to pardon Cressida for her ... youth and impetuosity," Lady Eleanor said calmly.

Charles Edward laughed derisively. "She is not impetuous, Lady Eleanor. Her reason for refusing my offer of marriage is that she has a hard, practical head. Impetuous women ... marry ... paupers." He rose, indicating that the discussion was over. Lady Eleanor also rose, visibly distressed.

"May I wish a you safe journey ... and a victorious return from the Peninsular Campaign, Mr. Ruthven?" she said gravely, extending her slender, cool hand. "May we look forward to seeing you at home then?"

He bowed and barely touched the hand, afraid that the touch would ignite tactile memories of another Courtney sister.

"I thank you, Lady Eleanor ... but I would prefer not to visit your home again."

Eleanor de Courtney stood before him for a long moment, looking at his anguished face. In her study of Greek Classics, she had read of Greek tragic heroes going to wars. Charles reminded her of just such a tormented man. If he should die ... Eleanor checked back a spontaneous cry and took his hand in hers, bringing it to her lips. "May you return safely," she whispered, tears springing to her eyes. Then, turning abruptly, she fled from the room.

Charles Edward watched her leave in utter amazement. As soon as he recovered, he rushed out of the room, to call her back but was in time only to see her spring into the coach. He watched the coach glide over the road, past clipped hedges, spreading trees and park railings until it disappeared in the shaded square beyond.

Charles Edward Ruthven fought bravely in the siege of Badajoz and received a medal to reward his valour. The Duke of Wellington noticed that this young officer had a capacity for reckless daring that few men possessed. It was as if Charles Edward was looking for a glorious death on the battlefield.

The Peninsular War ended in 1812, but young Colonel Ruthven stayed on in Spain, assisting in the interminable proceedings to restore the incompetent and obscurantist Spanish Bourbons to the throne of Ferdinand and Isabella. Privately, he thought Joseph Bonaparte a more able man than the stupid Charles IV while the lascivious Queen was more an embarrassment than Julie Clery Bonaparte, whose only passion was dresses and jewels. In Madrid, he heard of the rout of Napoleon's Grand Army in Russia and its disastrous return across vast snowy wastes. Unable to delay his return any longer, Charles Ruthven came to London in the spring of 1813, just as the allied armies of England, Prussia, Austria and Russia prepared to destory the remnants of the Grand Army at Leipzig.

Homecoming held a great surprise for Charles Edward. He found, on his arrival, his father ensconced at Cavendish Square. Speechless, he stared at the old man of seventy-eight, dressed in the clothes of the 1780s, white haired, stooping and emaciated. The once vivid bue eyes gleamed momentarily on seeing his third and least-loved son.

Sensing trouble, Georgiana rushed in and said, "Your father has been here for several months now. We will be going to Scotland in summer. He needs rest ... and peace."

Alexander Ruthven looked at his attractive, ageing wife. Her corn-coloured hair was almost silver now, but her figure was still firm and full, like a late, lingering autumn rose. For a moment, Alexander Ruthven's blue eyes flashed in memory of the blind passions she had roused in him thirty years ago. Then he stared at his son; tall and handsome, the harsh Ruthven features tempered by the Courtney breeding and the Manham vitality. He remembered his other son, the well-loved Andrew, who had been his very image, so like a Ruthven that none might guess he was born of a Moghul mother. And Claude, dark haired, hazel eyed like his lovely, gentle Liselotte, though more tenacious and astute, like his godfather General Claude Martin. Both gone, as were their mothers.

"Tell him why I am here!" Alexander commanded his wife. Georgiana sat down next to her husband, her hand on his gnarled, shrivelled ones.

"Charles ..." she began in obvious uncertainty, "Your father is here ... to ... hand over ... and instruct you ... regarding his ... estates and ..."

Charles Edward was surprised. "Indeed? Why? Is Claude not competent anymore? Or has he also fallen from grace?'

"Dead!" Alexander Ruthven cried hoarsely. "He died in an epidemic that swept Calcutta. But I ... lived!" His voice broke in despair.

"I ... am sorry ... for you," Charles Edward murmured, staring at the broken old man.

"Are you, Charles Edward?" Alexander Ruthven asked grimly, his blue eyes glittering. "Do you truly feel pity for one who has wronged you all your life?"

Charles Edward did not speak. It was difficult to know the truth, even of one's own heart.

"Or are you glad that I am punished? Yes, that must be so. Glad you must be. Claude could not have been a kind and generous brother ... though Liselotte was a sweet soul."

"I ... have nothing against Claude or his mother," Charles Edward said coldly. "They have had reasons to resent me ... and my mother. We ... were the intruders."

Alexander Ruthven let out a hoarse cry of grief ... for all the sorrows he had caused — to Shirin, to Liselotte, Georgiana, and to his sons by those women. Yet, he had loved them all, each in a different way. Except Charles. He had never cared much for this boy yet it was now Charles who must take his place.

"I have come to make you my heir, Charles Edward," Alexander announced. Charles Edward stared at his father in surprise. Even the news of Claude's death had not prepared him for this announcement. His astonished gaze moved to his mother, as if to seek confirmation. She returned his gaze, fearfully, nodding assent.

Charles was twenty-eight years old now. For twenty years, he had experienced the neglect and indifference of his father. — ever since Andrew Ruthven had died in Mysore. Andrew Ruthven — the favourite son of Alexander and the lover of Georgiana. Savagely, Charles pushed back the memory of that blazing day in Calcutta when Lord Cornwallis' emissary had brought the news to the vast mansion. He remembered his father's wild grief and his mother's secret stormy tears. His father had lost his beloved child and his mother an ardent lover. That day Charles had hated them both. From that day on, he had felt his father's dislike of him, springing from the fact that he was the child of a treacherous wife. Not once in twenty years had Alexander Ruthven displayed the least interest or affection for him.

"I do not wish to inherit your fortune, Sir," Charles Edward said coldly.

Georgiana almost leapt up from the chaise longue. "Don't be ridiculous!" she muttered fiercely, going up to her son. "This is the most fortunate thing that has happened to you. It will open all doors to you, and give you wealth, importance, success. You cannot refuse the inheritance!"

"I am refusing it," Charles said loudly so that his father could hear.

Georgiana regarded him with blazing eyes. "You will not refuse your inheritance. You will accept it," she said in a low, ferocious voice. I have endured many indignities for you. You will not deprive me of my reward!"

Charles Edward moved back a step, perturbed by the subdued violence of her manner. "I will not permit you to refuse the inheritance!" she said grimly.

"I am joining the Duke of Wellington's army shortly," Charles Edward told his mother. "I may not see you for some time."

Georgiana's heart smouldered in fury. "Foolish boy!" she muttered. "This fickle pride will leave you alone and bitter in a world where men are measured by success."

"I will follow my own inclinations. Ma'am," he said and left the room.

Alexander Ruthven stared after him. "The boy has spirit," he muttered.

"He is a Ruthven after all," Georgiana taunted, "but I shall tame him, as I have other Ruthvens."

London society was curious to see the aged "nabob" who had returned home after almost sixty years in India. The son of a fugitive rebel had returned in triumph. Georgiana changed her strategy overnight. She shed all resentment of her husband and decided to project him as an extraordinary man, emphasising that with daring and enterprise, the rebel's son became in turn a rich trader, then a commander of a royal Rajput army and the ruler of a jagir. "No man without great qualities could achieve so much," she often told her guests, whenever Charles Edward was near.

Princess Lieven, wife of the Russian ambassador and Princess Esterhazy, wife of the Austrian envoy, were Georgiana's friends. They assisted Georgiana in her plan. Suddenly, invitations flooded the Ruthven house at Cavendish Square. Georgiana entertained ceaselessly, as if her lost beloved had returned. Alexander Ruthven was sought after, endowed with the glamour of a condottiero.

Charles Ruthven was both bewildered and troubled by his father's remorse, his fits of gloomy despondency and entreaties to his son. "Let the feud end, my son," he said one day. "I have little time left. Let my efforts not have been in vain."

"You lived grandly," the son replied. "There is no need for more." Charles Edward was nevertheless caught in a predicament. He fought against the lure of India, which drew him and whose memories filled him with an inexplicable dread.

It was Lord Moira, now designated as the future Governor General of India who, on Georgiana's plea, put forth the proposition that Charles should join his staff in Calcutta.

"No, my lord. I am not made to be a bureaucrat. I prefer the army," Charles replied.

"Ponder over it, Charles," Lord Moira suggested. "You may find the task a challenge." He paused. "Your father met the challenge. Perhaps you can continue the tradition."

"The tradition of Plassey, Buxar, Seringapatnam, Laswari and Assaye?" Charles Edward asked. "But I have Badajoz and Jena to my credit."

Lord Moira did not possess infinite patience but he had promised to help his dear Georgiana. So now he replied patiently, "No, Charles, tradition is something more than the march of armies. It is the desire to bring law and justice, peace and order to a great and troubled land. It is a difficult task and I, nearing my sixtieth year, am not unafraid. Yet it is a task I cannot refuse."

Charles Edward met the nobleman's steady, challenging gaze. A slow smile lightened his melancholy face. "I will not refuse either, my lord," he said quietly.

Lord Moira nodded and caught Georgiana's radiant smile. The year 1813 drew to an end and the social season began before Wellington assembled his army at Brussels for a decisive encounter.

Georgiana Ruthven vied with Princess Esterhazy and the Duchess of Devonshire to give a ball for the departing warriors. She was importuned by mothers of debutantes for an invitation. Georgiana complied happily; it was a great triumph for her now to smile condescendingly on the grand ladies who had slighted her earlier. Standing beside Alexander Ruthven, she watched the procession of wealth and title as well as the mating rituals of the young.

Charles Ruthven seemed to be enjoying the ball as much as his mother, as he swept one maiden after another on to the polished parquet floor to execute steps of the swift new waltz.

"He asked Lady Cressida twice," the dowagers murmured to

each other. "That is as good as a declaration."

"And who can blame him?' Georgiana chuckled. "Cressida is prodigiously pretty."

"Had you not one day hoped to marry Cressida's father, my dear?" one old dowager asked Georgiana who nodded and said softly, "Indeed, I did, Ma'am, but that was long ago ... before I married my 'nabob'." She fixed glittering eyes on the old lady. "I am glad I went to India." She paused and glanced at the present Countess of Ashville. "I should have hated to languish in Ashville."

The old dowager cackled. "Yes, Georgiana dear. Ashville would have been too small for you." She turned to scrutinise the handsome man with red-gold hair who was making Cressida simper and smile, pout and dimple in turn. "Aye, she is a beauty and a hoyden," the dowager said, "but no doubt Charles Edward finds her agreeable."

Georgiana nodded again but this time there was a glimmer of malice in her smile. And Charles Edward's face, she noticed, looked enigmatic as well. He seemed amused by the gorgeous Cressida's antics.

"Am I forgiven, Charles darling?" Cressida asked, lips parted in invitation.

"You are irresistible," he replied quietly.

"Must you go to Brussels in the Duke's entourage? I'd rather you stayed behind ... to enjoy the summer at Ashville."

"Perhaps we can persuade Bonaparte to wait until autumn?" Charles asked ironically, causing Cressida to flush, though not retort. Charles was now a wealthy nabob. She would exact her price after the wedding bells had rung.

Just befor supper, Georgiana said she had an announcement to make. Everyone looked at Charles Edward and smiled, anticipating the announcement. It was, however, old Alexander Ruthven who spoke in the crowded but hushed drawing room.

"It is my great joy to announce today the betrothal of my son and heir, Charles Edward to Lady Eleanor de Courtney."

There were exclamations of surprise from the guests, a rush of whisper, and movement, as everyone began looking for Eleanor, who was nowhere to be seen. Charles nodded knowingly and went towards the conservatory where the scent of orange blossoms, jasmine and mimosa filled the warm air. He paused to gaze at the slender figure seated on a bench, bent head resting on a clenched fist.

"Lady Eleanor," he said solemnly, "My father has announced ... our betrothal. The guests would like to meet you."

Eleanor de Courtney rose from the stone bench and stared at Charles Ruthven. "It is wrong," she whispered, her voice quavering. "It is Cressida who should be your ... wife. It is she whom you ... love... not me... you hardly know me!"

Charles Ruthven smiled but did not contradict her. It was Cressida whom he loved but who he knew was both desirable and inconstant whereas Eleanor, the elder sister, would cause him neither pain nor joy; bring him neither glory nor shame.

"Well?" Eleanor asked, almost inaudibly. "Do you wish to go through with this charade?"

"Lady Eleanor," he said, offering her his arm, "I shall be honoured if you will accept me."

"And Cressida?" Eleanor asked hoarsely.

"That is over, Eleanor," he said gravely. "Quite over." He paused. "When you came to see me that afternoon two years ago, I realised that it was with you that I could find serenity." He paused again. "It is a bliss I have seldom experienced after the age of eight." He took her arm. "Let us go, my dear."

Eleanor de Courtney nodded, struggling against tears of mingled joy and pain as she placed her hand on his arm and went into the glittering drawing room to receive felicitations. "He has chosen me instead of Cressida," Eleanor mused, as people wished them happiness. "And Cressida, most of all, cannot understand."

Georgiana Ruthven kissed Eleanor, daughter of the man whom she had once dreamt of marrying. "My son has chosen wisely," she mused. "May he be happy."

If Georgiana's fashionable friends were surprised by Charles' betrothal to the plain, sensible Eleanor, they were also glad. This daughter of Lord de Courtney was known to possess a cultivated mind and an amiable disposition.

Courtney House in London, however, was the scene of storms and recriminations as young Lady Cressida raged and wept at Charles Ruthven's perfidy and her half-sister's "sly, scheming conduct." In tears, Eleanor explained that she had at first declined Charles' offer but he made it clear that under no circumstances would he marry Cressida. Both Georgiana and Lord Courtney had urged her to accept Charles.

"Very well!" Cressida told her half-sister. "Marry him but remember you cannot engage his heart. That belongs to me! He is taking revenge on me for jilting him earlier but he loves me nevertheless!"

Eleanor gazed in misery around her, acknowledging the truth of Cressida's words. Yet she could not refuse Charles Ruthven. "I have loved him for many years ... when he was without promise or hope. I will strive to make him happy."

They were married soon afterwards at St. George's church in Hanover Square, amidst a gathering of lords and ladies, directors of the East India Company, soldiers and merchants. As the rich, heavy tones of the organ filled the church and young sunbeams fell on the two figures kneeling at the altar, Alexander Ruthven thought of that terrible day almost seventy years ago when Georgiana's father Walter Manham had marched into their village and killed his father James Ruthven. Now, Alexander thought, the blood of the Manhams and Ruthvens had mingled in Charles and would flow on in the children borne to him by Eleanor. He asked himself whether it had been foolish to pursue a vendetta. Because of that I lost my beloved Andrew and must bequeath to Manham's grandson, all that I built and achieved. Surely this was the jest of the gods!

Georgiana nudged him into wakefulness, but his mind turned back to Culloden and the burning village in the highlands, until he could feel the smoke curling into his nostrils, banishing the scent of orange blossoms. He could hear the cry of the wounded rise over the sweet, sonorous strains of Handel.

The apocalyptic visions vanished; before him stood Charles Edward, composed and aloof, as a Plantagenet prince. And beside him was Lady Eleanor, her face illumined by joy. She curtsied and offered her cheek, murmuring, "Father, bless us."

"Child, my dear child," he said, unsteadily, moved by her soft voice and the touch of a gentle hand. He kissed her proferred cheek and shook his son's hand, before they proceeded down the aisle to a burst of music.

"Hanover Square," Alexander Ruthven muttered to himself. "How far from Culloden!"

Alexander Ruthven turned to glance at Georgiana, swathed in pearls, lace and satin, smiling around her in triumph. She had conquered them all. But he could not share her exultation in its entirety, because his mind raced back from the grandeur of Hanover Square to Culloden.

The wedding was over. The last guests left Cavendish Square and Courtney House. Charles Edward and Eleanor stole away to share a few days together before the bugles of battle called him to Brussels and Waterloo.

Alexander Ruthven set off for the highlands, stopping his carriage now to gaze at the purple glow of heather, or to watch the sun break through a veil of mist over Loch Lomond. Finally, he came to his native village where only ruins remained of his father's cottage. Looming over the hills was the laird's castle, sombre and grey. "Deogarh," he murmured, and then shook his head. "No that is far away. I am in Scotland. I have returned home — after seventy years." He thought of the journey of his life over seven decades, across many countries and seas, through episodes of pain and glory. What a long adventure it had been! He rose, trembling and exhausted. The alien cold was seeping into his blood, hastening his end. Alexander Ruthven was now ready to extinguish the lights. He was home at last.

17

Dawn Over the Ganges

Charles Edward Ruthven stood on the deck of a panchway, *Aurora*, as it rolled over the turbulent waters of Sagar Dwip where the rushing Ganges and the Bay of Bengal met in frenzied waves. Beyond lay dark forests, and young coppice woods interspersed with ruined cottages and barn-like buildings. The amber water moved landwards every year, causing merchants to abandon rude huts constructed to serve as storehouses. Charles Edward felt the thrill of homecoming; memories of Calcutta and the Bengal countryside washed over him, so that he turned in a spurt of excitement towards Lady Eleanor.

Nothing in London or Ashville had prepared her for the scene flowing past her now. She stood near her husband, watching fruit boats laden with bananas, grapefruit and coconut float past. Several large boats from the Maldive islands glided alongside, carrying dried fish and special seashells called cowries that served as currency. The Sunderbans were swampy and dark with feverish exhalations. As dusk fell with startling abruptness, Eleanor Ruthven drew her cloak around her. The swamps, the sudden flare of marsh gas and aroma of decaying vegetation reminded her of Dante's Inferno. To soothe herself, she began reciting in Italian —

I found that I had strayed into a wood
So dark, the right road was completely lost
How hard a thing it is for me to tell
Of that wild wood, so rugged and so harsh
The very thought of it renews my fear ...

Charles Ruthven turned and regarded her with some surprise.

"You know Italian?" he asked.

"I know a little Dante," she replied, diffidently.

He was silent for a moment. "I had thought you knew only French, embroidery, dancing and drawing."

Eleanor smiled. "I know them too but Dante has been a friend for many years."

"Indeed? Is he not a sombre poet for a young lady of fashion?" Charles asked lightly but with hidden interest.

Eleanor stared ahead at the darkening scene, as fearful as Dante had been of the Inferno. "I do not regard the Divine Comedy as sombre. On the contrary, the poem holds out hope ... for redemption ... and a belief in ... a perfect love."

Charles Ruthven stood motionless beside her, conscious of her warm scent and the desires surging within her slender form. He vaguely guessed at the intensity that lay behind her green eyes, sometimes translucent with joy, at other times opaque with melancholy. Her intensity and ardour troubled him — placing on him the obligation to respond. Quick to sense her feelings, Charles Edward realised very soon that the transient union of flesh alone would not satisfy Eleanor. "She wants what it is not in my power to give ..." he had thought, followed by a more unsettling thought; that it might have been easier with Cressida. She was gay and vivacious, full of saucy talk, relieving him of the need to communicate except through the flesh. Eleanor's quiet impeccability chilled him, making him retreat into a relationship strained by restraint.

Eleanor shivered. Charles had not responded to those two awesome words, 'perfect love'. Feeling foolish, she murmured, "I shall go inside — to the canopy. It is damp here."

"I shall bring a lantern there. Mosquitoes are more active in the dark. Would you care to taste the lentil soup prepared by the Serang's cook?"

"Yes ... if there is nothing else. We have not eaten since last night." Her voice was toneless.

"There are some biscuits in the hamper," he offered but she shook her head and went inside the canopied area, to stare out at the velvet darkness and the brilliance of southern skies. Her eyes traced the shining outline of the Great Bear, Cassiopeia's Chair and Orion's belt and sword. "At least these shall remain in the heavens, wherever I am," she consoled herself.

She slept fitfully, careful not to touch her husband, who reclined on a bench beside her. His touch made her hungry for an ardour she knew she could not arouse in him.

The early morning sunlight illumined the bronzed, well-formed bodies of boatmen and peasants as they toiled in land and river. Fields of upward thrusting rice and swaying coconut groves were left behind as they approached Diamond Harbour, lined by ships. Huts, warehouses and shops sold all manner of things intended to delight vagrant sailors, especially toddy, the indigenous liquor made from palm juice. As the panchway neared the harbour, many more ships, shops and brigs were visible until the river seemed to be a forest of masts and sails. Eleanor gazed at the glittering river, awed by its vast splendour.

The Ruthven mansion in Alipur seemed alien, even to Charles Edward, as he descended from the carriage to gaze upon his first home, after an absence of sixteen years. Lady Eleanor acknowledged the salaams of the bare-legged postillions who sported large whiskers, red turbans, and blue jackets fringed by yellow lace. Then she gazed upon the edifice built by her father-in-law, half a century ago.

It was not unlike the dazzling white mansions she had seen at Garden Reach and Khidderpore though this one was larger and more imposing with bay windows, a vast pillared portico and veranda, its baroque facade and newly painted latticed windows.

A strange stillness pervaded the interior, "as if the ghosts are waiting to see us," Eleanor reflected with a shiver, as she observed the light, elegant furniture of the 1780s, which had been brought in by Georgiana. Liselotte had done nothing to alter the classical grace of the rooms, content only to add her water colours to them. As a last gesture of her Gallic humour, Liselotte had left behind three oval miniatures: of Begum Shirin, vast and splendid in Moghul dress, of Georgiana in an extravagant dress of brocade and lace, and of herself in a simple gown, with flowers woven around her brown hair. Above the three miniatures was the inscription, 'Three Sisters'. Below them were eleven smaller miniatures of the progeny of Alexander Ruthven: Andrew, Alice, Clarice, Beatrice, Allan, Claude, Lucille, Alexina, Deirdre, Charles, Adrianne.

Charles Ruthven flushed upon seeing this open testimony of his father's profligacy. He turned to his refined wife, mortified and ready to apologise. Lady Eleanor, however, smiled. "Handsome family," she murmured. "The men are like falcons, the women like swans. Your father chose wisely."

"Eleanor!" Charles Edward exclaimed, astonished by her nonchalance. "I thought your delicacy would be repelled by ... all this!"

A swift flush came and fled from her cameo face. "Your father knew how to live ... and love. I am inclined to admire such a man," she replied, and swept past him to the back terrace, beyond which lay the wild garden and the folly.

Charles nodded and followed her remembering the unclouded days of childhood he had spent there until the fateful evening when his sister Deirdre had led his father to the folly where Georgiana lay in Andrew's arms. The unkempt garden seemed to symbolise the unhappy disorder of their lives thereafter.

The young Ruthvens settled down in the big mansion, trying to harmonise with the past that surrounded them at every turn. Eleanor supervised the cleaning of the massive crystal chandeliers, tall ormolu clocks, carpets, porcelain ornaments and silver — all fallen into disuse after the death of Claude Ruthven some three years back. She ordered the laying out of the garden, not as dictated by Georgiana but as advised by the head mali, the gardener. It soon became a lush place with banks of jasmine and tuberoses, groves of bamboo, clusters of champa set against the old mango and rain trees, statues of nereids and nymphs. Fountains of white marble were installed where ravens and nightingales splashed without diffidence. There were a dozen women to sweep, dust and swob, wash and press clothes, prepare baths, while ayahs were present to attend to the lady and her future children.

Her efforts with the numerous servants invariably ended with concealed laughter. Lady Eleanor could not remember the difference between chobdar (messenger) and akbar (water cooler) or the subtleties between khansamah (butler) and sherabdar (wine server) or khidmatgar (footman) though she knew the sardar who was the major domo and the sarkar who was Ruthven Saheb's agent and spoke English. Many had been trained by Georgiana, whom they held in awe. Some were retainers from Begum Shirin's time, and still owed their loyalty to her. But, in time, all of them gave their affection to the plain and frail young woman who was their new chatelaine. They had admired the brilliant and gorgeous Georgiana, and liked the easygoing Liselotte but they began to feel a deeper emotion for Eleanor, who spoke in a low, melodious voice, and sang softly; who moved through the house as lightly as a flower. "She is not beautiful, this bride, but she is Lakshmi," the Hindu retainers said. "Khusbud," the Muslims assented, charmed.

The elite of Calcutta was equally impressed by Lady Eleanor Ruthven. While the handsome Charles Edward cut a dashing figure, he was not so different from some of the other young men who were making a name for themselves in British India. Eleanor, however, was different from the traders' or soldiers' wives or the "young hopefuls" who hoped to garner a rich husband. Her birth and breeding set her apart from the boisterous and the pompous, while her keen, enquiring mind enabled her to analyse the complexities of the society in which she had been placed.

In this she had a friend in the Governor General's wife. The Governor General, Lord Moira, had been made Marquis of Hastings after his successful war against Nepal in 1815 and he viewed the Indian scene with some conflicting emotions. As a soldier, he had opposed Wellesley's aggressive policy. As a gambler, courtier and bon vivant he had displayed little interest in politics except to provide the grasping Prince Regent with adequate funds. Once thrust upon the turbulent "gaddi" of the Governor General, the man of fashion became a statesman with an acute awareness of the task awaiting him.

Lord Hastings propounded these views at the first dinner given in honour of the Ruthvens. "My predecessors," Lord Hastings said testily, "have left me with seven quarrels on hand, each likely to demand the decision of arms. We have already settled one of these. Nepal will no longer pose a threat. As you know, the campaigns of Ochterloney through the Terai or thick forested foothills, led to Kathmandu, and won for us the hill state of Kumaon, Garhwal and Simla. A British Resident at Kathmandu will ensure that the Ranas of Nepal do not encroach beyond their lines." He paused and smiled. "Some of our officers stationed there have begun to sing praises of the snow-capped hills and fine, scented air. Kennedy, our agent in Simla, is contemplating building a house there."

Charles Ruthven nodded, his mind's eye drawing a line around the Himalayas, which would now be under British colours. "What are the other quarrels, my lord?" he asked the Governor General.

Lord Hastings glanced around the splendid drawing room of Government House with a wry smile. "I ought not to sit here and criticise the man who built this palace, but it is he who has left me the legacy of unfinished battles."

"Marquis Wellesley?" Lady Eleanor asked involuntarily, causing her husband to frown.

The Governor General nodded. "The same. He expanded British territory by a series of wars but left a power vacuum in place of vanquished enemies. Maratha power has not been extinguished nor has its ambition diminished. The Sindhias are threatening Bhopal while the Peshwa's court at Poona is a hotbed of intrigue. The Raja of Baroda's envoy has been murdered by the Peshwa's favourite, Tumbakji. The Bhonsle Raja has asked for a British subsidiary force. And amidst this chaos, the Pindari tribesmen are devastating Central India with their violence and greed."

Charles Ruthven had no love for the Marquis of Wellesley. He had been rude to Charles' mother, referring to her as "that blonde Begum".

"Is it not ironical, my lord, that we glorify Wellesley for his conquests while we condemned Bonaparte for the same deeds?" Charles asked.

The Governor General's lady stirred uneasily in her seat, her astute eye flitting past the guests, who were now all alert. Eleanor smiled nervously. Lord Hastings' handsome face registered surprise and then amusement. "You amaze me, Ruthven. Did you not fight under Wellington in Spain and at Waterloo?"

"I did and admired him. Yet I cannot reconcile our contradictory attitude. We condemn Bonaparte as a brute and warmonger while Wellesley is considered a hero. Both sought to bring order to troubled and fragmented lands. Further, Bonaparte was of Europe whereas Wellesley was an alien to India."

The assembled guests held their breaths while the flapping of the huge silk fans above emphasised the vibrant silence. Lord Hastings wondered if he had erred in taking Ruthven into his establishment. The young man, he reflected, had neither Nabob Ruthven's cool, calculating mind nor Georgiana's alluring tact. "Yet, that is why I like Charles better than his parents," his lordship mused.

"Quite so, Mr. Ruthven. Perhaps we will learn the difference one day — in hindsight." The Governor General then alluded to his 'dear politicals' Elphinstone and Metcalfe and to their valuable help in assessing the prevailing situation. He hoped Charles Edward would endeavour to emulate them. "Indeed, Ruthven," Lord Hastings said thoughtfully, "it might be worthwhile for you to meet Metcalfe in Delhi and discuss the situation in the Punjab. We must not forget the Sikhs while focusing attention on the Marathas."

"Delhi ?" Lady Eleanor asked, turning from a rumbunctious trader at her side. "I should love to see the Moghul capital!"

Charles Edward's eyes narrowed. His wife, he was discovering, had a habit of listening in to masculine conversation while feigning interest in feminine fripperies.

Lady Hastings took control. "Dear Lady Eleanor, you will not go to Delhi until the winter is over, and we have explored Calcutta together."

Lady Hastings paused. "There is, of course, a superfluity of social occasions. You know, dinners and dances, fetes and picnics. Yet we remain unaware of the world in which we live, or perhaps we are unwilling to see it."

Eleanor waited until after dinner, then asked her august hostess, "Pray, what happens in the other world, my lady?"

Lady Hastings drew her countrywoman aside, pretending to show her the moonlit garden. Standing thus, the Governor General's lady said, "The rule of the Company has excited hostility in India. Their arms have won vast territories but dominion has not been accompanied by a corresponding concern for the welfare of the people." She paused, hesitating, and then resumed, "The heyday of the nabobs is over, Lady Eleanor. The Europe that encouraged that ethos has changed. The French revolutionary armies have implanted seeds of discontent and rebellion in subject races in Europe. It will not be long before the conquered people of India stir. We must not resemble the Ottoman Turks in our rule."

Lady Eleanor Ruthven smiled and impulsively took the Governor General's lady's hand. "You remind me of the great Whig ladies I knew in childhood, Ma'am," she said warmly. "It will be an honour to learn under your tutelage."

Eleanor Ruthven was kept busy by Lady Hastings thereafter. Visits to orphanages and convents, charity schools and mission hospitals were obligatory for those who did not wish to be rebuked by the peppery marchioness. She liked the open carriage ride past Chowringhee and the Esplanade, where the Town Hall and other government houses were located. They had the classical elegance of buildings in Rome and France. Leaving behind the "Saheb Para", the European neighbourhood, Eleanor often drove into Tank Square and Dharmatala, which was the residence of Armenian traders and Eurasians, and from there to north Calcutta with its narrow, crooked streets, houses of Hindu merchants and bankers where woodsmoke and the smell of clarified butter thickened the air. She sometimes wandered up to the bamboo and coconut groves of Salt Lake. In the south, was a stream that flowed into the Ganges. Eleanor had heard that three centuries ago, Portuguese galleons had sailed up that stream, then a wide, unsilted part of the Ganges.

Lady Hastings organised weekends at the pretty country retreat in Barrackpore, which had grown into a cantonment area. Here, Eleanor liked walking on the thick turf girding the river, bordered by flowering trees and shrubs. The river had a poignancy in this area, as it took a turn and flowed on, skirting the neat Danish settlement on the opposite side.

Eleanor found Charles Edward more relaxed here, though she wondered if her husband ever totally let down his guard. She noticed that he seemed sensitive to every subject. If Lady Hastings mentioned the plight of Eurasian orphans in the school at Circular Road, young Ruthven would stiffen, even though his half-Moghul half-sisters had long ago disappeared into the noble houses of Lucknow and Aligarh.

"It is most trying for these children," Lady Hastings said at dinner one night. "Not only are they between two worlds but they are illegitimate as well. The Military Orphan Asylum is ready to take children of all classes and creeds but insists on legitimacy."

"That is how it ought to be," Charles burst out. "There should be no compromise."

Lord Hastings glanced at his aide in surprise and embarrassment but Lady Hastings continued, "Dear Mr. Ruthven, have you considered the cruelty of righteousness? Suppose you had been illegitimate? Would you have held the same views?"

Charles Edward coloured in fury, sensing that the Governor General's lady knew all about Claude and the fact that he had been Alexander Ruthven's heir. Eleanor sat tensely, staring at the candles.

"I would have held the same views, my lady," Ruthven said grimly.

Lady Hastings changed the subject but noted that Mr. Ruthven was an intolerant young man. Her attitude hardened when she heard that instead of staying the night at the Governor General's country house, Charles Ruthven had decided to drive back to Calcutta through dark woods and past swampy lakes, with a protesting Lady Eleanor.

"You react too easily, Charles," Eleanor said gravely as they began the long drive back to Calcutta.

"I detest these arched comments of her ladyship!" he retorted.

"She means no harm, and certainly did not intend to offend you! The problem of illegitimate children is very real. I have been to these schools with Lady Hastings, and have seen their plight. Sometimes they are sent to England — to relations willing to have them. Sometimes they are married off to petty traders or sailors. Others ... sink into iniquity."

"I forbid you to visit these places!" Ruthven said abruptly.

Eleanor glanced at his chiselled profile, lit by the lantern at the side of the carriage. His blue eyes were afire. "You do not have to see the degradation of others!"

Her mood quickened into indignation. "It is necessary to see what kind of society we live in. It will serve no purpose if we close our eyes to reality."

"I hope you heard, Eleanor. I forbid you," he said, through clenched teeth.

"I will ignore so arbitrary an injunction!" she replied hotly.

The coachman was told to stop, in the middle of a coconut

grove. Owls and nightjars hooted in the darkness and shuffled from branch to branch, surprised by the intrusion. Charles Ruthven turned to his wife, who sat staring rigidly ahead.

"Can it be that you intend to carry out your intentions?" he asked coldly.

She did not reply. His fierce countenance chilled her anger. "I will not be defied — in my own home, and by my own wife. Please understand that, Ma'am," he said quietly.

Eleanor's patience snapped. "You are quite intolerable!" she whispered. "Had I known of your disagreeable temper, I would have declined your offer of marriage. Cressida would have known how to deal with you!"

He looked at her just once before leaning forward to order the coachman to proceed. They drove in silence for hours past illumined Arab and Portuguese ships, under the starry skies until a faint gold and lilac light fringed the horizon and then touched the river. The woods fell behind and the river banks on both sides suddenly came alive with the votaries of the Ganges, who came to bathe in the cold water and recite the Gayatri mantra. Once more, Charles Edward asked the coachman to stop and sprang down to the ground. Walking slowly over the bushes, he reached the river bank and stared at the bathers and devotees whose steady chanting hum was audible even to Eleanor who sat watching him, no longer angry but tired and depressed.

"He hates his legacy," she reflected. "He detests any reminder of Alexander Ruthven's profligacy and of his illegitimate brothers and sisters. Yet he could not, in the end, reject this opulent inheritance. He is a man divided against himself."

Charles Edward Ruthven slowly returned to the carriage and wearily climbed in. "I ought not to have returned," he muttered. "I cannot accept or admire the legacy left by my father. Sometimes I wish I had not been born to him and Georgiana Ruthven."

Eleanor's heart contracted in pain for him. Laying a hesitant hand on his, she said gently, "You have accepted, dearest, and cannot turn back now."

Surprised by her tone, soothed by her touch, he took her hand in his. She continued, "It is a grand legacy, Charles, and one to cherish."

"Do you truly think so, Eleanor?" he asked dully.

"Indeed I do, dearest. Your father's triumphs should make you proud."

"And his corruption and cruelties? His scandals? His treatment of the women he took and discarded?" Charles' tone was derisive.

"I think you judge him harshly. He was thrown into a time of tumult. He had either to perish or succeed. And as for his women, he was good to them in his own way. Each of his children has been well provided for."

Charles Ruthven sighed and beckoned to the whiskered, bewildered coachman to start once more. As the coach gathered speed, the houses came closer together and bullock carts laden with grains, fruits and vegetables trundled past from the northern suburb of Cosipore and Chitpur. An early carriage clattered over the hard, dusty ground.

"One day, Eleanor, I shall tell you of my half-brother, of my mother ... and of how I escaped the stigma of illegitimacy by a hair's breadth." His voice sounded gruff, as if he strove to hide a deep pain.

"Is ... that why you are ... afraid to bring children into this world?" Eleanor asked, almost inaudibly, as her cheeks flamed into a deep blush. She had suffered so intensely when he retired to his own room, on the pretext of reading despatches while she waited on the vast, silken bed, for a husband who had ceased to be a lover. He came into the room only when he was certain that she was asleep and rose to go horseback riding before she was awake.

Charles Edward wondered why he was afraid to possess her, why he dreaded the possibility of kindling a passion that he could not fulfil or satiate. Was it the dim, yet agonising, memory of a seven-year-old boy seeing his mother on the brocade sofa, locked in a terrifying embrace with a dazzling young man who looked so like Alexander Ruthven, yet was half-Moghul and half-Scottish?

He had heard their cries, and seen their bodies convulsed by a force that seemed as elemental as a Baisakh storm; a force that had then been unknown to him. Bewildered and stunned, he had run to Tara-bibi, his nurse, demanding an explanation for what he had seen. The Hindusthani woman had hugged him tightly and whispered, "Charles baba, you must forget what you have seen. Papa will kill you all if he hears of this."

Thereafter, Charles Edward had watched his adored mother with a tormented jealousy, and scrutinised his mother's lover who was his half-brother, Andrew. He still did not understand what lay between them, what made them look at each other with raw hunger or why his mother became excited and anxious whenever his father returned to Calcutta. He had turned in distress to his sister, Deirdre, then a precocious girl of nine, the child born out of hatred and violence, who knew of her mother's indifference, indeed distaste, for her. So Deirdre had watched, and she who had been entrusted to the care of ayahs, had learnt early. She had finally led her father to the folly, where Georgiana and Andrew satisfied their insatiable thirst, and let loose hell on a luxurious, laughter-filled home.

"I ... am afraid ... Eleanor," Charles Edward said, staring dully at his wife's agitated face, at the green eyes which were dark with pain and pride.

"You cannot be afraid of me!" she whispered. "I cannot and do not have the power or desire to hurt you. I would ... rather die before I cause you pain! I am not Georgiana Manham or Cressida de Courtney. I am Eleanor and I am yours, Charles, entirely yours!"

Charles Edward pulled her close, and kissed her fiercely, bruising her lips, and dismantling her long, carefully coiffured, chestnut hair. She responded gently, whispering caution as they were nearing the Maidan beyond which lay the stately government mansions in the Esplanade.

A golden winter sun played light and shadows on the Aubusson carpet in their room as Charles Edward Ruthven discovered his wife afresh. Her pale, fine-featured face was aglow with joy as he stroked the chestnut tresses on her neck, explored her slender, almost virginal body and buried his red-gold head on her small white breasts.

"Eleanor, you are unsullied and untouched ..." he murmured, lying next to her, staring at the gilt ceiling which Alexander Ruthven must have seen as he lay thus, after enjoying his various women. "I want to find peace and harmony with you. Our children will be happy and tranquil creatures. Would that be enough for you?"

Eleanor nodded, her arm around his broad, muscular chest, her slim legs pinned down by his strong limbs. "I will take what you offer, my love," she whispered, aware that he did not, even now, after such joyous closeness, mention love. Yet, she knew that Charles Edward would soon be bound to her, through his desperate need for her gentle touch and by the children she would bear for him.

18

Shadows of Ratangarh

Charles Edward accepted the Governor General's suggestion to go to Delhi and discuss the prevailing situation with Charles Metcalfe, the Resident of Delhi. The journey with Eleanor was long but the crisp winter air speeded him across the Gangetic plain and over the Doab, the land between the rivers Ganges and Jamuna, and on to Delhi, the city that had once been the capital of Vedic India, of Hindu India and then of the Muslim Sultans. The Residency at Delhi was comfortable and pleasant, set against the low banks of the grey-blue waters of the Jamuna.

Charles Metcalfe was almost the same age as Charles Ruthven, "but the similarity," Eleanor noted, "ended there." As ugly as Ruthven was handsome, Metcalfe referred to his visage as "an ugly phiz". He was a Classics scholar at Eton and had come to India at sixteen — the age when Charles Edward Ruthven left the nabob-style ambience of his home to become an Englishman. While Metcalfe discovered India, flitting through the princely states of India and parried with Wellesley on classics, Ruthven had been trying to imbibe British ideas and thoughts. While Metcalfe was sent at the age of twenty-three to deal with the great and astute Maharaja Ranjit Singh of Punjab, Ruthven joined the Hussars to fight Bonaparte — across Spain, Germany and the Netherlands.

Now both met, and tried to find out what they had in common. Little, Ruthven thought. Metcalfe, mused Eleanor, was like tempered steel. Fifteen years in India had turned a cheerful, prank-loving youth into a man of wisdom and resolve. Walking along the Jamuna at twilight, when the pale windy skies turned violet, and the violet jacarandas became roseate, Metcalfe spoke of his 'mission' in India and his duty to the Indians.

"It is our positive duty to render them justice, to respect and protect their rights and study their happiness. By the performance of this duty, we may allay and keep dormant their innate disaffection, but the expectation of purchasing their cordial attachment by gratuitous alienation of public revenue would be a vain delusion."

Charles and Eleanor listened intently. Charles had heard of his father's adventures and escapades as a condottiero. He knew of his mother's dilettante participation in the activities of the Asiatic Society. To him, India had been the backdrop to a brief, happy childhood and bewildered adolescence, of devoted servants, the scent of mangoes and the cries of parakeets and ravens. But India had been, in a deeper sense, terra incognita. Now he felt the tremors of this alien land and the dimension and dilemmas of the task that faced the British.

"I found Delhi and its environs in a state of chaos," Charles Metcalfe said, pausing to stand before the river embankment, Charles Ruthven and Lady Eleanor also halted, expectantly. "Delhi is supposed to be the kingdom of the Moghul king, but he ruled only in the Red Fort. While I pay him the deference due from a Resident, I must administer an area the size of six counties of north England. Crime has to be put down without merciless punishments. I have sought to suppress slave trade, and the burning of widows as also to offer viable employment to criminal tribes."

"You have succeeded so well, Mr. Metcalfe," Ruthven said quietly, "that Lord Hastings sent me to learn from you. It is learnt that revenue has risen from rupees four lakhs to rupees fifteen lakhs, because there is tranquillity for the cultivator while the zamindar is kept in check, unlike in Bengal, where Cornwallis made him a virtual ruler."

"Cornwallis ought to have been retired after Yorktown," the Resident replied. "Generals, especially defeated ones, make poor rulers."

"Lord Hastings seems to be an exception," Ruthven said with a smile. Metcalfe sighed and shrugged. "Let us hope so."

They walked on, discussing the charms of Delhi in the winter and spring, and of its sanctity as the scene of the epic battle of Kurukshetra. On Eleanor's urging, Charles Metcalfe promised to show them some special places. They dined early and then the Resident bade them good night at the veranda of the Residency and waited for them to repair to their rooms. Charles Edward was deep in thought, reflecting on the achievements of the young Resident and comparing them with his own circumscribed life.

"I ought to have stayed in India," he said, sitting on the sofa in their room. "Then I could have spent my youth learning the work. Instead, at thirty-one, now I have to begin again. My battles with Bonaparte have not prepared me for the tasks in India. Metcalfe, on the other hand, is already a part of the landscape, and has assumed control of his turbulent region. What have I achieved?"

Eleanor did not reply. She stood at the balcony, staring at the thickset figure of the Resident, striding briskly through the grounds towards a copse. There was something eager and purposeful in his manner, which arrested her attention.

"Eleanor, did you hear me?" Charles Ruthven asked, puzzled by her absorption in the scene outside. Finding her silent, he rose and came to her side and followed the direction of her intent eyes. "The Resident interests you considerably, I see," he said tartly.

Eleanor turned to meet his grim face and burst into a low laugh. "Indeed he does, my love. I wonder if he is going to that lovely house set amidst a wood, where his high-born Sikh wife and three sons live."

Charles Edward stared at his wife. Eleanor nodded. "Lady Hastings had told me. Mr. Metcalfe married the lady when he went to the court of the King of Punjab. They have three sons, but they live in seclusion."

"What prevented him from marrying a high-born Englishwoman?" Charles Ruthven asked in a cold voice.

"His heart was engaged," Lady Eleanor replied softly. "He could not marry for convenience."

Charles Ruthven turned away abruptly to increase the flame of the lantern. Eleanor wondered why he reacted so sharply to relationships between Indians and Britons. Was his father's life a perpetual anathema to him or was he afraid for some other reason?

The Resident showed the Ruthvens the Red Fort built two centuries ago by Emperor Shah Jahan, a sprawling citadel of red ramparts along the Jamuna, behind which nestled exquisite palaces, pavilions and mosques. An audience was arranged in the beautiful Diwan-i-Khas before Akbar II, the phantom emperor who was a virtual prisoner in his palace. His opium-dulled eyes flickered momentarily upon seeing the tall, slender Englishwoman with large, luminous green eyes, but his interest soon vanished. Opium soothed him better than any woman.

Metcalfe took the Ruthvens to see the palaces and mosques of the once-grand city. "The ruins of grandeur," he said quietly, "extend for miles and fill the mind with serious reflection. The palaces crumbling into dust, the vast mausoleums which convey to futurity the deathless fame of its cold inhabitants, are usually passed by unnoticed."

Eleanor, however, was thrilled by all that she saw. The melancholy rose gardens skirting tombs, the ramparts of once-proud citadels appealed to her lively imagination. "I can imagine the great Moghuls receiving emissaries from China and Persia here," she enthused.

"And from our own Queen Bess," Metcalfe said, smiling indulgently at the woman whose mind eagerly responded to her environment. "That is how it all began — with the visit of Thomas Roe to the court of Jahangir."

Agra was more entrancing than the phantom capital. This city too had been a capital once though now it was the setting for the famed Taj Mahal, which they hastened to see, soon after arriving, at dusk.

Lady Eleanor stood motionless before the exquisite mausoleum, the central cupola of marble aflame with the coral rays of the setting sun, the minarets tinged by gold, the spandrels of the arches a darker gold, the canal in front a sheet of liquid coral. She went slowly from one chamber to another, passing screens of lapis and jasper, inlaid arabesques of cornelian, jade and coral, latticed walls of agate and amethyst. Candles burnt over the two tombs, turning the bas-relief of marble to gold.

Charles Edward stood back watching her as she groped with new discoveries. Approaching motherhood had given a new roundness to her lean body, and a glimmer to her calm eyes. She turned to find him quietly scrutinising her. "The beauty of this place ... overwhelms one," she murmured. "Is it because of the ... presence of a ... great love ... still in the tombs there ... ?"

Charles Edward nodded, troubled by the tears brimming in her eyes. Eleanor's heart cried out for such a love that could make marble whisper and glow after flesh had turned to dust. "Will I ever know such a love?" she questioned herself inwardly.

He turned to gaze upon the Jamuna turning purple in the winter dusk. "Come," he murmured, "it grows dark."

"Afraid, Charles?" she asked tensely.

He laughed. "Of ghosts, my dear?"

Tears spilled out of the wide, anguished eyes. "Yes, the ghosts of your past! Memories of love." Images of Charles wildly kissing Cressida in the woods of Ashville stabbed her. As his eyes darkened, Lady Eleanor wondered if she had revived his pain. She was surprised by his slow, sad smile.

"The ghosts are safely laid, my dear," he said.

"Are they? Last night ... you cried her name in your sleep!" Eleanor's voice broke into a sob. "How you must regret that it is not Cressida beside you in this memorial to love."

Muezzins cried from the minarets above, as if summoning the stars. Charles Ruthven's face paled and seemed to become a part of the shadowy, marbled ambience. Eleanor knelt before the marble sarcophagus, covering her face. Slowly, he went and knelt by her side. "Eleanor, I have married you, and put aside that world. In you I know I can repose my honour and trust." He paused and asked with a wan smile, "Is that not enough?" She raised her face and wished to cry out, "No, I want more! I want your heart entirely." Instead, she sighed and murmured, "Yes, it is enough."

They rose and he drew her close, resting his cheek against her tear-streaked one. "I will not build any memorial to love, Eleanor, for I do not understand its inconstancy, but I will never dishonour your trust." They walked in silence towards the vaulted outer arch, now turning to dazzling silver in the gathering moonlight, paused and descended the glimmering steps towards the river.

Charles Metcalfe watched them wistfully, envying the simplicity of their lives, thinking of his beautiful beloved from the land of five rivers, and of his three sons growing up to face a troubled heritage.

Back in Delhi, they met Sir John Malcolm, the soldier and administrator who had served the armies of the East India Company for many years now. Travelling across the wild desolation of Central India, this hardy soldier had come carrying a recommendation to the Governor General. But first he wanted to discuss the matter with Metcalfe, his junior of fifteen years with whom he had shared the glitter of Wellesley's reign.

While logs crackled in the stone fireplace and cold Himalayan winds blew in from the north, shaking sturdy deodars and chinars, Eleanor and Charles listened to discussions about the Pindari brigands in Central India where Maratha power had eclipsed, leaving the Afghan mercenaries free to despoil village after village. From Malcolm, Charles Ruthven received advice on what the duties of a Resident should be.

"He must stimulate the first minister to improve the state of the country and of its inhabitants. He must impress him strongly with the idea that his favour with the English government is in proportion to the activity of his exertions to this pursuit." He paused to take a sip of port. Two spots of colour flushed his weathered face. "Go to any state, ruled by a raja or nawab and judge for yourself. The ruler is usually a melancholy madman, his minister a man of low birth who owes his power to British authority and is therefore subservient, almost servile. Where power is without pride, there can be no good government."

"Do you recommend the end of the subsidiary system?" Charles Edward asked the august soldier.

"It will run its course and fail. As Lord Hastings has said, the spirit of independence cannot be extinguished."

"Independence!" Charles Edward exclaimed. "Surely we do not contemplate giving independence after annexing half the country."

Sir John considered Charles Edward Ruthven with an amused countenance. "Did we not annex and rule the American colonies? Did not Bonaparte hold sway over almost all of Europe? Yet, what became of these vast dominions?"

Abashed but not silenced, Ruthven continued his argument. "But this is India, not America or Europe. Indians require discipline and authority. We have given them that."

Sir John Malcolm smiled. "Indeed we have. India, especially Bengal, has surely paid for our protection. Gold pagodas of £ 450,000 from the revenue of Bengal are used to support our oriental embassies and provide for the investment of the tea trade in China. Revenue from the fertile lands of Bengal and from valuable raw materials is sent to England. Bengal has also defrayed a considerable cost of the wars. In all, half a million pounds are sent to England — an amount that had remained with the people of India before they paid for our laws, justice and soldiers."

An uncomfortable silence fell upon the assembled guests. Charles Edward was acutely conscious of the fact that his father had benefited from trading privileges. The mansion in Calcutta, with its massive Antwerp chandeliers, paintings and ornaments, the silk factory at Murshidabad and the villa at Garden Reach had been the result of bridled commerce. "It is no house of the nobility," he thought bitterly. "Not like Courtney Hall, which has been a part of England's ordeals and glory. We are alien adventurers playing at being nawabs, shaking the pagoda tree until it is denuded."

Eleanor fidgeted with the fichu of Valenciennes lace around her shoulders, afraid of her husband's grim countenance. "Some good must have come out of British rule," she said timidly. "I hear Mr. David Hare, a renowned scholar and Sir Hyde East, the Chief Justice of Calcutta, have established a Hindu College offering western education to young Indian men."

John Malcolm smiled at Eleanor. He realised that the plain but refined lady stood in awe of her protean husband, yet could not be subdued. He liked her quiet resolve. "Indeed they have, Lady Eleanor," he said. "A school for Indian girls has also been established by a Mrs. Wilson of the Missionary Society. Even Brahmins are sending their daughters there." He paused and sighed. "These are, however, minor compensations for steady impoverishment. The renewal of the Company's charter in 1813 was unwise."

"Pray, Sir John, how do we impoverish India?" Charles Edward demanded with a hesitant hauteur, that seemed intended to disguise his uncertainty before the cool, austere John Malcolm.

"You must be aware of the process better than I, Mr. Ruthven," Sir John replied coldly. "The East India Company holds the monopoly of trade in India. The pernicious policy of trading privileges has impoverished the Indian farmer and craftsman alike."

Saying this, John Malcolm gave an impassioned account of how India's textile industry, famed for almost two millennia, had been almost destroyed by the Company policy. Spinners and weavers of cotton and silk were bound to the Company as bonded labour and could not work for other manufacturers or even themselves until the stipulated quantity of yarn had been delivered to the commercial Resident of the Company. These yarns were then sent to the mills of Paisley and Manchester, whose survival and prosperity depended on Indian raw material. Cotton and silk cloth manufactured in these mills was sent back to India, to be sold at exorbitant prices.

"Had Indians been free to retaliate," Sir John said sombrely, "they would have imposed steep taxes on English finished cloth but such an act of self-defence is not permitted. Instead, prohibitive taxes are imposed on Indian goods in England, thus discouraging purchases. Yet, no one will deny the superiority of Indian goods." He paused, studying his long thin fingers before continuing. "In fact, we brought these facts to the notice of the Parliamentary Committee in 1813 — but neither Sir Tom Munro nor I could persuade the Committee to change its policy. There were fierce debates and concern for India but the protagonists of British trade won. As you know, the Charter of the East India Company has been renewed to promote the prosperity of British trade — at the cost of Indian welfare, if necessary."

When the first purple buds appeared on the jacaranda trees, the Ruthvens prepared to leave Delhi, before the heat of north India made travel difficult. However, a message came from the Governor General suggesting Charles Edward Ruthven visit the Rajput states to gauge the temper of those princes, and find out their attitude to the Pindari menace.

Charles Ruthven was bewildered. "What do I know of Rajputana?" he asked John Malcolm. "Even less of the Pindaris! Why should his lordship ask me to visit the Rajput princes when you and Metcalfe are here?"

Malcolm spoke with asperity. "Neither Metcalfe nor I have the advantage of having a father who became a jagirdar of a Rajput state."

Charles Ruthven's face became tense. The last thing he wanted was a reminder of Alexander Ruthven's oriental legacy, of his jagirs, begums and their mixed progeny.

Metcalfe sensed this and interceded kindly. "Lord Hastings wants a war and wishes to have an independent assessment. We have already given ours. Central and Western India are in turmoil. The wars of Wellesley left a patched up peace with the Marathas, leaving the Rajputs to fend for themselves. These chiefs set out after the monsoons to plunder their neighbours with the aid of Pindari mercenaries."

Ruthven nodded. "Wellesley's wars have left the British as

legatees of anarchy. The unifying authority of the Moghul is gone. Neither the Marathas, nor the Rajputs, nor the Sikhs can fill the vacuum. So anarchy reigns from the Sutlej to the Krishna."

Metcalfe smiled. "British rule seems the alternative to anarchy. And the Lord Saheb wishes to extend it. But before that, Ruthven, he wants to ascertain his allies. Go to Ratangarh where your father attained glory and persuade the Ranas to be our allies."

"Yes," Lady Eleanor mused. "It will be a delightful trip."

"Do you intend to come?" Ruthven asked sharply.

Eleanor's smile was beatific. "Can you envisage me travelling alone to Calcutta?"

Charles Edward and Eleanor set out for Rajputana. Behind them lay the dying imperial city, its ruined mausoleums and palaces overgrown with ivy and creepers, its ramparts and keeps the haunts of bandits. The broad, flat plain was deserted, and poorly cultivated. Pale green patches of wheat and barley sprouted between fields of vivid mustard flowers. Clusters of churail, neem, shal and dhok trees formed patches of shadow in the relentless sunshine. Gradually, the villages grew smaller and more scattered and the lands more sparse. The pot-holed highway was deserted. The only travellers were rough hewn farmers on carts drawn by camels, who proceeded through that formidable territory with a stately condescension. Reluctantly, Eleanor rode in a closed carriage with women attendants.

Charles Ruthven paused on his horse to study the picture of desolation as his guide explained, "The cultivator has no hope of improvement and fears extortion from the marauding gangs. The merchant fares no better though he keeps bribing the robber barons. And the hapless man who has nothing but despair soon swells the ranks of these robbers and murderers whom he once feared."

Charles Ruthven nodded, suddenly afraid. 'We are facing a different enemy now," he thought. "Not enemies of a great intrepid emperor but thugs, dacoits and possibly those terrifying Goshais and Bairagis who kill in the name of gods and goddesses."

His guide, Vikram Lal, read his fear. "Let us turn back, Ruthven Saheb. The Burra Lat knows enough about this part of the country.

We can tell him nothing new. Besides ... we have the Lady Saheba to consider."

"Foolish woman!" Charles Edward thought, cursing himself for allowing her to come on this journey.

Charles Ruthven glanced around the darkening plains, and the wooded Aravalli ranges ringing the terrain. A red-gold winter haze softened the harsh contours, as the sun sank over the rims of fields and fronds of date palms. "Yes," he thought, "I would like to return but cannot. After all, I am a soldier." He sat upright and gave orders to camp under a cluster of neem trees, whose bitter leaves kept away insects. The campfire burnt brightly in the unrelieved darkness. While the men slept, Charles Ruthven stared at the dark outlines of the Aravalli hills, trees and distant huts, with Eleanor beside him, calm and unafraid. By day, the other worldliness vanished as the reconnoitring party travelled for several days across vast, silent and deserted countryside where men had fled at the sound of advancing horse hooves. Everywhere were reminders of Pindari raids on fields and villages, which Ruthven paused to scrutinise with a grim countenance.

"What desolation!" Charles Edward murmured, staring at burnt huts, and fallow fields, with no sign of any inhabitants. Skeletons of men and animals lay scattered on the parched ground, bleached by the sun. "This is how Chengiz Khan must have left the lands he overran."

Lady Eleanor shivered, not daring to show her fear.

After many days of travelling, they came to Ratangarh, and began the climb up the low foothills dense with broad-leafed churail and filigreed fans of neem, interspersed with crimson splashes of bougainvillaea. As the road ascended, the leguminous trees fell behind and the prickly dhok and kumat took over, standing gnarled and resilient on the sandstone hills. As they climbed, the fortified walls began their slow, tortuous ascent towards the citadel.

Ratangarh fort loomed over the pink-brown sandstone hills, a formidable cluster of high stone walls, battlements, towers and crenellated ramparts. Massive cannons were trained on the plain below from vast circular platforms. Charles Edward rode slowly along the walled road, past Suraj Pol to the high, arched gates of the citadel. Caparisoned elephants and camels stood in the courtyard in front of a line of Rajput warriors.

They scrutinised the young firingi with his red-gold hair and sea-coloured eyes, and the old men remembered his father, "Senapati Ruthven" or "Leader of the Army Ruthven" who had led Ram Singh's army to victory. Now Ram Singh's grandson waited to greet the man who he hoped would organise the Rajputs to challenge the Pindaris and Marathas once more.

Dismounting, Charles Ruthven assisted his wife to alight from the carriage. Together they walked up the steep road towards the citadel-palace, a series of sombre towers above and filigreed courts below with graceful chatris, cupolas, on either side.

Ruthven bowed before the tall, aquiline-featured man, aged about forty. The yuvaraj, the crown prince, could not have been more than eighteen years old. Their wide, heavy-lidded eyes held a mute plea. The Rana rose, a giant of a man, and held out his hand to the foreigner, but hesitated upon seeing Eleanor, dusty and dishevelled. Charles hurried to introduce her, "My wife, Lady Eleanor."

"We welcome you both," the Rana said. Charles bowed. Eleanor curtsied.

"Thank you, Highness," Charles said, suddenly overwhelmed by the grandeur of the castle, the graceful durbar hall and the warm salutation of the ruler. He no longer felt like a reconnoitring imperial officer but a humble vassal of this proud giant. "I have been sent by the Governor General to study the situation here."

The Rana's eyes narrowed. "Is the Burra Lat contemplating war against the Pindaris or does he wish to teach the Marathas obedience? It is time authority and order are established here."

Charles Ruthven nodded assent. "Yet, what prevented Your Highness from joining with other rajas to curb the unruly hordes?" he asked.

The Rana sighed. "Your father could have told you. We Rajput princes have vied with each other and allowed Sindhia, Bhonsle and Holkar to encroach on our lands. They were our feudatories before. Now they seek to be our masters." His moustaches rose as he disdainfully twisted his lips. "Those low-born bandits, lusting for our lands and treasures!"

"Yet they alone dealt with the Moghul empire," Ruthven said ironically.

Anger flickered in the prince's eyes and went out as abruptly. "Shivaji was a great man. He could have led Hindusthan today ... but his heirs are cowardly debauchees ... as our princes are a travesty of the great Rana Pratap." He paused and said wearily, "I am glad you have come, Charles Ruthven. Lead my army ... and those of my allies. We can evict the Pindaris and check the Marathas. Your father's valour did just that."

Charles Ruthven shook his head, smiling sadly. "I am not a ... mercenary commander, Highness. My loyalty is to my government. I can only serve that authority. What you can do is to cooperate."

The Rana bristled. "A pity. I had expected more from our Ruthven's son ... Tell us how we can cooperate — without losing our freedom." His eyes fell on Eleanor. "Rest awhile. Ride across to Deogarh ... and then tell me what we must do."

Charles Ruthven's protest died on his lips. Deogarh ... to see it ... after all these years. "Thank you, Highness," he said. "My wife and I feel honoured to be your guests."

A courtier led them to the white villa, perched on the domed hill, where Alexander Ruthven had spent five years as the commander of Ratangarh's armies. Charles stood still in the hall, hardly breathing as his eyes moved from carpets and ornaments to the paintings by Liselotte Fremont on the walls. "Almost half a century has gone by," he said, moving slowly around, pausing before a picture or book or map outlined by Alexander's strong hand. "Yet I can feel the presence of my father and Mademoiselle Fremont here." The garden, though not Liselotte's domain, retained, nevertheless, the swing made for Alexander's illegitimate son, Claude. In the children's room still lay Claude's French Primer and English notebook. Charles turned away, overwhelmed by the burden of past griefs. Eleanor stared at everything, mesmerised.

Charles and Eleanor rode across the wooded hills and an intervening plain to Deogarh. It was not as imposing as Ratangarh, but it was substantial enough to have provided satisfaction to an ambitious younger son in more settled Moghul times. Charles Ruthven gazed upon the citadel, its brooding towers pink in approaching dusk, its fortified walls softened by the mellow light. Slowly, they rode up to the walled road and dismounted at the courtyard. Over the high arched gate was carved, "Alexander James Ruthven, Jagirdar of Deogarh."

Admiration, love, pity and remorse surged within Charles Ruthven. "The son of a rebel crofter from the Scottish highlands ... and he wrested power and glory in an alien land ... and lived as lustily as any conquistador. How hastily I chose to judge my father!" Charles murmured, while Eleanor gazed on in awed silence.

The retainers bowed low, some came to touch Charles' dusty Hessian boots. Others murmured, "He is truly Sikander's son!" Moved by their salutations, Charles Ruthven allowed them to welcome him with garlands, coconuts, an earthen lamp encircled around his face and a vermilion tilak on his forehead. A joyous laughter bubbled within. He had never felt so much at home since his return to India after seventeen years.

The people surged forward to take him and Eleanor through the gate and into the vast audience hall. There, in a voluminous gharara, sequinned bodice and yards of gauzy veil stood a tall and stately woman of middle years, her dark auburn hair bound by pearls, her eyes a vivid sapphire. Charles Ruthven stood transfixed, as if he had seen his own reflection. Eleanor too was bewildered.

"Beatrice Begum," a retainer whispered.

Charles continued to stare at his half-sister, Beatrice Ruthven, widowed wife of a minor nawab.

"So you have come at last," she said in clipped English. "I wondered when you would come to take this castle. Andrew's castle!"

Slowly, he advanced, with a heavy heart, noticing how the hauteur of her exquisite face changed to anguish at his approach. She bit her lip to choke back her sobs.

"My sister," he murmured, taking her hand. "Forget the past. I am as innocent of the past as you are. Our mothers fought, suffered and paid their prices. Let us not get caught in their webs. We can still befriend each other."

Beatrice clutched his hand and began to weep. "You, my youngest brother, are as old as my grief ... when our father banished my mother and us to please your mother. He did not even dream then that the woman for whom he renounced us, would one day, destroy him too."

Charles Edward closed his eyes, as Beatrice's warm tears fell on their joined hands. He could still recall that terrifying scene when Andrew Ruthven had knelt before a broken Alexander to ask forgiveness and he remembered even now, after twenty-five years, the blazing day when news of Andrew's death in battle had reached their father ... and the banishment that had followed.

"My mother paid the price ... and so did I. My father never cared for me. Until the end, he was indifferent ... but a man like him needed a son ... and I am the only one left to carry the burden of his dreams."

Beatrice glanced up at Charles Edward's anguished face, and felt a stirring of tenderness for her only remaining brother. Slowly, she raised his hands to her lips and kissed them, bringing unbidden tears to his eyes. He embraced her closely, while the retainers and soldiers watched, as moved as he. Then slowly, he turned to Eleanor standing silently aside. "My wife," Charles said, offering Eleanor his hand. "Daughter of a noble house of England." Beatrice gazed at Eleanor and nodded with a faint smile. "So different from my father's wives," she thought. The two women gravely embraced each other.

Later, they talked, sitting on the rough balcony where once

Liselotte had painted and Shirin had taken the air, and from where young Andrew had surveyed his little principality. As her bitterness slowly evaporated, Beatrice seemed like a trusting child to her more complex brother. She listened wide eyed to his accounts of the Napoleonic wars, of London, and his present assignment. Dinner was served and cleared away and more wine served, as the night deepened. At last, Beatrice summoned a young man. Tall and fair, chestnut haired and blue eyed, he came and stood silently near them.

Startled, Charles Edward stared at the familiar face with incredulity. Speechlessly, he turned to Beatrice, who smiled sadly and said, "You said you were the only male heir of our father — to carry the burden of his glory. But there is another left."

"Who is he?" Charles asked, almost inaudibly.

"Andrew's posthumous son ... brought by his mother's relatives from Mysore." She paused. "Andrew loved once more before his death ... not the golden English girl of his dreams but the daughter of a Mysore Muslim nobleman. My other half-brother Claude had refused to acknowledge the boy ... but after Claude's death and Father's departure for England, the boy's relatives brought him to me at Lucknow." She paused. "It was too late, however ... Alexander Ruthven did not see his beloved son's child."

Charles Edward stared at the youth in tormented silence, suddenly aware how much he wanted to carry the burden of Alexander Ruthven's dreams. Beatrice's sapient eyes softened into a smile. "The boy is untutored; he grew up wild and uncared for, after his mother died. Young Sikander cannot carry his grandfather's burden. That is your privilege. But let him live here ... in honour." Tears filled her eyes. "God has chosen to take Andrew and my husband. Let Sikander be the comfort of my loneliness."

Sikander's bewildered gaze moved restlessly from his 'uncle' Charles to Lady Eleanor, at a loss to understand the significance of their visit. He had been a vagabond too long to fear dismissal but he was obviously afraid of the uncle who could banish him. As if sensing Sikander's fears, Charles Edward said, "Our father's legacy must be shared, Beatrice. You and Sikander must stay on here." Beatrice Begum bowed before her brother in homage. Following her example, young Sikander did the same.

It was past midnight when they suddenly became aware of a sudden commotion within the citadel. Charles Ruthven was alert at once, reaching for the pistols that rested in his coat pocket. Begum Beatrice rose, grim faced. "Those screams," she said, "belong to the Pindaris."

Lady Eleanor too rose, and glanced anxiously from one to the other. "Pindaris? So close to us?" she whispered.

Begum Beatrice looked at her half-brother. "Is it fate, Charles Edward, that you were sent by Allah to protect Deogarh?"

Charles Ruthven wanted to cry in protest "No! I do not wish to fight for these legacies! I am an officer of the Company — not an adventurer!" Instead, he went to the battlements and looked down to see the dark silhouettes of men on horses pouring into the plains below, merging with the trees and bushes. They carried flaring torches and curved swords, and rode as if they were moulded to their agile horses.

The citadel was roused from its slumber by the shrieking Pindari tribesmen as the soldiers gathered arms and torches to meet the thundering foe outside. Beatrice was no longer a veiled Begum; she flung aside her beatilah and commanded the gates to be closed and cannons to be trained on the bastions. "Our summer crop will be ruined," she said gravely. "These hordes will search our fields."

Charles Ruthven turned around to see the advancing Pindari hordes and then faced his half-sister. "I will meet their attack," he said.

"No !" Eleanor cried, clutching her husband's arm. "You have no need to fight these terrible tribesmen. Let them do their worst!"

Charles gripped his wife's shoulders. "Compose yourself, Lady Eleanor. Did your ancestors not fight in the crusades and against the Armada? Can these unruly hordes frighten you so?" Releasing his hand, he hurried down to where the soldiery of Deogarh waited for orders.

"So, Father," Charles Ruthven murmured, "you want me to defend your jagir? By Jove, I shall do just that! I, whom you loved less than Andraz or Claude."

Suddenly forgotten were the homilies of the Governor General as well as his own resolve not to be drawn into the affairs of the princely states. Suddenly, after all these years, he wanted to defend Deogarh and protect what his father had won by adventure and struggle. Throwing himself into the turmoil, Charles Ruthven swiftly supervised the positioning of cannons, cauldrons of hot oil and huge catapults, to resist the Pindari onslaught. The sight of the flame-haired officer in shirtsleeves and breeches heartened the soldiers.

Begum Beatrice watched her half-brother, son of the hated Georgiana, defend her domain. She moved swiftly from arrow slit to bastion, watching Charles Ruthven resist the Pindari attack.

All night the cannons roared, while the Pindaris hurled flaring torches over the fort walls, setting fire to trees, haylofts and huts. The arsenals however, remained untouched as they lay deep within the citadel walls.

Surprised by the unexpected resistance they met under Charles Ruthven, thwarted in their effort to storm the fort, the Pindaris began to retreat, in a bid to plunder the countryside and the hapless peasants who tilled the lonely fields.

"We will pursue them," Charles Ruthven announced. The fever of battle ran high in his veins now. "The Pindari chief must be taken captive — to teach his followers a lesson!"

Beatrice kissed his hand, beaming. "You are truly my father's son, Charles Edward! Braver, any day, than my dear Andraz or Claude!"

Exultant with the praise, Charles gave commands for the pursuit. Eleanor came to him in the courtyard, rage simmering within. "You are reckless!" she cried. "You cannot take on an army of assassins with these rusty soldiers of Deogarh."

Ruthven held her hand, impatient to be off. "Stay with my sister ... and pray for our success. I must go."

The Deogarh contingent rode out of the fort, pursuing the Pindaris, as they left the arid scrublands and penetrated deeper into the wooded terrain, cut by gorges and ravines. At one place they paused for breath.

"They are luring us into their hideout," the old commander of Deogarh cautioned. "We should return before they encircle us."

"We must capture their chief," Ruthven insisted. "He is an evil man."

"Ruthven Saheb, how can a handful of men deal with an army of ruthless cut-throats? You need an army for that!" the old soldier exclaimed, exasperated.

Charles Ruthven's face was set. "Not long ago, I chased the well-armed soldiers of Bonaparte with the help of handpicked Spanish guerilla soldiers. Are the Pindaris superior to that splendid army?"

The old commander sighed, looking around him in despair. The sun rode high overhead, casting no shadows, as cicadas strummed a solitary refrain.

"We will rest here and follow the tracks at dusk. The Pindaris' hideout is not far away. We will smoke them out of their hideouts."

But its was the Pindaris who returned at dusk, stealthily, swiftly, to take the Deogarh contingent unawares. As soon as they reached close, they descended on Ruthven's men with bloodcurdling cries, revelling in the ensuing violence and bloodshed. Twenty soldiers were shot, dragged and beheaded; and each severed head was held aloft by the chief with a roar of laughter. Charles Ruthven's arm was injured but he managed to gather the remaining men for a retreat. In the desperate flight back, Ruthven was glad to have the old commander who led the men over a little known route, thus throwing the pursuers off the scent.

It was dawn when they arrived at Deogarh, exhausted and dejected. "The old soldier was right," Ruthven thought, miserably. "One needs an army to destroy the Pindaris. I have failed to catch the chief ... and good men have died. But Deogarh is safe."

Begum Beatrice awaited her half-brother at the gates of the citadel, a tall, stately figure in a blue beatilah. Charles Ruthven dismounted and held the hands outstretched to him. Tears sparkled in her eyes.

"My noble brother! How I have wronged you all these years!" Beatrice Ruthven Hidayatulla murmured. "And how I blamed myself for letting you go in pursuit of those evil hordes." She paused and looked gravely at him. "Your wife, the Lady Eleanor, is quite distraught. Go to her and calm her. She is ... with child."

Charles Ruthven stood dazed, gazing at the ramparts bathed in morning light. The legacy he had spurned and yearned for had suddenly caught up with him. Cavendish Square seemed far away, as did the Pyrenees. He felt strangely at home here and wondered if his father's spirit was pleased with him at last.

A warm welcome awaited them in Ratangarh. The Rana came to the Sun Gate to meet Charles Ruthven. Beside him stood the crown prince, Nahar Singh. News of Ruthven's defence of Deogarh and pursuit of the Pindaris had travelled swiftly to Ratangarh.

"Now you know what turmoil surrounds us," the Rana said.

"Yes. And only the Company's army, assisted by you princes, can bring order to this troubled territory," Ruthven replied. They rode back, united now by a common purpose.

The evening shadows had lengthened over the hills and towers, when a slender shadow fell across the palace terrace where Charles Ruthven and Eleanor sat, gazing at the distant turrets of Deogarh. Both turned to see a girl in a voluminous gharara, and a long silken veil swathed across her head and shoulders. A tremulous smile hovered on the girl's face, as she joined her palms together in greeting. "Have you decided to stay on then to defend Ratangarh?"

"Who are you?" Charles asked abruptly, unsettled by her question. Lady Eleanor stared at the girl, wondering why she felt a shiver of foreboding pass over her. Standing up, she drew the light shawl she was wearing closer around herself.

"I am Urmila, daughter-in-law of the Rana of Ratangarh, and

wife of Nahar Singh." She looked intently at Ruthven. "We have been waiting for you for some time now."

"Waiting for me?" Ruthven echoed, surprised. "But why?"

The princess offered another hesitant smile. "There is no one else. The Rana is crippled by gout, and his son ... will one day ruin Ratangarh with his rash valour ... and the Pindaris wait below... waiting to sweep through our domain." She shivered. "When they do, I shall leap from a tower rather than perish in the flames."

Eleanor Ruthven stared wide eyed at the princess, feeling an icy hand pass over her warm pulsating body. Impulsively, she reached out to take her husband's hand but he was looking intently at the princess.

"You are too young to think of such matters. Why, you ought to be playing with dolls in your apartment," Ruthven said quietly.

She smiled and shook her head. "I left the dolls behind in my father's palace. Here I must think of others ... and Ratangarh ... so that my sons may rule here one day."

"Why, she is but a child herself," Eleanor murmured. "Yet she speaks like an old woman."

The princess shook her head. "Half my life is already gone, lady. And I have still so much to do. That is why I am glad you came, Ruthven Saheb. I will not be afraid anymore."

Glancing up at her husband, Eleanor was troubled by the anxiety in his eyes. "I have already told the Rana that I can do nothing, except on the orders of the Company."

"No!" the princess replied fimly. "You cannot turn away now." She removed a jewelled bracelet from her slim wrist and placed it in his hand. "This is Rakshabandhan, the bond of chivalry. Long ago, a Rajput princess sent a bracelet to the Moghul emperor to ask for protection ... and he protected her ... even from his own lust."

Charles Ruthven stared at the bangle and then at the dusky face with its eloquent eyes.

"Will you protect Ratangarh on a day of peril?" the princess asked. He nodded, defeated by the urgent plea in those eyes. She smiled and flinging the silken veil over her head, sprinted like a gazelle back towards the zenana palace.

"Let us go away from here," Eleanor whispered, gazing up at the star-scattered sky, wondering why she felt as if someone had walked over her grave.

19

Maratha Wars

The plans for war against the Pindaris began to take shape in the winter of 1817. Lord Hastings hoped not only to clear Central India of the chaos caused by the tribesmen but also to intimidate the Maratha powers in a single operation since it was in their territory that the Pindaris operated. A hundred thousand troops were raised, and divided into two groups. One group stretched along the Ganges-Jamuna line and was commanded by the Governor General himself. To the south-central were posted four divisions under Sir Thomas Hislop. A division each was placed under Sir Thomas Munro at Madras and at Gujarat to cut off lines of escape by sea.

Charles Ruthven returned to Delhi by June of that year, as the blistering sun and blanket of dust made Delhi a veritable inferno. He had left Lady Eleanor behind in Ratangarh, where the Rana promised to ensure her health and safety. Lord Hastings had travelled to the capital too, to plan the forthcoming campaign with his generals, Sir John Malcolm and Charles Metcalfe. The Governor General listened to Charles Ruthven's description of Pindari methods and manoeuvres. He did not rebuke him for his escapade, indeed, he thought it had been a useful exploratory trip. "I am glad to hear that the rulers of Rajputana wish to cooperate, though the Marathas do not," Lord Hastings observed. "But we shall bring them to obedience eventually."

"I advise caution with the Marathas," John Malcolm said. "They should be won over rather than fought."

"So that they may spread chaos?" Lord Hastings retorted. "Our Resident at Poona does not agree with you."

Malcolm said nothing then but on the way back to their rooms in the Residency grounds, he spoke with derision. "Lord Hastings wishes to have a splash of sunset glory. He is, after all, a mediocre soldier striving to become a great general, a fashionable courtier trying to become a statesman."

"He may yet succeed," Ruthven replied. "You see, he believes in himself."

In September, after the rains, the combined army of the East India Company advanced from the north, west and south, driving the Pindari marauders to their haunts in the Narmada valley in Central India. The states of Gwalior, Indore and Bhopal were asked to cooperate and offer safe conduct to the Company army. The British Residents in each state had their soldiers ready, to deal with refusal.

Ruthven had his doubts about the success of this strategy. "We are scattered forces operating from isolated posts. Should the Marathas combine, our armies will be routed.'

"Precisely," said Sir John Malcolm. "But Sindhia's dislike of Holkar is equal to his dislike of the British. They will not unite."

"If they did they could have made short work of His Lordship's strategy." Charles Ruthven paused, scanning the line of soldiers marching behind. "Bonaparte dealt with such a situation, when the combined forces of Austria, Prussia and Russia engaged the French armies at Austerlitz."

"Rest assured, Ruthven, there is no Bonaparte here. If there was, we would not be waging this war."

In October, faced with an ultimatum from Hastings, Sindhia agreed to cooperate against the Pindaris. The ruler of Bhopal soon fell into line, provided his existing territories were recognised. Holkar did not agree readily. The Pathans in his court were in no mood for surrender. The two armies met for an encounter at Mahidpur.

Here too, the victorious armies of the Company swept through the kingdoms of Sindhia, Holkar and Bhonsle. The Maratha chiefs rued the day that they had accepted the Pindaris as partners.

The campaign continued through the ensuing summer months. Dust and sunlight mingled together to form a grey screen and the sun itself became a burning orb of dust. The terrain was barren and arid. Years of depredation had devastated the countryside. The army passed empty, scorched fields and burnt villages strewn with skeletons of men and cattle. Wells had dried and rivers were thin, muddy trickles through the parched land. They marched across hostile Maratha territory, stopping at night in the shadow of sparsely wooded hills from whose craggy towers hostile chieftains watched their progress with belated understanding. Sometimes, as Ruthven lay on the hard, dust-packed ground, staring at the brilliant clarity of stars and sky, a strange sensation stole over him.

"I feel the presence of something great and enduring. Is it God? Or someone nearer — the presence of a great spirit?" he wondered. "Why does this country rouse these sensations within me? Why was it not the same in Badajoz or Leipzig? It is ... as if ... I have returned to my ... home."

By day the armies of Hastings and Hislop drove the Pindaris and their Maratha suzerains to their craggy domains or forest retreats. One of their main retreats was in the forest fastness of the Chambal valley in the heart of Bhonsle territory, under the leadership of the robber baron, Mulkari. Like the Parthians of old, Mulkari had a corps of arm bearers who kept alive the supply of ammunition for the cavalry, which was thereby free to advance and retreat according to convenience. This strategy enabled them to make sudden, unexpected attacks on the more predictable Company forces, inflicting heavy casualties on them. The Pindaris had little regard for rules of warfare and even less consideration for the hapless people who fell in their path.

While General Hislop's troops moved across the territory between Nagpur and Baroda, the Pindaris from the Chambal valley swooped down on the Company troops, and sent them into retreat, as the General was reluctant to face a direct confrontation in unknown terrain. Charles Ruthven, however, refused to retreat. Moving swiftly with his group, he pursued the Pindari contingent with heavy fire, relying entirely on his cavalry officers. Like the Parthians of old, the Pindaris fired as they retreated but Ruthven followed, grimly determined.

It took Ruthven three days to locate the valley where the Pindaris held sway, and when he did, the combing out operation was done thoroughly. The dacoits and thugs who had terrorised Central India for three decades were now on the run as the heavy artillery of Hislop's army battered upon their hideouts. Charles Ruthven rode ahead, anxious to avenge the death of the Rajput soldiers who had accompanied him in the exploratory expedition from Deogarh.

The Pindaris scattered under the onslaught, unable to cope with Ruthven's strategy of scattering his men and firing from all directions to confuse the prey. In their flight, countless Pindaris were killed, but Ruthven rode on, determined to find Mulkari, who fled at the approach of the crack cavalry. Ruthven pursued him relentlessly, across the ravines and streams of the forest fastness until he was finally shot and lay bleeding on the ground, gasping for breath.

"Did you say no one returns alive from the Chambal?" Ruthven asked the bandit chief.

The dying man swore obscenities as blood clotted on his lips.

"Well, I've smoked you out at last, scoundrel, and taken fifty of your followers."

Mulkari grimaced and closed his eyes.

Hislop's army marched on across Central India, over the territories of the Maratha princes who had allowed their domains to be used by the Pindaris. Finding Ruthven resourceful, General Hislop sent him to Poona, where the final encounter with the Marathas was being planned.

Mountstuart Elphinstone was then the Resident at Poona. He

had trained at the College of Fort William where he had learnt Persian and Sanskrit, thus adding to the impressive list of languages he knew. His favourite reading, however, was the Greek Classics. In that dawn of the British imperial age, the Briton found an easy affinity with the creators of another great empire. Indeed, Horace and Cato bore resemblance to the assurance of Samuel Johnson, while Cicero was not very different from Edmund Burke in his eloquent thunder.

Elphinstone learned his work under veteran Sir Barry Close and was soon dragged from his books to ride with General Arthur Wellesley at Assaye. Between battles, he read Homer and Hafiz, and gossiped about great events over a breakfast of figs and wine. He was appointed Resident to the Bhonsle court at Nagpur at the age of twenty-four, and undertook a mission to Kabul when Lord Minto wished to counteract the Napoleon-Alexander alliance after Tilsit. Though the mission was a failure, Elphinstone collected material for his book on the history of Afghanisthan.

In Poona, Elphinstone had both the time and the opportunity to scrutinise the Peshwa, Baji Rao. He found him addicted to both pleasure and power, though lacking in the capacity to exercise the latter.

Charles Ruthven arrived in Poona to find that Sir John Malcolm had preceded him, and told both the Chief Political Officer and the Resident the purpose of his visit.

Sir John Malcolm was thoughtful, as if treachery evoked other thoughts. Elphinstone said, "We must be careful of treachery, Sir John, not only among the Pindaris but in Poona as well."

Malcolm shook his head. "I think we should give the Peshwa a chance. His intentions may be amicable. With our armies in Nagpur and Malwa, he would not risk a confrontation. Besides, only by ensuring his neutrality can we have a free hand with Sindhia and Holkar. If they combine, we have no chance. Indeed, to foster an atmosphere of trust, I recommend the removal of our troops from Poona."

They argued. Charles Ruthven kept quiet; the episode at Chambal had shaken his certitude. Yet he was inclined to agree with Malcolm that the removal of troops would generate a sense of amity between the Peshwa and the British, facilitating the process of diverting him from joining his Maratha comrades.

Within a few days of Ruthven's arrival, a carriage came trundling up to the Residency, escorted by armed guards in yellow Rajput costume. Elphinstone came out to the veranda to see a heavy, weary woman alight from the carriage. Struck by the air of distinction in her bearing despite the dusty and dishevelled exterior, he went forward to bring her in.

"I am Eleanor Ruthven, Sir," she said in a low, tired voice. "I hear that my husband has returned from his battles."

"Indeed he has, Ma'am," Elphinstone replied, offering her his arm as they went inside.

Charles Ruthven was astounded by his wife's arrival. Tight lipped before the Resident, his anger broke forth in private. "Are you mad to leave the security of Ratangarh and come to Poona in your condition?" he stormed at Eleanor.

Eleanor sat with eyes closed, breathing heavily. His greeting, devoid of joy or kindness, had mortified her. But she held back the tears and reproaches that surged within her until his fury had spent itself and then she spoke with effort.

"I want to be near you ... when our child is born ... if I should die ... Ratangarh is too far ... and alien."

"The Marathas, you think, will be more familiar? Do you not know that we may have to encounter an attack from them any time? What shall I do with you then?"

Eleanor did not reply. She realised now that it had been foolish and reckless to leave the well-guarded citadel for this threatened villa but if she were to die, this was where she wished to be. Charles Ruthven did not berate her further. After having a room arranged for her in the outer wing of the Residency, he left her alone with the women attendants while he went to confer with Elphinstone about the growing tension in the city.

A strange silence fell upon Poona. The clamour of the city died down. Even the temple bells ceased to ring. The Poonites began to leave; they did not want to get caught in a battle. The Peshwa, Baji Rao, had decided to act at last. He had realised too late that the British had broken the Maratha Confederacy by weaning Holkar and Sindhia from him. He had heard of the approaching British battalion under Colonel Burr. Elphinstone, being anxious to ascertain the Peshwa's intentions, sent Charles Ruthven to offer a truce to gain time.

Charles Ruthven rode down the hill, refreshed by the cool autumn air, and the sight of the hills ringing the city with verdant monsoon foliage. A lambent October sun lit up the distant hills, the spires of temples and the turrets of the Peshwa's palace.

There was a flurry of activity within the Peshwa's palace. Young Baji Rao had interpreted the growing power of the Company rule as a threat to his dominion. He knew the battles of Assaye and Laswari had already pruned Maratha hegemony but if his vassals remained loyal, he felt he could still retrieve Maratha power ... and perhaps even Hindusthan ...

"Shivaji," Baji Rao murmured, gazing out of the arched windows into the city of his great ancestor. "That is the person we require."

"You are his descendant," his Commander-in-Chief, Bapu Gokhale, reminded him grimly.

The Peshwa sighed deeply. "Descendant only in name ... not in spirit." He paused and glanced at the solemn faces around him. "Shivaji would not have allowed the firingis to spread their tentacles over our land. Shivaji shook the mighty Moghul empire and outwitted the most cunning of emperors. He had resurrected the pride and glory of Hindu rule, and the dream of an empire such as Ashoka and Harsha had ruled." The Peshwa fell silent, thinking of his own striving to unite Sindhia and Holkar and of how neither of them would acknowledge his suzerainty. If only they had adhered together in common purpose, he knew that that pale-eyed man would not have seen sitting on his hill-top villa dictating terms.

The doors of the audience chamber were thrown open as a courtier announced: "An emissary from the Resident Saheb seeks an audience."

The councillors and commanders were instantly alert as Charles Edward Ruthven came in and bowed courteously before the Peshwa. The usual rituals were observed and courtesies exchanged before Ruthven came to the point and said, "It is possible to make peace, Your Majesty. The Pindaris have been put down. It is not necessary to pursue the war further into Maratha territory if you agree to peace."

The Peshwa stared at the young officer with something between anger and astonishment. "Is he impertinent or is he merely a fool?" he asked in Marathi.

Bapu Gokhale watched Ruthven with cool, grey eyes. "No Sire, he is as devious as the rest of his race. They talk of peace when they are stalling for time. Perhaps their army is still far away."

"Tell him that we will not rest until the trading company leaves the borders of Maratha lands," the Peshwa replied in Marathi, not deigning to address a mere officer. Indeed, he hardly acknowledged Elphinstone's presence at audiences. "Tell the firingi that we will sue for peace after repudiating the Treaty of Poona!"

Charles Ruthven left the palace, uncertain of the Peshwa's intentions. That Lord Hastings' terms rankled was clear but how far they would go to repudiate the treaty concluded a year ago remained unclear. He told Elphinstone so on his return. The Resident heard him out impassively.

"In more tranquil days, I played chess with the Peshwa," he said softly. "I never won a game. He always made a surprise move. I wonder what he has in store for us this time."

"You are remarkably calm, Mr. Elphinstone," Ruthven replied

with asperity and rising unease. "Should we not evacuate our women and children at least?"

Elphinstone's pale eyes glittered a moment in anger, and then the wry smile returned. "Ah yes, you are anxious about the Lady Eleanor." He paused before saying, "The hurried departure of our women and children would provide the spark I must avoid."

"Am I to understand that you intend to do nothing? That we must wait for the Peshwa to attack?" Charles Ruthven asked coldly.

Elphinstone shook his head. "Not at all, I intend to entertain all of you at dinner, some dancing and perhaps several rounds of whist and backgammon to soothe our ruffled feathers. Come, Charles Edward — what a gloriously Jacobean name — let us start by sampling a glass of some excellent claret that my sister sent me. Pre-revolutionary, I am assured, and favoured even by Bonaparte."

Fifty Britons had taken refuge within the vast hill-top villa of the Resident, waiting in dread for a war. The atmosphere within the Residency was that of spurious nonchalance, punctuated by long silences palpable with apprehension. It became obvious when expert gamblers lost to novices, ladies accustomed to being courted were treated indifferently by their habitual admirers, and when gluttons, who normally did full justice to the table, only toyed with morsels. Only the claret was honoured, as if to fortify the inner spirit.

Lady Eleanor Ruthven sat in a corner of the balcony where phosphorescent shefali flowers and late jasmines gleamed against the October velvet darkness. The enormity of her folly had begun to dawn on her as she realised that her presence might affect the free movement of others. She was too terrified to tell Charles that she had already begun to feel a strange pain. "Perhaps my dream of dying will be fulfilled here ... perhaps death has lured me here," she thought in rising panic.

Charles Ruthven came to sit by her. "I trust you realise how you have imperilled yourself and others by coming here, he remarked sharply.

"I ask your forgiveness," Eleanor whispered. "I was afraid to die alone ..."

"Will it be better to die amidst a horde of Maratha soldiers?"

Eleanor put her hand to her face and began to weep. Elphinstone said, standing beside her, "We have not much time to lose. You and the ladies must leave for Matheran before daybreak. Our agent there will look after you."

"Matheran?" Eleanor asked, distraught. "But that is quite far ... in the hills. Will we get that far?"

"There is no other safe place," Ruthven said, turning away. "We can only hope that the route does not fall in the way of the Maratha army."

Before dawn, Eleanor Ruthven, a few women and a dozen armed guards left the Residency and rode swiftly to take the hilly road for Matheran. Human habitation thinned out as the road became steeper, with patches of coarse bajra and jowar growing tenaciously on the table-topped Deccan hills. The women sat in three carriages, with their children, silent and stiff with fear. Peasants who saw them pass, frowned in bewilderment and went on their way.

By afternoon, Eleanor could not contain her pain in silence any longer. "I must stop," she whispered to a woman seated beside her. "I cannot go on further ... let me lie here under the shade of the sugarcanes ... but you go on ..."

"Impossible!" the Englishwoman said,"We cannot leave you here! We must all reach Matheran."

Eleanor shook her head, bathed in sweat. "I shall never make it to Matheran. Let me get down ... I beg you."

Sadly, the women watched Lady Eleanor walk towards a pool of water where she bathed her face and arms and then lay down, under the tall feathery sugarcanes. Two peasant women came out of their thatched huts and saw the firingi woman lying exhausted on their land. They glanced at each other and then at the two carriages filled with women and children. The armed guards explained their predicament.

"Leave her here. We shall try to care for her. Come after a few days and take her away," one of the peasant women said.

The carriages trundled off. The hapless passengers hurried on, afraid to tarry on the deserted hillside.

Moti-bai, the younger woman, sat down beside Eleanor and scrutinised her briefly, before proceeding to loosen her clothes. "Come to our cowshed," she said briskly. "It is cool and clean there. The cattle have gone to graze and the men are away, with the Peshwa's army. No one will trouble you there."

Eleanor closed her eyes. It seemed incredible that she, daughter of the Earl of Ashville, was lying in a Deccan village, tended by Maratha peasant women whose husbands were in the army which was soon going to fight her husband and countrymen. "This journey," she whispered, "is more wondrous than Dante's celestial one."

"You said something, Bai?' Moti asked.

Eleanor caressed the rough brown cheeks so close to her. "Bless you," she whispered as she lost consciousness.

The Peshwa was under pressure from his own advisers. "The British are panicking ... they have sent their women off to seek shelter. Let us capture them ... or at least attack the Residency now!" the chief commander, Bapu Gokhale, urged his king.

"We lose our advantage with every passing hour!" the chief minister, Appa Saheb, cried. "Colonel Burr is on his way with a large force."

The Peshwa sat immobile on his silken divan. "If we are to emulate Shivaji in battle, let us emulate him first in other matters. He never allowed women of the enemy to be molested. That is an essential code of the Hindus. Further, it would be poor sport to engage those isolated men at the Residency. Let them be reinforced and then we will show them the might of the chivalrous Marathas."

Appa Saheb struck his forehead in exasperation, and was soon ordered out of the audience chamber. "Maratha chivalry," he muttered as he walked out. "For foxes and jackals!"

Three days later, the Peshwa heard that Colonel Burr had arrived with a force of three thousand men, both Indian and British. "Now we march against the traders," he said with contempt.

Charles Ruthven watched the unforgettable scene in a kind of trance, praying that Eleanor and her party had managed to get onto the road to Matheran with the armed guards. He turned now to Elphinstone, who was discarding his Kolhapuri slippers for a pair of boots.

"I think we ought to go now," Ruthven said tersely.

Elphinstone smiled. "Yes, it is time. Our horses are in readiness."

They barely had time to leave the Residency before the Peshwa's army came forward like a roaring, inexorable tidal wave. From their refuge on a nearby hill, Elphinstone, Ruthven and other British fugitives saw the supple Maratha soldiers rush forward on lithe, swift horses. Behind them came the ponderous gun carriages, rumbling ominously. Peasants fled from the fields and bullocks ran with yokes still harnessed to their necks while wild antelopes and jackals leapt up in fear, as they witnessed this spectacle of two armies moving forward, over fields of ripening jowar and bajra, levelling everything as they went.

The flames of the burning Residency were soon visible in the October sky. "My books and journals!" Elphinstone cried. Above his lament was heard the cry of the Maratha army — "Har Har Mahadev! Shivaji Maharaj Ki Jai" — Hail Lord Shiva! Victory to Shivaji the King!

Charles Ruthven felt a natural sympathy for his countryman, yet some strange voice, a survivor, no doubt, from the spirit of Culloden, asked him why a handful of Englishmen and Scotsmen wanted to rule this vast, alien, incomprehensible land. Did they have a legitimate cause or a moral justification to be here at all? Nevertheless, Ruthven turned to Elphinstone and said, "I must join my regiment. General Hislop is in Kirkee."

All his life he would remember the terrible stillness of the battlefields as the two armies measured each other's potential. A deep hush fell, broken only by the restless trampling and neighing of horses. Suddenly, spears and lances were brandished and held aloft. Flags of both nations fluttered on pennants. The bugle cry had hardly ceased when the two cavalries rushed towards each other. Charles Ruthven saw a blur of brown faces ... the Indian soldiers hired by the Company army to fight their Indian comrades. Even as he fought, fiercely and bravely, Charles Ruthven felt pity for the soon-to-be defeated people.

The Peshwa's men were defeated at Kirkee. They regrouped and pursued the British upto Koregaon, and then Ashti. Here, the Maratha commander, Bapu Gokhale, was killed in battle. Ruthven heard a cry of lament and despair. He knew, as did the Marathas, that the battle was over.

Yet, the Marathas did not give up. The reverses suffered by the Peshwa roused the rulers of Gwalior, Indore, Baroda and Nagpur. Had they joined together earlier, at Assaye, or even a year ago, the Company could not have snuffed out their independence as a strong breeze snuffs out feeble candle flames.

"They have united!" Ruthven exclaimed to General Hislop, when they finally met by the banks of the river Narbada in the cool, clear winter of 1818.

"It is too late!" Hislop retorted. "We will smash the Confederacy."

They did. The unconcerted, uncoordinated attacks could be met by the British. Peshwa Baji Rao surrendered to John Malcolm. The Raja of Nagpur had attacked the Residency and was repulsed. He fled to the Punjab. The Raja of Indore was defeated by Hislop, and the Raja of Gwalior agreed to peace with the Company.

From afar, he saw a familiar figure standing on the sloping terrace of the Residency. He spurred his horse into a gallop until he was before her, a pale, frail creature with a tremulous smile. "Eleanor. Oh Eleanor," he cried, drawing her close. "I was so afraid I might not see you ... that ... oh what fears I have fought, my dear!"

Eleanor stood in his embrace, glad of his strong, comforting arms around her, and even more because he seemed so happy to see her. "I too was afraid for you, dearest," she murmured, gently drawing away to look upon his lean, sunburnt face and the fiery hair bleached by the sun.

Charles Edward held his breath, afraid to ask about the child; afraid that it had died in the ordeal of the flight from Poona, and smitten by remorse that he had acted harshly, thinking of battles and not of the being who loved him so entirely.

"Come inside ... we have a room in the undamaged part of the villa ... where we stay. Mr. Elphinstone has been very kind."

Charles Ruthven followed her to a large room, bare except for trunks, a straw pallet and a wicker cradle. A sturdy woman with a wheat-coloured complexion and high cheekbones gently rocked the cradle. She rose upon his entry and bowing, left the room. Slowly, breathlessly, he went over to the cradle and saw a red-haired baby asleep in it. He watched the infant for some time and then turned to Eleanor, to take her hands and kiss each in turn, almost in homage — for her courage and endurance.

It took Eleanor all evening to describe her ordeal in the hillside village, the kind ministrations of Moti-bai, the birth of their son, and of the fate of the villagers. "It made little difference to them that you were an officer in Hislop's army and their men were in the Peshwa's," she said softly. "They only thought of me as a woman in distress, a mother with a child ..."

"They are a fine people," Charles Ruthven said quietly.

Eleanor looked at him with something like a challenge in her eyes. "Is it necessary to vanquish such a people? Do we have anything superior to offer to them?'

Charles Ruthven seemed troubled and was spared an answer by the appearance of the Resident, who had been strolling in the garden, admiring the unmolested jacarandas. Coming up to them, he said, "Damn the fellows for burning my books! At a time like this I should have liked to read Cicero's. "Carthage a delanda."

I feel what the Romans must have felt after the defeat of Carthage." He paused and murmured, "Make no mistake, Carlus Edwardus, we are the new Rome! The Company is now the paramount power. Neither the Moghuls, nor the Rajputs, nor the Marathas can challenge our power."

Now it was Ruthven's turn to laugh. "Mr. Elphinstone, you delight me. Indeed you do. If a man ever lived in Rome and Athens, it is you. Do you fancy yourself as a Roman Consul in far Carthage or Judae, executing the orders of Augustus?"

Pale fires glinted in Elphinstone's eyes and flared out as swiftly as they had ignited. "Ours will be a better empire than Augustus', for we have conquered India. Beyond lies the far Orient —upto Japan. To them all we will carry our torch of classical learning ... and the dignity of man."

He sighed and added briskly, "But we start with the peasant of Maharashtra; with farming and land revenue, law and order, justice and education."

"Humble tasks for a tribune," Charles replied with a smile.

"Aye. But if future Indians remember us —when we have gone, as we will surely go one day — then it will be because of our revenue manuals and legal codes and educational institutions, and the grandeur of Pax Britannica."

"I wish they may," Eleanor replied, disturbed by Elphinstone's fervour. "But do not disrupt their lives too much or ... diminish their gentle humanity." She paused. "They too have something to teach us ... in the realm of the spirit."

Elphinstone regarded Eleanor's intense face with interest. "Have you concluded, my lady, that I am indifferent to the gentle heart of the ordinary Indian?"

Lady Eleanor nodded. "You are all immersed in dreams of empires and conquests, of laws and codes. Do not forget the people who have lived and toiled and suffered here for several millennia. They will outlive you dreams."

Charles Ruthven took her arm and bowed to the Resident. "We must prepare for our departure."

Elphinstone nodded. A shadow of wistfulness, even loneliness flitted across his face. He could have loved a woman like Eleanor, he mused. Quickly, he bowed to the couple and went slowly down the slope of the garden, murmuring lines from Theocritus.

Oh foxes, oh bears hiding in the mountains, farewell! I, Daphne the herdsman, will climb in wood and grove and glade. Farewell, oh Arethusa and the Rivers.

Winter is a fairy-tale season in northern India. The ancient Aryans invented religious festivals for the other seasons which scorch the earth with heat or drench it with a relentless rain, but for winter they had no need for festivals, because the splendour of pellucid skies and marigold sunshine, the cool and astringent air, is cause enough for celebration. Fields are amber with the rabi or second crop, not as fertile as the kharif but yet sweetly aromatic. Chrysanthemums, dahlias, cosmos, marigolds and sunflowers splash every garden with colour. The delicate, patrician rose must retreat before such earthy profusion and wait for leaner seasons to shine. The farmer draws water from the well or river, spilling glittering drops on the land. Sleek cattle and well-fed children romp on the pastures, plump with the last spurt of rain, before the advent of the scorching sun.

The Ruthvens made the long journey from Poona to Calcutta in this season of flowers, observing how the aridity of the Deccan plateau changed to the verdant voluptuity of the Gangetic plain. Fields of jowar and bajra fell behind the table-topped hills of the Deccan, going towards the harsher contours of the Nizam's territories, where the stern Hindu ethos of the Marathas was replaced by an even sterner Islam. The cupolas of temples soon gave way to those of mosques.

The Ruthvens halted in dak bungalows, where scrumptious meals were concocted out of wild fowl, new rice and curds. The nights were animated — by singing mosquitoes, nightingales, as well as by village campfires, around which peasants guarding their stored grains, sang of ancient deeds.

Charles Ruthven felt he was journeying in time, across centuries, as he passed through Central India. Malcolm had but scratched the surface of the hard, unrelenting traditions that kept man bound in poverty, superstition and subservience. Could laws lighten the burden of rusted customs, the prejudices of ignorance, he wondered. The cities of Central India fell behind until he came to the princely city of Hyderabad, where an inept Nizam ruled his rich and chaotic people. The Resident usually rode a richly caparisoned elephant, escorted by two companies of infantry and cavalry.

Major Kirkpatrick received the Ruthvens amidst the grandeur of the Residency, and listened to the accounts of the battles against the Marathas with a supercilious smile on his theatrical face.

"It is heartening to note that Elphinstone has done what I did many years ago — brought the Indian rulers under British suzerainty. He ought to have done it earlier."

Ruthven's ire was roused. "The Maratha Confederacy was the paramount power in India until a few months ago," he reminded Kirkpatrick coldly.

The thick eyebrows shot up. "Then all the more reason for subduing it." He sighed. "I won the Nizam's territories for the Company in a single tour de force. You may have heard of my confrontation with an overwhelming force of 14,000 French trained sepoys."

"I have heard of that engagement from Elphinstone," Ruthven admitted.

Kirkpatrick smiled benignly. "I dare day he was impressed, as were many others. The Governor General — Wellesley — wanted me on his staff at once ... but I preferred the post my brother held here as Resident."

Charles Ruthven nodded with an expression of innocence. Elphinstone had told him of how a Hyderabadi noblewoman had declared her love to the young Kirkpatrick and he yielding to the passionate lady, had married her and lived with her in utmost felicity. The lonely, pavilioned Rang Mahal, set amidst spreading trees, was the zenana for the Lady Khairunissa or Mrs. Kirkpatrick, who refused to live in the male dominated Residency.

"You have built a beautiful Residency .... and the Rang Mahal," Eleanor Ruthven ventured. "It is said that the villa, however, is outshone by the gracious dweller within."

Kirkpatrick beamed as a man should, on being complimented for beautiful possessions. "Tell you what, Lady Eleanor," he said expansively, "I shall take you there to have tea with my lady."

The Ruthvens were struck by the attachment of Major Kirkpatrick for his Hyderabadi wife and the two children she had borne him, William and Catherine Aurora. As Ruthven drank tea and murmured appropriate responses to the talkative Resident's monologue, Eleanor's keen eyes noted that the British Resident dyed his hands and hair with the herb, henna, and outlined his eyes with kajal, kohl. The Moghul court dress and hookah were part of the picture as well. Sitting in the pavilion in the mellow winter twilight, Charles Ruthven wondered if his father had also maintained this Indian style of life with his first wife, Shirin Begum. Had Alexander Ruthven been as devoted to Shirin as Kirkpatrick was to Khairunissa? Then he remembered that his father had brought a French mistress to share his life and still later, had thrust Georgiana Manham on them both. Whom had his father loved? Or had they all been a part of his thirst for triumph?

After an audience with the Nizam (who asked Ruthven to assure the Burra Lat of his loyalty), the Ruthvens followed the road north-east towards Calcutta. Moti-bai had lost her husband in battle and had decided to join her fate with the Ruthvens' particularly little James.

The mighty rivers, Godavari and Mahanadi lay in between, calm and blue under a tranquil winter sky, girded by lands rich in rice, maize and sugarcane. One of Charles' escorts, an old Hindu sepoy, told him of how the great Rama, divine king of Ayodhya, had passed through these lands, on his way south when exiled by his stepmother.

"Here, Ruthven Saheb," the sepoy told him reverently, "Shri Rama spent idyllic days with his wife Sita, while a devoted Lakshman walked behind. Little did they know that their halcyon days would soon end and the princess Sita would be abducted by the demon king of Lanka."

Ruthven's acquaintance with the two great epics of India — the Ramayana and Mahabharata — had been cursory, derived more from hearsay than direct study. Sir William Jones, judge and Indologist, had gifted a few translated verses to his mother which Charles Ruthven mildly curious, had browsed through. Now Havildar Surdas' reverence aroused his interest again and on the long road over the river valleys, Ruthven heard by campfire, the immortal story of the Ramayana — of the stern honour of Rama, the devotion of brother Lakshman and the indestructible purity of the tragic Sita, who was abandoned in the forests, though her body was heavy with Rama's children, not because she was impure but because Rama put the wishes of his subjects before his own love and happiness.

Surdas wept on the closing scene, when Sita, mortified by Rama's desire for yet one more ordeal by fire to test her chastity, cried to Mother Earth to devour her.

Charles Ruthven listened, bemused, for the story of Sita had been similar to that of Helen of Troy's except in the characters of the two women. The Hindu story had insisted on righteousness to the point of cruelty while the Greek epic had brought the reward of human passion and folly. He wondered if the Ramayana and the Iliad symbolised the essential spirit of difference between India and Europe: one which accepted and acquiesced to suffering and the other which defied the pain decreed by fate until the end. Was this spirit of rebellion, the stubborn attitude of a Prometheus, the reason for the progress of Europe while India retreated before challenges?

Small towns fell behind as they took the coastal road hemmed by the Bay of Bengal. They took a detour to see the ancient Sun Temple at Konarak, whose splendid sculpture spoke eloquently of India's rich material and cultural tradition. Charles and Eleanor sat on a large boulder, silent and surprised, for having discovered an India that they never knew existed: an India as rich in stone as was Greece and Rome; an India lustrous with legends equal to the Iliad and Odyssey.

The sun set behind the rice fields, leaving the dark eastern sea and sky speckled by an early Venus, and her stellar attendants. A new world seemed to open before Charles Ruthven; a world he had kept at a distance all these years but which now burst upon him with a stubborn demand for love and understanding. "Was it this same spirit which I felt attending me as I rode over the Deccan plateau?" he wondered. "Has the land of my birth, though not mine own, claimed me at last?'

Darkness set in with the startling swiftness of a February dusk. Charles was roused from his reflections by the vesper ceremonies of a traveller; the pitching of tents and lighting of fires. Surdas, the singer of grandeur unconscious of the turmoil he had unleashed in his commander, was occupied with the roasting of fish over a fire, while others laid out their clothes and beddings in the main tent. Bhistis, the water carriers came back to camp from the nearby village, replenished with water. Moti-bai tended to little James and her own child.

After supper was eaten and everyone rested in their tents, Charles Ruthven lay awake, listening to the ceaseless roar of the breakers nearby. Turning to Eleanor, he whispered, "You are indeed my pole star, Eleanor."

Eleanor turned to see him better in the luminous starlight. "Why do you say that?"

"Because you were the one to first glimpse the grandeur of India — not in her past glory but in the dignity of her humble people. And I, who was born here have found it only now."

Eleanor sat up, wrapping the peignor around her. "Now that you have made this discovery, what will you do, Charles?"

"What will I do? he echoed, drawing her close. "I will try to be something more than a nabob, or a conquering soldier."

"I am glad," Eleanor whispered, and lay down again, warm and contented.

20

And the Twain Did Meet

Brajesh Chowdhury, the zamindar of Mayurganj, stood on the embankment of the sacred river, awaiting the bajra of Charles Edward Ruthven, as it glided over the rippling gold and blue waters of the replenished river, its fringed silk canopy fluttering in the fresh breeze of Sharat, the autumn. It was a big day in Mayurganj.

Brajesh had met Charles Ruthven at a meeting of the Atmiya Sabha, the Society of Friends, in Calcutta, where the celebrated Raja Ram Mohan Roy had presided. This society had been the Raja's creation, an inspired effort to reform Hindu society, free it from the shackles of superstitions and restore it to the pristine glory of the Vedic times.

Ruthven had attended the meeting, eager to meet the brilliant visionary who had had the courage to denounce Hindu orthodoxy, and advocate the reform of society.

In the aftermath of the Maratha wars, the Company government had expected a simmering resentment among Hindus since the Marathas were its militant protagonists. It was surprised, instead, by the efforts of men like Ram Mohan Roy to accept British rule.

Charles Ruthven had listened in amazement as the Raja had said, "British rule is a historical necessity. If the Company, instead of only waging wars and collecting taxes, becomes also an agent of progress, if it unites the chaos of kingdoms under a central authority, promotes tranquillity and imposes just laws — then India will benefit by foreign rule." He paused and glanced at his western friends, among them the Reverend William Adams. "We want a partnership with Britain."

The Indian aristocrats and merchants had listened with as much wonder as Ruthven. Brajesh Chowdhury, however, had not been surprised.

"Will adoption of British laws and customs benefit India entirely?" Charles Ruthven had asked Ram Mohan Roy. "I understand that India has an ancient civilisation, rich in mathematics, philosophy, and social organisation. Why should that not be revived?"

The Raja had smiled. "The richness of Indian civilisation is indisputable. Scholars in the last century, such as William Jones, Colebrook, Halhed and Wilkins, rediscovered the forgotten glory of our religion and literature. For centuries, Indians had forgotten the rich philosophical legacy of the Vedas and Upanishads. Invasions from the north west left Indians bereft of hope, pride and courage. They saw the desecration of their most sacred shrines and reeled under the furious iconoclasm of the invaders. In fact, Indians had retreated into their inner selves. Not only did the peasants and craftsmen of frontier provinces bury their grains and gold under a silent earth, the priests and princes buried their awareness and even identities under a thick veil of ignorance and arrogance. There was no other way to counteract the superior force and organisation of the invaders. India went inwards and eventually backwards to preserve a confused identity and a troublesome heritage. Intellectual and cultural activities dwindled in the atmosphere of insecurity that prevailed. The kings and princes who were the traditional patrons of artists and scholars were now interested only in nurturing armies to fight each other. Creative energies were stifled and living religion retreated to quietist sects, haunting temples and river banks. India began to die." He paused. "India must now be revived. Paradoxically, she must be revived by another foreign power who can open for us the world of modern knowledge which is changing Europe." He paused again and smiled at Ruthven. "I believe that Britain, the leader of liberalism and enlightenment, will help us."

Charles Ruthven did not reply. He could only remember his father who had grown rich as an unscrupulous private trader, and wrested a jagir from a hapless prince. "Liberalism and enlightenment," he echoed involuntarily, distressed.

The Raja nodded. "Quite so, Mr. Ruthven," he said, as if divining the cause of Ruthven's darkened countenance. "Your uncle, Reverend Arthur Latimer, was the embodiment of this spirit, as was his friend, William Adams. They first made me realise the potential of an Indo-British relationship."

Brajesh Chowdhury started. He had not realised that the aloof, handsome man was the amiable little boy he had met almost twenty-seven years ago in Ruthven House. He had been a boy of seven, on his way to join Mr. Sherbourne's School at Chitpur Road, on the urging of Fiona Latimer.

He got up and introduced himself to Charles Edward Ruthven, who stared at the young zamindar.

"Perhaps you do not recall our meeting many years ago?" Brajesh asked hesitantly.

"On the contrary," Ruthven replied. "I remember the day very well. We played with kites in the garden while the adults talked."

"What a prodigious memory!" Brajesh exclaimed. "My memories are vague."

Charles Ruthven did not reply. How could he tell this orthodox Hindu that it had been the summer of a domestic holocaust, when his father had discovered a liaison between his mother and half-brother. It was, in a sense, the end of innocence.

"So we meet again ... after so many events," Brajesh mused. "Our fathers are no more ... but Mrs. Fiona Latimer ... she lives. Have you seen her since your return?"

Charles lowered his eyes to contemplate his hands. "No, I have not. It has been remiss of me," he said quietly, once more reluctant to tell the Brahmin zamindar of the confusion Fiona Latimer's name caused, as well as about his father's fulminations against her.

Brajesh smiled. "Mrs. Latimer is my neighbour. Her son Ian

and I are disciples of William Carey and William Adams." He paused, once more hesitant to revive a dangerous connection and then plunged on, tantalised by the prospect of such a friendship. "It would give me great pleasure if you paid us a visit at Mayurganj ... and joined our efforts."

"Mayurganj," Charles Ruthven echoed. "Abode of peacocks ... How much I have heard of that place! It was there that my father made his fortune ... and ..."

"And where my father discovered both the goodness and cruelty of the British," Brajesh said softly. "Will you come, Mr. Ruthven?"

"As soon as you can receive us, Mr. Chowdhury."

The news of the impending visit was not welcomed by the zamindar's family. Brajesh's mother, Indumati, had reservations about beef-eating, wine-drinking foreigners. But her objections rather than being political nor religious, were more immediate and personal. She had never forgiven a firingi woman, Fiona Ruthven Dalrymple Latimer, for bewitching her husband.

Indumati had been a child-bride of thirteen when the affair had begun and by the time she was eighteen, Indrajit Chowdhury had parted from Fiona and had fallen deeply in love with his imperious and beautiful second wife. But Indumati had always sensed in him a lingering desire for the flame-haired foreigner, which had always disquieted her. She was not possessive by nature. Like many high-caste Brahmin zamindars, Indrajit had three wives and Indumati had not only learnt to co-exist with them but to love the older Bishnupriya and younger Kamalakshi. But Indrajit's passion for Fiona, she felt, was a thing apart, bound up with his dream world. Even after parting from Fiona, he had asked another firingi woman, Liselotte, to paint a portrait of Fiona. Indumati had hated the miniature that had reposed on his table. When Indrajit had died, she had banished the painting to the lumber room, though Fiona still lived on in the next estate, to torment her.

And now to hear that a nephew of that woman was coming to Mayurganj! She felt a strange and inexplicable pain, as if the anguish of the past was extending into the future; as if these wild and wilful Ruthvens were once again seeking to disrupt the peace of their world.

"No, Mother," Brajesh argued gently, reluctant to offend the person he admired most. "They do not come to disrupt our lives. On the other hand, they will enrich it with their ideas."

"We do not wish for that! We wish to be left undisturbed!" Indumati looked at her son. They will unsettle us ... and undermine our traditions. We have seen his father and another uncle ... cruel, grasping men. Let them not cross our thresholds!"

He took her fine, fair hands in his. "Mother, my adored mother, listen to me. They come as friends. Charles Edward is neither like Alexander Ruthven nor Henry Dalrymple ... he is quite different. Receive him courteously, I entreat you!"

So now Brajesh Chowdhury stood awaiting the bajra that would bring the Ruthvens to Mayurganj. Tenants of the vast estate, fisherfolk and artisans had found some excuse to be present nearby on that day. They were curious to see the son of Alexander Ruthven, the man who had almost succeeded in buying up Mayurganj during the terrible famine in 1770, when Indrajit Chowdhury had failed to pay the land dues. That event was fifty years old, but it lingered on in the minds and tongues of the older folk. Nor had they forgotten the indigo planter, Dalrymple, who had tortured his peasants and tenants. They had been glad when the man had died and his attractive young widow had become the mistress of the zamindar. It was in the capacity of Fiona's nephew that Charles Ruthven was now being welcomed by the folk of Mayurganj.

The large bajra drew up before the landing ghat, bobbing on the gentle swell of the autumnal river. Charles Ruthven stepped ashore, and bowed to the zamindar, who responded likewise. Then stepping forward, the two young men tentatively stretched out their hands. A firm handshake followed. Then Charles stepped back and reached out to grasp the thin and sallow-faced woman who waited in the canopied cabin. Gently, he brought her forward and almost carried her to the ghat.

"May I present my wife, Lady Eleanor Ruthven?"

Brajesh Chowdhury bowed deeply, gingerly touching the frail white hand offered to him. He had expected a beautiful wife for the handsome Mr. Ruthven. In contrast, Lady Eleanor was pale, almost ashen, and her chestnut hair was lustreless. There was, he noticed, breeding in the aquiline nose and firm lips, and an expression of pain in her large, green eyes. Her smile, however, warmed his heart; it was as vulnerable as a child's. He had hardly shaken her hand when another woman emerged from the barge — a being as different from Eleanor as the autumn from the monsoon. Indeed, her hair was golden as the October sunlight and the eyes were blue, like the sky. Her skin was the colour of cream and her ripe figure apparent to all. Brajesh Chowdhury stared at the apparition until Charles Ruthven said in a strange tone, "This is Lady Cressida, sister to my wife."

Brajesh bowed in silence while Cressida smiled sardonically.

At once, a chaos of sounds broke forth; drums beat and flutes blew, while young men danced something that reminded Eleanor of a highland jig. The zamindar led the couple to the open curricle that awaited under a huge ashwath tree. They seated themselves — Lady Eleanor in the main seat with the child and the two young men facing her. Two attendants in yellow costumes leapt up behind to hold two large, white, tasselled umbrellas over them. The short drive to the house past fields of ripening rice, sugarcane and mulberry bushes took ten minutes. All along, the carriage path was lined with shirish trees, spreading filigree branches and leaves into the glowing air.

It was with considerable trepidation that Brajesh Chowdhury alighted from the carriage when it stopped before the new wing. A hundred dreaded thoughts flashed through his mind, filling him with apprehension that the welcoming ceremony would go wrong.

Indumati stood at the doorway of the new wing with her daughter-in-law, who held a silver tray containing earthen lamps, coconuts, flowers and flaming blobs of camphor. The attendants fluttered their tongues to alluliate and blow on the conchshells. The stately dowager then pushed forward Annapurna, wife of Brajesh, to perform arati — the circling of a tiny silver lamp around the faces of the visitors.

Annapurna glanced at the guests with veiled interest — the flame-haired saheb and the two women who she presumed were his two wives; one glowing with health and the other weary and frail. Her heart was touched by the pathos of the plain wife. Sensing Annapurna's sympathy, Eleanor reached out to touch her hand.

Annapurna stiffened with apprehension. The touch of a mlechha was profane and necessitated an elaborate bath of purification. Before she could withdraw her hand, Brajesh Chowdhury's eyes admonished her to behave properly.

The ceremonies over, the Ruthvens were led inside the new wing by the proud owner. It did not take Eleanor long to realise that the furnishings had been bought at an exorbitant cost from the auction shops of Calcutta, where departing Europeans deposited their possessions. She felt guilty at once that their visit had necessitated such an expenditure. Yet, as the day progressed, with a visit to the riverside temple, and tea on the roof garden, Eleanor was unable to regret her presence.

Charles Edward and Brajesh resumed, it seemed, the spontaneous rapport of that distant summer day when they had lured nightingales to their snares and caught baby monkeys on lowering branches. Now, however, they sat in a more vast and tranquil garden, with the lush Bengal landscape glimmering around them, as they discussed the upliftment of Indian society with the catalyst of western ideas. They argued over the means and discoursed on the diverse schools of thought; the conservative approach of the Indologists like Sir William Jones and Warren Hastings, who did not wish to disturb Indian customs, and reformists like Malcolm and Lord Hastings, who wished to bring India into the mainstream of western civilisation. When they tired of these discourses, the two men walked on the bunds bordering vast fields of ripening kharif paddy, or sailed on the brimming river. In the evenings, they sat on the roof garden gazing at the moonlit panorama of the fields or the stellar designs in the brilliant sky, forging a bond that was as simple as the world around them.

Lady Cressida continued, however, to intrude on these discussions. Brajesh sensed at once that Charles had once been enamoured of the beautiful woman and that some residue of that attraction remained hidden behind a deliberate indifference. Cressida talked animatedly and often sharply, ridiculing both Indians and the British, and laughed at every oddity that caught her eye, making rude judgements on Indian servility and British pomposity.

Eleanor remained in the cool rooms of the new villa with her son James and Baby Catherine, pensive and withdrawn as she watched Cressida's witchcraft.

The half-sister had burst in on them one stormy monsoon afternoon, escorted by two raffish officers who had become her 'slaves' in Madras. In the five years since their parting, Cressida had married a rich, old, iron magnate whose fierce desire for a young voluptuous wife had hastened his death. Wealthy and free, she had journeyed to India "to see dear Eleanor" but in actual fact to win back Charles Edward, a task which Eleanor realised, was proceeding very well.

When Brajesh went to attend to matters relating to his estate, Cressida followed Charles like a panther stalking its prey. Her throaty laughter brought back memories of London and country houses, of dancing the quadrille or riding through clusters of ash and beech in sun-dappled English woods. Cressida's parted lips brought back a sensation of their taste. He was aware of her heady perfume, the mint-scented breath on his face, the sensuous pressure of silken hands on his.

"Do not stare at me so!" Cressida chided one day. "Give me a brotherly kiss if you must." And she pressed herself close, asking for surrender.

"Conduct yourself properly," Charles rebuked her, feeling, at the same time, a primitive desire to capture those full, heavy lips and possess that eager, yielding body.

"Truly, Charles?" she asked with a mocking smile. "Are you certain you do not envy the old zamindar who had three wives?" Charles Ruthven stormed out, because he had indeed envied Zamindar Indrajit Chowdhury for just that.

One day at dinner, Cressida provoked Charles to anger as she sat in a pink muslin dress, revealing the deep cleft between her swelling bosom, her golden hair loosely curled around bare, gleaming shoulders, her eyes bright with desire. Brajesh smiled as Cressida extolled polygamy of high-born Hindus. Charles coloured and Eleanor watched them in deepening melancholy.

"If Henry VIII had been allowed to take two wives, there would have been no fuss of the Reformation. Think of that, Charles!" Cressida said,

Charles did not reply, but Brajesh was delighted and teased Cressida by discussing the Reformation with deliberate solemnity, until she rose yawning, though she managed to lure Charles Ruthven out for a walk on the river bank.

Eleanor sat by the windows, weeping. She was surprised, suddenly, by the arrival of Indumati. "I have come with a woman who knows the art of massage," she said in Bengali, which Eleanor had learnt to speak. "She will put strength back into your limbs and bring the lustre back into your hair. Will you permit her to attend to you?"

Lady Eleanor glanced at the wizened woman with her nut-brown face. "Is she ... capable of such magic?" she asked with a wan smile.

Indumati smiled back. "Strange that you say 'magic'. We do indeed call her a witch, a 'jaduburi'. But she is a sweet old thing. Her wizardry is only in her hands."

While Lady Eleanor hesitated, Indumati's sapient eyes scrutinised her. Then, slowly, she said, "You are still young, Lady Eleanor, and have yet to bear more children. You must be strong ... and attractive ... for your husband. Men tend to stray with little excuses."

Lady Eleanor felt a hot flush on her face. Had Charles told his zamindar friend about Cressida? Or was Charles' indifference apparent to all?

Indumati carefully selected a folded betel leaf from her tiny silver paan box. "All men are the same. It is for women to take care."

For a week, Eleanor lay on her bed while the wizened old woman massaged her tired limbs with a concoction of oils, and washed her hair with a blend of herbs. She made her drink many glasses of ghol, a sweet butter-milk and honey concoction, to supplement the vegetarian diet from the Chowdhury kitchen. Charles Ruthven laughed and teased her though he, too, began to gradually see the change in his wife's figure and colour.

Cressida seethed in frustration at Charles' pussilanimity, but was soon diverted by an easier victory that she scored with the enigmatic Englishman across the estate.

Ian was Fiona Latimer's surviving son, a man as dreamy and vague as his father had been practical. He had inherited the parish from his father, where he continued the good works of the Reverend Arthur Latimer though with a lesser intensity. Ian's real guru was the Reverend William Adams, a friend of Ram Mohan Roy, whose home he frequented in order to listen to theological discussions by both Hindus and Christians.

He was informed shortly by a messenger from the zamindar of Mayurganj that his Ruthven cousins wished to visit him. He hurried from his study to inform his mother.

Fiona Latimer sat on the veranda of the old house, built seventy years ago by her first husband, soon after the battle of Plassey. She had long ceased to remember Henry Dalrymple, who had been dead for almost fifty years. But she thought often of the other two men in her life — Arthur Latimer and Indrajit Chowdhury — who had given her both affection and passion. Those two were also dead, while she, nearing eighty, lived on, heavy with memories. Smiling at Ian, her youngest child, Fiona said, "You must not be disappointed, my dear, if Charles Edward is not overly cordial. He may have inherited his Papa's disapproval of your Mama."

"Mother dear," Ian murmured, stooping to kiss the white head, "how could anyone disapprove of the kindest creature on God's earth?"

Fiona smiled at her son. "Dearest, you are so like your Papa," she murmured. "He too thought I was kind and gentle. But I'm not. I was rather wicked in people's eyes."

Ian flushed. These oblique references to her affair with Indrajit Chowdhury upset him. "Quite, quite. I dare say they did. But we know better. Now, when shall we invite Charles Edward and Eleanor to dine with us?"

"You must ask Matilda. She is now the chatelaine of Dubb's Point."

Matilda, Ian's wife, had been debating the matter for some time. It would be a social achievement to have the daughter of an earl for dinner and to make contact with the rich, influential cousin, Charles Edward. However, a grand dinner would involve heavy expenditure. The estate had not been doing well in recent years, thanks to Ian's preoccupation with theosophical predicaments. Instead of tending to the rich coconut plantation and rice fields, Ian journeyed frequently to Calcutta. Revenues had fallen and taxes were in arrears. That was where Charles Ruthven could help. She settled on a compromise. The Ruthven cousins would be invited to tea.

Not many days later, Charles Edward and his wife, accompanied by Chowdhury, came in the zamindar's open curricle to the nearby estate.

Hearing the clatter of wheels on the gravel path, Ian bounded down the veranda steps, in shirtsleeves and trousers, his fiery hair tousled. Stepping down from the curricle, Charles Edward stopped to gaze upon his cousin.

Fiona stood on the veranda, surveying the two men who resembled each other so closely in colour and features. Their differences, however, went deep. It was not merely because Ruthven was impeccably dressed and Latimer wore rumpled clothes. It was in the expression of their blue eyes; one had the cool resolve of Alexander Ruthven, the other the kindly gentleness of Arthur Latimer.

The moment of scrutiny over, the cousins embraced each other, laughing to hide their momentary embarrassment and unease. Then each called his wife to complete the ceremonies. Matilda was surprised by the amiable greetings offered by Lady Eleanor. Her gaze lingered on the lustrous pearls that had once graced the neck of a Moghul princess. "There is much to be derived from this relationship," Matilda thought with self -satisfaction, though she could not quell a stab of jealousy that fate had not given her as splendid a husband as Charles Edward instead of the disorganised Ian Latimer.

"Aunt Fiona!" Charles Ruthven greeted the white haired, stout woman who stood on the veranda.

She brushed away the memories. They came so frequently now that there was little of the future left to dream about. She greeted her nephew affectionately. Eleanor dropped a curtsey before the old lady, who kissed her while her eyes went to the other man in the circle — Brajesh, son of her dead love.

It was rarely that Brajesh came to Dubb's Point these days, because the visits brought on a strange depression. He liked to remember his father as a stern patriarch, an ascetic who fasted and prayed to expiate his sins, and the man his mother adored. Dubb's Point made him remember his father as the reckless, defiant man who had kept assignations in this very house with Fiona when she was a lusty, young widow. It had happened before his birth but somehow he felt as if he had lived through their tormented passion.

The tea was wholesome and tasty. Matilda knew how to make the best use of given resources. As the wife of an indigo planter, she could have commanded much more, had her husband not decided to become a vicar and theologian like his father. It irked her particularly now as she saw Charles Ruthven's opulent elegance and the aristocratic indolence of Brajesh Chowdhury as they sat around the trestle table under a spreading banian tree.

Conversation ceased with the arrival of Cressida, just as tea was ending. The high phaeton she had purchased in Calcutta clattered over the gravel path and lurched to a halt before the balcony.

Ian Latimer was roused from his musings by the apparition that alighted from the carriage and came forward in a flurry of muslin and lace, the high bonnet slung back to reveal a crown of golden hair. He stood up, wild eyed and muttered, "Ganges ... the goddess ... or is it Proserpine?"

Charles Ruthven stood up with reluctant courtesy, half-annoyed and half-amused. "No cousin Ian, she is Circe herself," he said mischievously. "Perhaps you have not seen Junos before, but they abound in England. Let me introduce you to my sister-in-law, Lady Cressida Busby."

Lady Cressida smiled at Ian, who dissolved before the magnetism of her ripe lips, the taut yet opulent figure, a gorgeous disorder of golden hair and eyes that held a feline charm. Matilda Latimer glared at the visitor in uncomprehending anger. Fiona Latimer beckoned to Cressida, who kissed the old woman's leathery cheeks.

"How extraordinary," Fiona murmured. "She is like Georgiana ..."

Cressida laughed. "Georgiana is my aunt, once removed, and almost became my mother, did she not, brother Charles?"

Charles Ruthven's face tightened but he said nothing.

"Have I come in time to hear you preach, dear Reverend Latimer?" Cressida asked softly, glancing at the low church tower nearby.

"Preach?" Ian echoed stupidly.

"Sermons," Cressida murmured.

"Oh! Yes... er ... if you are interested ..."

"Indeed, I am," Cressida replied. "I hear that you give singular sermons."

Ian stared at her, unable to speak. Cressida's laugh was a purr of delight. "I hear that you are a heretic ... that your Christian certitude has dissolved before your incursion into the Hindu faith?"

Ian nodded, failing to see the amused contempt in those flashing eyes. Though Brajesh Chowdhury laid a warning hand on his, Ian broke forth into an impassioned plea.

"Why should the two faiths be in conflict? Christ can be the son of God along with Krishna. But who is this God? The bearded patriarch of the Bible or the Divine One who is both formless and unknowable? Christ is part of this great universal soul which can absorb all mysteries and miracles in its boundless magnitude."

Charles Ruthven glanced at his aunt Fiona, mutely begging her to restrain his cousin from further indiscretion. The old lady rose and sighed. "Ian, my son," she said, "it is not your duty to unify the faiths but to propound the message of Christ, as your father taught you to do. Those who have found solace in the message of Christ and His promise of resurrection do not wish to be ensnared into the doom of the karmic cycle. Remember that when you speak to your neophytes."

Ian sighed, shaking his head. "You speak now, Mama, like that odious magistrate, Carruthers. He, too, admonished us to banish all interest in Hinduism."

"And very rightly so!" Matilda stormed, furious with everybody. "You disgrace me by dressing like a native and speaking like one!"

"Robert de Nobili did the same in South India and he won many converts," Ian hastened to remind his wife.

"He was a Roman Catholic ... Ian Latimer ... and did not pretend to be an Anglican!" Matilda's pale eyes swept over them all in anger and hatred. "But then your maternal grandfather was a papist and traitor to boot. How can you be different?"

Charles Ruthven had been watching the exchange with embarrassment. Now he turned to his cousin's wife and said, "Pray keep a civil tongue in your head about my grandfather, Ma'am. He was a brave and loyal man, and died for his beliefs. If Ian and I are half as noble, we shall be happy."

Matilda glanced around her, red eyed and red nosed. "Why, you all assume the airs of aristocrats but at heart you are traitorous Jacobites! Yes, I understand now! That explains your sympathy for these natives, these heathens!" She burst into tears and fled inside the house.

Cressida burst into ripples of laughter. "But how diverting!" she cried. "I do believe I shall extend my stay!"

"But of course," Brajesh Chowdhury declared. "You cannot go without seeing our Durga Puja."

"Indeed I shall not!" Cressida replied and then turning to Charles, whispered, "I am so partial to heathen customs, dear brother."

Brajesh pretended not to hear but Ian was alert at once. "Truly, Lady Cressida? Why, then I must take you to the fringe of our estate, the original Dab Tola, where tantric sadhus practise rituals. Would you like to see that?"

"Above all things!" Cressida enthused.

No one dared protest; Cressida brooked no interference in her plans. Watching her, Charles Ruthven wondered once again how it would have been if vibrant, reckless Cressida had been his wife. Would they have moved through life in a series of exciting discoveries? He felt a shaft of pain at the thought that perhaps he had deprived himself of great joy by spurning Cressida.

"And now ... it is too late. All I can do is watch her entice poor Ian," he thought in sudden misery.

Eleanor rose. "I must go in and thank Cousin Matilda for her hospitality," she said in a weary, dejected voice, as if she had divined her husband's thoughts.

An air of excitement descended on Mayurganj on the new moon night of October. The entire household rose at three in the morning to bathe in the river. Brajesh led the taperlit procession, followed by his brother Harish, their sons, wives, daughters and finally, Indumati. Servants waited by the water's edge with the flaring tapers, as the family bathed and the servants, in groups, also took a quick dip before hurrying back to the house where six Brahmin priests waited to read the 'Chandi Path', the litany of the goddess Durga. As the Chowdhurys and their guests and retainers sat on the roof terrace, under a canopy of stars, the priests recited the story of King Rama's quest for the great goddess shortly before his duel with King Ravana, who had abducted his wife Sita. Charles and Eleanor sat apart, listening to the litany.

Cressida waited at the point where the two estates met, staring at the fields and groves, thatched huts and irrigation channels glimmering in the starlight and thought of Courtney Hall at Ashville, where the de Courtneys had lived from the time that they came from Normandy with the French conquerors of England, its church of square, crenellated Norman towers, fields of barley and wheat, thick, green woods and gentle slopes. It seemed far, far away from this flat terrain of endless rice fields and coconut groves, on the banks of a mighty, majestic river. Here there were no ancient houses belonging to aristocrats; here, nothing had survived the ravage of invaders. The temples were low, round, as if designed to escape the eye of the invaders, and the bells were muted as if they were afraid of being heard.

The hurrying figure of Ian made her start. At first glance, he could be mistaken for Charles Ruthven; only on closer scrutiny did the resemblance vanish. But the tousled fiery hair gave her a stab of pain and quickened her desire.

"Lady Cressida! You are waiting alone? Are you not afraid?" he asked, coming close.

"Of what should I be afraid, dear Reverend?" she asked tartly.

"They say that Henry Dalrymple — my mother's first husband — still roams here as a ghost and chastises the peasants by crying, 'Damn you natives! I will make you blue in the face with indigo!'"

"He will not disturb me," Cressida replied, staring at Ian and wishing it was Charles. "Shall we go to witness the pagan ceremonies?"

"Yes ... if you are quite certain ..."

"I am ... now take my hand ... I cannot see in the dark."

The coconut grove was a dark smudge in the starlit landscape. In between the trees, sudden flares of fire could be seen as the ascetics performed strange and complicated rituals to worship Shakti, the goddess of power. Ian Latimer led Cressida closer to the grove.

"Who are they worshipping?" Cressida asked.

"Shakti, or the elemental force of nature, the essence of life, represented by a goddess." He paused. "Do you see the woman there? They will use her in the ceremonies ... as vestal virgins were used in pagan Rome."

Cressida moved closer, clutching Ian's arms, staring mesmerised at the rituals of worship of the sadhus, their frenzied invocation to the goddess and the transfiguration of the village maiden, who was disrobed and made to sit on the tiger skin spread before the sacrificial fire.

"What will they do to her?" Cressida whispered.

Ian hesitated before saying, "They ... satisfy their lust ... and then ... destroy her as a symbol of lust and evil."

Cressida shuddered but did not draw away. The strange incantations sent a thrill through her, and aroused a powerful hunger. The drums beat slowly, and the flames of the sacrificial fire rose higher.

"It is time we left," Ian muttered, unable to endure the mounting tension of the ceremony.

Cressida did not, however, move away. "I was a frequent visitor to the Hell's Fire Club in London ..." she murmured. "I am not afraid."

"No ... I dare say ... but it could affront your delicacy," Ian said.

"Delicacy!" Cressida laughed derisively, turning to him. "Do you imagine a woman of delicacy would come to watch such a scene? Would ..."

A thin, high scream rent the air, followed by a series of strangled cries.

Cressida turned swiftly towards the grove and saw the girl lying inert below her violator, who had, after taking his pleasure, snuffed out her life. The scene stirred her own thwarted hunger. Returning to where Ian stood, Cressida drew close and raised her face to his, ripe lips parted in invitation. He stared at her in terror and awe, incredulous of what was happening. Then, as he understood the clamour of his own senses, Ian Latimer led Cressida to the solitude of the last patch of the indigo, helpless before her relentless sorcery. He was like a man possessed as he dissolved in Cressida's body. Never had he known such wild pleasure. Never had he known such a carnal beauty, who gave him a joyous deliverance from all the doubts that plagued his existence.

From afar, they could hear the chanting of the priests in the Chowdhury mansion, indifferent both to the dead sacrificial maiden and the voluptuous woman lying in the field.

Oh divine lady of radiant beauty
who art clad in the image of motherhood
To you I offer my salutations

Oh divine lady of radiant beauty
who are clad in the image of love
To you I offer my salutations

Oh divine lady of radiant beauty
who art clad in the image of power
To you I make my salutations.

The dark sky had lightened perceptibly when a thin sliver of a new moon guided Charles Ruthven to the spot where Cressida lay asleep, alluring and dishevelled.

"Get up, in heaven's name!" he cried, shaking her roughly.

Cressida was awake at once and sat up. "Charles! Oh Charles," she murmured, "is it really you?"

"Go to your room at once," he retorted. "Let no one see you ... heartless woman."

"What is plaguing you?" she snapped, tossing her golden curls.

Charles Ruthven's face was grim. "Ian tried to drown himself a short while ago. Some fisherfolk found him and revived him. Are you quite satisfied now?"

Cressida stared at Charles, a slow smile touching her lips. "No, my love, I wish it was you who had tried to drown yourself ... in despair over me ... Ian Latimer is no prize at all!"

Charles Ruthven regarded her in derisive silence before turning away.

"Do you understand why I did not wish to have these alien beings cross our threshold?" Indumati asked her son in the sunlit brilliance of Mahalaya morning. "Is this the way to begin the sacred festival?"

Brajesh Chowdhury held a huge silver bowl while his mother and wife plucked red hibiscus flowers and starry white shefalis for the morning puja. "I am surprised at Ian's behaviour. Wonder what possessed him?" he asked no one in particular.

The imperious dowager glanced at her son. "What is wrong with Latimer Saheb? The same malaise that took your father... these unprincipled firingi women! No shame, no restraint, nothing but gratification of their cravings!"

Annapurna's pale cameo face was suffused with colour. Indumati went on plucking flowers, muttering to herself about the evils of foreign rule.

"Charles Ruthven is close to the Burra Lat Saheb," Brajesh said quietly. "He is sympathetic to the ways of our people and the need to reform the debris. Ram Mohan Roy holds him in esteem as an enlightened Englishman. He can do much good. Can you not for the sake of this larger good, be courteous to Ruthven and his wife?"

Indumati gazed at her son and smiled slowly. "I will sit with Lady Eleanor and tell her the stories of the Puranas — of the noisy gods who fight and intrigue, love and hate and are occasionally defeated by earthly opponents. Will that please her?"

Brajesh bent down to touch his mother's feet. Her hand pressed his bent head in fervent benediction. "You know, Mother, I do not have to seek the blessings of Mother Durga as long as I have you."

Indumati smiled, though tears came to her eyes. "Oh yes, you do, my son. She is your Eternal Mother while I ... am a transient one."

The festival began in Mayurganj on the seventh moon of October.

Cressida had been persuaded by Fiona Latimer to leave for Calcutta. "Do not torment my poor Ian," Fiona had rebuked. "You have no dearth of other admirers." So Cressida had left, leaving Eleanor to enjoy the pageantry of Durga Puja.

That evening, when Charles Ruthven came into the suite of rooms, he found Eleanor deep in thought. "I saw you talking to Ian," he said quietly.

"I feel as if a new world awaits us, Charles, a world of ideas that we had never dreamt of."

He laid a hand on her slender shoulders, glad that she was no longer thin and sickly. "It is a new world that we have to discover Eleanor ... a new civilisation." He paused and smiled. "Thank heavens I can talk to you, my love ... that you have a mind."

"Yet a comely form is so powerful," she mused.

"Not when you have learnt of its emptiness," Charles replied and added almost inaudibly, "as I have."

Husband and wife gazed at each other in the cool, lamplit room, filled with a sense of oneness. They had always possessed this gift of knowing the other's thoughts, even when pain and pride had lain between them. Perhaps it was this very knowledge of the other which sharpened the pain at times and now flooded them with a gentle tenderness. He came to her, lifting her light figure from the window seat onto the silk-covered bed, eager to explore the warmth of her newly rounded body. His mouth found her lips, the tips of her small round breasts, the curve of her slim waist and hips. He felt desire flow over him and reach out to her. She offered herself with grace and tenderness melting at his touch. As the Sandhi puja began, and the eighth moon merged into the ninth, to celebrate the worship of union, Charles and Eleanor celebrated their oneness as well.

21

Joint Ventures

The Ruthvens' visit to Mayurganj had been a revelation. They felt as if they had been allowed entry into a hitherto unknown world, a terra incognita peopled by men and women who belonged to a complex civilisation, fraught with predicaments. Returning to Calcutta, Brajesh Chowdhury invited them to his rambling mansion on Chitpur Road, built by Brajesh's grandfather, soon after Plassey.

Standing on the veranda skirting the upper storey, Brajesh told Charles how he had studied law and court procedure under Robert Fergusson, in order that he might deal better with his land and legal problems. In time, he had become a legal adviser to other zamindars and argued on their behalf in the Diwani Adalat, the district courts. There he had met leading British merchants of the day, Gordon, Calder and McIntosh, who had helped him trade in silk, indigo and saltpetre.

Charles Ruthven had nodded, glancing at the road lined with broad courtyards, where palanquins were carried past, followed by carts and coaches. As they walked around, the English guests saw the central courtyard vibrant with people and noises; the clamour of cows being milked, palanquins cleaned, coaches polished, stoves lit with wood and cowdung cakes. Women bustled around the house, heads no longer veiled as they attended to vital tasks, boys studied in the upper rooms, attended by servants who fanned and fetched for the young masters, girls sewed or read amidst whispered gossip and laughter. Clerks and accountants hurried from office rooms with leather-bound ledgers. Meals were served, according to status, in several rooms and in the still afternoon, one could hear a woman's voice recounting stories, children's laughter, the contented sighs of well-fed men. Dusk ushered in a burst of ceremonies — of the lighting of lamps, blowing of conchshells and the appearance of people dressed in style to defy darkness.

"You are a rich man," Ruthven told Chowdhury. "Why do you frequent philosophic societies in search of ... answers?"

Chowdhury regarded his guests with a smile. "I learnt something of the forgotten grandeur of India from the scholars of the Asiatic Society, who were Ram Mohan Roy's friends. At the Calcutta Unitarian meetings, I learnt about Europe." Brajesh paused. "These two streams could produce a great culture."

"Yes," Ruthven agreed, pensive. "That could be so."

Brajesh Chowdhury returned the visit by going to Ruthven House. His wife, Annapurna, accompanied him, protesting, while the dowager Indumati advised her daughter-in-law: "Keep your eyes open, Anu, and tell me what you see. I have so longed to see that house which your father-in-law once described as a palace ...." She paused and added, "a palace of vice and violence."

Annapurna flung aside her veil in a rare gesture of protest. "Then why are you permitting me to go, Mother?" she cried.

Indumati smiled sagely. "So that, unlike me, you are not taken unawares. Your husband and Charles Saheb are going to be friends. Ensure that you do not have to deal with a flame-haired firingi sorceress lurking in the gardens of Ruthven House."

Annapurna paled. Indumati continued, "The danger is there. You know ... about your father-in-law's involvement with Fiona Ruthven." Annapurna bowed her head in distress. "I am not certain I can do anything if your son ..." she began, but could not continue.

Indumati laid a hand on her daughter-in-law's shoulder. "Go, child, and see everything. If there is peril, let us act with wisdom."

The Ruthvens' welcome gladdened Brajesh but could not thaw

Annapurna who sat heavily veiled, silent but agitated. The tinkle of her jewellery was the only sound that indicated her presence. Yet, through the gossamer veil, her wide eyes took in all the details of occidental opulence. The gilt chairs, tapestried screens, chandeliers and ormolu clocks were not unknown to her. Brajesh had purchased such stuff at high costs in auctions. But Lady Eleanor's lady friends struck her as strident creatures who talked loudly, laughed shrilly and shamelessly exposed their bosoms.

Returning home in their smart new cabriolet, Brajesh listened absent-mindedly to his wife. He had been stimulated by the men he had met at the Ruthvens'. They discussed politics and new philosophical ideas. "I hope you will get to like them, Anu," he told his wife quietly, "because Charles Ruthven and I are going to be partners in a new venture ... involving both the mind and money."

Ruthven, Chowdhury & Co., a joint stock company, was formed in 1822. The combined wealth of the two men was put into far-flung ventures. Their company began exporting silk, sugar and saltpetre to Europe. They also shipped rum, aniseed and nutmeg to New York. At Valparaiso, their ship, *Endeavour* was loaded with copper. From Europe, they brought in finished cloth, furnishings, wines, steel and basic machinery. They maintained agents in New York and Philadelphia to assess the needs and demands of the local markets. They generated their own capital, while the new bank, the Calcutta Bank of John Palmer, and McIntosh's Commercial Bank also advanced capital for their enterprises.

In Bengal, the factories producing sugar, silk and indigo established by the daring Alexander Ruthven were modernised. Their partnership protected them from the impudence of British Company officials on the one hand and devious Indian agents on the other. Both maintained well-paid British managers in their estates and factories, who were instructed to put down any encroachments by other British entrepreneurs.

The two partners went every day to the Khidderpore docks to acquaint themselves with the latest news in trade — which company brought what, or sent what consignments and which of them were competing with their own. Several hours were spent in the crowded, humid warehouses where their merchandise was kept, secured from rain and sun by tin-roofing and gunnies. Clerks and coolies bustled around counting and carrying.

In Khidderpore, they supervised the building of barques and clippers, which would be added to their growing fleet. A Dutch engineer from Rotterdam, along with a local British shipbuilder, designed and constructed the light vessels that carried silk, muslin and spices to European ports, and brought back copper, steel and finished goods. Their ships were offered to the East India Company for transport of Company merchandise. Since they were faster and more methodically scheduled, the Company gave lucrative contracts to Ruthven Chowdhury & Co. The ships became an obsession for Charles. Their wealth burgeoned. Purchase of more ships was considered, while a more commodious office was found at Fairlie Place, on the Esplanade. Lady Eleanor devised a company logo for their flag — a ship and a sheaf of rice.

The lure of commerce, however, did not deter the partners from their interests in the intellectual ferment around them.

The departure of Lord Hastings brought in John Adams as the new Governor General — a man of narrow vision, quite untouched by the spirit of enlightenment that was flowing from England. He had little patience with the aspirations of educated Indians.

Glad to go into battle, Charles Ruthven followed Brajesh into the progressive circle. As prosperous and progressive members of society, Ruthven and Chowdhury were able to pinpoint the areas which would impede growth. They agitated against Company monopoly in some spheres and press restrictions which gave the Bengal government an arbitrary hand in many matters. Charles Edward drew up petitions on behalf of his partner, which were sent to the Governor General to repeal the press censorship imposed by the authoritarian Marquis of Wellesley.

Under the more liberal rule of the Marquis of Hastings, various Indian newspapers were launched. One was *Bangla Doot,* or Bengal Messenger, and *Bengal Hurkaru*. English newspapers such as *Bengal Herald* and *The Englishman* were also started. The *Englishman* which had originally been an aggressive British paper called *John Bull,* the eminent entrepreneur Dwarkanath Tagore bought up for John Stocqueler and renamed. The Serampore missionaries began a Bengali paper called *Samachar Darpan.*

Brajesh had another English friend in John Silk Buckingham, who wrote witty and erudite articles for the Calcutta Journal. Buckingham's acquaintance with Raja Ram Mohan Roy and Brajesh Chowdhury had made him realise the paradox of foreign rule. "A man who would have been considered an honourable and intelligent member of society in England is in India, a vagabond or a nuisance, a little better than a fool. What in an Englishman is called an independent spirit is in an Indian called presumption, arrogance and impudence."

The reactions of conservatives did not surprise Ruthven though they bewildered Chowdhury. "But why should Dr. Bryce, a minister of the church, oppose Buckingham's humane views?" he asked his partner. "Reverend Adams and Reverend Latimer were liberals."

"My dear Brajesh," Ruthven said gently, "you must realise that not all churchmen are liberals; some are champions of orthodoxy. Buckingham would do well to recognise this as well."

Buckingham refused to do so and made sarcastic rejoinders to the minister. "It is the duty of a journalist to admonish and criticise," he told the furious Governor General.

Brajesh hurried to the office of their company on Fairlie Street to announce to Ruthven that Buckingham was being deported and an ordinance prepared to allow vigorous Press censorship.

"We must protest," he told Ruthven. "I must meet Ram Mohan Roy, and organise a protest."

The draft was taken to Ram Mohan Roy, who amended it. "The British," he wrote, "have been regarded by us as deliverers from oppression and the arbitrary whims of our own rulers. We had hoped to be treated as British citizens under a common judicial code. This hope is now being belied."

The Memorial was effective; Lord Amherst was soon sent to replace Adams.

The next few years passed happily for the Ruthvens and Chowdhurys. Their lives seemed to follow a similar pattern. They had similar interests, not only in their joint company but in social reforms as well. Chowdhury rented a summer villa near the Ruthvens' at Garden Reach, where they retreated for brief holidays and where the numerous children of both families played without consciousness of their different races or creeds. Little James Ruthven and Sudhir Chowdhury were close friends.

The three Ruthven girls occasionally saw Gayatri Chowdhury but the little girl was not given the same freedom by her orthodox mother.

Late in 1824, Charles Ruthven suggested that he and Brajesh Chowdhury should go south to explore the possibilities of extending their commercial ventures in the Madras Presidency. Though the journey was known to be long and arduous, Lady Eleanor agreed to go, along with her four children. Brajesh decided to take his two sons. He did not ask Annapurna; such a journey would have been unthinkable for her.

The party set off in the cool month of November, across the deltaic region of Bengal, past the rich valleys of the Mahanadi and Godavari. On the way, they stopped to admire the famous Sun Temple at Konarak, before they proceeded along the Coromandel coast to Madras.

The area within the Fort St. George of Madras was clean and simple, the dazzling white St. Mary's church dominating other buildings. Simple and whitewashed, the church did not reflect the ornate Rococco style of seventeenth century architecture. Here, Job Charnock had arranged the christening of his daughters by his Hindu wife and here too Robert Clive had married Margaret Maskelyne. Elihu Yale, founder of the great university in America had donated fifteen pagodas for building the church.

They stayed in the house of Robert Clive within the fort, and made plans for their sojourn. But before that, they called on Sir Thomas Munro, one of the most celebrated British administrators in India and now the Governor of Madras.

The Madras Government House had been designed by John Goldingham, a Danish architect, and commissioned by the eldest son of Robert Clive it. With its classical Doric columns, sheltered. cool and spacious verandas which tempered the heat of Madras summers, it was an inviting place.

Sir Thomas Munro received his visitors cordially. "He does not possess the hauteur of other Bengal governors, though he probably knows and understands India better than all of them," Charles reflected as he urged the Governor to describe his early life.

Sir Thomas told them how he had come to India forty years ago, as a youth of twenty-three. He had since served in the Mysore wars, both as a soldier and intelligence officer. When the war ended and Tipu Sultan's territories were ceded to the Madras Presidency, Munro had attended to the survey and settlement work and the restoration of law and order.

"I opposed the imposition of Cornwallis' Permanent Settlement in the south, and urged the ryotwari system to remain, whereby I think we have saved the peasantry here from distress," he told his guests.

"You have brought prosperity to the south," Charles Ruthven observed.

"Indeed I have not. Madras, Mysore and Malabar were already prosperous kingdoms: their riches unplumbed," Sir Thomas replied. "We have only tried to organise the actual procedure of land revenue on a system."

"Do you not believe that progress will come only with British cooperation?" Brajesh Chowdhury asked.

The piercing blue eyes rested on the Bengali zamindar. "Do you truly believe that, Mr. Chowdhury? If you do, you have but a poor assessment of your own people."

Brajesh Chowdhury flushed in vexation as Sir Thomas Munro

continued, "European agencies are recommended as a cure for every evil. Yet, Europeans are not always more efficient than the natives. The native official can be trusted if he is as well paid as his counterpart." He paused and added, "We cannot expect to find in a nation fallen under foreign yoke the same pride and principles, as among a free people. Here in India, previous foreign conquerors have treated the people with violence and cruelty ... but the British have treated them with scorn."

Charles Edward stirred uneasily on the settee next to his wife. Munro's searching blue eyes now fell on him and then on the graceful woman beside him. "Your family has, I understand, been settled in India since Plassey?"

"That is so, Sir," Ruthven murmured.

"Trade is not per se to be decried. Indeed, a judicious growth of trade and commerce can benefit both the employers and the entrepreneurs. The interests of the people must not be ignored in the name of progress." He paused and said, "We should leave the Indians improved from their connection with us, so that they are able to maintain a free and regular government amongst themselves."

Charles Ruthven bowed slightly. "That would be the desire of all British in India," he said.

"Unfortunately not. Some come only to shake the pagoda tree, or to harbour erroneous notions about this country and her people. That is why I have recommended that junior recruits to the Company's service should live in the villages, speak the local language, and realise that they are neither superior nor inferior to the natives. History has placed us in a position to advance the welfare of a nation, an opportunity that should not be lost for selfish needs."

Sir Thomas Munro spoke with real affection about the people he had served. His guests noted that he used the word 'serve' and not 'govern' or even 'administer'.

Tea was served in the high, windblown third floor veranda of Government House, where ebony-skinned servants in gleaming white uniform brought in South Indian delicacies that the Ruthvens ate with more gusto than Brajesh Chowdhury. With a wistful smile,

Sir Thomas watched Lady Eleanor pour tea and told her in measured tones of his sorrow at being separated from his dear wife and children, who were in England.

Eleanor's ready sympathy and interest thawed the stoical Scotsman, who began talking about his past, his family and work. She responded in like manner, bringing a smile to his stern, aloof features, and a hint of the former glint to his wise, probing eyes. Charmed, the Governor invited the party to spend the following day, Sunday, with him at the Garden House in Triplicane. "Lord Clive paid a dear price for the improvements but I think you will enjoy a day in the sylvan setting."

They found Sir Thomas more relaxed in the retreat, with a fund of ready wit and humour, for which he had once been famous. He reminisced about Arthur Wellesley, now the great Duke of Wellington, and of how they had referred to his haughty elder brother, the Marquis of Wellesley as "old villainy". "Little did His Lordship realise," Munro said with a twinkle in his eye, "that he failed to frighten us with his hauteur. His conduct was too theatrical for that."

Lady Eleanor laughed, for at Courtney Hall she had seen as a child the haughty Marquis, fretting because he had been overshadowed by the growing splendour of "young Arthur", the presumed black-sheep of the family, who had ultimately become the hero of the Peninsular War and was soon to be the victor of Waterloo.

"I did feel sorry for him," Eleanor Ruthven said. "He seemed lost and lonely in a world that had no more use for him."

"Did you indeed, Lady Eleanor?" Sir Thomas Munro asked tersely. "I commend your tenderness. But bullies do not generally evoke sympathy in me." He paused. "Until Wellesley's time, there was no attitude of superiority towards the natives — the rightful inhabitants of this country. He initiated a new mood — an imperial mood. It did not accord well with our mission to modernise this country."

"The era of the nabobs was not beneficial to the Indians," Charles Ruthven reminded him.

"Yet in that era, we did much work here in South India," the administrator-turned-Governor said wistfully. "I would love to return to my districts any day. The pomp of office sits ill on a man accustomed to the exhilaration of those hot plains, swirling rivers, tranquil fields, and the splendour of tropical skies over the tents."

His gaze went to little James Ruthven, romping in the garden with his little sisters, under the watchful eye of their ayah.

"Should your son decide to continue the family tradition by staying in India, let him work in the districts and among the people. Only then can he grace a durbar."

Charles Edward and Eleanor listened intently. They would recall those words in the future.

Charles Ruthven and Brajesh Chowdhury made plans to establish a branch of their company in Madras, with a reliable English manager to look after the work. This was the mart for ivory, brass and spices, which would fetch a fancy price in Europe. While the partners located an office not far from the precincts of Fort St. George, Lady Eleanor visited the new St. George's church whose Ionic pillars and Romanesque facade reminded her of its namesake in Hanover Square in London, where she had taken her marriage vows.

As she came out of the church, a carriage drew up and Charles Edward sprang swiftly out of it.

"Whatever has happened?" Lady Eleanor asked, astonished by her husband's distraught countenance.

"Cholera has broken out in the suburbs. We must prepare to leave," he replied, hurriedly pushing their four children into the carriage, ignoring their protests.

Lady Eleanor looked at Charles Ruthven. "We have lived through epidemics in Calcutta. Why should we fly into a panic, especially as you have not completed your work here?'

"In Calcutta, we have Dr. Montgomery Martin to look after us. I know no one of his eminence in Madras. Nor do we have a home here. A circuit house is hardly an appropriate place to fall ill."

Eleanor glanced at the four little faces at the carriage window, flushed and vexed at their banishment into the carriage. "Perhaps you are right," she said as she got in after them.

When they went to take leave of Sir Thomas Munro, they were surprised to hear that he, Governor of Madras Presidency, was preparing to leave for Arcot where the epidemic was raging. No matter how much his officers pleaded with him, Sir Thomas would not listen. "Arcot was my first charge," he said. "I feel for that taluk and its people what a mother must feel for her first-born." His eyes rested on Lady Eleanor's agitated face.

"You cannot endanger yourself, Sir Thomas," Eleanor pleaded. "You have a family to consider."

"Unless I go to Arcot, there will be no one to protect those desperate people. I can organise relief work.'

Eleanor and Charles Ruthven, along with Brajesh Chowdhury, bade farewell to the Governor and drove to the çircuit house, where twenty servants were busy packing and loading the five coaches. Six-year-old James Ruthven and Sudhir Chowdhury got in everybody's way while the little girls, oblivious of the anxiety around them, waited for Moti-bai to tell them stories before lunch.

Charles Ruthven paced the narrow veranda of the circuit house. The heady aroma of a Madras mutton curry and appams wafted in from the kitchen. "Perhaps we can stay two more days to complete our work. The epidemic cannot be too virulent if Sir Thomas is emboldened to go there."

"Why not?' Brajesh Chowdhury asked. "Two more days will hardly matter."

Lady Eleanor did not argue. She went to the cook and told him to prepare a menu and make purchases for two more days. Then, as the two men went into town to negotiate and the children slept fitfully, Eleanor sat on the veranda of the circuit house, trying to concentrate on Jane Austen's last novel. But Bath in spring and dances in the Assembly Rooms seemed to be a distant world in the midst of the blazing sunshine that bleached and blackened at once, that turned the leaves to dust and the rivers into gulleys. The eerie silence of these glittering, hot afternoons disquieted Eleanor more than the dark, jackal-infested nights, because now nothing stirred. It was as if the city had died.

"And yet," she thought, "great kingdoms have flourished here — the Cholas, Pallavas and Pandyas, who sent their long ships to the far Orient and took Indian treasures and culture to them. How did they build their intricate temples in this murderous heat? How did they celebrate life so joyfully? What resilience they must have had!"

Two days later, Charles and Brajesh returned from town, distressed. Eleanor had been embroidering to soothe her taut nerves because terrible stories of cholera deaths had reached her through the servants' grapevine. And now, one look at her husband's face told her the stories were true.

"We leave before dawn," Ruthven said curtly, barely pausing to greet his wife, who turned to Chowdhury.

"Is it true then? Sir Thomas Munro died helping the sick?" Eleanor asked softly. Brajesh nodded, his eyes darkened by pain and something else which he himself could not understand.

Eleanor stared at the flamboyant colours of the sunset sky. "His poor wife ... and children," she murmured. "How bereft they will be!"

Brajesh shook his head. "No one can be more bereft than the people of Madras. Go into town, Lady Eleanor, and see their terrible grief."

"He was deeply revered and loved," Eleanor whispered, her voice leaden.

"It was more than that! Sir Thomas was the 'Daridra Narayan' of our scriptures, the god of the lost and lowly; friend of all who needed him."

"If only he had remained behind!" Eleanor cried, unable to check her tears.

"He could not ... that was not his way." Brajesh paused, and said, "Lord Buddha was entertained at the house of a poor man who gave him contaminated meat to eat. The Lord knew the peril of eating it but He ate it nevertheless — to make his disciple happy. Thomas Munro, like our great Buddha, was a man of compassion. Such lives are a gift of God to mankind."

Charles Ruthven sat alone that night, staring at the star-strewn southern sky, which seemed to be clearer and nearer than the northern one. The shock and pain of Munro's death was receding before a different sensation, a sense of pride and exultation that a boy from Scotland had come to India, not to enrich himself as a nabob, or acquire personal estates, but to demonstrate, through his work, the ideal of western compassion. How far I have come from the world of Alexander Ruthven, he thought.

As their commercial enterprises grew, Charles Ruthven and Brajesh Chowdhury initiated their sons into the excitement of ships and trade. Brajesh's son, Sudhir, and the Ruthven heir Jamie, loved accompanying their sires to wharves and warehouses, to the jetties jostling with people and the quays where they watched ships and barges float past. The partners took turns in having parties on their barge, *Neptune*. The nights were indeed tender and tranquil after the guests left and the boat flowed slowly downstream under a glittering canopy of stars. On either side, the banks were dark shadows with darker patches of trees and crops. On moonlit nights, the river was like molten silver, the shores eerie with the pale glow from above. A feeling of timelessness, of boundless distances and infinite peace suffused everything. On one such night, Charles Ruthven and Eleanor sailed alone, immersed in a world of their own. They came together as the moon slanted westwards over the fields, leaving the sky in a pearly glow. And when their passion cooled, they gazed upwards to stare at the heavens. They had never felt so united as now nor so much at peace. It was as if the elements had mingled together their blood and bones. They both knew it had been a moment of creation.

Julian Ruthven arrived on Christmas day in 1825. He was named after Charles' favourite Roman emperor, who had tried to revive the classical heritage of the Graeco-Roman world in the frenzy of nascent Christianity.

As the warm balmy rays of March slipped into the heat of

April, the Ruthvens moved into their summer villa at Garden Reach, built by Alexander Ruthven fifty-five years ago. It was still imbued with the spirit of Liselotte Fremont, who had lived there. After the death of Claude, her son by Alexander Ruthven, the villa had passed to her daughter, Lucille, who had left India after her marriage to a French army officer in 1796. Lucille and her Bonapartist husband now lived in retirement in Rome, leaving to Charles the possession of the family villa.

Brajesh Chowdhury lived in a nearby villa with a complement of servants and his son, Sudhir, who was also being trained as the co-heir of Ruthven Chowdhury & Co. Annapurna had refused to join him at Garden Reach, the riverside suburb full of unclean firingis and heretic Hindus like her husband, who had lost his caste by eating with them.

James and Sudhir loved Garden Reach, where they were free to explore the lush gardens full of mango and coconut trees, but most of all they loved the riverside where fishing boats bobbed on the swell of water; where ships from Diamond Harbour and Khidderpore dock sailed downstream; where the Ganges met the turbulent Bay of Bengal at Sagar Dwip.

One sultry afternoon, when the two households were drowsy with sleep, James and Sudhir slipped away to board a ship that was progressing downstream. "It is time to go and see Europe," James advised his friend. "If we don't go now, we will have to go to the school Papa talked about. Eton it was, I think. There they will cane us if we don't learn arithmetic."

By the time the boys dragged the dinghy out of its cradle and into the water, the sunlit sky had turned dark and sullen, and a strong wind churned up the slow flowing river into a choppy sea. Sudhir glanced up and frowned. "A Kal-baisakhi, Jamie," he said uneasily.

"Not to worry, we'll reach the big ship before the storm. Row fast, Sudhir."

The dinghy was tossed and turned by the wild nor'wester and the oars proved futile against the swelling water.

"Turn back, Jamie!" Sudhir cried. "We will not reach the ship!"

James Ruthven glanced wildly around him, finally afraid. "Yes," he said stoically, "we are in trouble. Let us get back."

As a gust of frenzied wind swept the boiling water over the dinghy, Sudhir cried out, "Bachao! Help!"

Three fishermen, returning hurriedly with their catch rowed swiftly towards the dinghy, amazed to see the two little heirs of Ruthven, Chowdhury & Co., struggling against the storm. One of them reached out his hand to Jamie, who made haste to leap into their larger boat. He swayed and slipped into the water. Sudhir plunged into the water after him. The fishermen leapt into the river and pursued the two boys.

It was twilight when the fishermen arrived at the Ruthven villa, where the entire household was in a state of panic.

As the fishermen approached the villa, Ramlal, a servant rushed out and then stopped. Watching him, Charles Edward ran out of the wide veranda, towards the dark figures silhouetted against the livid sky. He too stopped, unable to believe what he saw — James lay in the arms of one fisherman and Sudhir in the arms of the other.

Swiftly, Charles Ruthven felt Sudhir; the child breathed feebly and his pulse was thready. "Quickly — get Dr. Sullivan!" he cried to Ramlal. "And Memsaheb!'

Then he touched his son and recoiled in horror. The little body was cold and hard. Wildly, he groped for the boy's wrist to check his pulse. He placed his ear aganist the chest to hear silence. "Jamie!" he shouted. "Wake up! Jamie, open your eyes only!"

The fisherman gazed sadly at the father, and shook his head.

Eleanor had come out by then, a bottle of brandy in her hand. She stared at Charles and James, the two beings dearest to her heart, and then at the dark, tearful fishermen. She knew now what had happened. With a cry of wild grief, she dropped the bottle and seized her son from the fisherman's arms, and laying him on the rain-soaked ground, put her lips on his eyes, as stormy sobs convulsed her body.

The house that had been so joyful a day ago was now plunged

into despair. Eleanor had lain till midnight on the rain-soaked grass with the dead body in her arms, refusing to be separated from the cold, inert form until Charles Edward forcibly carried her, weeping, to the house. Ramlal followed, carrying the boy he regarded as his own for it was he who had cared for James during his brief life.

Brajesh Chowdhury came from his house after midnight, where Dr. Sullivan was struggling to save Sudhir, who was fast sinking. "Go home, Brajesh," Charles Edward said in a hoarse voice. "The child may need you ... there is nothing to be done here ... it's all over."

Brajesh bit his lips. "Let my life go ... but spare the boys ... so I prayed," he said in a broken voice.

Charles Ruthven shook his head. "God is deaf ... didn't you know? Go now ... help Dr. Sullivan — he may do what God failed to do."

"Yes ... I'll go," Brajesh muttered. "I came ... to see if ... I could do ... anything ... for you and Eleanor."

Charles Ruthven shook his head. The vigorous man of forty suddenly looked old and broken.

Eleanor surrendered to a grief that separated her from the world with a dark impenetrable veil. For days she sat alone or before the stone angel in the garden, beneath which reposed the body of her best-loved child. Charles Ruthven also came and sat for hours in deepest dejection, wanting to share his grief with Eleanor. She remained aloof and silent, unable to unburden herself, unable to console the distraught father. She took to wandering around the garden at night or sitting by the river by day, her hair unbraided, her dress crumpled, her eyes vacant and dull. Her rich chestnut hair began to grey.

Charles Ruthven decided to leave Garden Reach for the town house. The summer heat had abated and the monsoon hovered around the Bay of Bengal. He had once loved the season of life-giving rains; now the sullen skies reminded him of the Kal-baisakhi, the black April storm that had taken his son and heir. Calcutta would mean a return to routine and work, an escape from the grief that crippled him. Yet he wondered, "Will I be able to watch ship-building without remembering my Jamie and his plans to be the captain of a ship? Can we live in the house where Jamie played and laughed and frolicked in the garden? Shall I lie awake at night to hear him as a passing breeze or see him as a star amidst a host of clouds? Will he tell me to sleep and when I am asleep, will he enter as a shaft of moonbeam to kiss my weary eyes?"

The return to routine helped Charles Ruthven to recover from his grief, but for Eleanor there was no escape. "I want to die. Then everything will be all right," Eleanor used to whisper to herself, sitting on the balcony at night.

"She is going mad, Brajesh, quite mad! If I am not careful, she will drive me mad as well. Perhaps I ought to go away," Charles told his friend in despair.

"No," Brajesh Chowdhury said gently. "I will take Lady Eleanor away from all this. She needs a change of scene or else she will die."

Brajesh and Annapurna took Eleanor to their house in Mayurganj.

Annapurna hovered around Lady Eleanor with gentle concern, coaxing her to eat, or rest, inviting her out for walks when the monsoon tempests ceased and the whimsical sun broke with splintered brilliance over young rice fields, and green verdure. For Annapurna, the severest test of endurance came when Eleanor drifted to the vast roof garden of the zamindar's mansion, where she was performing the rigorous rituals. Pausing, Annapurna glanced at the pale, gaunt face of her guest and remembering Lady Eleanor's loss, she relented and smiled, then continued her worship of the whimsical monsoon sun god.

"Will it help if I perform these rituals? Eleanor asked.

"Help what?" Annapurna asked, puzzled.

"To ease this pain," Eleanor said in a husky voice, placing a trembling hand on her heart.

Annapurna was confronted with an alien problem. Pujas and rituals, fasting and prayers had been intended for the salvation of the soul, to free it from the sins and attachments of this life, flesh and desires, so that it could elude the doom of rebirth. She had already attained the highest state of being by birth as a Brahmin. She was a step away from Nirvana — redemption and eternal life. Where was the question of pain? Indeed, what was pain? She shook her head. Strange that pain had eluded her so far. "I have achieved moksha, liberation from both pain and joy," she thought.

"Let us take Lady Eleanor to Nabadwip ... where the spirit of the Saint Chaitanya may heal her wounds," Annapurna told her husband.

The party stopped in Nabadwip on the last phase of their trip. A quiet town now, it had once been the centre of proud learning and later the hub of the Bhakti movement, which swept over India in the fourteenth and fifteenth centuries.

Sitting near the ruined terracotta temple, where the mystic saint Chaitanya had once sung the songs of brotherhood and devotion, Brajesh told Eleanor about the Bhakti revival.

"India, particularly the north, was reeling under the impact of Turko-Afghani invasions. Those apocalyptic armies came, ravaging our land and people, intimidating all. Cities fell to the sword, kingdoms became their satraps, and the soul of India was almost extinguished. Then something miraculous happened. A tidal wave of compassion and devotion flooded this country. Saints and mystics sprang out of huts and palaces to proclaim the grandeur of God, be it Shiva or Krishna or Rama. But this devotion was not a solemn worship; it was filled with the ecstasy of love, of total identity with Him as friend and lover, father and brother, master and playmate. Lord Krishna emerged, not as the king of Dwarka or the preserver of the universe, but the consolation and refuge of all in search of an anchor and meaning in a terrible world."

Brajesh paused as the bells of the temple began to peal at the hour of arati, the welcome. Conches blew in the warm, humid night, summoning not only the devotees but the loved one as well, to accept human homage.

"Never had such a phenomenon taken place in India. The Rani

of Chittor, Meerabai, left her raja, palaces and jewels to search for her divine friend at Mathura — the place of the Lord's frolics. Tulsidas of Benaras gave up his position as court scholar to recreate the story of Rama for the ordinary people. There was Jayadev of Kenduli, not far from here, who heard the Lord dictate the lines of his immortal 'Gita Govinda', and the Muslim weaver, Kabir, who sought the image of the Universal God. And here in Nabadwip, was the saintly Chaitanya who, like Lord Buddha, left his home to search for God and answers."

The temple bells continued to chime in the warm night, merging with the soft lapping of water on the worn out steps leading to the river.

"Did he find the answers?" Eleanor asked gravely.

"Of course. He found life in all its grandeur and joy and celebrated the discovery by singing the praise of God. Whoever he may be, landlord or peasant, Brahmin or Shudra — all followed him and regained their dignity as God's children and not the Sultan's slaves. He changed the mood of despair and degradation. The strength of our faith reasserted itself once more.'

"Yet the oppression continued," Eleanor murmured dully.

"True. But that irresistible faith gave them weapons to fight back — like the Christian martyrs in Rome."

Brajesh Chowdhury glanced at the pale silhouette of the sad face. No star or moon could lighten that countenance, he thought. Nothing but an inner lamp would illumine that darkness. "What I am trying to say, Lady Eleanor, is that love can vanquish pain and death. And in love lies immortality."

Eleanor shook her head. "My little Jamie," she whispered. "Where will I find him?"

"Within yourself," Brajesh replied gently. "And in the great unknown."

Eleanor covered her face, convulsed by fresh grief as she imagined Jamie alone in the great unknown.

Charles Ruthven came to fetch her back.

"You will have to forget him, my dear. He is gone ... forever.

You must come to terms with death, so that you may put it behind you and look upon life once more. Cannot the others fill the void: Catherine, Margot, Valerie and little Julian? ... and I? ... I need you too, my dear."

Eleanor gazed at her husband mutely, at the fresh glowing complexion, at the red-gold hair, strong, vigorous body and face which showed no signs of despair. A strange resentment stirred within her. He had overcome the pain and wanted to resume life, and pleasure.

"Come with me, Eleanor. The Governor General has asked me to go to Ratangarh where the Rana is mobilising an army for Ranjit Singh of Punjab. He wants me to keep an eye on him ... as once my father did. A change of scene will do you good. You will forget ... there."

Resentment changed to anger now. She drew away from his gentle embrace. "Perhaps I do not wish to forget," she said in a low, cold voice. "Perhaps I do not wish to resume life and pretend that nothing happened!"

Charles Ruthven's tenderness and pity changed to exasperation. "Perhaps you are enjoying this life of self-indulgence ... and selfishness? It is so much easier to run away from life than face its ordeals with grace." His voice was low and hard.

Tears spilled out of the dull, green eys that glazed in momentary fury. "Is that how it appears to you? Self-indulgence? Have you any idea of ...? No you cannot! The Governor General calls ... the Rana has to be subdued into submission ... and one more victory for the Company Bahadur! Go in haste, Charles, to the scene of your father's plunder and glory ... but leave me in peace to mourn my child!"

Charles confided his predicament to his friend and partner. "I too need to recover, my friend. Can you not envisage what I have suffered? Alone? Without Eleanor's company or consolation. No ... I must go away — to escape this mood of gloom and despair which has begun to grip me."

Brajesh admitted the justice of the argument. Charles Ruthven had suffered by the death of his beloved son but he clung on to life and hope. There were many years still to be lived and not merely endured. Brajesh promised to look after their company and the Ruthven family while Charles was away.

22

Ruthven's Rani

Charles Edward Ruthven accomplished the journey through the storm-tossed Gangetic plains in September 1826. Behind him lay the vast, rain-soaked fields of rice, coconut groves and brimming ponds. As he travelled, he sought to leave behind the dark mood of melancholy that had settled over him.

The Rajput princes had accepted the suzerainty of the British in 1818, after the defeat of the Marathas. Nahar Singh, the present Rana of Ratangarh, had been reluctant to do so. With the threat of Maratha depredations being removed, he felt the superfluity of a British alliance. Indeed, he speculated on the possibility of creating a nascent Rajput power as Ranjit Singh had created in Punjab.

Any ambitious ruler would have been dazzled by the Sikh Maharaja. Lean, energetic, fair-skinned and white-bearded, this leader of the Sikhs welded together the disparate Sikh bands to form a militant state, stretching from Afghanisthan to Kashmir upto the borders of Delhi. He combined in his person the skills of a warlord with that of a diplomat, and was able to gather allies as he dismantled adversaries and bring into the folds of his homogeneous state, the talents of other ethnic groups, while keeping everyone bemused with his own enigmatic personality. No one was ever certain of Ranjit Singh's intentions. He dissimulated frequently, yet he could inspire loyalty as no one else in India could. In him lay the hope of integration. European generals, Brahmin theoreticians, Jat and Rajput soldiers and Muslim tacticians served him with an enthusiasm that only the great Akbar had commanded two centuries ago. In him, too, lay the dream of a resurgent India.

Young Nahar Singh of Ratangarh pondered over this dream for several years. His grandfather, Rana Ram Singh had nursed hopes of a powerful state; he had invited Alexander Ruthven to train his army, in order to resist Maratha encroachment and retrieve the territories he had lost to the Maratha chiefs. He had even hoped to outbid Madhaji Sindhia and become the custodian of the Moghul Emperor. These schemes had dissolved before the armies of Lord Wellesley. British power had become a reality, and an obstacle to Indian dreams.

Nahar Singh believed that where Madhaji Sindhia and his grandfather had failed, the Maharaja of Punjab might succeed. His father disagreed. "Let us live in peace," he had told young Nahar. "We have regained our territories and forts, our wells and fields. Let us not stir up a hornet's nest."

The young prince had regarded his father with a sardonic smile. "You have retrieved everything except your pride. We are no better off under the British than we were under the Moghuls or Marathas."

"So be it!" Rana Bharat Singh had retorted. "Our people are exhausted. There will be no more wars."

Nahar Singh fretted and dreamed. He thought of his great ancestor, Rana Pratap, who had refused to submit to the Emperor at Delhi and he began to correspond secretly with Sikh generals. General Ventura, the Italian general, Gardener the Englishman, Generals Allard and Court, both Frenchmen, were training the army of Punjab. Their artillery and infantry were superior, it was said, even to the Company's forces. "Such an army could vanquish the British," he thought. "If we can get the Rajputs and Sikhs to join ... even the Marathas would join us, for they have nothing to lose but their servility. What could we not achieve together?"

Rumours of the young Rana's fraternisation with the Maharaja of Punjab filled the Rajputs with excitement and disquieted the

British. The warlord, Lord Hastings had left in 1823; his successor, Lord Amherst was not a man for campaigns. Besides, his hands were tied with the Burma war and the mutiny at Barrackpore, in the heart of British India. Nevertheless, it was not a matter to be ignored. In India, "a cloud no bigger than a man's hand, could become the harbinger of a storm." There in Calcutta, immersed in his commercial activities, was Charles Edward Ruthven, whose protean father had been a hero at Ratangarh. Lord Amherst asked him to go there.

A fortress-palace loomed high above the pink-brown town of Ratangarh. Set against the wooded hills, its towers and ramparts were sombre silhouettes against a vivid sky. Charles Edward Ruthven halted, staring at the old citadel, built even before his Norman ancestors had conquered England. Everyone in his entourage watched his motionless figure on the chestnut charger. Beams of the dying sun touched the red-gold of his hair and turned his grey coat to gold.

Charles Ruthven spurred his horse towards Deogarh, to spend the night and inspect the jagir. Nine years had passed since he had last visited this estate, in the midst of the Maratha wars. Begum Beatrice, his half-sister, had remained as his representative, assisted by a Major Brunton to collect revenues from the peasants.

His practised eye passed over fields and huts, with some satisfaction. "Brunton has taken good care," he said aloud to his nephew, Sikander. "Matters had deteriorated greatly when I saw it last, nine years ago." Sikander beamed, as they rode past the fields towards the fortress of Deogarh, atop a high, craggy hill.

In the great hall lit by oil lamps, tapestries from Tournai and swords of ancient warriors hung on the walls. Beyond was a smaller chamber, where Liselotte had arranged French furniture of the Louise XVI period and Begum Shirin had installed Moghul-style divans, screens and paintings.

Charles Ruthven felt that familiar welter of emotions that effaced the present and revived the shadows of the past; of his father, and his Moghul wife, and their ill-fated son Andrew, of Liselotte and

Claude, and a host of Rajput princes who had lived and fought here, to halt the progress of Afghan invaders racing towards Delhi or the valleys of the Ganges. "What am I doing here?" Charles Edward wondered. "Why should I strive to bring Company rule to these proud, unfettered people?"

"Salam Ale Kum," a husky voice murmured from the shadows. Charles Edward turned around swiftly, and saw the stately figure of an ageing woman, her eyes still a vivid blue, but her copper hair streaked now with grey.

"Beatrice," Charles murmured, taking a long white hand in his. The dowager smiled. "So you remembered me, my brother. I thought you would never come again. Have you forgotton our father's dream?"

"This dream is to be bequeathed now to Sikander ... as our father would have wanted. He will administer Deogarh," Charles Ruthven said.

Begum Beatrice looked from one man to the other, and then slowly knelt before her half-brother. "You are a noble man, Charles Edward. I do not know from whom you inherit this generosity, for neither our father nor our mothers possessed it. Let your lineage flourish and illumine the family name!"

Charles Ruthven smiled and drew Beatrice close. "Take Sikander in hand," he said. "He has much to learn." He paused and looked around the sombre, ancient hall. "Let Father's wish be fulfilled. Let Andrew's line prosper here."

Beatrice nodded. "Now I can die, my brother. Now the ghosts will rest in peace."

The next day, as a coral dawn broke over the hills, Charles Ruthven set off for Ratangarh. He felt the same exhilaration as he had nine years ago, riding the winding road towards the magnificent fortress-palace, whose walls seemed to be carved out of the rock face. It reminded him of the Alhambra at Granada, though this was more harsh, more grim. Yet, it looked like Granada once he entered through the massive iron-studded gates, as soldiers and courtiers stood in silence, saluting the son of Alexander Ruthven.

He was led by courtiers to an inner courtyard, with carved

sandstone walls and graceful, ornate pillars. Fountains splashed in the centre and cascaded into stone channels which flowed into banks of flowers and grass. The fitful October sunshine glittered on the cascades and illumined the last of the monsoon clouds. Below, the plains lay in the pale green splendour following a bountiful monsoon.

From the ornate courtyard a flight of shallow steps led to the diwan-i-khas, where Rana Nahar Singh waited on a carved silver throne studded with precious stones.

Charles Ruthven bowed, placing a silver tray of gold coins before the Rana as a nazrana, a tribute. As he rose to glance at the prince, Ruthven was surprised by the tangible animosity in the young man's face.

"Your Highness," he said gravely, "it has been many years since I last saw you."

The young Rana nodded sombrely. "It was indeed a long time ago, Ruthven Saheb. My father tried, if I remember correctly, to persuade you to train our army."

Charles Ruthven remained standing. "Your army need not be afraid. There are no threats to Ratangarh now. The Company is your friend."

Nahar Singh smiled bitterly. "Friend? I do not need so dangerous a friend."

Ruthven stiffened. The boy he had come to chastise had grown into an intractable man. "Perhaps you prefer a friend such as Ranjit Singh of Punjab?" Ruthven asked tersely.

The courtiers stirred uneasily, watching now their handsome young prince and now the tall, flame-haired, imposing saheb. None present had seen but most had heard of the legendary general, Alexander Ruthven, who had trained the army of Nahar's grandfather, Rana Ram Singh. They felt a spontaneous attraction for this man who was that general's son. A white-haired man entered the durbar-i-khas and bowed low before the Rana. Then slowly, bending over a stick, he came up to the throne.

"Welcome him, my lord," Suraj Mal, adviser and banker to many Ranas, said to the present Rana. "Alexander Ruthven was a friend of your grandfather. He trained our army and made them defeat the Marathas and Moghuls ... he almost made us rulers of the Doab and custodian of the Emperor."

Nahar Singh smiled coldly. "Welcome then, Mr. Ruthven," he said with evident mockery. "No doubt, we shall be friends if you are as loyal to Ratangarh as was your father."

Charles Ruthven rose, gazing at the impassioned prince. "Amherst was right. The Rana aims to join Ranjit Singh and give him assistance to encroach southwards," he thought, though aloud he said, "Be careful, Your Highness, that your powerful ally does not annihilate you."

The dark eyes were inscrutable. "We want a strong Hindusthan, Mr. Ruthven. Let it be ruled by a Sikh, a Maratha or a Rajput ... but let it evict the Company's devious agents!"

Charles Ruthven bowed, colouring, despite his resolve to be composed. "I shall convey these er sentiments to the Governor General. I doubt if he will consider them as compliments." He paused and smiled drily. "In fact, in my country, duels are fought over such remarks."

"Ask the Lord Saheb to come to Ratangarh. Or I shall go to Calcutta. His life would be shortened by my sword." The Rana's voice was cool and menacing.

Charles Ruthven bowed again and left the hall, unable to be angry. He had begun to respect the courage of the young ruler. If only he could be persuaded to be a friend of Amherst instead of Ranjit Singh!

Standing in the central courtyard, he became aware of a veiled figure at the window of the diwan-i-khas. Puzzled, he mounted his horse for the ride back to Deogarh. Elephants paused in their ponderous steps to raise their trunks in salute. And then the ancient doors closed upon him.

As winter fell in the arid hills, news came that Ranjit Singh of Punjab was mobilising his troops to cross the Sutlej and proceed to Multan in Sindh, a domain of the Sindh Amirs. Rana Nahar Singh was clearly excited. He began gathering a small band of warriors. Hearing of this, Charles Ruthven sought and was granted an audience with the Rana though he received no assurance from the prince on his intentions. "I go to Jaigarh to visit kinsmen," the Rana told him, adding with a dry smile, "My Rani, Urmila-bai, is a princess of Jaigarh."

"Do you need an army to visit in-laws?" Ruthven asked ironically.

"Why yes, Ruthven Saheb. A son-in-law must go in full splendour to his wife's people. It is a matter of izzat, prestige."

Charles Ruthven regarded the young Rana with growing anger. "You will not, I trust, join with the Sikh army?"

Nahar Singh shrugged. "And if I do?"

"You will violate your treaty with the Company."

Nahar Singh's low laughter irritated Ruthven. "But Ruthven Saheb, surely I do not reject the Company's embrace if I watch the progress of the Sikh army?"

"Make certain that you do not become Ranjit Singh's pawn, Your Highness. After Multan, he may turn his eyes on you. Ratangarh has a strategic value — standing as it does between Delhi and the Rajputs.

A few days later, the Rana of Ratangarh stood at the vast central courtyard of the fortress, as royal priests chanted prayers and circled earthen lamps around the prince and his warriors, wafting incense over caparisoned horses and elephants. From an apartment above, showers of rose petals fell on the heads of the men, as ladies chanted invocations to Ganesh, the god of enterprise, from behind latticed windows.

Charles Ruthven watched from the rampart, his eyes following the clouds of coral dust raised by the horses' hooves as the Rana and his men rode westwards, towards, it seemed, the dipping orb of the sun. "How ironic," he mused, "that I should he here to curb the Rana's militant designs when my father stood here once to train the Ratangarh army."

A fresh, cold breeze sprang up from the hilltops, now illumined by winter's ochre light. He turned to go and saw a heavily veiled woman move past the crenellated ramparts towards him. The richly embroidered gharara and silk veil caught beams of light as she moved slowly, revealing narrow golden feet encircled by jewelled anklets, and a plait woven with a gold chain. Her hands held aloft folds of the silken veil, so that Charles Ruthven could glimpse fragments of her taut, rounded figure.

"You have forgotten me, Ruthven Saheb?" she asked in Hindusthani.

Charles Ruthven stared perplexed at the woman; the heart-shaped face, that was the colour of pale honey, the full figure and wide sensual mouth. And then he saw the hazel eyes with their strangely haunted look, which had struck him nine years ago. But that had been an unformed, awkward girl. "Princess Urmila," he said, bowing.

"No ... I am now the Rani of Ratangarh."

"Of course ... pardon me. I thought of you as 'the little princess'."

"You ... thought of ... me?" she asked, surprised.

Charles Edward nodded. "Yes ... I thought of you, Highness, and your lord, and Ratangarh."

Abruptly, she turned to face the plain below. The last shadows of twilight had been swallowed up by a wintry dusk, obscuring even the clouds of dust raised by the young Rana's departure.

"I implored him not to go! He would not listen!" Her voice trembled and Ruthven saw two tears glide along high cheekbones. "I warned him of danger!"

"Your lord does not heed advice ... or reality," Ruthven replied.

"But you ... you are wise ... perhaps you can guide him ..." There was an urgent appeal in her voice which touched him.

"If he will deign to listen," Ruthven replied.

The courtiers, especially old Suraj Mal, did not fail to notice that the Lord Saheb's emissary looked upon the Rani with a certain protectiveness, as if the lovely woman was still a child seeking assurance. They encouraged Urmila to invite Ruthven to the Jal Mahal, the water palace, for discussions.

Ruthven conferred with Suraj Mal, the financier and the Rana's ministers on the wisdom of joining the Sikhs, though news had come of their victory at Multan. Soon, the Sikh army would pour into Sindh ... and then cast their eyes on Delhi.

The older councillors of Ratangarh were in favour of a conciliatory policy towards the paramount power, the Company, which they felt was the only means of keeping Ratangarh free from war or annexation. The younger ones, however, influencd by their Rana and the Punjab Maharaja, felt that the day of reckoning was coming when Indians would have to choose between subjugation and struggle. "We must strike before they swallow us entirely," the younger men said. "The firingi traders have now become greedy for more. Profits are not enough to slake their thirst. They seek dominion as well."

Charles Ruthven listened intently, wondering how he could influence them to choose the Company as their ally, when their free existence was in jeopardy. That they listened to him at all, he knew, was because of his status as Alexander Ruthven's son.

Except the Rani. She listened because she found Charles Ruthven's maturity restful after the turbulence of her husband, though she would not acknowledge this even to herself. "His presence is reassuring," she told her ladies. "An emissary of the Governor General ... who is a friend."

"Of course," they responded eagerly. "And the son of the dashing Ruthven who once trained our soldiers."

"Yet," she asked herself, "is there not something else which draws me to this foreigner ... some instinctive trust in his chivalry, even though he is here as an agent of the British government?"

She tried to stifle the spontaneous joy that she felt on seeing him ride up the steep road into the central courtyard. Her ladies observed the sudden flush of colour, the suppressed gaiety, the unbidden laughter which came to her at the sound of his steps. "Is it wrong?" she once asked her old nursemaid, the only one who had accompanied her from her father's palace at Jaigarh. The old Rajput woman nodded solemnly. "It is unwise. You are the wife of a noble prince; you cannot behave like a milkmaid!"

Urmila stared at her effulgent self in the mirror. "The Rana, my husband, has never cared to give me his time. His interests have always been war or politics."

"He is a prince, not a court jester," retorted the old lady.

Urmila laughed and seizing the gauzy veil from her attendant, fled from her disapproving glances, to greet the foreign emissary who impatiently paced the veranda adjoining her apartment. Sometimes, they sat in the fountain-splashed garden, or strolled on the ramparts of the fortress. There, sitting under a graceful circular chatri, the young Rani regaled the Englishman with tales of Rajputana.

The cold season set in, a blue-grey haze at dawn through which a waning moon, flickering stars and a mellow sun made their claims. As the mist cleared from the hilltops, the winter sun burst upon the hill and fort, plains and waterfalls with an iridescent brilliance. Oranges and pomegranates ripened in the walled gardens of the fortress and roses filled the cold air with a heady fragrance.

Rani Urmila waited for Charles Ruthven's visits on cold, sunlit afternoons when the copper brazier in the audience hall burnt sandalwood logs and perfumed the air with a strange sensuality. Suraj Mal was always nearby, encouraging the princess to win over the Governor General's emissary.

"It is not proper," the old nursemaid told Suraj Mal. "My lady must not talk alone with Ruthven Saheb."

Suraj Mal smiled. "Our lady will win over the Saheb ... and get him to protect Ratangarh."

"How can he? He is an emissary of the Company!" the old nurse protested.

"That is where our Rani will do the needful."

Later, the old nurse bristled with rage. "You would use my lady?" she asked, outraged.

"Calm down. The Saheb will not harm the Rani. Indeed, he admires her." Suraj Mal's voice was silky.

Later, the old Rajput woman shivered in dread. No matter what she said, the young Rani laughed. "Ruthven Saheb is a friend," Urmila said. "He will protect me."

Their meetings were brief but frequent, as if they could not bear to remain separated for too long. Everyone watched with veiled eyes as the Rani and Ruthven walked around the woods, by the lake or sat on the balcony of the water palace.

Winter passed and spring made its overtures. The festival of spring, Holi, came, drawing revellers from the town and village. Courtiers and servants joined together to smear each other with vermilion and turquoise powder and splashed coloured water on each other. Veiled but agitated, Urmila demurely daubed Ruthven's cheeks with gulal, coloured powder, and he hesitantly did the same. They stood staring at one another, as if suddenly aware of their unworded relationship.

Urmila hurried away to the ramparts, to compose herself and banish the hot blush on her cheeks. Charles Edward followed her, no less agitated, and stood in silence beside her. Her breasts rose and fell, and tears glimmered in her eyes as she spoke.

"I am the Rani of Ratangarh," she said miserably. "I am therefore bound to my lord and to the code of honour that has chained me for life."

"I understand, my lady," Charles Ruthven said gently. "I never thought otherwise."

She turned to him, stormy eyed. "But I cannot deny that I love you and were I free and not a mother, I would ask you to take me with you."

Charles Ruthven stepped forward impulsively and clasped her hand. "Urmila," he whispered. "Is that so? If it is so ... let us flee from here ..."

Urmila smiled and shook her head. "We are doomed to be apart ... Go now ... before I disgrace myself."

Rani Urmila sat in her little pavilion near the ramparts, gazing at the moon, the hills and plains bathed in a golden light. The beat of dhols and cymbals reached her from the main palace. From the town below, wafted sounds of revelry. "A night for love," she thought with a desire that was a burning pain. "But I cannot, will not weaken!" She tried to banish thoughts of Charles Ruthven, but the desire that had lain dormant now became insistent. She had no son, only a daughter; the Rana seemed not to care. Perhaps he wished to take another wife or else an heirless Ratangarh would pass to the Company's rule.

Then, as her eyes drooped and the sounds grew fainter, shadows of galloping horsemen loomed on the hillside, Urmila sprang up with a cry. "The Rana has returned!" she exclaimed, as she ran to the rampart to peer at the figures that swept into the central courtyard.

At once, a chaos of sounds broke over the fortress. Dancers and singers, courtesans and soldiers left their revelry to hear the ominous news. Charles Edward Ruthven came into the courtyard.

"What is the cause of the commotion?" he asked quietly.

"Sir, our Rana has been held hostage by a son of the Sikh Maharaja. Prince Sher Singh wants Ratangarh's submission as ransom."

Rani Urmila froze. "Rana Nahar Singh a prisoner!" she whispered. "I cannot believe it!"

From the courtyard came a welter of sounds, of arguments and orders, disagreements and counter orders.

"Give up!" cried an old warrior. "We cannot endanger our Rana."

"We will fight the Sikhs! We cannot allow them to enter Ratangarh," responded a young warrior.

"They will kill the Rana!"

Charles Ruthven listened to their arguments in silence. The Sikh alliance had been perilous to Ratangarh. He had warned the Rana, to no avail. By his folly, Nahar Singh had now brought the Sikh forces towards the Doab — the goal of all rulers of India.

The sudden rustle of silk made everyone pause. Rani Urmila came in, unveiled, and stood before the foreigner, as instructed by Suraj Mal.

"Ruthven Saheb, will you lead our scattered soldiers and rescue our lord?" she asked.

Charles Ruthven turned to look at Urmila, and steeled himself to say, "You wish me to lead your army?" he asked. "But I have no locus standi. I am only an emissary of the Governor General."

"Your father led Ratangarh to victory and enabled us to retrieve our lost territories," Suraj Mal, the Chief Councillor replied gravely. "Rana Ram Singh gave him Deogarh as reward. Name your price, Ruthven Saheb, and it is yours."

Charles Ruthven glanced at the white-haired Councillor, the assembled warriors and courtiers, and then at the young Rani. He felt a shiver of dread once more, as he had experienced one evening nine years ago. Gravely he said, "My price is simple, Your Highness. In return for leading your forces, I want an assurance that a British resident may stay here henceforward."

"So high a price!" Urmila cried, even as Suraj Mal lifted a hand to caution the Rani.

"British presence for British protection. The Governor General will accept nothing else." His voice was cool, almost aloof.

The Rani's eyes were stormy with rage and pain. Pulling her veil across her head and shoulders, she swept out of the courtyard. Ruthven stared after the imperious figure.

"We accept," Suraj Mal said in a cold voice. "But bring back the Rana safely. Otherwise, the bargain is nullified."

Preparations began at once as Charles Ruthven took command, instructing the remaining commanders regarding the weapons to be taken, the cannons to be harnessed, and supplies to be collected. The tranquil beauty of the moonlit night was suddenly dispelled by movements of horses and soldiers, and the music of the ghummer was lost in the clank of swords and guns, as the remaining forces of Ratangarh prepared to march against the Sikh force at Multan.

Preparations continued well into the next day. Heavily veiled, Urmila received the commanders in her apartment, heard and approved their plans, sanctioned expenditure, disbursed monies and trembled inwardly at the enterprise. Suraj Mal and his fellow councillors came at dusk to tell her that all was in readiness. "Ruthven Saheb will set off tomorrow for Multan with the army of Ratangarh. May Shiva bless our enterprise."

Rani Urmila nodded. "We have so much to lose," she said bitterly. "Either Sher Singh despoils us ... or the Company!"

Suraj Mal nodded, grim faced. "The Rana would not listen. How often I advised him to accept reality ... but no, he dreamt of a Hindusthan freed from the foreign hand." Suraj Mal sighed. "The time for that has gone."

"Then why are we accepting Ruthven's terms?" she asked sharply.

Suraj Mal glanced at her speculatively, as if uncertain about her loyalties. "A British Resident in Ratangarh will be less evil than a Sikh prince."

The sounds of soldiers preparing for battle, the dragging of cannons, stomping of horses and bellowing of elephants vanished with the approach of dusk. Urmila returned to the water palace from the hilltop temple of the goddess Durga, where priests performed puja to obtain her blessings. Commanders were given prasad, which was in turn distributed to the soldiers, who then went to their homes in silence. Invocations to the goddess wafted down from the highest hill to the apartments of the Rani who sat alone, gazing at the hills bathed in moonlight, the flickering lights from the town. Silent and withdrawn, she discouraged her ladies from talking to her. They left her alone in the richly decorated chamber, as previously instructed by Suraj Mal.

Night had deepened when Rani Urmila heard a knock on the door. Slowly, she rose to open the door and found a pale, ghostly figure standing in the silent moonlit corridor. His red-gold hair was silvered and his eyes had the distance of stars. She stared at him in amazement.

"Forgive me, Your Highness," he said gravely, entering her lamplit chamber. "I too am bound by my duty to the Lord Saheb who sent me. He would not have accepted any other form of protection for Ratangarh."

"So you too bind me in chains!" Urmila exclaimed, bitterly.

"I will fight for you ... What more can I do in atonement?'

Urmila regarded Ruthven with haunted eyes. "If anything happens to me ... or my husband — will you promise to safeguard my daughter?"

"Nothing will happen to you," he said gently. "I will not allow anything to happen."

Urmila shook her head. "If my husband dies at the hands of the Sikhs... I will end my life ... honourably."

Ruthven stepped forward and clasped her hand. "No! You will do nothing like that!"

"When a woman becomes a widow, she has little to live for."

Ruthven regarded her intently. "Can you not live for me?"

"For you?" she whispered, startled.

"Yes ... I need you, my lady..." He was close now and held her gently. "Yes, my little princess. You have made me forget my pain at the loss of my son ... the gloom of my home ... you have made me thirst for life once more."

Involuntarily, she drew close and his arms tightened around her taut, slender body and then he bent his head to meet her parted lips. He felt her yield, as eager and hungry as himself. Swiftly they moved towards the high balcony adjoining her bedchamber which was suspended above the hill, where larks and eagles cried with the murmur of wind, the rush of the distant waterfall. Only the vivid moon and wisps of golden clouds witnessed the surrender of the Rani to the foreign emissary; only they saw him rain fierce kisses on her lips, neck and thrusting golden breasts, only they saw his wild journey over her eager, yielding body. The high wind drowned her cries as he possessed her in an explosion of desire. Then they lay, spent and satiated, while the moon slanted westwards towards the paling hills, as if afraid of what it had seen.

"I must start at dawn," Ruthven whispered hoarsely, holding her close.

"So soon?" she asked, shivering.

"Delay means danger to ..." Charles Ruthven could not proceed. How bizarre that he must go to fight for the Rana, whose Rani lay in his arms.

Urmila sensed his hesitancy. "A little longer," she murmured, her fingers caressing his long, high-bridged nose, the arched brows, wide mouth, and the tangled skeins of his hair. "Do not repent what you have done," she whispered sadly.

Charles Ruthven sat up slowly. "Do you repent, Princess?"

he asked with anguish.

Urmila shook her head. "I have always wanted to know this sweetness ... it has eluded me for ten years." She paused and said, her voice breaking. "I am glad I finally know it." Tears sprang to her eyes, and she bit her lip to stifle a sob. Ruthven pulled her gently down and wiped her tears with his lips. She shook herself free and rushed on. "It was always a war ... or a.... campaign ... or a plan ..." she said in a choked voice. "There was no time for joy ... or love ... there was only time for Ratangarh!"

Ruthven stared at the outline of the hills still etched by moonlight, remembering the Rani as a young girl pleading with him to lead the army of Ratangarh, and thinking now of the brave and proud prince whom he must betray and protect in one act of perfidy. "Is that where she has led me?" he asked himself, staring at her tender face. He pulled her close in anguish, which soon kindled into hunger and they rushed on, eager and desperate to coalesce their desire into one flaming form.

The lightening purple dawn nudged them into wakefulness. Ruthven bent over Urmila and said, "I must go now, Princess."

Urmila nodded, opening her eyes. "God speed you," she whispered.

As Charles Ruthven sat astride his charger in the central courtyard of the Ratangarh fortress, a shower of flowers fell from the latticed window of the apartments above. He raised his eyes to the veiled woman who stood there with her attendants to wish him good fortune. Imperceptibly, he nodded, clutching one flower in his gloved hand. Then he moved out of the massive brass-studded gates and onto the steep road girding the hills.

The newly organised army of Ratangarh rushed ahead over the springtime plains, passing town and village, on its way to Multan where the Sikh prince, Sher Singh, waited to march upon Ratangarh.

Charles Ruthven waited with the Rajputs of Ratangarh at Khairapur on the border of Punjab, some two hundred miles from Ratangarh. He had also mobilised from his own jagir of Deogarh, soldiers who had been trained by Major Brunton. Excited by the challenge, the retired officer had joined the fray with great enthusiasm. Now they waited for the army from Punjab.

Prince Sher Singh expected a fragmented army left behind by Rana Nahar Singh, with no commander worth the name. The Sikh prince had every hope of annihilating such a force on the sandy plains, before rushing on to storm the ancient citadel and capture its young Rani along with the little Rajkumari.

The Sikh army was unprepared for the onslaught of the small but dedicated army that stormed them, killing with pent-up ferocity. At their head was Charles Ruthven. Though fifteen years older and heavier than he had been at the battle of Badajoz, where he had seized French guns and officers in a daring raid, he plunged through the enemy lines, scattering them and screaming directions for attacks, and phalanx formations that completely bewildered Sher Singh's rowdy hordes. From strategic places, cannon-fire ploughed through the Sikh soldiers.

Unnerved by the carnage, the Sikh army withdrew and retreated westwards towards the Sutlej. Ruthven allowed them to retreat in peace and made a pretence of returning to Ratangarh. Two days later, after hard and swift marches, his Rajput army fell upon Sher Singh's forces at their night camp to execute a cold and calculated carnage, and then before riding back, set fire to cannons and tents.

From afar, people saw the swift, bloody battle and the flaming conflagration. No one knew what had transpired. No one cared. It was one more battle and still more bloodshed in a land that had known no peace for a millennia.

The first fierce winds of summer had begun to blow when Charles Ruthven returned to Ratangarh in May 1827. He was now riding to tell Rani Urmila of the return of her husband. Ruthven was content now; he could return to Lord Amherst in glory. Not only had Ratangarh been saved from a Sikh incursion, but a British

Resident was to be accredited to the Rana's court. It was more than he had hoped for. "And Urmila," he thought wistfully, "how will I learn to forget her now? But forget I must. Nahar Singh will return and I ... must return to Eleanor. I had quite forgotten her. Or had I deliberately shut out the memory of her grief so that my own sorrow could heal?"

Rani Urmila waited in the Jal Mahal on the lake below the fortress. The councillors rose as Charles Ruthven entered, dusty and weary after a week's hard ride.

"Ratangarh is safe," he said gravely in reply to their mute agitation. "The Sikh army has been forced to retreat to the Cis-Sutlej for the time being. I do not think they will attack Ratangarh." He paused before continuing. "The Rana has been released and will be returning soon."

Everyone bowed, murmuring gratitude but Ruthven saw that their joy at victory was dimmed by the realisation that once unvanquished Ratangarh was now the Company's vassal. They left, leaving their sombre-faced Rani to face Ruthven in her apartment.

Urmila shook her head. "Do you remember the rakshabandhan I gave you ten years ago? That talisman was to bind you to me — for protection. My ancestress sent one such to the Moghul Emperor... and he protected her kingdom ... even from his own ambition."

Charles Ruthven said nothing. He had stored away the jewel-encrusted bracelet among his papers, disturbed by its demands.

"I am no emperor, Princess, merely an emissary," he said sadly. "Forgive me if I have failed you."

Rani Urmila held her head between her hands and began to weep.

"Urmila," he said, "why do you weep? You cannot grieve for your husband's folly!"

"Oh no," she cried, raising an anguished face to him. "I weep for my folly!"

"Was it only folly?" Ruthven asked gravely.

Urmila did not reply. Ruthven sat beside her on the divan and drew her close. "Tell me it was something more, my love!" She closed her eyes and nodded, her lips on his, her warm, silken flesh igniting his smouldering desire. He glanced around the darkening gardens below. No one was near. Lifting her, he stepped inside and laid her on the low, gilt bed.

"What has happened?" he asked, agitated.

"I have borne a son — for Ratangarh," she whispered.

Ruthven stared at her. "My son?" he asked.

"A son — for Ratangarh," she said gravely. "That is all that matters. Now go, before the Rana returns."

Ruthven refused to go. "Come away with me," he said, fear running in his veins. "Let me take you away."

"No, I am now the mother of a future Rana. I am not afraid."

And there on the canopied bed, they banished fear in a frenzy of passion.

It was late when a troubled Charles Ruthven returned to the villa where his father had lived.

All night, he lay tossing and turning, wondering why his heart felt leaden, why his hands trembled. As the false dawn broke over the grey hills, he got up, agitated. Faint noises led him to the window. Down below, a line of people in yellow robes moved in slow procession, like jaundiced phantoms. Then a faint scream seemed to echo around the arid hills. Dressing hurriedly, Ruthven left the villa and began to run towards the yellow figures. The sight that greeted him seemed to freeze his blood.

A funeral pyre had been lit, and Princess Urmila stood before it, hands bound. Seeing Ruthven she cried out. "These fiends are going to kill me, my lord!"

"How dare you?" Ruthven shouted, running forward to break through the cordon of yellow-robed courtiers. They scattered like leaves at his coming but Suraj Mal stepped before Rani Urmila, attended by three armed soldiers. "The Rana has ordered this lady to be burnt. He will not come to Ratangarh until his honour is avenged."

"Honour?" Ruthven cried in rage. "What honour does the Rana

have? He was a prisoner of the Sikhs. I had to save him and his state from the Sikhs."

"In return for his wife," Suraj Mal replied.

Ruthven stared wild eyed at the princess, suddenly remembering that evening ten years ago when he had felt as if someone had walked over his grave. "But no, I will not let it happen ..." Moving swiftly forward, he addressed Suraj Mal. "I shall take the lady away and honour her as my own wife. Let the Rana publicly repudiate her. His great honour will be avenged."

There was a moment of silence. His eyes went to Urmila, who stared at him, her face transformed by a strange radiance. "My lord," she cried out. "Save me from these fiends! Take me with you. I want to live!"

Charles Ruthven rushed towards the Rani, his hands outstretched towards her bound and bleeding ones. Encircling her in his arms, he glanced around him at the phantom figures. "Let us go!" he commanded. None dared to defy him.

For a moment, he thought he would be able to escape with Urmila. But Suraj Mal cried out, "Save the Rana's honour!" The yellow-robed figures closed in, snatching the Rani from Ruthven's arms. Ruthven struggled, until a heavy blow on his head left him senseless.

Ruthven lay unconscious as the nobility of Ratangarh led their silent Rani to the blazing pyre. An early duststorm sprang up, sending the spectators hurrying up the hillside as it sped across trees and terraces, over towers and bastions, hiding all in its screen of darkness. When Ruthven regained consciousness, he ran to the pyre, and stared at the burning body of his once-beloved. He fell on the ground and wept — for Urmila, for Jamie, and the heir of Ratangarh. The desert dust mingled with the Rani's ashes, obliterating all semblance of life.

The Rana returned a few days later. All was still within the citadel that night. Lamps burned low, softly celebrating victory. Inside the palace, there was only the disconsolate weeping of a child and an old woman.

Charles Ruthven rode up to the heavy gates of the citadel and commanded the sentries to open up. Surprised but complying, the sentries opened the gates to admit Ruthven and fifty of his men from Deogarh.

Windows were flung open as the mounted men stormed into the courtyards. Charles Ruthven rushed into the Rani's apartment, where the little prince, Uday, wailed for his dead mother. Gathering the boy in his arms, he ran out and signalled to his warriors to commence their work.

An explosion split the heavy silence, followed by bursts of fire. Then, as flames ignited, the wind spread their tentacles to the citadel-palace. Ruthven's warriors barred the doors of exit. The cries of the inmates were smothered in the roar of flames fanned by the hot wind.

Charles Ruthven watched with grim satisfaction as the raging inferno swept over the citadel. People watched from ramparts and balconies, untill the flames scorched the palace walls and hissed over fountains. Terrified of Ruthven Saheb's wrath, they ran away to the hillsides to hide.

When all was silence again, Ruthven went to the untouched Jal Mahal and sat by the lake. In the dusty, smoke-filled dawn, he drew out a jewelled bracelet from his pocket and whispered hoarsely, "Now you may rest in peace, Princess." He flung the bracelet into the depths of the lake, in a final act of farewell.

23

Winds of Change

Charles Edward Ruthven and Lady Eleanor sat in silence as their smart barouche rolled across Wellesley Place, past the massive neo-classical edifice of the commander-in-chief's residence towards the taperlit magnificence of Government House. The main gate, straddled by a lion and resembling the triumphal arch of Septemevius Serverus, was open that night. The barouche trundled over the wide gravel drive and halted before the vast Romanesque facade supported by six Doric columns. At once, four turbanned and liveried footmen sprang down, two on each side opening the doors for their Saheb and Madame-Saheb, who then proceeded to mount the shallow flight of marble stairs leading to the reception hall, where six Adam-style windows were thrown open to admit the cool spring air.

"They walk distantly," the old footman muttered to his acolyte. "They held arms before."

"Vulgar, if you ask me," the young Oudh man retorted. "It is better to walk distantly ... as do our women."

The old footman shook his head, loath to share his knowledge of the unworded turmoil he knew existed in the Ruthven house. He had seen it all, thirty years ago in Georgiana Mem's time and hoped earnestly that such events would not be repeated.

Ruthven walked on, staring ahead, while Eleanor glanced at the lawns carpeted with flowers, guarded by dusty sentinels of silver oak, rain trees and the ubiquitous coconut palms. Incongruously, a military band played Scottish and Irish airs.

Charles Edward Ruthven had returned to Calcutta after the arrival of a new Governor General, to find that his Ratangarh mission had become the subject of a controversy in the Council, and a source of silent strife at home.

Lord William Bentinck, the new Governor General was a member of the powerful Whig aristocracy. His mother was a daughter of the Duke of Devonshire and his father the Duke of Portland. The Bentincks were originally from Holland, having accompanied the entourage of William of Netherlands when he became the king of England. They had never adopted the hauteur of the Anglo-Norman aristocracy of England and had, in fact, retained the frugal simplicity of their Dutch forbears, who had carried on a relentless war against the autocracy of Philip II of Spain. Perhaps it was the racial memory of this struggle which had made William Bentinck a champion of self-determination for subject nations, and a hater of wars of conquest.

"There is no need for us to intervene in the affairs of Indian princes," Bentinck told Ruthven when they first met. "It is sufficient if we concentrate on our commercial interests."

"Wars are necessary if we are to protect our territories," Ruthven replied.

Lord Bentinck turned around abruptly and looked at Charles Ruthven. "Do we want empires, Mr. Ruthven?" he asked gravely.

"We have slowly acquired one, my lord," Ruthven replied with a sardonic smile.

"Inadvertently," the Governor General rejoined.

"As inadvertent as wars of conquest," Ruthven retorted.

Lord Bentinck paced the grand room, his tall, portly figure bent as he formulated his thoughts. "The ambition of an empire leads us to wage wars, Mr Ruthven. But out of this we may achieve something else — a united nation moving towards self-determination ... and enlightenment."

"Under British tutelage, my lord?" Ruthven asked. His irony was lost on Bentinck.

"Under British guidance," Bentinck said gravely, and sitting down, gazed intently at his visitor. "In my youth, Mr. Ruthven, I formed friendships with members of the Carbonaros of Italy, intelligent men of the noblest characters dedicated to the cause of Italian unification and unity. My sympathies were at once engaged ... as are the sympathies of many Englishmen." He paused, scrutinising the man opposite him to gauge his response. "If Italy is worthy of such a dream, why not India? Do they not share the same proud past, the same sad, fragmented present?'

Charles Ruthven sighed and the Governor General saw the impassive face darken with pain. "We have no Company in Italy. So it is possible for us to be magnanimous with Italian aspirations."

The Governor General leaned forward and spoke intently. "The Company, Mr. Ruthven, can be the agent of change." He got up again and pointed a plump hand at a parchment map. "India is too vast to be ruled by a handful of British subjects." The vivid blue eyes twinkled. "India is too vast to be ruled by anyone but without Indian assistance, it cannot be ruled at all." Lord Bentinck halted his pacing. "I have been meeting eminent Indians — entrepreneurs, zamindars, scholars and have commenced discussions with them on the need for reforms to modernise Indian society. I want you, Mr. Ruthven, to join my endeavours."

Charles Ruthven stood up. "Do you, my lord? I understood that I was out of favour because of ... the episode of Ratangarh. Yet, had I not taken the initiative and lead the Rana's forces in defence of the principality, you may be assured that Ratangarh would have become a part of Sikh territory."

"I understand," the Governor General murmured hastily. "But ... the hostility of the Rana remains unabated."

"Nahar Singh is a mindless buccaneer ... without an iota of compassion!" Charles burst out. "He was quite content to allow an Englishman to defend his territories but refused to acknowledge his debts!"

Lord Bentinck thought it as good a time as any to broach the forbidden subject. "Perhaps he harbours a resentment for another reason?"

Charles Ruthven's impassive face was suddenly ablaze with fury. "He has more than avenged his resentment ... by the savage murder of his wife! Had he been a man, he would have called me out to preserve his honour!"

Ruthven turned away, images of that terrible dust-laden dawn returning with the smell of acrid smoke. "It seems I will never forget," he said, as if to himself.

The Governor General stood silent, watching the man he had judged so harshly and for whom he now felt a surge of pity. He understood now why some spoke of Charles Ruthven as a tormented man.

Ruthven turned to face Bentinck. "My acquaintance with Raja Ram Mohan Roy and Brajesh Chowdhury led me to believe in the rediscovery of the past glory of India ... but now I am prepared to put my fortune and service at the disposal of anyone who wishes to pull India out of the cruel debris of her past!"

Lord Bentinck came forward, the smile returning to his genial face. "Then we shall be friends, Mr. Ruthven, for that is what I sincerely desire."

Now Lord Bentinck stood at the head of the marble stairs and greeted the Ruthvens in his habitual amiable manner, letting those sapient delft-blue eyes rest a moment longer on Lady Eleanor's pensive face. Lady Mary Bentinck was, however, more effusive, her Welsh warmth asserting itself over the ceremonial of high office.

"They are all here," Lord Bentinck informed Ruthven. "Including the formidable Raja Radhakanta Deb."

There was a glint of battle in Ruthven's eyes. "I shall be delighted to cross swords with the Raja," he said with a smile as they went into the octagonal reception room.

It was lit by six chandeliers, whose coruscating splendour could only have been fashioned in Antwerp. Six columns lent a classical air to the room. Rich Kashmiri carpets covered vast expanses of the marble floors. The heavy ornate furnishings decreed by Wellesley had been replaced by the light, pale silk upholstery favoured by Lady Mary. The circular corridors had masses of potted plants while crayon sketches of local scenes lined the walls.

The scene that greeted the Ruthvens was indeed unique. Men in shervanis and kurtas, belonging to the north of India spoke with men in dhotis, whose embroidered shawls draped their shoulders. There were a few women in voluminous ghararas, draped in silken veils and others in brocade saris. Their complexions ranged from the ivory hue of the north to the dusky glow of the south. Aquiline noses and grey eyes remembered Alexander's Greek armies, while square faces and high cheekbones were a legacy of Scythian tribes. One saw too the fruits of the latest intermingling — the British and Indian, though it had yet to be woven into the tapestry of India.

The reception rooms sparkled, not only with the light of chandeliers, but the conversation of the assembled guests as well. Raja Ram Mohan Roy, the spearhead of the reform movement, sat discussing matters with kindred spirits. Raja Radhakanta Deb, the aristocrat who decried all reforms as heresy and subversion, listened in growing dismay to the programme for progress.

"It must be a sweeping one," Brajesh Chowdhury said enthusiastically. "We must not only banish evil practices but replace them with education, and a sound legal code."

Raja Ram Mohan Roy nodded with a smile. Brajesh had, he observed, proved a staunch supporter. "Mr. Macaulay is already looking into the matter. He can refer to the committee set up by Lord Amherst on public instruction, which had outlined the reforms to be effected in education."

"And then sati," Ram Mohan Roy said. "That pernicious custom must be made illegal, my lord." He paused, his face clouding. "I have seen it inflicted on my own grandmother — a frail, little woman who could not have endangered anyone's honour or interest. I have a passionate revulsion for the custom."

"It was a way out for women under the degradation of foreign rule," Raja Radhakanta Deb retorted. "Honour before life."

Charles Ruthven turned slowly, almost reluctantly, to the orthodox Raja. "Pray, who gave you the authority to take life which is given by the Almighty? Under which tenet of the Vedas does a mere man destroy the life of another being?"

A hush fell on the room. While the reformers nodded approvingly, Lady Eleanor met her husband's stormy eyes, and turned away in acute pain. "There is nothing more to be said or endured," she thought bitterly. "It is all there in his anguish. No matter what he pretends and I dissimulate, we cannot deceive each other anymore. He, my beloved, has drifted away."

Dinner was an ordeal for Eleanor. She had to force herself to listen to the enthusiastic ideas of Lady Bentinck seated opposite her and the gentleman at her side. Briefly, she became totally unaware of the conversation around her, as she remembered Charles' homecoming.

She had known, as he stepped into the vestibule, that a shadow had crossed their lives. He looked gaunt and weary, and greeted them with a forced geniality. Catherine, Valerie and Margot had greeted him with reproaches at his long absence while two-year-old Julian had burst into tears at the sight of the stranger. Charles Ruthven had gazed at his second son, remembering Jamie, and the grief that had driven him to Ratangarh. He had turned away abruptly, astonishing Eleanor. But it was later, in the solitude of the night, that Eleanor realised with her unerring instinct that something lay between them, something which made him awkward and aloof even while he tried to show a passion that he did not feel. She had left their bedroom to sit on the adjoining balcony, bewildered.

It was only later that whispers from Ratangarh had reached her. "He loved another woman," Eleanor thought in anger and pain. "While I struggled with my grief, looked after the children, and his ventures, he dallied with a princess." She remembered Urmila and realised why even ten years ago the young girl had troubled her serenity. "It is as if I already knew of the betrayal."

"Betrayal," she now whispered to herself, staring at her husband with haunted eyes. "How can I stay on? How can I pretend anymore? We have become strangers to each other. We have separate rooms, keep separate hours. Why continue this farce any longer?"

"Did you say something, Lady Eleanor?' Raja Radhakanta asked courteously.

Startled, Eleanor looked into his stern face. "No," she murmured, trying to compose herself. But everyone had observed her brooding countenance. "They all know," she mused. "They pity me."

They drove back in silence. Brajesh Chowdhury had refused Ruthven's offer of a brandy. "Nightcap?" the zamindar had laughed. "It is almost dawn! Must return home in time for Annapurna's morning dip in the Ganges."

So there was nothing to stop Eleanor from saying, "I believe that your ship *Resolution*, sails next month for Europe. I should like to go back with the children."

Charles Ruthven stared at his wife. "Go to England?" he asked. "Why?"

"Why?" Eleanor cried, on the brink of tears. "Oh heavens, you must know why!"

A gold and rose light suffused the rooftops of houses along the Esplanade and Chowringhee and shifted from one dusty plane tree to another. Milkmen with their cattle and pails, sweepers with brooms, grooms leading horses and early commuters in carriages made their way along the cool, silent streets of Calcutta. From the nearby Ganges, came the hoots of ships gathering steam before sailing towards the Bay.

Eleanor remembered a similar spring dawn twelve years ago when they had argued about a point and at the end of it, discovered their mutual need. And now, when that need was even greater, she was forced to part.

"Can you not forget, Eleanor?" he asked, denying nothing. "It is all over."

"So too is our marriage," Eleanor thought bitterly. The memory of the anguish in his face after his return, wounded her more than a rough dalliance would have. That Charles had loved the princess, that he had forgotten his grief in her arms, was what she could not forgive.

"No," she replied in a trembling voice. "I can neither forget nor forgive!"

A month later, Eleanor and her four children stood on the deck of the *Resolution* as the ship of Ruthven, Chowdhury & Co. prepared to sail with its cargo of silk, muslin, spices, indigo and tea to Europe. A pair of cabins had been specially prepared for the comfort of the Ruthven family and their retainers. Brajesh Chowdhury was on board, inspecting arrangements and giving last minute instructions to Captain Fontaine and other ships' officers on board. Then he came onto the deck, flooded by spring sunshine, where Eleanor stood gazing absently at the skyline of Calcutta.

"Come back soon, Lady Eleanor," he said gently.

Eleanor Ruthven regarded him thoughtfully. "To what, Mr. Chowdhury?" she asked desolately.

Chowdhury met her gaze. "To so much, Lady Eleanor. A beautiful home, great wealth, social position and a man who loves you. One day, you will understand what makes men commit folly and bring sorrow on themselves. Perhaps then you will forgive that man."

Her hands tightened around his ... "Mr. Chowdhury, I'm afraid! It's such a long journey ... what if ...?" Eleanor began to cry softly.

"Trust in the Great Mariner. Do you remember the boatman's song?

> I salute you, oh Divine Mariner.
> My journey begins.
> Let me not be afraid.
> Come storm, come wind or high tide
> I will sail with You.

The ship's siren hooted. The flurry of activity suddenly ceased. In the dock below, all noises and movements of porters, stevedores, boatmen and visitors were stilled, as if in anticipation of the ship's departure. Brajesh Chowdhury kissed Eleanor's hands, and blew kisses to the Ruthven children. Twelve-year-old Sudhir Chowdhury bade his friends and his "Aunt Eleanor" a tearful farewell. And suddenly, as if in a dream, Eleanor found herself sailing down the eternal river to an unknown land.

The year passed quickly, despite the loneliness of Ruthven House. Charles Ruthven threw himself into the reform movement with an intensity that only the Governor General and Brajesh Chowdhury understood. The Ordinance to ban sati was almost ready when Lord Bentinck, taking fright at the sudden turmoil among the Rajputs and Marathas, decided to seek the help of the Maharaja of Punjab, and with the intervention of Charles Metcalfe, concluded an alliance of friendship with the Sikh ruler on the banks of the Sutlej. Returning to Calcutta the Governor General pushed through the Ordinance, which took India by storm.

Once more the tall french windows of Government House were ablaze with lights as Lord Bentinck and his liberal Indian friends celebrated the fulfilment of their efforts. Bentinck moved among them, explaining that this was but a prelude. "Thuggis and their confederates have to be suppressed as well as other evil practices such as female infanticide and human sacrifice for worship. We shall bring order to the courts," he said. "The provincial courts shall be abolished and transferred to district judges and in time, Indian civil judges shall try cases."

"Do not proceed too swiftly, Your Excellency," Raja Ram Mohan Roy advised his friend. "The orthodox of India will be up in arms. Customs which have taken root and flourished for so long cannot be eradicated so swiftly."

After the reception, Charles Ruthven asked Brajesh Chowdhury to sail with him on their clipper. They sat on the deck gazing at the shifting patterns of celestial lights while fishermen dropped their nets and settled in for the night, singing mournfully.

"Are we on the brink of a new era?" Ruthven asked his friend. "Or is this one more tamasha for India, one more act in the endless drama of wars, famines and pestilence?"

"No, I feel it is a stirring of something new ... something that has not happened since the time of Lord Buddha ..." Brajesh replied.

Lord Bentinck soon sent Charles Ruthven and Brajesh Chowdhury as his emissaries to London to seek support for the reform bills.

Brajesh Chowdhury was thrilled with the Governor General's suggestion. "What a splendid opportunity!" he enthused. "To go to Europe and that too, as emissaries of the Governor General. Indeed, Charles, I could have asked for nothing better!"

A sort of subdued chaos descended over the Chowdhury mansion at Chitpur Road as news of the zamindar's voyage to Europe spread. Priests and astrologers came to warn and admonish; relations and servants pleaded against the voyage and Annapurna refused food, shutting herself up in her room. Indumati smiled at her son. "Come back soon, my child. I do not wish anyone else to light my funeral pyre. Morever, your company will not survive too long without you and Ruthven Saheb."

Brajesh Chowdhury went to take leave of Annapurna the evening before his departure. At first she did not open the door but his persistent knocking finally made her relent. She stood tearfully before him. "It is all untrue!" she said almost inaudibly.

"What is untrue?"

"About losing caste. These are all ruses to keep you back!"

Brajesh Chowdhury stared at her astonished. "Why should you wish to keep me back? You seem happier in my absence."

Annapurna shook her head. "I have been a fool, trying to attain perfection and merits to attain nirvana ... while life as passed by. I suddenly realised that my hair is greying! Soon I shall be old ... and ugly!"

Brajesh shook his head, smiling. "You will never be ugly or old in my eyes, dear one," he said. "There is no other woman I have loved."

Weeping, Annapurna went into his arms, after five years of celibate living, and gladly responded to his gentle desire. She could not conceal from her own heart nor deny to her body the knowledge of the pleasure that swept over her at his touch. Eagerly, tenderly, she responded to his passion, anxious and afraid as a bride on her wedding night. As his flesh joined hers, Annapurna wondered if the ecstasy she felt burst within her was comparable to the nirvana she sought in pain and self-denial.

As she lay awake, cradling Brajesh's head on her breast, listening to his even breathing and watching the moon sink below the western sky, she was aware now, at the hour of farewell, how deeply she loved her heretic lord.

Once more the *Resolution* ploughed the sea, this time to take Charles Edward Ruthven and Brajesh Chowdhury to Europe. With them travelled their personal physician, a Scotsman, Dr. Fergusson, Hindu servants and two cooks, a Hindu and a Muslim who were to teach many a haughty chef the secrets of the curry. As usual, the steamer also carried commercial merchandise from India to Europe.

After four months of travelling, the party reached London in April 1831, where they stayed at St. George's Hotel at Albermarle Street, until a more detailed programme was made. The next day, Charles Edward went to Ruthven House at Cavendish Square, accompanied by Brajesh Chowdhury.

He stood before the graceful baroque house built in the reign of King Charles II by a Scottish nobleman who had been executed and whose property had been forfeited by the Crown for participating in the Jacobite Rebellion of 1745. The house had been later gifted to Walter Manham, who had lost it to Alexander Ruthven as a gambling debt. Fate had restored it again to the Manhams, whose daughter and Alexander's second wife, Georgiana, had opened up the house in 1802, after leaving India. She lived there, a widow of seventy years.

Georgiana Ruthven rose from the upright Louis XV chair to greet her son after an absence of sixteen years, staring at him as if she was seeing a new and alien being. The grave, melancholy man of forty-six was not the cheerful, vivacious son who had bid goodbye to her in this very room.

"Welcome home, my boy," she said with a bright smile that failed to hold back tears. Charles Edward embraced her, and kissed her cheeks with suppressed emotion.

"Mama, it has been so long!" he murmured.

"Yes," she said crisply. "A long time, in which your flaming hair has turned to ash."

"I am ageing, Mama," he said quietly, regarding Georgiana with an ironic smile. She still wore the empire style dress of 1800, though her painted cheeks were now leathery.

"Do not stare at me, boy," Georgiana snapped, tapping her silk fan. "I may have aged but my bones don't rattle when I do a turn with the waltz. The Indian sun made me strong, unlike the gals who got buried in Indian soil." Her eyes fell on the elegant figure of Brajesh Chowdhury.

"Where have I met you before?" she asked sharply.

"I am Indrajit Chowdhury's son. Perhaps you knew my father?" Brajesh asked, bowing.

Georgiana nodded, a far away look in her bleary eyes. "So I did ... on a strange day. He and Fiona, I and Andrew ... we lovers sat and drank tea and abused Cornwallis."

Charles Ruthven turned abruptly to look at the square below but Brajesh only smiled sadly. He had no quarrel with the dead.

"Tell me about yourself, Charles. Have you fulfilled your father's dreams?" Georgiana asked. Charles Ruthven did not speak. Georgiana went on. "I have heard of your exploits. Why, my boy, you move in your sire's footsteps! He won Deogarh for himself. You seized Ratangarh for England! He made a fortune. Your ships ply the seven seas, flying your colours, and you sit in the Lord Saheb's Council." Her eyes glittered and her voice dropped again. "You loved a princess, of ancient lineage. Your father did not aspire so high. He would have been proud of you."

A strange stillness fell upon that baroque style room, furnished in the ornate style of the late seventeenth century, with echoes of a tempestuous, reckless, romantic age. Charles Ruthven had often yearned to hear those words. No matter how much he had deplored his father's unscrupulous methods and his mother's untrammelled quest for fulfilment, at heart he had admired them.

"Thank you, Mama. I hope you are right." He paused before adding, "I am now able to understand many of your dilemmas."

Georgiana stood on tiptoe to kiss her son. She did not have to be told what he meant; it was clear that pride in his rectitude had been diminished.

"Eleanor is in Ashville," Georgiana said meaningfully. "It may be wise to go there soon. But in the meantime, you and Mr. Chowdhury can move in here. I am partial to youthful company. We will talk of old times."

Georgiana did not, however, talk only of old times. Learning the purpose of her son's visit, she enlightened him about the current British situation.

"Fighting with Bonaparte has made the ruling class anti-Jacobin," she explained, drawing on a silver hookah while an ageing Salim fanned her. "Rural England is changing and everywhere you will see Blake's 'dark satanic mills'. The Luddites tried to break machineries but they were suppressed at Peterloo. But Wilberforce has roused the English conscience and Sir Robert Peel is enthusiastic about reforms. The callous temper of the wartime years is giving way once more to a spirit of enlightenment — and concern."

"Is the atmosphere congenial for propagating reforms in India?" Brajesh Chowdhury asked the dowager.

Georgiana put away the coiled pipes of the silver hookah. "You will find a better response among the Whigs," she said, and added, "Your brother-in-law, Lord Geoffrey de Courtney, is one of the protagonists of reform in the House of Lords. Persuade him to support you."

Ashville, thought Charles Ruthven, is immutable. The Courtney manor was as it had been for several centuries — half-castle, half-manor with a medley of medieval, Renaissance and late baroque styles. The garden was luxuriant and the lake was filled with young Courtneys, punting amidst laughter.

Charles Ruthven stood gazing out at the tranquil scene, breathing in the warm June breeze, scented with honeysuckle and azaleas as he remembered the turmoil of his youth in this very place.

The young people splashed water on the grassy verge as they drew in the punt. They sprang out, laughing, and stood before the lord who introduced them to their newly found uncle. Richard de Courtney surveyed Charles Ruthven with evident admiration, and flooded him with a barrage of questions about India, where he was determined to go. Then talking all at once, the family group went towards the house, leaving Charles standing by the lake.

It was some time before Eleanor came out. He sensed her presence at once and turned. She looked pale and thin, as if the watery English sun had failed to warm her flesh and blood. The grey streaks in her chestnut hair had extended from temple to crown.

He went forward and uncaring of who was watching, embraced her close.

"How I have missed you, my dearest," he said in an unsteady voice. "Will you come home with me next month? Life is utterly melancholy without you."

"Home?" she whispered. "India! What a strange place to call home ... but I love it ... only promise that you will not...."

Charles stopped her words with a kiss. "I promise. I am not as wise and strong as you, but I am yours."

They clung closely together, glad of each other's nearness, aware of a need to bridge the chasm of loneliness and resentment; to accept pain and acknowledge the imperfection of their love.

Slowly, they walked back to the ancient manor, where, many like them, had made their peace in the end.

Geoffrey de Courtney, the Earl of Ashville, was full of good intentions. He wished particularly to help sister Eleanor's husband so that their estrangement would end. Besides, one did not wish to alienate a powerful nabob. From the sylvan tranquillity of Ashville, they travelled to London where Lord Courtney introduced Ruthven and Chowdhury to prominent Whigs in both houses of Parliament.

"Raja Radhakanta Deb has met the Anti-Jacobin Club, comprising mainly of Tory landlords, to obtain support against intervention in the Hindu way of life. He has even got a few moulding orientalists to support him," a Whig leader informed Ruthven.

"Raja Ram Mohan Roy has been meeting the Prime Minister. You should both meet him and intensify your efforts," Lord Courtney told his friends. "Lord Melbourne is sympathetic as well but you need the support of the Privy Council."

The age of reform had begun in England. Preparations were afoot to pass the Great Reform and Emancipation of Slaves Bills. In this mood, Lord Bentinck's Ordinance banning sati was ratified. The Charter of the East India Company was renewed.

London, too, was in a state of excitement. Though Georgiana Ruthven was old, she was by no means inactive. Her home in Cavendish Square remained a salon for the gifted and famous.

"You must meet the famous men of England," the dowager said. "Staying in India has made you rustic."

Charles Ruthven forebore to reply. Besides, he was genuinely interested to meet Carlyle and Ruskin, to discuss the politics of reform and the poetry of Byron and Wordsworth. Cressida often came to these soirees, beautiful and restless, still infatuated with Charles Ruthven and jealous of her half-sister, Eleanor. That Charles Ruthven had, in the end, betrayed Eleanor, pleased Cressida, but what embittered her was that he had not surrendered to her. To tease him, she set about fascinating Brajesh Chowdhury, his friend. 'It will be a pleasure to vanquish this detached and austere Brahmin," Cressida mused. "It will also shock that tiresome moralist — my sister." But Brajesh remained impervious to her magic.

The *Resolution* was once more on the waves. This time, Eleanor stood joyfully beside her husband and four children, one protective hand on Sudhir. Brajesh Chowdhury stood a little apart, gazing at the mist-wrapped scene of Venice, as the sun rose over the spires of San Giorgio, splintered on the Byzantine cupolas of San Marco's basilica, lit up the Doge's palace and glimmered on the floating magic of Ca'doro and Ca'Pesaro. Gondolas and vaporettos of the nobility floated in from the mist.

"I have seen Europe," Brajesh thought. "I have been invigorated by contact with Europeans. I have seen the splendours of its past and heard the music of its future. They have not become prisoners of past grandeur — as we have. We too must move forward, with hope and courage. My own people will condemn me but I will be happy as an exile in my own land. I will not enter the prisonhouse of superstitions!"

Brajesh Chowdhury returned to India to find that a beautiful little daughter had been born to him and Annapurna. A daughter, Isabel, was born to the Ruthvens some time later. While the mothers hovered over their new infants, the fathers returned to their office on Fairlie Palace, to attend to their shipyards and warehouses. They were invited to the Governor General's Council which was now the nursery for reforms. The vibrations of the Reform Bill of 1832, which ushered in a new age in England, were felt across the sea in India.

The prophet of reform, Raja Ram Mohan Roy, died in the midst of these events at Bristol in 1833 and Lord Bentinck soon left for England.

At a farewell barge-party hosted by Ruthven and Chowdhury, Lord Bentinck sat with the guests, thinking of the vast and splendid land he would soon be leaving, with its diverse people and customs, its chaos and turmoil, its strange tranquillity and timelessness. Would one person, in one lifetime, ever understand India, he wondered. Lady Bentinck joined him. "We have been honoured to serve here," he said to her with the humility of a great man. "Let us hope that India will remember us with kindness."

Sitting nearby, sixteen-year-old Sudhir Chowdhury heard these murmured words. He felt a lump in his throat. With the pride of young manhood, he blinked back tears. Ten-year-old Julian Ruthven and five-year-old Dilip Chowdhury looked at their leader in mute query, trying to understand the import of these words. Julian saw Sudhir rise and joined him, followed by little Dilip. "My lord, Sudhir said unsteadily, "we will all remember you, not merely with kindness but with ... admiration."

"Yes, my lord," Julian echoed shyly. "We will remember." Little Dilip nodded, not fully understanding.

The Bentincks drew the boys close and bade them sit near, talking to them as friends, and not as visitors from another world.

One day, that scene would be remembered by all three, with sorrow and regret. Tonight, however, it was just one more ride in the barge, down the timeless river.

24

A Simla Summer

The Ruthvens were celebrating their daughter's eighteenth birthday. The ball at Ruthven House was one of the grandest that Calcutta had seen. Miss Emily and Miss Fanny Eden escorted their bachelor brother, the Governor General, Lord Auckland to the glittering occasion. They were fond of Catherine though Miss Emily found Lady Eleanor too solemn for her taste. She, however, enjoyed occasionally flirting with the enigmatic Charles Ruthven.

"Well, Miss Eden," Charles Edward asked lightly, "what are your other observations about Calcutta society?"

Emily Eden was a member of an illustrious Whig family. Like her brother, George, she was languid and gracious, but unlike her brother she had an insatiable curiosity and a great capacity for laughter. She was not bored as easily as the Governor General, though she shared his aristocratic dislike of pettiness and injustice. Not without hauteur, Emily Eden possessed, however, a sophistication and tolerance that made her a good observer. If she lacked Lady Eleanor's sensitive perception of the Indian scene, it was because she had lived too long in a different world. However, she shared Eleanor's view of the incongruity of a few hundred Britons ruling India.

"My observations, Mr. Ruthven?" the great lady asked with an ironic smile, her pale blue eyes sweeping over the colourful diversity of guests. "I marvel at the absurd rajas, the outlandishly dressed gentry, our own pushing officialdom and their incorrigibly flirtatious womenfolk. It would be a unique scene — anywhere in the world."

Charles Ruthven laughed, amused. He had little in common with the three Edens but he liked their gracious manners and ready humour.

"I hear you are to embark on your journey soon."

"Yes. George wishes to make a royal progress through the up-country." Her eyes twinkled as she added softly, "Poor George. He would rather be at White's making puns to delight Lord Melbourne."

"I dare say, the up-country people would enjoy them too."

Miss Eden laughed. "George would have to learn Hindusthani then. He might do just that — to pun in another tongue!" Her eyes caught Catherine dancing with young Richard de Courtney under a chandelier, its coruscating light glittering on her sequinned tulle dress. "Lovely child, Mr. Ruthven. How I wish I could take her with us. Would you consider it?"

"Take Catherine with you, Ma'am?"

"Yes. She would be a lively companion for me and Fanny ... and for George too."

"Kitty has never left home ..." Charles Ruthven faltered.

"I shall ask Lady Eleanor — if you are agreeable. It would do her good to see other parts of India." There was a hidden command in Miss Eden's voice that Charles Edward could not ignore.

Lady Eleanor was puzzled by the request "Well yes, Miss Eden, if you wish it, but Catherine is not the sort of demure girl you would like on attendance. She is restless and tends to provoke."

"I do not wish a demure girl on attendance," Miss Emily Eden declared. "Catherine is a dear, vivacious child, and will keep us amused."

The ball continued well into the night. Lord Auckland danced with his hostess several times and amused her with his witty repartees and frequent puns. She relaxed in the warmth of his languid presence. It seemed so long ago that she had been a girl like Kitty, in Regency England, dancing with Whig blades in Devonshire House or meeting the Lamb boys at Lady Melbourne's home. She had looked forward to a serene, happy existence, never imagining that passion for an impecunious Scotsman, son of a notorious nabob, would have led her to a different, stormier life. "Yet," she thought with a sigh, "I would not exchange my dear Charles for any lord or duke."

Across the room, where the tall neo-classical windows opened out into the wide circular balcony, Miss Eden was busy discussing a point in animated conversation with Brajesh Chowdhury. When the dance ended and Lord Auckland moved casually towards a giddy hoyden, Eleanor joined the group in the balcony.

Brajesh Chowdhury was describing to the Governor General's sister, the route of their proposed journey through the Indo-Gangetic plain. She listened with a meditative countenance. It gave her an odd feeling to hear Mr. Chowdhury's impeccable English accent, his acquaintance with European literature and history and his familiarity with the London scene and persons of mutual acquaintance. Miss Eden felt embarrassed that she and her people, beings from so far away, should try to rule this intractable country, of which she knew hardly anything while Mr. Chowdhury, a member of the governed people, should know so much about the rulers.

"Extraordinarily knowledgeable man, Mr. Chowdhury," Emily Eden said, as she strolled in the lamplit gardens of Ruthven House. Eleanor assented. "Seems a pity that such men could not rule this country. Why did we have to come here?"

Eleanor stopped under the spreading filigreed branches of a jacaranda tree, just beginning to unfurl purple blooms.

"Is it because they did not have armies to fight ours?" Miss Eden asked.

Eleanor shook her head. "It was not a question of armies, Miss Eden. It was a question of the will to succeed ... and because the people welcomed us as deliverers from chaos and misrule. Perhaps they regret it now, but it is too late."

Miss Eden sighed. "Yes. So it appears." Impulsively, she turned to the grave, elegant woman with meditative eyes. "Does it trouble you sometimes?"

"It troubles me often," Eleanor Ruthven replied quietly.

"I do so hate some of what I see," Miss Eden murmured.

Eleanor's eyes rested on Emily Eden's, urging her on.

"The other day I saw an English officer in the grounds of Government House — kicking his groom mercilessly. Would that be permitted in England? Yet he sits at my table, pretending that he is civilised, as if by assaulting a defenceless groom he had risen in status."

Eleanor nodded. "I have seen such incidents often, Miss Eden. It is painful. The ordinary Britons coming to India have no knowledge or respect for this country. They are so ill-equipped to rule. So how can they but stir disaffection in the people of this land?'

"That is why George thought of this journey up the country. To get to know the people, to greet them, as friends and allies." She paused. "I wish you could accompany us."

Eleanor Ruthven smiled and shook her head. "I have four children to care for. But let Catherine go and learn."

With verve and wit, Catherine described in her letters her flirtations with nawabs, the Prince of Orange and encounters with her fiance, Richard de Courtney, who continued to take leave from his regiment in Meerut in order to meet Catherine in Delhi.

Charles Ruthven found her epistles a cheerful change from the harangue of his cousin Ian's sons. Jeremy and Thaddeus Latimer came to ask their uncle Charles to protest against the abolition of rent-free lands that British settlers had enjoyed since the time of Clive. They were shocked to hear that Uncle Charles had joined forces with the reformist, Brajesh Chowdhury.

Jeremy Latimer had already met Chowdhury at the latter's mansion in Belgachia, where the zamindar had been mortified by the English army officer's attitude. "Can this arrogant man be the son of my gentle friend Ian?" he wondered. "No Englishman has ever behaved offensively with me until now."

Brajesh Chowdhury left his study to stand on the adjoining balcony. Below lay a garden designed by a Welshman — the first of the landscape gardens. There were clusters of mango trees set on artificial hillocks, and bamboo trees encircling a discreet pavilion. Stone benches were placed around a small pool in which pink and white lotuses floated. Here he had entertained his western and westernised Indian friends after returning from Europe. Though neither his mother nor his wife said anything, Brajesh had sensed their coolness to his idea of entertaining unconventional friends in the old Chitpur Road house. Chowdhury had, therefore, built a separate villa for himself and his friends in the sylvan suburbs of Calcutta.

Suddenly, he felt a revulsion for the western style house, the servants in livery, the English furniture and paintings, the sound of a piano being tuned. "It is all artificial," he said to himself. "I do not belong here. I am masquerading as a westernised man. Were I an Englishman, that slip of a boy would not have dared to insult me! Neither my wealth nor education, nor my friendship with exalted Britons protected me from the contempt of a rough, uncultured Englishman!"

A new pain stirred within him; a pain he knew could only be assuaged by one place. He gave orders at once for two carriages to be prepared for travel to Mayurganj.

Indumati, the old dowager, sat beside her daughter-in-law Annapurna, fanning her with a palm leaf, though the punkha-pullers kept the silk fans moving on the ceiling. The khuskhus, window screens made of rushes, had been sprinkled with water to cool the air that passed through. But Annapurna tossed restlessly on the bed. As soon as she saw Brajesh, she murmured, "Oh, it is you! I keep thinking you have gone abroad again."

"No, my dear, I am here ... trying to gain strength from you ... and Mother." Brajesh's voice was hoarse with unshed tears.

Annapurna's pallor frightened him. Her full, curved lips were bloodless, and her huge eyes were filled with an unnerving luminosity. His warm hands tightened around her cold ones.

Slowly, Indumati left the room, wiping away the tears of old age. "Strength from me?" Annapurna whispered, trying to smile. "Why, I am a feeble, frightened woman. What strength can I give you?"

"The strength of truth, of purity, of self-discipline," he replied.

Annapurna sighed. "Poor substitutes for a strong, happy woman who could have satisfied your love of life." She looked at him with steady eyes. "I have not been the wife you wanted, I know."

Brajesh Chowdhury laid his cheek on hers and whispered, "Dear love, don't go on like this. You led a fine life, worthy of a goddess. With your punya, I may be redeemed as well. And then, perhaps, we will be joined together in another life — in complete happiness!"

Her bloodless hands stroked his grey head. She felt the warmth and vitality of his being flow into her — fleetingly — before the eternal coolness came. "Do you believe then in another life, that we are born again?"

"I ... want to believe, Anu, in anything that will keep you close to me. You will not go too far, will you, my love? I could not stand that, I want to know you are near, like a beam of light ..."

"I shall be near," Annapurna whispered. "I cannot go yet to nirvana. The chains of maya, of attachment and desire, will keep me close ... to you ... and my children." She paused. "Be good to them — as you have always been ... especially to my little Radha ... she is so young, so helpless!"

Now Annapurna, who strove for detachment, wept for her children, particularly seven-year-old Radha, who, hearing her parents, came into the room. "Come, my precious," Annapurna whispered to the little girl with her pale gold skin, gleaming black hair, straight nose and full, chiselled lips. Her eyes were as large and luminous as her mother's, though she had inherited too the sparkle of her father's, his love of life and laughter. She sat between them, conscious of a palpable anguish.

She had known with the unerring instinct of a child that her mother was dying, and had drenched the pillows each night with her tears. When her father arrived a month ago, she had begged him to save her mother but he had only sat with his head between his hands, wracked by dry tears. Only old Indumati knew how to deal with Radha, explaining gently to her the inexorable pattern of life, death and rebirth.

"Will I see Ma again then — after we are reborn?' Radha had asked, pausing in her weeping.

"Yes, you will meet her. Love such as you have for your mother will pull you close together. Such love never dies." Indumati drew the dark, silken head to her robust bosom. "But if you cry and make your mother unhappy, she will be suspended between two worlds — in pain."

"I will not cry," Radha promised her grandmother. "I will bring peace to Ma."

Radha had kept her word. Throughout the stormy monsoon months, she had sat by Annapurna's bedside, telling the dying woman stories of kings and queens, of frogs that became kings and parrots who forecast the future. She was rewarded by her mother's soft laughter. To please her mother, Radha came in the evenings to chant the immortal lines from the Bhagavad Gita, the Song Celestial.

Now Radha came with an earthen lamp, sticks of incense and a silver bowl of jasmines which she made into garlands for her mother's still-black hair. Softly she intoned the sacred name, as her deft little fingers joined one jasmine bud to another. Brajesh and Annapurna watched their child, the exquisite being born out of their joyous passion on a golden autumn night.

It was autumn again — the season of pujas, festivals and gaiety, when the mother goddess Durga came in resplendent form to renew mankind's performance. Annapurna clung on to life and to love, eager once more to hear the beat of drums and blowing of conchshells, to smell the cooking of bhog, the oblation; scented rice and lentils, nuts and raisins, curds and sweets. She took part in these remembered rituals from her bed, Brajesh and Radha always by her side. Durga

Puja was followed by Lakshmi Puja and then came Diwali, the festival of lights. As the lamps of worship were extinguished, Annapurna left the world with the goddesses, redeemed at last from pain and desire.

Brajesh Chowdhury was forced out of his mourning by the question of the government's resumption of rent-free land. It was essential, he knew, to muster support from other landlords as well as Charles Ruthven.

Charles Ruthven, however, was more anxious about the trouble brewing in the north west. Persians had taken Herat and the Russians were marching towards Khandahar. It would soon be Kabul. A war would stir an upheaval in both Punjab and the Rajput states. He had been asked by Lord Auckland to use his influence in Ratangarh to ensure the neutrality of the Rajput princes.

"You must, therefore, manage the affairs of our company as well as the Bill for resumption of rent-free land," Ruthven told Chowdhury. "You will face opposition from European settlers."

"I have already faced unpleasantness from one," Chowdhury replied.

"I am ashamed of Jeremy Latimer's conduct. Allow me to ask pardon for his misdemeanour," Ruthven said.

Brajesh Chowdhury sighed. "Yet this misdemeanour is growing—imperceptibly. Is it the beginning of a new mood in the relationship between our peoples?"

"Jeremy Latimer must not be permitted to represent our people," Lady Eleanor said quietly, rising from the sofa to stand near the windows. "He is quite odious."

Brajesh Chowdhury sensed that Jeremy had upset Eleanor, who resumed, "Jeremy Latimer has inherited neither Aunt Fiona's generosity nor Ian's tolerance. He is indeed Matilda's son — petty and abrasive. He comes now to please 'Uncle Charles' because he needs help in the land question. But I cannot endure his manners."

Brajesh laughed. Eleanor, he knew, could assume an air of polite indifference that could be ignored only by the brazen.

"I wish he did not seek the company of my ... children," Eleanor continued, in a strange voice.

"The fellow is rough," Ruthven admitted, "but he tries to be amiable."

"Latimer should adhere to his own ways," Eleanor replied sharply. "His attempts at amiability are more grotesque than his rough manners."

The Ruthven girls found their second cousin to be singular and laughed at his ways. Julian, their brother, however, declared that Jeremy Latimer was like Mephistopheles.

"Dear me, who was that?" asked fifteen-year-old Valerie.

"Devil of a chap," thirteen-year-old Julian replied. "Tempted Dr. Faustus with eternal youth ... to win fair Marguerite."

"Heavens, Julian where do you read all this?" Margot asked, tinged by envy. "You ought to concentrate on geometry or else you'll fail to get admission to Eton."

"Shan't try to get into Eton. Prefer Sherbourne School any day," Julian replied. "Can fly kites and charm cobras in my spare time."

"That would hardly do credit to your race," a voice interrupted.

The five young Ruthvens glanced up to see the figure of Captain Jeremy Latimer. The blue eyes, sandy hair and sharp features would have made another man good-looking, but in Jeremy's case, there was another dimension that made him appear sinister to his second cousins. The girls shrank away, awed yet fascinated. Julian stood his ground, his eyes sparkling.

"My race, Cousin Jeremy? I regret I do not understand," he said softly.

"Your British inheritance, Cousin Julian. You cannot, with honour, fly kites and charm cobras when you ought to be learning about Greece and Rome, and of England's greatness."

The blue-green eyes glinted. "Greece and Rome had trade with India. Alexander took philosophers from here. They learnt astronomy and mathematics from India. Do you know that? As for snake charming — if silly old Orpheus had known that, Eurydice might have survived snakebite."

Valerie and Margot giggled, more to relieve their tension than from amusement. Catherine regarded Julian with new wonder. "The little brother is becoming quite a man," she thought, but decided to mollify the awful cousin.

"Do go and study, Julian dear. Margot is right. Your geometry requires more attention," she admonished with a smile.

Julian bristled. "My geometry is quite saitsfactory. Dilip and I built a mud fort on Sunday. If my geometry was unsound, it could not have withstood the river tide. It has." He fixed his eyes on Jeremy Latimer, bestowed a withering glance on him and then turned on his heels. Valerie and Margot followed their brother and as Catherine moved to join them, Latimer barred her way. His pale eyes moved from the profusion of red-gold ringlets framing the flushed face to the wide, sea-coloured eyes, and the sensual Courtney mouth, the slender white throat and swell of round breasts. He felt a constriction in his throat and chest, an urgency that he had never experienced before, not even his first time with an Armenian harlot in a squalid brothel of north Calcutta. Walking with leaden steps, Latimer went and stood before Catherine, who stood motionless by the piano, mesmerised by his wild look.

"Catherine," Latimer muttered thickly. "Little Kitty, why are you so maddening?"

"Don't be absurd," Catherine muttered, as fascinated as frightened by the naked lust in his face. "I must go ..."

The words were choked back by a stifled cry as Jeremy Latimer crushed her in an embrace and forced open her lips with his own. She felt his hand move over her throat and shoulders and then seize her breasts. The novel sensation within her suddenly altered as she felt him harden Catherine tried to release herself, suddenly repelled by his bared teeth and mad eyes. But he held her in a vice-like grip with one hand and flung back her head with the other, thrusting his mouth against her lips. His hand moved on, exploring her hips and thighs through the thin, sprigged muslin dress. Catherine struggled and then tore herself free, gasping in rage, and staring at him with hatred.

"Are you all right, Missy Baba?" Moti-bai asked, quietly entering the music room. Julian trembled beside the servant woman, hands clenched for assault but Moti-bai stayed him. "Don't soil your hands on a badmash, Julian Baba," she said with derision. "Come Kitty, your Mama calls you."

Catherine breathed in gasps, her cheeks as flaming red as her hair, and then fled from the room. Moti-bai followed, disturbed.

"Greece and Rome?" Julian shouted hoarsely. "You rotten disgusting fellow! Today I listened to Moti-bai, but another day... I will throttle you. Now get out and stay out ... unless you want to face Papa over your conduct!"

Jeremy Latimer stood staring at Julian Ruthven with palpable hatred and then seeing the rage in the boy's eyes, he calmed his own desire to hit him. But from that moment on, he dreamt of the day when he would be able to humiliate these haughty Ruthven cousins.

Caught in the excitement of the ensuing days, Julian Ruthven forgot to report cousin Jeremy Latimer's misconduct to his parents. The Calcutta papers were full of the news of Lord Auckland's order for war. And at home, young Julian heard his father's friends speak in support of the Governor General's decision. One of them, a Major Trevor Barclay of the 3rd Bengal Light Infantry, was most vociferous.

Charles Edward Ruthven glanced at his young friend. Major Barclay was a good soldier, but he saw everything in black and white. The tangled webs of Indian politics required an appreciation of chiaroscuro. "Peace with the Sikhs is a kingpin of British policy, Trevor. For thirty years, the East India Company has striven to keep Ranjit Singh west of the Sutlej. An alliance with Dost Mohammed would unleash them into the Indo-Gangetic plain."

"What is the alternative?" Brajesh Chowdhury asked.

"To countenance Russian influence in Kabul!" Major Barclay exclaimed.

"The Governor General wishes to keep the Sikh alliance and remove the Russians from Afghanisthan. He has just sent his emissary, Macnagten, to sign a tripartite treaty with Ranjit Singh. The Sikhs will move only with British assistance." He paused. "The Army of the Indus marches soon."

Charles Ruthven shook his head. "It will be a costly adventure, Trevor. Afghanisthan," he said, grimly, "is not India. It is a land of high, unpassable mountains, peopled by fierce tribesmen. No army has succeeded there."

"Except Alexander of Macedon's," Major Barclay said, with an exultant smile. "We carry his mantle."

Lady Eleanor served tea in the twilit drawing room of Ruthven House. Beside her sat Major Barclay's wife, Lavinia, a thin, sallow young woman, worn out by the Indian climate and malaria. Quietly, she passed around the Dresden china cups to the guests. Eleanor smiled at her encouragingly, remembering the travails of her own early years in India. But she knew that she could not calm Lavinia's fears for her husband's safety in the forthcoming war.

At one corner sat Catherine Ruthven, listening intently. Finding an opportunity after tea, she went up to Barclay. "Major," she asked in an urgent whisper, "will the Bengal Lancers be joining the Army of the Indus?"

Major Barclay glanced thoughtfully at the young woman with her effulgent Titian face. He wondered how she retained this opulent beauty while Lavinia had shrivelled and wilted. "Yes, Miss Ruthven. I hear they too will join. We will join up at Buxar, under Sir John Keane."

Catherine nodded, blue eyes darkening with fear.

Charles Edward Ruthven soon left Ratangarh, where his task as Resident was to persuade the young Rana and other Rajput rulers to resist from martial activities. "Take me, Papa!" thirteen-year-old Julian demanded. "I should love to ride from one fortress to another with you!"

Charles shook his head. "I shall go in a comfortable carriage, my son. I am no longer a young Hussar. And you must stay to keep the girls in order." He paused. "Especially dear Kitty. She is pining for Richard."

Julian held his breath. He wanted to tell his father of Jeremy Latimer's assault on Kitty but decided not to. After all, he thought, Cousin Jeremy had said good-bye and gone to join the Army of the Indus. He would not trouble Kitty again.

Meanwhile, Brajesh Chowdhury was embroiled in the proposed legislation to resume rent-free lands. He attended the scheduled meeting at the Calcutta Town Hall in November 1839 under the chairmanship of Theodore Dickens, a leading barrister, but refused to join Dickens, Prinsep or Tagore who condemned the move. "Many beneficiaries of these lands are poor," Dickens declared. "Let the authorities discriminate between the deserving and the non-deserving."

Brajesh Chowdhury got up to speak. "Let the Land-holders' Society cease this agitation for the moment. Let them look to their tenants and redress their grievances before we ask the government to redress ours. It is a powerful body, whose interests cut across racial and religious differences. It is well equipped to redress grievances. Let the Society advocate the use of vernacular languages in mofussil courts, and the grant of maintenance allowance to poor witnesses at these courts. Let stamp duty on official documents be reduced. Let the landlords not harbour the ruffians who terrorise the tenants. Once the Society accomplishes these tasks, it can ask for benefits."

He left the meeting in a triumphant and belligerent mood, and stopped at Ruthven House for a cup of tea with Lady Eleanor who was in the first floor sitting room with her children, reading a long letter from Charles Edward. Seeing Brajesh, she rose and took his hands. "Thank heavens you have come," she said. "I am so agitated. I have news that Charles has taken ill in Ratangarh and that Richard, Catherine's fiance, is missing."

Lady Eleanor dreaded the stay in Ratangarh but she had no choice. Her husband was ill and she was compelled to go, accompanied by Catherine and Julian.

The old fort, the graceful palace, the Jal Mahal by the lake, and Alexander Ruthven's villa — everything brought back to Eleanor the agony of remembering Charles Ruthven's passionate encounter with Rani Urmila.

Lady Eleanor felt strangely drawn to the young Rana. He was, she knew, Rani Urmila's son by Charles, though no one dared to say so. Uday Singh's existence kept the British from annexing the state. Eleanor had tried to hate the child born out of Charles' betrayal of her, but found instead a strange surge of tenderness. It was as if Uday, born a year after the death of Jamie, was the latter's reincarnation. "He is my son too," she mused.

The young Rana, Uday Singh, kept aloof from both the Resident and his lady. He was not hostile to Ruthven, because it was Ruthven who had protected him after the murder of his mother and the mysterious death of the Rana. It was Ruthven who had ensured that the throne passed on to him; yet Uday Singh could not banish the dishonour that had stained his mother.

It was during a visit to Deogarh that Catherine coaxed Uday Singh into telling her the entire tale of love, dishonour and tragedy.

"I still hear her anklets, my lady, as she used to run to meet the ... Lord Saheb's emissary. I can hear her hushed laughter and ... sudden sobbing ..." He turned to Catherine Ruthven. "Stay awake on the festival of Ghummar, and you too will hear her."

Catherine's eyes followed Charles Edward on the festival of the spring moon. As drums beat and dancers shook the fort walls with exuberance, she saw her father withdraw into a world of his own; taciturn and aloof, daring anyone to question him. She too sat alone on the terrace of the water palace, waiting for the sound of ankle bells, the shadow of a comely form rushing towards a rendezvous among the cluster of churail trees by the take. Though nothing stirred in the golden moonlight except the restless spring wind, the atmosphere of Ratangarh stirred her blood and made her thirst for romance.

After ensuring that the young Rana would not join the Sikhs, Ruthven took his family to Simla to recuperate — and if possible, to caution the Governor General against further involvement in Afghanisthan.

Simla had become a fashionable resort from the time of the Governor General, Lord Amherst. Britons roasting in the summer-scorched plains discovered this earthly paradise in the early years of the nineteenth century. Houses and hotels with white walls and sloping tiles, and shops and offices soon sprang up. Yet the beauty of Simla remained: the lofty hills, perennially snow-crowned, forests of pines and fir greening the stony face, tall red rhododendrons and slopes ablaze with banks of violets and irises. Gardens fashioned in the English style grew artichokes and asparagus, wild strawberries and plums. Tulips were grown as well. And cuckoos sang all day.

Lady Eleanor fell in love with Simla. A house had been arranged for them. Miss Emily Eden sent chintz cloth for curtains, damask for tablecloths and surplus asparagus. A hill-dweller brought a pail of foaming warm milk which Julian drank al fresco and took ill. The Kangra man materialised again, not with milk this time, but half a dozen servants to look after the Ruthvens.

"We received news of young Courtney," Miss Eden said casually. "I thought Catherine would like to see him."

While Catherine and Julian went exploring the resort town, Lady Eleanor sat in the little garden, gazing at the clouds that swept past her, cool and sweet after the heat of Ratangarh. She drank creamy tea, devoured peaches and strawberries and felt like purring in contentment. Charles Ruthven sat with Lord Auckland, discussing the deepening crisis in Afghanisthan.

"There can be no withdrawal," Macnatgen declared, while Charles Ruthven advised a slow, phased out withdrawal.

"We cannot keep Afghanisthan in subjugation. No one can. Neither Alexander nor Nadir Shah have succeeded. Let us fortify our borders and quit the impassable territory before winter comes," he said.

Sir John Keane, the Commander-in-Chief, now promoted to a baronetcy, disagreed. "The campaign must finish. We cannot withdraw! It would be shameful. We owe this to Shah Shuja!"

"We owe Shah Shuja nothing — neither money nor loyalty and certainly not the blood of our soldiers — Indian or British!" Charles Ruthven retorted.

Lord Auckland said, as gently as he could, "It is difficult to retrace our steps now, Mr. Ruthven."

There was no respite in Simla. Miss Eden encouraged dances, dinners, amateur theatricals, fete champetre. Wives of bureaucrats and army officers were eager to help and draw the notice of the Governor General. A delegation of Sikhs watched couples waltzing with astonishment. "That respectable women should dance thus!" they muttered.

A week later, Richard de Courtney arrived, battle-scarred but triumphant, a hero in the hillside resort. Catherine flew down the hill, hearing of his approach. Julian stood on the balcony and watched; he would always remember his sister's yellow silk-clad figure hurtling down the slope, like a windblown daffodil, her hair like leaping flames and her cry, "Richard! Dearest Richard!" He would always remember their hungry embrace under the pines, their reluctance to rise from the bed of violets where they sat, arm in arm, while great swirls of clouds hid them from prying eyes. He would always blame himself for not being more careful; for not heeding the wild desire in their eyes.

Eleanor and Charles Ruthven tried to be strict but could not enforce their will. Catherine refused to submit to rules and restrictions. Never docile, she now threw all form to the winds.

"Richard is back ... whom I never hoped to see. Don't you see how wonderful it is? Why, I can hardly have enough of him! And soon he will be gone. Do let me go for walks at least, Mama. No one can object to that!"

There were narrow bridle paths where they cantered on tiny horses, pausing to glance at the majestic sweep of the Himalayas reaching to the sky. Deliberately, they allowed the other riders to overtake them, so that they might enjoy each other's presence in solitude.

One day, Catherine came in at dusk to Lady Eleanor. "Mama,

a couple in the Governor General's entourage got married today."

"I know. Poor young things, they have to spend their wedding night in tents. I would have gladly offered them this cottage if Papa were not so tired."

"Mama ... let Richard and I be married ... before he returns to Afghanisthan." Catherine's voice was low but tinged with frenzy.

Lady Eleanor glanced quickly at her daughter, her sapient eyes noting the reddened lips and dishevelled hair. "Richard will return soon. Until then it would be ... unwise to marry," Eleanor said.

"Why?" Catherine cried. "Because you fear I might become a widow?"

"Hush, darling. Don't say such things!"

"But that is what you are thinking! Yet, I would rather be Richard's widow than someone else's wife. Do you hear, Mama?" Catherine cried, her voice rising. "I cannot wait so long!"

Lady Eleanor drew Catherine close and laid her cheek on her daughter's tear-streaked one. "Kitty, my sweet, you will have a splendid wedding. We shall go to London ... or ask Richard's parents to come to Calcutta ... and you both shall have a honeymoon anywhere you choose. Is it not worth waiting for — rather than a hurried wedding in Simla and a honeymoon in a tent?"

"No. I want to be with Richard ... in a tent!" Catherine said heavily.

Eleanor Ruthven shivered, despite the warm sunlight. The wild look on Kitty's face recalled to her a scene from the Ruthven family tales ... of Georgiana and Andrew rushing heedlessly to their nemesis. "I will speak to Papa," she said sombrely.

That night, Lord Auckland gave a ball for his newly married aide-de-camp. Richard de Courtney, a resplendent figure in white and scarlet regalia sporting the new medals for his valour in Afghanisthan, escorted Catherine in her debutante's dress of white tulle and Begum Shirin's pearls. People watched them, two youths so immersed in each other, so similar in looks; two impulsive and intense young aristocrats standing out starkly against the cluster of drab officials and their overdressed wives.

Miss Emily Eden watched them and murmured to her brother, "It would have been wise to have got them married with your other ADC."

"Dear Emily," her brother said fondly. "Ever the indefatigable matchmaker!"

"No, George," she replied, staring at Kitty and Richard. "I feel a presentiment."

Charles Edward Ruthven also watched his daughter. Despite his wife's suggestion, he stood firm. "My cousin and your brother, the Earl of Ashville, would misconstrue a hurried wedding as a ploy on our part to bind Richard."

The days slipped away, as elusive and fleeting as the sunlight glimmering on the pink-and white-capped hilltops. Catherine brooked no opposition to her rendezvous with Richard. Moti-bai packed a cold lunch one day, when they insisted on a picnic by their favourite waterfall skirted by irises and violets. Purple and green butterflies hovered over them and twinkled away. Catherine ran after them, deep into the pine woods. Richard followed her and soon the two stood gazing at each other until a wordless message drew them into each other's arms. There was no need for answers or questions, no doubts and hesitations as they lay on the mossy, resin-covered ground. Catherine offered no resistance to the hands that explored her hungry, eager body. Instead, she drew Richard close, and soon they both forgot their fears as waves of desire and longing carried them towards a frantic quest for fulfilment. He thrust through silken layers of flesh, until her cry of joyous pain echoed around the dark pinewoods and then they lay in exquisite delight, trembling, and gazing at the distant snowy peaks. They rose at twilight, to bathe in the glittering cascade by the violet-covered slope, and returned home under bright, silent stars and mist.

"I will return soon, my heart," Richard said, as they trudged up the slope to the Ruthven cottage.

"I will wait, dearest," Catherine whispered, choking back a sob.

25

A Reluctant Bride

Charles Ruthven was anxious to return to Calcutta as soon as the rain clouds appeared on the hilltops, so that by August the Ruthvens were back home. Catherine found Richard's letter waiting for her. He had received sanction for long leave in autumn, before the snows made travel impossible in the Hindu Kush.

"In the meantime, there is discontent among the Afghan chiefs," Richard de Courtney informed his fiancee. "The Company has discontinued its allowance to them, and dissension is ripe. In Kabul, we are three brigades of artillery and infantry comprising of 4,500 combatants but our Commander, General Elphinstone, though brave, is ill and old. The location of the stores and cantonment is vulnerable to attack. It is all worrisome."

Catherine sat with the letter for a while, rapt in thought, then went to her mother who was in the lawn waiting for tea. "Mama, I must go to Simla and await Richard there next month," she said in agitation.

Lady Eleanor looked up, startled by Catherine's tone. "Why Kitty, we have just returned! Richard will come before Christmas — when we plan your wedding. There's a good four months left. We can spend the time getting your trousseau ready, darling. I have such marvellous plans for your wedding!"

Catherine stared at the garden with unseeing eyes, a strange smile on her face. "That would have been lovely, dearest Mama, but I fear our wedding must not, cannot, be delayed beyond next month."

Eleanor Ruthven slowly rose to her feet, clutching a chair, her eyes wide with apprehension as they swept over Catherine's face and figure. "What can you mean, Kitty?" she asked in a hoarse voice.

Catherine regarded her mother with fear and distress. "I ... you must not be upset, Mama ..." the girl said in a strangled voice. "Richard and I love each other ... terribly ... and it will be all right. There is no ... sin ... in ... giving oneself to the man one loves, is there, Mama?"

Eleanor continued to stare at the lovely girl who was her daughter but who reminded her now of the girl's grandmother, Georgiana Ruthven, with the same reckless impulses for fulfilment. "Are you ... enceinte, Kitty?" she whispered.

Catherine nodded, a rueful smile on her face, her eyes bright with tears.

Eleanor collapsed into her chair, her head between her hands. "Oh Kitty!" she cried hoarsely. "My foolish child! Whatever shall we do no? Richard is in the midst of terrible turmoil. How can he return before Christmas?"

Charles Ruthven was informed that evening of Catherine's predicament. Distressed and anxious, he shut himself in his study till late at night, smoking intermittently as he stared at the stormy monsoon sky, remembering Rani Urmila and his half-brother Andraz. "Why, dear God, did Kitty not inherit Eleanor's steadfast character instead of our Ruthven traits?" he mused.

The next morning, he sent one of his couriers to Simla with an urgent message to Macnatgen, the political agent, requesting for a short leave for the Honourable Richard de Courtney to meet him at Simla.

Catherine waited for the reply as the monsoon raged over the Indo-Gangetic plains. She sat in her room, her hand over her slightly swelling belly, filled with a strange mixture of dread and joy. She often thought of the exquisite rain-washed afternoon when she and Richard had become lovers on the moss-covered slope, the iridescent light glinting on the frothing water, its murmur muffled by their cries of delight and desire. "Richard darling," she murmured, "I do not regret this ... but come soon so that we may be together."

News came in September end that Richard would be arriving next month. As Macnatgen had been taken into confidence, he acted promptly. Charles Ruthven informed his daughter grimly. Her conduct had distressed him and he seldom spoke to her. Meanwhile, Eleanor went ahead with preparations for a stylish wedding at St. Paul's Cathedral. Richard was her brother's son, a fine young man, who would make Kitty very happy.

One November evening, as the Ruthvens sat down to dinner, the head bearer, the khidmatgar, came to announce the arrival of "an army officer from Kabul." As Charles and Eleanor Ruthven heaved sighs of relief, Catherine sprang from her chair and rushed out of the dining room to the drawing room.

Her cry of "Richard, darling ... I ..." died in her throat when she saw Major Jeremy Latimer standing by the mantelpiece.

Jeremy Latimer's pale eyes regarded her with a strange intensity and dwelt with some surprise on the new heaviness of her breasts and waist. A momentary fury glittered in them, replaced by a cold satisfaction.

Catherine drew the Kashmiri shawl over her bosom, blushing. "Where is ... Richard?" she asked. "Has he not come? He is due home!"

Jeremy Latimer stared at Catherine's eager, anxious face, reading the concern and love, impatience and joy, at the thought of Richard de Courtney's arrival. He hesitated only a moment to let a shaft of pity pass over his bitter heart. Then calmly he said, "There has been a revolt in Afghanisthan ... the Shah's treasury plundered, the arsenal set on fire ... Alexander Burnes, the new political agent, his brother and ... Richard de Courtney ... were murdered."

"No!" Catherine screamed. "No! You lie! Richard is not dead!"

"Dead. Lying cold in a hurriedly dug grave in Kabul," Latimer insisted, triumphantly. Catherine screamed with pain and anguish and collapsed onto the floor.

Charles Ruthven and Eleanor rushed from the dining room to the drawing room, where they found their daughter lying motionless on the floor, with Jeremy Latimer looking on. At their entry, he told them the news. The Ruthvens carried Catherine to a sofa and called for water and brandy.

Julian Ruthven brought the water and brandy. Valerie and Margot fanned their sister, while their parents heard the details of the tragedy from Major Latimer. In stunned silence, father and son carried an unconscious Catherine to her room. Dazed, Eleanor and her three daughters sat with Catherine, while faithful Moti-bai tended to the unconscions girl.

A clear, golden morning dawned with sunlight glittering on the dewy grass and leaves. Charles Ruthven went out into the garden, staring with glazed eyes at the autumn brilliance so out of tune with the despair in his own heart. Eleanor joined him and sat by his side, taking his hand in hers.

"Why Eleanor? Why?" he asked in a thick, husky voice.

"Why? Because we come here to suffer, to repay old karmic debts of another life."

"I reject such a cruel explanation!" he cried.

"It would be far more cruel to say that Kitty is paying for her sins in this life ... the sin of love ... and joy."

"The sin of love ..." Charles Ruthven said brokenly. "Oh, Eleanor, have I set a bad example? Have I sinned greatly?"

"No, it's better to think that all this is part of an older design, of births and rebirths aiming towards the final liberation. Annapurna told me this when I grieved for our Jamie."

Charles Ruthven put his grey head between his hands, his body convulsed by sobs. Eleanor drew the grey head to her own and let their tears mingle. Slowly, he raised his head and gazed at his wife with red-rimmed, defeated eyes.

"Latimer and I were talking late into the night. He guessed Kitty's condition."

"Very perceptive," Eleanor retorted bitterly. "Did he recommend Christian charity?"

"He offered to marry Kitty," Charles Ruthven muttered.

Lady Eleanor stared incredulously at her husband. "Is he mad?"

Charles Ruthven shook his head. "I wonder. Or perhaps he loves Kitty better than Richard did. Why else would he want to marry her in such a situation?"

Eleanor was silent and bewildered. It was difficult to believe that Latimer was capable of such noble qualities as to marry a fallen woman. "What did you say?" she asked.

Charles Ruthven sighed wearily. "What else could I say? The child is expected in four months. Kitty would be ... ruined ..."

"So we have to be grateful that Jeremy Latimer is to be our son-in-law!" Eleanor burst into long held-back tears.

"Do not take it so hard, dearest. We have been caught in a bigger tragedy ... So many men have perished in Afghanisthan. Richard is one of those tragedies. I wonder if Lord Auckland would now agree that I was right when I advised withdrawal from Kabul."

He got up and took her arm. "We have to be strong, Eleanor, and guide Kitty. She must agree to the marriage ... for her own sake ... and that of Richard's child."

Catherine Georgiana Ruthven was married to Jeremy Latimer a week later in St. Paul's Cathedral. She wore the full taffeta, seed pearl-encrusted gown and veil of Valenciennes lace that Lady Eleanor had ordered for her wedding to Richard. Pale and stunned, Kitty took her vows to a man she did not love, while the child of her dead lover stirred within her. She had protested vehemently against marriage with Latimer but had realised the hopelessness of her situation.

Valerie, Margot, Julian and Isabel watched their sister from the front pews, each resolved to love wisely.

Jeremy took Catherine to the Latimer estate near Mayurganj

to enjoy a strange honeymoon with his pregnant bride. There could be no joy or even passion in their union; only lust on his part and despair on hers. Catherine lay with closed eyes, steeling herself against the rough, brutal hands that assaulted her painful body, the tongue that darted into her mouth.

"Fastidious, are we?" Jeremy asked thickly. "You superior bitch! Was it better with Courtney?"

"I hate you, Latimer. You married me because you have no shame."

"Ungrateful whore! Hate me, do you? For giving you respectability and your bastard legitimacy?" Latimer slapped his bride. Catherine struggled and tore herself free from his grip.

"Yes, I loath you. You married me so that you could satisfy your lust. You also wanted to share my wealth and connections. Did you not get a share of Ruthvẹn, Chowdhury & Co. as part of the bargain? Why, it is you Latimer who is the whore. I gave myself to Richard because I loved him ..." She paused, her eyes glittering with tears of rage and grief. "And because he loved me ... he had no need of my wealth or connections because he was a handsome, gifted and ..."

Catherine could proceed no further. Major Latimer dragged her from the bed and thrust her onto the floor, her arms pinioned under his. And then he possessed her with such force and roughness that she screamed in pain. "Kill me and my baby. We can be saved by death alone!"

Jeremy Latimer left for Afghanisthan soon after. The turmoil in that kingdom had deepened after the upheaval of November 1841. The Commander-in-Chief, Elphinstone, tried to deal severely with the rebels but failed. Kabul passed into the hands of Dost Mohammed's son, Akbar Khan.

In the meantime, neither Lord Auckland nor the political adviser, Macnatgen, gave specific guidance to the besieged officers in Kabul though they interfered at every stage in what was a military operation. Realising the futility of the situation, Macnatgen negotiated with Akbar Khan and agreed to relinquish Shah Shuja's claims.

Emboldened, Akbar Khan increased his demands. Elphinstone agreed to capitulation. As the soldiers began their retreat amidst winter snows, the wild Afghan tribesmen began to pursue them, killing their men and taking the women for Akbar's harem. More than three thousand men perished. It was the greatest military disaster the East India Company had suffered.

In February 1842, Lord Auckland was relieved of his post as Governor General. His military failure obscured the wisdom and tolerance of his domestic policy. In pursuing the fiat of the East India Company, Auckland had drained India of blood and revenues. When their policy met with reverses, the board of directors of the Company refused to accept responsibility and made Auckland an easy scapegoat.

Lord Auckland's departure was a cause of distress to those who had been familiar with him and his sisters. People like the Ruthvens and Chowdhurys, the westernised Dwarkanath Tagore as well as the orthodox Raja Radhakanta Deb lamented his departure. His sister, they claimed, had brought a patrician graciousness to Calcutta society. Emily Eden had deplored intolerance and arrogance. She had chosen to mingle with Indians and had learnt their customs with an untiring interest. More than anything else, she set an example to lesser British ladies on how to conduct themselves as emissaries of a great empire.

Lord Ellenborough, the new Governor General belonged to quite a different species from Lord Auckland. Cold and resolute, eager for action, his strategy reversed the defeat of the armies of the East India Company. He sent Nott and Polleck to Afghanisthan, where they sent the armies of Akbar Khan to flight and captured Kabul.

While the older Ruthvens returned to their leisured pace of life, Catherine fretted at Dubb's Point with her hated husband, who had taken long leave to stay with and torment his gorgeous wife. Julian was finally sent to England, to study and prepare for entry into an Oxford college. His parents feared that he had forgotten England altogether.

During the next few years, Brajesh Chowdhury remained active with his reformist work, and involved his eldest son, Sudhir, more and more in his commercial ventures. To provide a chatelaine for the household, Sudhir was married to a comely and accomplished girl whose father was also a part of Brajesh's enlightened circle. Rukmini, the new bride, strove hard to be the housewife and hostess that Brajesh expected his son's wife to be.

It was now in the Chowdhurys' villa at Belgachia that Charles Ruthven found serenity and a sense of purpose. His own house had become a silent storm-centre.

Brajesh Chowdhury understood his friend's predicament. "The strife will pass. Peace will come again. Nothing lasts, my dear Charles. We are all transient."

Lady Eleanor decided to take her three daughters to England—to settle them with proper husbands before they followed Catherine's example and earned her sons-in-law like Jeremy Latimer.

Brajesh Chowdhury asked Eleanor to take his fourteen-year-old daughter, Radha, along with her own daughters. "Find her an excellent governess, let her travel and widen her horizons. My son, Dilip, is also going. I have got admission for him in Cambridge. I want my children to belong to the future ... so that they can help take their country out of the past."

The proposed journey met with severe opposition from the Chowdhury family.

"You will imperil us all!" Harish, the second son, stormed. "You have crossed the black water, and intend your sons to do the same, but why Radha?"

Sudhir was calm, but annoyed. "Surely you will not take so ill-advised a step?"

"Why should I not?" Brajesh's tone was sharp and defensive.

"Why not? Because it is unthinkable for a Hindu woman to cross the black water."

"Radha is not yet a woman. She is a child, a motherless one

at that. I refuse to leave her behind, for the better part of a year."

"Would that not be infinitely better than having her cast aside as an outcaste? Have no illusions, Father, because that will happen if the word is bruited around. She will not be married if she goes abroad."

Brajesh Chowdhury paced the length of the Persian carpet, his forehead creased by a frown. "This is intolerable! A girl cannot see the wide world because of some obscurantist rules! I refuse to submit to them!"

"You have not submitted to them, Father. You have always defied them. Did you not refuse to do penance when you returned from Europe in 1830? That is why orthodox Hindus refuse to have you in their homes ... or give their daughters in marriage to us. But Radha need not suffer."

Brajesh Chowdhury sighed. "Radha will not suffer. I assure you. No one need know she is accompanying me and Dilip."

It was a journey of discovery for the young Chowdhurys. Eighteen-year-old Dilip travelled through Europe with wonder and awe and when Lord Lyndhurst, the provost of Cambridge, welcomed him and Brajesh, the young man felt that his dreams had indeed come true. Twenty-year-old Julian came from Oxford to welcome his boyhood friend and together they discussed myriad subjects.

For fourteen-year-old Radha, the trip was all that she had expected. Isabel Ruthven and she explored London together, while their fathers met reformers and scholars of Britain — Sir Robert Peel, Lord Brougham, Marquis of Lansdowne — all of whom were interested in the reform of India and were members of the British India Society. The visit to Queen Victoria at Windsor Castle was the high point of the trip. The young Queen's warm concern for India won her a devoted subject in Brajesh Chowdhury.

At the end of three months, both Charles Ruthven and Brajesh Chowdhury felt that their purpose of arousing interest and sympathy for India had been achieved. Lord Grey's reforms had prepared the ground for change and Gladstone's advent would quicken the impetus.

Then it was time to begin the journey to India from Marseilles.

Autumn had set in; gold and russet, with limpid skies and a sharp breeze. "On such a day, my father set off from Marseilles for India ninety years ago," Charles Ruthven told Brajesh standing with him on the deck of the *Bentinck* of the P&O line.

"Ninety years ago," Brajesh Chowdhury mused, "my grandfather, Ishwar Prasad Chowdhury, was burying his treasures under the rice field because the Afghan chiefs were threatening to invade our land."

"And my grandfather, James Ruthven, was killed by my other grandfather Henry Manham after the battle of Culloden — exactly a hundred years ago. That is why my widowed grandmother fled to Marseilles with her children." Charles Ruthven paused and glanced at Brajesh. "The Hindus are right. Time moves in a cycle, returning to the same point of departure."

"I hope he does not return," Catherine Latimer wished fervently as Jeremy Latimer packed his valise, before leaving for Ferozpur, along with his regiment. "I hope I never see him again."

"Well, my dear," Latimer said grimly, "try to behave while I am away."

Catherine regarded the long face, sandy hair and pale eyes with a contempt she did not attempt to hide. "There is no temptation in this ugly town and all the men are gone to battle," she said softly, enjoying the sudden rage in his pale eyes.

"You will always be a whore," he said through clenched teeth.

Catherine laughed. "And you, Major Latimer, will continue to tolerate me because you like my money. You will continue to crave for my body because you have no self-esteem."

Jeremy Latimer closed his eyes, remembering the night before when he had possessed her, in violence and rage, while she lay inert and cold. He had withdrawn from her hostile flesh, humiliated. "I wish I could kill her," he thought. "Only that would bring me peace." Without looking at her, he left the bungalow.

The cantonment town of Barrackpore fell silent as the army marched out, leaving behind a maintenance force. An air of gloom hung in the white mist of the November morning. Many officers had perished in the recent campaigns, leaving vacant bungalows.

Wives watching the scarlet-coated, turbaned sepoys marching wondered if their menfolk would ever return from the dreaded land of five rivers.

Lavinia Barclay stood at the gate and watched her husband ride away. The three children at her side clutched her hand. They were afraid now. Papa, the strong capable parent, had gone, and Mama, thin and sick, seemed to offer little solace as her sunken eyes stared in the wake of dust clouds.

"Bring them back safely," Lavinia murmured in a fear-choked voice.

Catherine Latimer sat inside, glad that her husband was leaving.

The Sikh army crossed the Sutlej on December 10 and ten days later, on the day of the winter solstice, they were crushed at Mudki by British forces commanded by Sir Hugh Gough. Henry Lawrence, Collector of Delhi, had sent men, weapons and food for the army of the East India Company.

The Sikh leader, Shyam Singh, realised that the hour of reckoning had come. Two of his generals, Tej Singh and Lal Singh had already informed Sir Hugh of the battle position and strategy. Now, the brave but doomed warriors rushed headlong into battle.

Major Barclay rushed forward, equally determined to win. As he prepared the bull-headed frontal assault preferred by Sir Hugh, Trevor Barclay was surprised by the valour and vitality of the enemy. "Seems a shame we must fight these people instead of winning them over," he thought as the 80th Regiment raced forward over the hardened earth.

The battle of Mudki was brief and bloody. By dusk on the shortest day of the year, it was all over. Shyam Singh lay dead on the battlefield. The Sikh army dissolved into the evening dusk. The British forces set up camp nearby in alert watchfulness. Sitting by their campfires, they heard the loud lamentations of Sikh women from across the battle lines. Barclay and his comrade, Latimer, walked through the starlit darkness to watch the lighting of a pyre as Shyam Singh's wife, dressed in bridal regalia, leapt into the flames, clutching the dead body of her beloved lord, now covered by his wedding garments.

"The best wedding I have seen," Latimer thought to himself. "If only all marriages could end thus!" He walked back to camp, thoughtfully, as if a new dimension of India had opened up before him.

The battle of Mudki was followed by that of Firozshah, Aliwal and then Sobraon, where the Sikh army was finally crushed in February 1846.

The question of Punjab plagued the Governor General in Calcutta. He decided to postpone annexation for the time being, in order to retain Punjab as a buffer state between Afghanisthan and British India. The treaty of Lahore trimmed the Sikh army to 20,000 infantry and 12,000 cavalry. Kashmir was ceded to the East India Company, which sold it to Gulab Singh for £1 million.

The Marquis of Dalhousie, a young autocrat of thirty-six, was now Governor General. Seeing the unrest in Punjab, he decided that the time had come for a final encounter with the Sikhs. "The Sikh nation has called for war, and on my word, Sirs, they shall have it with a vengeance!"

Once more Gough, now a lord, led the British forces across Punjab, and crossed the Rabi in November 1848, joined by those officers already in Punjab. Jeremy Latimer and Trevor Barclay fought in the decisive battles of Ramnagar, Chilianwala and Gujerat, where the Sikh army was destroyed. In March 1849, the Sikhs surrendered and Lord Dalhousie, tiring of incessant oriental treachery and political instability, decided to annex the land of five rivers.

"Water," Lavinia muttered through cracked lips.

Catherine poured a few iced drops into the woman's mouth and wiped her burning face. "My dear," she said softly, stroking the lank, tangled hair of the other woman, "drink a little of this coconut water. It will give you strength."

Lavinia shook her head. "No ... don't want ... native drink. Give me ... brandy."

Catherine sighed. Lavinia was a silly woman. And now she was dying, leaving behind three young children. "Brandy will upset your stomach further, dear. Coconut water will cool it. Do try it."

Lavinia turned her face away. Catherine sponged the thin arms and legs, and called the ayahs. "Fan the Memsaheb while I call the doctor. Our doctor has gone but there is one in Goalpara."

"How will you call that doctor? He lives quite far away," one ayah protested. "Doctor Saheb will not come."

"I shall ride there!" Catherine declared, tossing her head.

From Barrackpore to Goalpara was a rough ride over hard, sun-baked, mud paths. The morning sun soon turned pale and made Catherine shiver but she did not stop galloping until the huts of Goalpara loomed before her.

She soon found the doctor's dispensary, next to the little parish church, set amidst a cluster of huts of jute-mill workers. Suppressing a shudder, Catherine strode in, hat and riding crop in hand, as a dozen dark faces turned in amazement to stare at the flame-haired white woman in a fine riding habit.

The doctor was dressing a man's wound, his sleeves rolled up to reveal powerful forearms. "Yes?" he asked in Bengali, sensing a visitor's presence. "What is your malady?"

"I am well, thank you, but an English lady needs your help," Catherine replied in English.

Eric Blair raised his head and stared at Catherine in amazement. Never in his five years in India had he seen a white woman as gorgeous as the one who stood before him now. For a few vibrant moments he did not speak. Then, recovering, he pointed to the villagers who sat silently on the three benches in the thatched shack and said, "They need my attention, Ma'am. I am afraid I cannot come."

"My friend is dying! Can you deny her help?" Catherine's voice rose.

"Where do you live?"

"Barrackpore."

"There must be a doctor in a cantonment town?"

"There were three but all have gone to the Punjab. Lavinia's husband is a Major Barclay. She has ... typhoid ... and is dying," Catherine repeated.

Dr. Eric Blair continued to dress his patient's wound, while Catherine watched with fury, tapping the riding crop on her hand, until he was compelled to look up.

"Are you refusing a request to give peace to a dying woman?"

"No, I shall come — in an hour — after I attend to my patients."

"I shall wait," Catherine said, and sat down next to a coughing man.

They arrived at Barrackpore as the afternoon sun quivered before the winter wind. Reining in her horse, Catherine strode up the steps to the veranda of the Barclays' bungalow, where a child whimpered in fear. Eric Blair followed in silence until he saw Lavinia tossing on the bed. After examining her, he turned to Catherine standing nearby.

"Mrs. Latimer," he said in a low, urgent voice, "please leave. This lady is beyond help. She has caught the plague."

Catherine stifled a scream of fear. "Plague?" she whispered hoarsely. "Good God ... that is ..."

"Very bad ... and contagious. Leave at once. You have, you told me, three children. You must not endanger your lives."

"And you?" Catherine asked, suddenly concerned for this detached being.

"I?" Eric Blair asked with a wan smile. "I am a doctor. It is my duty to attend to the dying — as you told me this morning."

She regarded him in silence; the grave, pensive man with grey eyes and brown hair, a slim, taut body and a pair of dextrous hands that were already busy attending to the sick woman. She had not seen this variety of commitment before; not in her gifted father or uncles or acquaintances or even in that idealised figure of Richard de Courtney. Something inexplicable rose in her, something akin to pain — the realisation that grandeur of man lay not in bold words and dashing deeds but in an unobtrusive nobility that sought to bring relief from pain and desolation.

"I will stay and assist you. Trevor Barclay asked me to look after Lavinia," she said slowly.

"Not when you can contract the disease yourself," he replied brusquely.

Catherine was suddenly unafraid of dying. She wanted to be near this brave, compassionate man. Slowly, she began to assist him, preparing mixtures, sponging Lavinia, and lighting candles as the abrupt dusk of Bengal winter fell over the cantonment town. She instructed the Barclays' servants to prepare a simple meal for them all, fed the children and put them to bed. Then, coming to Lavinia's candlelit room, she found Eric seated by her, reciting a prayer from Thomas a Kempis' "Imitation of Christ".

Lavinia had ceased to toss but the hectic flush of fever had been replaced by the pallor of death. She was, however, serene, a hand held in Eric's warm clasp, listening to his gentle voice.

Catherine sat down unobtrusively at a distance, afraid of dispelling Lavinia's tranquillity.

"I am not afraid, Dr. Blair," Lavinia murmured faintly. "Do look after my little ones until my Trevor returns."

"I will. Mrs. Latimer, too, will help."

Lavinia's laugh was almost a sigh. "Yes. She has a kind heart ... despite her hoydenish ways."

Eric Blair said nothing but sat in silence, holding the patient's hand and stroking her head until she fell asleep. Rising, he saw Catherine sitting motionless in a chair in the shadow-filled room.

"Some unexpected people have courage," she said in a low voice. "I would not have expected Lavinia to be calm in the face of death.

She was so ... agitated ... about little things in life."

Eric Blair nodded. "I have seen many instances of that as well," he said in a grave voice. He looked at Catherine with sapient eyes. "I did not expect you to be .. good at a patient's side ... or with children."

Catherine laughed softly. "Because you thought me a hoyden?"

Eric shook his head and walked into another room, troubled by the effect Mrs. Latimer was having on his own serenity.

They stayed by Lavinia's side that night and the next, when her condition deteriorated. Catherine assisted Eric in every way to lessen Lavinia's suffering, and when the stars paled and it was evident that the woman was dying, she brought in the children to say good-bye to their mother.

The next day passed in utter melancholy. Eric Blair arranged the funeral and took charge with his quick competence, while Catherine tried to cope with the grief-stricken children. The well-ordered cantonment town was polite and kind but the anxious women who had stayed behind did not wish to endanger themselves or the lives of their children with the dreaded contagion. They kept away, sending polite excuses, peering through chintz curtains to see the cortege move past pretty bungalows, neat gardens and parade grounds. The Indian servants stayed, afraid of losing their posts.

"This place is terrible!" Catherine cried, as they sat in the veranda after the funeral. "I must get away — to Calcutta — or I shall go mad!"

Eric Blair nodded. "Yes. I have also found cantonment towns singularly unattractive. The British live in ignorant isolation, convinced of their superiority ... and invincibility. They have no awareness of India. How can they? Their contact with India is through sepoys, shopkeepers and servants. They know nothing of men like Raja Ram Mohan Roy and Dwarkanath Tagore, leave alone the cultural heritage of India."

Catherine gazed at him in astonishment, and then smiled, as if to acknowledge to herself that she had guessed he was different. "Why did you come to India, Dr. Blair?" she asked softly.

The young doctor gazed into the twilit horizon. "It is a long story, Mrs. Latimer — and possibly a tiresome one. I would not weary you with it ... not today at any rate."

"Another day, then? Perhaps if I come to Goalpara?" she smiled entrancingly. "I can bring a picnic basket."

Abruptly, he rose. "I think I shall leave tonight. I have left my parish for three days already. It is time I went back." He made a move to go. Catherine rose and stood in his path. Darkness had settled like a velvet mantle over the cantonment township.

"Afraid, Dr. Blair?" she asked, green eyes glittering.

He nodded. "Yes, Mrs. Latimer. I do not wish to ... do anything that might ... diminish ... us."

Catherine put out her hand to him but Eric stood frozen as a statue, until she took a few steps towards him and laid her head on his shoulder. Slowly, his arms encircled her soft, voluptuous body. She raised her face to his sun-bronzed, clean shaven one, to the calm, grey yes that were alight now with a new warmth.

"Can we not diminish ourselves ... and forget the world ... for a while ... when death stands in our way? Tomorrow, I may be as stiff and cold as poor Lavinia."

"No!" Eric exclaimed, drawing her closer. "No, you are meant to live ... a glorious life ... full of joy and laughter ... and love ..."

His mouth sought hers and his hands caressed the body that she offered so joyously. Her fiery tresses seemed to burn his hands, the glittering yes kindled a long forgotten fire within him and the warm flesh seemed like rose petals. His kisses grew more frantic and her response more frenzied, until the church bell began to toll slowly in memory of Lavinia.

Eric tore himself free from her ardent arms and lips, and rushed out to the veranda where the cold, damp air lashed his face. "God forgive me," he murmured, gazing at the silhouette of the church spire against the starlit sky. "And yet ... could it not have been ... ?"

Catherine watched Eric Blair leave, in the meagre light of winter stars. No plea or blandishment had detained him again. Yet she did not feel desolate at his departure. It was as if she had, after five years, looked within herself once more. "I am not yet dead ..." she thought. "I can hope and dream again. The life I have been leading need not be the only one ... something splendid may happen yet!"

Taking her children as well as Lavinia's, Catherine left for Calcutta a few days later. If Eleanor was glad to have her eldest child back, Charles Edward was anxious about the effect his volatile daughter might have on his ordered home and on his youngest daughter, Isabel.

"She is changed," Eleanor told Charles Edward. "There is a new serenity in her. Perhaps it has been caused by Lavinia's death. Perhaps, she is growing up at last!"

Charles Ruthven watched his daughter closely, hoping his wife was right. He still sensed a certain turbulence in her, which lay under the surface calm. "A legacy of the Ruthvens," he mused.

He was not far wrong. After a few weeks of pensive domesticity, Catherine embarked on a life full of romantic escapades once more.

PART III

JULIAN RUTHVEN
1847 — 1867

CHARACTERS

Julian Ruthven
Isabel Ruthven
Catherine Ruthven
Afraz Ruthven

Radha Chowdhury
Dilip Chowdhury
Prince Uday Singh

Jeremy Latimer
Thaddeus Latimer
Eric Blair
Trevor Barclay
Carolyn Barclay
Stephen Reynolds

26

Beyond the Seven Seas

For five years, the Ruthvens sought to make a merchant prince out of their heir — to no avail. After completing his studies at Oxford, Julian refused the Grand Tour of Europe and six months to enjoy the pleasures of country houses and the London season. Instead, he applied for a civil servant's post in the East India Company.

Charles Ruthven was furious. Why should a young man with assured wealth and position wish to work as a humble official in the East India Company? Lady Eleanor reluctantly supported her husband. It was the old dowager, Georgiana, who backed her grandson. "Of course you shall serve in India. Your grandfather, Alexander Ruthven, would not have liked his empire to be abandoned."

"The empire, Grandmother," Julian said earnestly, "is a sacred trust and possession. Duty and honour require that it should not be administered as a precarious acquisition."

The bleary blue eyes twinkled. "Bravo!" she cried, laughing.

"Lord Wellesley's words, not mine," he replied with gentle malice.

"Aha, that horrid fellow. Called me a 'blowsy blonde begum' once," Georgiana muttered.

"Will you recommend me to your friends in the Court of Directors?" Julian asked anxiously.

"Why not? Few can have your claims," she paused, dropping her banter. "You are serious, then, about 'serving India'? It is a hard life, Julian."

"I am serious, Grandmother."

"Very well. Prepare to go to Haileybury then. That is where they teach you to be an official of the East India Company."

Two years passed in Haileybury. Julian spent his time studying Sanskrit, in love with the Rig Veda and Kalidasa. Monier Williams, the authority on Sanskrit, was pleased by Julian's prowess. He learnt Persian, Hindusthani and Bengali as well. Malthus, Ricardo, and Adam Smith were taught by Richard Jones, while Melville taught Law and Ethics.

On holidays, Julian visited his grandmother, whose stories of India fascinated him. He avoided the smart set of his sisters, Lady Margot and Mrs. Valerie Davenport where "butterflies" or debutantes gleamed in candlelight.

"Have an affair, Julian," his grandmother advised. "It isn't decent for a man of two and twenty to be celibate. Pick on a ripe female. Nothing like a worldly woman to teach you the art of making love in a carriage, keeping assignations in a library and giving gifts with little money but prodigious sentiment."

Julian laughed. "Did you do all that, Grandmother?"

Georgiana Ruthven chuckled. "I did all this and more ... my escapades shocked both Regency London and Hastings' Calcutta." Suddenly, she sighed. "But it was poor compensation for losing the two loves of my life — Robert de Courtney and Andraz Ruthven."

Julian studied her painted face, the thin body loaded with fabulous jewels and felt a surge of love and esteem for the brave, old woman. Georgiana eyed him too. "I hear your cousin Lady Amanda de Courtney is pining for you. Are you going to offer for her?"

"No," Julian replied gravely. "I do not wish to settle down yet."

"Sow your wild oats first, eh? But Amanda is a fine catch."

"Maybe," he replied, non-committal. "Anyway, it will be time to leave for India soon." Julian took Georgiana in his arms, a thin stick of a woman dressed in satin and diamonds, incongruous and bizarre but for those jewel-bright eyes. "Dearest Grandmother, take care of yourself. I will return to England for a holiday and regale you with stories."

"Of course. I shall be waiting. And Julian, my boy..."

"Yes Grandmother?"

"Avoid a begum or rani when it comes to loving. Choose someone more original."

Julian laughed. "I shall bring back a nautch girl or a devadasi."

The ship was crowded with a variety of passengers — army officers stationed in Malta, Aden and India; traders, bankers, and clerks ekeing out livelihoods in the east; a few missionaries, bravely travelling to heathen lands, carrying the message of the gospel. Julian surveyed them all with curiosity, wondering about them, and their reaction to the country of their destination. Among this crowd, yet curiously detached from it, was a young woman who seemed to be brooding over some inner pain.

The captain, Angus Macfarlane, invited Julian Ruthven as a permanent guest at his table, while other passengers were selected by turns. Julian enjoyed meeting the different kinds of people and if he found some of them lacking in the polished manners and cultivated minds to which he was accustomed, he forebore to show his aversion. What did amaze him were the many fallacies that the Britons carried with them about India and Indians. Most of them, like Reverend Paine, thought Hinduism was no better than a set of Red Indian rites. "They are, after all, all Indians!" he conceded generously.

Julian regarded the missionary with incredulity. "Surely you cannot be unaware of the ancient traditions of India or the philosophical wealth of Hinduism."

Reverened Paine fixed two glassy eyes on Julian. "I understand you are a civil servant of the East India Company, Sir?"

"You are correctly informed on this matter, at least," Julian replied with a condescending smile.

Captain Macfarlane coughed and called loudly for his best hock as Reverend Paine's face flushed into a warm, purple hue. "I cannot believe that the East India Company selected you, Sir!" he said grimly.

Julian Ruthven leaned forward, his lively temper aroused. "Not only one director, Reverend, but all the directors recommended me. Furthermore, I was judged the best probationer at Haileybury. My proficiency in Sanskrit, the language of the gods, was considered meritorious. My grasp of Persian, the language of the Muslim Sufi mystics, is not prodigious but tolerable and my command of Hindusthani and Bengali is excellent." He paused. "I was born in India, Reverend, in a room where the Ganges breeze baptised me first. My family have been there for almost a century now... These are the reasons why I was unanimously recommended. If you wish to succeed in India, you may well remember that you are dealing with a complex race, rich in culture, fierce in their devotions but fickle in loyalties, and as prone to chaos as Italy. Do not offend their souls if you wish to win them for Christ."

Captain Macfarlane stared at the young man with a strange smile. The others remained silent, including Reverend Paine. Only one voice was raised — that of the brooding, young woman.

"What would you suggest, Mr. Ruthven, for those who go to India with the intention of spreading the gospel, bringing succour to the sick, and educating the ignorant?"

Julian Ruthven glanced sharply at the woman. She was very young — not more than twenty, but her fine grey eyes were dark with visible pain. The nose was straight, the mouth tight. Her pale, blonde hair was drawn tightly back into a chignon, without ringlets or fringe, and her thick serge gown almost succeeded in concealing her white neck, full breasts and slim waist. Her hands were fine but red and a thin gold band encircled the third finger of her left hand.

"What do I suggest, Ma'am? A spirit of tolerance — that is all. Do your good work; you will receive gratitude — even gifts, but do not expect loyalty or easy conversion. Hindus are an obdurate people. Islam could not subdue them nor could Buddhism."

"Can we win them with compassion and tolerance?" the woman asked.

Julian smiled. "They can be subdued or defeated, they can be bribed, but I do not know if they can be won over. Many have tried."

A silence fell over the table. Captain Macfarlane's hock had run out. Passengers on other tables had their eyes riveted on the captain's table, where the attractive young man held forth. While Macfarlane offered Havana cigars and wondered how to dismiss his guests, his perennial friend, the sea, came to his aid.

The ship began to roll and pitch. "Ah," he said, blue lights in his eyes, "I think we have entered the Bay of Biscay. A winter storm, most likely."

The announcement had the desired effect: the passengers hurried out, anxious and restless. Only Julian stayed back to finish a quarter of Madeira.

The Bay remained rough throughout the night. Julian stayed up, reading the Odyssey. Ulysses' dilemmas seemed suddenly like his own. The next morning, he went onto the deck to find it brimming with water. He joined Macfarlane on the bridge. The sea was a grey fury. Julian wondered idly whether they would be shipwrecked.

"Stirred up a hornet's nest, you did, young sir," the Captain said, chuckling.

"Yes, I apologise. But the conversation saved your wine. Otherwise, the artillery boys would have drunk much more. Shall I stay away, tonight, Captain, Sir?" Julian asked, laughing.

"They will all stay away. No one will come to eat for days! The Bay hits them and for weeks they're green and yellow. Then comes the desert wind. Yes sir, a rum journey it is!"

"Yet you do it every time, month after month, year after year!"

The captain puffed on his cigar. "Ever known a nasty beauty?" he asked.

Julian laughed. "Never. My mother is an angel, and my sisters ... well they're fine girls underneath all their foolish ways. But my granny — ah, yes, she must have been a challenge in her days."

"Well sir, the sea is like that. A challenge. Can never leave her till she submits. Now let's take a stroll over the deck."

Julian later returned to his cabin to read and then went to lunch at the captain's table. The dining hall was empty except for the young woman. She sat erect, waiting for the captain, who came in rubbing his hands. Julian spoke little, except to make polite observations about the journey ahead.

She was still there on the deck in the grey and purple dusk, staring at the frothing waters. Julian was about to turn away when her eyes caught his. Reluctantly, he went over to the chair where she sat.

"Rather rough for an airing, isn't it?" he asked.

"Very exhilarating ... after the cramped cabin," she replied.

"Oh, I am sorry. Is it uncomfortable?"

Her grey eyes were as wild as the sea, but she seemed composed. "It is extremely uncomfortable. And the company makes it more so."

Julian hesitated, uneasy: "I have not met your husband," he said.

The woman's face darkened. "I am not travelling with my husband. He returned earlier — to his station in India, but arranged for me to travel with his acquaintances." Her mouth tightened. "Mrs. Dorothea Paine is my ... chaperone."

"My sympathies," he said softly.

"No! She is not bad at all. Rather a kind, if confused woman. Even Reverend Paine is not bad. He means well."

"He is a bore, and rather an ignorant one at that," Julian retorted. "I apologise if I offend you. No doubt your husband's friends are yours too."

"Yes," she agreed dully.

Her misery was so obvious that he felt obliged to cheer her up. She seemed a lost and lonely soul in this crowded ship. He drew up a deck chair nearby and said, "Is this your first journey away from England?"

"Yes ... unless you count a few weeks in France and Italy with my employer," she said.

Julian nodded. He had not expected a woman of her type to be "employed". She seemed rather genteel. "Were you happy there?"

She gave him an ironical smile. "As happy as a governess can be with three difficult children to manage."

"Yes, of course, I understand," Julian responded quickly.

"Do you, Mr. Ruthven?" she asked, once more sharp. "Can a man of your background understand the life of ... less fortunate people?"

Julian said nothing. He could not envision such a circumstance. Poverty was unknown to him.

The young woman gazed at the sea, the high waves, the creaking rigging and masts. "I am ... afraid of India. I am not sure if I am going to endure it."

"You will, if you make up your mind. My mother went to India as a bride ... and she loved it then as now."

"I ... am ... also a ... bride," she said softly.

Julian looked at her and wondered why her husband had gone ahead. Divining his thought, she said, "My husband had to join his regiment early... and I had to settle my sisters with an aunt before I could come. You see ... we lost our parents early."

"I am sorry," Julian said.

The meagre afternoon light dwindled with the rise of mist and spray of water. "Care for tea?" he asked and led her to the deserted dining room, where they talked about India until supper, for which no one came. Even Captain Macfarlane was delayed on the bridge. He was concerned by the sight of an approaching storm. After a desultory dinner, Julian went to the deck, to watch a Biscayne storm and ponder over Carolyn's story.

They met often during the next two days when the decks stayed deserted. Carolyn was pleasant company; she had an interested mind and a moderately good education and seemed an accomplished pianist and housewife. "You will make an excellent soldier's lady," he told her, sitting on the deck on a dark, rainy night.

Carolyn's face clouded. "Yes. I expect I will," she said. Then she looked at Julian and he saw something in her eyes which disturbed him. No woman had looked at him with such frank passion as did this girl, the bride of a soldier. He had not sought this nor evoked it consciously. Unsteadily, he rose to his feet. "Mrs. Barclay, let us return inside. You will catch a chill. I ... have some reading to finish ... and letters to mail. Tomorrow we hope to reach Gibraltar. My father's friends will be there to take the letters."

Carolyn stared at the sea. "Please attend to your work, Mr. Ruthven. I will stay here a little longer ... until Mrs. Paine completes her devotions."

Gibraltar loomed high over the ship on a bright February morning. The clouds had vanished and a gold sunlight flooded the ancient fort of the Spanish Moors. Julian prepared to go ashore and explore the town. He found Carolyn standing on the deck, looking at the harbour with yearning.

"Not going ashore?" he asked pleasantly.

"Mrs. Paine is unwell and will not go down. She says Spaniards are lewd and untrustworthy."

Julian laughed. "One glance at Mrs. Paine and they will all be virtuous!"

Carolyn's eyes were cool. He stopped laughing. "Well, buenos dias, Senora ... I must go."

"Have a nice day, Mr. Ruthven." Her voice was desolate.

He was about to go when he stopped. "Would you ... care ... to come?"

They explored Gibraltar, dined at a tavern on paella and peaches and a rough, local wine. Julian told Carolyn about the conquest of Spain by the Moorish general, Tariq, in the eighth century, and the subsequent predicament of rich Moorish Spain and the austere Visigotho-Roman north, of Ferdinand and Isabella, the sad Hapsburgs, Philip II and the stupid Bourbons. Carolyn listened, rapt, flushed by the warm sun and an overwhelming attraction for the auburn-haired, blue-eyed young man at her side.

He took her back to the *Bentinck* untouched and unfulfilled. The ship entered the Mediterranean and steamed towards Naples, where it was to halt four days. Julian walked and read, saw Carolyn at meals and stayed on the bridgehead to talk to sailors at night. At Naples, he went ashore, alone, to see the beautiful city once more. Prince Torlonia, the European agent for Ruthven, Chowdhury & Co. sent emissaries to meet Julian and see to his comfort. He was put up at a hotel on the road facing the Bay and Mount Vesuvius.

On the third day, a commotion began in the town. Students and young men came out of colleges and homes crying, "Italia! Viva la Risorgimento! Viva la Mazzini e Garibaldi!"

Julian watched a group of Austrian soldiers on horseback appear on the scene, followed by King Ferdinand's gendarmes. They fired at the students, mowing down the front line. Then the youth went wild. As they surged forward, the Spanish Bourbon army scattered back to the fort and the townsfolk rose with them. The Revolution of 1848 had now filtered down from Milan, Paris, Frankfurt, Vienna, Venice and Rome to Naples.

An air of excitment gripped Naples as news came of the French king, Louis Philippe's abdication, the deposition of Ludwig of Bavaria, and the fall of Metternich. The restored ancient regimes, bolstered up at the Congress of Vienna, had been finally swept away by the resurgent spirit of liberalism.

As Julian walked back to the hotel in the evening, he saw Carolyn desperately asking for a carriage to take her back to the harbour but the Italians, mistaking her for an Austrian, cried, "Tedesca! va via!" — German woman, go away! She tried to explain. "Io sono Anglaise ..." but they refused to believe her. "You are an Austrian, a spy, sent by Metternich!" they insisted.

Julian rushed across and grabbed her hand. "Come, let us return to the ship," he said, and half-clutching her, leapt into his waiting carriage.

There was commotion at the dock. Captain Macfarlane wished to set sail by night to avoid any trouble in Naples. Passengers hurried into the ship. Julian took Carolyn to his spacious cabin to offer her a brandy to soothe her nerves.

As night deepened, many of the revolutionaries went home to recharge their batteries, but an atmosphere of tension and suspense hung in the air. Julian Ruthven stood on the deck, gazing at the bay in the distance and at the shadow of Vesuvius rising against the starlit spring sky. Sighing, he found Carolyn at his side. Tentatively, she placed her hand on his reposing on the railing.

"Mrs. Barclay," he said, looking at her with a troubled face.

"Julian," she murmured with a plea in her eyes. "Can we forget everything for one night?"

"It is never as simple as that. People get caught," Julian thought, though he did not say so. Instead, he drew her close and kissed the lips that were offered so eagerly, so humbly. She came close to him, her breasts trembling against his chest, her hand caressing his hair and neck. He carried her into the candlelit cabin and laid her on the bed. She lay still, watching him as he sat beside her. "You are a bride, Carolyn. Why do you want to do this to your husband?" Julian asked gravely.

"Because I do not love him ... because he loves his dead wife ... because he married me for convenience and I married him for security ... and ..."

"Yes?"

"Because I want to know what it can be like between a man and a woman before I forget my dreams of passion."

Julian sat beside her and stroked her pale hair, her supple neck and shoulders, and then let his fingers glide down to the cleft between her plump white breasts, which stiffened at his touch. Flinging away her chemise, he laid his cheek against her quivering flesh, and put his lips to her offered breasts. Her hungry, eager body roused his desires, impelling him to explore and caress until she led him deep into her. As they moved together in a frantic rhythm, Carolyn cried out his name and he paused, troubled by her intensity, until he too forgot everything in the pursuit of quenching his desire. As they shuddered in fulfilment, he felt her tears on his body before he fell into a tired slumber. Carolyn lay awake, whispering of her love.

All her life, Carolyn would remember the idyll of those weeks. Nothing that happened before or after would ever equal the joy of that spring of 1848. That Julian Ruthven did not reciprocate her sentiments was not unrecognised by her though she loved him more for not deceiving her with false promises or declarations. He brought to the illicit relationship a quality of honesty by treating it for what it was: Carolyn's longing to taste a tender passion before she buried herself with the elderly soldier, whom she had married for security. He felt her frustration and loneliness and gave her a transient warmth and tenderness.

It was not easy to arrange their meetings. Fortunately, Mrs. Paine was sick and Carolyn, pleading a need for fresh air, declared her intention to sleep on the deck. Using this as an excuse, she was able to spend the nights in Julian's cabin. They drank wine, talked and made love. Carolyn knew that her vigorous young body pleased Julian and if his love making lacked the mad ardour she desired, it gave her no less pleasure. When he fell asleep at dawn, the hour of departure, Carolyn sat in bed staring at his long, muscular body, the tousled copper hair, the fine features reposing in tranquillity. A wave of tenderness washed over her, filling her with a longing for him that the wildest coupling could not satisfy. "Yet, this is all I can ever hope for — all I can ever have," she thought, stifling a sob. "If only some good fairy had let him see me before I married ... but no ... I must not go into fancy ..."

She would, nevertheless spend hours, imagining being his wife, living in a lovely house in a lonely spot in India, bearing him children and making a nice home for him. She knew of his background and wondered if Lady Eleanor would have accepted a governess as her son's wife and if Charles Ruthven would have approved. Would she have ever been gladly received at Courtney Hall or Ruthven House? "Ah, it's all fancy, that can never be! Just enjoy these golden moments before you go into exile!"

Julian Ruthven often thought of his grandmother's advice. "This is not what Grandmama envisaged," he thought ruefully. "She wanted me to conduct a discreet, elegant affair with a rich, sophisticated, accomplished woman of the world, who knew the rules of the game. Would she approve of Carolyn — lost, lonely and yearning for love?"

Carolyn understood that Julian had no desire to continue the affair, though she had hinted that she would be prepared to follow him anywhere. "No, Carolyn, that cannot be," he said gently. "This was a ... divertimento ... for us both. Your husband awaits you, as does my work. We have our different paths to follow."

At Sagar Dwip, Julian Ruthven stood stiffly on the deck as Carolyn walked slowly forward, her white, muslin dress billowing around her in bridal splendour. The pale hair which he had caressed was now drawn severely back into a chignon. Her face was ashen. Beside her walked a familiar figure: sandy-haired, blue-eyed and erect despite a limp. Julian Ruthven was chilled by a strange dread.

"Why, Julian! It is a surprise to see you!"

The young man stared at the middle-aged soldier, who had frequented his parents' house in Calcutta during the Afghan war. In a daze, he extended his hand. "Major Barclay," he said with spurious composure, "I am glad to see you!"

The older man laughed, raising a hand in protest. "Not major, Julian! I am a colonel now. Survivor of Sikh wars." He indicated his lame leg.

"Colonel," Julian murmured, bewildered, as he glanced at the shortened leg and at the scar across the genial face.

"Now then, I hear you travelled with my new wife?" the Colonel asked.

Julian stared wildly at Colonel Trevor Barclay. "Your ... wife ... Lavinia ...?"

Trevor Barclay sighed hoarsely and his eyes grew suspiciously red. "My... Lavinia ... died two years ago." He paused, fighting for composure. "Your sister, Kitty, was with Lavinia ... at the end. Bless her."

Suddenly, he pulled up his drooping shoulders, and threw back his head, glancing at the ashen-faced woman beside him. "Carolyn ... and I were married recently ... in England."

Julian nodded, braving a glance at Carolyn "I wish ... you ... happiness, Colonel Barclay," Julian muttered.

Momentarily, the colonel's eyes darkened, as they moved from Julian to Carolyn. Then he summoned a bright smile. "Thank you,

Julian. I am sure we shall be happy." He touched Carolyn's cold, stiff hand and bowing, led her back to the cabin.

Julian Ruthven stared after them. "Barclay's wife," he muttered to himself. "How was I to know?" He felt a surge of anger at his own conduct.

The ship lifted anchor, sped up the Ganges and ran into a late monsoon storm. Carolyn lay beside her sleeping husband, staring at the low ceiling of the swaying cabin. Trevor Barclay had taken her, not with tenderness, but with a fury that had frightened her. Then he had turned aside, as if shunning her. Carolyn heard the roaring storm outside and wondered if Julian was in his cabin. Her body ached for his and her heart seemed leaden in her breast. She could feel the quickening of life within her. "Good-bye, my dear, sweet love," she thought. "How will I bear it now?"

Suddenly, she could not endure it. Springing up, she flung a thick cloak around her and without thinking, rushed onto the deck. A grey and orange dawn was breaking over the turbulent river. She moved forward and then halted. She knew their affair was over, because Julian Ruthven stood at the railing, gazing at the water-logged landscape in ecstasy.

He had obviously forgotton the turmoils of the day, as he stood there watching the mighty, perennial river. As she watched he began to softly chant a Sanskrit hymn to the Ganges:

> Oh redeemer of the perditioned
> Thou flowest through stones
> Fragmented by thy touch
> Mother of the pure hero Bhishma
> The three worlds sing thy praise
> Thou who wash away death, disease,
> Grief, sins ... and even dreams.
> To thee, great river,
> I offer my salutations!

27

Fires of Spring

Julian Ruthven sat under a spreading banian tree, staring at the yellow-coloured house, its ugly precincts encircled by a bamboo fence. Tall and noble were the trees that gave it shade and cool at that blazing hour.

"So this is where my grandfather, Alexander Ruthven, began his career as a privateer and trader under the auspices of the East India Company ..." where the Ruthven fortune was built ... where he lived with his Begum and charted out a future for their son Andrew-Andraz." Julian mused, forgetting those around him. "How brittle are human dreams! How inexorable our little fates!"

"Saheb, it is time," said his sheristedar, a humble functionary who, nevertheless, held sway over his bailiwick.

Julian rose, shaking the grey-brown dust from his jodhpurs and boots. He had come recently to Bishnupur, as sub-divisional magistrate. The change from life at Ruthven House in Alipur to this silent and remote sub-division town had been overwhelming. He remembered the night he had arrived from Calcutta in dak-gari, with two valises of clothes and books. Despite Lady Eleanor's entreaties, he had refused to take the linen, cutlery, pictures and carpets that she had insisted would soften the rigours of mofussil life. The functionaries of the sub-division town had lain awake, in wait for the "SDO Saheb," but had not anticipated his arrival in a creaking dak-gari. It was only when he alighted from the little box-like carriage that they recovered sufficiently to blow on bugles, bow and cry welcome. Wearily, with every joint aching, Julian acknowledged their greetings and went inside the bungalow assigned to the sub-divisional magistrate — a crude house with an extensive garden. Two mahogany-skinned servants bowed deeply, as they murmured the greeting "Good night, Saheb," with the studied mannerisms of Lucknow courtiers.

"Good morning," he had replied, glancing at his watch. This response had evoked considerable speculation about his nocturnal habits.

The next morning, Julian went on horseback to the district magistrate's house, an edifice of brown brick, with pseudo-Gothic towers. Two sentries paced up and down outside. Four chaprasis, footmen armed with swords and shields, stood on the steps, ready to defend the district magistrate, Major Gerald Adams, an officer of the Guides called upon to discharge civil duties. He greeted the younger man and each silently assessed the other. Major Adams was of medium height, sandy-haired, and weathered, with enormous moustaches. He had wanted a rough-and-ready assistant. Looking at the tall, elegant figure of Julian Ruthven, the district magistrate wondered if this man would be able to discharge the duties of SDO of Bishnupur.

"Come last night, did you?" Adams asked by way of greeting, extending a hard paw.

The long, white hand that clasped his, Adams observed, was surprisingly powerful. "That's right. Saw no lights at your bungalow, Sir, nor I suppose was it an appropriate time to call."

"Go to sleep when we can," Adams replied tartly. "There's no saying when we are roused to cater to an emergency." He paused. "Used to more lively evenings, I suspect? But that won't do here."

"Yes, I realise that," young Ruthven replied with an indulgent smile at his senior. "Of course, I shan't expect dances and dinners here but I can catch up on my reading."

"Didn't you do enough of that in Haileybury?" Major Adams snapped.

"Not enough," Julian replied. "We did mostly languages and law."

The sandy eyebrows shot up. Fastening his pistol to his belt, the district magistrate said coldly, "Here, you'd better learn to catch thugs and collect land revenue.'

"Oh that too," Julian said casually, glancing at the sword on his hips, the one Charles Ruthven had worn at Waterloo.

Major Adams led the way to the district court: a large, roughly furnished room full of Indian clerks sitting on a carpet. They rose and saluted as the two men entered. Charge reports were brought in by the sheristedar, the head clerk. Julian signed and "took charge" formally. Thick, brewed tea was served to everyone after which the SDO went to his room to begin his duties.

The task of trying petty cases of assault, theft, civil suits of moneylenders and debtors gave Julian Ruthven an idea of the social climate of his bailiwick. He became acquainted with the current laws.

He also toured his bailiwick extensively, observing the conduct of the mustagirs, who went from one village to another to collect taxes. Julian followed them and stopped in each village to inspect the state of land, irrigation and yield of crops. Summoning the peasants, he sat in the village square, under a huge banian tree and coaxed them to talk.

A magistrate saheb who behaved thus was a phenomenon, particularly one with the name of Ruthven. Dimly, they recalled tales of another flame-haired saheb who had despoiled Bishnupur, eighty years ago. They sat around him, curious and sceptical, wondering why he was interested in their situation.

"The mustagir collects too much from you," Julian declared, hoping to provoke them.

Paan-blackened teeth were bared in smiles, and grizzled old heads were scratched. But they did not confirm the allegation. The magistrate saheb was a remote boon whereas the mustagir or bailiff was an ubiquitous curse.

"You bear a heavy burden," Ruthven tried again. "The mustagir and zamindar tax you beyond your capacity."

Gradually, tongues loosened and a peasant said, "Yes, Saheb, our thin shoulders carry the fat bailiff, the fatter zamindar and then the Company's weight. Do you wonder why we are bent and bow legged?"

The words were said in mocking jest but Ruthven felt something tighten within him. "It is the Company in the final analysis that is doing this," he thought. "Cornwallis' Permanent Settlement."

"Look at our lands," another peasant said, spitting scarlet betel-juice onto the ground. "We have hardly any water for channels. If we cut in a little from the river, the mustagir puts up the rent. He gives some of it to the zamindar and keeps a portion. He builds another house and the zamindar goes to Lucknow or Calcutta to squander it on fancy women." He paused. "Every drop of our sweat enriches them."

"What do you do when they raise the taxes?" Julian asked. "Do you not go to the mofussil court in appeal?"

"Hai Ram! Cursed destiny!" the peasant exclaimed, slapping his forehead, where his pitiful fate was allegedly writ. "We cannot get redressal in court! Who will listen? What do we know of rules and laws? One of us protested when the mustagir gave tax remission to his friends. He came and razed our crops. He has the ears of the thana, the police station, Sir."

Julian Ruthven gazed around at the village scene with deepening gloom. Clusters of thatched huts stood huddled together. Clumps of bamboo, mango and jackfruit grew around them. The fields were fallow, awaiting the rains. The villagers ate coarse rice and chilli sauce, unless they caught a fish to spare. There was no surplus money to buy clothes or implements. Even the seed grains were liable to be eaten in a lean year. "A century of Company rule," he mused. "How little there is to show for it!"

He stayed there that night to accept the villagers' hospitality. Cattle returned in the "cowdust" hour, when the dust from their steps mingled with woodsmoke and cast a pall over the trees, and fields. Somewhere a flute piped, in immemorial echo of Lord Krishna, as the village women hurried home, laden with water. The brief dusk dissolved into night, a time for peace — or was it oblivion — from an endless and accursed fate? But the flute played on, and a thin, reedy voice invoked god in tender homage.

At dawn, the lowing of cattle roused him from the bed of hay, where he had elected to spend the night. Washing by the well, Julian ambled along to the riverside to watch the sun rise. He did not, however, venture too close because sitting on the ghat was a stocky man of swarthy mien, laughing and teasing the womenfolk who had come to collect water.

"The zamindar," murmured the office peon. "He has an eye for the comely young women."

"Droit de seigneur," Julian muttered derisively, and was about to turn away when the swarthy man rose and bowed deeply, with an extravagance that belied the salutation.

"SDO Saheb!" the zamindar greeted him. "It is a pleasure to meet you."

Julian bowed perfunctorily, feeling an inexplicable revulsion against the man who could have been, with a lighter skin, mistaken for a Prussian Junker. They exchanged pleasantries but Julian had no doubts that the zamindar, angered by Julian's enquiries about yield and assessment, was following him in his journey. But Julian moved on, determined to prove that the assessments were higher than the yields and that the condition of rural Bengal was steadily deteriorating as the peasantry reeled under unsupportable taxes.

It was inevitable then that Julian Ruthven flung himself headlong into a collision course with the local zamindar. Scrutinising land records and assessment figures of crops, he muttered, "Too much tax. This calls for revision. A peasant records he has paid three hundred rupees but there is receipt for two only. Where is the rest? We must, henceforward, assess demands on actual yield on lands."

The village officials listened, exchanging covert glances with each other. Unaware of the cross-currents, Ruthven rode back to his own bungalow.

Dusk was falling over the flat plains and farmers were gathering in the harvest in the light of bonfires, as they sang poems of praise to the rain god and the earth goddess who had given them a good harvest. Julian reined in his horse, gazing at the purple horizon embroidered by stars, and the silhouettes of dark figures, sugarcane plumes and coconut fronds. Cowherds returned home, with their cattle, playing on their flutes as a film of coral dust rose in the chill, dry air.

The farmers came to Julian's bungalow after sunset to invite him to join their feast. Julian readily agreed; his mind was not on his despatches today. In the village headman's house, there was new rice boiled in thickened milk, sandesh, a kind of toffee made of milk and new molasses, bananas and coconuts — all served on gleaming leaves of plantain. The villagers thanked the goddess of plenty, before commencing the feast. Julian felt at peace. He was almost reluctant to go to Calcutta for Christmas.

When he returned from Calcutta on a starlit January night, he stopped his horse, filled with a sudden sense of foreboding.

The village was silent, as if spent of its very life force. When he went out into the village, a spectacle of devastation greeted his eyes. The huts were burnt and the crops had disappeared. There was nothing left but the old banian trees. Seeing the SDO Saheb, the villagers materialised from scorched hovels to tell him of their ruin.

"Better you had left us in a lesser misery, Saheb," Mondal, the peasant cried. "In this land, those who protest, perish. See the price of your protest! We are finished!"

"Ruined forever!" Kar wept. "A beggar once more. And my wife crazed by grief ... my daughter raped before our eyes ... my sons maimed. Oh Ruthven Saheb, why did you not let us endure our lot?" Kar sobbed, beating his chest.

Julian Ruthven stood dumbfounded for a long time. Then his anguish turned to rage. "Harpal Deo will pay for this! I assure you!"

"No!" a peasant screamed. "They will not pay. Men like Harpal

Deo are your accomplices. You sahebs have created these laws!"

Julian felt his body wracked by fury. "They will pay," he muttered, mounting his horse and riding madly towards the zamindar's house.

The news of the zamindar's arrest and trial stunned the sub-division town. They came to watch the proceedings in stupefied silence. The almighty Harpal Deo in handcuffs! Standing before the flame-haired magistrate, who read out a sentence of imprisonment! "Cornwallis may have erred in land settlement," Julian said, concluding his verdict speech, "but Macaulay redressed the wrong by offering laws. There is a system of law now in British territories."

Mondal wept loudly. The zamindar had offered to pay for the losses in return for his release, but Julian had refused. "He will recompense from jail."

The village and townsfolk stared at each other, bewildered. "It is," said one, "like the stories of our scriptures — where even the god Indra is punished by a sage."

"Incredible!" muttered another. "It is as if the sky had turned upside down. Zamindar-babu going to prison for burning low-caste Mondal's crops!"

Harpal Deo fixed Julian Ruthven with wild eyes as he was led away by the doffedars of the court. "One day, firingi, you will pay for this! On my father's ashes, I swear!" he shouted.

Julian Ruthven nodded. "We shall see," he retorted quietly and turned away, strangely disquieted.

Ruthven's triumph, however, was short lived. The news of his action frightened the men at Writers' Building, who saw disruption of an accepted pattern of livelihood. Many British officials depended on errant zamindars for their luxuries. Radicals like Ruthven had, therefore, to be taught a lesson. The interested group contrived to have the young officer transferred from Bishnupur and sanctioned privilege leave, which was, in effect, compulsory waiting "until further orders."

Lady Eleanor and Charles Edward Ruthven felt both pride and concern for their son's attitude. Already, word had gone around about young Ruthven's insubordination and headstrong conduct. His ability and lineage made it difficult for his detractors to dismiss him as a wayward radical. He had, therefore, to be cajoled into submission.

Submission was the only thing Julian Ruthven refused to consider. He was young, gifted and wealthy. He meant to fight for justice and order.

He was, however, diverted from the fight for justice and order by the attractions of the Chowdhury mansion. The ostensible reason was the magnetism of the lively, gifted family presided over by Brajesh Chowdhury.

"A Renaissance atmosphere prevails there," Julian confided to his sister, Isabel. "Everything is discussed there from land reforms to Franz Lyzst. Everyone is charged with ideas and sentiments."

"It sounds almost like Cavendish Square," Isabel said archly.

"Absolutely!" Julian enthused. "Dilip has just returned from Cambridge and we discuss the revolutions of 1848; philosophers who are one day going to change the world."

Indeed, the young men went further. They wondered when India would aspire for freedom, as Italy and Poland were doing. Dilip particularly was agitated over this. "How are we different from Italy or Greece? Have we not experienced the same chaos and upheavals, invasions and plunders? Have we not the same proud past? Why should we be ruled by another nation?"

Julian was disquieted by this query. "The liberal traditions of England will prepare India for her liberation. Everything, even freedom, needs preparation."

Dilip glanced at his friend. "A revolution is like the Ganges in full spate. It comes and sweeps away everything from its path. There is no preparation. It just happens."

Discussions were followed by lively dinners, where the luminaries of Calcutta came to grace Brajesh Chowdhury's generous table. Here a haughty Lord Dalhousie could be seen with the patrician, Debendranath Tagore. Erudition and wit enlivened the evening. Julian listened, exhilarated. "We are present at the creation of a new age," he once told Dilip.

"To be alive in that dawn ..." Dilip murmured.

After dinner, guests strolled in the lamplit gardens or sat on the terrace while music emanated from a room within. And after dinner, Julian waited for the real reason for his frequent visits.

Nineteen-year-old Radha Chowdhury had left the seclusion of the antah-mahal, the ladies' apartments, to appear before the world. Julian Ruthven had seen her all his life — as a sad child weaving jasmine garlands for her mother, as a shy girl discovering England with wonder-filled eyes. And now she was transformed into a beautiful young woman who sang ragas in a rich, soft voice, who played Chopin on the piano, who laughed a great deal behind latticed windows, and whose wide, luminous eyes made the blood quicken in his veins. He had seen her after many years on a spring morning when she had been reciting the hymn to the sun god on the roof garden.

"Seven mares draw You, oh lord
In Your chariot, oh sun divine
Oh radiant One with hair aflame
Radiant above the world of men
Blazing and luminous like fires.

Radha had turned to see Julian standing nearby, watching her with a smile.

"Be aware, fair maiden," he had said. "The sun god often comes down to seduce his devotees. Remember the story of Kunti?"

Radha saw winter sunlight glint on his auburn hair and twinkle in his sky-coloured eyes. "Why, you look like the sun god," she murmured, and then trembled at her own words.

"I have no chariot or seven horses, or else I would have taken you into the kingdom of clouds," Julian replied, his eyes moving over her graceful figure, clouds of long dark hair, dancing eyes and full, firm lips.

"You are, I see, an accomplished flirt," Radha laughed, making a move to go.

He caught one slim, golden arm. "I have come to your father's house many times in the hope of seeing the disembodied being who sang and laughed unseen. Now that I have seen you, I wonder how I shall ever go back to earth."

Radha laughed, despite herself. "In your chariot, Mr. Ruthven."

"Come then in my pakshiraj," Julian said. "It waits outside."

Radha leaned over the balustrade, smiling. "Your pakshiraj is a beauty," she said. "But will it fly over clouds and take me to see strange new lands?"

Julian had regarded her intently. She was so different from the young women he knew; the married ones he flirted with at Government House parties, the calculating members of the "fishing fleet", the pretty, simpering debutantes who were Isabel's friends — yes ... even that strange young bride, Carolyn Barclay. Radha was radiant and innocent, tender and joyous as a spring dawn.

They met often after that, but always in the company of others. Radha accompanied her brother, Dilip and Julian when they sailed on their barge, or rode with them to the Botanical Gardens, or met at each other's houses. No one seemed to notice their mutual enchantment until a reception at the Chowdhury mansion.

The beautiful baroque pile at Belgachia was illuminated by a thousand lamps that spring evening in 1851. Nature contributed to the splendour by offering roses, dahlias and late chrysanthemums, whose scarlets and golds gleamed in the effulgent lamplight. Inside the rectangular reception hall, carpets had been rolled away to reveal veined marble floors contrasting with the opulent furnishing. At one corner, a band of musicians, mainly Anglo-Indians, played a medley of Strauss' waltzes. In the adjoining dining hall, a sumptuous feast had been laid — cold salmon, pressed ham, caviar, pate de foie gras, chicken in aspic, truffles, olives and melons, ices of all kinds, pastries and cakes. On another table rested twenty types of wines and champagne.

Barefooted liveried footmen went around with silver salvers bringing food and drink for the guests — the Indian and European elite of Calcutta. There were members of the old landed gentry of Bengal, officials of the East India Company, military officers, rich entrepreneurs of all colour — Armenian, Jewish, British, Dutch, Portuguese and Indian. Renowned scholars from Europe and their Indian counterparts talked in the garden terrace, while members of Government House stood stiffly, decorous and silent, listening to the Governor General.

Lord Dalhousie had condescended to come. He felt comfortable with this gracious "Hindu gentleman", of distinguished background, who believed in the benefits of British rule.

Brajesh Chowdhury was progressive but his mother still would not permit Radha to participate in the dancing. So Radha stood in the gallery above, wistfully watching the swirl of crinolines to the lilting cadence of waltzes. "How unfair!" she protested to Evans, her governess. "Why am I not permitted to dance?"

"Silly, if you ask me," Delphinia Evans retorted. "You ought to be permitted to join the Miss Ruthvens below."

Thwarted, Radha watched the guests below, in particular the tall, auburn-haired young man.

"Let me pretend .... for one night," she thought to herself. "Let me imagine myself in his arms ..." She closed her eyes and began to turn and whirl in time to the music.

Minutes passed. The music rose to a crescendo and stopped. She too stopped and opened her eyes ... to find Julian Ruthven standing before her, gazing at her flushed cheeks and uneven, quick breathing. She glanced around uneasily; Miss Evans had vanished. Only he stood there, resplendent in evening clothes, tense and grave. Slowly, he bowed and stretched both gloved hands towards her. "May I have the honour?" he asked in a low voice.

Radha stared at the chiselled bronzed face, and the sea-coloured eyes that regarded her with grave tenderness. "I ... dare not ..." she whispered. "They ... would not ... permit."

"We shall see," he replied, and taking her hand led her down the curving staircase and entered the hall where a waltz was in progress. Without ado, Julian led her to the floor and began guiding her over the mosaic floor to the tune of a new waltz. She felt his hand on her waist, and shivered and stiffened. The pressure of his hands increased, drawing her close.

Radha could hardly breathe now but her feet moved swiftly and lightly with his, as if they were one. Their eyes were held by the others; as they danced, profoundly disturbed yet exhilarated by their mutual discovery. An astounded audience watched in silence.

The music stopped. Julian released a breathless Radha and bowed, his unwavering gaze on her. "You see, we dared," he murmured.

A hush fell upon the room as Julian Ruthven led Radha to the terrace. Vigilant eyes watched their progress, but no one could summon the courage to speak to the defiant, young man or the radiant, young woman who whispered, laughed and became strangely restless in turn.

Undeterred, Julian continued to see Radha — at the Chowdhury villa, in the Mạidan where they kept their assignations on the pretence of riding or in the Ruthven villa at Garden Reach, where Dilip Chowdhury and Isabel Ruthven acted as chaperones.

There, by the riverside, while fisherfolk sang mournful dirges, Julian and Radha discovered each other. It seemed as if they were part of the timeless scene, a fragment of eternity, and that everything around them was conspiring to make them joyous. They had no thoughts of the past or future, but only of the moment that was so full of delight.

One evening, as the sun disappeared and shadows lengthened over the vast river, Julian drew Radha close, and bent his head to hers. He felt her lips quiver under his, and the sudden thawing of all resolves. Then they drew away, to stare at each other and ascertain the reality of that fragile embrace, which caused such turmoil of mind and body, to understand better this beautiful and terrifying revelation.

"We must make plans," Julian said gravely.

Plans however had already been made by the Ruthvens and Chowdhurys — to thwart their defiant progeny.

Julian was posted on "special duty" in the establishment of Sir Henry Lawrence, the Chief Commissioner of Punjab. On receiving the written communication one morning, he burst into the library where Charles Edward Ruthven sat with Lady Eleanor, waiting for the storm to break.

"This is absurd!" Julian exploded. "I am not a member of the Punjab civil service! Why should I go there?"

Charles Ruthven heard a past echo: of Alexander Ruthven banishing Andraz for misdemeanour. And he was now doing the same — not in anger but out of concern.

"You go as Lord Dalhousie's special emissary, Julian," his father said gravely.

"Lies!" Julian stormed. "His Lordship cares tuppence for me!! I go as part of a conspiracy ... to separate me ... from ... the woman I wish to marry!"

Grimly, Charles Ruthven now rose in anger, but Lady Eleanor stepped between her husband and son, with tears streaming down her cheeks. "Please, my love," she whispered to Charles, "please let me explain." She turned to Julian who stood grim faced. "Darling, listen to me," she said gently, "you cannot marry Radha. She is a high-born Hindu ... and would be ostracised by her people if she married you ... and you too would be ... an outcaste."

"Damn her people and damn mine!" Julian cried, "We have no need of anyone ... but ourselves!"

Eleanor Ruthven paused, and then said, "Radha has been betrothed ... to a zamindar ... and will be married shortly."

"No!" Julian exclaimed.

"Yes ... it must be so, dearest. Accept it," Eleanor pleaded, her hands taking his trembling ones.

Julian Ruthven snatched his hand from his mother's and flew down the staircase, until he came to the portico where his horse waited. Spurring his horse, he gallopped to Belgachia, in shirtsleeves and breeches, fury in his heart, stopping only at the Kali temple to obtain the vermilion powder that annointed foreheads.

The Chowdhury household stared at him in astonishment, when he arrived, unable to move or speak. Ignoring them, he questioned Miss Evans, who said Radha was near the lake. He walked swiftly across the vast garden and towards the lake where Radha sat, sombre and sad. A crackle of twigs made her look up, startled.

"Is it true?" he asked, grim-faced. "Are you marrying some zamindar?"

Radha was silent.

"How can you do this terrible thing?" he asked harshly.

"Where would we go?" she whispered, gazing up at him in misery.

"To paradise, which is waiting for us. Are you afraid, Radha? I would protect you with my life's blood."

"I am afraid ... of the unknown," she whispered again. "I am afraid of what they could do to us."

Julian pushed her gently away. "Radha, my love, you shall not marry the zamindar they have chosen for you. Neither he nor anyone else. Do you understand? You belong to me." With one hand he brought out the tiny packet containing the vermilion powder. Swiftly, before she could move, he inscribed a bindi on her forehead and put the powder in the parting of her hair. Radha trembled, and stared at him. "What have you done?" she asked hoarsely.

"I have done what only a Hindu husband is permitted to do to his wife," he said gravely. "Remember, you are bound to me now. This vermilion I obtained from the Kali temple."

The sound of advancing footsteps made him look around. Indumati was approaching, with her hand-maidens, reproach writ large on her face. She was remembering an episode older than her grief, when a flame-haired woman had threatened her world. Now, it was being repeated again. Another flame-haired Ruthven was bringing disruption into their lives.

"Julian Saheb," she said coldly. "It is not right for you to dally here with my granddaughter." She paused and added, "Radha is promised — to a man of our world."

Julian's eyes were blue fires. "Indeed, ma'am?" he asked, agitated and defiant. "That promise is broken then — because she is mine now ... just see the vermilion in her hair and on her forehead." He looked at Radha. "Wait for me, Radha, I will come back to take you with me."

Radha held his hands. "Come soon. I fear they will separate us," she whispered.

He laughed harshly. "Let them try!" He paused and looked with entreaty at Indumati. "Help us, Ma'am. Surely you cannot want her unhappiness!"

Indumati turned away, afraid of what she saw, on the road ahead.

28

Land of Five Rivers

Carolyn's sojourn in the glittering metropolis was short lived. She had barely time to see the palatial mansions of the exalted and wealthy and visit the shops that lined Chowringhee, displaying wares more diverse and opulent than the ones she had seen in Market Drayton or even in London. The imposing offices on Esplanade had a vitality rivalling London's and the clamorous "Strand" on the Ganges testified to Calcutta's position as the emporium of the Orient. The visit to Government House excited her; she had never seen a marquis before and Lord Dalhousie's aristocratic hauteur succeeded in unnerving her. She spilt tea on her faded satin gown, causing her husband to fix a pair of cold, tawny eyes on her in disapproval.

The hotel in Middleton Row where she was living, was small but comfortable with a colourful garden and delicious cuisine. It was here that she and her new husband renewed their acquaintance after a separation of a year, since their marriage in London. Colonel Trevor Barclay was now forty years old; he had been a widower for three years. The fresh, firm appearance of his second wife gladdened him, though he had doubts about whether the twenty-year-old girl would be able to cope with his household.

"You will have to meet my children," Colonel Barclay told her the first morning, as they shared a chota hazri, a petit dejeuner, on the balcony of their room. The ravens and koels had begun an early concert under the jackfruit trees.

"Yes ..." Carolyn replied, "I ... should like that."

Colonel Barclay stared at the papaya slices before him, remembering how poor Lavinia had hated "pawpaw." Would she understand and forgive Carolyn's presence? "My eldest son, Timothy, is in England, as you know. He is fourteen."

Carolyn nodded. It was when Barclay had gone to England to put Timothy in school that they had met at a house where Carolyn was governess.

"That leaves Lucy and Linda, aged thirteen and eleven. They are now staying with Mrs. Catherine Latimer ... at Ruthven House."

Carolyn dropped the papaya onto the table, and glanced up to meet her husband's inscrutable eyes. "Mrs. Latimer was a friend of my ... Lavinia ... and is daughter of Lady Eleanor and Charles Edward Ruthven."

"Oh," Carolyn murmured, colouring at the fateful name.

The ravens and parakeets screamed over a luscious, ripening jackfruit. Carolyn pretended to be absorbed in their quarrel. Barclay watched her with brooding eyes. "Yes," he thought, "I was not mistaken." Aloud, he said, "We will collect them and proceed to Punjab." He paused. "I have a short leave. War brewing there now."

Carolyn's glowing complexion turned a shade paler. "A war, Colonel?" she asked.

"A war — against the Sikhs," he said tersely. "While I go to battle, you will look after my home ... and children." The soldier rose heavily. The excitement of possessing a fresh, young bride had suddenly chilled in the discovery he had made. He could not resist a retaliation. "That is why I married you."

Carolyn stared at the garden, remembering Julian Ruthven's polite indifference and her own aching love. It had not gone. Barclay could not hurt her more than Julian's indifference had. "I understand, Colonel," she said quietly, blinking back tears of pain and humiliation. "I will try to be ... a good ... housewife."

Trevor Barclay felt a surge of tenderness for the girl, half his age, and with it a strange anger at his own hunger for her. Clumsily, he patted her head. "You will make a fine one," he said gruffly.

Lady Eleanor's gentle scrutiny unsettled Carolyn completely. She stared at the large, pensive eyes which were so like Julian's, while Charles Edward seemed a heavier, older version of the son. But it was Catherine, auburn haired and sea eyed, who made her start. She was Julian all over again. Except in the manners. Catherine Latimer put everyone at ease, even the brooding Trevor Barclay. Yet Carolyn was glad when the tea party was over. She was filled with a terrible restlessness in the home of the man who had become her lover on the sea voyage to India. It was as if his very presence invaded her. She dreaded betraying herself before her gruff, taciturn husband with his tawny eyes.

Catherine tried to smooth over Carolyn's gaucheries while she studied the new Mrs. Barclay, comparing the robust, fresh-complexioned girl to poor, silly Lavinia. The two motherless girls stared at their young stepmother with open hostility. Kitty's amusement at Trevor Barclay's second marriage suddenly turned to pity and concern. As impulsive as always, she decided to go to Punjab with Carolyn.

"A campaign is going on there," Lady Eleanor reminded her.

Catherine shrugged. "Just as well, Mama. I am bored here in Calcutta. The interesting men have all gone to fight."

Punjab was once more in turmoil. In April 1848, the Governor of Multan took up arms after two British officers, sent to install his Sikh successor, were murdered. General Gough advised Lord Dalhousie that punitive operations should be delayed until after the monsoons. Sir Henry Lawrence, the Resident, was on leave and young Herbert Edwardes raised levies of "cut throats to cut any throats for a price." But the revolt spread. The Barclays arrived on the borders of Punjab as the conflagration grew.

Carolyn was terrified by the spectacle of hordes of dusty soldiers moving under a broiling sun, led by British officers. They stopped at Ambala where Colonel Barclay met his regiment, and waited for a decisive direction. "Edwardes was a fool to attack Mulraj," he stormed. "This has only provoked the Sikhs to revolt ... and it looks as if the contagion is spreading."

"What will happen?" Carolyn asked, almost inaudibly.

Catherine Latimer laughed. "My dear, you must not take fright so easily. We are, after all, soldiers' wives. We must be brave."

"Yes ... of course," Carolyn muttered, glancing around the lantern-lit room buzzing with pre-monsoon insects.

Carolyn crossed the threshold of her new home with surprise. The low, rambling, whitewashed bungalow was bare and stark crates of crockery and furniture were stacked in one room, waiting to be reassembled for use. Slowly, hesitantly, she began unpacking. Colonel Barclay watched, as if he was seeing the reassembling of the fragments of a previous existence, and was wondering what the new pattern would be. But there was little time for speculation. News soon came from Calcutta. Lord Dalhousie decided that the Sikhs were "unwarned by precedent, uninfluenced by example," and that "the Sikh nation has called for war and on my word, Sirs, they shall have it with a vengeance!"

General Gough was placed in command of the avenging army. Colonel Barclay's Bengal Lancers and Latimer's Bengal Infantry joined the main force as it crossed the Ravi in mid-November.

Events in the Punjab soon replaced personal preoccupations. Catherine went to the officers' mess to collect news of the army. The splendid avenging army, well supplied with cavalry, draught animals, ammunitions and men seemed invincible. Yet it met with a serious setback at Ramnagar on the banks of the Chenab. The second action at Sadoulpur was no better. The Sikh army retreated from the Chenab to the Jhelum. Lord Gough was forbidden to advance by the young Governor General until, on a cold January day, he decided to act.

Colonel Barclay wrote to his new wife, "The Duke of Wellington said that if there is anything more sad than a battle lost, it is a battle won. The battle of Chilianwala was just that. Our infantry advanced recklessly towards the Sikh army and faced the fortified enemy in an exhausted condition. The crossfire of Sikh marksmen resulted in a hasty retreat and terrible loss. A brigade of cavalry with support from the rear fared no better. Our guns were so placed that they could not fire a shot in support. A retreat began in the midst of confusion and the 14th Dragoons bore down mercilessly on our own men, refusing mercy even to doctors. By evening, we counted a total of 2,350 dead or wounded. I hear this terrible episode is beginning to be called a great victory!"

Carolyn read the letter carefully, touched by the excitement of battle and the fear of loss. Trevor Barclay may not be Julian but he was, certainly, home and security. "Let me not lose him now!" she prayed, while her two stepdaughters watched her. She set about to bake a cake, plant a bed of champas and embroider a few cushion covers to while away the fear-filled days. Her anxiety was also bound up with her own condition. She was heavy with child — a fact not observed earlier due to the voluminous crinoline but very evident now to Catherine's discerning eye.

Catherine came across from her adjoining bungalaw, to chat and discuss the war. She too heard from her husband, of his exploits and daring at Chilianwala but her anxiety was not for Jeremy Latimer but the young major who was political agent in a small state and who now sought to keep peace in his jurisdiction, along with men in similar predicaments. Catherine did not mention the name of this man, who steered a perilous course somewhere on the banks of the Indus, but she hinted to a stunned Carolyn that Jeremy's death would leave her free to marry him.

Neither Trevor Barclay nor Jeremy Latimer had sufficient time to remember their wives in the turmoil of preparations for the next battle, which was not long in coming. Spurred by criticism and the threat of supercession by Napier, General Gough summoned all his skills. With a force of 20,000 men and 100 guns, he attacked the Sikhs numbering 50,000 men. Advised by John Cheape of the

Engineers, the Commander kept himself in check until the artillery had done its best. Sikh resistance was demolished. But even after their guns were silenced, they fought recklessly until they were routed and forced to surrender.

Colonel Trevor Barclay was present with Gilbert at the scene of their surrender — when thirty-five chiefs laid down swords, matchlocks and shields on a growing heap of arms. Trevor Barclay felt the pain of the vanquished when after laying down arms, the Sikhs had to part with their beloved horses.

"This is unjust," Barclay muttered. "The fallen warriors must be allowed to return on their chargers."

Jeremy Latimer's reply was like a whiplash. "So that they may ride forth again? Let them go back on foot — like any Jat peasant!"

Barclay regarded his old friend with surprise. "We are soldiers," he said gravely. "Let us leave the job of hating to politicians."

"In India, our roles blend one into another. Look at the Lawrence brothers, or Edwardes. We must be both if we are to succeed," Latimer replied. "The Indian needs a complex adversary."

As the surrender ended, an anguished cry of "Ranjit Singh is dead today!" filled the sunlit plain. The victors turned their backs on the melancholy sight and headed towards their garrison towns.

Julian Ruthven arrived in Lahore, in the midst of this turmoil, where the chief commissioner, Sir Henry Lawrence, was trying to bring order to the land of five rivers. Punjab was very different from Bengal, where British authority had been safely established and enjoyed the prestige of power. In Punjab, Julian observed that the Englishmen were imbued with the frontier spirit — of a people standing on the brink of time, a step away from eternity. There was, nevertheless, a sense of certitude — a belief in Christ — that sustained them against the rigours of a merciless existence.

If Julian was sent by Lord Dalhousie to find fault with Henry Lawrence, he became, instead, his admirer. Everywhere he saw the attempts made by Lawrence to conciliate the warring people of the region. Lord Dalhousie had ordered annexation of Punjab — a step abhorred by Henry Lawrence. Many British officers, however, welcomed the step, particularly Henry's brother, John, who was a believer in Dalhousie's policy of annexation. An administrative board was set up to deal with the aftermath of annexation.

Lahore was a pretty city, of parks, pavilions and houses that bore the look of transience, as if this border town, an outpost of Moghul and British India, was forever prepared to dismantle and retreat into the vast hinterland. The mood too was one of brittle gaiety, as of men and women who flit through life in subdued frenzy.

No one could exemplify it better than Julian's sister, Catherine Latimer, who had left the stately pleasures of Calcutta for the rough excitement of Lahore. That her husband, Jeremy Latimer, fumed in helpless anger when she went about her romps and flirtations only added piquancy to the enterprises. She treated Jeremy's missionary zeal with contempt.

Sitting in her bungalow one afternoon, when a duststorm raged over the city, Catherine poured out iced tea and spoke to her brother. "These men believe they are instruments of Providence or Divine Will. They race across this vast land believing they are its saviours. They collect taxes, demarcate lands, put down thugs and dacoits, chastise wild Afghans and other intruders into their domain. Very fine and noble, no doubt — from their point of view. But is it all for the greater glory of God and Britain? Or is there a craving for glory and mastery over lesser men, a yearning to see themselves as conquerors of another race?"

Jeremy Latimer looked at his wife with fury. If he could, he would have liked to wring that long, white neck and detach it from those gleaming, bared shoulders. "Is that what you think?' he asked thickly.

There was a knock on the door, and the orderly ushered in a couple into the cool, dark drawing room. Catherine glanced at them and smiled. "Dear Carolyn ... and Colonel Barclay ... what a surprise! When did you return from Ferozpur?"

Carolyn Barclay stood petrified as her eyes fell upon Julian Ruthven who rose and bowed to the colonel and his young wife. "Why Julian," Barclay said cordially, "what are you doing here? Weren't you last heard jailing a zamindar?"

Catherine's laugh was pure delight. "You may well ask! Poor Julian has now been banished because of a forbidden affaire de coeur. The young lady is ..."

"Kitty," Julian murmured with menace in his voice. Catherine pur a finger on her full, ripe lips. "Not a word more, darling ... though it is such a marvellous thing to relate."

Trevor Barclay laughed, as if in relief to know that Julian's attachment lay elsewhere. Carolyn held her cup of iced tea with trembling hands, not daring to lift her eyes. "He has found someone to love," she thought with a pang.

"I heard you speaking just now," Colonel Barclay said, taking a comfortable seat. "It is not that we wish to conquer and rule. We have a mission in India and you see it taking shape in Punjab. My regiment came from Bengal to evict the Afghans and then to subdue the Sikhs. This region was the playground of domestic tyrants and foreign plunderers. Our army has brought peace through the efforts of our brave soldiers."

"I met such an officer of the Guides on my way from Delhi," Julian Ruthven said. "He is the political officer in a remote, arid place called Pannu and lives an unquiet existence."

"Yes, indeed," Colonel Barclay said warmly. "That must be young David Sandys. An intrepid officer.

"A flamboyant popinjay!" Colonel Latimer exploded in a manner that surprised both Barclay and Julian.

Only Catherine, they noticed, said nothing. Her cheeks were flushed and her eyes were lambent with suppressed emotions. Carolyn, who had heard of Catherine's affair with Sandys, fidgeted with her bonnet, afraid of her own secret.

"Flamboyant popinjay is hardly a description for a man who dares to bring law and order to the wild Muzbi and Afridi tribesmen," Julian retorted.

Trevor Barclay frowned, wondering what hornet's nest he had stirred up, but Julian continued, "In fact, I have told Sir Henry Lawrence that there is little I can learn from his office and would like to stay with Captain David Sandys — to better observe frontier conditions."

Çatherine stood up abruptly. "Do that, darling," she said to her younger brother. "You will learn more from David than from a regiment here! And now I must get some more cakes from the pantry," she said, disappearing into the interior.

Jeremy Latimer's face was a mask of rage as he watched her go. "It is time to teach that harlot a lesson," he muttered through clenched teeth.

No one but Barclay heard, and his tawny eyes rested on his young wife who sat uneasy and restless, staring at the dust outside.

It was with a sense of relief that Julian left Lahore for Pannu. Catherine's revelations about her affair with David Sandys disturbed him. Somewhere, an old woman's forecast seemed to ring in his ears — that Kitty, voluptuous and vivacious, would bring only bad luck to her lovers. He tried to admonish her but to no avail. "I will try to join you," she told Julian. "It is ages since I saw David."

More disturbing than Catherine was Carolyn, whose eyes said more than he wanted to hear.

Travelling across the newly annexed Punjab, Julian saw the work of the Administrative Board under the guidance of Henry Lawrence. Revenue collection was organised and the local police force improved for prevention of crimes. Nests of desperadoes were cleared, canals and bridges were built and village schools begun.

After several days, he reached his destination. Pannu was situated in a wild, inaccessible region where neither Greek nor Scythian had ventured to come. A tribe of Afridis lived here, as rough and resilient as the very rocks around them.

Here, the indomitable Captain David Sandys had plunged into the work of "taming the shrews" of Pannu. He had forced them to lay down arms and grow corn instead of raiding farmers to get their food. When the Afridi tribesmen told him that they had never grown crops, Sandys threatened to starve them to death. Now, Julian saw the fields sway with tall jowar.

"After this, we shall draw up a code of conduct for these noble savages," Sandys announced.

"A momentous change for people who consider murder their birthright and rapine their sport," Julian observed.

Sandys laughed. "We will do more. We will even tame the Afghans! But before that, I have orders from Colonel Sleeman to search for nests of outlaws. The Thuggies have left a trail of terror running from Bengal, Oudh and upto Punjab. We must keep them out of Punjab, where there is enough underlying violence, and where demobilised soldiers are ready to join such gangs."

The Afridi tribesmen accompanied Sandys and Julian on these explorations. Julian found these reconnoitring journeys exhilarating, as they rode across deserted hills, forests and ravines where no human settlements were visible, and the wind bent the tall grass with an endless murmur. "It is as if we have discovered a new land," Julian said.

"Or stepped back into another time," David replied.

A few days later, they set off to search for the Thuggies, accompanied by a handful of sepoys. The terrain was rough and the going slow. The wind blew around them, making eerie noises among the trees and ravines. Attuned to every sound, Sandys paused now and then to listen. "Strange, I hear footsteps," he said, frowning.

Julian glanced around, unable to hear. "I see no one," David shrugged his shoulders. "Perhaps it is the wind or ground animals ascurrying for cover as dusk falls." He paused. "I think we should go forward — until we come to a clearing before camping."

"You said the caves would make good camps in the bitter cold," Julian observed.

"No ... not tonight. Cold winds keep one alert," Sandys said. They rode on, but the terrain grew more and more difficult until it was too dark to proceed further. Bizarre hootings of owls and the low moans of animals drifted towards them. The group halted to set up camp.

While the sepoys made chapatis and roasted potatoes, the young captain and Julian talked of many matters. It was incongruous to talk of England, military college and Haileybury in that desolate countryside, but it diverted their minds from a sense of unseen danger. They soon turned in for the night.

It was late when David Sandys awoke with a start. The sound of footsteps was now clearly audible, and silhouettes of figures could be seen by the light of the campfire. Accustomed to danger, he felt, nevertheless, a sudden unreasoning fear. Julian felt Sandys move and sat up. Seeing the furtive figures move forward, he reached for his pistol and waited. At a curt command from Sandys, the sleeping sepoys sat up, poised with their rifles.

The group was thrice the size of Sandys' handful of sepoys and it surrounded them in no time. "Where is the Saheb of Pannu?" a man, obviously the leader, asked.

"Who are you?" Sandys asked.

"That is a secret. I have come in search of you, and now I have found you," the leader replied.

Again, Sandys felt that quiver of fear. "You could have seen me in my headquarters. Why did you follow me here?"

The chief's laugh seemed lurid to Julian as he moved slowly towards him.

"Come with me, Captain Saheb, I have work with you," the chief said.

In reply, Captain Sandys fired at him. The bullet barely missed the chief. The others moved in, slowly but menacingly.

Sandys and Julian fired on them in rapid succession. Several fell; others moved forward, only to be felled down. The four sepoys too fired, uncertainly, not daring to use up all the ammunition. When their bullets were spent, the chief Thuggi moved in with his comrades and dragged David Sandys away from the campfire. Others held Julian in a vice-like grip. The sepoys scattered like pigeons before a cat.

The Thuggi chief brandished a knife and then held it on the fire for a moment before walking to where Sandys lay struggling with his captor. "Now, my gallant captain," he said, "here is an act that will deprive you of your manhood."

A terrible scream followed, ricocheting around the hills. Julian struggled and tried to break loose from the vice-like grip that held him. "You fiends!" he shouted. "What are you doing?"

The Thuggi chief's laughter was indeed fiendish. "What am I doing, you ask? Something which will stop the golden-haired captain's gallantries in Lahore! He turned to his brigade. "Come let us go. Our work is done. We have to now claim our payment!"

Julian watched the men ride out before rushing to where David Sandys lay, bleeding and in agony. "Finish the work," he groaned. "Shoot me if you have a bullet. I cannot endure the pain!"

Julian washed and dressed the wound and carrying David, laid him on the quilts by the campfire. "End it all," Sandys groaned again.

"You will feel better soon. Drink this entire cup of brandy and the pain will be dulled. We will camp here for a few days until you can ride," Julian said gently, trying to sound calm.

David opened his eyes with an effort. "Who hired these fiends, Julian?"

Julian Ruthven did not reply. He could only guess. Raising his eyes to the stars, Julian called down a curse on Jeremy Latimer.

After several days, they slowly made the journey to Pannu, and there David Sandys was looked after by his Afridi tribesmen, who attended to him with care and concern.

Julian stayed with David Sandys for several months, while the latter recovered from the horror of what had happened to him. Captain Sandys withdrew into himself, his gaiety gone, his vigour sapped by his constant brooding about his emasculated condition. He rode once more to hunt for Thuggis and demarcate lands but without any real zest. As the blistering heat of Pannu intensified further, Julian urged David to go with him to Simla, the summer capital.

"No, I have finished with that life forever," Sandys said grimly. "I shall remain here, with my savage companions who are kinder than civilised Englishmen."

Julian Ruthven hesitated before saying, "Let Kitty come to visit you. That is the least she can do."

David Sandys laughed bitterly. "Kitty will have no use for a maimed man. You will find her in Simla, on her happy hunt."

The Simla officers' mess was the scene of merriment and camaraderie that year. Punjab was settling down, and Lord Dalhousie had come personally to bless the efforts of John Lawrence's men. The officers of the Guide Corps, the Bengal and Madras regiments, the scarlet and gold of the Hussars, white and green of the Engineers, the dull brown of the Guides, made a patiche of colours, outshining the pastel muslins, lace and tulle worn by the leathery-skinned matrons and maids. The men, too, showed fewer signs of stress despite the rigours of their existence in the arid and stony mountains or burning plains. They danced exuberantly, drank until comatose and flirted with anyone willing and able. The cool hill air went to their heads. The women, too, blossomed in the coolness, and for a while a semblance of freshness and health returned to their wasted faces and forms. Their frantic energies surprised Julian; the Briton in India seemed alien to him. They seemed to have a heightened impulse to drain the cup of life to its dregs, as if tomorrow was far away.

Carolyn Barclay met Julian Ruthven on the many bridle paths where Memsahebs took the air. Clouds swirled around them, leaving tiny particles of mist and the scent of moist lilacs and violets on the hair and cheeks.

"You have taken care to avoid me," she reproached gently.

"Mrs. Barclay," he said stiffly, "what happened is best forgotten. There are men like your husband and David Sandys who are risking their lives to bring law and order to a troubled region. The least you, my sister and other women can do, is to think of their safety ... and welfare." He bowed stiffly and walked away.

Colonel Jeremy Latimer was in good spirits. He stayed in Ruthven Cottage but did not make any demands on Catherine. He returned home late from dinners, and was busy during the day with John Lawrence.

Catherine went through the social rounds with a brittle gaiety, until she heard of David's fate from her brother. For a few days she shut herself up alone in the Ruthvens' cottage and then flung herself into the merriments once more. Julian watched, astounded by her indifference. In disgust, he returned to Pannu, to see primitive men toil on a stern land, battling with elements under the command of a man who had turned his back on civilisation. Julian watched the tribesmen attend to him, and saw with dismay the transformation of David Sandys — from a self-assured empire builder to a bitter recluse who found solace with the very savages he had sought to civilise. In time, he became like them, gaunt and withdrawn, with an Afridi tribesman for a lover. It was hard to believe this was the same David Sandys who had once courted Kitty Latimer with Petrarch's sonnets.

29

A Ceremony of Innocence

A procession moved slowly up the long drive of the Chowdhurys' Mayurganj estate, led by red-liveried and white-turbanned men, some playing vigorously on dhols while others played flutes. All the front windows of the mansion flew open, as members of the family and servants strained to see the new district magistrate arrive on a caparisoned black charger. Uniformed sepoys with rifles slung on their shoulders, marched behind him in measured tread.

Julian Ruthven stared ahead, determined to appear distant and detached. He had returned to Bengal after a year's sojourn in Punjab, to be posted as magistrate of the district in which Mayurganj was situated. So now he came to the Chowdhury estate, triumphant yet afraid.

For a year, he had had no news of Radha. The conspiracy of silence was complete. "She is gone," he thought miserably. "Married to that zamindar. Heavy with child-bearing. Enslaved and despoiled. They have succeeded in their scheme to separate us."

As the procession drew up, Julian dismounted before the round-pillared portico. Sudhir Chowdhury came forward to greet the new ruler of the district. At his signal, his wife Kumudini appeared with a gold tray bearing a small earthen lamp, blades of grass, rice and a coconut. She circled the small tray around the magistrate's face in arati, welcome. Another lady blew a conchshell while the other women alleluiated with their tongues. The liveried musicians broke into a scherzo of drums and dhols.

Julian Ruthven tried not to show that he was moved by these ceremonies. He had come to pay an official visit as guest of one of the eminent gentry. Gravely, he shook hands with Sudhir, Harish and the younger men, and joined his palms together in namashkar to the women. His eyes moved swiftly over the veiled figures, in search of a particular form. He failed to find her. "She is gone," he thought dismally. "I will not find her here."

Julian Ruthven was led upstairs to the circular veranda, where Brajesh Chowdhury sat in a low armchair awaiting his honoured guest. On hearing a light, firm tread, he stood up. Julian came towards him, wondering how he should receive homage from this venerable man who had been "Uncle" to him all his life, and his parents' dearest friend. Brajesh Chowdhury stood up, poised for ceremonies. Impulsively, Julian embraced him, murmuring, "It's good to see you, Sir!" Tears rose to Chowdhury's eyes as he returned the embrace. "Welcome Julian," he said in an unsteady voice.

The entire house was geared now to entertain the district magistrate. The retainers rushed around, settling the sepoys in the outhouse, scyces stabled the district magistrate's horse, the musicians were given a place to rest and eat. An apartment on the second floor was allotted to the district magistrate.

In the veranda, the dhoti-clad Chowdhury retainers brought in a silver tea service and breakfast delicacies, prepared by the Goan chef from Brajesh's Calcutta villa, while half-veiled ladies supervised the serving. Sudhir offered his father's best cigars while his valet came in with the ceremonial silver hookah.

Everyone was taut, awaiting an outburst. Brajesh Chowdhury, however, pretended not to notice his guest's tension or his sons' discomfiture. "I received letters from Charles and Eleanor," he said, drawing on the hookah. "They are in London now. The London season," the zamindar murmured, staring at leaves swirling in the capricious sunlight. "How far away it seems ... the women in beautiful gowns, like animated dolls, and their gorgeous menfolk ... and the lovely little Queen, who stopped my heart with her radiant smile. I thought I was in paradise."

Julian smiled. "Why do you not join them in London and Ashville once more? The change would do you good."

The zamindar sighed. "The changes here are doing me good. Dalhousie is bringing order and progress to India. Three universities in the Presidency towns are to be established, offering western education to our youth. We wil achieve what we sought in our youths — a cultural synthesis."

Julian regarded his host gravely. "Do you truly believe in cultural synthesis?"

"Of course! What else have I been working for all these years?" Brajesh Chowdhury asked indignantly.

"How deep is your belief, how strong your emancipation?" the magistrate asked, relentless.

Everyone held their breaths. They knew that Julian Ruthven had come to Mayuraganj with a purpose, as a Ruthven always had: Alexander to trade and grasp land, Charles Edward to build bridges of understanding and Julian ... what did he want in Mayurganj? This official visit, with the accompanying panoply of power, was not just a gesture of friendship.

"My commitment?" Brajesh Chowdhury asked. "Surely, Julian, you have seen it all! I have believed and worked for an India enriched by contact with the west."

Julian sighed, reluctant to argue, unwilling to accuse this distinguished man of hypocrisy. His parents were no less to blame.

The morning passed in rituals of sociability, as the young magistrate was shown the improvements that had been brought about in Mayurganj. The zamindar and his sons discussed the latest books with Julian, as well as recent events. They talked guardedly about Punjab, to where Julian had been banished for a year.

The afternoon brought in a summer storm, that darkened the sky and twisted trees, that roared and rattled windows. Julian Ruthven awoke from his siesta and went into the adjoining balcony. He was startled to see a slender figure, standing motionless and grave, watching him.

"Radha!" he whispered. "Is it really you? I had given up all hope of seeing you again! I feared ..." His gaze went swiftly to the parting of her hair, where there was a smudge of vermilion. His chest tightened. "You are ... I see ... married."

"Yes," Radha said softly. "I am married ..."

Julian came close and grasped her hand in his, taut and angry. "To whom? Where is your ... the man you married?" he asked, staring in pain at the face whose radiance and tenderness reminded him of a Raphael Madonna. The luminous eyes darkened.

"And you?" she asked evenly, "Did you do great things in Punjab? Did you ... meet suitable women of your world in Simla?"

"I had to go to Punjab. It was an order ... and a scheme to remove me from ... your path. I see that they succeeded."

Radha frowned. "Why have you come, Mr. Ruthven?" she asked.

His eyes were now dark with pain. "Why? Because I wanted to see if you ... were still ... free ..."

"You came to see me?" she cried. "I was told you had forgotten me ... in the rush and excitement of work ... amongst golden-haired women ... and I was advised to ... forget you as well."

Julian came close and held her. "Forget you? Of course I tried ... I had enough temptations ... but no one engaged my heart. I immersed myself in work, determined to return and find you." He paused, grimfaced, glancing at the vermilion in her hair. But I see I have come too late."

Tears glimmered in Radha's eyes as she laughed. "No, Mr. Ruthven. This is the vermilion *you* gave me. I wear it ... in defiance ... of them all." She paused. "When they pressed me to marry a rich and powerful zamindar, I told them that I considered myself ... bound ... already."

Julian embraced her, laughing, feeling the vibrance of her body close to his own, the fragrance of her skin, the turmoil and tenderness that matched his own. "And I ... felt bound to you ... so there could be no other ..."

They regarded each other now, with joy and apprehension. "We must go ... before ... they make another ruse," Julian said.

"I ... cannot offend ... my father. Can we not get his blessings?" Radha whispered.

Julian sighed, releasing her. "Let us try."

The storm that greeted Julian Ruthven's proposal to marry Radha Chowdhury matched the Kal-baisakhi storm raging outside. Her elder brothers declared it was pure madness. The Ruthvens had already pronounced such a union ruinous. Brajesh Chowdhury was in a terrible predicament but in the end, was persuaded to give his approval.

"Go away soon ..." he said, "before you are stopped. I cannot hold things together too long."

The next day, preparations began as more dark clouds rushed in from the Bay of Bengal, bringing rain and wind to swell the river and drench the hungry earth. Thatched roofs of huts and cottages quivered and then were torn from their bamboo frames to be flung across the leaden sky. The last mangoes and jackfruits fell and scattered their pulp on the ground. Even the strong iron gates of the Chowdhury estate swayed and creaked in the frenzied wind.

No dhols or drums were beaten this time, no conchshells blown, no chatelaine performed the arati. Dilip Chowdhury received his friend in the vast, damp hall with a grave countenance. "Everything is in readiness at the temple," he said.

The temple was wrapped in the sepulchral gloom of a stormy monsoon dusk. A Brahmin priest had lit all the one hundred and eight lamps before the shrine of Shiva and his consort, Parvati, the divine couple whose devotion kept the universe in order. Jasmine and champas were heaped in a gold plate and on a gold tray, were laid the offerings of coins, silks and fruits to the deities. Incense burned, its sweet fragrance hovering over the temple and making everything visible only through a screen of smoke.

Julian Ruthven entered and took off his shoes. He wore a well-tailored suit of superfine cloth. Radha, too, was dressed in bridal regalia — a red Benarasi sari, ornaments of diamonds and rubies that her father had made for her long ago, in anticipation of a different kind of marriage. Her long hair was now bound in a plait, woven with threads of jasmine buds. Brajesh Chowdhury awaited them, sombre faced.

They sat across each other, while the priest murmured incantations and threw ladles of clarified butter onto the small yagna, the fire of sandalwood logs. Brajesh sat beside his daughter, ready to do the kanyadan, the giving away of the bride ... "Begin, Purohit Thakur," he said anxiously.

The old Brahmin sighed. "To think a daughter of yours ..."

"We are waiting, Thakur," Dilip said curtly.

The ceremony was brief but charged with the power of a Vedic rite. The priest was bewildered to find Julian repeating the Sanskrit lines clearly, invoking the gods of sky, wind, water and earth as witnesses. Radha's sari was tied to Julian's coat as they walked seven times around the sacrificial fire. Their union was now forged by the five elements, only Yama, the lord of death, could sever the bond.

Dilip and Brajesh Chowdhury stood aside as Julian looked at his bride with a sense of unreality. "Dearest love," he whispered, putting vermilion powder in the parting of her hair and inscribing a bindi on her forehead. Radha bent down to touch his feet but Julian withdrew. "No, my love. I want no submission from you. "You are ... my pole star."

Thunder boomed outside, making the stones of the temple tremble. The priest looked troubled. "This is godhul lagna," he said, the hour when cowherds return home.

"So it is," Dilip murmured, glancing into the tempest, and then tried to suppress his sense of foreboding with a jovial countenance.

"Julian," Brajesh said, "our bajra is anchored nearby. Radha's trunks have been put on board, as well as all the presents given to you both. The retainers will serve food and attend on you. By dawn, you will reach Narayanpur, and then an hour later, Tussore." He paused, trying to suppress a cry of pain. "Look after our ... little girl. Her happiness is in your hands. She has been a great joy to us ..."

"I will never fail her," Julian murmured, gazing at his bride.

"Then go ... and forgive us this brief ceremony. Had our family members permitted, we would have lit up Belgachia with a million lamps, called Lord Dalhousie to dinner ... and ..." Dilip Chowdhury could not continue.

"No matter," Julian replied, gently. "This is sweet enough."

Thunder rumbled outside and lightning now lit up the temple's interior. Radha did pranam — touched her brother's feet. Julian embraced his new brother in-law, and taking his bride's hand, stepped out into the fury of the wind and thunder. The brightly lit bajra was anchored on the bank. In a minute, they ran and entered it. Two retainers followed and drew up the plank. Dilip stood at the temple entrance, sombre faced. Tears sprang to Radha's eyes as she waved to the figure on the land. Julian Ruthven stood by, watching the temple recede into the distance as the bajra sailed up the river towards Narayanpur.

A monsoon storm hit the bajra shortly after, swinging it from side to side. The river swelled with the downpour; the benign life-giving Ganga became destructive, hurling down trees and river banks, twisting frail boats, washing away fragile seedlings of rice. Lanterns in the large, comfortable bajra swayed and twinkled but continued to give a steady glow to the main hall, where dinner was laid by a Muslim khidmatgar. Silver candlesticks and crystal shone on the table. In the main cabin, Radha's old nurse, Mukta, laid out things she thought would be immediately needed and made up the bed. She had brought along a basket of jasmines to strew on the nuptial bed. She then lit a lamp and went to the kitchen to keep an eye on the cooking, but in reality to talk to her familiar colleagues. The tall, fair saheb frightened her to distraction. She wondered how her "little mother" was going to live with the "Angrez" gentleman.

Julian and Radha sat opposite each other, silent and pensive, as they pretended to eat. He poured out a glass of wine and offered it to her. She declined. Tureens of food came and went back, untouched. He rose and led her to the lamplit cabin, fragrant now with jasmines.

They slept fitfully on the nuptial bed as the bajra rolled and pitched on the churning water. The wind howling over the river awakened them, and made them draw close, as they lay still and silent thinking of the future. Then, as the violet light of a monsoon dawn broke over the banks, they rose and saw the barge approach the sleepy sub-division town with its small, sturdy buildings on the "Strand", the cluster of thatched houses beyond, the little church with a modest steeple and crucifix and further beyond, the ruins of a former nawab's palace.

Eric Blair was at the bank to welcome them. He shook hands with Julian Ruthven but his eyes were fixed on the wooden door of the bajra. As it opened, he ceased to converse with Julian and stared at the figure that emerged — of medium height, slender, with willowy grace, a pale-gold complexion and a face that glowed with wonder and innocence,

"Why, she is exquisite!" he exclaimed softly.

Julian smiled at his friend, both with gratitude and pride, and then turned to watch his bride alight, hesitant yet radiant.

Eric recovered and stepped forward. Welcome, Mrs. Ruthven," he said gently. "It is a pleasure to meet Julian's dear wife."

Radha gave him a tremulous smile, but Julian realised that beneath her calm, she was taut with apprehension. Without delay, he helped her onto his barouche which had driven from Mayurganj and along with Eric Blair, sped to the church, where they were married once more by Christian rites.

The bajra moved slowly over the white turbulent waters of the Ganges. The timid sun god peeped from between banks of heavy, dark clouds to survey the scene, as if preparing for an encounter with Varuna, the rain god. Radha sat on the bed watching the river scene, the distant water-logged paddy fields, bent trees and rain-lashed huts.

"Today, the sun should have shone," she thought, glancing at her husband. "Today, the sun should have blessed us. Is it an inauspicious sign? Have we begun a ... sad journey?"

When Julian Ruthven had conveyed the news of his marriage to the Bengal government at Writers' Building, he was not surprised to find himself abruptly posted from the Mayurganj area to a remote district in Bihar, whose headquarters lay on the vast bosom of the Ganges. The townsfolk gathered on the river-bank to see the "Angrez Magistrate Saheb" and his Hindu wife come ashore from the bajra.

"The sun god and Lakshmi," a bystander said, staring at the handsome couple.

"Your mythology is confused," replied another, "but there is no denying that they look splendid. Hear she is of illustrious lineage."

"Must have been disowned by her folks. No decent Hindu marries a mleccha," observed a dour Brahmin.

"The plague take you!" retorted one of the magistrate's servants. "Many high-born women have married Europeans ... take Job Charnock and his Brahmin wife, Metcalfe Saheb and his aristocratic Sikh wife, and ..."

The dour Brahmin turned away. "That does not make this less disgraceful! Such renegade women should be outcaste ... and burnt."

"Say it before the Saheb. He will have *you* burnt!" snapped the orderly.

"Will he dare?" someone asked, interested at the prospect of a tamasha.

"His father dared," the orderly whispered. "Be careful of this red-haired clan!"

The European populace, consisting of the commanding officer of native regiment, the garrison engineer, the civil engineer, the district surgeon and district police officer and their wives were equally curious about their new magistrate and his Indian wife. The men soon overcame their reservations in admiration of Radha's beauty of face, voice and manners. If they had expected a gorgeous nautch girl, they were surprised to find a woman as refined as any English lady, who made the gloomy old bungalow of the district magistrate a place of charm. The women were less enthusiastic, seeing in Radha Ruthven a threat to their own positions. If their menfolk fell prey to these exotic native women, what would happen to those "young hopefuls" who came in the fishing fleets from Britain to marry British soldiers, traders and administrators?

Julian and Radha remained cocooned in their private idyll. Julian Ruthven could never clearly remember the incidents of that time in sequence, but only as images of pain and joy against the backdrop of the sleepy district town. He remembered the old rambling house on the banks of the Ganges with its wild, unkempt garden that was soon brought under order. Servants were set to work on floors and ceilings. Then the walnut furniture, silver, silk curtains, Sevres and Staffordshire china, and Bohemian crystal, gifted by Brajesh Chowdhury, transformed the gloomy bungalow into a gorgeous abode. Julian Ruthven went about his duties as district magistrate but his mind was never far from the tender, exquisite being who had illumined his home. He would always remember how he galloped his horse on the last stretch of the road from the district office to his house, impatient to see Radha, and how she, pretending to be busy with the roses and nasturtiums, stood motionless in the lengthening shadows until they moved into each other's arms. There they would remain until a discreet cough and the clink of silver announced that tea and the retainers had arrived. While he read despatches and gave dictation, she embroidered or read and after dinner, sat in the balcony of their room, watching the clouds move over the river. As thunder boomed and rattled the windows and doors, or as clouds drifted across the moon, they discovered one another with a sense of joy and wonder. Each moment was a celebration of life.

"Will it always be like this?" Radha asked one dawn, as hesitant sunshine broke through banks of clouds and the warm air was drenched with the scent of jasmines.

Julian kissed her gently. "I hope not. Let us endeavour to become a dull and decorous pair," he paused, to enjoy her quick laugh and said pensively, "lest the gods get jealous of our happiness."

He took her on his tours around the district; she in a small carriage and he on a bold chestnut horse. Radha enjoyed new sights and people, and was eager to see her husband at work in his bailiwick. At night, they stopped at dak bungalows, ate delicious food concocted by Muslim cooks and lay on charpoys in the garden to sleep under the stars. Mukta hovered nearby while guards marched up and down.

Once, caught in a storm, they were forced to stay in a village for several days. Radha whiled away the time by telling Julian the story of the great musician, Tansen, who could move the clouds to rain with his raga, Megha Malhar. "Tansen was in love with his guru's daughter, and would not work hard at his music. The guru finally asked his beautiful daughter whether she wanted Tansen to be immortal or whether she wanted his love. There was no other alternative. 'Go away, and tell him you do not care,' the guru said. The girl left Ujjain, telling Tansen she loved another. In grief, Tansen took refuge in his genius and became the greatest musician of his time."

Julian smiled. "Did they never meet again?"

"Many years later, when she told him of what she had done."

"Was it worthwhile?' Julian asked. "To lose his beloved for fame?"

"Tansen is immortal," Radha replied. "No one would have known him otherwise."

"Love is the road to immortality ... to be forever in someone's heart," Julian said. "But you Indian women revel in sacrifice and martyrdom. Perhaps that is why you lend yourselves so readily to oppression."

Radha looked at him intently. "Were you ever in such a predicament, would you not expect me to ... renounce you?"

His eyes became dark. "Never," he whispered, drawing her close and laying her silken head against his broad chest. "Never renounce me, Radha. I have no use for fame or success without you."

Radha burst into tears ... of joy and relief ... of an ache that she could share with no one, an awareness of the transience of all things.

The rains began in earnest, no longer furious but steady and relentless, turning the fields to lush splendour. Flowers and shrubs sprang up in a frenzy of creation making the earth sweetly fragrant. But the river became a raging creature, sweeping away great clumps of earth and washing away fields of new grains and frail huts. As the floods began, Julian Ruthven prepared to organise relief for those caught near the delta. Radha watched him with apprehension. The executive engineer and the assistant engineer went with him. "Get the boats from the cloth merchants," he told the assistant Engineer, as he put on his solar topi and mackintosh.

"They have hidden the boats, Sir."

"In the bamboo thickets, near the burning ghat. It's their old trick. Tell them you have my orders to seize them!" His voice, now cold and imperious, sounded alien to Radha.

The food relief operations took more than a week. Julian Ruthven seized all available boats and personally supervised the rescue of stranded villagers from the treetops and rooftops. He went on horseback, scouring the submerged countryside for stranded persons. Ten miles away, in Narayanpur, the river had burst its banks. Julian went there to assist the new SDO who depended mainly on Eric Blair. Together they had tents put up further inland, on whatever high grounds were available. They organised community kitchens to feed the hundreds of homeless, and provided shelter to those whose homes had been washed away by the river. Eric Blair worked with a hard-pressed team. He went to another village where only the river remained. Everything else had floated away! Huts, cattle, trees, and bodies of villagers. Julian gazed at the desolate scene with a sense of impotence. "So much for plans and strategies, of storing seeds and waiting for the rains to sow a few acres of land ... all to await this terrible destruction!" he muttered.

Returning home he said, "The elements must be harnessed. I will visit the chief engineer at Patna to ask him to advise us on building a dam. If the Dutch can keep out the sea, we can channel a river!"

Radha smiled and brought in tea. She felt a sense of power and will emanating from him. "Is this the quality which makes him and his people triumph over others?" she wondered. "This refusal to be vanquished by stars and sun?"

The new year came and progressed; a crisp winter followed by a fragrant and balmy spring — of pellucid skies and glittering stars filled with promise, reminding Julian and Radha of the spring, five years ago, when they had discovered one another. March followed with its whimsical winds, shaking dry leaves and swirling dust. In April and May, the flowers began to wilt in the garden and the river became slow and thin.

In the midst of a June storm, Julian Ruthven was interrupted in his work in a village by a peon, who came to announce that he must return to headquarters at once.

"Why?" Julian asked, feeling a sudden chill within him.

The peon forgot his station and laughed gleefully, "Because, Saheb, you have now a beautiful son ..."

Julian Ruthven rode hard over the water-logged countryside, driving his horse as fast as he could; wet and weary, but driven on by an exhilaration so deep that neither his stiff, aching limbs nor the fury of the rain impeded his progress. Arriving at Tussore, he headed towards his bungalow, where the banana and coconut trees were bent by the wind and rain, but the scent of jasmines and tuberoses permeated the moist air. Doors opened, a host of figures bowed and salaamed but Julian Ruthven rushed up the stairs, oblivious to all, until he flung open the doors of his room.

Radha lay spent and frail on the high, four-poster bed, her hair in two plaits, looking more like a fourteen-year-old than a woman of twenty-three. Julian came slowly to her side and knelt by the bed. In silence, he took her hand and put it against his lips, and gazed in wonder at the infant lying in a froth of lace and silk beside its mother; a little face with perfect features and an alabaster colour. Downy, dark auburn hair brushed the head. The eyes were a deep blue.

"Marcus Aurelius Ruthven," Julian said, lightly touching the little clenched hands, "may I welcome you to us?"

Julian gazed at his wife. There was no need for words. She understood.

Julian and Radha were now even more bound than before, by the tangible bond of their son, who was their chief delight. A year later, a daughter was born whom they named Rowena, an old Scottish name in memory of the Ruthven homeland. The bungalow by the river became a place full of laughter and cries, of games and scoldings, where the two children and their parents lived in a perpetual idyll.

Julian was more busy than ever before.

Subduing Punjab, Lord Dalhousie had turned his attention to development and quickened the life of the empire. He began by reorganising the Central Secretariat at Writers' Building, Calcutta. A lieutanant governor was placed in charge of administering the huge state of Bengal so that the Governor General was free of this duty. A powerful and well-funded department of public works was organised to execute and implement Dalhousie's construction programme. An agricultural country like India needed water, and irrigation, he realised, was imperative. He earmarked a large sum — £ 1,400,000 to complete the mighty Ganges canal, which flowed over the vast Gangetic plain. The Grand Trunk Road, constructed by Sher Shah in the sixteenth century, connecting India from Peshawar to Calcutta, was modernised. As chief architect of British railways in the 1840s, Dalhousie was equally enthusiastic about connecting India through a network of railways, that would facilitate defence, commerce, transport. Communications of other kinds were also introduced, including telegrams and a reformed postal service.

Economic development needed educational development, to provide trained manpower for building roads, bridges and canals, and evolve a middle class of doctors, lawyers and administrators. Lord Dalhousie sponsored Sir Charles Wood of the Board of Control to promulgate a new education policy, stressing primary education in the vernacular, and the expansion of colleges through the grant-in-aid system. The first engineering college was begun in Rourkee, and the first university in Calcutta.

Dazzled by the aura of that imperious Governor General, young administrators like Julian Ruthven were impelled to emulate his example by working hard as they too dreamt of a progressive India. Visiting Writers' Building in the winter of 1854, Julian felt the presence of that dedicated man. The atmosphere at the Central Secretariat was charged with the same energy that the ailing Dalhousie was pouring into his work.

Caught up in the excitement of those years, of hurrying from Calcutta to Tussore with designs for bridges or plans for a dam, Julian Ruthven was not troubled by the other events which made north India restless. The princely Jhansi was taken over in 1853, and Nagpur in 1854. "Gilded relics" scoffed Dalhousie, when misgivings were raised. "These states are an anachronism in a modern India. Misgovernment should not be excused." Once the legal heirs died, the doctrine of lapse gave him the right for outright annexation. Though such cases produced a tremor among the nobility of India, they were, for a few years, submerged.

Julian Ruthven felt, as did many others, a sense of commitment to the task of governing India and drawing her out of her medieval conditions. India had become a moral responsibility. It was no longer a pagoda tree to be shaken and plundered. It was this awareness that made Julian work hard through hot days and steamy nights, inspecting fields, assessing crop yields, choosing sites for bridges over tempestuous rivers, irrigation channels over parched land, and the establishment of schools in his district. His efforts were not always successful: resources were limited and government spending frugal. He tried to interest private traders to participate in these schemes but they preferred the secure profit from silk, jute, indigo, tobacco and saltpetre to such large-scale ventures.

It was always a delight, however, to return home after days or hours, and find Radha waiting for him with Marcus and Rowena. He walked in the lush garden with his wife, talking of events, while Mukta walked sedately behind with the children. Sometimes, looking at his children playing, Julian felt as if Marcus and Rowena were indeed a synthesis of his world and Radha's.

"Do you suppose Marcus and Rowena will grow up to be a truly cosmopolitan man and woman?" Julian asked Radha as they sat in the roof garden of the district magistrate's bungalow, under a cloudless, moonlit autumn sky.

"They ought to be," Radha replied, smiling, "if they inherit all the affinity between us."

Julian gazed at her pensively. "Yes," he murmured, "India will be no mystery to them, nor a riddle to be unravelled. Its rhythm will be in their blood. Nor will Britain be an alien country." He paused. "That was how the Roman citizens of Spain, Gaul, Asia Minor and even Egypt were a synthesis of two worlds. Their origins were no longer important. What mattered was that they were proud to be Romans." He paused and murmured, "Civic Britannicus Sum. I hope one day it will be as truẹ as Civic Romanus Sum."

Both parents glanced at their children and laughed at their premature anxieties for the future, which, at the moment, seemed full of promise. Pandora's box remained unopened.

30

The Gathering Storm

The wedding of Isabel Ruthven and Stephen Reynolds, an Oriental scholar from Oxford, was celebrated in December 1856 with due pomp and ceremony, as if in defiance of the gradually darkening mood. It was also the occasion for Julian and Radha to leave their remote idyll to visit their respective families. They were saddened by the change of atmosphere in both Ruthven House and the Chowdhury villa at Belgachia. Charles Ruthven and Brajesh Chowdhury, who had embodied in themselves the enlightened liberalism of the Bentinck era were now relegated to the background while the protagonists of resistance gained ground on both sides.

The room which had been the scene of lively debates, and the nursery of reformist programmes, where Lord Bentinck, Raja Ram Mohan Roy, Dwarkanath Tagore had discussed ideas with Brajesh and Charles, was now the scene of differences between Dilip Chowdhury and Julian Ruthven. While Dilip condemned Dalhousie's policy of annexation, Julian upheld the Governor General's programme of progress. As they argued, both men felt anguish for the lost camaraderie of their youth.

"Have we searched in vain for a synthesis, Charles?" a bewildered Brajesh asked his old friend. "Have we dreamt of unreal utopias — of an India enriched by the west?"

Charles Edward gazed at his friend with pain. "I feel desolate to think that our efforts were in vain ... that our cherished wish to see the two peoples united in a common endeavour has resulted only in bitterness."

"Have a vanquished people ever come together with the victors?" Dilip asked his father bitterly.

"What is Europe but the result of Graeco-Roman conquests?" Julian persisted. "Did they not have an idea of an imperium — of a single state with equal citizenship for all?"

"The standard bearers of this imperium are most inspiring," Dilip said with a sardonic smile. "The missionaries who consider our religion barbaric, the soldiers who treat our sepoys with contempt, the traders who bleed our resources, and yes ... the humble, young hopefuls who come in fishing fleets to secure husbands and become intolerably arrogant Memsahebs within months. Yes, they would have made a Nero happy."

"What of men like Bishop Heber and Tom Munro, and humbler instances such as Eric Blair ... and yes, even myself, who love and work for India?" Julian asked in rising anger.

Lady Eleanor, grey and tired before her time, entered the room, as if sensing the brewing tension. "This is a time for renewing ties, not for severing them," she said, admonishing both Dilip and Julian with reproach in her eyes. "Tomorrow, I shall expect you all at our home and expect you young men to behave."

The scene at Ruthven House, however, was worse. It was as if the older Ruthvens had been forced to abdicate, giving place to a man like Jeremy Latimer, now a colonel in the Company army.

That winter, Jeremy Latimer came down from the Punjab to visit the Ruthvens in Calcutta. Catherine met her husband with an air of contempt but she noticed that it no longer irked him. She soon realised why — he had diverted his craving for assurance and dominion into a more satisfying channel. It was about this that he spoke, with an intensity that disturbed even the blase Catherine.

"Taught the fellows the meaning of obedience!" Colonel Latimer exclaimed, slicing a papaya with superfluous force. Isabel noted that her brother-in-law enjoyed viciously cutting everything. "Caught a rebel Sikh. You know what I did, Julian old chap?"

Julian shook his head as he looked away at the garden. Not discouraged, Colonel Latimer sat back with a sigh of pleasure while Catherine moved the Jacobean silver coffee pot on the rosewood table. He glanced at the three women, particularly his "Jezebel of a wife."

"Cut him in half, I did, from skull to crotch, as I rode past on my stallion." His laugh was pure mirth. "Better than pig-sticking, if you ask me."

No one spoke. Radha stared at the bowl of jasmines and seemed to see splashes of blood on them. Catherine's skin paled under a golden tan. Julian and his father exchanged glances. Only Catherine glanced at the gaunt-faced man of forty-seven, whom she had resisted for fifteen years and thought, "Why, he is worse than I thought! He is not just distasteful! He is a fiend!"

"This Sikh," Latimer resumed, "had fought against us with the Afghans. I recognised him at once. There was another fellow as well. John Nicholson. I ordered them to be tied to mouths of cannons and watched them fly." Latimer laughed once more. "What a splattering of offals there was!"

Radha closed her eyes in distress. Julian Ruthven rose, white with rage. "That was a vile thing to do, Latimer," he said in a low, hard voice. "I am amazed you confess it ... and that too before women!"

"Hah!" exclaimed Latimer shrilly. "These Ruthven women are resilient, Julian old chap." His eyes glittered as they rested on Catherine. "Especially my lady wife. Resembles her grand-aunt ... my grandmother Fiona. They can cope with blood."

Julian's jaws tightened. "You will have to atone for this Latimer ... with blood. But what is so terrible is that your hatred will destroy us as well!"

Radha rose and before Julian could stop her, she ran down the shallow flights of steps to the lawn and beyond to the lily pond where the children's ayah was singing —

What a vision of sweetness
Did I see in my Lord Krishna
As I fetched water from the Jamuna
What mercy and kindness was there
In my gentle, dark Lord!

Radha sat beside her, venting her fear in rasping sobs. The ayah glanced at her, alarmed. "Why do you weep, my lady?" she asked.

Radha shook her head and whispered, "What a terrible vision I see by our sweet Jamuna!"

A few days later, Isabel and Stephen Reynolds set off for Lucknow, where he was doing research on Indian history. "In this heartland of India, in the rich land of the Doab, between the Ganges and Jamuna, I will discover the India I seek," Stephen told Julian.

"May you prosper and succeed," Julian replied with a vague ache in his heart, that came from knowing Stephen Reynolds was a dreamer.

"Come with us," Stephen urged his brother-in-law. "I am new to India and would like you to guide me in my journey of discovery."

"You have your new bride," Julian reminded him.

"Yes, of course, but she, bless her heart, has no interest in medieval history." Stephen paused. "Perhaps your wife could join us. We would make a happy foursome."

The matter was settled by Lady Eleanor, who decided that she wanted to have all her grandchildren with her, particularly the hitherto undiscovered ones — Marcus and Rowena.

The Ruthvens and Reynolds thus went to Lucknow, where General Outram, who was Resident, extended hospitality to the family of Charles Edward Ruthven. The young people, however, stayed with a relation, Charlotte Levina, a granddaughter of Alexander Ruthven through his mistress Liselotte Fremont, and therefore half first cousin to Julian and Isabel. Charlotte's mother had received a handsome settlement from Nabob Ruthven, and had stayed on in Lucknow to enjoy the luxury and decadence of that fabled city. Madame Charlotte's house was not far from Farad Baksh, the fantasy house built by her putative great-grandfather, General Claude Martin. It was filled with the paintings of Liselotte, that Georgiana had swept away from the Calcutta mansion, as well as the memorabilia of Nabob Ruthven's escapades as a private trader and mercenary general.

Charlotte stood back, enjoying Isabel's wonder. "Come, ma petite," she said chuckling, "you must not be mesmerised by Grandpere's presence."

"I never knew how varied was our family tree," Julian replied, smiling at his older cousin.

"How could you? Madame Georgiana sent us all away from Calcutta and then my uncle Claude died, leaving everything to be enjoyed by my other uncle, Charles Edward."

"Was it very unfair to you?" Isabel asked anxiously.

Charlotte laughed. "No, ma chere, it was not too bad. We had our house in Lucknow, and plenty of money. We, the half-French Ruthvens, were not meant to be illustrious like the English Ruthvens."

Charlotte showed them around the city in her smart carriage. Lucknow had become a city of luxury, of glittering palaces and parks where exotic animals were caged. The river Gomati was illumined by barges at night and every day was a festival with processions by day and fireworks by night.

"The bordellos," Cousin Charlotte informed a blushing Isabel and Radha, "are the most exotic in the world. Every vice and perversion can be sampled in return for high payment. The Nawabs of Oudh have been servile before the Company Bahadur. The present one has given the right tribute and lends himself to extortion by any unscrupulous hesident."

"We hear so much about the present nawab, Cousin Charlotte. What is he like?" Julian asked.

The plump lady smiled. "Perhaps you would like to see Wazir Ali Khan?"

"Do you ... know him?" Radha asked with interest.

Charlotte nodded with an enigmatic smile. "I know him well, proverino. He is a kind man but cannot cope with the burden of a crown. But you will like him."

The men tried to dissuade their wives, but to no avail. Charlotte took them to the splendid palace where Wazir Khan, the last of a line, ruled or rather, misruled. His tawny eyes rested speculatively on the beautiful Radha and the young Memsaheb whose flame-coloured hair and sea-green eyes provoked from him a burst of poetry in Persian. Radha blushed and Isabel fidgeted uncomfortably but Stephen was delighted, and even added a few lines in Persian to the Nawab's couplets. Thus encouraged, the Nawab summoned his boon companions — fiddlers and buffoons who swarmed the gorgeous palace. While they beat on dhols and fiddles, the Nawab executed a few dance steps, singing in a rich, untrained voice.

Radha laughed, but was sobered by the strange expression on her husband's face. When the audience was over, the Nawab clapped his hands, whereupon his minions brought him a parcel.

"For you, Saheb," the Nawab said to Stephen. "I hear you understand Persian. This was brought by Emperor Humayun from Persia — a manuscript copy of the Shah-Namah by Firdausi.

Stephen gazed at the brittle pages, full of exquisite calligraphy but shook his head. "How can I, Your Majesty? This is a priceless gift!"

Wazir Ali sighed and shook his head. "It will soon be destroyed ... or taken by a greedy officer." He paused, looked around and whispered, "This fellow, Jackson, is a terrible thief ... the severe Outram was at least honest. Now, take it Reynolds Saheb, and when Oudh is swallowed up in the Company's domain, remember Wazir Ali, whose one fault was his love of poetry and music!" The Nawab wiped his tears with a plump, bejewelled hand.

Julian was silent as they sailed in the barge that night. "Avadh," he mused loudly. "The ancient Ayodhya of the Ramayana. The glory of Muslim culture. How sadly has it fallen!"

Charlotte nodded. "Oudh is ready for dissolution. Wazir Ali

is living on borrowed time. Sleeman has sent a report to the Governor General. Sati, infanticide, slave trade — everything is going on. The Company extorts from the Nawab who in turns bleeds his peasantry ... but who cares?"

"Is there no remedy?" Radha asked.

Charlotte smiled. "You are young, my cousin, and believe in remedies. But some things have no remedy. Oudh has gone too far. It is ready for the final dance of death. Dalhousie's men will soon be here."

"A pity," Stephen remarked. "I have a love for this chaotic old India."

From Lucknow, the party went to Deogarh, to see the domain of 'Nabob' Alexander Ruthven, their grandfather. Here, they met an enigmatic kinsman, Afraz Ruthven, great-grandson of Alexander Ruthven and Begum Shirin.

Afraz took little pride in his British blood. "A Scottish fugitive-cum-robber on one side and a Moghul princess on the other," he said sarcastically to his British cousins, "which would you choose?"

The reply came unexpectedly from Radha Ruthven. "I would choose the nobler of the two ... the more heroic ... the one who rose by his own efforts."

Afraz Ruthven turned to stare at the woman with the darkly luminous eyes, and a figure of sensuous grace. Something awakened within him, which he dared not name — a vague plan for avenging an ancient wrong. "Indeed, Radha devi?" he asked. "Can a woman of Hindusthan be so bold? Your natural ally would be Shirin Begum."

Radha turned away, suddenly embarrassed. Feeling a chill of dread, Julian took her arm and said, "We are visitors here, Afraz, come to see our common ancestor's domain. There is no need to dwell on the past. It is best forgotten."

"Forgotten?" Afraz cried indignantly. "Why should it be forgotten? My Moghul ancestors ruled Hindusthan. You are the intruders here ... until the day when ... we ... regain what is ours."

There was a moment of oppressive silence, broken by Julian

who spoke gravely. "The Moghul emperor is a phantom ruler. Do not set much store by that, Cousin Afraz. You will find few supporters for this theory."

Afraz Ruthven laughed. "Think you so, dear cousin? Go to Ratangarh and ask your father's former ward and your friend, Rana Uday Singh ... who too waits for the time when past dishonours can be redressed."

"Uday owes his childhood safety to my father," Julian replied grimly.

Afraz's smile was sardonic once more. "He was endangered due to the ... conduct ... of his mother, Rani Urmila, who ... but there, I am sure you know that terrible tale ... of your father and the Rani."

Isabel and Radha turned away, troubled and embarrassed. Both knew what Afraz was referring to. Julian, however, went on. "Yes, the tale of chivalry; of a solitary man defending another man's throne, and the reward of violence and cruelty."

Antagonism between the Moghul Ruthven and the British Ruthven was palpable. Radha turned to her husband. "It is time we saw the view from the ramparts — which your father has told me of. Would Cousin Afraz take us there?"

Afraz Ruthven bowed with courtly exaggeration. "But of course, Radha devi."

A high wind was singing in the towers of Deogarh when the group stood surveying the grey-pink hills tinted by a coral twilight, the fields turning brown, the bougainvillaea vivid splashes in the arid background. Set amidst a patch of green were the tombs of Begum Shirin and her progeny.

"Why do I feel a sense of impending peril?" Radha asked her husband, who reached out to draw her close and found her trembling.

"This wild and melancholy place is not conducive for a genial holiday. Let us return home — to our house on the bend of the Ganges," he said gently.

On the return journey, they met Colonel Trevor Barclay and his wife Carolyn, in Lucknow, at a palace soiree. Carolyn could only stare at the beautiful Indian woman.

"Julian's beloved," Carolyn's heart cried out in anguish. "The one he married by defying the world, the one for whom he accepted banishment ... for whose sake he spurned me! So this is she, the one fated to cause me pain! Oh, fortunate woman, if only I could be in your place for even a day — to receive the homage of such a love!"

If Julian Ruthven was troubled by Carolyn's unconcealed misery, Radha showed no sign of discomfiture by Carolyn's strange manner and seemed not to notice the misery in Carolyn's countenance as she watched Julian Ruthven with his wife.

As if enjoying his own pain, Colonel Barclay invited them to his house. It stood in the midst of a grassy plain encircled by silver oaks, where Carolyn had once more assembled a home from the residue of her predecessor's possessions; the same chintz covers, glass-topped tables, squat cupboards and spartan charpoys. She had made no effort to change Lavinia's legacy. She had learnt to endure the silence around her, to bear the scorching heat of summer and dry cold of winter. She had grown accustomed to this place where the dried, dusty leaves swirled around the house by day and the wind howled by night. Sleepless, beset by a vague sense of loss, she thought of her brief idyll.

And now, the focus of her fantasies, stepped across the threshold of her house, not as a fugitive lover, but the husband of another woman, courteous but distant. While Isabel, Stephen and Julian discussed the Nawab and the Resident with Colonel Barclay, Radha conversed with a tongue-tied Carolyn. They had barely proceeded beyond formalities when Carolyn's seven-year-old-daughter, Marina, ran into the room.

Radha stared at the girl, and wondered why she seemed so familiar. Her eyes moved the from girl to Isabel and then to Julian. She had the same gentian-blue eyes and copper hair. And then, as Radha saw Carolyn's expression, she understood.

"Let us return home," Radha told her husband as darkness fell around them. "This city makes me uneasy."

"Tomorrow," Julian promised, equally glad to leave the

atmosphere of suppressed passions.

That night, Carolyn went to play on dead Lavinia's piano. "She knows that Julian was once mine, that I bore his child before she did. Her happiness cannot be perfect now."

Trevor Barclay came to the dark room where she sat plucking out wild tunes. "You tried to destroy their harmony ... but you did not succeed," he said harshly. "Theirs is a stronger bond."

Catherine Latimer joined her sister, Isabel, in Lucknow and suggested that they visit Kanpur. "But why Kanpur?" Isabel asked. "We must return to Delhi."

"I wish to meet Dhondu Pant, or Nana Saheb as he has styled himself. I hear he is fascinating," Catherine replied with a strange look in her eyes.

They found Kanpur no different from Meerut or Lahore; there was the same regulated social hierarchy, and procedures, the dull and interminable formal dinners, the evening parade of carriages in the Mall.

The collector and magistrate came in their buggies preceded by Indian troopers with two armed sepoys behind. The chaplain followed in his smart carriage, with liveried servants. At a smart pace behind him came the doctor who tried to forget what medicine he had learned at Glasgow but suggested drastic remedies for trifles. The drive would end at the Bandstand, where a medley of Scottish airs and Neapolitan melodies vibrated in the cool, crisp air. As the north Indian winter darkness fell with a shower of brilliant stars, the European populace gathered at the Assembly Rooms, an imposing building with Romanesque facades and Doric columns.

"It is so tedious," Catherine protested to Isabel. "I sometimes think I am back in Bath, except for the dark servants. Really dear, I do think Stephen should not bring us here to be ogled by florid, heated men and their silly women!"

"But everyone comes to the Assembly Rooms, Kitty!" Isabel

exclaimed. "They are the best in north India!"

"Fiddlesticks!" Catherine retorted, her eyes narrowing. "I came here to meet Nana Saheb. Ask Stephen to procure an invitation!"

Isabel fanned her face nervously. "Very well ... but Kitty... do not ... that is to say ..."

The blue-green eyes narrowed even more. "Isabel, you need not come, you know. I can go alone. I want to meet this son of the Peshwa."

"Of course we will come! It would be ... improper for you to go alone ... Colonel Barclay knows Nana Saheb ... they once played billiards together."

Catherine laughed in pure amusement. "Darling Isabel, you are still so innocent! I love going alone to meet interesting men!"

A swift flush stained Isabel's milky skin. "I am not innocent, Kitty. I am ... afraid of your ... restlessness."

Catherine laughed harshly. "Call it promiscuity, darling. And don't be anxious for me, child. I am happiest when I have a man afire with desire for me ..."

Isabel closed her silk fan with a snap and glanced coldly at her sister. "That will do, Kitty," she retorted softly. "I shall not listen to this anymore. I do believe you enjoy debasing yourself!"

Nana Saheb was delighted by Mrs. Catherine Latimer. A connoisseur of women, this adopted son of the last Peshwa and titular head of the phantom Maratha Confederacy assessed Catherine. "A patrician whore," he thought to himself as he bent slightly to kiss her hand. "But she, unlike the other firingi women, does not crave for gifts." He had just parted with a shawl to one lady, a bolt of silk to another, a diamond-studded bracelet to a third. Their husbands had grinned, delighted by the gifts.

"Charmed, Mrs. Latimer," Nana Saheb murmured, as Catherine scrutinised him with an enigmatic smile. He gazed into the blue-green eyes and saw the rage for life in them. The prince drew back, uneasy. It was easier to deal with the silly flirts. "This one," he mused, "is dangerous. This one likes to subjugate her victims!"

Nevertheless, he could not refuse Mrs. Latimer's request to be shown around the palace, where valuable Meissen china, Chinese jade and ormolu clocks jostled for place with Lucknow silver and Jaipur enamel. Catherine's practised eye took in the treasures, lingering, in turn, on a translucent jade bowl, an exquisitely painted, gold-framed miniature and a silver statue of Lord Nataraj. The Peshwa saw her gaze and smiled sardonically.

"You favour my humble trinkets, Madam?" he asked, the dark eyes full of mischief. The firingi women he had known were as bold as the girls of Chandni Chowk in Delhi. "May I offer you a memento?"

"Later ... when you are ... pleased," Catherine replied, her green eyes narrowed like a feline stalking its prey. "But let us see your palace first."

They drifted through the congerie of halls and rooms furnished in western style, where damask and plush, satin, wood and marble lent a subdued opulence. Catherine stopped at a bend in the palace corridor. "And there, Your Highness? What lies beyond those latticed walls?" she asked, pointing to the zenana with a thin hand.

"My inner apartments, Madam ... and my own world." Nana Saheb replied in a strange voice. Catherine looked up at him, startled.

"Does that mean we ... your British friends, are not part of your own world?"

The dark eyes were opaque now. "Can you, a race of intruders, ever be part of our world, Madam?" he asked sombrely. "We meet by mutual need ... but not by mutual inclination."

"I thought you welcomed your British guests very cordially," Catherine replied with a frown.

Nana Saheb shrugged his shoulders. "It amuses me to hear their compliments and fawning remarks. It amuses me to lend them my carriages, and make gifts of jewels to their women. Apparently, great wealth can condone the position of an inferior race," he said in sarcasm.

Catherine's cheeks were delicately tinted now. She wondered if he sought to insult her. "You are a prince," she said in her low, husky voice. "Who would dare to be condescending to you?"

Nana Saheb's lips tightened and Catherine saw his pale, jewelled hand clench into a ball. "I am more than a prince! My adoptive father, the last Peshwa, Balaji Rao, was a king! His territory was equal once to Belgium or Italy. But your government has sought to deny me the title of Peshwa or the pension due to a Peshwa's son. Why? Because by obliterating the symbol of Maratha kingship, the British seek to extinguish the last flicker of Maratha resistance!" He paused and stared out into the starlit, velvet darkness of a January night. "But perhaps it will be the last flicker that will ignite a conflagration," he added softly.

Catherine shivered, with the sudden realisation that this man was not a mere entertainer or hedonist. She felt the vibrations of his rage and ambition. It made her quiver with a strange anticipation of desire. Nana Saheb felt her throb of excitement flow towards him. He stared at her through half-closed eyes, which moved slowly over her white neck, the full breasts which, taut with desire, trembled beneath the low neckline, and the red, ripe mouth that had recently been bruised by a lover's rough kisses. Then his cold eyes met the fiery challenge in hers.

"Come," he said gruffly. "I will take you to my other world."

Isabel waited in the reception hall below, restless and anxious, while Stephen chatted with other guests, drinking vintage champagne. She listened to the hushed, excited chatter of the women, the raucous laughter of men and wished she had never come to meet this strange prince, who emanated a sense of power and silent antagonism. She was no longer embarrassed by Kitty's extravagance; she was afraid for her sister.

A man stood for a moment at the head of the stairs, watching Isabel. As if aware of his presence, she turned and saw Dilip Chowdhury. The sight of a familiar face made her move towards him until she saw a change in him. Shorn of western attire, Dilip looked different but it was the expression of his face that was alien. Slowly, he came down, a taut, austere figure in a white dhoti and kurta, and made his way towards her.

"Isabel," he asked gravely. "What are you doing here?"

Isabel's smile was tremulous. "Visiting, with Kitty." She paused and asked, "What are you doing here, Dilip?"

Dilip considered the matter as his gaze rested on her flushed cheeks and the auburn curls framing her face. Once, in his boyhood, he had fancied little Isabel. The thought made him smile now; the bonds of Ruthven, Chowdhury & Co., had ceased to bind them together.

"I, too, am visiting, Isabel."

"With ... Nana Saheb?" she asked timidly.

"Yes."

Isabel's fan fluttered in her hand. "You ... do not ... belong in this milieu."

"I belong here more than in Ruthven House," he replied grimly.

Isabel's colour heightened. "That is an unfair remark," she retorted in a quivering voice. "You are like a ... son of the house... as your sister is a daughter of the house."

Dilip shook his head. "My sister's presence is tolerated ... and my presence is welcomed on condition of obedience." He looked at the cluster of guests enjoying the Nana's promised fare of strawberries and peaches.

"Fancy, in winter!" observed a brick-faced Englishwoman.

"Well, I never!" responded another incoherently, mouth full of the delectable berries.

"These people, dear Isabel," Dilip said quietly, "are intruders here. We suffer them because we ... have not yet found a means of resistance. But one day we shall ... in the person of a great leader."

"What ... will happen to us then?" Isabel asked, bewildered by the distance between herself and the man she had regarded from infancy as a friend. "Will you ... drive us away?"

Dilip lifted his hand to touch hers, briefly. "When and if that day comes, little Isabel, I will ... be there to help," he said in a voice of such anguish that it brought tears to her eyes.

A hush fell upon the vast reception hall and vestibules as Nana Saheb, taut but composed, appeared at the head of the grand, gilded staircase with a pale and perturbed Catherine Latimer by his side. Isabel noticed that an exquisite jewel-encrusted locket was now on her bosom. She stared at the pair so intently that reaching her sister's side, Catherine whispered harshly. "Isabel! What on earth is the matter with you?"

Nana Saheb regarded the white-faced younger woman with an enigmatic smile. "I hope to make your acquaintance tomorrow if you will accompany your sister to dinner. A diva from Milan will sing and there will be dancing, of course. And for your scholar-husband, I have a rare manuscript ..." His words were checked by Isabel's anguished expression. "Madam?" he asked, now disturbed by his lovely guest.

"When ... the time comes ... Your Highness," Isabel whispered, "I trust you will be merciful?"

"Isabel!" Catherine hissed, but Nana Saheb's unwavering eyes were on the trembling woman, as if in some point, their future had already met in the present.

"Who knows, when our paths will cross, Mrs. Reynolds. But if they do ... I will remember you and Mrs. Latimer."

Nana Saheb glanced questioningly at Dilip as Isabel stifled a cry and fled to the security of her husband's presence.

Isabel and Stephen returned to Delhi, to their house of many gables where the terrace sloped down to the silvery sands of the river Jamuna. Here, Stephen Reynolds taught at a college, while Isabel set about to decorate her new home. Catherine was a frequent visitor; in fact, she was happy to escape to Delhi from Lahore, where Colonel Jeremy Latimer was now posted. In Delhi, Catherine found ready admirers with whom she caroused under the stars near the Kutub Minar or had moonlit picnics near the Taj Mahal in Agra. Sophisticated and sociable, Catherine also made friends with the Chief Commissioner of Delhi, Sir Theophilus Metcalfe and his daughter Emily. Catherine's daughter by Courtney was now a pretty girl of sixteen who found Emily agreeable and the aide de camp, Richard Lawrence, even more so.

In the Easter of 1857, Jeremy Latimer came to Delhi to see

his wife. He called on Metcalfe, accompanied by Catherine, Isabel, and Stephen Reynolds.

Stephen hesitated before speaking. "There is unrest, Sir, in the cantonment towns, and a growing dissatisfaction among the sepoys. As it is, they have been fuming over the stoppage of double batta on the Sindh, Burma and Afghan campaigns. Many of them have found it difficult to return to their homes and villages after crossing mleccha or alien territories."

Latimer had been listening with barely concealed impatience. "Soldiers must go where they are sent!" he snapped before Metcalfe could speak.

"Not when they are assured otherwise," Stephen retorted.

Latimer's pale eyes glittered. "Assurance, Stephen?" he asked in evident excitement. "With what insolence do the natives ask for assurance? Is it not enough that we pay them for their services, such as they are?"

A hush fell over the lamplit drawing room of Metcalfe House as the guests laid down their cups and ceased individual conversations to listen to the two officers with utmost interest. Only Sir Theophilus seemed distressed by the verbal duel. Isabel Reynolds tried to catch her husband's eye but to no avail. She sat stiff and silent before an untouched plate. Catherine Latimer, however, seemed amused by the altercation.

"The government, Colonel Latimer," Stephen replied, "pays the sepoys for their services; the services which have helped us to win vast territories in India — their territories, in fact. The sepoys do not fight for us for love. They are mercenaries. As long as we keep our word, they will continue to serve us well. We can claim no more and offer no less."

Sir Theophilus Metcalfe interceded before the anticipated outburst. "Mr. Reynolds is right, of course. Our officers must display proper discipline in order to command the respect of those serving under them."

He glanced around the gleaming table, at the opulently dressed women and men who were so certain of their positions and destinies.

"Our officers and even soldiers have become accustomed to extravagant lifestyles and luxuries, which cannot be supported by their pay. They are often in debt to moneylenders or their own havaldars. Worse still, I have known cases where British officers have preferred to forget their debts and punished their subordinates for reminding them."

"Surely not!" a guest protested. "No British officer would stoop to such self-abasement!"

Sir Theophilus gave the prosperous merchant a cool, level glance. "Indeed they do." He paused. "Perhaps this is a residue of the older times and traditions when British and Indian officers and soldiers enjoyed a certain camaraderie and mutual respect. But when the British can no longer treat his sepoy as a friend, he should at least maintain the dignity of distance."

Spring ended early in 1857. The jacarandas bloomed along with mango blossoms under pale, windy skies. A hidden turmoil simmered in Ruthven House at Calcutta. Lady Eleanor, now aged sixty-five, was aware of the fact that her husband and son spoke softly and broke off when she or Radha entered.

"What is the matter?" she asked the two men sharply at dinner one night.

Julian hesitated, glancing at his mother, silver-haired and stately, and at his lovely young wife. "There has been trouble nearby. The sepoys have become restive upon hearing about the beef-fat being used for cartridges of the new Enfield rifles. The army has withdrawn the order and will take back the cartridges. But a feeling is gaining ground that the British government is determined to break faith with the sepoys and officers. Firstly, the breaking of word regarding compensatory allowance for serving beyond present boundaries, then Dalhousie's coercive measures to send soldiers to Burma and now this affront to their caste and religion. Despite General Hearsey's assurance that those cartridges will not have to be used, the damage has been done." He lowered his voice. "There is unrest, nocturnal meetings, masked men moving from hut to hut and burning arrows being aimed at thatched roofs of officers' bungalows ..."

"There is something else," Lade Eleanor said gravely. "Tell me!"

Julian glanced at his mother and said, "Very well, I shall tell you. There has been trouble with the 34th Native Infantry at Berhampore. A sepoy called Mangal Pandey tried to kill a British officer. General Hearsey ordered him to be hanged. But the smouldering resentment has not disappeared with Pandey. These mysterious fires in barracks, storehouses and telegraph offices are continuing and enigmatic messages are being communicated through chapathis. The disbanded soldiers of the 34th Native Infantry are back in Oudh, telling their tale of woe ... and relating the faithlessness of the British. There has been trouble in Meerut with the 3rd Native Light Cavalry. The soldiers refused to use the cartridges and eighty-five of them have been court-martialled and sentenced to imprisonment. General Hweit has remitted the sentence but ... I am afraid."

An air of deceptive calm hung over the Bengal Presidency in April 1857. Julian Ruthven felt the vibrations of this lull as one hears the rumble of a distant drum but he was reluctant to acknowledge the implications. Before leaving for headquarters, he and Radha went to visit the Chowdhurys. They talked about the disbandment of the 34th Native Artillery, which was intended to discourage other regiments which nursed plans of mutiny.

Dilip regarded his British brother-in-law with a strange smile. "It is not a mutiny when a people rise against their oppressors. It is a rebellion — a revolution ... like that of France in 1789 and England in 1642."

The punkah-bearers slowed their movements. The attendants paused in their serving of sherbets.

"My dear Dilip," Julian said evenly, "when soldiers revolt, it is a mutiny — pure and simple. When a people rise, it is revolution. No people, as such, have risen. Mangal Pandey and his comrades were soldiers."

"It will be a rebellion," Dilip murmured, staring at the stark summer landscape outside.

Julian looked at Dilip with concern. "Take care that you are not involved. It would be a pity if the efforts of your family over a century ... were to be destroyed." He paused. "I would hate to take action against ... a kinsman."

Dilip raised his eyebrows. "Kinsman, Julian? How can a ruler and ruled be kinsmen?"

No one spoke. The punkah-bearers flapped the huge peacock fans. Radha glanced in concern at her husband and brother and then lifted her eyes to the sky in silent prayer.

Julian Ruthven looked at his friend with evident distress. "What you say before me will not endanger you. But take care how you express yourself before others ... who can harm." He paused. "The price of rebellion, Dilip, is retribution ... to see one's home burnt, one's village razed."

"Are there no laws then for the ruled? Or does the Pax Britannica stop at Garden Reach?" Dilip sighed and shook his head. "It has all been a mirage, Julian, and a myth; the myth of British liberalism and justice. But those myths have taken root in our hearts. How will you pluck them out?"

Brajesh experienced a palpable pain, as if Dilip's words had brought to the surface a thought that had troubled him for long. But he could not, dared not, acknowledge it even to himself. "Would you advocate a return to the chaos and violence that India experienced before British rule, when every raja was at the other's throat, leaving the frontiers unprotected for wild hordes to loot and rape this country? Is that what you want? Do you know what those six centuries of violence did to India? And you want now to fight under the symbol of a decadent old man, whose only claim to rule is that a few drops of Akbar's blood flows in his veins — assuming of course that in the debauchery and intrigues of the court, the royal women remained chaste!"

"Bahadur Shah is a mere symbol," Dilip replied. "There are others to lead."

Julian felt his patience snapping. "If you join the rebels, Dilip, I will have no choice but to place you under arrest. No bond of family loyalty or friendship will deter me. Do you understand?"

Dilip nodded with a bitter smile. "Oh yes, I understand you clearly, my friend. It is indeed your duty to arrest me since it is you who introduced me to the 'liberty' of John Stuart Mill, to the writings of Mazzini and the liberalism of Europe which Europe applies only to itself." He paused. "Let me tell you also, Julian, that if I find you on the opposite side, I will give you no quarter."

Radha left the room and stood on the terrace, which had been her favourite retreat in childhood. Her gaze travelled with the swirling, rustling leaves to the river where Julian had declared his love for her.

"Had it not happened," Radha thought. "If only we were all free and unfettered by those warring loyalties!" She remained on the terrace, filled with a nameless dread.

Feeling a hand on her shoulder, Radha turned to find Eric Blair beside her. "Your father is not to be disturbed. He is not well. If he is uncomfortable, give him the medicine I've left on the table." Eric Blair attended to the zamindar whenever he came to Calcutta.

Radha nodded, trying to fight her distress before this calm, compassionate man who had become worn out by the years of hardship in service of the poor of India. "Dr. Blair," she murmured in a hoarse voice, "I am so miserable! What can I do to stop this bitterness between us?"

Eric Blair sighed. "If I only knew, my dear! If only I knew! It seems as if people have gone mad. Heaven knows there's enough suffering in this country without calling out for more!" He paused to glance at Radha's bent head. "Follow your heart, child. Nothing can guide you better!"

"My heart?" Radha cried. "But it is breaking in half!"

Charles and Eleanor Ruthven came later that day to visit Brajesh Chowdhury. Each pretended it was a temporary au revoir, but each was aware of impending turmoil. They had been close friends for forty years. They had had a partnership in trade, and their blood had mingled in the children of Julian and Radha. It was as if the British and Indian had almost become one ... and yet a storm was gathering momentum, threatening to destroy their world of comradeship.

"Forty years, Charles, and yet it seems but yesterday that we met to discuss the unity of the universe. And between us, we reconciled many disparate forces. Am I being unduly proud of our achievements?"

"No, Brajesh," the Englishman answered, gazing with full eyes at the Bengali aristocrat. "We brought many ideas and people together. We have ... yes, it is boastful of me to say it, but we have created an age."

"Will it be destroyed?" Brajesh asked sombrely.

"No, I do not think the spirit of an age can be destroyed." He paused. "Come to England with us, Brajesh. The sea air will do you good."

The zamindar's eyes regarded his friends. "Why, Charles? Afraid that I will be caught in what comes after? That you will not see me again?"

Charles Ruthven got up abruptly and went to embrace Brajesh. "Dearest friend, we will meet once more, here or there. We cannot be apart for long."

The two men sat in silence. The time to say good-bye had come.

The scarlet gulmohur blossoms were vivid against the black clouds as the Ruthven's bajra waited to take the four Ruthvens down the river to meet the P & O Liner anchored downstream. Reluctantly, Julian had agreed to let his parents take Marcus and Rowena with them to England. "Let the children not be caught in a turmoil between their two peoples," Lady Eleanor had entreated Julian and Radha. A dark April storm was brewing in the Bay of Bengal, ready to break the sultry heat of the Bengal summer.

Heavy, ripening mangoes were suspended from lowering branches, their fragrance sweetening the hot, inert air. Jasmines grew in profusion in the Ruthven villa at Garden Reach. Lady Eleanor stood gazing around her in anguish. Charles Ruthven walked slowly around, looking at every detail of the old villa and its grounds, as if he would never see them again. Radha embraced her children, again and again, in such evident agony that looking at her, Julian almost changed his mind. But the bajra pilot was growing restless. "Ruthven Saheb, the storm comes nearer," he cried. "Let me get the passengers to the big ship before that!"

Radha stood motionless, transfixed by those words. Lady Eleanor and Charles Ruthven took a tearful leave of her. Rowena, heedless of what was happening, happily kissed her mother and joyfully entered the bajra. Only Marcus stood aside quietly. "Come soon, Mama," he said softly, as Radha pressed him close, dry-eyed, her voice choked. They were like that for a long moment until Julian gently guided Marcus to the waiting barge. It set off with the cry of oarsmen.

Radha walked along the grassy slope, keeping pace with the slow flowing barge, as thunder growled and lightning flashed through the lowering clouds. Then as a few drops fell, she raised the anchal, the end of her sari, over her head. Marcus stared at her, until the image of a beautiful, veiled woman, under the gulmohurs, by the eternal river, was seared forever in his mind.

Eleanor took his hand and remembered a little boy just like him, whom she had lost to the river. "Jamie," she whispered, "Good-bye once more."

31

Mutiny

Catherine awoke, heavy headed after the champagne she had drunk at Metcalfe House. The hot May morning did nothing to soften her headache. "Rosie!" she called to the ayah. "Bathe me!"

Rosie, a woman from the Himalayan foothills, was in actuality, named Rati. She was a pious Hindu woman, but if the Colonel-Madame insisted on calling her Rosie, she could do nothing but respond. Slant-eyed Rati brought in two drums of cold water and a bowl of rose petals, which were thrown into the stone tub along with the water. It was Rati's task to soap and sponge the Colonel's Memsaheb while her brother, Rang Bahadur, poured clean pitchers of Jamuna water over the lady. Catherine enjoyed seeing the young man's face, taut with craving as he poured water on her. "If Jeremy could only see his sepoy serving me!" Catherine chuckled to herself. She smiled and handed a towel to Rang Bahadur, whose next duty was to rub the lady down. "One day," Catherine mused wistfully, "he will gather enough courage to violate me. But until then I must be content with his touch."

Rati scolded her mistress often. "One day, Memsaheb, you will be ashamed of yourself — when your son learns of your ways," she said. But Catherine always laughed. "Frigid old woman," she teased the ayah. "Your brother is also made of ice."

Rati shook her head. There was no point telling the lady-Saheb that her brother copulated with two wives but was too terrified of the colonel to even glance at the white lady.

"Where is Bahadur?" Catherine now asked, as Rati prepared her bath that hot May morning.

"He has gone to the lines. There is talk of unrest there," Rati said absently.

"They do love to gossip, these sepoys! He ought to be here, serving me!" Catherine snapped, missing the sight of the virile, young man. "Hurry up and bathe me, Rosie," she said impatiently. "I have a guest coming."

"In this heat?" Rati snapped back.

Catherine chuckled. "Why not? We do not intend to dress for the occasion!"

The door opened as Isabel Reynolds came in, cool and elegant in a pale green muslin dress, with scalloped lace neckline and sleeves, her auburn hair tied by a velvet ribbon as green as her eyes. "Kitty, do come to church with me," she said in some agitation.

"I had enough of the pulpit yesterday," the elder sister retorted. "I do not need to hear a sermon today ... even if I sinned last night."

Isabel sighed. "Very well. Deirdre and I will go then. We shall be back soon. Do be ready before breakfast, Kitty."

Aunt and niece walked leisurely under the shades of their silk parasols while two servants, Dhulan Singh and Abdul Rahim, walked behind, armed as per their Saheb's instructions. "Why are we going today, Aunt Isabel?" sixteen-year-old Deirdre asked, striding ahead at times, her white organza dress billowing around her.

Isabel glanced at her niece, already as tall as her mother, with the fine-featured beauty of the Courtneys and the vigour of the Ruthvens. The girl's red-gold hair glistened under the harsh sun and the green eyes were filled with laughter.

"I feel ... uneasy, Deirdre dear. I keep having dreams of your uncle Julian wading in blood and of you ..." Isabel stopped short.

"And of me ...? Deirdre asked, frowning. "What about me?"

Isabel tried to smile. "I dream of you, darling, in white satin and lace, being led to the altar by Richard Lawrence."

Dierdre laughed. "Splendid, Aunt Isabel! I do hope it happens thus." Tears filled Isabel's eyes. "I hope it does, my child," she whispered.

Deirdre clutched Isabel's arm. "Auntie, let's go back. You are in no condition to walk. Come, let us go home! Mummy did say you have become melancholy since the baby began."

Isabel shook her head. "No dear, I am all right. It's the heat, I expect. We will feel better inside the church."

St. James's church was a baroque edifice built by Colonel James Skinner of the Light Horse, to commemorate his recovery after a battle. Its cool sepulchral gloom was welcome after the blazing sunlight.

They sat at the front, as the church was deserted, except for a few worshippers whose Sunday devotions had spilled into Monday. No sooner had they sat when a muffled roar reached them. Startled, Isabel glanced at Deirdre. "What is that?" she asked. Deirdre rose from the pew. "Let me have a look. Sounds like a commotion." Isabel clutched her niece's arm, fighting the waves of terror that washed over her. "Dierdre, let us go ... by that little door to the woods beyond ..." The young girl shook free the hand. "Shan't be a moment ... wait here, Auntie."

Isabel stared at the ivory crucifix, and the altar where yesterday's flowers were wilting in the heat. With a piercing shock, she realised after a while that it was this church, this scene, that she had seen in her terrifying dreams. "No!" she cried as she rose, trembling all over. Tottering from dizziness and an inexplicable terror, Isabel ran down the aisle. Before she reached the door, her servant, Dhulan Singh, ran in and clutched her. Stunned, she opened her mouth to scream but was prevented from doing so by his hand on her mouth. Her eyes, however, remained open and she saw a group of men set fire to buildings in the distance, their shouts drowned by the rattle of gunfire and the ragged cries of people in pain.

And she closed her eyes as she saw a sepoy brandish his sword over an Indian doctor's head. She struggled as the orderly dragged her away towards the belfry door. Tearing herself free, her green eyes blazing, Isabel cried, "How dare you do this to me!"

Singh sighed jerkily. "Memsaheb," he whispered hoarsely, "please come with me. I cannot let you go there ... the mutineers are ... killing Christians and Europeans."

Isabel stared at the orderly. "My niece ... my Deirdre ... I must call her!" She made a move to run but he held her in a tight grip. "No Memsaheb, you cannot go there now... the Missy Saheb is... already dead."

"Dead?" Isabel asked hoarsely, incredulously.

Dhulan Singh nodded and caught her as she fell into a heap of pale green muslin on the cool stone floor. Slowly, he picked her up and carrying the inert body, hid in the woods beside the church, waiting for the screams and shouts to cease. He stared at the woman lying on the hot, dusty ground, her dress stained and hair darkened by the grey dust. "God," he said brokenly, "how will I answer my Saheb if his lady is murdered here? Yet, how will I escape with her?"

A crackle of dry twigs caused him to draw up his rifle when he saw Abdul Rahim standing before him, his sword as bloodstained as his clothes. In his other hand he held aloft a severed, turbanned head. "Missy Saheb's murderer," he muttered.

Singh turned away, shuddering. "Let us get my lady home, Abdul," he said dully.

"After dusk. The Meerut mutineers crossed the Jamuna and arrived in Delhi this morning. Some have gone to Red Fort to order the Emperor to declare war against the Company Raj. Others have begun to ransack the houses of the Europeans at Darya Ganj and nearabouts. Memsaheb must not be seen. They will kill her," Rahim spoke grimly.

Singh listened in great agitation. They sat down, beside their lady-Saheb, carefully laying her hat beneath her head of copper ringlets and wondering how they would escape the frenzied mob from Meerut. They waited in anguished dread for her to regain consciousness. At dusk, Isabel stirred and opened her eyes. "Water," she whispered.

"We must go home, Madam Saheb. Can you walk? It is only a short distance."

Between the two soldiers, a dazed Isabel was escorted under cover of darkness, through deserted paths, to the house of Professor Stephen Reynolds. At the gate, the two servants and the woman stood still with shock. The rambling bungalow on the river bank had been burnt, and ransacked. The well-laid flower beds had been trampled upon, the grass plucked out. Furniture and pictures, clocks and carpets were littered around.

"My God!" Isabel whispered brokenly. "What have you done, my God?"

Rahim turned to Singh. "Stand there, by the shadow of the trees while I go inside and see ..."

Isabel tore herself free from her guardians and ran frenziedly towards the house, tripping and stumbling. "Kitty!" she screamed. "Where are you?" She stopped short, seeing the crouched figure of Rati in the vestibule. The slight figure rose, trembling, and came towards Isabel who stood before her, dusty and dishevelled. The two servants stood behind her, motionless.

"Rati, my dear, where is my sister and the children? Where are the other servants?" she asked in panic.

Rati shook her head and covered her face with the anchal of her sari. Isabel gripped her shoulders and said, "Tell me, for heaven's sake!"

"The Meerut sepoys came here soon after you and Deirdre Missy left for church. Kitty Memsaheb was still in her bath when ... they... violated her ..." Rati's voice broke.

Isabel shook her violently. "And then? Tell me!" she cried.

"Memsaheb lay there ... until my brother Bahadur and a few of our sepoys burst in and fired on them ... killed three, my brother did, and sent them packing ... but the ... two children... could not be saved."

Now Isabel clutched the woman for support as waves of dizziness washed over her. Sensing Isabel's condition, Rati dragged her to the couch and made her lie down, then turned to the two servants. "We must get away soon. The mutineers will return at dawn again. The Emperor is keeping them busy at the moment. Bahadur has taken Kitty Memsaheb to the woods nearby. We must procure a boat and leave by the river while it is dark." She paused and said with a sob, "Bury Master Maurice and Missy Harriet ... in the garden ... under the jacaranda tree where they played."

"What will happen when Stephen returns from Lucknow?" Isabel cried. "What will he find? No, I will stay and wait for him."

"No Memsaheb, we must go," Dhulan Singh replied. Isabel rose, trembling but resolute. She assisted Rati in packing a few clothes and hats, a sack of rice and potatoes, and a small chest of jewels from Kitty's cupboard. The servants gathered as much ammunition as they could carry. Together, they stole out of the burnt-out house towards the woods. The hot May night was ablaze with stars, whose glow illumined the unbeaten path through the clusters of trees. Leaves rustled continuously as animals moved for cover and birds fluttered restively from one branch to another, as if they too were aware of an impending conflagration. From a distance came the glow of flames, the muffled roar of the rebels near the Imperial Palace at Red Fort and the crackle of fire as houses of Europeans and Christians in Darya Ganj burned.

At last, Isabel and her escorts reached the spot where Rang Bahadur sat, rifle loaded, with Catherine next to him. She did not speak or move as Isabel knelt by her and pressed that red-golden head to her anguished heart. "Kitty," Isabel whispered, but Catherine did not respond. She lay impassively in her younger sister's embrace, bereft, it seemed, of life itself. Rang Bahadur took Isabel aside and explained that Memsaheb was behosh, unconscious. The murder of her children had affected her thus. "She has not spoken ... since the Master-baba screamed."

Isabel turned her face and wept silently. It would not be possible to tell Catherine about Deirdre, whose mutilated body was lying in the compound of St. James's church nearby. "Can you ... bury my niece?" Isabel suddenly asked Singh, who nodded. "It has been done, Memsaheb. I left word then itself to one of my comrades to ... bury Missy Saheb with her brother and sister ... under their jacaranda tree. They will do it in cover of darkness." Singh offered her his canteen of water. "Now, Memsaheb, we must go."

The party of three retainers and three women stumbled across the woods until they came to the bank of the river Jamuna, where Rang Bahadur's comrade had kept the Reynolds' sailboat in readiness on the dark, smooth waters.

The sailboat sailed briskly down the Jamuna as the three sepoys rowed and Rati joined her palms in prayer. Catherine sat glassy eyed, petrified by an insupportable grief while Isabel gazed tearfully at the banks, peering into the starlit night to try and get one last glimpse of her house by the river, where the dhobi-woman used to wash clothes on stones and sing: "What a sweet vision did I see by Jamuna's bank." Isabel sobbed brokenly as she remembered.

The imperial city stood silhouetted in grey against the paling pink sky, its turrets and towers luminous in the first light, and the row of still burning fires. The mutineers had stormed the precincts of the palace, where princes and British agents had once genuflected before the Emperor of India. Now that hapless old man, with his empty title and purse, had been forced to sanction the spreading insurrection.

The journey from Delhi to Mathura took two days on the boat. The fugitives stopped at night to boil rice and drink their fill of the river water. Isabel bathed and washed her clothes, while Rati sat nearby as chaperone but Catherine refused to move from the wooden bench on the boat. Her hair had become a mass of brittle tangles, her magnolia skin burnt like a lobster's scales. Rang Bahadur gazed at her with pity, begging her now to sleep, now to eat, but her blue-green eyes remained fixed in a glassy stare. At night, she slept, exhausted, groaning at times as if in pain. Isabel sat silently by her, remembering Kitty's wild, dissolute life, her indifference to the children and contempt for the life that could have been peaceful, if not happy. Could the grief for Richard Courtney have led her to such excesses? Now nothing remained of that passion; even Deirdre was dead.

"And I? What will I do with myself if anything happens to my Stephen? How will I bring up his child alone?" Isabel fought hard against panic and despair. "I will survive," she promised herself, "I will not die!"

Mathura, the birthplace of Lord Krishna, was restive. News of the Delhi mutiny had reached the crowded city, where people were particularly restive about the tales they had heard about the sacrilegious cartridges. Here the fugitives alighted, and by selling the first instalment of Isabel's jewellery, procured a hackney carriage to take them northwards to Kanpur, a cantonment town with a large European colony. The journey took them days in the blazing heat of May, the servants and ladies crammed together in the box-like coach.

"I cannot bear it anymore," Isabel thought. "I will die." But Rati remained calm and concerned, feeding them with a mother's care and cradling them as they slept, leaning on her shoulders.

Then the white-walled city of Kanpur stood before them, like a haven of safety.

Kanpur was taut with tension, though no sign of disaffection was visible. However, General Sir Hugh Wheeler KCB, a veteran soldier of Indian battles, had been ordered to prepare accommodation of a European force and "to let it be known." The general was afraid of arousing the suspicion of the sepoys and of indirectly insulting them by undertaking such measures that questioned their loyalty. Hearing rumours of the move, the 2nd Cavalry became restive.

The Ruthven sisters arrived in the midst of this tension. The rest of the European population, anticipating a dreaded event, had already begun to engage boats as a preparation for departure. None of the ladies known to Isabel were thus willing to take responsibility for a pregnant woman and her obviously demented sister. Isabel went to Mr. Hillersden, the Resident Magistrate of Kanpur, who offered them a room at the Traveller's Bungalow, but advised them to move as trouble was expected. As they sat in the Bungalow, an Indian gentleman came with a message from "the Raja of Bithur".

Exhausted, hungry and suffering from a mild heat stroke, Isabel threw all caution to the winds and accepted the invitation of Nana Saheb. She did, however, send a note to Charles Hillersden, who readily agreed to the plan. "The Raja is a trusted friend," he wrote back. "I am contemplating taking his assistance to guard the treasury and, if necessary, to entrust the women to his care should the native troops rebel. You will be safe in his care."

Two carriages came to take the sisters and their attendants to the prince's palace set amidst gardens, not far from the broad Ganges. When he came to see them in their cool, well-appointed suite, he was shocked by Catherine's condition. Not a flicker of recognition lit her eyes as he bowed slightly in greeting. Isabel, six months pregnant, curtsied with difficulty, as she watched the Maratha prince stare sadly at the woman who had caroused with him in that now-far-away winter, six months ago. Drawing him aside, Isabel related the events that had occurred in Delhi and then burst into tears.

Nana Saheb gazed at Isabel, deeply troubled and unable to console, yet moved by the grief he saw in that lovely, pure face. "You must rest ... and then move to safety," he said grimly. "No harm shall come to you."

The sisters and their attendants recovered physically from the ordeal of their journey. Rati threw away Catherine's bloodstained clothes and bathed her body and hair, washing away the traces of that terrible morning. Mrs. Hillersden, the magistrate's wife, sent a few loose muslin gowns for the ladies to use. Isabel walked in the gardens, pensive but alert, fully aware of the growing tension in the city. She had felt it when she went to visit her friend, Carolyn Barclay. Nana Saheb sent 200 cavalry, 400 infantry, and two guns to guard the district treasury containing £100,000.

The sepoys waited, watchful and tense, while the British, too, waited for their revolt. Large bands of marauding Gujars had begun streaming in, ready to loot in the midst of a mutiny. The Entrenchment and Magazine, brick-built barracks, were ear-marked as protection in the face of trouble, making it clear to the sepoys that they were not trusted. Their resentment was heightened when a drunken officer fired at sepoys of the 2nd Cavalry. The officer was court-martialled but set free, "This is the injustice of the Saheb-logs," the sepoys muttered. "Had we Indians fired on Europeans, we would have been hanged."

In the meantime, the British troops of Her Majesty's 32nd Regiment were sent back to Lucknow, where too growing unrest was obvious. The sepoys mutinied there, the capital of Oudh, on 30th May, leaving Sir Hugh Wheeler feeling insecure. The British civilians departed once more for the safety of the Entrenchment, taking with them provisions for a month and rupees one hundred thousand from the treasury. The sepoys decided to rebel before British enforcements from Calcutta arrived. The 2nd Cavalry was joined by the 1st Infantry. In panic, General Wheeler ordered his batteries to fire upon the sepoy lines, whereupon other regiments too joined in the revolt.

Isabel paced the carpeted floor of her room, exchanging anxious glances with Rati. "What sort of prison have we entered?" she asked. "It is rumoured that Nana Saheb may join the mutineers. They have asked him to join their cause to retrieve the kingdom denied him by the British."

The frantic speculations ended at dusk when Nana Saheb came, dressed in the full regalia of the Peshwa's costume and carrying a long, curved sword. His dark, almond eyes rested briefly on Catherine sitting silently in a plush armchair, before he turned to Isabel standing at the door of the balcony, the topaz twilight blending with the copper hair gathered in a plait. Her thin face seemed even more ethereal than ever, her sea-coloured eyes fearless and lit by resolution.

"Mrs. Reynolds," he said, "the time has come for us to bid farewell. The pride and honour of my house demands that I join my compatriots in an attempt to free our country from foreign rule."

He paused, his brooding eyes directed once more at Catherine. "However, my ... esteem for you and your sister compels me to send you away from Kanpur before you are caught up in the violence which must follow."

Isabel regarded him in surprised silence for a while. "Then it is true? You are joining the mutineers?"

"Do not call them mutineers, Mrs. Reynolds. They are fighting for freedom — from foreign rule. There is no shame in that. Yes, we want to cleanse ourselves of the degradation of alien rule."

Isabel nodded. "Where will you send us?" she asked, her voice choked.

"To Allahabad — by boat. There, your escort will ensure your journey to Calcutta. Go home soon, Mrs. Reynolds. The rebellion against the British is spreading."

"Why are you so concerned for us, Your Highness?"

A strange smile lit his inscrutable face. "Perhaps there would have been no bitterness if all Englishmen and women were like you." He turned away abruptly, as if in pain. "Please be in readiness to leave within an hour, after darkness falls." He turned again to glance at Catherine and bow before Isabel.

Night fell, bringing only slight relief from the burning heat. Isabel and her party stood waiting at an antechamber below for their escort. As a shadow fell in the lamplight, Isabel stifled a cry of surprise. Standing before her was the tall, slim figure of Dilip Chowdhury in Moghul dress.

"Dilip!" she exclaimed. "It cannot be! You too cannot have joined ... the mutineers!"

"I have joined those who seek to free my country from the injustice and dishonour of foreign rule," Dilip replied sombrely.

"Dilip," Isabel said in considerable agitation, "do not join with those people. They are not of your kind ... you are like us!"

"They are more of my kind than you are, Isabel," Dilip replied grimly. "We have nothing to share."

Isabel shook her head. "That is not so! We share memories...

of growing up together ... of the same values ... the friendship of our fathers ... the marriage of your sister and my brother ... we are ..."

Dilip closed his eyes as if he wished to speak no more. Then he sighed deeply and said, "Let us go. The boat for you waits in readiness. I shall go down the river for a while with you ... and from Allahabad you can go to Calcutta."

At midnight, Dilip Chowdhury signalled the boatmen to start the hundred-mile journey down the Ganges towards Allahabad. He followed in a smaller boat, aloof and withdrawn as if some inexorable force was drawing him towards his destiny.

Julian Ruthven, meanwhile, was making every effort to treat the mutiny as a military matter with which the army should deal. Whenever any conversation arose among the district officers, Julian used all the authority of the district magistrate to quell all thoughts of retaliation.

"The sepoys have been disgruntled for some time," he said, "and our own officers have set poor examples of discipline and decorum when they opposed Bentinck's and Dalhousie's efforts to curtail their extravagance and expenditure. Boys from impecunious homes in England and Scotland came to India and began behaving like sultans, keeping countless servants, getting into debts and allowing bania moneylenders to pay for their escapades, while imposing rigorous discipline on the sepoys. Let the army, therefore, deal with the sepoys. We are not involved."

"Mutiny is illegal and has to be punished!" Colonel Thorpe declared. He commanded the local garrison.

"Certainly — in a military manner," Julian Ruthven retorted. "It is not as if there have been no mutinies in our own history. Did not the troops of King Charles I betray him so that he lost both his kingdom and his head?"

May passed; the scorching heat interspersed with the violent, cooling nor'westers and hailstorms that dislodged ripening mangoes from trees and brought back blades of green grass to the baked earth. The district was as watchful and alert as the rest of India, waiting for more news.

It came, in early June, first as a whisper and then like a scream of outrage. Julian could not believe the account of the Delhi and Kanpur massacres. "It cannot be!" he exclaimed, staring at Colonel Thorpe, who was preparing to leave for Lucknow, where British soldiers were urgently required.

"I am afraid it is so," the colonel replied grimly. "We have first-hand reports." He paused before continuing, "You must prepare yourself for a shock, Mr. Ruthven."

Julian clutched the arms of his chair as he heard Thorpe's low, grim voice. "What is it, Colonel?" he asked quietly.

Colonel Thorpe stared down at his large red hands. He had withheld the information for some time, in order to ascertain the truth, but now there was no doubt of its veracity. Professor Reynold's trusted servant had asked a British officer to inform Ruthven.

"Mrs. Reynold's bungalow in Delhi was set on fire on the morning of 11th May ... and ..."

"Isabel? Was she there?" Julian instinctively asked first about his favourite sister, then added, "And Kitty? What happened to them?"

Colonel Thorpe's brown eyes were solemn. "They ... were able to leave Delhi with the help of Professor Reynold's trusted servants."

Julian Ruthven loosened his grip on the chair arms, leaning back to release a long-held breath, but was surprised by Colonel Thorpe's unwavering, almost pitying gaze.

"Is ... there ... something else, Colonel?" Julian asked, almost inaudibly.

The colonel nodded, reluctantly. "Mrs. Latimer and Mrs. Reynolds left Delhi alone."

Julian Ruthven did not speak. His throat ached. The colonel went on, "Mrs Latimer's daughter was ... murdered by the Meerut mutineers."

Julian remained sitting. Before him wavered the picture of Deirdre; innocent and lovely, as eager for life as Kitty though with greater restraint. He felt a searing pain, touched with a growing fury.

"How ... has ... Kitty taken this, I wonder?" Julian said hoarsely.

Colonel Thorpe sighed. "I hope she is ... alive, Mr. Ruthven. You see, they left Delhi in the hope of finding security in ... Kanpur."

"Kanpur?" Ruthven cried. "But ... there has been a ... siege there!"

Colonel Thorpe nodded. "That is so. We are going to organise reinforcements to relieve the besieged people in the Entrenchment." He paused. "Will you join us, Mr. Ruthven?"

Julian Ruthven started. Colonel Thorpe regarded him with a silent challenge. "How can I? I am a magistrate, a civilian."

Colonel Thorpe rose, hat in hand. "That is for you to decide, Mr. Ruthven. Civilians have taken up arms in Kanpur. There is a dearth of British fighters. We are a force of 38,000 and they are 200,000. Most of the Bengal army is stationed in Punjab. There are hardly any Europeans between Calcutta and Meerut."

Julian Ruthven rose and handed the colonel his pistol, which reposed on the table. "I will consider your suggestion, Colonel," he said tersely and inclined his head to accept the colonel's salute. Then he sat at his desk in silence for a long time. He did not call for his horse that evening to return home but walked through the warm coral dusk, stopping now and then to gaze at the river where fragile fishing boats floated down towards the sea and where women drew water in brass pitchers while children frolicked in the cool water after the scorching day. "Everything goes on as before," he thought. "Nothing seems to change in this country. "Nothing seems to stir her from her colossal indifference. The pain and struggles of her people are so elemental that they have no fire left for other causes. Injustices and humiliations have been borne by them for centuries. They have lost the habit of protest. Then, why this upheaval? Surely it cannot be the work of the defenceless, humble people of India who pass from life to eternity without a cry? And yet ... I am expected to take up arms against these poor people ... for whose enlightenment my parents strove, for whose sake I have toiled ... How can I fight these people who are like my own?"

Resolutely, Julian walked towards the rise where his bungalow stood, surrounded by a cluster of forest trees. An empty swing hung down from a high branch, reminding him of Marcus and Rowena, who were in England now, and then of Kitty's daughter who had perished in the Delhi riots. No matter how he tried, their faces returned to torment him.

Radha watched her husband as she supervised the laying of tea in the garden, where a breeze had sprung up. She had noticed his abstraction lately and felt a veil fall between them. She had been trying to remove that constraint. Once, unable to sleep, Julian had walked out into the grounds, listening to the rustle of the coconut fronds; he had stared around the hot starlit darkness, at the river flowing in its milky path. Radha had joined him, afraid.

"What happened in Meerut," he had said, staring at the river, "has nothing to do with us. Do you understand, my love?"

"No," she had replied, miserably. "It has everything to do with us. We married because your family and mine were friends... but now, my people have called war on yours."

"No," he said with a strange intensity, "we married because we believe in the same things ... because I loved your people as well. The action of a few sepoys and rajas does not alter this. My ... attachment ... for you transcends all that."

"Julian!" she had cried, flinging her arms around him and uttering his name for the first time. "I am so afraid!"

Julian had drawn her close. "We must not be afraid. We must not let external events disrupt our happiness together! This upheaval will pass ... we will remain together. We must not lose our sweet world, nor forget our dreams for Marcus and Rowena."

Now, Radha knew that external events had caught up with them. Julian was more distracted today, and barely had the servants gone when he told her the news about Catherine and Isabel. Radha trembled as she put the tea-pot back on the table, and stared unseeingly at the jasmine bowl before her. Julian rose and wandered off to the riverside. Today, Radha did not join him, but remained sitting until the sky darkened and the first monsoon storm swept over the countryside. She knew then that the idyll was over.

They awaited news of the besieged at Kanpur with a heavy heart. While Radha prayed indiscriminately before both the crucifix in her husband's study and Lord Krishna in her puja-ghar, Julian went through the routine of his own work — hearing civil and criminal cases, granting land awards, inspecting irrigation channels, opening a telegraph office here, a dispensary there. The superintendent of police commented that "the district magistrate's indifference was shocking," but the district surgeon and district engineer agreed with the district magistrate that a military outburst was not a cause for reprisal against the hapless civilians on the other side.

Then, one day in July, news came. The besieged in Kanpur had been offered safe conduct by Nana Saheb. The fugitives were to be conveyed in boats down the Ganges to Allahabad, the sacred city of the Hindus, where the Ganges met the Jamuna. However, just as the boats got ready to leave, soldiers fired upon them, killing men, women and children on the burning waters.

Julian Ruthven returned home early, to the consternation of his wife. Grimly, he told her the news. "Kitty and Isabel must have perished in that massacre," he said quietly, though Radha could see the agony in his eyes as he turned and went over to the back veranda, where they normally watched peacocks parade at dusk, and nightingales settle on branches for their musical soirees. He spoke with his back to her. "I must join the Bengal Army. Reinforcements are needed at Lucknow and Allahabad."

Radha moved forward, clutching his arm, and forced him to face her. "You said you were not involved! That this was a military matter ... that ..." her voice broke.

He laid a hand on her shoulder. "So, I did, my love. But things have changed. You understand, don't you? I cannot remain detached when my sisters ... my flesh and blood ..." Now Julian's voice broke, "I must avenge their ... deaths."

Neither slept that night. They lay still and separate, listening to rains lashing the bamboo groves and mango trees and replenishing the river once more. Windows rattled in the other rooms but no one closed them. Julian got up and opening the balcony door, went out to stare at the deluge, remembering his sisters with fresh pain. Radha followed him, and stood there quietly until he turned and embraced her in anguish and despair.

"If you die, what will I do?" Radha asked. "I will die too. What will happen to our children? We cannot survive without you. Oh, my life and love, don't go! Revenge cannot bring back those ... who are gone. Think of the living, Julian!"

He released her abruptly. "Radha, sometimes we have to think of the dead ... to set their souls at rest."

Radha stared at him with a strange uneasiness, as if this wild-eyed man before her was not the calm and strong Julian Ruthven she had known all these years, the resplendent sun god of her dreams. "He has drifted away," she thought with sudden desolation. "I must leave leave now ... before our love dies."

Radha Ruthven felt that the world she had treasured had been destroyed in one night ... or had it been destroyed on the sacred river, where innocent blood had been spilt? Whatever it was, she no longer wanted to be a burden to Julian. "He must be free to return to his world, to his people ... and yes ... avenge the bloodshed of my people. Our life together, so sweet and perfect, is over."

Julian did not notice her stealthy preparations for departure, because he was living in an inner hell of his own doubts and dilemmas. When he returned home one evening a few days later, he knew at once that something had happened. Hesitantly, fearfully, the major domo gave him a sealed letter. It was from Radha.

"I am going so far that you will not find me. It is better this way. The fragile world we lived in has been splintered ... by an episode on the river at Kanpur ... that same river which has been the spring of our lives. You are free now, my dearest. Do what you must. Never cease to dream for Marcus and Rowena for they now have only you. As events are shaping, I would be a burden to them as well. One day, when the blood and tears are washed clean by this same river, remember me with love."

Julian Ruthven went into the empty bedchamber with leaden steps. He unlocked a cupboard and drew out a jewelled sword and gazed at it. Charles Edward Ruthven had used it at Waterloo and before him, Alexander Ruthven at Plassey, and even before that, James Ruthven at Culloden. "I thought I had laid aside this heirloom forever," Julian murmured hoarsely, "but fate has decreed it otherwise. I must unsheath it now — to raise it against those very people whom I sought to love ... to prove my loyalty to another people! It is like severing myself in two!"

32

Siege

"We will raze the rebel strongholds to the ground, and teach them the price of mutiny! And now, Colonel Barclay, commence disarming your soldiers!"

Colonel Trevor Barclay stared at the massive Irishman who sat on a charger, his granite face suffused with zeal. Then he looked around at the vast gathering of sepoys and officers in the Ambala Parade Ground, who heard the command with astonishment.

Trevor Barclay frowned. "Disarm my soldiers, Nicholson? On what grounds?"

"The grounds are evident — even to an idiot," Nicholson replied.

Barclay's jaws tightened; for a moment he contemplated flinging a glove in Nicholson's face. But there was too much to lose. "Pray enlighten me," he said quietly.

The sepoys watched uneasily as Nicholson rode slowly towards Barclay. "I should have thought it was quite obvious. These sepoys cannot be trusted."

"These men," Barclay replied tersely, "have fought shoulder to shoulder with us in the Afghan and Sikh wars — at the cost of their lives. They have served us loyally. Is this dishonourable disarming to be their reward?"

Nicholson's square face was a mask of fury. "Mercenaries do not need to be rewarded," he retorted.

"Then mercenaries cannot be accused of mutiny. They come and go as they like," Barclay replied.

Nicholson's face was suffused with blood. Barclay's calm, quiet air of assurance incensed the man of the hour. "Disarm your men — or I shall do it for you," he said through clenched teeth.

Colonel Simpson, a man grown old in the service of the British-Indian army moved close to Nicholson. "I plead for a reconsideration, General Nicholson," the old soldier cried, "I can answer for my men with my life."

A smile twisted Nicholson's face. "Your life cannot be worth much then," Nicholson said before turning to Barclay, "Disarm your men."

Colonel Barclay, sat as motionless as a Roman equestrian statue. Only his eyes moved from one sepoy to another, and they looked up at him with a mute plea. Then, in a hoarse voice, he gave the command: "Lay down your arms, my men!"

There was a long moment of stunned silence as sepoys and officers stared at each other in misery, remembering the campaigns in Kabul, Sindh and in their own homeland; of shared ordeals and triumphs, of camaraderie and obedience. General Nicholson watched them all, painfully aware that as great a soldier as he might be he would never command the hearts of his men. As the silence lengthened, however, Nicholson grew uneasy. The sepoys stared at the grim Irishman defiantly. Nicholson turned to Barclay, whose sombre face was lit briefly by a sardonic smile. "Afraid, General Nicholson?"

"Damn you, do something!" Nicholson muttered fiercely.

Barclay drew in a deep breath. Then swiftly, he drew out his pistol and held it up in the air for all to see. "Lay down your arms, my men, as I am doing!" he said, and flung first his pistol and then his rifle onto the ground before him. A long drawn out sigh rippled through the ranks of the sepoys — a sigh of despondency and resignation. Then one by one they began to fling their arms onto the ochre, sun-baked earth until they grew into a massive pile.

Barclay turned to John Nicholson. "Should Dost Mohammed sweep down from Kabul with his wild tribesmen, may you feel the same satisfaction. But remember only, that then these sepoys will not be available for bloodshedding and cannon-fodder!"

"We shall see," Nicholson retorted, tight lipped, but it was clear that the same fear haunted him as it did the other British soldiers in Punjab.

That night, while Nicholson read the Bible in his tent and vowed vengeance on the heathens, Trevor Barclay paced the dry, hard path in front of his tent, reflecting bitterly on the events which had brought dishonour to the 5th Cavalry, which he had loved to the exclusion of all things.

John Nicholson had been called by the commander-in-chief to relieve the beleaguered garrisons between Delhi and Patna where British authority had collapsed by July 1857. Punjab, itself, simmered with a latent violence and the dual danger of an Afghan attack or Sikh uprising. While officers like Barclay and Simpson counselled caution, Nicholson was determined to preclude rebellion by disarming Indian regiments, ignoring the resentment this would cause.

Sweeping across the vast valleys of the five rivers, John Nicholson seemed to the people of that land like a veritable horseman of the apocalypse, as he disbanded one suspected regiment after another, never pausing to fear or even consider the consequences of such drastic action.

"Abandon Peshawar if necessary," he told an exasperated Sir John Lawrence, "but we will not countenance a mutiny. We will deal separately with the Afghans too, should they decide to attack us from the north. But I think not. They have learnt to respect our strength after our last engagement with them. As for the Sikhs, they will not revolt; a restored Moghul empire will not be to their benefit. Memories of Emperor Aurangzeb and his treatment of the Sikh gurus is still fresh in their minds."

Indeed this was so. The Punjabi sepoys remained disciplined, not because they were more loyal to the British than were the sepoys of Delhi, Oudh and Kanpur but because three successive Sikh wars in a previous decade had left them bloodless and weary. Thus they accepted Nicholson's humiliating methods without protest, and formed part of the formidable column which moved south to relieve the siege of Delhi.

In September 1857, a combined assault of four columns arrived in Delhi. Brigadier-General Nicholson commanded the 75th Regiment, the 1st Bengal Fusiliers and the 2nd Punjab Infantry, planning to storm the breach near the Kashmir Bastion and escalade its face. The second column under Brigadier Jones consisted of the 8th Regiment, 2nd Bengal Fusiliers and 4th Sikh Infantry. The third column was commanded by Colonel Campbell and the fourth by Colonel Reid. Trevor Barclay was under Nicholson, with his own 2nd Punjab while Major Julian Ruthven marched in the Reserve Column under Brigadier Longfield.

Both sides waited restlessly throughout the warm, humid night, firing now, shelling again, and splitting the darkness with constant flashes. Heedless of this preparation for carnage, the birds in Kudsia Bagh, the palace of an imperial Moghul princess, kept up a steady twitter as rain fell intermittently and the fragrance of roses prevailed over the smell of sulphur. On a signal from an officer, the British opened fire just as the sun rose like a scarlet orb over the mossy tombs of the Bagh. Julian Ruthven watched in anguish as his men fell around him but he pushed relentlessly through the moat, firing with one hand as his other hand clawed over the wall until he was inside the Bagh. Running recklessly over the parapet, Julian stopped upon hearing an explosion. The Kashmiri Gate had been blown open. A sepoy, bruised and bleeding, tried to stop Julian and his men from advancing by firing. Julian closed his eyes and murmured, "Forgive me for slaying an injured man," and then shot the rebel soldier.

Nicholson's column moved relentlessly forward, capturing the Mori Bastion, the Kabul Gate and the Burn Bastion. There the British met the stoical determination of Indian sepoys, who were prepared to die rather than permit a British advance. Impatient at the halt of progress, John Nicholson arrived on the scene. "Forward!" he shouted to Major Ruthven. "Why have you stopped?"

Burnt by the sun, bruised by injuries, Julian glanced wildly around him in the twilight. "How to go forward ... we are surrounded!" he shouted. "My soldiers are falling like pins!"

"Let them! That is what soldiers are for!" Nicholson shouted in rage. "Follow me!"

As the young conqueror strode forward, an Indian officer rose from behind the rampart. His lean, patrician face was distorted by grief and rage. The two men stared at each other, remembering an episode that had occurred seven years ago, when John Nicholson had humiliated the officer's father, a patrician zamindar from Bengal.

"We meet again, Nicholson," the rebel officer cried over the roar of gunfire.

"My God!" Nicholson murmured, "protect me!"

The rebel officer who had followed the dreaded Nicholson for months, lifted his Enfield rifle to his shoulder and taking aim, fired directly ahead. John Nicholson's massive figure swayed and his convulsive hands caught Julian's steadying ones. Then, as blood bubbled up from his mouth, he fell with a crash to the dusty ground. Julian Ruthven dragged the body, still pulsating, towards a cluster of trees and laid it to rest. Trevor Barclay came there to see the fallen hero lying in the dust.

"Nicholson," Colonel Barclay muttered to the death-mask, "you could inspire fear but never loyalty, and now you inspire only pity." He paused and seeing the shocked soldiers, shouted a command, "Forward! We must take Lahore Gate!"

Julian Ruthven, however noticed that the Indian officer was very familiar, and he left his soldiers to pursue the man who had felled the dreaded Nicholson. The Indian officer moved swiftly, pausing by a wall or column to remain undetected. Then, finding the path clear, he moved swiftly towards the riverside. Julian followed, his heart hammering, until the Indian came to the burnt house whose terrace sloped down to the river. It stood now, wrapped in the monsoon dusk. The officer turned upon hearing Julian's footsteps, and stared at the Englishman.

"Julian!" he cried, raising his pistol. "Do not come closer!"

"I am sorry to see you, Dilip," Julian said grimly. "I had hoped better sense would prevail. You can be arrested — as a rebel and inciter of mutiny," Julian said in the same grim voice.

Dilip nodded and smiled at the Englishman. "Will you hand me over to your justice?"

Julian stepped closer, fury in his heart. "Don't mock our justice, Dilip. We do not massacre women and children!"

"Neither do I. In fact ..." he hesitated for a moment before continuing. "I left Catherine and Isabel in Allahabad with their friends ...before the ... Kanpur episode."

"You ... saw them ... after the Delhi riots?" Julian cried, clutching Dilip's arm.

"They came to Kanpur where Nana Saheb gave them shelter and then asked me to see them to safety at Allahabad," Dilip said quietly.

"Then they are safe!" Julian cried, surprised and agitated.

Dilip nodded. "They are, I am informed, now in Calcutta." He paused. "Isabel has given birth to a son."

Julian regarded his one-time friend with terrible anguish. "Leave now, Dilip. Go away before you are caught or killed. Return to Calcutta," Julian urged. "I will never mention what I know. Let us be friends again! We shared a splendid world!"

"Slaves share nothing with their masters," Dilip replied bitterly and then smiled at his old friend. "You will let me go, Major Ruthven? Did you not warn me that if I became a rebel, you would not hesitate to arrest me?"

"I did, indeed. But I am now in your debt. You saved my sisters," Julian spoke gently.

Dilip nodded, grim faced. "And I spared you this afternoon because you are my sister's husband. He turned to peer at the river. "I must go — the boat is here."

As Dilip half-ran towards the river where the boat bobbed on the swollen waters, an explosion burst the silence of the night. Dilip wheeled around, hand clutching his chest and swayed before falling to the ground.

Jeremy Latimer stood in the shadows. "Thought you could escape, eh, Chowdhury? Not while I am alive!" His fiendish laughter filled the dark night. And then, as suddenly as he had appeared, he was gone.

Julian knelt by Dilip's body and covered his face. "My friend," he murmured, "and now my foe. Where did it all begin to go wrong?" Slowly Julian lifted the body and walked towards the river bank, where the boat stood waiting. A muffled, turbanned figure stepped out to stare at Julian Ruthven carrying Dilip Chowdhury's body.

"Let us give him the proper rites and scatter his ashes on the Jamuna. He was a noble man — in every sense." Julian got into the boat and sat there with the bleeding body on his lap, while the boatman rowed the boat past silhouetted turrets and towers to a lonely spot.

Watching them was like recalling Siegfried's journey down the Rhine, on his way to a distant Valhalla.

The young body was consigned to flames under a sullen monsoon sky. Only once the clouds parted to reveal a brilliant but tortured moon, as if it wished to bestow a benediction on the young man. Then, as the body disappeared in the flames, the boatman and Julian gathered the ashes and scattered them on the river.

Julian remained standing by the riverside remembering a thousand episodes bound up with that friend with whom he had shared the joys of youth, of sailing on the turbulent Ganges, of riding on the springy turf at Mayurganj, of glittering balls in London, and genteel soirees at Calcutta, and of the woman so dear to them both. His reveries flowed on, until the leaden sky lightened and the towers and minarets of imperial, battered Delhi loomed before him.

Fighting continued in Delhi for several days more. Julian Ruthven's group poured into the streets, near the famed Jama Masjid, not far from the palace where the last of the Moghuls waited with his Begum and sons for the grim finale of an event which they hoped would turn the tide of history. As the British forces moved deeper into the city, the last Moghul realised the futility of their hopes. The old Emperor and his sons fled from the palace of his forefathers and took refuge in the beautiful mausoleum of Emperor Humayun.

The next day, Colonel Hodson set off for Emperor Humayun's tomb across the city to accept the surrender of Emperor Bahadur Shah. The bruised and bleeding city lay silent, almost like a ghost town. The Moghul Emperor was taken prisoner and his sons, who had been in the eye of the storm, were executed by Hodson before a horrified populace.

"We will leave no rallying point for a future rebellion," he announced, replacing his smoking pistol.

The surging populace of Delhi was stunned by the spectacle. For a minute, the multitude stood in a shocked, ghostly silence. Then, a cry of terror arose. "Fly! The Saheb-logs will kill us all!" The crowd dispersed like a tidal wave in retreat. They ran to their homes and snatching up absolute essentials, began a vast exodus out of the battered city. "Nadir Shah's hordes have come once more," they told each other. "Let us escape their savagery!"

Hodson ordered a celebration in the Elysium of the Diwan-i-Khas in the Red Fort of Delhi. There, candles gleamed on lustrous marble walls and exquisite arabesques. Toasts were drank in warm claret and laughter reverberated around the once-proud citadel of Moghul power.

Standing apart from the exultant crowds, a fair-haired young officer with hollow eyes watched the scene with a strange smile on his handsome, weary face. His blue eyes rested now and then on Jeremy Latimer, who had a cluster of junior officers around him. As if aware of someone's close scrutiny, Latimer looked at the young major with a frown. "Who is that?" he asked one of his admirers, "I can't recall the name." The officer turned and saw the man still staring at Colonel Latimer. "Haven't a clue, Sir, but from his colours, I expect he must be from a Punjab

Regiment."

The revelries went on late into the night. Colonel Hodson did not attempt to check the merriment of his officers. They frolicked in the once-forbidden precincts of the imperial Moghul citadel. Julian Ruthven went out into the sultry September night, to get a breath of fresh air, and reflect on the transience of glory. Sitting on a stone bench and gazing at the starlit silhouettes of mosques and minarets, he thought of the great Moghul emperors who had ruled their vast domain from Red Fort. "Who knows when our day will end here as well?" he thought.

The sound of two voices speaking with a strange urgency disturbed his musings. Rising, Julian Ruthven followed the sound until he was in one of the pavilions of the garden. There, Jeremy Latimer stood motionless, as the fair-haired officer held a pistol levelled at him.

"You have been misinformed," Latimer cried. "I never left you to die ..."

Major David Sandys shook his head. "No, Colonel Latimer, it is you who arranged the episode ... to have me mutilated... as revenge for having engaged the affection of your wife."

"No!" Latimer cried, retreating from the wild-eyed Sandys. "I ... did not know ..."

Sandys advanced slowly forward. "You should have called me out for a duel and killed me with honour. I deserved that ... but not this horrible mutilation which has left me half a man."

Latimer began to tremble. "Forgive me ... I sinned ... forgive me ..." he whispered.

"You destroyed me ..." David Sandys replied in an even voice, "and must pay ..." He cocked the pistol. "My life has been a long penance for a foolish escapade."

"No!" Latimer screamed, eyes protruding in horror as he stared at the young Guide officer who had been Catherine's lover and whose mutilation he had arranged at the hands of Thuggies.

David Sandys lifted his hand and pulled the trigger. A burst of fire hit Latimer but he did not fall. David Sandys fired again and again, until Latimer's body was riddled with bullets.

Julian Ruthven stood watching the scene in a daze, unable to move or speak. Laughter from the Diwan-i-Khas drowned all sounds of the firing.

David Sandys turned around. For a moment he stared at Julian Ruthven. "I killed Kitty's husband," Sandys said, quietly, by way of an explanation. "He was an evil man. He had me mutilated... as a penalty for loving Kitty."

Julian Ruthven nodded. "I remember," he said grimly. "I am glad. He killed my dearest friend as well."

"But will that bring back my youth ... my vigour ... my need for wife and children?" Sandys cried out to the dark, sullen sky. "No! I am only half a man ... half dead! It is better I end this miserable existence!" Before Julian could stop him, David Sandys raised his pistol once more and pointing it to his head, pulled the trigger. He swayed and whirled before falling onto the muddy ground.

•

Carolyn Barclay fanned her sick daughter in a small room at the Lucknow Residency, and occasionally dipped a rag into a bowl of tepid water to lay on the child's burning forehead. It was three months since the siege had begun. Outside, the battery of guns continued to shell the high walls of the Lucknow Residency.

Sir Henry Lawrence was besieged with the British population in the Lucknow Residency. His courage as well as that of his wife, Honoria, inspired the others within those walls. Carolyn assisted Lady Honoria with the sick and in the kitchen, where meals for the humbler folk were cooked. She was astonished at first to find that the upper echelons of the besieged consoled themselves with moselle and pate de foie gras, while the others had to make do with coarse grains. "This is hardly a demonstration of Christian charity!" Carolyn exclaimed to Sir Henry's wife.

Honoria Lawrence regarded Carolyn gravely. "We must not

quarrel, Mrs. Barclay. It would be futile to tell these people to share their goods with others."

"Water is becoming scarce. The wells are yet to fill. But moselle and claret are flowing in certain quarters," Carolyn observed grimly.

Lady Honoria sighed in resignation. "We cannot ask them to share, unless they themselves wish to do so."

The rains came in late July just as the rebels renewed their shelling of the Residency. Sir Henry Lawrence took command of the resistance, ordering retaliatory fire, the use of ammunition and defence of the area. The officers and soldiers readily assisted. But it became evident that the defence could not continue for long. Sir Henry could not conceal his despair as the rebel batteries continued to pound on the walls.

"I trust Lord Dalhousie will hear of this in London," he said grimly. "A policy of reconciliation with the people we seek to rule is an essential condition for our continued presence. Our government's failure to do so has brought us to this ... !"

The thunder of guns drowned Sir Henry's bitter lament but every officer reflected on the truth of his words. Lawrence gazed with weary eyes at the leaden sky. "It seems incredible that we came to this very city for pleasure!"

Now, in November 1857, Carolyn knew that all hope of resistance was over. Sir Henry Lawrence had been killed during heavy shelling. Food stocks had dwindled and water was scarce once again. Two months ago, General Havelock had set out with a force of 2,000 soldiers from Allahabad to relieve the besieged at Lucknow but he had been unable to attack the Indian strongholds. The besieged waited for the inevitable. Carolyn was worn out with nursing the sick in the Residency, and by the spectacle of swift deaths. Gazing with red-rimmed eyes at her own child, she wondered how she would bear life without Marina. She needed no doctor to tell her that her child was dying of typhoid. "Take me also, my Lord," she whispered to the crucifix on the wall, "I have no wish to live anymore."

A thunderous noise reverberated around the silent Residency as Sir Colin Campbell entered Lucknow with reinforcements from Calcutta. Carolyn rose from the sick child's straw pallet and peered into the sunlit courtyard outside, where the last of the soldiers stood, straining their ears to ascertain that they had truly heard the rumble of an advancing army. The spontaneous cries of hope were at once drowned in another burst of thunder as the Indians returned fire on Campbell's advancing forces.

Julian Ruthven halted before the Residency, staring at the fallen rebels on either side; the men who had offered a determined resistance against the might of an irresistible power, in the name of freedom and honour. He sat motionless on his horse, staring around him in horror at the desolation of death all around him. The Residency was shelled and holed, its manicured velvet lawns uprooted, its noble trees demolished. Slowly, he entered the gates, his anguished gaze resting on the hurriedly-dug graves, the abandoned posts of officers, burnt cannons and blackened pillars of the portico. The stench of death thickened the cool autumn air. Suddenly, the palpable silence exploded into cries as crowds of gaunt men and women rushed forward towards the thickset figure of General Campbell.

Leaving behind the chaos of sounds, of wailing children, women and indignant men, Julian entered the cavernous hall of the Residency, which had once been a glittering room meant to awe and impress the wild Nawab of Oudh. He remembered an amusing evening he had spent here long ago.

The chandeliers were now thick with dust and the heavy plush curtains had been removed to facilitate the firing of rifles from the gilt-arched portals. A muffled cry reached him and disturbed his reveries. Moving swiftly, he ran towards that single anguished sound, which was soon lost in the roar of the relieved crowd outside. He came to a small room and stopped abruptly. "Carolyn!" he exclaimed, staring at the gaunt woman sitting beside the dying child.

Carolyn raised her glazed, grey eyes to Julian, who came towards her with a sudden urgency and knelt beside her on the floor. He gazed with a pitiful expression at the woman and child and then impulsively reached out for the cold, little hand that was clenched over a ragged quilt. Marina's eyelids fluttered as she looked at the unfamiliar man beside her. "I hear thunder," the child said hoarsely, "I am afraid."

There was something in the child's demeanour which stirred old memories in Julian, of his sister Isabel as a little girl, with blue-green eyes and auburn hair. He raised his eyes to find Carolyn watching him intently. Then, their eyes met in comprehension. Julian stared incredulously at the mother and then at the sick child lying on the pallet. He stepped back, stunned.

"Is ... Marina ... ?" he could not complete the fateful question. Carolyn nodded with sudden fury. "She is your daughter ... created in that sea voyage nine years ago. Hence the name — Marina... of the sea."

"Why ... did you not tell me ... ?" Again, Julian found it difficult to continue.

"Did you truly wish to know?" Carolyn asked bitterly. "You had no desire to continue our ... relationship in India. In Punjab you spurned me. I wanted to tell you then ... but you were indifferent. After that ... I was afraid that you would despise me, that public knowledge of Marina's birth would jeopardise my life with Trevor Barclay. He outwardly ... accepted her ... but never loved her ... as he did his own children." She paused, her face distorted by pain. "It is of no importance now ... my Marina is going!"

Covering her face, Carolyn began to weep brokenly. Slowly, reluctantly, Julian knelt down once more by his new-found child, staring at the grey face with its sunken eyes and lank red-gold hair. He thought of the long sea voyage nine years ago, when his desire and Carolyn's passion had created this star-crossed child under a star-strewn Mediterranean sky. He took the child's cold, inert hand in his.

Marina's eyes fluttered again as she felt his warmth and perhaps the affinity of flesh. A tired smile flitted across the little face as she met her father's bewildered gaze. Then, with a little tremor, she drifted into the final sleep.

Carolyn knelt beside her child, still holding her hand, until, feeling no pulse, she began to cry, softly at first, and then in tearing sobs. Julian lifted the child's motionless body and cradled it in his arms, experiencing a strange sensation as the cold flesh met his own, as the clammy red-gold hair brushed his hand. "My poor child," he whispered, dropping a kiss on the ashen forehead, "I am so sorry."

"Sorry?" Carolyn screamed hoarsely, clutching both her child and her child's father. "Why should you be sorry? You never even knew of her existence ... or your bond with her ... she was of no consequence to you ... you can feel no pain."

Julian laid Marina back on the pallet, his eyes on the tormented woman who had borne this child. Tentatively, he held her hand and drew her close, while she sobbed and beat her fists on his chest. He held her tight, accepting those blows of misery and grief, as if in atonement for his unwitting sin. "Carolyn, my dear," he murmured, "do cry and let me share this pain with you. Tell me how wicked and cruel I've been ... tell me all you want ... let me take away some of your misery ... please, my dear."

Carolyn ceased to cry. The feel of Julian's strong body so close to her, his lips not far from her own, his hand caressing her aching head, filled her with a searing need for him — the same agony of desire that had created poor Marina nine years ago. She remembered, in the midst of this present agony, the ecstasy of those months on the ship, and the mixed thrill and fear of discovering his child growing within her.

"I loved Marina so much because she was yours," Carolyn whispered, now weeping again and drawing closer to Julian. "She was my tie with you ... a remembrance of all that had been between us ... oh, Julian, I am so bereft ...!"

Julian was silent. He could feel her hunger and pain, as her weary body nestled close to his, seeking warmth and satiety.

"Julian," she whispered, "save me from this terrible emptiness!"

His hand left her head and she could suddenly feel his distance.

"Carolyn," he said gently, "that would betray both Trevor Barclay... and my ... wife."

Carolyn withdrew abruptly, looking wild eyed at him, her dusty cheeks stained with dried tears. "Your Radha ... yes, she is worth ten of me ... I understand ..."

Carolyn rose, her head reeling, and covered her face with trembling hands, as fresh sobs broke from her. Julian rose as well and once more drew her close, as if to absorb somewhat the rage and grief of her heart. And this time she laid her weary head on his chest and sobbed in despair, because there was no one else left to love.

The Lucknow Residency was relieved at last. Arrangements were hastily made to tend to the sick, who were then dispersed. The British officers compared notes with the besieged, but no one really listened. Each was bent on telling his own tale of woe to anyone who might care to listen.

"We will avenge Kanpur!" one of the officers cried. "Nana Saheb will pay for his crime!"

Julian Ruthven looked up to scrutinise the officer. "Have you not already avenged Kanpur?" he asked curtly. The young officer shifted in his seat as the steely Ruthven eyes swept over him. Julian continued, "You were with Neill at Allahabad. As was my friend, Colonel Trevor Barclay. He told me of the terrible massacre perpetrated by Neill's men after storming the fortress. Unarmed men, women and children were butchered — indiscriminately.'

The officer thrust out his chin defiantly. "What if they were? Did not Nana Saheb butcher our women and children? Why should not these natives pay for their rajas' sins?"

"Enough has been paid ... and done. It is time we learnt to forget," Julian said, and left the hushed hall.

Sir Colin Campbell stayed behind to settle Lucknow. Major Julian Ruthven stayed back with other officers to "mop up" the countryside of Oudh, where the seeds of the insurrection had really sprouted. Carolyn Barclay left for Calcutta with a large group of women and children, escorted by armed guards.

33

End of a Dream

Carolyn Barclay returned to Calcutta after ten years. It was no longer the happy metropolis of 1848 but a solemn, imperial capital where both sides measured each other's potential. The atmosphere matched her own mood. She had barely recovered from the loss of her child, Marina, when news came of Trevor Barclay's death in the fateful battle of Gwalior. Alone and adrift, she came to take refuge with her friend, Catherine Ruthven Latimer.

It was a silent Ruthven House that she entered. Catherine was still in a daze and did not utter more than half a dozen words a day. The death of her three children in Delhi had stunned her. Isabel was in a happier condition; her child had been safely born and she had had news that Stephen Reynolds, her husband, was safe and on his way to Calcutta.

In contrast to Catherine, who sat glassy eyed and silent, looking out of the windows, Carolyn made herself useful. On the suggestion of Eric Blair, she volunteered to work as a nurse in one of the hospitals overflowing with wounded from the front lines. She admired Dr. Blair's competence and compassion, and wondered what force drove him on in this selfless task. He told her wistfully of his little hospital in Narayanpur, where he treated the rural folk.

"Calcutta offers more scope for a man of your talent," Carolyn said.

"Does it? But I prefer the serenity of the mofussil where I tend the sick without the bitterness that attends me here."

"You are more needed here now," Carolyn observed.

"There is something in all this that repels me," Dr. Blair said. All this talk of 'bloody natives,' and 'vendetta' is not only tragic but foolish as well. Yet I am forced to tend to these demented beings. I loath men of violence; they undo my work in moments."

Carolyn sighed. "If only you had seen Kanpur and Lucknow. I wish I had succumbed as well instead of living this empty life."

Eric Blair scrutinised her with his grave, grey eyes. "No life is empty, Mrs. Barclay. You have a capacity for kindness which should pave the way for a purpose."

"Purpose!" Carolyn exclaimed bitterly, "I came to India — to find security and happiness. I found only disappointment ... in marriage to a man who still loved his first wife's memory. And I lost the child who had given me a sense of purpose. Now I am alone ... all alone ..."

Dr. Blair watched her closely before saying, "You would find life less burdensome if you lived for others; sometimes, the pursuit of our own pleasure is a big burden ... and the cause of pain."

Carolyn smiled sadly. "We are humble people, Dr. Blair. We are not noble and selfless like you. I wonder what stuff you are made of. How can you spend a lifetime tending to others without wanting a home and family of your own?"

Dr. Blair looked away. "I led a merry existence in England—until one day, as happens to all of us, I wondered what it all meant. And then, my search for purpose and meaning led me to India."

Carolyn laughed harshly. "My search has ended. My life has ended. When I have saved up enough, I shall return to merry England and become a governess once more, after a gap of ten years."

"Help us tide over this chaos. Maybe events will sort things out," Dr. Blair said, and added, "and perhaps you can help Catherine as well."

The silence of Ruthven House was broken by the arrival of Stephen Reynolds. He had managed to leave Delhi and travel across turbulent territories, anxious to be with his wife and infant son.

"It is a miracle you are safe!" he told Isabel with joy. Isabel nodded. "I am safe and you are here now. But my heart aches for dear Kitty. She is so bereft."

Stephen Reynolds sighed. "There is more to tell. Are you strong enough to hear?"

Leading Isabel, Carolyn and Dr. Blair to the library of Ruthven House, Stephen unfolded the story of Jeremy Latimer, Dilip Chowdhury and David Sandys.

None of them noticed Catherine standing in the shadows, listening.

"David," she whispered to herself, "oh, my poor David! What a price you paid for a little pleasure!" Catherine stood motionless, still unseen, staring at the starlit darkness outside. "Can it be that I am cursed .... to lose all whom I love? But no ... not all ... Jeremy Latimer is dead! What a liberation!"

Suddenly, she rushed out of the room in a frenzy and flew up the fluted staircase to her room. Moti-bai, her old nurse, looked up from her sewing to scrutinise her beloved Missy Baba flinging out one gorgeous dress after another until she found a gown of bright velvet. Snatching up a heap of gold and pearl jewellery, she uncoiled her fiery hair and ran down the stairs. The servants watched her in astonishment.

Laughing, she flung open the library door. Eric rose, clutching the back of his chair at the sight of Catherine's grotesque flamboyance. Isabel and Stephen stared, bewildered.

"How is this for mourning?" Catherine cried, still laughing. "Do I honour the memory of my late lamented husband?" She reached for the bell rope. "Call for champagne! We must celebrate!"

"Kitty ... my dear ... Jeremy was ... killed in the siege of Delhi," Stephen said in an effort to restrain Catherine.

"Killed?" Catherine screamed. "Don't lie! He was murdered by David! I heard you! My poor David ... if only he had come back to tell me of his deed ... I'd have married him now!" Catherine's glazed eyes leapt into a glitter, as she lifted her glass. "I drink to Latimer's infernal memory!"

Eric and Stephen rose. Isabel hurried to Catherine's side. "Kitty darling ..." she said, but Catherine brushed her aside. "I am glad!" she screamed and draining the glass, burst into wild, rasping sobs. "If only Jeremy had died in Kabul ... instead of my Richard! If only he had not ruined my life! He has left me nothing ... not even happy memories! My Deirdre... gone! Dear heaven, how sure is your retribution for our little sins!" Catherine wept until she lay exhausted on the sofa. Moti-bai came and helped her to the sanctuary of her room.

"Someone will have to inform the Chowdhurys ... of Dilip's death," Eric Blair said as he left that evening. "How will Brajesh Chowdhury bear this after Ṛadha's disappearance?"

The summer sun beat down on the scorched plain. Julian Ruthven tried not to think of his raging thirst as General Rose's columns pushed north. Almost a year had passed since the relief of Lucknow. From there, General Campbell's army had moved south to Gwalior where the Raja contemplated raising the standard of rebellion.

Julian had disappeared for a while, searching the area around where he heard Radha had last been seen. He rode like one possessed in quest of the being who was dearer to him than all others. Only then, as he traversed one village after another, did he realise how precious Radha was to him, and how necessary for his happiness. His efforts were in vain. Radha could not be found. She had, it seemed, vanished in an India gone mad with blood-lust.

"And if you find her?" Trevor Barclay had once asked. "What will you do?"

Julian had stared at the burning plains around him. "If I find her, I will ask for discharge and take her with me to her seaside estate where no one will find us. I have no use now for vainglories."

"Yet you let her go away," Barclay had mused. "You would not heed her pleas." Julian Ruthven regarded his comrade in misery. "I did not know then what griefs this mutiny would bring us! I have suffered enough and wish I had not joined the battle lines."

Julian Ruthven returned to his regiment to find that the Raja of Gwalior, the descendant of Madhaji Sindhia had decided not to expose Gwalior to the fury of the British who had warned him of reprisals. The rebels, led by Tantia Tope, retreated from Gwalior to Indore where the Holkar Raja welcomed them. "The Marathas must combine!" he exhorted his people. "Lakshmi of Jhansi, Nana Saheb of Kanpur, the Bhonsles of Nagpur, and I will drive out the foreigners!"

Julian Ruthven saw, first-hand, what the Indians, united, could achieve. Throughout the winter of 1857 and the spring of 1858, he fought them, pausing often to admire their desperate courage and resilience, before moving forward again to subdue those he had once considered his own people. As spring advanced, so too did the armies of the rebels. Tantia Tope regained lost territories in desperate battles.

Campbell retired, and was replaced by the wily Hugh Rose, who decided that a bold move was necessary, because the rebels were gaining ground. In March 1858, he laid siege to Jhansi, the domain of the beautiful young Rani Lakshmi, who, when threatened by Dalhousie, had retorted. "I will never relinquish my Jhansi!" Julian stared at the formidable fortress and wondered if the indomitable young Rani was like the one his father had loved. The siege lengthened into weeks and Sir Hugh Rose finally ordered the walls to be breached.

"Poor lass," Colonel Trevor Barclay had murmured. "Now we shall see who will relinquish Jhansi!"

Jhansi was stormed and taken, but the young Rani was not to be found. She and her soldiers escaped from under the very eyes of the British and rode west towards Gwalior. There, her forces joined with those of Tantia Tope and took the massive fort of Gwalior. The Sindhia Raja fled in panic to the British camp. Nana Saheb was installed as the Peshwa. The dream of a liberated Hindusthan was slowly becoming a palpable one.

Hugh Rose conferred with his officers. "The north has been quelled but the Marathas elude us. We must take Gwalior and crush the rebels once and for all. Nana Saheb must be taken!"

So now Julian Ruthven rode towards the seat of the Sindhias, across the vast plains and forests of Central India, as wild and untrammelled as they had been from the beginning of time, except for some kingdoms carved out by ambitious condottieros. Interspersed amidst wooded hills were fortresses of chieftains or haunts of bandits. All watched in silence as General Rose's army moved towards Gwalior, under the burnished skies of a searing summer.

The fortress was formidable, built, as it had been, by a prince to terrify those who questioned his might. It was here that Rani Lakshmi and her generals conferred on the strategy of resistance. Gwalior of the Sindhias was a symbol of the resurgent Maratha spirit. "It is from here that Madhaji dreamt of making Hindusthan one. It is from here we must once more drive out the foreigners," the young Rani said.

The vast army of General Rose camped in the plains below. Julian and Trevor Barclay wondered how long the Rani would hold out. A siege could go on forever. The Rani decided to meet the British forces in battle.

The Maratha army stormed out of the massive gates with cries of "Har Har Mahadev", led by their imperious young Rani, clad in armour, sword in one hand, pistol in another. She rode recklessly, disregarding the formidable array of General Rose's forces massed on the plains. "Let us drive out the foreigners from our soil!" she cried.

Behind her rode an immense cavalcade of warriors, the combined forces of the Rajputs and Marathas in yellow and ochre turbans and tunics. The formidable phalanx fanned out across the entire plain, keeping the Rani encircled in a protective talisman.

Julian Ruthven sat on his horse, watching the advancing army of Lakshmi Bai, poised to penetrate the phalanx and capture the imperious princess. As the Maratha-Rajput forces advanced, Julian and his sepoys rushed forward, in a headlong encounter with the enemy. As they charged through the ranks, bullets fell on them in a fiery shower but they rode on towards the yellow-robed hosts. "Let us turn back," the sepoys cried, reeling under the onslaught. "Go forward!" Julian shouted and the sepoys followed him grimly in implicit obedience.

The battle raged all morning and into the afternoon. Julian and his soldiers advanced and retreated, in a futile attempt to find a breach in the formidable phalanx that surrounded the Rani. The azure sky changed to lead and then to a sullen grey as the sun disappeared behind rumbling clouds. Frustrated by efforts to penetrate the circle, Julian pondered how to proceed next when he remembered the stories of Alexander Ruthven and the strategems of highland chiefs that he had taught the Ratangarh army seventy years ago. It struck him that the circle around the Rani was following the same strategy. Once more he advanced with his men, determined this time to break the ring of warriors.

Then, amidst the smoke and screams of battle, he saw Rana Uday Singh of Ratangarh following the Rani, a thickset but stately figure in the yellow "marana poshaka", the robes of death.

Julian thought swiftly as an idea formulated itself in his mind. "Uday Singh!" he cried hoarsely, over the roar of guns, "I thought you were our friend! Why are you fighting with the Marathas? Your place is by my side, my friend!"

For a moment, the stillness of utter surprise reigned. The Marathas paused to glance suspiciously at their Rajput ally, who stared at Julian Ruthven in fury. Then, lifting aloft his sword, the Rana cried, "Let us settle our friendship with blood, Julian Ruthven!" He rushed forward to meet the man who had once been his friend and now faced him as a foe.

Julian Ruthven's ruse succeeded. As the Ratangarh forces broke away to pursue Julian Ruthven's contingent in a headlong gallop across the burning plain, the magic circle broke and General Rose's cavalry rushed in to encircle the Rani of Jhansi.

The encounter was brief and bloody. A cry of desolation swept across the plain followed by shouts of exultation from the British officers. "Lakshmi Bai has fallen! The Rani of Jhansi is dead!" the soldiers cried in one voice.

Rana Uday Singh halted, and turned back to see the Rajput and Maratha forces scattering. He charged towards them, in a desperate attempt to prevent the fatal tendency of soldiers to disperse once the commander falls. "Reassemble!" he screamed. "Return fire!"

The valiant Marathas reassembled once more but the spectacle of the dying Rani on the battlefield broke their will and sapped their determination. They offered the forces of General Rose the desperate resistance of those who have lost everything but their honour. The British-Indian forces ploughed through the desolate Maratha-Rajput ranks, mowing down their vast numbers in a relentless assault. Before dusk of 20th June, the fortress of Gwalior had been taken by General Rose. The blood-soaked plain below was a testimony to the terrible carnage.

"Tantia Tope must be captured!" was General Rose's command when he stormed the fortress capital of the Maratha resistance. "Take the Rana of Ratangarh!"

Major Julian Ruthven, who knew the terrain well, volunteered for the task. He rode with his depleted force as the leaden sky split open into the first monsoon storm of the year. Before them, between thickets and woods, rode the ubiquitous retreating army of the Rana of Ratangarh with Tantia Tope. The pursuit continued for two days through a pouring deluge, until they were within sight of the fortress of Deogarh on a grey, rain-sodden morning. It was the one hundred and first anniversary of the battle of Plassey.

Julian Ruthven ordered his soldiers to camp on the rain-drenched plain while he and his officers planned the assault on Deogarh and Ratangarh, where Uday Singh had taken the Maratha commander,

Tantia Tope. Sitting in the tent, Julian wracked his memory to remember the layout of the Ruthven jagir. Where were the bastions for the guns? Did the cannons rest on the ramparts? Where did grandfather Alexander Ruthven build the arsenal? "I have seen them, yet I cannot recall clearly ... because I never imagined that I, a Ruthven, would have to attack the Ruthven estate!"

It was late when Julian heard swift horsehooves rushing towards the camp. Snatching up his rifle, he stood poised for an encounter, but to his astonishment, the rider dismounted and stood before the astonished eyes of everyone in the camp. The burly figure in mud-splattered yellow robes advanced towards Julian.

"Your Highness!" Julian exclaimed.

"Master Julian!" Uday Singh replied in a hoarse voice, as tears brimmed over his heavy-lidded eyes. He stepped forward, hand outstretched, remembering the boy he had taught to ride bare-back and hunt with falcons, the boy whose father had loved and dishonoured his own mother. Then he remembered the present and retreated. "Take me prisoner if you must.... but spare Ratangarh," the Rana said through stiff lips.

"Where is Tantia Tope?" Julian asked quietly, also troubled by memories.

The Rajput prince lowered his eyes. "Tantia Tope has raced ahead."

"Or he is in Ratangarh," Julian said grimly. "We must then take it by force of arms."

"Would you hurt the city your father and grandfather loved?"

"Mutiny is a hurtful business, Your Highness."

For a moment, the Rana's dark, weary eyes flared into life. "This is no mutiny, Master Julian. This is a revolt of Hindusthan against firingi rule! You have put it down today because our own brothers have betrayed us. But one day, under one great man, we will unite and force you to leave."

A bitter smile lit Julian's face. "I hope you may. But until then ... where is Tantia Tope?"

The sky darkened, and rain fell in a fine drizzle. The horses neighed and shifted. Uday Singh advanced forward until he was able to feel Julian's breath on himself. His eyes were steely.

"Do you wish to pursue Tantia Tope or rescue your wife?" the Rana asked, almost inaudibly. Julian Ruthven started. The Rana's grim voice and countenance precluded any doubts.

"My wife?" Ruthven asked, his voice rising involuntarily. "How can you know where she is, when I have scoured this damned area for months in a futile search?"

The Rana's expression remained grim. "The lady Radha has been residing close by for months now. Afraz, your kinsman, abducted her as she was returning to Calcutta after leaving you."

Julian listened, wild eyed. "Abducted? Is she safe? Where is she now?" Suddenly he clutched the Rana's arm. "Tell me, where can I find her?"

"Listen well," Uday Singh said grimly. "I will help you to rescue Radha devi, but you must not touch Ratangarh."

Julian looked intently at Rana Uday Singh who stood stiffly, as if in anticipation of some untoward event.

"Why have you told me about my wife?" Julian asked grimly. The Rana smiled wanly. "Perhaps it is a ruse — to divert you elsewhere away from pursuit of Tantia Tope or Nana Saheb."

Julian's eyes were fixed on the Rajput prince, as if to bore into the other's soul. Slowly, he shook his head. "I would not fear such treachery from you."

The Rana bowed, mocking and bitter. "Such trust in Rajput chivalry? I salute you." The Rana paused, his smile gone. "Go soon, if you are to find the lady Radha. Our kinsman, Afraz Ruthven, might do something hasty." Julian frowned at the word "our".

The Rana understood and shook his head sadly. "Julian — go soon. Do not waste time on me. I am dead already and have nothing more to do. But you ... I want you to be happy. I owe ... our father that."

Julian grasped the Rana by the shoulders. "Tell me ... what are you trying to say?"

The Rana's dark eyes now bored into Julian's, grim and anguished. "Very well, hear me then. I am the son of Charles Edward Ruthven by Rani Urmila. That is why the Rana, Nahar Singh had her burnt — to avenge his honour. But he could not disown me because then, without an heir, Ratangarh would have passed to the British. Your... our ... father kept up the charade for everyone's sake. For my sake he left me to be a Rajput ... and never laid claim on me as a son."

There was a long, stunned silence.

"Why did you join the rebels?" Julian asked at last.

"I had no choice. "He paused and smiled wanly again. "Had I been born on the other side of honour as the Rana's true son or as Ruthven's legal heir, I would have stayed aloof. But I, the imposter ... the usurper ... the half-firingi ... I had to prove my legitimacy before other Rajput princes." The Rana's voice broke.

Julian drew him close, embracing him tightly, trying to smother the tears that pricked his eyes. "Go away, Uday," he murmured hoarsely. "I have neither met nor seen you. Go in haste ..." Julian withdrew and stood stiffly.

The Rana nodded, struggling with emotions, "I will lead you to Deogarh. And then I shall ... disappear."

Julian gave curt instructions to his men and rode towards Deogarh.

A storm began, darkening sky and earth, as if aiding Deogarh to conceal itself from the determined eyes of the foreign commander. But Julian rode in the storm, climbing the steep road skirted by dhok and churail trees, which led to the gateway of the fortress. Ratangarh's yellow-robed warriors followed.

A wave of green-robed soldiers descended from the fort of Deogarh. "Who comes?" their leader asked.

"A messenger from the Rana of Ratangarh," Uday Singh replied. "Tell Nawab Afraz Ruthven that it is imperative for me to meet him. The British forces of General Rose are on our trail. They are searching for Moghul noblemen involved with the Emperor's sons."

The Deogarh soldiers reflected on those ominous words, then

went back to receive orders. Afraz Ruthven came out to stand on the ramparts.

"Rana Saheb," he called to Uday Singh. "What have you to say?"

"Open the gates, Nawab Ruthven, so that my men and I may shelter in your fort. Ratangarh is no longer safe."

Julian Ruthven stared at the copper-haired man standing on the ramparts, resembling so closely a portrait of Alexander Ruthven that Julian wondered if his grandfather had returned to earth. "My kinsman, and my foe," he thought. "I must teach him a lesson."

Afraz Ruthven's laugh echoed off the stone walls and floors. "Go back to your hideout, Rana Saheb. My fort is closed. There are too many foes around."

Julian realised now that it was Afraz Ruthven he had seen in Delhi, attending the Emperor's sons before they were executed by Hodson. "So, the great-grandson of Alexander Ruthven is a rebel as well," he thought. "That makes my task easier."

It was dusk when Julian Ruthven stormed Deogarh fort, the last of the rebel strongholds. The insurgents fell or scattered as Ruthven's sepoys ploughed through them, until Julian stood before the barred doors of the main building.

"Open, in the name of General Rose!" he shouted.

The doors remained closed. Julian ordered his sepoys to blow up the entrance. He waited for the smoke and debris to settle before entering the dark, cavernous hall. Then taking up lighted torches, Ruthven and his soldiers poured into the rooms and balconies, searching for Afraz Ruthven, who was nowhere to be found.

"Have I been misled by Uday Singh?" Julian wondered as he searched one room after another. "Was it a ruse to make me give up the pursuit for Tantia Tope?"

He flung open one more door and stood transfixed. There, standing by the window was a woman in a saffron sari, her hair in one long plait, her anguished, dark eyes vivid in the pallor of her face. She stared at the tall, flame-haired man in his mud-splattered uniform. It seemed as if she had seen him last in another lifetime, when an ineffable radiance had lit their lives and had as swiftly turned to darkness.

Julian Ruthven advanced slowly into the lamplit room, flinging down his rifle, arms outstretched towards her. "Radha!" he whispered. "Is it ... can it really be you ... for whom I have searched so long ... or am I dreaming?"

They remained in each other's embrace, incredulous and confused, but with a sudden, blinding revelation that they had found each other again, and that what they had feared to have been destroyed in the bitterness and bloodshed of their peoples, was intact and preserved within them like a magic fire.

"My dearest love," Julian cried again and again, his lips on her eyes and lips, his hands caressing her with a tenderness that was an ache. "I had given up hopes of ever seeing you! Oh my darling, why did you leave? Why did you not wait at home for me to return ... oh, why have you put me through such misery?"

"Because you had drifted away from me ... because my love was not as strong as your anger ... because I did not want that bitterness to be turned upon me ... I couldn't have borne that, my dearest!" Radha spoke gravely, clutching him, as if afraid that he would vanish.

"I was crazed by grief for my sisters ... you understand that, don't you, my love?" he asked in a hoarse voice, adding "but they are safe ... your brother, the rebel, saved them."

"Oh, I am glad! So glad! Tell me, dearest, that you will not quarrel with Dilip again ... that you will not argue and break my heart ... that we ..."

Julian pressed her head close to his chest, choking back a sob that rose within him at her plea, because she believed her brother to be safe and alive, because she knew not that his ashes were now merged with the sea.

"I promise, my angel. We will never argue again." He paused, gazing into her face, more ethereal and tender than it had been even on their stormy wedding day. "I vowed that when I found you, I would leave the army and return to our old life. I intend to do just that."

"To our old life, dearest? But that time can never come back ... so much has happened ..." Radha said.

"We will go to Sonagram ... or Mayurganj ... and I will look after the family enterprise. We will get back Marcus and Rowena ... and determine our own destinies ... we have suffered enough for the folly of others! No more!"

Radha lifted a radiant face to him. "I only dreamt of this, my love ... I never believed it would happen ... that you would find me. I am afraid that I will awake and find that it is a dream after all ..."

"No," Julian murmured, leading her back to the divan where they sat, huddled close against the monsoon storm that raged outside. "It is not a dream. We are together ... as we have been fated to be ... through many lives."

The storm raged unabated that night. Julian Ruthven went out into the windswept, rain-lashed courtyard to give instructions to his soldiers of the march that awaited them at daybreak. Tantia Tope had to be pursued, and then he would be free from the bonds of bitter loyalties that held him in battle.

Julian and Radha tried to hold the moments together as time slipped away into the lightning-streaked darkness. He related to her the events that had occurred in Kanpur, Delhi and Gwalior and spoke of the desolation and devastation that had possessed India. She listened in anguish, her hand tightening on his as she told him how on her way to Calcutta, she had been abducted by Afraz and brought to Deogarh as hostage.

Julian regarded her intensely, trying to find traces of dishonour in her face. He dared not ask, yet a cold fury rose within him at the thought that Afraz might have violated her while holding her captive. Radha saw his grim expression and understood. "No," she said softly, "he did not insult me; he kept me here as hostage to lure you here. I fear you have stepped into his trap."

Julian sighed. "I came of my own will — to find you. It has been a torment not knowing where you were." He paused before continuing, "The news from Kanpur maddened me. I realise how deeply I must have offended you ... for you to leave without a word of farewell."

"I went away because I wanted to set you free," Radha replied.

He drew her close, resting his weary head on her shoulder. "Do you remember the vow we made on a stormy dusk such as this?" he asked.

"I remember," Radha whispered, thinking of that dream world that seemed to belong to another life.

"If our lives are bound up in eternity, we have to surmount these events. All this will pass ... and we will still have each other."

The darkness deepened, the wind scattered vagrant clouds and brought in a fresh deluge. Then they forgot, in each other's arms, the turmoils which had separated them as they experienced anew the deep and tender passion that had bound them irrevocably to each other. For a while they dissolved in each other, sharing not only the joy of reunion but their secret sorrows as well, as they clung to each other not only in passion but in wordless anguish as well. Never had they felt closer than they did now. Never had their need for each other seemed so strong. The idyllic early days seemed brittle beside the passion that drew them together now, and coalesced their forms in an incandescent joy.

"Sleep now, my love," Julian murmured. "Tomorrow we must plan our next move. Somehow, I must contrive to send you to Calcutta."

"Will you return soon?"

"As soon as I can ... and we will go where conflicts and strife will not touch us. Is that not worth waiting for?"

"Oh yes," she murmured, nestling close and smiling sadly. "Till eternity."

A series of explosions shattered the silence of the grey dawn.

The ancient walls shuddered and collapsed under the impact, while debris covered the drawbridge and doorway. With a roar, the masonry of the fort began to crumble.

Julian leapt up from the divan, pulling Radha to her feet. They stared at each other, horrified.

"Go to a safe place and stay there until I return! Keep away from windows and balconies," Julian said urgently, holding her close for a moment before rushing to the main hall of the fort where his soldiers now poured in from the courtyard. The acrid smell of burning timber and horseflesh assailed him. Glancing swiftly around, Julian saw that many of his men had perished. "Get into the ramparts and fire on the rebels," he commanded grimly, leading his sepoys.

Thus it came to pass that two Ruthvens exchanged fire. Their mortal duel brought down the stones of the old citadel, stained with the blood and tears of Ruthvens gone before. From a hillock above, Afraz kept up a relentless fire. He was not fighting a mere "angrez"; he wanted to destroy the grandson of Georgiana Ruthven, the angrez woman who had destroyed the descendants of Shirin Ruthven. "With the death of Julian Ruthven, I, descendant of Alexander Ruthven and Begum Shirin, will regain all that was taken from us by the firingi usurpers in the family."

Julian Ruthven's depleted force reeled under the relentless onslaught of the Deogarh soldiers. He stood on the ramparts with his men, directing the retaliation, until the enemy soldiers finally retreated further into the rocky terrain below. "We must rout them," Julian thought, "otherwise I cannot rescue Radha."

Leaving the sheltered alcove where Julian had left her, Radha came to the ramparts where her husband was engaged in grim battle, filled with a terrible presentiment of disaster. "This place is cursed," she thought. "Nothing good can happen in this fort of tears." No sooner did she think this than she saw Julian cry out in pain, hand on his chest, before he staggered and fell on the rain-drenched stones. She rushed out into the rain-lashed rampart, and sank beside him cradling his bleeding body in her arms. "Help me to take him inside!" she cried out to the sepoys.

She raised her eyes to the hillock where Afraz Ruthven stood, exultant. He lifted his rifle once more, to take aim at Julian as if to ensure the work of destruction before the sepoys could remove their commander to safety. In one swift movement, Radha bent forward, covering Julian's body just as her own exploded into splinters of flesh and pain.

When the sepoys came at last, they found the two bloodstained bodies locked in a final testimony of unity.

The Chowdhury house was silent, as if in preparation for grief. It fell to Eric Blair to break the tragic news to his patient and friend, Brajesh Chowdhury.

The Bengali aristocrat stood motionless, staring at the English doctor, unable to grasp the calamity that had befallen him. "My son ... my hope ... Dilip ... killed by a hate-consumed man! My Dilip, who was a votary of western civilisation ... killed by an Englishman! How can this be? Have I been living under delusions all these years?" Brajesh Chowdhury's body was convulsed by sobs. The doctor helped his patient to the chaise longue, wondering how to break the news of further disasters.

Brajesh seemed not to hear about Radha and Julian. His eyes were glazed, his breath uneven and fast as he stared at Eric Blair. Before him floated fleeting images of the past ... of the halcyon years when he had entertained visions of a regenerate India; of travelling to England with his favourite son, Dilip, who had become a scholar at Cambridge, of his darling Radha rushing headlong towards disaster.

Conchshells blew to herald the vesper hour and Brajesh's daughters-in-law brought in incense for the evening worship. Suddenly, he rose and shouted, "No! Not tonight! I cannot bear these rituals tonight! Why call in Lakshmi? She has fled from my house!" The broken old man sat huddled, staring at the sky, thinking. How I wish I had not exposed my son and daughter to the west! If Dilip had not been inspired by western revolutionary ideas, he would now be sitting in Fairlie Place, running the family business. He would not be a speck of ash floating on the Jamuna. And Radha ... had she not entered Julian Ruthven's world ... would have been a protected woman instead of dying in a remote fort in the midst of violence. My world, my visions and all those I loved best, have been destroyed by hatred and violence.

"Eric," Brajesh Chowdhury murmured hoarsely at last, "I have no reason to live anymore. Let death come now to end my pain."

That night, as the breeze wafted in from the Ganges, and stars glittered in the winter sky, Brajesh Chowdhury left the world, in search, he murmured, of those beloved beings who had gone before. The world which he had loved had become a dark prison for his soul, which now flew beyond the confines of a weary body towards liberation and eternal life.

34

To Begin Again

Chestnut and hawthorne blossoms scented the spring air as Julian Ruthven rode through the sun-dappled woods of Ashville, the medieval seat of the Courtneys. "How different this is from Bengal," he mused, glancing around the gently undulant land, the fields of barley and wheat and the lush water meadows fringed by watercress. A sudden longing for the hot, sun-baked land which he loved, suffused him. "I must forget ..." he told himself, though he knew it would not be possible.

"How can I forget?" he often asked himself, riding along the lush Berkshire downs, or at night, when Courtney Manor was silent, and the ghosts of his past joined the leagues of medieval barons and knights, who had left their shadows in Ashville. His ghosts, however, were more immediate, almost palpable. He lay awake, or went out into the grounds, trying hard to banish the sights that had seared his eyes.

He remembered coming to consciousness to find officers and soldiers of General Rose's column hovering over him, congratulating him for "single handedly destroying a rebel stronghold."

Julian had risen swiftly, though in pain, to search for his beloved

Radha. "My wife," he had muttered hoarsely, "she must be in the apartment ... where I told her to hide ... how is she ... have you found her?"

It had been the gaunt expressions around him that had alerted him. "What is it?" he had asked, "How is she?"

No one spoke. There must have been something wild and desperate in his expression that had intimidated the officers and soldiers, who must have feared a fresh convulsion if he learnt the truth.

Julian had closed his eyes, trying to remember, until a wispy memory of Radha rushing into the rain-lashed rampart returned, filling him with dread. "Is ... my wife ... wounded?"

No one answered. Julian strode then to his faithful orderly, Shyamlal, and shook him violently. "What has happened to Radha-bai?" he shouted.

The old faithful burst into tears, and indicated to the next room. Julian had gone hurriedly and found his Radha lying on a bier, her saffron sari encrusted with blood, her long hair spread around her waxen face. Someone had put desert flowers around her in homage. Falling beside Radha's body, Julian had cried out in agony, clutching her hands, her fair, narrow feet, raining kisses on her cold lips. It was then he had found the bullet lodged in her stiff, cold body. He had risen and unsheathed his sword, eyes bursting in their sockets. "I will kill Afraz ... right now!"

"He is been taken prisoner," an English officer had said quietly. "We captured him in Ratangarh, whose Rana has vanished ... with... Tantia Tope.

Julian had knelt beside his beloved once more, wracked by sobs, calling a curse on his fate.

Later that evening, Shyamlal had arranged the cremation of his master's wife, not far from the place where Begum Shirin Ruthven had lain buried for sixty-five years. As Julian had watched his beloved being consigned to flames, he had remembered Radha as a little girl building sand castles at Mayurganj, reciting English poems to impress him; he remembered her laughter and her voice, her beauty, and the tender, steadfast heart that had been his. He thought of that fateful dusk when they had married and sailed away to what they thought had been their Arcadia and which had become a Calvary, ending in this arid, hilltop fort.

"I will take her ashes home," he muttered to Shyamlal. "We will not scatter them on the river but plant them in the earth at Garden Reach ... flowers will sprout from them, and my Radha will live again."

"No Saheb, a Hindu's ashes must go to the Ganges ..." Shyamlal sobbed, "only then will she find peace."

And Julian had stood by the river offering Radha's remains to the Ganges.

Peace was proclaimed in July 1858. The Mutiny had ended. Peace had been proclaimed, though no pardons were given. One sultry morning, the local rebels were brought before the fort for execution. Julian watched from the ramparts as his kinsman, Afraz, came trudging in, hands bound. "A kinsman," he thought, "can I let him die like this?" Then he remembered that Afraz had killed his beloved and turned away. A rattle of gunfire announced that Afraz Ruthven was no more.

Then began the long, tortuous journey back to Calcutta. All along the highway from Ratangarh to Patna, on the water-logged highways and pools, among the vivid blossoms of the scarlet gulmohurs, Julian saw gibbets from which the bodies of rebels hung in the steamy heat. Vultures fluttered in legions, and jackals attended, faithful to their task. Village after village suspected of harbouring rebels, had been burnt to the ground. Palaces and forts, mosques and temples were treated no differently. Humble folk who had neither rebelled against the rulers, nor resisted the rebels, were also made victims of wrath.

Julian Ruthven rode on over the Gangetic plain, as anguished by the severity of British revenge, as by the accounts of brutality perpetrated by the Indians. "Neither side observed the restrictions imposed by humanity. This battle has been fought by men driven mad by hatred on one side and fear on the other," he thought in despair.

Kanpur, Allahabad, Patna stood like ghost towns, stunned and devastated. "How can we remain here against a popular upsurge?" he asked himself again and again. "Do the Indians then want us to leave? What of the order and stability we brought to this troubled land? Do they want back their freedom at any cost? Perhaps Indians do not want progress and western ways thrust on them. Why not leave them to their fate? For a century, my family worked in India and no one spared us ... all I have left are patterns of grief ... and terrible loss. Yes, I must go ... I do not belong here anymore. I must become an Englishman again!"

Julian Ruthven decided that this could nowhere be better accomplished than in Courtney Manor, where his middle-aged cousin Jonathan was the Earl of Ashville, presiding over a large family and army of retainers. Lady Eleanor accompanied Julian there, afraid that the Courtney cousins might seem alien after all these years. She was relieved, however, to find that her nephew, Jonathan, and his wife, Lady Cynthia, received Julian with every sign of affection. The lavish gifts from India — bolts of Benaras silk, jewellery from Bengal and Jaipur, ivory from Mysore and silver from Madras— warmed their hospitality. The younger Courtneys were thrilled to see Uncle Julian, who had become as fine a legend as grand-uncle Charles Edward, who had fought in the Mutiny and whose "princess had died defending their castle." They doubted that their little cousins, Marcus and Rowena, were the princess' progeny because the children were fair with dark auburn hair and dark blue eyes. Lady Eleanor had not elucidated. When news of the Mutiny had reached England in the autumn of 1857, she had, in sorrow and fear, ceased to remind her grandchildren of their troubled heritage.

Now, seven-year-old Marcus recalled little of the shadowy figure that had been his Mama, except for the texture of her satin-smooth cheeks against his and the scent of jasmines in her hair. Rowena, aged five, remembered even less. Lady Eleanor's generous heart soon filled the void.

Julian's advent threw the children into confusion. They asked for Mama and were told that she had gone to the angels. Marcus stared with tears at the miniature photograph of Radha on her father's table, and Rowena shook her head, bewildered. But the conspiracy of silence gradually banished Radha from their memories.

Lady Eleanor allowed this to happen, with pain, and only because she felt that the truth should be revealed later, after the children had been accepted and established in their father's world. But the shock and horror of Radha's death troubled her. "What is it in the Indian earth and air that makes women renounce life?" she repeatedly asked her husband. "Is it that they are taught to be selfless, placing the happiness of others before their own? Or is it that they rejoice in the act of martyrdom as the final step to freedom?"

Charles Ruthven did not reply. Three decades had not effaced the memory of Rani Urmila.

While Julian recuperated at Ashville, his two sisters, who were settled in England, conspired to match-make. "'Tis a pity that Cousin Amanda is recently married — otherwise she would have been fine," one of them said. Lady Amanda had been smitten by Julian many years ago but he had left for India in 1848 without offering for her.

Julian's main refuge now, however, lay in his cousin Lord Courtney's house at Knightsbridge, where Lady Cynthia held comfortable soirees twice a week. That summer, the Neapolitan campaigns of Garibaldi were of primary interest. Wagers were made as to how the Prime Minister, Lord Russel, would react if Garibaldi marched into Rome. It was hotly debated whether Austria would tolerate this open violation of the Vienna Settlement.

"Italy must be united and freed from both the Hapsburgs and the Bourbons," a Liberal MP declared.

Julian listened absently, remembering with anguish a young rebel, his brother-in-law, protesting that while Britain was aiding

Italy to evict alien rulers, Indians were being blown from the mouths of cannons, because they wanted British rule to end.

"What do you think, Mr. Ruthven? Has the Mutiny made you a bit of a reactionary?" asked another gentleman.

Julian Ruthven stared around the well-appointed room, at the flushed, happy people, warmed by champagne, and reassured by the security of British power over seven seas and the steady flow of wealth from her far-flung empire. Suddenly he felt as if he had strayed into another planet. This room, overcrowded with furniture, chandeliers, knick knacks, velvet and plush, stifled him. Putting down the pack of cards he had picked up, Julian said, looking evenly at the guests, "Yes, I have become a bit of a reactionary. I believe that Indians should be bound in chains to us forever. Rebels and mutineers should be blown apart from the mouths of cannons and villages harbouring such men should be razed to dust. And men like Cobden and Bright who say that 'Britain has committed a century of crime against the docile natives of India' should be clamped into prison or exiled!"

The guests glanced uneasily at Julian and at each other, not certain whether Ruthven spoke in earnest or in sarcasm. His remote countenance precluded any further questions. Silently, uneasily, they sat down to play cards while Julian, tight lipped, dealt a hand.

When supper was eaten and more brandy had been consumed, the men drew closer to Julian and asked about India. Tired and desolate, he told them. They listened intently, their faces expressing now surprise, now indignation, now shame, now pity. Julian's bruised heart was soothed by their responses: "We did not know," or "It is a pity that the situation was so clumsily handled without respect for the natives of India," and "Let us hope that the new regime under the direct rule of the Crown will be better." He returned home to Cavendish Square, lighter in mood, to find Marcus and Rowena waiting up for him in his room, though everyone else was asleep.

He sat down in a deep armchair and placed them both on his lap. "Why aren't you asleep, my darlings?"

"You said you'd be back by supper time," Rowena chided him.

"So I did, dear heart. But some gentlemen delayed me. Now that you know I am back, will you please go to sleep?"

Rowena was already asleep in his arms and Marcus dozed, wearied by his vigil. Julian carried them to their room where Nanny waited in despair. Relieving her with a cheerful goodnight, Julian sat by their beds gazing at the lamplit street outside, deep in thought.

England, he reflected, was the citadel of liberal thoughts and political ideals, the sanctuary of exiles fleeing oppression in Europe, the paradise of free thinkers. Here, in the cavernous spaces of the British Museum, a philosopher was composing Das Kapital in order to change the fabric of capitalist society and call into question the very empire which sheltered him. Here Jews were making fortunes, and Russians discussing a never-to-be Utopia while exiled Bonapartists dreamt of a Third Empire. Surely this wise, generous England would understand that India was not Wales or Scotland, to be treated as an appendage, but a vital country to be befriended, cherished, and if possible, made a Rome to her Greece?

Julian had long talks with his father as the two men strolled in nearby Regent's Park, followed, at a slower pace, by Marcus who looked around to see if his friends were visible. Driving slowly in an open landau, Lady Eleanor smiled at the three generations of Ruthvens, wishing that both Radha and Georgiana could be present to see them too. But both were gone, one before her time and the other in the fulness of a century, having seen her great-grandchildren.

"India is in the throes of change, as is Europe," Charles Edward Ruthven told his son. "The old order made its passionate and convulsive protest against the inexorable changes brought on by British rule. Now that old order lies inert and desolate, awaiting the wisdom and comprehension of its new rulers. If we are to succeed, a sagacious policy will have to be evolved." Charles Edward paused to draw breath. At seventy-five, he was still strong, though the damp, cool air of London had given him a permanent catarrh. "Go back without bitterness, Julian," he said. "Don't give up the civil service. I want you to make something more than a fortune in jute or tea with Ruthven, Chowdhury & Co. I want you to achieve what my privateer buccaneer father and I , a confused reformer and empire builder, could not accomplish." Charles Edward's eyes rested on Marcus. "You have a legacy to pass on to your son."

Julian clasped his father's hands. "Father," he said gently, "I will try."

The three Ruthvens walked slowly over the springy grass to the carriage, where Eleanor waited with Rowena.

Julian Ruthven lay in the master suite of Ruthven House in Calcutta, staring at the ceiling, remembering the last time he had been there with his wife, never dreaming that he would be alone and bereft so soon. To make the agony of the first night more bearable, Julian had made his children sleep on either side of him. But their gentle breathing and milky breath failed to act as a talisman against relentless memories. Their presence, in fact, only enhanced the poignancy of Radha's absence.

Catherine proved inept in handling her nephew and niece. They reminded her of the children she had lost, and in some way, she resented their intrusion into the silent, sedate pace of Ruthven House.

Julian's plans to show them around Calcutta one day were upset by a summons from Writers' Building, where the Secretariat had now moved, after the dissolution of the East India Company, which had built it in 1760.

The chief secretary had called some of his officers to discuss the outbreak of a severe famine in the Bihar-Bengal border, due to failure of the monsoon. Looking at Julian from under his bushy eyebrows, he said, "You dealt with one famine in your sub-division, Ruthven. I see from the reports that it was well handled."

Julian Ruthven did not speak. His stony expression conveyed that he was not susceptible to compliments. Anxious to enlist his cooperation, however, the chief secretary said, "You did good work, Ruthven, and showed considerable initiative in transporting wheat from Dehradun."

"I am glad my services are remembered," Ruthven replied coldly.

The chief secretary nodded, "Your record is exceptionally good."

"Perhaps that is why I have been posted as survey officer in the Arakan forest?"

The chief secretary's astute eyes met Julian's steely ones.

"I am asking the Governor permission to rescind that order and post you as district magistrate of Motihari ... to organise relief... and after that I want you in the Secretariat in the legislation department." He paused again. "Men like you, who have an understanding and respect for India, can alone heal this bitterness which has been generated by the Mutiny. Not all of us were in favour of what happened."

Julian sat rigid, staring ahead at the rain-bearing clouds overhead. He could almost hear Radha singing Tansen's Megh Malhar. Tansen's beloved and the song of sacrifice by the riverside. That was what had ruined it all.

"I will prepare to go to Motihari, Sir," Julian said quietly, rising. The chief secretary also rose. "Good. I am glad to have you back, Julian," he said.

Motihari was the haunt of indigo planters. Over a century, indigo plantations had usurped the land earlier utilised by peasants for rice, mustard and pulses. The indigo plant, which had a capacity to sap the fertility of the soil, had gradually impoverished the area and made it famine-prone. Confined to till narrow patches of land, the peasants had no margin to cushion shocks. One meagre monsoon was enough to bring them to the verge of starvation.

Julian Ruthven arrived in the full regalia of a district magistrate, with an impressive procession of liveried orderlies, clerks, and turbanned guards with red sashes across their tunics. Dhols were beaten, bugles played. The district superintendent of police rode behind the district magistrate on his frisky, black horse.

Samuel Baldwin, the most powerful indigo planter of Motihari met the procession in his carriage. "Come for breakfast, Ruthven Saheb," he said, puffing at a cigar.

Julian's eyes were steely. "Who is this man?" he asked the police officer but did not wait for a reply. "Ask him, first, never to smoke in my presence and, second, not to accost me on the roadside. He will have to make an appointment to see me — at my office." Spurring his horse, the Magistrate Saheb cantered forward, satisfied at having given a set-down to one of his potential adversaries.

Marcus sat in the carriage, staring at Nimai, his father's Man Friday. "Is Papa angry?" he asked in English since he had forgotten Bengali during the three years he had been away in England.

"Papa angry with planter man. Wicked man," Nimai elucidated in pigeon English.

Rowena peered through the windows, giggling. "Look at the wicked man," she said in a clear, carrying voice. "He is as red as a tomato!"

Mukta pulled the child down. "Rowena-baba! You cannot behave like this!" she chastised.

Rowena laughed even louder, a clear tinkling laugh, that brought tears to Mukta's eyes. "My Radha laughed like that," she said. Sighing, she looked at Nimai, "How long can these children go from place to place like gypsies? Why doesn't Master Julian leave them behind in Calcutta with their aunt?"

Nimai shook his head. "The aunt is morose lady. How can she cope with these live wires?"

"Still ... what a way to bring up two high-born children!"

Julian Ruthven summoned the district officers to his vast high-roofed office the next day, to take stock of the prevailing situation. He asked about the number of tanks and wells which had dried up, the untilled acres, the acres where crops had withered after sowing. The figures were alarming. "Let me have information on the acres under indigo plantation," he said in an ominous voice. In the afternoon, he rode over ten villages to assess the extent of drought and hunger. Returning late at night, he found Rowena sleeping, fully dressed, on the drawing room divan and Marcus dozing on the dining room table, books spread out in disarray. Wearily, he undressed them with Mukta's help and put them to bed in his own room. The following day was even more gruelling. The July sky was cloudless, and dust swirled over the withering heads of paddy and pulses. Villagers rushed out to tell him their woes; women came out to show him their starving children.

The next morning, he began the relief operations. Centres were set up in the affected areas. The Bengal government had provided the district magistrate with a sum for the purpose. Julian now "invited" the indigo planters to contribute. Since most of their illegal activities depended on the district magistrate's acquiescence, they came forward with sums equal to the amount given by the government. Julian rode hard for several days to reach the granaries of Burdwan where wagons of rice, wheat, pulses, potatoes and onions were being loaded. Placing an official in charge of every convoy, he rode back to Motihari, just as the first starvation deaths began.

A hot, dry wind blew across Motihari, but the ravages of a famine were temporarily averted. People trekked across the parched, blazing fields to thank the Magistrate Saheb who had saved them and their children. Even now, they knew, he sent his trusted tahsildars to purchase grains from Burdwan and Birbhum in Bengal to be released if the supplies ran out.

In the meantime, Digvijay, a learned priest, was asked by the British magistrate to organise a puja, a worship to appease Varuna, the rain god. That Ruthven Saheb defrayed the cost of the ceremony from his own purse did not go unnoticed. A famous singer from Calcutta came to sing the melodious Megh Malhar, in an effort to split the clouds, as the great Tansen had once done.

Motihari went festive that day, despite its precarious proximity to hunger and death. Baldwin, the formidable indigo planter had been "asked" to provide a shamiana, a cloth canopy to accommodate the huge audience. It was full by early afternoon. The singer arrived as the blazing sunlight slanted and lengthened over the brown fields, and the darker smudge of indigo estates yonder.

The singer sat down, with his accompanists, who immediately began to tune their instruments. Suddenly, he cleared his throat, and frowning, said, "Why, there is no idol! We must have an idol of either Ganesh or Lakshmi here."

Some consternation followed, until Julian took out a cameo from his briefcase. "Treat this as a sacred image," he said, placing the ivory cameo of Radha next to the small sacrificial fire. The singer frowned and would have protested. How could a firingi lady's cameo be used? But the district magistrate's eyes dared him to protest.

He began to sing, slowly at first, then as the rich timbre of his voice gathered volume, like the breeze that stirred the dry, rustling leaves on the surrounding trees of shal, ashwath and banian. His voice rose and dipped, like a scherzo, frivolous and playful. The villagers stirred restlessly. The man sang well but the sky remained a cloudless, velvety blue even as the shadows lengthened. The singer too grew pensive, pausing to glance anxiously at the treacherous sky. It did not seem as if it would rain tonight or even tomorrow.

Julian Ruthven sat at some distance from the others, his two children by his side. Marcus listened, wide eyed, and agitated. "That is what Mama used to sing!" he cried out, "Yes, I can remember it now!" Rowena gazed at her brother and her grave father, distantly aware of something that she had forgotten. She nestled closer to Julian's side, clutching his arm, as the music rose higher with the flames.

The singer was wearying. "A hundred rupees for an hour," he had laughed when Julian's emissary had come to see him. "Of course I shall come — rain or no rain!" But now he wished he had not come. He paused to take a deep breath, his eyes straying to the cameo. "If you are a good lady, help me," he pleaded. "I cannot leave in shame. I cannot leave these people in despair!"

The raga of the clouds tore across the fields like a fierce wind, soaring up to the sky to touch the swollen, grey clouds that had gathered now over Motihari. As the singer poured all his will into his voice, a rumble of thunder shook the town and its environs. The singer paused and slapped his chest, to gather strength, and sang on, wildly, passionately, almost in a frenzy, until the first hot drops fell on the cracked fields. The audience shouted and rushed out in the twilight, but the singer remained, to weep at the rain god's mercy. Julian sat with his children, eyes closed, to resurrect a beloved face. Tansen and his beloved lived on forever in India's tears and pain.

Motihari was green again. Farmers and landlords rushed out to prepare the soft earth to plant seeds. Julian ensured that plenty were available, that manure was gathered, and the sowing accomplished. It was then that he ran into trouble with the powerful indigo planters.

Baldwin, as usual, led the movement, attended by half a dozen indigo planters who, in effect, controlled the district.

Julian, cold and arrogant, met them in the sepulchral gloom of his office.

"We have a complaint, Sir," Baldwin began, deliberately shifting his feet to indicate his weariness and desire to sit. The magistrate ignored his gestures.

"What is your complaint, Baldwin?" he asked curtly.

"Is it true that you have told the peasants to grow rice and pulses on land reserved for indigo?"

"True."

The terse, staccato reply took the planters by surprise. "But why?" one asked indignantly.

"Why?" Julian Ruthven asked, his eyes narrowed in disdain, "Because you coerced the former raja to hand over these lands or 'dilat' to you, and then coerced the headmen of the villages to sign documents, agreeing to grow indigo on one-fourth or one-third of their lands. You have forced them to carry the indigo to your factories, and deducted money if the quantity of indigo fell short. The farmers have grown deeper in debt to you planters, while their soil keeps getting thinner, thanks to this pernicious black weed that earns you your fortune. All these so-called agreements will be reviewed in open court."

The indigo planters were in uproar. "This is impossible!" Baldwin shouted.

"Insufferable!" shouted another. "We won't tolerate it."

Julian nodded to the six turbanned dalayats, the orderlies who stood at the end of the vast hall. "Remove these men," he said in chaste Hindi. He paused and looked at Baldwin. "If I hear of any episode of coercion or assault on the villagers in my domain, perpetrated to cow them into submission or to serve your infamous greed, I promise to clamp you all in jail."

The planters stared incredulously at the grim-faced man on the dais. There was something ominous in his deep voice, and the cold blue-green eyes, that suppressed their furious retort. With his auburn hair and bronzed face, he looked like a furious Viking warrior. Baldwin felt his spacious stomach turn at the tales he had heard of Ruthven's deeds in the Mutiny. "The man is savage," he said softly, "Let us leave."

The monsoon passed, leaving the fields replete with rice, pulses and mustard. The lands where indigo had been planted, now grew a hardy millet for lean times. The planters had to rely on their own estates to produce indigo. Villagers came from remote corners of the district to touch the magistrate's feet, and offer bananas and coconuts in oblation, as to a deity. Julian accepted their thanks and a fruit in token. He was a harassed man now, working sixteen hours a day to modernise Motihari in agriculture and irrigation. In addition, he had to prepare estimates for a district hospital and school, decide on compensation for lands to be acquisitioned for railway lines and work out the resettlement of indigo lands.

Marcus and Rowena, however, became a problem. They refused to eat wholesome food, or to stay indoors in the afternoon. A dip in the pond became a regular pastime, followed by a swift ascent the jamun tree, where parrots and monkeys had acrimonious debates over tenancy. Tutors were tormented and sent packing. The Magistrate Saheb's children ran wild. If admonished, they had a ready rebuke and threat. "We wish to return to England. We are lonely here."

Though Julian wondered how he could care better for his motherless children, he was reluctant to part with them once more by sending them away to his old parents in England.

It was with relief that he learnt of his impending transfer to the Secretariat at Calcutta.

35

Roses from Ashes

"It is good to be back," Julian said, wandering around Ruthven House with Marcus and Rowena in tow. Neither could remember the holiday they had spent in the family mansion in the winter of 1857. It was all new to them, though sometimes Marcus felt the intrusion of an unexplained presence. Catherine watched them sadly, and Julian's expectation that she would look after the children was shaken by her announcement that she would be leaving for Narayanpur.

"Narayanpur?" Julian asked. "What can you possibly do there?"

Catherine stirred uncomfortably, colouring. Julian noticed that in the year that he had been away, Catherine had become more like herself, and seemed to have emerged from the trauma of the dark events of 1857. Her silences were less frequent, her smile more visible though she could never be, he knew, the vibrant, volatile Kitty he had known.

"I ... want to go for a change of air ..." Catherine replied, blushing like a shy girl, "and to try to help ... Dr. Blair."

Julian regarded her with sudden interest. "Could Kitty finally be in love, this woman who had once plunged into affairs in her search for fulfilment?"

Catherine met her brother's scrutiny with a sad smile. "You do not think it possible — that I, the high-stepping trollop, could find peace with a solemn man dedicated to his work?"

Julian took her hands in his, stirred by the greying hair and the lines around her eyes and mouth. "I believe it is entirely possible, dear Kitty. You have always possessed a talent for joy and love."

Catherine hugged Julian in relief. "I began to love Eric long ago ... but I was already married to ... Latimer ... oh, why did I not meet Eric earlier ... even before Richard? How different my life would have been!"

Julian turned away, remembering young Kitty in a yellow dress, flying down the hills in Simla to meet Richard de Courtney. "What a world of pain we would elude, Kitty, if things happened differently. But, for you, it is not too late. You will find happiness at last... perhaps the best is yet to come."

"Wish me joy, Julian," Catherine whispered, the ghosts of hope returning.

"Yes, I wish you all the happiness in the world," he replied, gazing sadly at his ageing sister.

Catherine and Eric Blair were married soon after, in a simple ceremony in St. Paul's Cathedral. The hard life of a doctor had taken its toll on Eric, but he worked on, regardless of the strain. Catherine joined him, though she too found the routine hard.

Visiting them, Julian arrived at a plan. On his return from England in 1860, he had found himself owner of Dubb's Point as Thaddeus Latimer had died soon after his brother, Jeremy, and neither had any heirs of their own. According to Fiona Ruthven Latimer's will, the estate had passed on to the Ruthvens.

Julian did not want Dubb's Point; his possessions were many and his needs few. He felt that Catherine and Eric should enjoy Dubb's Point and since they had no children, the estate could later pass on to Isabel and her children.

Catherine was happy indeed to go to Dubb's Point and begin a new life with Eric Blair.

Julian's life was outwardly calm. He admitted eight-year-old Marcus to La Martiniere School, where Nimai took him in a carriage everyday. Six-year-old Rowena received lessons at home with an elderly tutor. The old Ruthven retainers ran the household smoothly, but they could not fill the place of a chatelaine such as a Lady Eleanor or a Radha.

Isabel came to visit her brother's family whenever she found time from her busy schedule. Stephen Reynolds now taught at Scottish Church College and her hands were full with two children.

Julian immersed himself in his work, as an antidote to loneliness and occasional moods of futility. There was, after all, much work to be done.

The Mutiny had shaken the old order, which had continued, with modifications, from the time of Warren Hastings. Queen Victoria's Proclamation of 1858 set the tone for the new era of authority and conciliation. She stressed the need for justice, welfare and improvement. The intelligent members of the British ruling class recognised the need to avoid past mistakes and mollify the princely classes. The Government of India Act of 1858 ended formally the rule of the East India Company. The place of the president of the Board of Control was taken by a secretary of state for India, who became the source of authority and director of policy in India. A Council of India was established with fifteen members, who were first appointed for life and then for ten to fifteen years. They were men who had served in various capacities in India and possessed considerable knowledge in their own spheres.

The Governor General became the Viceroy — a direct representative of the Crown. Queen Victoria took a personal interest in the governance of India and managed to convey this interest to her civil and military servants and to the people of India.

One of the first reforms was the replacement of Cornwallis' Permanent Settlement with the Bengal Rent Act which gave occupancy rights to tillers and both security of rent and tenure, thus protecting them from the vagaries of zamindars. The three outstanding men in the Viceroy's council — Sir Bartle Frere, Samuel

Laing and James Wilson — listened with interest when Julian Ruthven told him of his experiences in Bishnupur and Motihari.

In the two years that followed, Julian Ruthven, together with others, was immersed in the shaping of the new era. He spent hours over the proposed Indian Council Act of 1861 in which the executive Council was expanded. The Cabinet system was introduced by allotting portfolios of departments to individual members. Cases of doubts or differences went to the whole Council. A central government began to emerge, with the Viceroy as the head.

As an official who had wide experience in famine relief work, Julian Ruthven was asked, among others, to formulate a Famine Code to act as a guidebook for officials in similar situations. Lord Canning took a personal interest in this after seeing the ravages of famine in the previous years.

Julian brought home papers to study, browsing through countless documents, scrutinising drafts, and suggestions of lawyers and jurists which could be discussed exhaustively at the Law Commission.

In the solitude of Ruthven House, Julian worked hard, while everyone slept. Sometimes unable to sleep, he went from the library to the music room, furnished ninety years ago by his grandfather's mistress, Liselotte Fremont. Her old clavichord brought from Bremen and grandmother Georgiana's pianoforte faced each other in eternal conflict, while Radha's veena, on which she had played Tansen's ragas, stood silent in one corner. Tentatively, he picked it up and plucked a few vagrant strains and then feeling a sudden anguish, left the room. Sometimes, he played snatches of Bach, revelling in the challenge of the music to his skilled but tired fingers. It was as if by learning to accept the harmony of Bach's music, he was trying to believe in a harmonious order. Sometimes, he gave up the effort and lay on the library sofa in a kurta and pyjama, letting the rustle of the wind on palm fronds lull him to sleep.

The Famine Code became a legal document in 1861. The Law Commission had been set in motion in 1830, under the stewardship of Thomas Babbington Macaulay. It had collected rules, laws and customs and codified them in a systematic manner. The great achievement of the Law Commission now reached its climax in the enactment of two great legislations. The Indian Penal Code became law as did the Criminal Procedure Code. Indian life was now bound by these two great Acts, making all men equal before law. No longer was it possible for the mighty to dispense justice according to their whims and caprice. Pax Britannica became the law of the land.

India was astir with excitement. Nowhere was this growing optimism more evident than in the homes of enlightened Indians in Calcutta. The new legislators were hailed by both the liberal British and the Indian populace. The lawmakers were described as new Solons who had brought India into the mainstream of western law and progress. The Viceroy, Lord Canning, received acclaim from Britain. After three years, the bitterness created by the Mutiny was beginning to be laid aside.

Julian visited his old friend Sudhir Chowdhury, after two years. Radha's death had at first put a barrier between him and the Chowdhurys — as if his love and loyalty were being cleaved in half by two elemental forces. But now he felt he had made peace with the land of his birth and could take up the threads of old friendships.

The Chowdhury villa was still charged with the intangible presence of Brajesh Chowdhury — his vitality, sympathy and quest for enlightenment. There was once more a cluster of both Indian and British scholars, lawyers, doctors and litterateurs in the drawing room where conversation, centred around Lord Canning's momentous reforms, sparkled like the champagne that Sudhir served to his guests.

"Our fathers should have been here ... to see the fruits of their efforts," Sudhir said, as he and Julian strolled in the gardens of the villa.

Julian stopped, his eyes on the scarlet blossoms of the gulmohurs encircling the lake where he had once, in another lifetime, discussed doctrines with Dilip and made entreaties to Radha. "If only these reforms had begun earlier ... Dilip and Radha would have been here," he said quietly. "I hope they forgive us."

Sudhir too stopped and regarded his friend with a gentle plea. "Events shaped themselves into tragic dimensions. Who can be blamed for the conspiracy of history?" He paused. "I believe Radha would be happy if she knew you were devoting your life and talent to the progress of India."

The atmosphere of the Chowdhury house was candidly western, from the wood-panelled walls, crystal chandeliers, silver candelabras, Staffordshire porcelain and Sheffield cutlery. Hock and moselle was served to enliven the discussion on the imposition of income tax on non-agricultural produce and enhancement of salt tax.

The capo de lavore of Julian's work in the Law Commission ended in 1862, whereupon he took time off with his children to visit his sister Catherine and her husband, Eric Blair, at Dubb's Point.

Stopping his carriage on the boundary, Julian surveyed the former indigo estate, now bathed in the rain-washed glitter of autumn. The old house looked the same, but the grove of coconut palms, which had been the haunt of the formidable tantrics, was dotted with huts. Three swings were suspended from the jacaranda tree—a memorial to Catherine's children, killed in the Mutiny.

As Julian's carriage drove up the long track, he noticed the changes that had been effected in one year. The brooding stillness of Dubb's Point had been replaced by a hum of activity. Hearing the sound of the carriage, Eric Blair hurried out of the house and came down the wooden porch to great him. Catherine stood behind, smiling at her brother, who was startled by the change in the once-voluptuous and volatile beauty. Though her hair had greyed and the opulent figure was now lean and spare, there was a serenity in her face which had never been there before. The scars of the Mutiny had begun to fade from her countenance. Julian came forward and held her close and then embraced Eric Blair.

"Isabel and Stephen have come too with their children," Kitty informed her brother. She paused and aded, "It is nice to have children here again."

Hurricane lanterns were lit as dusk settled over the dark groves of coconut and neem trees beyond. Awed by the sudden stillness, Isabel's girls nestled closer to their ayah, while the more intrepid Marcus and Rowena stood on the wooden porch, listening to the hooting of owls and watching lamps flickering in the row of huts across the garden.

Eric took Julian and his children walking around the garden as the women sat on the veranda. "The huts are dormitories for my students, Julian," he informed his brother-in-law. "I have selected twelve boys from the nearby villages, who will be taught here and prepared for higher education in Calcutta."

Julian paused to look at the four neat cottages, where boys were studying by the light of lanterns. "Do you have the means to educate them?" he asked.

"Not really. I have applied for grants-in-aid for my school. Lord Dalhousie gave a boost to the education system by introduction of this measure, and Lord Canning promoted it further. Now, colleges and schools are sprouting all over India, to prepare students for the three new universities."

The two men walked on in silence until they came to the chapel at the edge of the estate. "I have added a dispensary," Eric said, as the two men stood looking at the small edifice, with its twin, square Norman towers, that had been built eighty years ago by Fiona Latimer. "I can now practise medicine without other worries."

Julian Ruthven stopped, and gazed around him. Despite the heat, and the droning of mosquitoes, he felt a strange peace envelop him. It was as if Dubb's Point had finally found peace as well. "Neither the rage of tantric sadhus, nor the ghost of Henry Dalrymple whipping indigo peasants, nor the brothers Latimer will haunt Dubb's Point again," he said, almost to himself.

"Thanks to you and Kitty," Eric Blair replied.

Julian shook his head. "No, Eric. All this is due to you. Kitty lived here before but she could do nothing to lay those dreadful ghosts at rest. In fact, she was, in a way, drawn into its whirlpool of violence."

"Not the same Kitty. This Kitty is different," Eric said, shyly but resolutely. "She has immersed herself in caring for these boys, in medicating the villagers, and visiting those who are in distress."

"How strange to see Kitty so altered!" Julian observed, and immediately regretted his thoughtlessness in making such a remark. But Eric did not seem to resent it.

"Is she really so different, Julian?" Eric asked intently. "Didn't she always possess a great capacity for loving and giving?"

Julian did not reply. He could only remember Kitty's wild escapades and relentless search for pleasure and excitement.

Dubb's Point was a busy place during the daytime as Eric and Catherine Blair moved between the school and the dispensary. The day began with morning worship in the little church. A few villagers came, more to please the "Doctor Saheb" and his "Mem" than because they were drawn to the austere creed. However, if the chiming of church bells at five in the morning was regarded as a salutation to the sun god, Eric did nothing to contradict this view. By six, husband and wife breakfasted and were in the long, thatched hall that served as a school for the twelve boys on the estate and others from the village. Lessons continued until eleven, when the "residential students" went to bathe in the river and Eric and Catherine repaired to the dispensary to treat and medicate the sick. In the long, warm afternoons, Eric read and Catherine attended to household chores. A young Bengali who served as the manager, discussed accounts over tea with the "Doctor Saheb", while young children played among the coconut palms flourishing on the land which had been used a hundred years ago as an indigo plantation by Henry Dalrymple.

Marcus and Rowena explored the estate on their own, revelling in the river and shaded coconut groves. Once, while the adults took their afternoon siesta, they slipped away to the riverside and persuaded Nimai to row them downstream. As they passed the grey-stoned temple of Shiva at Mayurganj, Marcus felt a strange magnetism emanating from it.

"Who lives in that huge house?" he asked, pointing to the Chowdhurys' mansion set back from the river.

Nimai hesitated. It would have given him a thrill to tell his wards about their dual legacy but he held his silence. Knowledge of what had happened might bewilder them now. "A fine zamindar used to live there once," the old servant said at last.

"A king?" Rowena asked, ever ready for the dramatic.

"Yes, little mother, if you wish ... and he had a daughter who was beautiful and charming."

"Like me?" Rowena asked, with a mischievous smile, spreading out her hands. Nimai gazed at her, struck suddenly by the close resemblance Rowena bore to her mother. Watching him, Marcus knew that there was something more to Mayurganj than a mere fairy-tale.

Unable to cope with Rowena, Julian Ruthven advertised for a governess to care for his daughter. It was with astonishment that he met the applicant one morning in Ruthven House.

"Carolyn!" he exclaimed, staring at the woman in a plain linen dress, her pale hair tied severely back, her fair skin tanned by the sun. "I did not know you were in Calcutta!"

Her grey eyes regarded him calmly. "I have been here since I left Lucknow, first working at Lady Canning's hospital, then at a school." She paused. "I expect you know that my husband, Trevor, died in the siege of Gwalior?"

Julian nodded. "We were together in that battle. Then I went in pursuit of Tantia Tope ... to Deogarh ... where my wife was killed."

"I heard," Carolyn murmured, afraid of glimpsing his grief and the turmoil within him.

Julian turned away, staring out of the windows at the garden. "I have had trouble with my children after they left England. I do not know if you can manage them. They are both wilful and turbulent." Carolyn nodded, grave faced. "My Marina was the same. It must be the Ruthven blood."

Julian turned back to look at her, startled. Marina hovered between them like a reproach and now, a strange, inexplicable bond.

"Very well," Julian said stiffly, "you can see for yourself."

Marcus and Rowena Ruthven were called down to meet their prospective governess, Mrs. Carolyn Barclay. Nine-year-old Marcus was polite and distant, but seven-year-old Rowena was interested by the prospect of company.

Carolyn stared at them in silence, remembering her child by Julian Ruthven as well as the beautiful woman who had borne Julian these children — in love and joy. And now Marina and Radha were both gone, leaving Carolyn childless and these children motherless. Was there a pattern in life woven out of grief?

"I hope you tell nice stories, Ma'am!" Rowena said, breaking the spell. "I like dancing as well." She paused to glance at her father with mischief-filled eyes, and added, "I hope to be a ballerina one day."

"We will do all that after our lessons," Carolyn replied gently.

Carolyn Barclay was governess to Julian's children for a year. Because they knew that if this experiment failed, they would have to leave their father and go back to England, both children co-operated, and there were fewer tantrums and caprices. Indeed, Carolyn felt strangely drawn to them. "Is it because they are Julian's flesh and blood? Or is it because I see in their eyes and their tousled auburn hair, their voices and laughter, echoes of my own lost child who was their half-sister? Or is it because I need to love, for I am terribly alone?"

Marcus kept his distance, attending school during the morning, playing games in the afternoon, and only in the evening, entering Carolyn's domain of homework, piano lessons and supper. Rowena took up almost all of Carolyn's time, exhausting her and leaving her no time for herself, as she slowly began to substitute her in the void left behind by an unknown mother.

Julian Ruthven, however, took care to avoid Carolyn Barclay. He breakfasted with his children, and dined alone or with friends, while Carolyn had supper with her pupils. He spent long hours in the library immersed in his work, trying to shut out memories and sensations. Sometimes, he heard Carolyn teaching his children to play the piano in the music room. Sometimes, she played at night when the house was still. Memories assailed her as well — of a sea voyage fifteen years ago, of a star-crossed child dying in Lucknow, of hot, windy nights in Punjab, when leaves swirled outside under the gaze of lonely stars in a vast sky. The muted frenzy of Liszt conjured up lost idylls, while the music trembled in the wind.

Julian sometimes felt an impulse to join her and unburden his desolation to her but he always resisted it. He was afraid of coming close to Carolyn and of the carnal cravings that could neither satisfy nor assuage his pain.

It was not long before Rowena began match-making. "If Papa married Mrs. Barclay, we could have a mother," she told Marcus, who bristled at the idea.

"How can she be our mother?" he retorted. "Our mother is dead!"

Rowena frowned and drew closer to her brother. "Do you remember our Mama?"

Marcus nodded, sapphire eyes bright with tears. "She left us by the riverside, when we were little," he murmured.

"Was she a lovely Mama?" Rowena queried. "Did she tell stories and dance and sing?"

Marcus regarded his sister pensively. "There is a closed room upstairs where ... Mama's portrait stands, and her things lie. Shall we get Nimai and Mukta to open the secret room?"

"Yes! Oh, yes!" Rowena enthused.

"Papa should never know. He has ordered the room to remain closed."

The room was opened when both Julian and Carolyn were out.

Marcus and Rowena stared into the dust-filled, cobweb-hung chamber and then walked resolutely forward. It was a beautiful room, overlooking the sun-dappled garden, with the pale walnut furniture favoured by Georgiana and flowered, pastel silk curtains and upholstery. On the white and gilt dressing table reposed Radha's brushes, combs, pins and jewelled nets for her hair, kajal for her eyes and vermilion for her hair. A carved chest at the foot of the bed held her clothes. Marcus and Rowena went around touching each article and then stopped before the gilt-framed water colour on the wall. A woman sat by a stream, her hair swirling around her like clouds, with a face that was at once gentle yet compelling. Julian Ruthven had captured his beloved forever in that picture.

They stared at the portrait, moved and agitated. Marcus touched the portrait, a surge of pain rising within him.

"Mama!" he whispered, "Mama, I have found you at last!"

Julian Ruthven was furious when he found that his orders had been flouted and demanded an explanation from the old retainers. It was Marcus who spoke, grave faced. "I opened the room. I wanted to find my mother. Why has she been banished to this secret room? Why does no one tell us about her?"

Wearily, Julian Ruthven sat down on the library sofa. "Come," he said gently, summoning his children to his side, "let me tell you about your mother."

It was late when Marcus and Rowena left the library for their rooms, their cheeks tear streaked, eyes swollen, yet strangely satisfied that "Mama" was no longer a shadowy figure but a real, vibrant, beautiful woman whose memory their father cherished. It had been decided that the secret room was now to remain open, the cobwebs bainshed by flowers and lamps of worship. "Mama" was now an angel in heaven.

Julian sat in the candlelit library, spent and sad. Outside, a monsoon storm was gathering momentum, shaking old trees and rattling windows. Radha's story had been told to the children. There was no need for secrecy or silence anymore. But the recital had brought back the buried anguish, now touched with a deep remorse.

Julian suddenly felt utterly lonely, as he pondered the transience and futility of all things.

Carolyn entered the library hesitantly. "Would you rather be left alone?" she asked.

Julian sighed. "I am alone." He looked at her intently. "Does one never overcome this emptiness? Time does not heal — it only deepens the anguish, and makes one realise the dimensions of the loss."

Carolyn sat on an armchair nearby. Candlelight gleamed on her pale hair, and shadowed her tired face. "One learns to accept the pain ... and to forget both the joys and sorrows," she replied quietly.

Julian rose from the sofa, to look at the rain-lashed garden. "If only I could forget!" he said in despair. The storm reminded him of the one that had raged in Deogarh fort, when Radha had died. Suddenly, he wheeled around and faced Carolyn. She was no longer the naive and passionate girl he had possessed on a sea voyage long ago. She was a woman who had, in solitude, accepted grief as the price of living. He wanted to be close to her, to draw strength from her.

"Help me forget ... these monsoon storms conjure up terrible memories," he said, his hand extended to her. Carolyn rose and took his hand while he drew her close, until she could feel his heart beating against her own. He led her to the sofa, where he studied her in silence for a moment, as if to compare her with another. Then as the wind rose higher, and the candle flames trembled and were extinguished, Carolyn was aware of flames leaping within her, the flames she thought had surely been extinguished by deaths and defeats. She was aware of the sensation of hunger and desire as Julian explored her, not with tenderness, but with an intensity that was new and stirring. Flesh dissolved into flesh, whispers became cries lost in the howling wind outside and thunder seemed to accompany their wild and desperate effort to banish emptiness in a carnal explosion.

It was almost dawn when the storm abated. Julian Ruthven looked around the sombre room, filled with memories of the past, and then at the woman asleep in his arms, her face in happy repose. For a moment he felt panic wash over him, accompanied by a desire to flee. Then, as she stirred, her warm flesh against his, he resolved to be calm. Carolyn awoke, startled, and rose from the sofa, momentarily confused. Julian held her back, taut and trembling.

"Help me ... to rebuild ... our lives," he whispered hoarsely. Carolyn stared at him, unprepared for this declaration. Her dreams of being his wife had long been smothered in ashes.

"It is not much I am offering," Julian Ruthven said sombrely, "but I cannot make false promises to you, Carolyn." She looked at him with a surge of tenderness and compassion.

"You never have, dear Julian," Carolyn murmured. "I will accept your terms now ... but one day ..." Her voice quivered and she could not continue.

Julian glanced at her startled. "What will you want, Carolyn?" he asked.

"So much, Julian," she replied intently. "A right to share your dreams, a place in ... your heart." She paused. "Can you not give me a fragment of what you gave Radha?"

Julian turned away, agitated by the entreaty in Carolyn's eyes. "Give me time," he murmured.

She did not reply. Fourteen years ago, she had sailed up the Bay with Julian in the *Bentinck*, wondering if they would ever meet again. And now he wanted her to make a home for him and his children. Had roses bloomed from ashes?

They were married on a sunlit autumn morning in St. Paul's Cathedral. Eric Blair performed the ceremony while Catherine, Isabel and Stephen Reynolds looked on. In the front sat Rowena and Marcus and Isabel's little girls.

While Eric read the simple, eloquent words, Julian and Carolyn replied gravely. In between, Julian remembered the Vedic prayers uttered on a stormy, monsoon dusk that had bound him to joy and grief. Now, a vagrant beam of sunshine from the high, stained-glass windows fell on their joined hands, like a benediction, promising peace.

Epilogue

Of Knights and Nuns

Sir Marcus Ruthven stood on the moonlit river bank, his eyes fixed on the distant shadow of a boat that loomed over the luminous horizon. Slowly, he let out a sigh of relief as the hull of the vessel moved silently forward, and turned towards the old villa built by his great-grandfather almost a century and a half ago ...

He thought of that protean ancestor who had founded the Ruthven fortune, and who had been elevated by the family to the realm of legends. The enlightened Charles Edward and dedicated Julian had followed, bringing to India their particular passions. Then they too had left India, the land of their birth and love, for a cold and loyal exile in England, the land decreed to be their home. Only he, Marcus, had stayed behind, he who was regarded as the best and the most British of the Ruthvens. Plucked out from Bengal at the age of nine, Marcus had undergone the stipulated curriculum at Eton, Oxford and then at Gray's Inn, where he learnt to gasconade on justice and jurisprudence. He had returned to India as a barrister, sombre and aloof, as a future judge should be. This did not, however, prevent him from slipping away to Afghanisthan to see the spectacle of a British debacle at the hands of Pathan tribesmen, or the death of Pierre Cavagnarri. Nor could the preoccupations of the Calcutta High Court keep him from visiting Madras, to report on the terrible famine of the 1870s, or prevent him from taking part in the agitation for the repeal of the Vernacular Press Act, passed by Lord Lytton, "an arrogant ass of a Viceroy". The advent of a new viceroy gladdened Marcus.

Lord Rippon arrived in 1880, embodying all of the best traditions of British liberalism and humanity. Marcus Ruthven became, as did many Indians, his ardent admirer. It was a time of reforms and lawmaking, in which Marcus wholeheartedly participated. The Famine Code, the First Factory Act, the Local Government Act were enacted during these years. Lord Rippon's regime culminated in the foundation of the Indian National Congress. It was paradoxical that this Viceroy gave his imperial benediction to the Congress.

The celebrations at the Chowdhury mansion heralded a new upsurge, led not by rajas and nawabs, but by the rising bourgeoisie, which, paradoxically had been created to serve an imperial purpose. It was this class that had imbibed the intellectual gifts of the west, which now began to man the administration and fill the cloisters of colleges, vaulted courts and corridors of hospitals. It was they who lent support to the imperial crown until they chose otherwise. It was this age that produced men like Rabindranath Tagore, his brother Satyendranath, Bankim Chatterjee, Surendranath Banerjee, Vidyasagar, and most vital of all — Ramakrishna Paramahamsa whose message, and disciple, Vivekananda, transformed the soul of India.

Marcus Ruthven was the archetypal, liberal Englishman, who gloried in the contribution of British rule to India, and who put his vast fortune and name at the service of the British empire. He even put aside his love for a Bengali cousin to marry Arabella.

"Under British guidance, India will move forward," was Marcus Ruthven's reply to his Chowdhury kinsmen. British rule will be the catalyst for these changes, as it has indeed been for the last century."

No one contradicted Marcus. No Chowdhury told him of the exploits of Alexander Ruthven and his partner Henry Dalrymple, of their silk farms and factories, where thumbs of the famed weavers of Dhakai muslin had been cut off to prevent them producing cloths, of demographic disasters brought on by famines because vast lands were given over to the cultivation of the prized and pernicious indigo. Nor, indeed, did they reclaim their lands seized by an avaricious Alexander during the famine of 1770. Certainly, no one mentioned the murder of Dilip Chowdhury by an arrogant, "native-hating", Englishman, Jeremy Latimer. The Chowdhurys wanted to forget that grim past. They were now, after all, collaborators of the British, and Marcus Ruthven was one of its best representatives.

But as it often happens, someone is always willing to resurrect the past. It was a daughter of the Chowdhurys, a woman very different from the tender, selfless Radha. This woman, Ramola, had attracted Marcus during a holiday at Mayurganj, when he had briefly fallen captive to her subdued passions and sensual beauty. It was probably to avoid such dangerous liaisons that Marcus brought home a pretty bride, fresh from a debutante's world. But by then, Ramola had informed him of his infamous legacy, and taunted him for his liberal pose. Mortified, Marcus had returned to England, to complete his legal studies.

Rowena, his sister, was also well established in England. Seeing her subdued under a stepmother's tutelage, her aunt, Lady Margot had taken her away to be brought up as an accomplished lady of fashion. Under Aunt Margot's vigilant care, Rowena had blossomed into an exotic beauty, with all the qualifications necessary to be accepted in high society. She had enjoyed the admiration of many suitors before accepting a dashing young Hussar, whose aristocratic lineage was tempered by a lean purse. Rowena poured all the ardour of her heart on the Right Honourable William Stafford and felt she had found Arcadia.

After many years, Marcus went to Scotland to see the old family village, from where the Ruthvens had sprung. Even after a century and a half, the burnt cottage of James Ruthven remained as it was. The highland village was bleak and barren. The rebels' families had abandoned homes for a safe fugitive existence in France or Holland. Some had gone to India. The Hanoverian dynasty had left the ruins intact, as a reminder to Stuart loyalists of the price of rebellion. The tomb of James Ruthven, rebel to the English, martyr to the Scots, remained lichen-covered in the neglected churchyard. "Here lies James Ruthven, who died in Culloden for the liberty of Scotland" was inscribed on the grey stone.

Marcus Ruthven had spent several days in and around the highland village, trying to learn about James Ruthven, whom the Ruthvens themselves had forgotten. Tramping through hillsides bristling with gorse and heather, gazing at mist-covered lochs, Marcus went to Culloden, to sit on the battlefield where Scottish liberty and Stuart dreams had ended and where James Ruthven had brought disaster upon himself.

And the son of that man had gone to India, not as a tormented fugitive but as an adventurer, to seize lands from helpless Indian peasants and princes alike, to dishonour women and dominate men, to lie and cheat, betray and torment those who loved him dearly. James Ruthven's son had become a glorious nabob, and helped to consolidate an empire for a dynasty which had annihilated his father and his homeland.

Marcus tried to shake off the spirit of Culloden. "The past," he mused, 'is best forgotten. Neither the grim tales of Mayurganj nor of Culloden will allow me to go forward."

Soon after returning from England, Marcus received intimations from the saffron trail. His brother-in-law, the Right Honourable William Stafford had gone to fight for Britain in Sudan under General Gordon. At Khartoum, Colonel Stafford had been massacred by the Ma'hdi's men, along with his commander, General Gordon. Rowena was shattered. Leaving behind the glitter of the London she revelled in, Rowena came to India to assuage her grief. At thirty-two, it seemed as if her life was truly over. Deprived of her mother at infancy, distanced from a father soon after, removed from a familiar world, Rowena had dared to dream and hope once again with the dashing William Stafford. And now, he too was dead and she was desolate.

One of the many subjects she heard discussed at Ruthven House, was that of the great mystic and saint, Shri Ramakrishna

Paramahamsa, who had died a few years earlier. Rowena went to Dakshineshwar to visit his sanctuary. There, she met Swami Vivekananda, who gave her practical advice on how to overcome grief and emptiness. "Serve others," he told her. "In that alone is there escape from sorrow and futility."

In response, the beautiful, life-loving, vivacious Rowena put away Worth gowns and donned saffron robes, shore off her long copper tresses and performed her own funeral rites. Rowena Ruthven Stafford was dead. Her place was taken by Sister Radhika, vowed to poverty, chastity and service.

For Marcus, nothing changed outwardly. He went from success to success, achievement to achievement and one glory to another. His family flourished with numerous, well-bred progeny. His career flowered with acclaim and the Ruthven fortune swelled. In 1897, during the diamond jubilee celebrations of Queen Victoria, Marcus Ruthven was knighted for his services to the British empire. In time, it was expected, he would be made a baronet or lord. Lord Marcus Ruthven of Deogarh? It was a project to nurse, a goal that even Alexander Ruthven would not have dared to dream about.

Within him, however, raged a new storm, the kind that had made a prince two millennia ago, leave his palace to seek enlightenment. In Marcus' quest there was no search for truth. He had arrived at the truth; at the realisation that the glories in which he had revelled were gaudy tinsel, that he was enacting a role imposed upon him by the family tradition, that he had never thought for himself about life and beyond.

It was on an August morning in 1905 that his well-ordered life disintegrated within himself.

Lord Curzon, the Viceroy, had ordered the partition of Bengal—between Hindus and Muslims. The province simmered in rage and protest but an unarmed people could do nothing against a formidable empire. Rabindranath Tagore, the great poet, led a mammoth procession through the streets of Calcutta, singing a hymn to Mother Bengal, which he composed as he went along.

Let your children be one
Let your soil and air be blessed
Mother Bengal, may you be fulfilled.

Tagore went to Nakoda Masjid and there, calling the chief imam, tied a rakhi on the imam's wrist in a bond of brotherhood. Hindus and Muslims embraced and went together to protest to Curzon, who sat fuming in his crumbling citadel.

The age of revolt had begun. A revolt not spearheaded by disgruntled mercenaries or self-seeking princes but by men and women, prepared to sacrifice their lives, prepared to sing Bande Mataram as they mounted the gallows. A spate of violence broke out as Bengal, Maharashtra, Punjab awoke to the danger of the imperial design. "Terrorists" blossomed in every city, particularly in the British Indian capital. They plotted and killed in bewildered rage, and then destroyed themselves.

Sir Marcus Ruthven did not join in the clamour for brutal repression. He was curious to see the outcome of this upsurge. Were a few terrorists going to shake the mighty British empire? There had been mutinies and revolts before, and India periodically made attempts to rid itself of the British yoke.

One of these rebels was Aurobindo Ghose, who after a fine western education, had decided to join the efforts to end British rule. His trial was held in Alipur district court in 1907, a stone's throw from Ruthven House, with Chittaranjan Das leading the defence. Sir Marcus Ruthven had declined to join the formidable team for the prosecution but he attended court to watch the proceedings.

He sat mesmerised by the young man, Aurobindo, who seemed not to know fear or self-interest. After a trial of seven months, the "terrorist" was acquitted by the British prosecution. They did not wish to create martyrs.

Sir Marcus sent a secret emissary to Aurobindo, to ask what assistance he could offer. Aurobindo and his disciples told Sir Marcus what they needed to prepare for the day of reckoning.

The revolutionaries needed arms, and funds to finance purchases. The French at Chandanagar were only too eager to provide armaments from the factory at St. Etienne in France notwithstanding the signing of the Entente Cordiale with England. Sir Marcus agreed to give the necessary assistance.

And now Sir Marcus Ruthven, a knight of the British empire, stood at the riverside in Mayurganj, awaiting the boat from Chandanagar. Behind him stood a cluster of young men, ready to take the arms consignment and flee to their nearby sanctuary in Dab Tola.

The boat moved like a cloud over the luminous waters. Sir Marcus turned to peer at the grey stone temple, where his English father had married his Indian mother. Set back from the river was the Chowdhury mansion, where its present master, Bijoy, sat, plotting to become a knight as well. Bijoy Chowdhury, the district magistrate, who wanted to earn plaudits by apprehending terrorists. How ironic it all was! Bijoy wanted to live in the very world that Marcus detested: council meetings at Government House, mingling with haughty empire builders, going to London for "the season"; deliberating on imperial policies. How much he would have liked to spend his days in Coconut Grove, watching the river flow past like a perennial life force!

The boat loomed near the shore. Men leapt into the swirling water to carry ashore the consignment. Sir Marcus moved forward to scrutinise and make payments. Suddenly, the muffled, hushed conversations ceased as the figure of Bijoy Chowdhury stood etched against a milky sky. The conspirators melted away into the darkness.

Sir Marcus stood transfixed, staring at his distant kinsman. Bijoy moved slowly forward, equally astonished to stumble onto this strange discovery. "Was it ... can it be you ... who has been the ringleader of the gunrunners at Mayurganj? I can hardly believe what I see!"

Bijoy paused, and moved forward again. "Tell me it is not true, that Sir Marcus Ruthven, my ideal, is not involved in all this!"

Marcus' eyes were fixed on the filigreed shadows of the Coconut Grove, trying to ascertain whether his fellow conspirators had escaped to safety.

"Don't be absurd," Marcus said at last, "Now put away your revolver and stop asking foolish questions. Why should I join this unkempt group of gunrunners?"

"But you have," Bijoy replied in a daze, "incredible as it seems."

Marcus Ruthven nodded. "Yes, incredible as it seems," he said softly, pulling out his own revolver and aiming it at his adversary. "You will not understand my motives, young man, since we stand on different banks of the river as once our common ancestor Ishwar Chowdhury stood opposite Alexander Ruthven. You dream of power and plaudits, whereas I seek peace."

"By gunrunning?" Bijoy taunted.

"In atonement for old wrongs," Marcus retorted softly, and began stepping backwards, towards the boat which swayed on the water. He remembered every step of the river bank, from the unfettered days of his childhood. Gaining the boat, Marcus leapt in and cried, "Return to your plans of glory, Bijoy, but do not cross my path again. Your life is the forfeit.'

As the boatman lifted the oar, a hail of bullets flew towards the boat and found its target in Marcus' body. He slumped down on the wooden floorboard of the boat, stifling a cry of pain.

The boat sped on, over the turbulent river, illumined now and then by a burst of moonlight. Marcus lay on a bench, gazing at the sky, remembering episodes from a troubled past ... of Alexander's exploits and Charles' endeavours, of Julian's dedication and dilemmas, of Dilip's rebellion and Latimer's violence, of those wilful, passionate women who had brought joy and pain to these men. He thought of his happy innocence by the riverside as a child, mingling with the humble folk. He remembered too the vague, almost shadowy figure of his Indian mother, as she stood by the riverside bidding him farewell; that lovely, tender mother he had never seen again but who had remained the secret spring of his dreams. Was it for her that he had turned his back on the road to glory? He wondered as an image recurred again and again of a charred Scottish cottage, and the moss-covered tomb of a rebel, who had given his life's blood for liberty. Had all the Ruthvens, in their quest for glory, and imperial zeal, forgotten that solitary tragic figure? And was it his fate to remember Culloden and help Indians to revolt? Was it his fate to atone for the sins of his forefathers?

A stormy dawn broke over the river as the boat dropped anchor by a sheltered grove, where Sister Radhika lived with the other sanyasinis in the ashram.

Marcus Ruthven lay, as if suspended between life and death, between dream and reality, between pain and numbness. He smiled at the graceful figure in saffron who hurried towards him, her sari the colour of the dawn light. In anguish, she exclaimed, "What has happened? What have you done?"

"My dearest!" whispered the knight of the empire, "I have found myself at last."

Rowena searched for the wound in panic. "We will take you to Calcutta ... the wounds can be healed ..."

"Rowena, my dearest sister, let me go in peace ..." he said hoarsely, as she cradled his head on her lap and held his hands in hers. "I cannot return to Ruthven House. They are well off ... some of my fortune is placed at the disposal of the revolutionaries. I have burnt my bridges ... and am glad." He paused for breath. Rowena pressed his wound with her saffron sari. "Will you see to the arrangements? I have made you my executrix."

Rowena nodded.

Marcus sighed slowly. "There is peace in finding oneself, is there not? No more searching, no more quests, no more pursuit after mirages." Tears gathered in the nun's eyes. She had renounced the world to obliterate its pain, but she had found that pain had still not eluded her. It had come again with this gallant knight, her brother. He had been the solace of her sorrows, the comrade of a lonely childhood. Now he lay dying in her arms. Could one ever renounce pain? She was different from the other Ruthven sisters. She was no Deirdre to incite revenge, no Fiona to flaunt traditions, no Catherine to shock the world. Marcus stirred. "You are like the mother earth which cradled us, the father sky which looks over us." The knight was hushed by pain. Pale, gaunt, he gazed at his sister. "Dearest Rowena ... or is it Sister Radhika?"

"It is both," Rowena whispered, choking.

"You will ... find me there — in the other world? You will not be too great a saint to abandon your human brother?"

Rowena nodded, eyes brimming over.

Marcus held her hand tightly before releasing it. Then he closed his eyes.

The sun rose in an aureole of clouds as the boat sailed over the eternal river towards a timeless destination.